W9-BNG-139

"He mixes real with historical characters . . . in clever ways."
MARGARET CANNON,
The Globe and Mail

"One of Gutteridge's gifts—others include swift plotting and blessed wit—is to lure us into a world of smugness, treachery, crime, despair, and of course murder through fresh, outsider eyes, so that as Edwards discovers the complexities, subtleties, and brutalities of Upper Canada, so do we."
JOAN BARFOOT,
The London Free Press

"Too bad most school history teaching lacks the wit and sparkle of this tale."
Quill & Quire

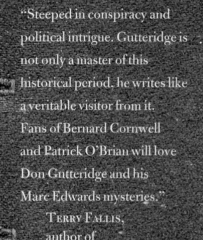

"Steeped in conspiracy and political intrigue. Gutteridge is not only a master of this historical period, he writes like a veritable visitor from it. Fans of Bernard Cornwell and Patrick O'Brian will love Don Gutteridge and his Marc Edwards mysteries."
TERRY FALLIS,
author of
The Best Laid Plans

"Don Gutteridge has created a fascinating cast of historically accurate characters as he follows a trail of murder and political intrigue with a bit of romance thrown in."
DAVID CRUISE and
ALISON GRIFFITHS,
authors of *Vancouver*

RICHMOND HILL
PUBLIC LIBRARY

SEP 1 3 2012

CENTRAL LIBRARY
905-884-9288

BOOK SOLD
NO LONGER R.H.P.L.
PROPERTY

Other Rebellion Mysteries by Don Gutteridge

Dubious Allegiance

Coming August 2012 from Touchstone

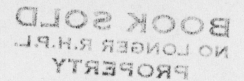
BOOK SOLD
NO LONGER R.H.P.L.
PROPERTY

THE
REBELLION
MYSTERIES

TURNCOAT

SOLEMN VOWS

VITAL SECRETS

DON GUTTERIDGE

A Touchstone Book
Published by Simon & Schuster
New York   London   Toronto   Sydney   New Delhi

Touchstone
A Division of Simon & Schuster, Inc.
1230 Avenue of the Americas
New York, NY 10020

This book is a work of fiction. Names, characters, places, and incidents either are products of the author's imagination or are used fictitiously. Any resemblance to actual events or locales or persons, living or dead, is entirely coincidental.

Turncoat copyright © 2003 by Don Gutteridge
Solemn Vows copyright © 2003 by Don Gutteridge
Vital Secrets copyright © 2007, 2011 by Don Gutteridge

All rights reserved, including the right to reproduce this book or portions thereof in any form whatsoever. For information address Touchstone Subsidiary Rights Department, 1230 Avenue of the Americas, New York, NY 10020.

This Touchstone export edition June 2012

TOUCHSTONE and colophon are registered trademarks of Simon & Schuster, Inc.

For information about special discounts for bulk purchases, please contact Simon & Schuster Special Sales at 1-866-268-3216 or Customerservice@simonandschuster.ca.

Designed by Akasha Archer

Manufactured in the United States of America

1 3 5 7 9 10 8 6 4 2

ISBN 978-1-4516-8694-4

Each of these titles has been previously published individually.

RICHMOND HILL
PUBLIC LIBRARY

SEP 1 3 2012

CENTRAL LIBRARY
905-884-9288

For John and Kate,
my Right Readers

ACKNOWLEDGEMENTS

I would like to thank Jan Walter for her wise editorial advice and Beverley Slopen, my agent, who has been with this project from the very beginning. Thanks also to Alison Clarke and Kevin Hanson for their continuing support.

CONTENTS

BOOK 1

TURNCOAT

AUTHOR'S NOTE

Turncoat is wholly a work of fiction, but I have endeavoured to convey in it the spirit of the period and the political tensions that led to the Upper Canada Rebellion of 1837. The statements, actions, and character traits attributed to actual historical personages referred to in the novel—Sir John Colborne, William Lyon Mackenzie, Peter Perry, and Ogle Gowan—are fictitious, and readers will have to make up their own minds as to whether such characterizations are consistent with the historical record. All other characters are the invention of the author, and any resemblance to persons living or dead is coincidental.

Toronto and Cobourg, of course, were and are real towns. Although Crawford's Corners is imaginary, many hamlets or postal drops like it could be found along the Kingston Road in 1835–36. The political issues raised in the story—the Clergy Reserves and the question of rights accorded to American immigrants—are presented as they would have appeared to those adversely affected by them. The Hunters' Lodges were an actual underground movement for the liberation of Upper Canada, but I have moved their activities up two years to facilitate the plot. Many such "secret societies" existed or were perceived to exist during the stress and paranoia of this turbulent period in Ontario's history.

A number of books provided useful background information and serendipitously suggested ideas that made their way into the story. Edwin C. Guillet's *Early Life in Upper Canada*, E.C. Kyte's *Old Toronto*, Frank Walker's *Sketches of Old Toronto*, and Percy Climo's *Early Cobourg* provided specific geographical and sociological detail; Sam Welch's *Recollections of Buffalo* was, among other things, an inexhaustible source of interesting names; G.C. Moore-Smith's *The Life of John Colborne* and Charles Lindsey's *The Life and Times of Wm. Lyon Mackenzie* offered close-up, contemporary accounts of the 1830s; and Gerald M. Craig's *Upper Canada: 1784–1841* brought some bracing scholarly balance to the task of interpretation. Any errors of fact in the novel, deliberate or naïve, are exclusively my own.

PROLOGUE

In 1836, Upper Canada is a colonial province in turmoil. William Lyon Mackenzie, sometime member of the Legislative Assembly, editor of the radical *Colonial Advocate*, and a left-wing rabble-rouser, has just sent the Assembly's Seventh Report on Grievances to the imperial government in England.

The farmers in Upper Canada have many legitimate complaints—domination of the political and financial spheres by an aristocratic elite known as the Family Compact, the Clergy Reserves law that sets aside every seventh lot in a concession to support the Anglican church, the Alien Act (recently repealed but whose spirit lives on) whereby American immigrants were limited in their property rights and freedom to hold office, and a governor-appointed Tory Legislative Council that has turned down dozens of bills from the Reform-controlled Legislative Assembly. The province is plagued by political gridlock, firmly in the hands of a military governor. Dissident farmers have pinned their hopes on the Reform Party, but are becoming more and more militant. Whispers of rebellion are in the air.

American-syle republicanism is seen as a possible resolution of the grievances, and its support among the populace is abetted from the United States by the Hunters' Lodges, an organization dedicated to the annexation of Upper Canada by the Republic. Other American groups, like the Lofo Foco Democrats, are likewise sympathetic to their cause. To make matters worse, drought struck the province in 1834 and 1835, bringing many farmers to the brink of starvation. The Family Compact and their Tory counterparts in the legislatures have turned a blind eye, branding as disloyal all critics of the regime, while claiming as their due all the privileges and entitlements of their class.

Amidst this and the possibility of insurrection stands a small garrison at tiny Fort York in Toronto, the provincial capital. It is a town of only three thousand souls, a dozen taverns and half as many churches, plunked down in the mud and gravel of ten blocks by five. The fort itself is a series of jerry-built structures erected in haste following the War of 1812. To add to the general uncertainty, Sir John Colborne, the lieutenant-governor, has just been transferred to Quebec, where rebellion of a different kind is brewing.

All that is needed now is some spark to ignite the flames of civil war.

ONE

Toronto, Upper Canada: January 1836

The message that was to change Ensign Marc Edwards's life forever was simple enough. It was relayed to him by a chubby-cheeked corporal as Marc came out of the Cock and Bull, a tavern frequented by officers of His Majesty's 24th Regiment of Foot.

"You are to report to Government House immediately, sir," the corporal said nervously.

"But I'm due back at Fort York within the hour," Marc said. "Colonel Margison is expecting me."

"It's the governor, sir. He wants to see you, personally. I've got a sleigh waiting around the corner."

"Very well, then." Marc tried not to let his excitement show, but after eight long months of barracks life and daily military routine in this far-flung colony of the British Empire, the possibility of something—anything—out of the ordinary was enough to set a young man's heart racing.

Government House had once been the country residence of a local grandee, a rambling wooden structure sporting several ornate verandas and a dozen chimney pots above its numerous wings and belvederes. It was set in a six-acre park at the corner of King and Simcoe streets, well out of view of those who might be envious of its splendour. As Marc was driven through the park and down a winding, snow-packed lane at breakneck speed, he tried to guess what was so urgent that an ordinary ensign like himself had to be summoned into the august presence of Sir John Colborne. But he had come up with no answer by the time he was ushered through the foyer into an office on the left-hand side of the carpeted hallway.

The lieutenant-governor's office was not the luxuriously appointed room Marc had expected. It was small, with a single window and a plain desk, upon which several neatly stacked piles of papers were strategically arrayed, like figures on a model battlefield. Beside it stood a simple table, cluttered with notes and binders—the secretary's desk, now unoccupied.

Behind the larger desk, in a wooden captain's chair, sat the man himself. Sir John was a veteran of the Peninsular War and the decades-long fight against Napoleon, culminating in Waterloo, where he had been instrumental in securing the allied victory. As Marc was shown in by the duty corporal, Sir John rose and offered a brief, tight smile of recognition and welcome. For a moment his tall, austere figure and intelligent, appraising gaze left Marc speechless. He had, of course, chatted with Sir John several times at various galas in the fall, and most recently at the New Year's levee, where the governor had gone on at some length about Marc's uncle Frederick, who had served under him during half a dozen campaigns on the Continent. But Marc knew he had not been summoned here for polite chit-chat about his uncle.

"Come in, Marc—I'm going to call you that, Ensign, if you don't mind—and take a seat. We have much to discuss and too little time in which to do it."

Sir John began without further ceremony.

"I will tell you as much as I know and am able to reveal to you at this time. As you are probably aware, having been abroad in the countryside on several occasions last year, I have numerous agents and correspondents in the districts who keep me informed on a regular basis of matters pertinent to His Majesty's interests in Upper Canada. Joshua Smallman was one such man."

"The chap who used to run the dry goods store on King Street?"

Sir John smiled, as if some portion of his judgment had been confirmed. "Yes. He packed up and moved off to Crawford's Corners, a hamlet near Cobourg about seventy miles from here, after his son died, to assist his daughter-in-law and her brother in the operation of their farm. A Christian gentleman and a loyalist through and through. For the past twelve months he has been sending me sealed letters that have provided me and His Majesty with invaluable information regarding agitators and would-be insurrectionists in the Cobourg region—men who would have us yoked with the United States and its insidious republicanism."

It was little wonder, Marc thought, that Britain was hypersensitive to the threat of democracy from the south and the passions it stirred among the disaffected in Upper Canada. She had lost her Thirteen Colonies in the Revolutionary War, and then had barely hung on to the remaining ones up here during the American invasions of 1812 and 1813.

"And I needn't remind you that that area is Perry terrain," Sir John continued.

Peter Perry, Marc recalled, was a leading light among the radicals in the Legislative Assembly—Reformers they were called—and an outspoken critic of the governor and his conservative administration.

"You think, sir, that Mr. Perry may have gone over to the annexationists or the Mackenzie republicans?"

"He's been conspiring with Willy Mackenzie on this

latest so-called Report on Grievances cooked up by the Legislative Assembly. But no, it is not Perry or Reformers like Rolph or Bidwell or Baldwin I am concerned about—troublesome though they may be. In fact, it is precisely the inability of old conservatives and Tories like Allan MacNab or Orange fanatics like Ogle Gowan to discriminate between a loyal dissenter and a committed seditionist that has caused so much of the present confusion and discontent. Even Mackenzie does not concern me: he abides and caterwauls not half a mile from this office. His movements and nefarious doings are reported to me before they occur, and quite often when they don't." Sir John, whose military bearing dominated any room he chose to grace, glanced up from the papers on his desk to see what effect his modestly ironic sally might have had on the youthful ensign.

"Joshua Smallman was not among the fanatics," he said emphatically. "He was a humble citizen of the Empire endowed with common sense and a strict but not strident adherence to duty."

"Was?"

"He died on New Year's Eve. And I have good reason to suspect that he was murdered."

Marc's surprise registered clearly on his face.

"As you may already know," Sir John said, in the same straight-ahead, matter-of-fact tone, "I have been unavoidably busy with packing my books and belongings in the past week."

"Then it is true that you are leaving for Montreal," Marc said.

"I am. Simply put, I am needed more urgently in Quebec, where open rebellion may be nearing. I am to lead the troops there. My sovereign has called me, and the long and short of it is that all of us, major general or drummer boy, must do his duty."

The manner in which Sir John first looked down and then glanced furtively back up alerted Marc to the sudden change in his own fortunes about to be announced, and the necessity of an unwavering obedience.

"I have here," Sir John continued, picking up a letter from his desk, "the last report that Joshua Smallman sent me. It is dated December 28, almost two weeks ago. It came into my hands after New Year's Day, but I must confess to you—and upbraid myself yet again—that I let it idle amongst more trivial messages and petitions until yesterday evening."

"He wrote you, then, three days before his . . . death?"

"That's right. Naturally I was informed of that tragic event within the day by courier. The district magistrate, who is a staunch supporter of the government, sent me the news, and three days later I received from him and from the sheriff of Northumberland County at Cobourg a summary of their findings and the results of the inquest."

"Murder?"

"Death by misadventure."

"I don't follow, sir."

"According to Sheriff MacLachlan's report and the minutes of the inquest, Smallman, for reasons undeterminable, set out on horseback from his daughter-in-law's house on New Year's Eve. He told her that he was doing so in response to a message, but she doesn't remember seeing any note and swears no one came directly to the house that evening, other than neighbours invited in for a quiet celebration. Nor would he tell her where he was going, despite her earnest entreaty and her expression of fear for his safety." Before Marc could interrupt, Sir John said, "The weather was inclement in the extreme: below zero with squalls of snow and a strong wind off the lake. But away he went."

"Worried? Anxious?"

"One would assume so," Sir John said with a rueful smile, "but apparently not. He was described as rather excited, eager even, with not the least suspicion of danger. In fact, his last words to the young woman—Bathsheba—were: 'When I return I may have some news that could change our lives forever.'"

"How, then, did he die?"

"Presumably he headed east along the Kingston Road, turned off on one of the newly surveyed concessions—he was seen to do so by a reliable witness—and kept going towards the lake. Fortunately the snow stopped completely before midnight and the wind soon died down, so when a search party was organized the next morning by Philander

Child, the magistrate, and the supernumerary constable
for Crawford's Corners, one Erastus Hatch, the trail left by
Smallman's horse was still traceable. They soon heard the
wretched beast whinnying like a sick child from the woods
nearby. They found it tethered and near death, and a few
yards farther on they came across the frozen corpse of Smallman himself."

"Surely he couldn't merely have lost his way. Not with a
horse to lead him out."

"True. But he had donned snowshoes and trod straight
into a deadfall trap set years ago by the Mississauga Indians
and long since abandoned."

"Could it have been re-rigged more recently? For other
ends?"

With each question or comment from Marc, Sir John
grew more assured that, despite the beardless and callow
countenance of the youth sitting in near-solemn attentive-
ness before him, he had chosen the right man for the task he
had in view.

"No," Sir John said. "The entire area was thoroughly
scrutinized by Sheriff MacLachlan and Constable Hatch.
However, I expect you'll want to see for yourself."

"But what can I hope to discover that they have not?"
Marc said, genuinely puzzled.

"Why I am suspicious of murder, you mean?" Sir John
said dryly. "Well, I wasn't, not until I read Smallman's report
last night." He held the paper up as if he needed to consult

its contents, whose import and detail he had committed to memory. "Among other things, not relevant to our concerns here, he hinted near the end that he had grown weary of playing secret agent, that he had started to have doubts about his own sentiments in regard to the grievances so recently raised by the Reformers in the Assembly."

"He doubted his own loyalty?"

"Not at all. That he could never do, whatever the provocation. That is the very reason I trusted him. Even the frank expression of such fleeting doubts endeared him the more to me and further validated his probity in my eyes. When you have commanded men in battle as I have, or attempted to administer justice among colonial grandees driven by deceit and self-serving ambition, then perhaps you will better understand what I mean. No, I doubted not, nor do I now doubt, Joshua Smallman's loyalty. But he did go on to inform me that he felt that his role as a 'spy'—his characterization, not mine—was close to being exposed, that his daughter-in-law's increasing sympathy for left-wing causes was becoming public knowledge and threatening to compromise him. He was beginning to feel torn between his patriotic duty to His Majesty and his Christian duty to his son's widow and her family. Finally, he said that while he had no firm evidence yet, he felt matters were coming to a head on several fronts."

"Did he suggest he was in any physical danger?"

"Yes. Not directly, mind you. I'll read you what he wrote:

'There are men in these parts who are growing more desperate by the week. Many of them I have mentioned in previous reports, all of whom, until quite recently, I would swear still held to legislative and lawful means to achieve their purposes. At this moment, I don't know whether there is more danger in my being thought to be a true-blue member of the Family Compact or a Tory-turned-Reformer under the influence of his son's wife. In either case, I fear my usefulness to you is at an end. I do not lack courage, but I must admit that I was shaken last week when a young lad from a radical family on one of the back concessions was found tarred and feathered and bearing a sign that labeled him a turncoat.'"

"Upsetting, but not evidence of a threat against him personally," Marc ventured.

Sir John replied, with some of the steeliness that had earned him such respect on the Spanish Peninsula and later at Waterloo: "Joshua Smallman would not have left his home in the midst of a New Year's celebration and ventured out into a blizzard upon a fool's errand. He was born and raised along that portion of the lake, he knew every brook and ravine. His horse was found tethered, not roaming frantically on its own. He was going somewhere in particular and in earnest. And even though the surgeon testifies that he died in the manner suggested by the circumstances in which he was found, neither he nor the constables knew that Joshua was my agent, and friend. Nor will they." He held Marc's eye long enough to settle that point, then said,

"They have no reason to suspect that he may have had some clandestine and possibly life-threatening motive for being out alone on the last day of one of the saddest years of his life."

"But we do," Marc said.

"Precisely." Sir John shuffled several papers on his desk, then looked up. "Please send your report directly to me in Quebec."

Marc nodded. "When do you want me to leave for Crawford's Corners?"

"In half an hour." Sir John kept his appraising gaze on the nephew of Frederick Edwards.

Marc gave him the answer he was looking for: "Yes, sir."

There had been little more to say, then, except to sort out in their brusque, soldierly way the mundane details of Marc's departure and, as it were, his marching orders. Sir John went over the contents of the special governor's warrant that would allow him to interview witnesses and otherwise invoke the governor's authority to investigate the suspicious death of Joshua Smallman. Marc was given a bundle of notes and papers that might be pertinent to his efforts and told to read them over before he reached his destination. Colonel Margison, his commanding officer, had provided a swift horse and was to concoct a suitable story to account for Marc's absence from Fort York.

So it was just before three in the afternoon that Ensign Edwards set off down King Street on a secret and possibly dangerous mission into the troubled countryside of Upper Canada. He still had no idea why he had been chosen.

As Marc trotted along the main thoroughfare of the province's capital—past its self-important little strip of shops, offices, and taverns—he was pleased that the sun was shining. It highlighted the scarlet and grey of his regimental uniform, most of it dazzlingly visible through his unbuttoned and wind-buffeted greatcoat. But his initial sense of excitement soon gave way to consideration of what faced him seventy miles east on the Kingston Road. Even if murder had actually occurred—and there was no guarantee that Smallman's death had not been a bizarre accident—his chances of resolving the matter were slim. He knew no one who might be involved in the affair or was in a position to provide useful information. Perhaps a studied disingenuousness, combined with the secret information supplied by Sir John and his own observation skills, would be his best hope.

Someone waved a mittened hand at him from the doorway of Miss Adeline's dress shop, and a feminine cry sallied up. Marc kept his eyes front so that his quick smile went unappreciated. The brisk winter breeze chilled and stirred him. He felt physically alive, acute, like some exotic woodland creature that was both hunter and hunted.

Only one discordant note threatened to disturb the pleasure he was feeling, and he fought hard to suppress it. By the time he got back to Toronto—even if he were to be spectacularly successful in Crawford's Corners—his role model and benefactor would be in Quebec. Sir John's replacement as lieutenant-governor was already on his way from England: Sir Francis Bond Head, a man with not a single battle under his belt or laurel to his name, a scribbler of travel books and sonnets for the titillation of ladies-in-waiting among the petty gentry of Toronto and York County.

As he crossed Simcoe Street, Marc's eye was drawn to the red-brick silhouette of the two-storeyed parliament buildings a block to the south. Their glittering glass windows and cut-stone pilasters gave them an air of permanence and pertinence. Like their counterparts along the Thames in London, these legislative halls were in his mind mere houses of words, monuments to bombast and hyperbole. He had seen the originals at Westminster, at first in awe as a child at the side of Uncle Jabez (as he called his adoptive father, Jabez Edwards), and later as a law student at the Inns of Court when he was old enough to judge for himself. Even now, even here, a thousand leagues from all that mattered in the world, men slung epithets as if they were weapons: to sting, incite, confuse, and corrupt. But in the end it was the soldier who had to set things right, risking body and soul.

Marc was so deep in thought that he didn't notice crossing Yonge Street or seeing the Court House or St. James' Church farther east. Before he realized it, he was easing Colonel Margison's second-best horse back to a walk as

they began a slow descent to the Don River. The few sporadic clearings on either side of the road indicated that the
industry and mercantile zest of the capital city was reaching well beyond its civic borders. He breathed in the yeast-
sweet odour of Enoch Turner's brewery before he spotted
its outbuildings and brewing stacks. Just below it lay Scaddings Bridge, as it was still called by the locals, even though
Scaddings and the original structure were long gone to grass.
Ignoring the bridge, Marc tugged the horse down the slope
and onto the frozen surface of the river itself. The recent
snowfall allowed him to spur his steed into a lusty gallop,
and together they charged across the wind-swept, treeless
expanse as if it were the perilous space separating the armies
of Wellington and the Corsican usurper. As he plunged
through knee-deep drifts up the far bank, a fur-capped trapper stood up to take notice, then waved enthusiastic approval. Marc tipped his plumed shako hat with elaborate
politeness.

At the top of the rise he paused to rest the horse and
check that he had not overheated it. The trapper held up
one of his trophies as if to say, "Both of us are having a good
day, eh?" It looked to Marc as if the drowned creature (missing one leg) was what the locals called ermine, which in
truth was merely a fancy word for stoat or common weasel, a
canny predator who could, like a turncoat, adjust the hue of
his skin with the fickle swing of the seasons. Even the hares
in this alien landscape went white with the snows.

And it was alien territory that Ensign Edwards—late of the shire of Kent and the Royal Military School—was heading into. He had no reason to believe that affairs in Crawford's Corners or the nearby town of Cobourg would be much different from the querulous, mongrel politics he had done his best to ignore here in Toronto: with its raving and moderate Tories, rabid Reformers, and ordinary Grits, annexationists like John Rolph and William Lyon Mackenzie, out-and-out Yankee republicans recently arrived from Detroit or Lewiston, and Loco Foco Democrats insinuated from Buffalo or Oswego. His own brief dalliance with the study of law had taught him to be logical and analytic, though he hadn't persevered there long enough to learn the trick of deviousness. His subsequent career as a soldier, so much more to his liking and talent, had taught him to be direct and ever poised for precipitate action.

Marc emerged from the woods and once again headed east along the Kingston Road. The sun was well past the high point of its daily arc but still shone bravely in a cloudless sky. The weather appeared promising. He would take his time, he would savour the liberal air and pleasing sensation of his body moving with the rhythm of the horse's stride.

When Sir John had suggested that he go directly to Crawford's Corners, where he felt the answers, if any, to the puzzle of Smallman's death lay, he had assured Marc that he would find ready allies there to assist him, should he have need: in particular Magistrate Philander Child; Major

Charles Barnaby, an ex-army surgeon; and James Durfee, local postmaster and innkeeper—sensible gentlemen and true Tories all. Moreover, the supernumerary township constable, Erastus Hatch, was also the miller for the region and a man whose honesty and bluff friendliness should prove invaluable. It seemed he always had a spare room for allies in the cause and a not-unhandsome daughter inexplicably unattached. And, most conveniently, Hatch's hostel was situated right next to the Smallman farm.

Marc's plan was to arrive unannounced at the miller's place sometime the following afternoon (after a satisfying supper and a feather bed at the Port Hope Hotel), discreetly explore the site of the "murder" with Constable Hatch's assistance, and then interview the members of the victim's household before his presence in the area became generally known and speculated upon. He would then pronounce himself satisfied that everything connected with the death was just as it had been reported. From that point he would fabricate some plausible excuse for remaining in Crawford's Corners (the handsome, unengaged daughter of miller Hatch?) and then, using leads generated by Magistrate Child or other loyalists, he would keep his ears pricked for the undertones of sedition he was certain would provide him with the motive and, if God were a monarchist, deliver up the treacherous assassins themselves.

It seemed like a sound strategy. However, his wide reading in military history had left him with the disconcerting conclusion that most generals were astonished to discover their impeccable schemes for battle starting to unravel at the opening volley. With such thoughts still contending in his head, Marc sighed with relief when, late in the afternoon, he spotted in the near distance the square-log building he knew would be the popular wayside hostelry of Polonius Mitchum.

As he rode up to the primitive log structure, he found himself whistling.

TWO

We don't get too many of your kind this far out." The tavern-keeper chuckled as he dipped a tin cup into the barrel under the counter and poured the contents into a mug that had seen happier and kinder days. "Least not in the daylight." His whiskers quivered to underline the wit of the remark.

Marc dropped a threepenny piece on the unvarnished pine board and stared straight ahead. "I'm on the King's service," he said. "I'd be grateful if you'd have your lad see to my horse. It'll be getting dark in an hour or so, and we've got a ways to go yet."

"Indeed, sir, it's always a pleasure for Polonius Mitchum to serve a servant of His Majesty. Even though I ain't had the honour of shakin' his hand, I'm told the King's a decent sort of German gentleman."

Marc lifted his mug and took a man-sized swallow of the liquor.

Mitchum swivelled his heavy body to the right and yelled towards the curtained alcove behind him: "Caleb! Drag your lazy arse outside and see to this gentleman's horse. Now! Before I tan the hide off ya!"

A lazy scrabbling sound was heard from the murky recesses, and a moment later a door opened somewhere and the winter wind whipped gaily through the premises. "Jesus Murphy," Mitchum roared. He seemed about to bend his entire bulk around, then changed his mind and, instead, swept the coin off the counter and fetched up a fearsome grin. "That ain't my lad, thank Christ, though he calls my wife 'Mother.'"

"And this isn't whisky," Marc said, peering up and fixing Mitchum with a quizzical eye.

"Thought you'd never notice," Mitchum said. "I don't serve Gooderham's rotgut to gentlemen of quality, and I can see plainly you are that, sir, if nothin' else." He reached across and laid the grubby stub of a finger on the sleeve of Marc's tunic. "Now that's real quality, sir, even if it do make you look as temptin' as a guinea hen in a coopful of foxes."

"This tastes very much like rum from the garrison stores," Marc said quietly.

"Upon my word, young sir, you wouldn't be accusin' Polonius Mitchum, Esquire, of breakin' the law or encouragin' others less fortunate to do so?" Mitchum's eyes bristled with friendly menace.

"I merely remarked upon a suspicious coincidence," Marc said.

"As indeed have many of your fellow officers who are wont to frequent this establishment to quench their thirst— and other appetites."

The rambling outhouses behind the tavern itself were reputed to be places where a libidinous bachelor with an instinct for gambling could indulge both vices with a minimum of inconvenience. Marc's repeated refusal to join his comrades-in-arms on their nighttime excursions, out here or closer to home, was a source of wonder to them and, for a few, a cause for resentment. Marc himself could scarcely find reasons for his reserve in such matters, though the scars of a youthful romance cruelly broken up had not perhaps healed as fully as he had hoped.

"Even so," Marc said to Mitchum after finishing off his draught, "the importation of Jamaican rum into the province, directly or surreptitiously through the United States, without paying the excise on it, constitutes a crime under the statutes, as does the purveying of bootlegged army rations."

"Smugglin'?" Mitchum said, as if the very utterance of the word was horror enough for any respectable citizen.

"Aye."

Mitchum refilled Marc's mug. "On the house," he said.

Marc dropped a shilling on the counter. "That'll cover the drinks and the ostling," he said.

"I ain't had truck with any smugglers," Mitchum said. "But there's plenty of 'em about for them that's inclined to be unlawful. Most of them Yankee peddlers up from Buffalo or across the ice from Oswego are rum-runners, or worse."

Marc sipped the rum, grateful for the warmth it imparted.

"Why, I seen a pair of 'em earlier today, headin', they claimed, for the bright lights of Cobourg. And if they was tinkers, I'm the Pope's bum-boy."

"You tell that news to the sheriff of York," Marc said, reaching over and grasping the bib of Mitchum's apron. "I'm on serious business, and the governor's warrant."

Mitchum mustered an ingratiating grin. "No need to do that, now, is there, sir? Gentleman soldiers need their little bit of fun and relaxation, don't they?"

Marc released his hold. "How far is it to the next hamlet?"

"That'd be Perry's Corners: eight miles, give or take a furlong. You can make it before dark, if the weather holds." Mitchum dropped his grin. "'Course, there ain't an inn with a decent bed between here and Port Hope."

Marc pulled his greatcoat back on. "Tell your wife's boy to bring my horse around to the road."

"I'll do that, sir. And I'll remember you to your mates this evenin', shall I?"

THE WEATHER DIDN'T HOLD. MARC HADN'T gone half a mile when the prevailing northwesterly abruptly died, replaced seconds later by a southeasterly pouring in from the cold expanse of Lake Ontario. Huge nimbus clouds gathered in the wake of the wind. Marc took off his stiff-brimmed shako with its green officer's tuft, pushed it into his saddle-roll next to his French pistol, and pulled on—with more urgency than ceremony—the beaver cap so prized by Canadian voyageurs and woodsmen. He wound his scarf several times around his throat and collar and leaned forward as far as he could over the horse's withers.

He had not long to wait. The wind-driven snow struck horse and rider like a loose flail. The road vanished, and the treeline, no more than twenty feet away on either side, fluttered and swam. Marc felt the horse's panic and heard with alarm the stunted wheeze of its breathing. In a minute it would rear and bolt—somewhere. Marc leapt off into the packed snow of the road without releasing his grip on the reins. The startled horse shied and then spat the bit. But Marc, whose own fear was rising, wrenched the frenzied animal sideways, then hauled it, step by stubborn step, into the sheltering pines on the lake side of the Kingston Road. They halted under a tall jack pine, itself shielded by a hedge-like ring of cedars. Marc laid his cheek against the beast's shoulder and stroked its neck. After a while they both stopped shivering.

When the wind dropped, they got back on the road. It was covered with a foot of fresh snow, and no track or rut was visible, either to the east or the west. The wind had eased off and only decorative little eddies of snow spun intermittently at the horse's hooves. Less than half an hour of light remained. It would be pitch dark before he could reach even the unwelcoming hamlet of Perry's Corners. Port Hope itself, and a hearty fire, was at least twenty miles farther on.

Suddenly, from a bend just ahead of him came the sound of horses pounding and snorting, accompanied by cries of human merriment. Marc drew to the side just in time to avoid collision with a four-horse team and a massive sleigh whistling along behind it. The driver waved a friendly mitt in Marc's direction and clamped a smile around his pipe, but did not slow down. Weller's thrice-weekly mail coach sailed past, leaving its fur-wrapped passengers only a moment to cheer his presence and admire his perseverance. One of them, apparently female, stood up, swung around, and held up a silver flask, as if offering a toast to the ensign. Such was social nicety among the self-professed gentry of the Upper Canadian bush.

Marc felt a pang of disappointment that the coach had not stopped, even though he knew the storm meant that both it and he had to get to their destinations as soon as possible. Marc had been quick to observe how the Upper Canadians went about preparing themselves for comfort and survival during winter. Snug in his saddle-roll were extra blankets and underclothing, a large square of sailcloth, and three-days' rations, in addition to his army kit and pistol. Colonel Margison, who had arrived in person with the horse for Marc, had persuaded him at the last minute to include his sabre. It lay in its scabbard, which was attached to the saddle, not his belt, where it would have been handy but too conspicuous. His Brown Bess musket, however, stood in its rack in the officers' quarters at Fort York.

A short time later, one of the landmarks that had been mapped out for him came into view. Here the roadway veered so close to the lake that its icy expanse could be glimpsed through a screen of leafless birch and alder trees. He was three miles or so from Perry's Corners, where, if he was lucky, he would find a cold meal and space by the postmaster's fire. A steady canter would put him there in less than half an hour, despite the deep snow, the rapidly descending darkness, and a weary mount. He looked up in time to see the single star in the southern sky swallowed by cloud. The east wind, bringing no good, was cranking up for another blow.

Not a person to repeat his mistakes, Marc cajoled his horse into the woods on the right, knowing that the cliff above the lake would deflect some of the fury of the approaching squall and send it screeching over the trees. He soon found a suitable spot, tethered the horse, spread the canvas out at the base of a stout pine, covered this with a wool blanket, and sat down to wait out the worst.

IT WAS AN HOUR LATER WHEN, with no sign of the storm abating, Marc made the decision to camp somewhere in the shelter of the woods. There, the snow was not yet deep enough for him to have to strap on his Indian snowshoes (if he did, it would be his maiden excursion on them), but he couldn't walk far. His feet were nearly frozen: he needed a fire and some boiling tea—soon. He had noticed earlier, just to the south of him towards the lake, a small rise in the land that had kept the drifts from accumulating on its leeward side. He thought he might erect a makeshift lean-to there.

After giving the horse a shrivelled apple and a reassuring pat, he trudged through the snow towards the ridge. Within a few minutes he had reconnoitred a sort of den formed by the ridge and the exposed roots of a large tree. With the sail-cloth for a roof and a ground sheet from his army kit under him, he would be as snug as a hibernating bear, with plenty of brushwood for a smudge fire. He was in the midst of congratulating himself when he saw the smoke.

He stood stock-still, cursing himself silently for having trod so noisily into an unknown area with no thought for his personal safety. He was unarmed: his pistol was in his saddle-roll, his sabre in its scabbard. He spoke no aboriginal tongue. He was shivering and, to his consternation, found himself nearer exhaustion than he had been willing to admit. But his mind remained alert: he listened for the slightest sound and was certain now that he could hear voices. The smoke itself continued to pour upward in thick whorls not twenty yards to his left, its source hidden by a knoll and several squat cedars. This was no campfire smoke, or if it was, it was of no kind Marc had ever seen.

He had two choices: he could return to the horse and risk being heard (one nicker from the animal would ring like a rifle shot through the silence of these woods) or get close enough to the murmuring voices to discern if it would be safe to approach whomever it was and ask for a warm place by their fire. He chose the latter strategy.

Taking one slow, muffled step at a time, he edged towards the knoll and the coils of woodsmoke. When he was within a few yards, he eased himself up the slope of the ridge. Then he crawled along its height until he was at last able to look into the wintry glade below him. What he saw was a log hut, no more than ten by ten, windowless (on the two sides he could see), but sporting a lime-and-straw chimney—in active service. A trapper's cabin.

"Well, sir, don't just sit up there like a frozen cod, come on down and join us." A face poked out from behind the chimney. "You look like you could do with a wee drop of the craychur."

• • •

"NINIAN T. CONNORS AT YOUR SERVICE," said the big Irishman with the Yankee-accented brogue and the ready smile.
He handed Marc a cup of whisky and urged him to move
his feet (unbooted, with much effort and more pain) closer
to the fire. "My associate, Mr. Ferris O'Hurley, and I are always pleased to oblige a gentleman of the officers' fraternity,
whether his coat be blue or scarlet."

"And I'm the fella to second that," added the other one,
as dark and wiry and toughened as his partner was florid and
generously fleshed. When he drank his grog, he gulped the
cupful entire, squeezed his eyes shut as his whiskered cheeks
bulged, and then blinked the rotgut down his gullet like a
toad with a stubborn fly.

"I am most grateful for your kindness," Marc said, sipping
at his drink and wishing it were hot tea. His horse stood at
ease outside the cabin, keeping a donkey company and sharing its feed. When Marc had offered to pay, Connors had
taken exaggerated umbrage: "The laws of hospitality in this
savage land are as strict as the ones in ancient Greece, and
necessarily so. It is we, sir, who are obliged to you for hon-
ouring us with your unexpected but worthy presence."

"You headin' for Cobourg?" O'Hurley asked between
gulps.

"In that direction," Marc said, taking the slice of bread
and cheese held out to him by Connors.

"What my associate means," Connors said, with an impish twinkle in his blue eyes, "is that we seldom see an officer of His Majesty's regiments travelling alone on the Kingston Road."

"You know it well, then?"

"Indeed we do, though you have no doubt surmised that we are citizens of a neighbouring state."

"We're up from Buffalo," O'Hurley said.

"Peddling your wares," Marc said evenly.

"We don't do nothin' illegal," O'Hurley said, then he glanced at Connors as quick as a cat.

"What my confederate means is that we are not mere Yankee peddlers, as noble as that profession might be. Mr. O'Hurley here, whose father was as Irish as mine, is a bona fidee tinker, a tinsmith and artiste of the first rank. You, good sir, are drinking from a recent product of his craft."

The tin cup held by Marc looked as if the donkey had tried to bathe in it, but he refrained from comment. His toes had thawed out, the crude meal and whisky were sitting comfortably on his stomach, and the mere thought of curling up in his own bedroll next to a fire was beginning to warm him all over.

"Mr. O'Hurley here travels these parts—highway and back road alike—several times a year. He not only sells a grateful citizenry household items unattainable in the British half of America, though commonplace in the great Republic to the south, but he repairs anything constructed of metal, and where repair will not suffice, he fashions original works with the touch of a true master—an impresario, you might say, of tin and copper."

"You have an established itinerary, then?" Marc lit his pipe with a tinder stick and puffed peaceably.

"Well, not what you'd really call regular-like," O'Hurley said.

"Which is to say, we improvise," Connors said, leaning over to allow Marc to light his clay calumet with a fresh tinder, "as occasion dictates." He sucked his tobacco into life and continued. "As a man of the world, I'm sure you know there are people in this distant dominion of King William who, notwithstanding the intent and principle of His Majesty's law so recently and justly amended—"

"You are referring to the repeal of the Alien Act? Naturalized citizens from the United States can now keep their property and participate fully in political life," Marc asserted confidently.

Connors squinted—part frown and part smile—then grinned and said, "Yes, but many of your countrymen persist in believing that any resident of this province who hails from the United States of America—however long ago and however naturalized since—is a primee fashia blackguard and potential seditionist. A Yankee spy under every rock, to use the vernacular."

"So you move about . . . judiciously," Marc offered.

"How well put. You seem uncommonly schooled for a soldier, sir."

Marc acknowledged the compliment with a nod. "And are you a smithy as well?"

O'Hurley coughed and spluttered into his cup.

"I, sir," Connors declaimed, "am a smithy of words and subordinate clauses, of tracts and contracts—monetary, fiduciary, and commercial. I draw up bills of sale and bills of lading, deeds of property and dunnings of debt. I drum and I stake and I capitalize; I minister and mollify."

"A solicitor, then."

Connors reeled back as if struck by a blow as cowardly as it was mortal. "You jest, sir. If I am to be vilified by that name, it can only be in the generic sense. I do what lawyers in my country do, but without the handicap of education or licence. In brief, young sir, I am what the Republic hails as its quintessential citizen: an entrepreneur." He leaned back, laid his gloved hands across his mustard waistcoat, and smiled without a trace of guile.

"He does the thinkin'," O'Hurley said, "and I do the craftin'."

"The perfect partnership, you might say," Connors added.

"And you travel together, then? Both of you on a single donkey?"

"Not literally, of course, like Yankee Doodle or our Good Lord on Palm Sunday. I come up by myself to scout out new territory and solicit orders, and once in a blue moon I get the urge to hit the open road for a spell. Then Ferris and I set out in tandem."

Assuming he had been tossed a cue, Ferris blinked sleepily and said, "Ninian's got a sister up here he likes to visit."

"And where does she live?"

"Now you've gone and done it, Ferris old friend," Connors sighed. "You've flat out embarrassed me." He turned to Marc and slowly raised his downcast, abashed eyes. "The visits to my dear sister are, sir, acts of kindness towards that poor impoverished soul and her wretched children, and Ferris knows full well I do not wish to have broadcast those acts of Christian charity that should be executed privily for their own sake and not for the public aggrandizement of the perpetrator."

"I think it's time for me to turn in," Marc said.

"You'll not have one more drink, then?"

Marc yawned and shook his head.

"Surely one toast to His Majesty."

"Just two fingers, then," Marc said.

"Why don't you give him a swig from the canteen?" O'Hurley suggested.

Connors shot him a look that was part reproving, part resignation, then managed to attach his smile to it in time to say, "Splendid thought! We keep a modest dram of superior spirits to mix up a syllabub now and then." He drew what appeared to be a regulation army canteen from under his jacket and poured each of them a toddy.

"To King William the Fourth!"

They drank to the fount and guardian of the British Empire.

"Your toast, good sir."

"To honest men everywhere!" Marc said.

The liquor slid silkily down Marc's throat: overproof Jamaican rum.

As soon as horse and donkey had been made as comfortable as possible, the three men set about arranging their bedrolls around the last glow of the fire. When Marc went back out to relieve himself, he slipped his sabre from its scabbard and tiptoed back inside. All was dark and quiet.

For a long while, Marc lay awake, despite the demands of his body for sleep, waiting for the telltale snoring of the peddlers, who, graciously enough, had given him pride of place next to the fire. While checking his horse earlier, Marc had given the donkey and its packs a searching look and decided that these men carried no weapons of any size. Nor did he see anything that resembled contraband goods among the pots and pans of their tradesmen's gear.

Some time later he opened his eyes wide. How long he had slept he did not know, but he soon knew what had wakened him. Connors and O'Hurley were both upright, huddled against the door and fumbling for the latch.

"Jasus, it's cold. We shoulda stayed in Buffalo."

"Well, I gotta take a piss and I'm not fouling my own nest."

"Me too, dammit." O'Hurley was jerking at the latch in the dark.

Then Connors whispered, "Sorry to wake you, Ensign. Ferris and I have got to answer a pre-emptive call of nature."

The door opened, colder air drifted in from outside, and the peddlers vanished. Seconds later the air hissed with their exertions, but they did not return. Marc reached over and felt for the saddlebags, his own and his hosts'. Both were still there. Once again he fought against sleep—thinking hard.

O'HURLEY HAD HIS EAR AGAINST THE door. "I don't hear no snorin'."

"Let me have a gander, before my balls freeze solid and drop off." Connors eased the door open a crack. The unexpected onset of moonlight allowed him a partial but clear view of the ensign wrapped in his bedroll, his fur cap pulled down over his face against the biting cold of a midwinter night.

"Edwards," Connors said in a low, amiable voice. "You awake?" No reply. "We're just gonna move the animals to the other side of the cabin."

"He's out for the night," O'Hurley said nervously.

"The rum did the trick."

"We gonna go through with this?"

"Of course we are. We can't take any chances."

"He seemed like an okay fella to me."

"You wouldn't last a week on your own," Connors said without rancour.

The decision had been made after they had relieved themselves in the brush at the foot of the knoll, though not without several minutes of furiously whispered argument.

"I bet that horse's worth fifty bucks," O'Hurley said, warming to the task at hand.

"It may be too risky to take," Connors said.

"If only the bugger'd not asked so many questions."

"Here," Connors said, and he held out a stout log frozen as hard as an iron bar. "Get on with it."

"Why me?"

"Your turn, old boy," Connors said, smiling. "Besides, it was you that blabbed about the rum and my sister."

With the weapon shaking in his grasp, O'Hurley inched the door farther open, shuddering at every creak it made. But exhaustion seemed to have claimed the redcoat utterly. He would never see the blow that killed him. Perhaps there would even be no pain: he would simply not wake up.

O'Hurley stood over the silent, unsuspecting sleeper, his eyes riveted on the ornate haft of the officer's sabre just peeping above the army blanket. He could sense Connors watching in the open doorway behind him. He raised the log, hesitated, shut his eyes, and brought it down upon the fur cap. He opened his eyes just in time to see the entire bedroll spasm and grow still. There wasn't even a moan. Thank God.

"Jasus Christ and a saint's arse!" Connors yelled. "You can't kill a man with a fly-swat like that!" He ripped the club from O'Hurley's grasp and slammed it down on the rumpled cloth. "And may you rot in Hell like every other English bastard!"

"Go ahead and hit him again, if it makes you feel better."

The assassins wheeled about in confusion, then dismay. Ensign Edwards stood in the doorway—bareheaded, coatless, unshod—with a loaded and primed pistol in his right hand. "I can only shoot the liver out of one of you, but I assure you I will kill the other with my bare hands."

Even the smithy of words could find none suited to the occasion.

"I followed you out when you went to take a leak," Marc said by way of helpful explanation, "and heard everything. You've gone and made a mess of my hat."

"What're you gonna do?" Connors was able to say at last.

"I want you to hop on that donkey and hee-haw your Irish arses out of this province."

"Now? In the middle of the night?"

"Now. You're lucky I don't haul you into Fort York and have you hanged before sun-up. Get going before I change my mind."

The peddlers tripped over one another scrambling out the door. Connors fell into a drift and lost a glove, but he didn't stop to retrieve it. They skedaddled to the donkey as if expecting at any moment to feel a lead ball between their shoulder blades. The tinkling of copper and ironware and sundry animal grunts were loud enough to rouse every wintering creature within ten miles.

"Hey," Connors called back from his precarious perch on the donkey's rump, "what about our saddlebag?"

"You can pick it up sometime at the Crawford's Corners post office, if you've got the courage to show up there!"

"You bastard! Our life savings are—" The sentence went unfinished as the donkey foundered in the snow and Connors tumbled off.

"If I see or hear of you two anywhere in this province, you won't have a life worth saving!"

Remounted, cold, wet, and dishevelled, the tinker and the wordsmith cursed the donkey forward, towards the Kingston Road and Toronto.

Marc took one step in their direction, raised his right arm, and fired the pistol. The ball went where it was aimed, into a thick branch just above the fleeing duo.

"Giddy-up, ya jackass! We got a maniac behind us!"

The donkey, true to the breed, slowed down.

That felt good, Marc thought, damn good.

MARC JUDGED IT TO BE ABOUT four o'clock in the morning. The three-quarter moon was shining in the windless, star-filled sky. He saddled up the horse, packed his gear, tossed the peddlers' saddlebag across the withers, and led his mount back to the Kingston Road. He would ride steadily until he reached Port Hope, rest a few hours, and proceed to his destination early the next afternoon.

He knew he should have taken half a day to escort the would-be murderers to Toronto, but Sir John's warrant and instructions outweighed all competing considerations. Nor could he ride into Crawford's Corners with his pistol primed and a pair of cuffed miscreants clanking the news of his arrival everywhere. Instead, he would have to be content with giving their names and a description to Constable Hatch, who would forward the information east and west by the first available coach or courier. Besides, two bumblers who connived to clobber you with a makeshift club in the middle of the night were dangerous only if you allowed them to be. Still, he would like to have known what their motive was.

As he veered onto King William's high road and let the horse settle into a canter, it occurred to Ensign Edwards that, in a very real sense, he had just experienced his first skirmish in the field, fired his first shot in the heat of battle, and lived to tell the tale.

THREE

U p here, about a hundred yards," Erastus Hatch hollered back to Marc, pointing to a trail of sorts.

"You'd have to know it was here to find it," Marc said,
catching up and drawing his horse to a halt beside the constable's.

"Joshua Smallman was born and raised in these parts. He
knew where he was going all right." Both men nudged their
horses forward into the drifts between the trees.

"Then you don't accept the story that he became disoriented in the blizzard and wandered into the deadfall in a fit
of panic?"

"You've been reading the magistrate's report," Hatch grinned. They had met less than an hour before, but Marc was beginning to like him already and, prematurely perhaps, to trust him. "I don't think Child himself believed what he wrote there. But it was the only conclusion that made sense."

"You think he met with foul play, then?"

Hatch waited until Marc was abreast of him and they had paused to let the horses rest. He turned to look directly at him before answering. "To be frank, I don't. Major Barnaby, the surgeon, came out here with Child and me on New Year's Day after the alarm was raised. Barnaby's an ex-army man and a good tracker. We were able to pick up Joshua's trail despite a little overnight snow, and it led us where we're headed right now. The three of us found the body. Charles looked him over real careful here at the scene and later at his surgery in Cobourg."

"He died when the deadfall struck him?"

"Possibly, but more likely some time afterwards. His neck wasn't broken. Poor bugger probably froze to death."

"But why was he out here?"

"I said I didn't think there was foul play, but I also figure he didn't trot out to this old Indian trail to enjoy the scenery on New Year's Eve, leaving his daughter-in-law and guests to fend for themselves."

"So you do believe he was coming to meet someone. A secret rendezvous, of some kind."

The horses plunged forward again, wheezing and protesting.

"Or he was out here in search of something."

"It would have to have been bigger than a moose to be seen in this stuff."

Hatch laughed, as he had often since their meeting at his house earlier in the afternoon. By temperament and build, the man had been destined to become a miller or smithy. He had a broad, wind-burnished face with a raw, unfinished look to it. That was true of so many of the native-born out here, Marc thought, even though their parents most probably had been undersized, underfed émigrés fleeing famine and persecution. Even their accents vanished, it seemed, in a single generation.

"Don't make sense, does it?" he said.

They dismounted and, with some difficulty (most of it on Marc's part), laced on their snowshoes. The horses had done all they could.

"This is where we found Joshua's big roan," Hatch said. "Despite last night's blow, you can still see where the poor beast thrashed about."

"Nothing had been taken or tampered with?"

"Nothing. And Joshua was carrying no money, according to his daughter-in-law."

"Bathsheba Smallman."

"Everybody around here calls her Beth. You'll get a chance to ask her yourself. The Smallman farm's right next to the mill. What she told the inquest, though, was that Joshua told her he'd got a message and had to go out. Nothing more."

"You found no note or letter on him?"

"No. And neither Beth nor any of the neighbour guests at the party remember any note being delivered."

Marc took his first giant steps on the raquettes, amazed to find himself on top of the snow. He felt the same light-headed exhilaration that might have come from waltzing on a cloud or striding over a Cumbrian lake—that is, until he tipped sideways into a drift and had to be hauled out by the grinning Hatch.

"You can't tell a snowshoe how to behave," he said, not unkindly. "Let it take you with it and you'll be fine."

"You could still follow Smallman's trail this far on that morning?" Marc said once he was upright and moving again.

"Just faintly, but clear enough. Till we came round this cedar."

They stopped. A few feet ahead the massive boles of several trees formed a natural aisle that any hunter or wayfarer would be foolish not to enter. Even now the scene before them was peaceful and innocent under the fresh snow: except for the huge log that stuck up odd-angled out of the drift at the base of the arch. They moved cautiously towards it, as if its murderous power were still somehow extant.

"Was there any sign that the contraption had been recently re-rigged?" Marc said, staring down at the brute log and the tangle of rawhide rigging that had provided the trigger for its lethal drop.

"None. As you can see, it's the kind of trap the Mississauga Indians used to make when these were their prime hunting grounds. The rawhide is old and quite dried out. Joshua was just unlucky, I figure. Nine times out of ten this rope'll snap when it's hit and leave the deadfall in place. Still, the log is designed to fall when the shim is given the slightest shock."

"You searched the area all around here for other footprints or signs of human disturbance?"

"Yes—once we'd recovered from the shock of seeing one of our dearest friends lying there dead and stiff."

"I'm sorry," Marc said. "I must remember he was no stranger to you."

"As soon as he came back to help out on the farm after his son's death last year, we took him into our company. He was one of us. He joined us every Wednesday evening he could."

"Us?"

"The magistrate, the major, me, and Durfee, the postmaster. He was supposed to be with us on New Year's Eve over at Child's. It's a sort of gentleman's club, made up of like-minded citizens, you might say."

"Loyal Tory gentlemen," Marc said with a slight smile.

"That's right," Hatch said, taking no offence.

"You were all there, then?" Marc said, more abruptly than he'd intended.

"Could one of us have been floundering about out here, you mean? Lurking in the shadows like Madame Guillotine?"

"No, of course not. Anyone else would have had to come in along the same route that Smallman did, and that means tracks—deep hoof marks or snowshoe tracks." He was staring back at the turbulence his own raquettes had left in the snow. "And you found no tracks beyond the trap?"

"We went carefully on ahead for a good twenty yards or more. Then we fanned out in a circle twice as wide. Nothing. Not even a rabbit track. Our friend died out here alone, looking for someone or something. Even so, who could have known or predicted that he would take this particular route? Or that the damnable device would work, if someone were obliging enough to blunder into it? It hadn't been touched for years."

After a pause Marc said, "What's beyond that ridge up there?"

"That's the rim of the cliff before it drops down to the lake," Hatch said, suddenly more alert.

"The frozen lake," Marc said.

THE TWO MEN STOOD ON THE ridge and stared out at the endless, ice-covered stretch of Lake Ontario, more vast than most of the Earth's seas. A little farther to the east, it would be frozen completely across its thirty-mile breadth, and on any Sunday afternoon you would be able to see cutters and sleighs and homemade sleds sliding merrily in both directions between the American republic and the British province. Families pulled apart by borders and politics and memories of the War of 1812 reconvened as soon as the lake froze, as if humanity was meant to be without division or dissent.

"You figure somebody may have come up here from the ice?" Hatch said.

"It's thick enough to hold a horse, even a sleigh. And the highway at Crawford's Corners can't be more than a quarter of a mile from the shoreline, can it?"

"True enough. That would explain why we only found Joshua's tracks coming in here. But how would anybody coming up along the lakeshore know exactly where he was? You'd have to be an Indian or a wolf."

"What's that down there? To your right. Looks like an inlet or a little bay to me."

Hatch's eyes lit up. "That's Bass Cove, a favourite fishing spot in the spring."

Marc began to move along the ridge in that direction, raquettes in hand. Then he stood straight up and didn't move until Hatch had joined him. He pointed to a shadowy indentation in the escarpment just below them on the wooded side of the ridge. "I think we've found our rendezvous," he said.

Together they scrabbled down to a ledge that was invisible from above but easily seen from the woods just below. They pushed through a dark entranceway into a low, cramped, but otherwise habitable cave. They waited until their eyes had adjusted to the murky, late-afternoon light before commenting.

"We aren't the first visitors here besides the bears," Marc said.

"These ashes were made by more than one fire," Hatch added, holding up a tin cup and a blackened soup spoon.

"And something's been stored here at some time or other," Marc said from his crouching position at the far side of the cave. "I can see the ridge-lines in the dirt: crates or barrels, I'd say."

Outside again, Hatch said, almost to himself, "Still, we don't have the foggiest idea of whether anybody was waiting here for Joshua Smallman two weeks ago. And if they were, they might just've been as friendly as hostile. Until we know why he came out here, we're just spittin' in the wind."

But Marc was already edging along away from the mouth of the cave, bent low like a hound on the spoor. Hatch was tempted to chuckle at the ensign's antics but didn't.

"Come over here, Constable Hatch."

"Only if you call me Erastus, or just plain Hatch. I'm only a part-time, supernumerary constable, and under duress to boot."

From their vantage point they had an unimpeded view through the evergreens to a spot somewhere on the trail they themselves had made: their tracks were clearly visible.

"That's the trail all right," Hatch said, puzzled. "But the deadfall's farther down."

"On the other side of that patch of evergreens. You can just see the limbs of the big oak it was attached to."

"But if someone was standing here that night—in his snowshoes—looking down and waving Joshua on, he would've come straight up this open stretch and missed the trap."

"Look at the size of the drifts down there," Marc said. "They're deep, but not deep enough to cover the trees that've been knocked down by storms or something. See how they're blocking the way?"

"Knocked down by lightning," Hatch said, spotting the telltale blackened branches and stark, splintered trunks poking through the snow. "You figure somebody stood here and encouraged Joshua? Maybe even pointed to the left, knowing the Indian trail went that way and—"

"Knowing that the deadfall was just ahead at the next bend."

"Possible," Hatch said slowly. "Still, it sounds a bit farfetched. Two maybes don't make a certainty."

"Could a person who was really expert on snowshoes have gone down to the trap from here, come back up again, and then whisked away all signs of his tracks?"

"Oh, I think so, 'specially if there'd been some additional snow to cover the brush marks. But you're forgetting one important thing: anybody meeting Joshua here that night might just as easily have been a friend."

"Then why didn't he walk down to the trap to help the man? He couldn't have been sure that Smallman was killed outright. And that horse of his would have been making a hell of a racket. They can smell death, I've been told."

"That's so, but we're still guessing that somebody was actually here."

"Not now we aren't," Marc said. He was hunched over a place where the ledge broadened slightly. Hatch leaned over his shoulder. The webbed signature of a pair of raquettes stared up at them as clean-edged as a palm print. The sheltering rock had kept it almost free of drifting snow and untouched by the recent squall driving off the lake.

"And look at this," Hatch said. "A stem broken off a clay pipe, right beside it."

He handed it to Marc, who gazed at it thoughtfully, then tucked it into his tunic.

"Every man and most boys in the township've got a pipe like that."

Marc was still thinking. "What are the odds of any two residents of this county being out in such a godforsaken place in the dead of winter on separate and unrelated errands?" he said.

"You know what all this means, then," Hatch said solemnly.

"I do," Marc said. "We've got a murder on our hands, or something damn close to it."

•   •   •

THEY MADE A MORE THOROUGH SEARCH of the cave with the aid of an improvised torch but found nothing more of interest. The place seemed to have been used over an extended period of time, months perhaps, as a temporary storage depot for whatever it was that needed to be hidden, possibly guns or rum. Access to it would have been via the ice-bound lake, where the slope, being exposed to frequent snow squalls, would leave no trace of the traffic over it. Marc himself scrutinized the deadfall trap, but there was not a piece of bark bared or twig snapped off to indicate any tampering had been done to ensure its working on cue.

"I have to believe you're right," Hatch sighed as they turned west onto the Kingston Road and headed back towards Crawford's Corners. "Someone, a smuggler or an insurrectionist, was standing up there when poor, unsuspecting Joshua came up the Indian trail. There doesn't seem to be any other reason for a man to stand on that exposed ledge and puff on a pipe except to get a view of the trail and anybody on it. And if he didn't intend to kill Joshua, then he left him in the snow to die, which amounts to the same thing in my book."

"And His Majesty's," Marc said.

"How do you plan to proceed with this?" Hatch said, alluding to the lieutenant-governor's warrant that Marc had shown him. "I gather you don't intend to involve Sheriff MacLachlan in Cobourg?"

"Not right away," Marc said. "Now that we're almost certain we have a crime of some sort here, wouldn't it be wiser to let people think everything's all right as is, especially those with something to hide?"

"But you'll have to question folks, won't you?"

"When I know a lot more than I do now."

"You'll have to tell Beth Smallman," Hatch said, in a tone halfway between command and entreaty.

"Probably. I'll work that out when I see her."

"You can walk over there in the morning, if you like. And tomorrow being Wednesday, I can just cart you along to the weekly meeting of the Georgian Club, as we call it. You'll get all the background information you need there. In the meantime, it's getting late, and a man of my girth and wit requires a regular intake of his daughter's cooking."

"Better than army rations?"

"What isn't?" Hatch laughed. "And you'll be wanting to meet my Winnifred. She'll be back from the quilting bee by now and wondering where the hell I've gotten to."

The not-unhandsome daughter, Marc mused. Would she prove handsome enough to account for the prolonged stay of a visiting ensign—perhaps one of her dead mother's distant cousins from the Old Country?

On their right as they passed the intersection of the highway and the Pringle Sideroad, Hatch pointed to a quarry-stone house just visible through a screen of trees. "That's

Philander Child's establishment. He's a county magistrate, but most folks just call him the Squire. We'll be going up there tomorrow night."

"And that must be the local tavern." Marc indicated a square-log cabin of considerable size, gabled like a true inn. Nearby were several semi-detached sheds and one rambling livery stable.

"One of them. The respectable one. Run by James Durfee and his wife. You'll meet James tomorrow night."

"He's the postmaster?"

"That's right."

"Then I'll need to meet him now," Marc said.

AFTER INTRODUCING MARC TO DURFEE SIMPLY as a visiting gentleman from the garrison and a protégé of Sir John Colborne's, Constable Hatch took his leave and rode across the intersection, or "corners," towards the mill and his house next to it. If James Durfee was meant to be impressed by Hatch's remarks, he restrained himself admirably. He was a plain-speaking man, born in Upper Canada but of Scots extraction, with a ready smile qualified only by a pair of watchful dark eyes.

"We don't get many soldiers on furlough this far from Muddy York, as we used to call Toronto before she took on those citified airs," he said. "Despite the obvious attractions hereabouts."

Marc smiled as he was expected to. "I'm here on official business," he said, accepting with a nod the wee dram offered and seating himself on one of the wooden chairs scattered about the outer room, which no doubt served as the principal drinking quarters of the inn. A plank bar and tapped keg of beer stood nearby. At this moment, Marc was the only customer.

"Business of a pleasant sort, I trust," Durfee said.

"I'm not at liberty to say much about it at the moment, but Hatch is bringing me to your club meeting tomorrow night. I'll have a lot more to say then."

"Ah," Durfee said, downing his whisky. "You'll be most welcome. But it's not been the same club without Joshua Smallman."

"You knew him well?" When Durfee gave him a quizzical look, Marc said quickly, "Hatch told me about the tragic accident."

"I see. And tragic it was. Joshua and me grew up in the Cobourg area, you know. Joshua went off to York when he was twenty, married, and did well in the dry goods trade. Then when his son, his only child, turned his back on the business, there was a falling out of sorts. Jesse, poor bugger, came here when this township was first opened up—to become a farmer and show his father he could make it on his own."

"Hatch mentioned that the young Mrs. Smallman is a widow."

Durfee again seemed puzzled by how much information

this casual visitor had managed to cajole out of the usually discreet miller. But there was an openness, naïveté even, about the beardless young man before him that begged his confidence and trust.

"Jesse died a year ago December," Durfee said. "That's why Joshua came back. And why we done all we could for him and Beth these past months."

Marc waited quietly until Durfee whispered, "He hung himself. In the barn. His wife found him."

EMMA DURFEE PRESSED MARC TO STAY for supper, but he assured her that Winnifred Hatch was expecting him to dine at the mill within the hour. Mrs. Durfee, as round and plump as her husband was spare and gnarled, smiled as if she were privy to some mutual conspiracy. "Ahh," was all she said, but it was meaning enough. When Marc failed to take the bait, she added with feigned reluctance, "Well, there ain't a man in the district brave or foolhardy enough to ignore the wishes of the handsome Miss Hatch."

Marc was beginning to wonder if "handsome" was part of Miss Hatch's Christian name, in the manner of the pilgrims' "Goody."

When Emma Durfee left the room to tend to her own cooking, her husband leaned forward and said to Marc, "You must've had some other reason for droppin' by than to say hello and sample my finest."

"Hatch tells me you have a safe."

Which turned out to be an understatement, for the iron box that governed the otherwise modest space of Durfee's office (itself adjoined to the taproom by a sturdy oak door) was roomy enough to have housed a successful brood of chickens and intimidating enough to have kept them safe from a regiment of foxes.

"It's been in the wife's family for years. We sledded it over the lake last February." Durfee fiddled with the dial and then drew the door open slowly, like a proud jailer who has no doubt about his dungeon's impregnability. "What've you got that needs protectin'?"

Marc dropped the leather pouch he had taken from the Yankees' saddlebag onto Durfee's rolltop desk. Then he gave the innkeeper the same abbreviated and carefully edited version of his encounter with Connors and O'Hurley he had given Hatch.

"I'm surprised to hear that," Durfee said, letting his breath whistle through the pair of wooden teeth on the left side of his jaw to emphasize his point. "Them two've been sidlin' about the province for several years now, and they're like most Yankee peddlers we get here—quick with the lip and about as trustworthy as a bull in a field of heifers. But they've never been known to do violence to anyone: all bluster and no delivery."

"I kept their saddlebag as security," Marc said. "As an agent of the Crown, I'd like you to witness my opening it, and then keep it in your safe until I can deliver it personally to Government House or the sheriff of York. I'm going to write up a description of the two renegades and have you send it off to Toronto tomorrow."

"I'll put it on the special courier comin' out of Cobourg at noon," Durfee said, and he stood beside Marc while he unbuckled the pouch and shook its contents onto the desktop. A wad of papers secured by a lady's pink garter fell out.

"A souvenir of the peddlin' wars," Durfee said dryly, giving the garter a playful snap. "But this ain't the profits from tinkerin'," he added.

"It's money of some sort," Marc said.

"American banknotes," Durfee said, riffling the two-inch wad.

"They look brand-new."

"They are new. Hundred dollar notes of the Second Bank of the United States."

Marc nodded to Durfee to place the confiscated money and the pouch in the safe.

"Guns or grog, I'd say," Durfee said as he gave the dial a spin.

"I'll let the sheriff know about it," Marc said. "I've done all I can for now."

"That you have," Durfee said, but his watchful eye suggested otherwise. "Now you best be trottin' across to the miller's. The handsome Miss Hatch don't like to be kept waitin'."

• • •

As Winnifred Hatch poured her guest his second cup of tea, she watched the hot liquid flow into the china cup as if it might, unfettered from her strict supervision, dash off towards some other cup. The tea settled obediently where it was directed. Miss Hatch had, of course, asked the table if it would prefer another round—"You'll have another cup, then?"—but it was only nominally a question.

Thomas Goodall—the angular young man who, Marc learned, assisted in the milling during the season and managed the modest farm as a sharecropper—swallowed his second cup in two gulps and said, "Well, I'll be off, then. Got three cows to milk."

The chatelaine of the house stopped the progress of her own teacup several inches below her thin, unrouged lip.

"If you please, ma'am." Thomas dropped his eyes and slid noisily off his chair.

"For God's sake, man, go to your cows." Hatch laughed. "They'll be popping their udders."

Mary Huggan, the Irish serving girl who had, in the strange custom of the country, joined them after her initial duties, giggled into her apron, then sneezed to compound her embarrassment.

"As you can see, Ensign Edwards, we don't often have ladies or gentlemen in to dine," Winnifred said.

"One lady in the house is more than enough," Hatch said with a grin.

"That was as fine a meal as I've had since I arrived in York," Marc said.

Winnifred Hatch accepted the compliment with a curt but not ungracious nod. Either she had not bothered to change her clothes following her return from the quilting bee near Port Hope, or she always dressed in a manner designed to display her widely acknowledged handsomeness. Her magenta blouse, of silk or some such frilly fluff, hugged her tall, Tudor neck almost to the chin, flaring downward around long and elegant arms and outward to suggest subtly the curving of a robust bosom. Her purple, fluted skirt was pleasingly cinched at the waist by a lavender sash that might have seemed overly bold, tartish even, were it not for her regal bearing.

"And just how long have you been with us?" she said in a voice that a Milanese contralto might have envied.

"About eight months," Marc said. "I arrived at Fort York last May."

"And you have been discovering some of our quainter customs, I trust?"

The miller's eyes were dancing delightedly at this turn in the conversation. His daughter, meantime, let her considerable gaze linger on their guest, expecting, it appeared, something more than a polite reply but giving no intimation on which side of the question she herself was situated.

Marc smiled in what he took to be his most winning manner (the one that had such a volcanic effect on the female gentry of Toronto) and said, "I am a soldier, ma'am. A man of action. We have little time to concern ourselves overly much with the manners and deportment of His Majesty's subjects, scattered as they be over the whole of the globe."

Hatch chortled, but he was brought up short by a glance from his daughter. The quickened anger in her reproof, followed immediately by a softening look that bespoke daughterly indulgence and forbearance, roused in Marc another sort of quickening. An image of the handsome Winnifred—her burnished mahogany hair loosed from its coiled bun, her Spode-white flesh gleaming in the moonlight—popped lasciviously into his head and made him feel foolish and abashed.

"We are doubtless a source of constant chagrin—and some sport, I suspect—for those raised within calling distance of the Throne."

"I was raised in the countryside," Marc said, as evenly as he could manage.

"Is that a boast or a whinge?" The onset of a smile trembled on her upper lip, and stilled.

"I have found much to delight me in Canada and little that has been discomfiting."

"Well said, lad." Hatch laughed. "Now let's go in to the fire and have a wee toddy so Mary can clean up the mess we've made."

Marc was only moderately surprised when, several

minutes later, Winnifred joined them in the parlour, taking her place in one of the leather chairs arrayed around the blazing hearth. And he tried not to look too "discomfited" when she drew a clay pipe from under her shawl and clamped it like a sailor between her flawless white teeth. He recovered sufficiently to realize that she was waiting, ladylike, for him to reach across with his lit tinder and assist her in igniting the plug she had just tamped down. The look she gave him as he did so was inscrutable, though mockery, raillery, and mischievous glee all came to mind.

As MARC REMOVED THE WARMING PAN from under the quilts on his bed and slipped on his nightshirt, he tried to stave off exhaustion long enough to reflect on what had been accomplished in the thirty hours or so since his departure from Government House and Toronto. While congratulating himself on having so expeditiously and discreetly confirmed the existence of a crime only suspected by Sir John, and having set in train at Durfee's the means of dealing with the peddlers, he tried not to think of Commander-in-Chief Colborne preparing for what would surely be an armed insurrection in Quebec before the year was out, leaving behind his favoured ensign. However, a speedy and successful resolution of the matter at hand would, if the world were just, guarantee his promotion and, more important, a place somewhere in the thick of the coming battle. This cheering thought was interrupted by the more mundane recollection that he had brought with him only two changes of linen and one additional blouse. A speedy resolution might well be a necessity.

More happily, the mattress was a feather tick and the quilts thick and soft. Erastus Hatch, who seemed to have enjoyed every aspect of Marc's company, had given him the best bedroom, the one he himself had used when his wife was still alive. The miller now slept in a smaller room at the front of the house next to the dining area. Some time earlier, Marc had heard the two women, mistress of the manor and scullery maid, enter the room across the hallway from his, chatting in low but amiable voices. He found this amusing to recall, but before he could summon a smile, he was asleep.

HE WOKE WITH A START, SUFFERED a moment of disorientation, then rolled over onto his side and listened hard. A door had just closed. He heard the soft tread of bare feet on the pine boards of the hall—moving away towards the square-log cabin attached at the back of the stone building. This, Hatch had told him, had once been his parents' home—the first building on the property. There was a summer kitchen back there and several cubicles where, apparently, Thomas Goodall kept house.

Marc pulled his door open in time to hear a stifled giggle from one of the shadowy recesses beyond the hall. Young Mary doing a little night riding in the hired man's bed? Well, some practices changed little from one country to another.

Would that notion please the handsome Miss Hatch, or dismay her?

FOUR

Any euphoria generated by Tuesday's events had evaporated by morning. Ensign Edwards awoke slightly disoriented, his spirits benumbed.

Winnifred Hatch arrived at the table moments after Marc, swathed in a taffeta kimono that flattered the shapely figure beneath it. Still, Mistress Hatch carried herself with such confidence that she could have come clothed in diaphanous veils and still retained an air of rigid respectability. Winnifred Hatch had not learned to blush. In a straightforward manner she asked Marc if he had slept well and refilled his cup with coffee. This kindness was interrupted by the arrival of Thomas and Erastus from the barn. The whiff of manure, muted somewhat by the winter chill, blended uneasily with the aroma of coffee and the tang of fried pork.

"How is the Guernsey doing?" Winnifred asked Thomas. He mumbled something positive but kept his eyes on his plate. Behind them, Mary Huggan sang softly over her stove.

"We'll take our coffee into the parlour and talk," Erastus announced.

"FIRST OF ALL," THE MILLER SAID, "we need to dream up an excuse for you poking your nose about Crawford's Corners. Then, whatever else we find out between now and Saturday, when I've got a meeting with Sheriff MacLachlan, has to be made official. After that, you and the sheriff can decide between you how to execute the governor's warrant. Fair enough?"

"Agreed," Marc said. The hot food, the coffee, and the bracing sight of the two young women were working wonders on his mood. The prospect of facing the challenges of the day revived and excited him. However he realized, somewhat reluctantly, that the ruse of his courting the miller's daughter would not do to explain his continuing presence.

"I've got a suggestion on the first score," Hatch said. "Every year about this time your quartermaster comes through the county, looking to buy surplus wheat or fodder. We can tell folks you're one of his advance men reconnoitring the region. I've got a silo full of grain, my own and others', that will most likely end up at the garrison in any event. Once I drop the hint to Thomas or Mary, the news'll be all over the district by nightfall."

"I've already accompanied him on a similar foray, in December," Marc said, brightening perceptibly. "We're buying extra grain against the coming of troubles in Quebec."

"Splendid," Hatch said, restoking his pipe.

"I know what to ask. And it'll give me an excuse to visit the local farmers and snoop about without raising suspicion. I've got more than a hunch that the man we're looking for will be found amongst the left-wing zealots and Reform fanatics along the back roads." Marc knew that Hatch was waiting for elaboration, but he was not prepared to tell anyone, yet, about Smallman's role as Sir John's secret agent in Crawford's Corners. After all, this was the trump card that would give him the edge he required to sift and assess every tidbit of information that might come his way in the days ahead.

"Well, then," Hatch said, getting up, "I guess it's time for you to meet Beth Smallman."

"Don't bother Thomas about getting my horse ready," Marc said. "I'll just walk across to her place."

"You going to tell her what we think we know?"

"I haven't really made up my mind," Marc said truthfully. "I need to talk to her first."

"That's a good idea," Hatch said, approving the instincts of this tunicked officer half his age. Then he grinned and added, "Beth Smallman is no ordinary woman." It was as ambiguous a remark as Hatch was likely to make.

THE SMALLMAN FARM, WHICH HAD WITNESSED much tragedy in the space of twelve months, lay adjacent to the mill on the north side. Taking Hatch's advice, Marc followed a trodden path towards Crawford Creek that took him past the outbuildings of the mill where Thomas and a stableboy no taller than the fork he wielded were mucking out the cattle stalls. The colonel's horse whinnied at Marc, but he kept on walking until he came abreast of the mammoth gristmill itself, its water wheel stilled by the ice of the creek. Two impressive silos made out of the same quarry stone as the main house stood as testament to the growing prosperity of the young province. Land was currency here, Marc thought, and the great leveller.

Beyond the silos he found a well-trampled path that meandered along beside the creek. So this was how the locals travelled by foot when the roads grew impassable—to spread all the news worth embroidering. Marc pictured a network of spidery filaments from house to barn to neighbouring house, indifferent to woods, weather, and other natural impediments. He went north on the path a hundred yards or so, enjoying the briskness of the early-morning air, until he spied through an opening in the evergreens on the riverbank the pitched roof of a clapboard barn, and above it, a little farther on, wisps of woodsmoke.

Next to the barn, a log hut with a plank door and single window sat hip-deep in drifts. The meagre smoke from its stovepipe slumped and frayed along the roofline. The door below it opened with a jerk.

"Got yourself lost, mister?"

Marc stopped, hid his surprise, and said, "Ah, good morning. My name is Marc Edwards. I've come from Constable Hatch's place—to see Mrs. Smallman, should she be at home."

"Officer Edwards, is it?" The old man, for he seemed indisputably old even by the gnarled norms of Upper Canada, glared fixedly at the interloper, blocking the footpath.

"I'm here on official business."

"Are ye now?" The old fellow gave no ground.

Marc met his stare, then for a moment he almost laughed as the impudent oaf stooped into what was meant to be a fearsome crouch but resembled nothing so much as a petulant crayfish, for he was all bony angles, his ungloved fingers were stiffened into arthritic claws, and the beady peppercorns of his eyes wobbled in rage.

"On Governor Colborne's warrant," Marc snapped. He had already said more than he had planned, and he held his tongue now with mounting impatience.

"The governor that was, you mean?"

That the news of Colborne's reassignment had travelled so far and so fast surprised and momentarily stunned Marc.

"Is Mrs. Smallman home or not?"

"Where else would an honest woman be?" There was a rasping, spittled quality to the voice that skewed whatever outrage might have been intended.

"I demand that you give me your name, sir, and then stand out of my way!" Marc reached down for the familiar haft of his sword and came up empty.

"No need to lose your temper, lad. There's plenty of daylight left." And he scuttled sideways into the corral beside the barn, where he appeared to execute a crab-like jig.

Marc walked with a dignified pace towards the house twenty yards ahead. The old fart was still jabbering to himself, or to some animal willing to grant him equal status.

Up ahead, the Smallman house was more typical of Canadian rural residences than was the stone structure of the miller Hatch: a notched, squared-timber block, caulked with limestone cement, small windows of murky "local" glass that let in an impoverished glow, a pitched roof over a cramped second storey, and a snow-covered stoop. Marc strode past the windows along the north side, one of which was draped with a swath of black crêpe, put one boot on the porch, and raised his fist to knock. The door swung inward and fully open.

"Nobody knocks in these parts," a light, feminine voice said from the shadows within. "I've been expectin' you, Mr.—"

"Edwards," Marc said. "Ensign Edwards."

"I TAKE IT YOU'VE MET ELIJAH," Bathsheba Smallman, known to all as Beth, said to Marc. They were sitting opposite one another in the parlour area—marked off only by a braided rug and an apt arrangement of hand-hewn chairs made welcoming by quilted seat pads—balancing cup and saucer with accompanying bread and jam (the bread fresh out of the iron pot over the fire, the jam homemade).

"Yes, but I'm afraid he wasn't overly helpful," Marc said just as a spurt of jam struck his chin. He rubbed at the offending blob, then licked it off his finger.

"Huckleberry," Beth said. "Grows like a weed in these parts."

"It's delicious."

"Elijah's harmless," Beth said. "He's very protective of me and Aaron."

"Your brother?"

"That's right. You'll meet him when he gets in from collectin' the eggs, if he doesn't get lost first."

When Marc looked concerned, she smiled reassuringly and said, "Sometimes he gathers more wool than eggs."

Marc could not take his eyes off Beth Smallman, even though he was aware of her discomfort as she glanced away and back again only to find him helplessly staring. As she did, sunlight pouring through the window behind her lit the russet tints of her unbound hair and framed her figure. She was as small and trim and wholesome as Winnifred Hatch was tall and hot-tempered and daunting. And he was charmed by the teasing lilt of her voice, with its exotic accent.

"You're in the district to look at buyin' grain for the garrison, you say?"

Marc blinked, took a sip of his tea, and forced his gaze past her to the petit point figure of Christ on the wall beside the window. "That's correct. I'm merely lining up possible sites for the quartermaster's inspection later this month."

"Elijah tells me we've taken in more Indian corn than our cows can eat."

"I'll take a look before I go, then." The tea was consumed, and the bread and jam with it.

"I'm sure Elijah will oblige you." Beth smiled. She was wearing a plain blouse and heavy skirt with a knitted cardigan tied across her shoulders. A white apron and cap lay on the pine table near the fire, waiting.

"There's somethin' else on your mind, isn't there, Ensign Edwards?"

"Yes, there is, ma'am. And I apologize for being so roundabout in approaching it."

She caught the sudden seriousness of his tone and looked intently towards him, willing him to speak.

"I have some disturbing news," he began.

"I can think of no news that could be more disturbing

than what I've had to bear these past weeks." She steadied her voice. He turned away briefly, but she had quietly composed herself, except for a slight glistening at the edge of her blue, unblinking eyes.

"And December last as well," he said softly.

Now he had her full attention and more: something sharp and suspecting entered her look—at once vulnerable and hardened by necessity.

"Why have you come?" she said. "Who are you?"

"I have been ordered here by the lieutenant-governor to investigate your father-in-law's death."

"Investigate?"

"Yes. And I have already reached the conclusion that Joshua Smallman was in all likelihood murdered."

A thump and a scraping clatter from the kitchen area forestalled any immediate reaction to Marc's news. Beth rose to her feet, a look of concern flashing across her face. "It's Aaron," she said.

Into the centre of the room came a tall, thin young man with an unkempt mane of reddish hair. He dragged one foot along behind him and, with a lurching effort, swung a basket of warm eggs up and onto a sideboard. As he did so, the left half of his face stretched. "I d-d-didn't break any," he said with a lopsided grin. Then he spotted the visitor and froze.

"I didn't expect you would," Beth said. "Say hello to Ensign Edwards."

Marc rose.

"Mr. Edwards, this is my brother, Aaron McCrae."

Aaron simply stared, not in fright but in fascination at the scarlet frock coat, many-buttoned tunic, and glittering buckles so abruptly and magically set before him. "Where's your s-s-s-sword?" he asked.

"I am pleased to meet you," Marc said, "and my sword's tucked safely in my saddle-roll."

"Aaron's goin' to be sixteen next month," Beth said.

The lad nodded but seemed more interested in shuffling an inch or two closer to this mirage in his parlour.

Beth touched him on the arm. "Mr. Edwards and I have some important business to talk over. Go out and help Elijah with the feed, would you?"

Reluctantly the youth shuffled himself out the back door.

"He was born like that. With the palsy. He's not really simple, but it's a strain for him to talk. With us, though, there isn't much need."

They sat down again.

A log rolled off its andiron, spraying sparks into the air, and the brief flare sent a wave of heat to the far side of the large room where they were seated, reminding them how cold it had become. Beth pulled her cardigan on with a shy, self-conscious gesture, but Marc had already averted his eyes.

"Murder is a terrible word, Mr. Edwards," she said at last.

"Does it surprise you to hear it used in association with your father-in-law?"

She did not answer right away. "I didn't believe the magistrate's findin' for one minute," she said slowly. "Father wouldn't have got himself lost out there, even in a blizzard."

"More experienced woodsmen have," Marc said. "Or so I've been told," he felt constrained to add.

"The horse he was riding was the only one we've ever owned."

"Your . . . husband's?"

She nodded. "All he had to do was drop the reins and Belgium would've carried him home safe and sound."

"You told this to the inquest?"

She smiled wanly. "I did."

"Mrs. Smallman, I'm certain you are right."

If she found this remark unexpected or patronizing, she gave no sign. "He went out there for a reason, that much I do know," she said.

"And I believe that that reason, when we discover it, will lead us to his murderer."

"You forget that he walked into a bear-trap," she said. "That was . . . tragic, but not murder." She swallowed hard, fighting off tears, and suddenly Marc wished he were any place but here.

As quickly and tactfully as he could, Marc told her what he and Hatch had found the previous afternoon out near Bass Cove.

"You're saying someone just stood up there and watched him die?"

"Yes. And that is tantamount to murder, especially if your father-in-law was deliberately lured out there."

She turned and looked closely at him. "Joshua Smallman was a lovable man. He could not bring himself to tell a lie. He had no enemies. He gave up his business in town to come back here and help me run the farm." Her voice thickened. "He was the finest man I've ever known." The pause and the candidness of her glance confirmed that she was including her husband in the appraisal. "If he was called out on New Year's Eve, it was to assist a friend or someone in need."

Marc hesitated long enough for Beth to discern that he had absorbed and appreciated the reasonableness of this claim. After all, it coincided with everything he had heard so far about Joshua Smallman. Still, someone seemed to have wished him harm, or at the very least colluded in his death. He pushed ahead, gently. "Would you tell me as much as you can remember about that evening? If it's too painful, I could return another time."

"I'll make some more tea," she said.

"WE WERE PLANNIN' TO HAVE A little celebration here to mark the end of the year, it bein' also a year to the day since Father'd arrived. You understand, though, it couldn't've been entirely a celebration."

"Yes. Your . . . husband must have been uppermost in your thoughts."

"Still, we were preparin' a small party, with the Huggan

girls, Emma Durfee, Thomas Goodall. We'd even asked Elijah to join us, but he'd already dashed off to visit Ruby the cook up at the squire's."

"Philander Child's cook?"

"Yes. Father felt strongly that we had an obligation to these kind people, whatever our own sorrows might be. About six o'clock, right after milkin' and supper, one of Mr. Child's servants came to the door and said they were expectin' Father at the gatherin' of the Georgian Club—"

"I know about that," Marc said. "Had your father forgotten about the New Year's celebration up at Child's?"

"He said—rather mysteriously, I thought—that he was through with all that frivolousness. I know he'd missed a few meetings of late, and he seemed to be growin' a bit weary of their whist games and political chatter, but I was still surprised when he suggested that we plan our own celebration. Anyway, he sent the servant back with a polite refusal, and we started to get ready for some mulled wine and a few treats Father'd brought us from Cobourg."

"Did he seem upset or agitated?"

"No. I could see he was sad, of course, as I was, but we were both tryin' very hard not to be. Mary Huggan and her sisters were due to come over at seven. Father'd even hauled his violin out of the trunk."

"What happened, then, to call him so suddenly away from all this?"

"I can't say for sure. Just before seven, he went out to check on the animals for the night."

"A regular routine?"

"Yes. Once in a blue moon Elijah gets into the liquor and so Father always checked the barn with him, or on his own, before comin' in for the evenin'."

"As he did that night."

"I can only assume so. Father was gone a little longer than usual, I think, but the girls had arrived at the front door gigglin' and carryin' on, so I can't say for sure. But when he did come in, he was a changed man."

"Describe him, please, as precisely as you can."

"As I told the magistrate, he was excited. Not pretendin' to be happy as he'd been before. 'I've got to go out, Beth, dear,' he said. 'Just for half an hour or so.' When I looked amazed, he smiled and told me there was nothin' to worry about . . ."

Despising himself, and beginning to feel more than a little resentment at the predicament in which Sir John had so cavalierly placed him, Marc forced himself to ask, "Did he have a note or letter or paper of any kind in his hand or on his person?"

"No. But he said he'd gotten a message, an important one that could change all our lives for the better."

"Those were his exact words?"

"Yes," she said. "I've been unable to forget them."

Marc pressed on lest his nerve fail him utterly. "But you saw no letter, and he never said or hinted who had sent this message to him?"

"I told the inquest that I heard what could've been paper

rustlin' inside his coat. But he'd been doin' the year-end accounts earlier in the day and so there was nothing surprising about that."

"The surgeon says no papers of any kind were found on him."

"I know. I could've been wrong. I was so shocked to hear him say he was headin' out into that awful weather and just abandonin' his guests, I wasn't thinkin' too straight." She sipped at her tea, found it unconsoling, and said, "But he seemed genuinely excited. Happy, even. I heard him ride out on Belgium twenty minutes later."

"If there was a note, with instructions about a rendezvous and some bait to lure him to Bass Cove, could anyone else here have read it?"

Beth Smallman peered up at Marc with a look of puzzlement, pity, and the beginnings of anger. "I'm pleased you are takin' such an interest in Father, and I would like some questions about that night to have better answers, but my husband's father was an honest and well-loved gentleman. If somebody deliberately killed him, then you'll have to come up with something less fanciful than notions about secret notes and mysterious footprints in the snow. You've got to hate or fear somebody with a passion before you can kill them. If there was a note, I was the only person here that night capable of readin' it. Unless you suspect Emma Durfee."

Marc got up and made a stiff bow. Beth's features softened, and in other circumstances he was confident she would have smiled. "I have inconvenienced you long enough and imposed unconscionably on your hospitality," he said, wrestling his way into his greatcoat.

Beth took an elbow and helped him complete the task.

At the door she said, "You will let me know what you find?"

"I can do no less, ma'am."

"Call me Beth, please."

He touched the peak of his cap and left.

MARC WAS GRATEFUL FOR THE SLOW walk back to the mill, one that didn't include a further encounter with the misanthropic Elijah. He needed a few quiet moments to mull over what he had learned before rehashing it with Erastus Hatch.

He was convinced that a note had been delivered. Joshua's decision to leave the house had been made sometime in the half hour or so in which he was checking out the barn. Most likely as he was returning to the house, someone gave it to him—a servant or stableboy on foot or someone who had ridden in from farther afield specifically for the purpose. The need for detailed directions and some elaborate "hook" strongly suggested written instructions, but a personally delivered oral message, though riskier, was not out of the question.

At some point he realized he was going to have to interrogate Elijah about when he had left for the Child estate and whether he had seen his master beforehand. But deep down he was certain that, until some motive became clear, little beyond informed speculation was possible. Nevertheless, he was still in possession of a salient fact known only to him: Joshua Smallman was an informer for Sir John. No one in the region, not even a friend like Hatch, was aware of this. But had someone discovered or guessed at the truth? Some rabid annexationist or firebrand among the apostles of the rabble-rousing Mackenzie? Even so, the area was thick with Tories and loyalists, any one of whom could be (and likely was) viewed as a spy with a direct link to the powerful Family Compact in Toronto or the government itself. You'd have to arrange for the deaths of a lot of locals to assuage that particular fever, Marc thought. At the moment, the most plausible premise was that Smallman had discovered some critical information, the revelation of which presented a real danger to a particular individual or cause. Such information may have been revealed already (Sir John would not be above withholding "politically sensitive" material from his investigating officer), prompting a revenge killing.

It was far too early to tell anyone what he knew about Joshua's relationship with Sir John. That he must, at some time, tell Beth Smallman that particular news filled him with dread: she obviously worshipped the father-in-law who in less than a year had become "Father." Any suggestion that he might have been leading a secret life and had perhaps used her political activities to gather information on her associates might prove devastating. Then again, Beth Small-man did not appear to be a woman easily devastated.

AT THE MILL, THOMAS GOODALL INFORMED Marc that Constable Hatch had been summoned to Durfee's inn to settle a dispute between two patrons over a bar debt. At the house he found no one in the parlour or dining area. Hearing voices from the summer kitchen, he walked down the hall and peered through the barely opened door.

Mary Huggan and Winnifred Hatch were bent over a washboard, their faces as steamed as a Christmas pudding. Winnifred's attire was more serviceable than it had been yesterday, a shirtwaist and voluminous skirt, but still she looked more like a lady-in-waiting who has discovered she must do her own laundry and has decided simply to get down to it without complaint. On a clothes horse set up beside an iron stove throbbing with heat, Marc saw the linens and stockings he had abandoned on his bed—now scrubbed white. Just beyond it, where a curtain had been pulled back and fastened, he noticed that the quilts on what had to be Thomas Goodall's bed were rumpled from recent sleep and other nocturnal activity.

Edging backwards, Marc eased the door shut.

FIVE

The evening being clear, cold, and still, Marc and Erastus Hatch decided to walk the quarter mile to Deer Park, the estate of Magistrate Philander Child. They could have taken the route south along the Miller Sideroad to the highway, then east past Durfee's inn and Dr. Barnaby's house to the stone gates Marc had observed from horseback the previous day. However, since no snow had fallen to blur the "gossip trail," as Hatch called it, they ambled along its meandering, well-travelled way through a pleasant winter wood, most of which, Marc learned, was the property of the wealthiest man in the township. As they walked, and between puffs on their pipes, they found ample opportunity to exchange the news of the day.

Marc summarized his interview with Beth Smallman, omitting only his subsequent speculations. Then he recounted his successful subterfuge of the afternoon when, to establish his cover story, he had ridden east along the second concession to the farm of Jonas Robertson, a loyal Tory whose grandfather had once represented a rotten borough in Shropshire before the family's fortunes had declined. Ensign Edwards had gone through the motions of examining the surplus bags of the finest maize in the county and confirming their producer's own assessment. During this exchange of mutually flattering pleasantries (even now, Marc marvelled at his guile and the ease with which he had been able to prevaricate), Robertson had disembowelled the reputations of several "republican" farmers along the Farley Sideroad, whose seditious behaviours apparently threatened the political stability of the province and even the health of the local grains. Marc had begun to realize why Sir John had placed so much trust in level-headed men of goodwill like Joshua Smallman. Could such qualities, as valuable as they were rare, provide motive for murder in and of themselves?

Hatch had spent the afternoon in Cobourg, where he had given Sheriff MacLachlan the names and description of the Yankee peddlers. As agreed beforehand, he had mentioned Marc's presence without revealing the real purpose of his visit, as, after all, the sheriff had supported the magistrate's finding of death by misadventure. Hatch told Marc that no one had admitted seeing the Irishmen since the autumn. Hatch himself, on his way home, had stopped at several of the taverns that Connors was known to frequent on his sojourns in the district and had learned nothing of importance.

"I think it's safe to say that your assumption about Connors and O'Hurley hightailing it across the nearest ice to the home state was the right one," Hatch said as they swung a little to the south towards several columns of smoke visible above the treetops. Marc had raised a chuckle earlier when he'd described the pot-rattling donkey skittering up the Kingston Road towards Toronto. "That pair of weasels won't linger a minute longer on the King's ground than they have to," Hatch continued. "The roll of banknotes, though—that may be of real interest to Sir John or his successor. I don't like the smell of foreign money."

"At the moment I consider it merely a distraction," Marc said. "It's hard to make any connection between a couple of scoundrels like that and Smallman's misadventure."

When Marc finally felt constrained to mention his standoff with Elijah, Hatch found the episode more amusing than suspicious.

"Don't worry," he said, "you won't have to put the screws to him. I questioned him very carefully myself, and Mac-Lachlan had a run at him as well. After a lot of coaxing and a little threatening, he admitted that he had not been with his employer to do the rounds that evening, nor had he seen him since supper at six, because right after he'd eaten he'd beetled off to raise a glass with Ruby Marsden, the squire's cook. Ruby backs him up. And, of course, everybody in the township knows the old codger slips up there every chance he can get. Why do you think this path is so easy on the feet?"

"So Smallman was out of the house and alone for at least half an hour before he came back in with the news that he had been called out, as it were?"

"I'm afraid so, with no way for anyone to find out who he might've seen or talked to."

"None of the guests coming to the New Year's gathering saw or heard anything?"

"We questioned them all before the inquest. Nothing. And Emma Durfee didn't arrive until well after he'd ridden off."

"Well, we know for certain he got a message from someone," Marc said, with an effort to hide his disappointment.

Hatch stopped. He placed an avuncular hand on Marc's shoulder. "You have to remember, lad, we've only got Beth's word on that."

MARC HAD SEEN NOTHING IN UPPER Canada to match the opulence of Deer Park—not at Government House, nor even in his illicit glimpses, from anterooms and vestibules, of Family Compact residences in Toronto like Beverley House, Osgoode Hall, or the Grange. Dozens of trees had been hacked down to allow those entering the estate by carriage to appreciate the Georgian proportions and Italianate façade of the manor house itself. Even now, in midwinter, the terraced gardens and housebroken shrubberies undulated elegantly beneath the snowdrifts. In the foyer, lit by an ornate candelabrum, Marc thought, for a sinking moment, that he was back in the entrance hall of Hartfield Downs in Kent, or that he had merely dreamed his secondment to North America and was just now waking up. When a pretty parlour maid took his hat and curtsied, another, more stabbing memory intruded. He quickly suppressed it.

"Maybe you should've stuck to the law," Hatch said, chuckling at Marc's open-mouthed amazement, just as Philander Child, King's Counsel, trundled forward to greet them with a great welcoming guffaw.

Hatch had prepped his new young friend for the evening at hand. Only charter members of the Georgian Club would be present on this occasion, at Hatch's request: he and Marc would be joined by their host, Philander Child, and by Major Charles Barnaby and James Durfee. Joshua Smallman had been among this number, though, understandably, his attendance had been irregular during the harvest season. Occasionally associate members or invitees were added to make up two whist tables or, when ladies were included, to enliven the card games and provide a pretext for music and dancing.

Winnifred Hatch, brushing Marc's freshly steamed frock coat earlier that evening, had winced at her father's reference to lancers and galops, prompting Hatch to add, "You'd think you'd never kicked up a heel or hopped to a jig, girl, but I know better, don't I?" Then he'd winked at Marc.

"You spend too much time living in the past," Winnifred had snapped with more impatience than anger.

"Well, all I know is a person shouldn't spend all their days doing good deeds."

"Like taking care of them who can't help themselves?" She paused, then shot him a telling look.

When she pulled Marc's coattails down, it was with a brusque, dismissive gesture: he felt the steel in her touch, the merest hint of contempt.

"She'll never find a husband," Hatch had said as soon as they'd left the house. "God knows there've been many who've tried."

"I'm surprised," Marc said graciously. "Your daughter is a handsome and . . . efficient young woman."

Hatch glanced warily, hopefully, at Marc. "That she is," he said.

That hers was also a cold beauty did not need to be uttered.

"You'd be alone, would you not, if she were to marry?" Marc said, probing gently.

"I'm afraid that's how she looks at the matter." Hatch sighed. "But then, I've been alone since Isobel died."

•   •   •

PHILANDER CHILD WAS AN ENGLISHMAN WHO had arrived
in Upper Canada as a youth of eighteen, and in his subsequent thirty years in the colony had not permitted a whit
of his God-given Englishness to be weathered away. His
prosperity was evident in the layers and folds of his cor-
pulence, and though he had grown fat upon the land, his
mind had not forgone its lean and hungry motive. Having
reaped a modest but irritatingly slow profit from farming
(more accurately, from instructing others how to farm
for him), he had turned to the law. The reliable flow of
conveyancing fees bestowed by grateful associates and confederates of the ruling clique and the magic of compound
interest had made him rich. Finally, appointment to the
Legislative Council by the former lieutenant-governor, Sir
Peregrine Maitland, yeoman's service to the fledgling Bank
of Upper Canada, and eventual retirement to Deer Park
as magistrate for Northumberland County and superinten-
dent of its quarter sessions had secured him a well-earned
and affluent old age.

This much Marc had concluded by the time the ceremonial cigars had been smoked, the first snifter of brandy consumed, and the blaze in the magnificent fieldstone fireplace
had died down to a warm, conspiratorial glow. Coggins, the
footman-cum-butler, poured each of the guests a second
glass from a crystal decanter, bowed in the direction of a

portrait of Squire Child in his hungrier days, and discreetly left the room.

"So, young man, Sir John was not entirely impressed with my report of the inquest into dear Joshua's death?" Child said, still en rôle as the affable jurist, the epitome of good breeding, exemplary manners, and moral probity. And not, Marc thought, unlike his guardian Uncle Jabez, or their more illustrious neighbour in Kent, Sir Joseph Trelawney of Hartfield Downs.

"He asked me merely to double-check the evidence," Marc said diplomatically. "Smallman was a man he knew well and admired much."

"Certainly, certainly," Child said. "A gentleman could do no less, and Sir John Colborne is every inch a gentleman."

"Sir John intends to leave you here in the province, then?" asked Major Barnaby, retired army surgeon, who had sawed the limbs off many a brave man on the killing grounds of the Spanish Peninsula. His Scots burr was a faint echo of the speech he had heard but little since leaving home at age eleven. His big-boned ruggedness was somewhat offset by deep-browed eyes that twinkled with humour yet gave away little of the thought and feeling stored up behind them.

"Like most young men," Marc said, "I joined the military to fight under the Union Jack."

"So you think there will be insurrection in Quebec," Child said, catching Marc's unhappiness at Barnaby's assumption.

"I have been led to believe so."

"And what is your assessment of the situation in this province?" Child asked Marc, opening a silver snuffbox.

"I don't really know, sir. I'm just a junior officer."

"Surely in the seven or eight months you've been here—in the confidence of Sir John himself, Hatch tells me—you've formed some opinion of the hurly-burly of our politics?"

"I was hoping to learn more about that this evening," Marc said, waving off the offer of snuff.

"It looks as though Sir John thinks there may be a political motive behind Joshua's . . . death," Hatch said helpfully.

Child smiled indulgently at Marc. "All three of us were there," he said. "No one preceded us. Charles examined the body carefully, on the scene and back in his surgery."

"Died of a massive skull fracture," Barnaby said. "Knocked insensible, but could've lingered for some while, alas. Rigor had just passed off, delayed by the cold. My best guess is he died sometime between nine and midnight."

"Which jibes with Beth's account," Hatch said, looking at Marc.

"There were no other injuries, no torn clothing, and no note or paper was found among his effects," Child said.

"And with no witness to corroborate Mrs. Smallman's suspicion that he had received a message sometime after seven o'clock, and no sign around the scene itself of any other disturbance or presence, we had no other choice than to make the finding we did." The magistrate spoke without the least note of defensiveness. His was the kind of dispassion Marc had come to respect among the barristers and judges of the Old Bailey, whose precincts he had haunted as a twenty-year-old articling clerk playing truant from his firm of lowly London solicitors.

"However," Barnaby said in his more humoured, laconic style, "Durfee here informs me you have a detail or two to add to our investigation."

James Durfee, who had followed the dialogue closely with an encouraging nod from time to time (while managing to devote a good deal of attention to his brandy and cigar), smiled sagely.

"Erastus gave me a quick account of your trip out there yesterday afternoon," Child said, "but we'd all appreciate hearing you yourself describe it for us."

Marc could detect nothing but curiosity in the faces of the four men whose attention was now fully focused upon him. He sensed that the next few minutes were critical to any success he might have in his mission. Without the wholehearted co-operation of these influential figures, he had no hope of proceeding one step farther. Moreover, to complicate matters, Sir John would not condone any unnecessary ruffling of feathers among the friends of the government. Why, then, had he—novice and interloper— been chosen? Suppressing any inadequacies he might feel, Marc plunged ahead. As he related the events in the exact sequence in which they had occurred, Marc found the energy he'd experienced the previous day returning, and with it the confidence—conviction even—he had felt in winning Hatch over to his theories.

"And so you see, gentlemen, one is compelled to face the incredible coincidence of two men being in that peculiar vicinity on discrete errands, along with the cogent question of why a respectable gentleman like Joshua Smallman would, on a whim as it were, ride out there in a snowstorm while the New Year's Eve party he was hosting was about to start."

For a full minute no one spoke.

It was Barnaby who broke the silence. "Well, in the least you've added to the number of questions we haven't been able to answer," he said dryly.

"Ensign Edwards thinks that we must try to discover the motive for any possible foul play, and work backwards from there," Hatch said.

Durfee turned a concerned and pained face to Marc. "We four have spent a good deal of the past two weeks going over and over that question in our minds. Joshua was a generous, likeable man. He had no enemies. He was a loyalist more than he was a dyed-in-the-wool conservative like us. I've heard many a professed Reformer in my pub speak respectfully of him when they would rather have cursed him for his views."

"It was suggested a while ago, Mr. Edwards, that Sir John

thought politics might be at issue here," Child said. "Joshua Smallman was not directly involved in politics. That he voted Tory puts him in league with hundreds of others in the county, many of whom have been more vociferous and a lot less tolerant. Why was it not one of us lured out there in his stead?"

"Sir John does feel politics might be involved," Marc said. "He told me he had good reason for thinking so, but, alas, he was not at liberty to give me chapter and verse."

"What did he think you could discover here on your own, then?" Barnaby asked, not unkindly.

"I guess he thought we could help," Hatch offered.

Marc paused, then plunged ahead. "I didn't press Mrs. Smallman on the matter, but I understand that her father-in-law accompanied her to a number of Reform rallies following his return here."

"Mrs. Smallman, I am sorry to say, having produced no children in three years of marriage, seemed unable to find anything else useful to occupy her time," Child said. "She spouted the contemptible opinions of Willy Mackenzie in public places in the most unseemly manner."

"And she is a Congregationalist to boot," Barnaby added.

"Never set foot in St. Peter's after the nuptials," the squire huffed. "The poor devil of a husband would drop her off at that tumbledown hutch they call holy and then drive alone to his father's church."

"Well, I blame him in a way," Durfee said, ignoring the

glare of his fellow Georgians. "I don't like to speak ill of the dead, but Jesse Smallman was dabblin' in dangerous waters near the end, if you ask me."

"That was a year ago," Hatch said. "As far as I can tell, Beth was involved in trying to get redress for the same grievances her husband and a thousand other farmers are pressing for—through the appropriate channels."

Child turned to Marc, adjusted his girth into its most magisterial posture, and said, "You've no doubt heard all the nonsense about these so-called grievances: the Clergy Reserves, the Alien Act, the evil monopoly of the Bank of Upper Canada, the stubbornness of the Legislative Council and the Executive, who rightly refuse to yield to the demands of the mob. And so on."

"I'm hoping to learn more about them as I go," Marc said.

"Well, son, the first thing to remember is that ninety per cent of what you hear, on both sides, is hot air, bombast, and rabble-rousing rhetoric. As long as the levers of power and the will to rule remain safely entrenched, as they are now, we can tolerate a great deal of invective and vituperation. I've been here for thirty years and have an intimate knowledge of Northumberland County and the province as a whole. Most of the populace is British to the core, and now that Sir John has almost doubled the population with needy immigrants from the motherland, the brief threat of American outcasts overwhelming us has abated. We are confident also that the next election will see a Tory majority in the Assembly."

"You'll get a chance to hear some of the rant for yourself," Durfee said.

"That's right," Hatch added. "Mackenzie and Peter Perry and all that gang will be in Cobourg for a Reform rally on Saturday afternoon."

"We're expectin' fireworks," Durfee said with a boyish grin.

"Only if the Orangemen arrive with them," Hatch said.

Looking mischievously at Barnaby, Durfee said, "Fanatic monarchists of the likes of Ogle Gowan and his anti-Catholic Orange Lodge make Mackenzie's lot look like schoolboy debaters."

Barnaby snorted. "I let go of that monarchist nonsense years ago. It doesn't sit well on a Scot's stomach, even though they do claim to defend the Crown and the integrity of the Empire." He paused and added, "I defended them in my own way."

"These are men, I've been told, who will resort to violence to further their cause," Marc said.

"Head-bashing in a donnybrook, tar-and-feathering a Papist or two," Hatch said, "but not, I think, a cold-blooded assassination."

"Quite so," Child said. "Though that gang is quite capable of leaving a man to die in the snow—if it served their purpose."

"What can you tell me about the Hunters' Lodges?" Marc asked, shifting the subject slightly.

Again, the room went unnaturally quiet, and one by one the members of the Georgian Club scrutinized the young officer, as if they might have overlooked something critical.

Child answered for his associates. "They are a secret society, organized very recently in New York and Pennsylvania, whose members, we presume from the little hard evidence we possess, swear an oath that they will help overthrow the British government of Upper Canada and link up with resident dissidents, republicans, and annexationists, with a view to forming a new, liberated republic. Most of them appear to be malcontents from the Loco Foco Democrats of Buffalo, with a few Irish incendiaries tossed in for leavening."

"I'm told that Mr. Mackenzie has for some years now promoted republican and annexationist doctrines in the *Colonial Advocate*," Marc said.

"Indeed he has," Child said. "Yet he was elected the first mayor of your city, takes his seat in the Assembly, and continues to swear the oath of allegiance. His infamous and dastardly Seventh Report on Grievances, which, as you know, helped unseat your own Sir John, was legally enough drawn up and, though sent by an unorthodox and clandestine route to Lord Glenelg in London, was nonetheless a powerful indication that, outside of his blather and rant, Mackenzie is still willing to work within the very system that has nurtured and tolerated his kind of dissent—often to its own detriment."

"And neither Joshua Smallman nor his daughter have been involved with Orangemen, Yankee extremists, or

secret societies. Surely that is the point of all this speculation," Barnaby added.

"Lookin' back over the past months," Durfee said, "the
only thing I can truly say is that my boyhood chum attended
a number of meetings and public rallies connected with the
Grievances Report. And since everybody 'round here knew
he was a loyalist and a Tory supporter at the polls, they realized he only went along to escort Beth. After all, she was a
widow, she couldn't very well run off to a public gathering
by herself. Who else was there to go with her? Elijah? The
crippled lad?"

"Surely Joshua's duty was to persuade her not to debase
her character by attending the kind of meetings God intended for men," Child said.

"He could've tied her to a chair, I suppose," Barnaby said.

"With a second rope for her tongue," Durfee added, and
laughed.

"You're all forgetting," Hatch said, "that Beth was carrying on the efforts that Jesse had made in regard to the Grievances before he got so depressed and . . . did what he did."

"It is conceivable, then," Barnaby said carefully, without
looking at Durfee, "that in an attempt to understand his son
and perhaps even to comprehend the reasons for his taking
his own life, Joshua did begin to become enamoured of the
Reform position."

"Even so," Child said, "and I'm not granting your premise
for a moment, that is no cause for the man to be murdered.
Turning your coat in political matters may lose you a friend

or some custom, but not your life."

"I have to agree, Your Honour." Barnaby smiled.

Only Durfee did not laugh. The brandy-whetted scarlet of his cheeks had suddenly paled.

"Are you all right, James?" Barnaby asked.

"I've just had a frightenin' thought," Durfee said. "Suppose some people did think that Joshua's goin' to all them meetings and rallies was in earnest, whether it was or not. And suppose someone or other at the rallies got the notion into his head that Joshua was pretendin' to be a convert—because of Jesse's grievances and so on—but was actually an informer."

Marc held his breath, and his peace.

"Preposterous," Child said, circulating the cigar box and serving with his own hand a generous round of brandy. He gave the slumbering fire an aristocratic poke with one of the irons.

Hatch became animated. "Not so, Squire. It makes a kind of sense, especially if you were a member of one of the fanatical fringe groups in the Reform party—a Clear Grit or whatever. Think of it from that point of view: a retired dry goods merchant comes into the district, a known Tory and occasional associate of the lieutenant-governor. Suddenly he starts showing up at Reform political dos everywhere with his daughter-in-law, a known sympathizer. Jesse campaigned over in Lennox for Perry, remember, and wrote up a petition that went to Mackenzie and the grievances committee in the Assembly."

"Aye, that's quite plausible," Barnaby conceded, and even Squire Child nodded meditatively.

Marc was buoyed by the drift of the conversation. Here was the one motive for murder he found to be the most compelling and for which he had inside knowledge he could not reveal. And now he would not have to. He tried to appear only casually interested.

"I see your point," he said, fingering his brandy glass.

"Nevertheless," Barnaby said, and he paused at the deflationary effect of that word. "Nevertheless, we are still faced with the same sort of question as before. What information would an informer—Joshua in this case—be able to gather, from ordinary political meetings and speeches, that would be seditious enough to pose a threat to some treasonous cause or specific persons espousing it?"

"Exactly," Child said. He turned to Marc like a wigged justice about to lecture the novice petitioner before his bench. "All you need to do is scan one issue of the *Colonial Advocate* or the *Cobourg Star* to realize that no rally, camp meeting, hustings debate, or underground pamphleteering goes unreported for any longer than it takes to set the type. One side inflates the rhetoric with hyperbole and bombast, the other edits and distorts at will—but no one's opinion, view, prejudice, or bigotry remains private for more than a day in this fishbowl of a province."

"True," Barnaby said. "There's a lot of bush out there, but not a single tree that would hide you for an hour."

"What we're saying," Hatch added, "is that the information would have to be truly seditious—like facts about proposed actions—not the empty-headed threats we see in the press every week."

For a minute or so the weight of this conclusion silenced the group, and fresh cigars were clipped and lit.

Barnaby spoke first. "I think we're agreed that truly treasonous information would not likely bubble up at the meetings Joshua and Beth attended last summer and fall. But what if those meetings were not the source?"

"What else could be?" Durfee said.

"You said yourself that Jesse Smallman was treading dangerous waters near the end."

"I only meant he was flailin' about—angry, in despair—at what was happenin' to him because of the Clergy Reserves. And how he kept repeatin' that there didn't seem to be any political party capable of gettin' anythin' done."

"Is it possible, conceivable even," Barnaby continued, "that Jesse joined or thought of joining one of the annexationist groups, one of the secret societies, and that he might have been privy to treasonable information?"

"Now we're really grasping at straws," Hatch said.

"The man's also been dead for twelve months," Child said.

Barnaby, who was beginning to enjoy himself wholeheartedly, persisted. "What if Joshua discovered this information? Among his son's effects, for example? And was thought to be an agent as well?"

"You've got a surfeit of 'what ifs' in that hypothesis," Child said.

"There's only one way to find out," Durfee said. "Only one person is left who can shed any light on Joshua or Jesse."

"You're not suggesting Beth might be involved in anything unsavoury?" Hatch said sharply.

"I think he's merely implying that some of the answers to our questions lie in the Smallman household," Barnaby said. "For the sake of the reputations of two men no longer able to defend themselves, I think it behooves us to engage in some hard questioning, indelicate as that might prove."

They all turned to gaze, with expectation and much relief, at Ensign Edwards.

The arrival of Coggins with a tray of cheeses and sweetmeats and decanters of wine stinted the flow of serious conversation for some minutes. However, as soon as the sighs of satisfaction had abated, Philander Child picked up a thread of the previous dialogue.

"While I concur that we must press Mrs. Smallman as forcefully as her delicate circumstances permit in order to eliminate any possibility that Joshua Smallman might have been an informer or that Jesse was anything other than a misguided Reformer, I would advise young Marc here to aim his investigation in more obvious directions."

"To those in the county already known to be fanatics," Marc said.

The squire smiled patiently. "My years on the bench compel me to consider facts before hypotheses. Someone has to ascertain, among the living, whether there was any actual contact or real acquaintance between Joshua and known extremists. We need facts, dates, notarized statements, sworn information or affidavits. No one gets himself mur‑ dered—and even that assumption is still conjecture, remem‑ ber—without coming into contact, in some discernible way, with his assassin."

"So, I need to find out whether any such extremists knew Smallman or were seen with him over the past twelve months."

"And I can suggest two or three likely candidates," Child said.

Marc smiled. "Azel Stebbins, Israel Wicks, and Orville Hislop," he said, recalling these names from Sir John's notes.

"Sir John has been well briefed," Child said.

"When will you begin, then?" Durfee said.

Marc smiled. "I already have."

JAMES DURFEE AND CHARLES BARNABY LEFT together shortly after ten o'clock, because the doctor was tired after nine hours in his Cobourg surgery and Durfee wished to help Emma clear up after the chaos of the afternoon stage stop and the brisk evening trade of local elbow-benders.

As the remaining three were finishing their nightcaps, Hatch happened to mention to Child that Marc had man‑ handled a couple of Yankee peddlers on his way to Craw‑ ford's Corners.

"You are a soldier, young man." Child laughed apprecia-
tively. "And a damn good one."

"Marc has reason to think they were involved in smuggling rum," Hatch said.

"What puzzles me," Marc said, "is why anybody, peddler
or freebooter, would bring tariffed spirits into a province
where whisky itself is duty-free and there seem to be more
local distilleries than gristmills. Grog's a penny a cup at
every wayside shebeen."

"A fair question," Child said, nodding towards Hatch.
"But these smugglers are 'importing' high-quality spirits and
wines: rum from the West Indies, bourbon from the Caro-
linas, Bordeaux and Champagne from France, port from
Iberia—and all of it, you can be sure, pirated or hijacked at
some point along the way. They peddle it only around the
garrison towns—Kingston, Toronto, London, Sandwich,
Newark—to establishments that cater to a higher class of
citizenry and that, in addition to cut-price vintage spirits,
offer the further comfort of a warm bed and willing flesh."
The squire, long a widower, shook his head sorrowfully, as a
man who has seen much folly and never quite accustomed
himself to it.

"But that means tuns, barrels, packing cases," Marc said.

"Oh, the peddlers don't do the actual smuggling," Hatch
said. "They're just petty advance men, order-takers, messen-
gers, and the like. Peddling door to door is a perfect cover
for the work. The county is crawling with them, summer
and winter."

"Erastus and I apprehended one of the blackguards a while back," Child said. "What was his name now?"

"Isaac Duffy," Hatch said, and his face lit up with pleasure at the memory. "Caught him trying to sell a bottle of His Majesty's finest sherry to Emma Durfee, an item he'd most likely pilfered from some smuggler's drop he knew about."

"He's in irons down in Kingston," Child said, "but before we shipped him off, he gave us a lead to two scoundrels in the area we'd long suspected of actually hauling the stuff across the lake on the ice."

"Jefferson and Nathaniel Boyle," Hatch said. "Brothers who operated two so-called farms out past Mad Annie's swamp."

"Hatch and I hopped on our horses and rode right out there like a pair of avenging angels." Child laughed, and Marc did too, at the image of Magistrate Child's two hundred and fifty pounds of pampered flesh astride and agallop.

"Without a sheriff or constables?" Marc asked above Hatch's chortling.

"I'd been after them Yankee cattle thieves for years," Child said with sudden vehemence. "I had a pistol tucked in each side of my waistcoat, and Hatch here had his fowling piece. My God, I can still remember every moment of that ride."

"By the time we got there," Hatch said, "they'd already skedaddled, as they say in the Republic."

"Those sewer rats can smell authority a mile away." The squire sighed. "I hate smugglers of every stripe. They undermine the fragile economy here, flout the King's law, and offer incentives to others to do the same. And when they're Yankees to boot, I detest them as much as I do a traitor or a turncoat."

"All we found were two abandoned wives, just skin and bone, and a dozen half-starved youngsters," Hatch said sadly.

"Well, they haven't been seen since," Child said with some satisfaction.

"And when I took Winnifred out there with some food and clothes at Christmas," Hatch said, "the women and children had packed up and gone. The whole lot of 'em."

Marc had witnessed the effects of grinding poverty on the streets of London and never become inured to it, or to the callow disregard shown towards its victims by the prosperous and the morally blinkered. The thought of Winnifred's charity warmed him in ways the brandy, cigars, and stimulating company had failed to.

Philander Child wished Marc well in his efforts on Sir John's behalf, complimented him on his good manners, and offered his assistance if it should be required. Walking back to the mill, grateful for Hatch's companionable silence, Marc went over the evening's conversation. He concluded that he had been told much that had been intended and some that had not.

Coming up to the house, Marc suddenly said, "Who is Mad Annie?"

Hatch snorted. "You really don't want to know that long, sad story." He placed a fatherly hand on Marc's shoulder and said with mock solemnity, "I'll give you the gory details in the morning."

MARC LAY AWAKE FOR A LONG while that night, mulling over what had been said or not said. What was really keeping him from sleep was the dread of interrogating Beth Smallman about two men whom she loved and who had been taken from her in the most horrific manner imaginable. At the same time, he was not prepared to discount any suspect, even an attractive and vulnerable one, in advance of the facts. But he was happy that the four gentlemen with whom he had just spent a most pleasant evening had themselves been together during the critical hours of New Year's Eve. He was just about to drift off upon this comforting thought when he heard a door open and a familiar footstep in the hall outside his room.

He waited several seconds before easing himself out of bed, slipping the door ajar, and peering down the dark hallway. This time he caught a glimpse of white nightdress and a fleeting image of the female form undulating within it before the door to the back section of the house shut it out of sight. Then came the same giggle he had heard the previous night, the only difference being that the figure he'd just seen animating the nightdress was a head taller and a good deal more Junoesque than Mary Huggan's. It was undoubtedly the handsome Miss Hatch.

SIX

"Well, lad, what did you learn of value last night?"
Hatch said to Marc, stabbing a sausage.

The question startled Marc, not because it was impertinent or sudden but because he had been absorbed in close observation of Thomas Goodall and his mistress, Winnifred Hatch. That they were lovers, and by all the evidence frequently and consensually so, could not have been inferred from the cool and formal intercourse between them over the Thursday morning breakfast table. Winnifred moved briskly about, neither smiling nor unsmiling, until the three men had been served, then sat down next to Marc across from her father and began her own meal. Mary Huggan soon joined her, and the two women exchanged pleasantries. Goodall, as was his custom, kept his eyes locked on his food, which he consumed rapidly but mechanically, as if eating were a duty. Like the miller's, his hands were large, roughened by cold and searing sun, and shaped to the plough and axe-handle.

Was it possible that the proud Miss Hatch was ashamed to admit her attachment to such a plain and taciturn man? Or had it more to do with a sense of obligation to her father? Marc had begun to realize that he had much to learn about the ways of these country folk, and that such knowledge might be necessary to unravelling the mystery of Joshua Smallman's death.

"Did we give you anything useful?" Hatch asked again, and he nodded towards the two women as if to say, "Keep it general."

"Yes," Marc managed to say. "Yes, you did. You gave me something definite to ask the gentlemen whose farms I plan to visit today."

"That's good, then." Hatch reached across the table and, with Mary Huggan's consent, tipped her uneaten egg and sausage onto his own plate.

"Thank you, Mary," Hatch said, and the girl blushed to the roots of her pale hair. Winnifred gave her a sharp look, and she blushed anew.

"We'll have to get that blush of yours repaired one of these days," Hatch said impishly.

"Leave the lass alone," Winnifred said, and before her father could recover from the rebuke, she turned to Marc and said, "You're likely to find most of the surplus grain among the farms on the Pringle Sideroad north of the second concession."

Marc suddenly found her face, with its strong bones and dark, perceptive eyes, no more than a foot from his own, and he could hear the whisper of her breathing beneath the taut bib of her apron. Across the table, Thomas uttered a satisfying belch and pushed his chair back.

"Oh, why is that?" Marc said.

"They're good Tories, of course," Winnifred said, and Hatch let out an approving chuckle. "The Reformers on the Farley Sideroad," she continued, "are too busy organizing petitions to get a decent crop in, or keep it from the thistles when they do."

"Winnifred keeps all the accounts here," Hatch beamed. "She knows the worth of every farmer in the district to the nearest shilling."

"Don't exaggerate," Winnifred said, nudging Mary Huggan, who jumped up gratefully and began clearing away some of the plates. Goodall had already stumped out to his chores, unremarked by anyone.

"I'll take your advice to heart," Marc said gallantly.

"It would be more useful in the head, I believe."

Mary knocked over a cup; Hatch reached out, caught it, and handed it back to the girl.

"Go put some more water on," Winnifred said firmly to Mary. "I'll finish up here." She rose and began stacking the dishes. There wasn't an ounce of self-consciousness anywhere in her body. "I wish you good hunting, Ensign Edwards," she said with cool solicitude as she went back into the kitchen.

"Don't mind her none," Hatch said. "She's a bit set in her ways."

And her straightforward, no-nonsense ways were certainly not those of the young ladies Marc had encountered at the mess parties and the soirees of Government House, ladies whose "aristocratic" breeding and overwrought manners seemed barely able to tolerate the indignities of mud-rutted streets, slatternly servants, uppity tradesmen, and stiff-fingered seamstresses.

"She's quick with figures, mind—like her mother," Hatch was happy to add. "And a handsome lass, eh?"

Summoning his own good manners, Marc said, "Most men would describe her so."

MARC WAS LOOKING FORWARD TO THE challenge of eliciting essential and perhaps incriminating information from Israel Wicks, Azel Stebbins, and Orville Hislop—the trio of suspected extremists passed on to him by Sir John. But he was not anticipating with any pleasure the imminent interview with Beth Smallman. The death of a loved one—especially a parent—was devastating. And while he himself had been a mere five years old when both his parents had died of cholera, he could still recall the numbing sense of loss, the abrupt rupturing of the world he had believed permanent and incorruptible, and the long, bewildering absence that followed and would not be filled. More immediate perhaps was the love he felt for "Uncle" Jabez, who had adopted him and raised him up in ways that would have been inconceivable had his parents survived. Beth Smallman had seen her husband hang himself out of some deep despair, the roots of which Marc knew he must probe, and barely a twelvemonth later she had suffered the unexplained death of a father-in-law she had come to revere as much or more than she had her husband. How and why that affection had grown, and its consequences, were facts he had to learn, if his investigation was to be rigorous and objective.

Taking a deep breath, Marc turned onto the Smallman property.

"You again, is it?"

"My visiting your mistress is no concern of yours," Marc said when he had recovered from the shock of Elijah's sudden materialization—this time from behind the manure pile in the stable yard. He realized immediately the ineptness of such a reprimand here in the bush, but not before Elijah had guffawed with his own brand of upstart contempt.

"The missus and me'll decide what concerns us," Elijah said. "We ain't impressed by no fancy uniform."

Marc ignored the remark and switched tactics. "When did you leave your cabin and walk up to Philander Child's place on the day your master died?" he demanded in his best drill-sergeant's voice.

Elijah's eyes narrowed, and his ungloved fingers squeezed more tightly around the handle of his pitchfork. "And who wants to know?"

"The lieutenant-governor," Marc said, bristling.

But Elijah had already turned away and was now ambling towards the barn. As he went in, he called back over his shoulder, "Don't tha' be long up there. I won't have ya up-settin' the missus."

So much for imperial authority.

"You're wonderin' why I'm not draped in widow's weeds," Beth Smallman said.

In truth, Marc was silently noting not the absence of mourning attire but the arresting presence of a plain white blouse, brown woollen skirt, and an unadorned apron that might have been stitched together out of discarded flour sacking. Once again her flaming russet hair was behaving as it pleased.

"Well, there's no one would see them, is there?" she said, once again seated across from him in the tender light of the south window. "Besides, grief goes much deeper than crêpe or black wreaths upon doors."

"I apologize, ma'am, for the necessity of this interview—"

"Please don't," she said. "I'm as eager to learn why Father died in the way he did as you and the governor are." Her face was grave but not solemn. She struck Marc as a woman who would do her weeping at night—more Scots than Irish. "Livin' with 'whys' that never get answered is as hard as grievin' itself."

That she was alluding to her husband's death as much as to her father-in-law's was not in doubt. But Marc was not ready to take up that cue. Not yet. "It is the why, the motive, that I need to discover," he said quietly. "And to do so, I must learn as much as possible about your father-in-law's thoughts and feelings and actions over the past few months."

"I understand," she said. Her voice was breathy and low: she would be an alto in the Congregationalist choir, he thought. "I'll help in any way I can."

"My task is made somewhat easier by the fact that until your husband passed away a year ago, your father-in-law lived and worked in Toronto. We need to focus then on those activities he took up here subsequent to his return."

"He was born here," she reminded him, "and grew up on a farm near Cobourg. When his father died, he sold the farm and moved to Toronto—it was still York then. He enjoyed the country very much, but his talents lay in business, in the life of the town."

"And your husband's?"

Beth paused, smiled shrewdly, and said, "They did not share similar interests."

Marc decided it was politic to sip at his tea and sample a biscuit before he spoke again. "Jesse was not enamoured of dry goods?"

"While his mother was alive, he pretended to be. When she died seven years ago, Jesse took the money she left him from her own father's estate, moved back here where they were just opening the township, and bought this farm." She looked down at her tea but did not drink. "He felt he'd come home."

The scraping of a boot along floorboards announced the entrance of Aaron. Marc waited patiently while Beth fussed over the boy, tucked a biscuit into his twisted mouth, did up the top button of his mackintosh, and escorted him back outside, whispering instructions into his ear as if she were not repeating them for the hundredth time.

When the tea was replenished and she was seated again, she said, "You'll want to know how we met."

"Pardon me for saying so, but you don't look as though you've been a farm girl all your life."

"You're very observant for one so . . . young," she said. And so coddled and pampered and protected from the true horrors of the world, she implied with her single, taut glance. "But these are genuine calluses." She showed both her palms while the cup and saucer teetered on her knees. "You learn how when you have to, and quickly." That she herself was younger than he appeared to be of no relevance.

"You met your husband here, then?"

"My father was the Congregationalist minister in Cobourg. We came up here when I was eight, after my mother died back in Pennsylvania."

"But your husband was Church of England," Marc said.

Once again he was raked by that appraising gaze. "A venial sin," she said. "Congregationalists are a tolerant lot. And democratic to boot." She watched to see the effect of this last remark.

"Would you say that relations between Jesse and Joshua were strained?"

"Did Father come to the wedding, you mean?"

"Did he approve of the . . . way his son's life was going?"

"He came down for the wedding at St. Peter's in Cobourg."

"And that was . . . ?"

"Almost four years ago. Jess and I came directly here."

"Did his father visit?"

Each new question seemed to disconcert her just a bit more, but the only outward sign of discomfort was the length of the pause before she could answer. When she did, Marc could see no indication that she was reluctant, withholding, or evasive.

"Only at Christmas. And once at Easter."

When the thorny issue of whose church to attend must have complicated matters.

"Perhaps if there had been children . . ." Her voice trailed off.

"But there weren't," Marc prompted, uncertain now of his ground.

Her smile was indulgent but nonetheless pained. "No miscarriages, no stillborns, no infant deaths," she whispered. "Nothing."

"But Joshua came immediately when he was needed," Marc said with feeling, "and he stayed."

"Yes."

"And gave up dry goods to become a farmer."

Her "yes" was just audible.

Marc was grateful for the sudden arrival of Mary Huggan through the kitchen door.

"Oh," she said to Beth, "I didn't know anybody was with you." Mary seemed to have arrived in a state of some turmoil, but when she saw Beth's face, she looked bewildered and began backing away. "I'm sorry, I've come at a bad time."

"It's all right, Mary. Ensign Edwards and I have some distressing but necessary things to talk over."

"Of course," Mary said, then whirled and fled.

Beth called out, "Come over after you've served dinner!" She had drawn a cotton handkerchief from her apron pocket. "I'm ready to go on now."

"If your father-in-law made an enemy, even one he didn't know he'd made, I need to find that person—or group."

"As in political party."

"Or faction. Erastus Hatch and others have given me a

rough sketch of the various parties and factions contending in the county. He also mentioned that—"

"I dragged my Tory father-in-law off to Reform rallies in five different townships when I'd be servin' my monarch better by mindin' the house, lookin' for a husband who could give me babies, and helpin' to raise enough corn to keep the bailiffs out of the barn."

"Something of that order," Marc managed to reply.

"I also read newspapers, and I helped Jess write two of his petitions to the Assembly."

"I've been led to believe that Joshua accompanied you to Reform rallies as a means merely of seeing you properly chaperoned."

"He was a gentleman."

"Was he not in danger of being . . . embarrassed or otherwise discomfited? After all, his Tory leanings, his former business in the capital, the friends he selected here upon his return—these would be well-known."

"Everything is eventually well known in Northumberland County."

"Did he participate in any way when he accompanied you?"

Again the indulgent smile, with just a touch of scorn in it. "I see you haven't attended the hustings or any of our infamous political picnics."

"As a soldier I have other pressing duties."

"So I've been told." This time her smile was warm,

accepting. "But if you had, you'd know that opponents of every stripe show up and pipe up at every opportunity. The give and take of public debate is another way of describin' the shoutin' matches and general mayhem. Sometimes it takes fisticuffs or a donnybrook to settle on a winner."

"No place for an unescorted lady, then." For a brief moment he pictured her dependent upon his strong, soldier's arm.

"You want to know, I think, but are too polite to ask, if Father became embroiled in the debates? The answer is no. He was a friendly but reserved man." She paused. "He was that rare thing among men: a listener."

Marc got up and walked to the window. He drew out his pipe and, receiving silent permission from his hostess, began stuffing it with tobacco from the pouch on his belt. When he turned back, Beth was beside him, a lit tinder stick in her hand. She watched him closely—with the same kind of marvelling intensity he himself had once used when observing his uncle Jabez shaving—as he got the plug going. With a start he realized she had done this many times.

"My feeling from what Sir John told me of Joshua, and what I've learned here thus far, is that there is more likelihood of his listening to what was being said, of taking it in—"

"Than bein' taken in by it?" she said quickly.

"That too."

"Well, I can say one thing for sure: he began more and more to understand what it was like—is like—to try and eke out a livin' from the land when so much of the province's affairs are run from Toronto by gentlemen who've never hoed a row of Indian corn and who think every person with a rightful grievance is an insurrectionist."

"You said a moment ago that some folks thought you should stay put on the farm to help keep the bailiffs away. Did you mean that literally?"

"Almost. If it hadn't been for Mr. Child extendin' us a mortgage, Jess and me might well've lost everything."

"Philander Child holds your mortgage?"

"He did. And when the second drought brought us to our knees, he kindly offered to buy the farm from us, for a lot more than it was worth."

"He doesn't look like a farmer to me."

Beth smiled indulgently. "You can be interested in agricultural land without wantin' to hoe beans or muck out stalls."

"Point taken. But you were not tempted by his offer."

"I was. But not Jess. He was not about to admit failure to his father."

"But then—"

"Then he died. And it was me that vowed never to sell. Then Father arrived and paid off the mortgage."

"I see."

"Mr. Child also arranged for Elijah to help Jess and me out that last year." She caught Marc's wince of disbelief. "Elijah's a miserable old coot till you get to know him, but he worked for his board and what little we could pay him at harvest time. He's got no family."

"Is he a local?"

"No. Some crony of Mr. Child's in Toronto was lookin' for a safe home for him and he ended up here."

"But the land around here appears to be extremely fertile," Marc said. "And you've already cleared most of your acreage by the look of it."

Beth took hold of his arm. "Let's go for a walk. It's time you learned somethin' about farming in this province."

As they made their way to the door, Marc caught sight of a brass bedstead behind partly drawn curtains. On either side of the bed, a pair of tall shelves listed under the weight of books. The title of one leapt out at him: Thomas Paine's *Rights of Man*.

Following the direction of his gaze, Beth said, "My own father's bed—his legacy, along with his library. I left the religious tomes back in Cobourg, for the Reverend Haydon." When Marc continued to stare, she said, "You enjoy readin'?"

"Very much," he replied, uncertain of the question's intent. "I spent two years as a law clerk."

She smiled. "I guess that counts."

Outside, the sunshine and cold air made walking a pleasant exercise. As they passed the barn to veer southwest towards the farm's fields and pastures, they could hear Elijah mucking out the pigpens and singing vigorously. No recognizable word emerged from his song, though the hogs joined in as they were able.

"Does Elijah have a last name?" Marc said.

"I suppose so," Beth said. "But he's never said and I've never asked."

A few yards beyond the barn Beth began to point out to Marc the location of fields, all alike now under two feet of snow, and their pertinent features: this one already bursting with winter wheat though you couldn't yet see its green sprouts; that one to be seeded with maize in April; this one lying fallow; that one an alfalfa field waiting for spring rains. The snow-packed trail they were following appeared to Marc to be shadowing Crawford Creek but at a consistent distance of thirty yards or so.

"Wouldn't this path be more scenic if it were closer to the creek?" he asked when they stopped at a field where tree stumps and random branches jutted brutally through the snow—a familiar sight, even to a newcomer like Marc, in a country whose arable land was still nine-tenths forest.

"It would," Beth said, her gaze upon the stump-scarred field in front of them, "if we owned the land next to it."

"Where we've been walking is your property line, then?"

Beth murmured assent. "This was the last of our fields to be cleared. We worked on it all one summer and fall. It was the last thing Jess and I did together."

Marc offered his arm in a comforting gesture. She did not lean upon it, but he could feel the pressure of her fingers and found it pleasantly disconcerting.

"From what you've just told me and from what I've seen of your livestock, you appear to have a prospering operation here."

"It must look that way now," she said, staring ahead. "The land was cheap so long as we cleared our quota and did our bit on the roads. The mortgage was mostly for the new barn, the cows and pigs, and some machinery that needed replacin'. We even had a team of oxen once."

"Surely two or three good crops would have seen you solvent," Marc said, as if he actually knew what he was talking about.

"True. But just as we needed them, as I said earlier, the drought struck."

"But you've got a creek over there twice the size of most rivers in England!"

"I'm not talkin' about the kind of drought you get in a desert or the kind that drove Joseph into Egypt. It only takes three or four weeks of little or no rain in June or July to weaken a crop. The thistles and blight get in, and the kernels shrivel up so you're lucky to get ten bushels to the acre."

"And that happened three summers ago?"

"And the summer before last, too. If you look back towards the barn from this high point where we're standin', you can see that the main section of growing land is very low. In the spring, it's actually swampy, and difficult to plough and seed. We had two wet springs in a row."

She said this as if rain and drought were the whims of a fate determined to tease and madden, the kind that brought plagues to the pharaoh and mindless ordeals to Job.

"The squire next to us back home had swamp ground like that, and he drained it with tile," Marc said.

"But we don't own the land next to the creek," Beth said.

"But the creek is right there," Marc persisted. "There's nothing but bush on either side of it, no one is using it. It's the same creek that drives Hatch's mill and feeds half the wells of the township." He was trying to keep the note of impatience out of his voice, any sense that he was instructing the naive or the unreasonably discouraged. "Nobody'd give a tinker's dam if you drained your swamp into it or drew water out of it for irrigation. Hatch says a quarter of the farmers here are still squatters, and no one pays the slightest bit of attention."

"That's exactly how Jess used to talk," Beth said. She turned and trod through the snow towards Crawford Creek. Marc floundered behind her. When he caught up, she gestured towards the frozen ribbon of water and the hardwood forest fringing its banks.

"Under those trees is prime farmland, rich soil, good drainage, a sugar maple woodlot, shade to protect the cattle . . ."

"You couldn't afford to buy it? Not even the part of it that includes the creek on this side?" Marc's eyes followed what he could now see would be the unalterable survey line that made every farm a rectangle, or set of contiguous rectangles, regardless of topographical caprice or nuance of Nature. The bow in Crawford Creek took it away from the

straight boundary line that marked the western limit of the
Smallman farm, when the curve of the creek itself cried out
to be the natural border between the adjacent properties, assuring each a precious share of the creek's water.

"We couldn't buy it," Beth said, "even if we had the
money."

Before he asked why, Marc had to suppress the unsettling
thought that Joshua Smallman had been a wealthy man
by provincial standards, having established his lucrative
business on "fashionable" King Street and paid off his son's
mortgage, and that his daughter-in-law, so recently restored
to his affection, would surely inherit whatever remained.

"What you see over there," Beth said, "and all along this
side of the creek, is a lot owned by the Crown. If and when
the government ever decides to sell it, the proceeds will go to
the clergy."

Light dawned. Inwardly Marc winced at his own obtuseness, his failure to see how Beth Smallman had been leading
him patiently towards this conclusion. The Clergy Reserves
had topped every list of grievances headlined in Mackenzie's
Colonial Advocate. This was a phrase flung like a goad against
the worthies of the province and the governor's appointed
Legislative Council.

"Ah. . . yes. Every seventh lot to be reserved for the use
and maintenance of the Anglican clergy," Marc said, the
legalese slipping easily off the tongue. "But surely the assignment of such lots is not random and self-defeating. Surely

both parties, the Church of England and the farmers, stand to gain by the rational allotment and sale of such reserve lands."

"The surveyors laid out these lots ten years ago and applied the grid plan they'd been given by the Executive Council. It's the same for every township in the province. The disposition of lots is decided in advance. What's actually on them or not on them is irrelevant."

"That's preposterous!"

"Mr. Mackenzie himself used that very word."

"Even so, can no one buy that lot over there?"

"Clergy Reserve lots are bought and sold all the time. Archdeacon Strachan and his cronies in the Council trade them—like marbles. But only when the value's been raised or it appears convenient or necessary to their interests. That one over there will be sold when all the property 'round it is cleared and improved and a concession road cut out to the north of it. It'll be worth ten times what it is now—to someone. Our farm and it would make a natural and very profitable pair."

"But couldn't you and your husband have run your tile down to the creek and set up some irrigation pipes in the interim? You could've put a squatter's shack on that piece by the bank, for God's sake!"

"We could have. But what's to stop the leaders of the Anglican Church with influence in the governor's Executive Council from suddenly decidin' to sell that lot to one of their friends, and that friend then comin' in and rippin' up our tile—leavin' us high and dry like we were in the first place? Not a thing."

"They don't have to sell at public auction?"

"Not if it doesn't please them. And don't forget, Jess and me were Reformers through and through."

Recalling Joshua Smallman's friendship with Sir John Colborne, Marc said, "But perhaps your father-in-law could have petitioned the Executive Council on your behalf?"

"He didn't believe in that kind of shady dealing," she replied, with more pride than regret. "He was too honourable."

"But you're not suggesting that the government would let politics influence the conduct of its responsibilities?"

The ingenuousness of the question surprised and amused Beth Smallman, but she suppressed a laugh.

"All this has been set out in the Report on Grievances that Mackenzie sent across to Lord Glenelg?" Marc continued.

"The Seventh Report on Grievances."

They walked slowly back towards the barn, Beth ahead, Marc behind. At the point where the path dipped south towards the mill property (that, as chance would have it, straddled the creek down its full length), Marc prepared to take his leave. He took Beth's hand and brought her mittened fingers to his lips, a gesture ingrained by long habit and prompted now by something more than courtesy.

"Thank you for being so candid and forthcoming," he said formally. "And good day to you."

She left her fingers where they lay for a second or two after Marc released them, and she looked steadily at him, as if he were one of her father's books that might possibly deserve reading.

"I intend to find out what happened to Joshua," he said.

"I believe you will."

He watched her until she had passed the barn and disappeared into the summer kitchen attached to the rear of the house. Then he turned to make his way to Hatch's house, but a banging noise brought him up short. He stopped to listen. Somewhere a door was flapping freely in the light breeze. He checked the barn, then swung his attention to Elijah's cabin near it. The old goat had left his door unlatched and, if the wind picked up even slightly, it would soon blow off its leather hinges. Reluctantly, for he did not wish the pleasant afterglow of the interview with Beth to be disturbed, Marc walked down towards the cabin.

He grasped the plank door by the knob, but before fastening it, he decided to have a look inside, in case the wretched fellow had fallen or taken ill. In the grainy light that illuminated the interior, Marc could just make out the unmade and unoccupied bed, an empty chair, and a makeshift desk cluttered with papers. Marc stepped back outside and peered around for any sign of Elijah. A movement up beyond the house caught his attention: someone was trundling across the road and into the woods on the far side, where the path led up to Squire Child's estate—Elijah What's-his-name scuttling, quick as a dog in heat, over to call upon his lady friend, Ruby Marsden.

Marc latched the door and turned to leave, then suddenly wrenched it open again and stepped boldly inside. He moved swiftly over to the desk and sat down on the rickety chair in front of it. The desk was a mass of jumbled newspapers, pamphlets, and broadsides, speckled with ash and shards from cracked pipe bowls. For a man reputed to be illiterate, Elijah had chosen some unusual recreational materials. One by one Marc held these up to the dim light that fell through the window. On every item, passages had been underlined or crudely circled with charcoal. The subject of each marked passage was instantly clear: political statements, whether they were in the reports of the minutes of the House of Assembly, a manifesto in broadside or tract, or a hyperbolic claim in the capitalized line of a poster. And each of them bilious with the rhetoric of the left—the bombast of the radicals. Among this detritus lay a single leather-bound book, the Holy Bible.

Gently Marc opened it, and he peered at the fly-leaf. A name was scrawled there, faded but legible. The word "Elijah" was readily decipherable, but the letters of the last name were tangled and blurred. After some minutes, Marc deciphered them as: c ‑ h ‑ o ‑ w ‑ n.

Elijah Chown.

So, Elijah had secrets to keep. He was a furtive reader and a closet Reformer. Little wonder, then, that he had been so protective of the Smallmans. But why the secrecy? Beth herself did not know he could read—or else she had lied about it yesterday when she had implied that only she among the New Year's guests was literate, a conclusion he now rejected out of hand. And what else might he have to hide? Somehow, Marc thought, he was going to have to find a way of interrogating the prickly old misanthrope. He needed to know much more about what was really going through the mind of Joshua Smallman in the weeks before his death. And he needed to hear it, unfortunately, from someone less partisan than his daughter-in-law.

At any rate, the hired hand would bear watching.

SEVEN

J ust as Marc rounded the north silo and turned towards the miller's barn, he heard a high-pitched squawk that rose to a terrified shriek, then stopped, as if an organ-pipe had been throttled with a vengeful thumb. Before he could even hazard a guess as to the tortured source of the sound, the elongated and fully engaged figure of Winnifred Hatch emerged from between the barn and the chicken coop. In the vise of her left hand, the silenced but thrashing body of a bulb-eyed, dusty-feathered capon struggled futilely against the inevitable. In her right hand, she clutched a hatchet. The miller's daughter—garbed in sweater and skirt and an intimidating leather butcher's apron—marched to a stump near Marc, one that had been set firmly in the ground for her purpose. She plopped the lolling head of the doomed creature upon it and brought the hatchet blade down with the zeal of a Vandal. Blood burst everywhere. Marc leapt back, then stared down at the crimson spatter on his boots and the gaudy petit point etched suddenly in the snow. As Winnifred jerked the decapitated fowl up by its feet to let the blood drip out, she noticed the spectator for the first time.

"Around here we do our own killing," she said. Then she wheeled about and strode into the barn. At the base of the stump, the creature's dead eye was wide open.

Marc scrubbed his boots in the snow and carried on. At the door to the back shed, he noted the probable cause of Winnifred's scorn, if that's what it was. Standing just inside, obscured by shadow, Mary Huggan was twisting a cotton hanky in her fingers and doing her best to hold back her tears.

"It's all right now, Mary," he said in what he hoped was a soothing tone. "You can go on over there. Beth's expecting you."

Mary sped away, carefully skirting the blood-drenched path beside the coop.

AFTER A MIDDAY MEAL OF CHEESE, cold ham, and bread, Marc and Erastus Hatch walked down to the barn, where Hatch asked Thomas Goodall to saddle their horses. They continued on to the mill and sat smoking in the tiny office the miller kept there, more as a sanctuary than a place of business.

"I could go out there on my own," Marc said.

"I'm sure you could, son. But this ain't England, you know. That tunic of yours is more likely to raise the bull's hackles than to instill fear, or even generate a modicum of respect." He was chuckling but nonetheless serious.

"I do know that," Marc said. A mere eight months in the colony had taught him to disregard the graces and rules of the society he had been raised in. In Great Britain there were dozens of offences for which a man who forgot his place in the unchangeable scheme of things might be hanged—and frequently was. Here in Upper Canada, you had to murder a man in front of ten unimpeachable witnesses before the scaffold was brought into play. And dressing down an insubordinate or an offending citizen was just as likely to get you a string of retaliatory oaths as a cap-tugging apology. Even women who professed to be ladies smoked pipes in public and were known to utter a curse or two when provoked. It was only at Government House and at the few mixed gatherings of the officers' mess that his scarlet tunic and brass set tender hearts aflutter or elicited respect amongst the enlisted men and servants. That he had been the son of a gamekeeper was neither here nor there, especially if no one were ever to find out.

"I'll just ride on out ahead of you," Hatch said, "and let

Wicks and Hislop know you're coming, and why. Then I'll leave you to them."

"That's extremely kind of you."

"Still, even if they accept you as an advance man for the quartermaster, I don't quite see how you're likely to bring the conversation around to a death almost everybody in the township believes to be an accident."

"I don't rightly know myself," Marc said. "But I think I've learned enough to improvise something. It shouldn't be hard to start a discussion of Joshua's accident: there's certain to have been lots of gossip and speculation about it. All I need is a cue to ask whether or not these people ever knew or met him. I might suggest that I knew him a bit back in Toronto. None of these men will know precisely when I came here or how long I've been in the garrison at Fort York."

"You could even mention you're going to make an offer for the two hogs Elijah is fattening up for the spring."

"Am I?" said Marc.

"I'm sure your quartermaster would approve," Hatch said, laughing.

HALF AN HOUR LATER THE TWO men were riding up the Farley Sideroad towards a group of farms locally dubbed "Buffaloville." Hatch had just suggested that Marc pull his horse into the protection of some cedars while he went on up to the Stebbins place to prepare for Marc's arrival and secure his cover story, when onto the road in front of them swung a two-horse team and cutter. Moments later, the vehicle went whizzing past them at full trot. A curt wave from the fur-clad driver was all the greeting they got as he raced down the concession line.

"Azel Stebbins," Hatch said. "Prime suspect."

"Where would he be going in such a hurry at one in the afternoon?"

"By the looks of that harquebus sticking up behind the seat, I'd say he was going hunting. Some deer were spotted up that way yesterday."

"Is everyone around here armed?"

"Well, they all hunt."

"I take it we can write off Stebbins for the day?"

"Unless you'd like to spend the afternoon watching young Lydia Stebbins bat her big eyelashes at you."

As GOOD AS HIS WORD, HATCH did go on ahead to the farm of Israel Wicks to prepare the ground for an official visit from the regimental quartermaster's emissary. When Marc rode up the lane alongside a windbreak of pines, he spotted a tall, bearded fellow sporting an orange tuque waiting for him in front of a low but extensive square-log cabin, onto which a number of ells and sheds had been added over time. Behind it stood an impressive barnboard structure, several smaller coops and hutches, and a split-rail corral where a pair of matched Percherons idled in the cold sunshine.

Wicks held out a friendly hand when Marc dismounted, and led him into the house. "Erastus says you're from the garrison in Toronto, scoutin' for grain and pork."

"That's right," Marc said. "I'm authorized only to line up potential supplies, to save Major Jenkin time when he makes the rounds of the eastern counties next month."

"We'll have some coffee and a shot of somethin' stronger before we talk business," Wicks said, pulling off his coat and scarf. He hollered towards the partitioned area at the rear of the house, "Moe, come out here. We got company!"

Wicks appeared to be about forty-five years of age. He had a grizzled beard, grooved brow, and deep-set eyes that revealed the confidence and the anxiety that comes from prolonged experience of life's vicissitudes. He took Marc's greatcoat and draped it carefully over a chair beside the fire blazing in the hearth, above which a brace of Kentucky shooting guns were on display.

"Ah, Maureen."

Marc turned to be introduced to Mrs. Wicks, a spare, fretting little woman who reminded him of a nervous songbird that's forgotten to migrate and seems perpetually puzzled by the consequences. She stopped abruptly when she sighted him, as if bedazzled by the blast of scarlet before her.

"Say hello to Ensign Edwards, Moe."

"Ma'am," Marc said, but his bow was missed by the averted eyes of his hostess.

"We don't get much company out here—in the winter," Wicks said.

"I'll fetch us some coffee," his wife said. She scuttled back into the safety of her kitchen, and the clatter of kettles on an iron stove was soon heard.

"You've no children?" Marc said.

"Two lads," Wicks said, in a voice strong and rich enough to grace a podium or the hustings in the heat of a campaign. The vigorous health that is the gift of an outdoor life shone through his movements and ease of bearing. Marc suffered a pang of envy and felt suddenly ashamed of his deception. "They're both out doing road duty for a couple of days."

Maureen Wicks flitted in with a tray of coffee and biscuits and flitted back out again. Wicks tipped a generous dollop of whisky into the mugs, and the two men drank and ate.

"I've got about fifty bags of wheat in storage at Hatch's mill," Wicks said and, looking closely at Marc, added, "but then you already know that."

Marc finished chewing his biscuit before replying. "Erastus hasn't written down the amounts for me yet, but he's suggested I see men like yourself because he knows you may be interested in any offers."

This answer seemed to satisfy Wicks. "I'd be willin' to sell half of that, as grain or flour when the mill starts up again. Hatch can vouch for the quality."

"Any livestock?"

"Half a dozen hogs fat enough by April, if that's okay. Do you need to see them?"

"The state of your buildings and the neatness of your house tell me all I need to know about the fastidiousness of your farming," Marc said, hoping he was not overplaying the flattery card, "and, of course, what Hatch has already told me about you."

They chatted informally about potential prices, the prospects for a good spring, and the severity of the past two winters before Marc said casually, "Hatch tells me the winter's been hard on his neighbour."

"Mrs. Smallman," Wicks said, eyeing him closely.

"Something about her father-in-law getting killed in a freak accident."

"A tree fell on him. New Year's Eve."

"What kind of fool is out cutting trees on New Year's Eve?" Marc said, feigning incredulity.

Wicks eyed his guest carefully, then said, "Joshua Smallman was no fool."

"You knew the man?"

"Just to see him," Wicks said with calculated offhandedness. "I knew his son Jesse a while back. The father was a merchant from your town—an old Tory, I'm told, but a good man all the same."

"Not the dry goods man?"

"That's right. He come back here to run the farm after Jesse died."

Marc smiled. "And I take it that you are not a Tory?"

Wicks laughed, and the tension in him dissolved. "I see that my good friend Constable Hatch has been praisin' more than my ploughin' techniques. In this province, once an American, forever a Yankee." The laughter faded. "I'm more the fool for thinkin' that'll ever change."

"My quartermaster doesn't distinguish between Yankee wheat and English corn," Marc felt compelled to say.

"That is quite true," Wicks said, pouring them each another whisky. "And it's one of the many reasons I've chosen to stay here and raise my family. Though I still have days when I wonder if I'm crazy to do so."

Marc shifted in his chair.

Again, Wicks's smile was as broad as it was enigmatic. "You haven't been in this country long, have you?"

"A year or so," Marc said.

"So far I bet you know mostly what you've been told by the self-serving grandees around you, includin' a lot of lies and exaggeration about the Yankee settlers doin' all the agitatin', or secretly yearnin' for the democracy they so foolishly abandoned."

"I've heard that kind of talk," Marc said. "You think I shouldn't believe it?"

"I'd be astonished if you didn't," Wicks said. "But you've

been given a chance—bein' sent out here to the untamed countryside—to see for yourself. Which is somethin' the Family Compact—with its rectors and bankers and lawyers—and the toadyin' members of the Legislative Council in Toronto have never bothered to do."

Marc seized his opportunity. "I did see for myself only this morning the tragic effects of the Clergy Reserves policy—on the Smallman farm."

"You can multiply that by a thousand," Wicks said, seemingly without rancour. "But since you are interested and may be young enough to learn somethin' new, let me tell you a bit about the so-called Yankee troublemakers in this province."

"I would be happy to listen," Marc said, barely able to contain his delight.

"I was a Yankee born and raised up, like so many of us who came up here after 1815: free-spirited, happy-go-lucky, fearin' no man and certainly no government, genuflectin' to nobody. My parents had carved out a farm in the Ohio Valley and helped to push the frontier towards the Wabash. But when they died, what they left me was not peaceful fields and prosperous towns. They left me Indian wars and military service and all the horror and lawlessness that comes with social chaos and the seductive power of sudden riches."

Mrs. Wicks, detecting perhaps some sea change in the familiar rhythms of her husband's speech, poked her nose around the partition.

"I was forced to serve my three months with the Ohio Volunteers during the Indian wars. I was at the Battle of Frenchtown on the River Raisin. A slaughterhouse it was. I saw the great warrior Tecumseh up close before some tomahawk clubbed me unconscious. I was one of the lucky ones: I got dragged back with my unit when we retreated. Several hundred of our wounded were massacred later that night and their bodies tossed into the bush to be eaten by bears and coyotes. And later on, when we got a chance to get our own back, we did: I watched women and children hacked and slashed like butchered swine. I myself held torches to houses, some of them with people still inside, refusin' to leave. I still wake up at night, screamin' with the agony of it."

"War is sometimes an unpleasant necessity," Marc said lamely.

Wicks did not hear. He stared into the fire for a while, then said, still looking down, "Most of us came up here for a little peace and stability, a little law and order, and a chance to prove we could be good farmers and better citizens. When Governor Peregrine Maitland called us aliens and sought to have us barred from holdin' office or a seat in the Assembly, we had no choice but to do the very thing most of us were tryin' to escape: get embroiled in politics. For a time even our property rights were threatened."

"So you joined forces with the radicals in the Reform party?"

"Who else was goin' to look out for our rights?"

"And so you met Jesse Smallman, who also had his grievance."

"And dozens of others—local-born, Scotchmen, Irishmen, a few fair-minded loyalists. And we got the alien question settled once and for all."

"But I've been told that a new petition of grievances is in the colonial secretary's hands at this very moment."

Wicks had lit his pipe and was now puffing contemplatively at it. "I do read the papers, young man, including the *Colonial Advocate*. But my property is now secure. My two sons, who can't remember any other home but this, are out doin' public service on the King's Highway. My own concerns are no more than the weather and the price of grain."

"I'm most happy to hear it," Marc said, rising. "Thank you sincerely for your hospitality and your frankness."

As Marc was buttoning his greatcoat at the door, Wicks said, "When you make your report to John Colborne, be sure and ask him how keen he'd be to repeat the carnage of Waterloo or Toulouse."

Riding away, Marc was still too flummoxed to notice Maureen Wicks's angst-ridden face in her kitchen window, like a winter moon with all the harvest-blood drained from it.

EIGHT

Marc continued north along the Farley Sideroad towards the last farm before the serious bush began, though to someone not familiar with the Upper Canadian landscape this frozen twelve-foot swathe bordered by cedar, pine, and leafless birch would seem more like a logging road in a wilderness than a neatly surveyed thoroughfare. At the moment, the isolation and silence suited Ensign Edwards, who was deep in thought.

He guided the horse through a gap in the evergreens and was astonished to see before him a very large area, perhaps a hundred acres, completely shorn of trees and seemingly of all vegetation. Not a bush or vine peeped above the rumpled counterpane of snow. At the far edges of the clearing Marc could see a ragged fence of uprooted stumps and charred limbs. Three buildings interrupted the horizon: a low, ungabled log house with oiled-paper windows; a ramshackle barn whose wings, ells, and jetties seemed to be patched together; and beyond that a sort of lean-to fashioned of cedar poles and layers of bark or wind-stiffened sailcloth. From the house a limp plume of smoke rose out of a crumbling chimney.

Marc rode up to what he deduced to be the front door, dismounted, and, failing to find a hitching post or ring of any kind, wrapped the horse's reins around one of the protruding log ends. The door itself drooped on stretched leather hinges and boasted a number of gouges and splinters where a boot or fist had met it in anger. Marc gave it a tentative rap, fearing he might knock it irreparably askew.

A booming voice that might have been female answered from the depths inside: "For Chrissake, don't just stand there pickin' at your scab, open the goddamn door and come in!"

Marc did as he was bidden. Seated in the centre of the room in a horsehair chair of princely proportions was a woman of ample dimension and extraordinary presence. Marc recoiled visibly, as if unable to take in the image of her all at once.

"Cassie, get off your plump rump and take the gentleman's hat! Buster, vacate that chair this instant or I'll take a strip off yer arse and turn it inta a red bandanny!"

The fire in the hearth, fitful and smoky, flung a dim glow through the almost windowless room. Cassie came meekly out of one of its shadowy corners: a young woman clad only in a shift and moth-eaten sweater, whose beauty was marred—or perhaps made more exotic—by a glassy walleye and a mole at the base of her throat. Staring at Marc, abashed, from her one clear, blue eye, she stretched out a trembling arm for his coat and shako cap. She continued to stare at his uniform.

"You keep yer eyes on the floor, milady!" the girl's mother—as Marc assumed her to be—roared with an accompanying guffaw that shook the room with the vehemence of a fart. "Young Cassie's got a thing for soldiers. Come militia day, and we gotta lock her in the pigpen!"

"Good day, madam. My name is—"

"I know what yer moniker is, young gentleman. I've been forewarned, ya might say, and I know why you're here. Take that chair by the fire. Buster, get yer greasy paws offa it! You get the loo-tenant's uniform dirty and he'll take you outside and shoot you silly with his Brown Bess."

Marc smiled reassuringly at young Buster, who seemed deaf to his mother's entreaties and more intent on looking for any sign of said gun. Marc sat on the edge of the chair.

"I'm Bella Hislop," the woman said, "as I'm sure you've figured out already. You met Cassie, my oldest and prettiest—don't blush, girl, beauty's not a gift to be sneezed at, the good Lord only doles out so many talents—and

Buster there, with the gawkin' eyes and big nose, my eldest of the bollocked variety. And up there the other six are skulkin' and tryin' to keep outta my reach, aren't ya, ya little buggers!"

On this last note, Bella Hislop wrenched her thick torso a quarter-turn, which allowed her to gaze up into a huge loft that covered almost half the house at the north end. Several titters and much rustling ensued, and Marc could just make out in the gloom a row of dirty children's faces peering down with curiosity and trepidation.

"Mr. Hatch has been here, then?" Marc said.

"Indeed he has, the old crook. I damn near run him off the place."

"He has wronged you somehow?" Marc said, unable to hide his surprise or his irritation.

Bella Hislop rose in her chair, lifting her heavy flesh into a posture of indignation and contempt, like an overweight marionette whose slack strings are suddenly jerked upwards with a singular flourish. Her voluminous dress went dangerously taut, threatening to burst. Her jowls quivered stiffly and her eyes blazed.

"He merely swindled my husband outta twenty barrels of flour, that's all. And us with eight mouths to feed and me still teat-feedin' the young'un. 'Full of chaff and tares,' the bastard says to Orville, right in front of half the neighbourhood. That's all he's got to say for comin' up twenty barrels short on our millin', our whole summer's harvest. Well, we got our pride if we got nothin' else. My Orville just turns and walks away, real dignified, like the gentleman he was brung up to be."

"I'm sure the miller is not a man to cheat his customers," Marc said.

Bella gave him a withering look, then abruptly relaxed, her flesh and bones sagging thankfully back to their accustomed position. She emitted a thunderous chuckle. "You are a young man. You know little of the ways of the world and its thousand iniquities. All millers are cheats and mountebanks. If they were honest men, they would till the soil themselves instead of feedin' off the sweat of their fellows. And what redress have we got anyways? You think my sweet Orville—as honest as Esau, as upright as Solomon—can trot along cap in hand to the constable to swear out a complaint?" She burst out laughing. "Is that bugger Hatch gonna arrest himself?"

"There is a sheriff for the county," Marc pointed out. "And a magistrate a stone's throw from the mill."

"Randy-the-dandy MacLachlan, you mean!" she roared, and the shock wave made the peering faces in the loft bob. "I wouldn't let my six-year-old Susan near him. And who do you think is a charter member of that faggots' club up at the squire's?"

"I would be most pleased to forward any written complaint or petition on your behalf," Marc said, not for a second believing Bella's charge but nevertheless feeling some obligation to demonstrate the absolute objectivity and probity of British due process.

"What makes you think Orville and me got any surplus to sell to the English army of occupation?" Bella said, and she pinned him with a stare.

"That's what I'm here to find out, ma'am. I'm merely an emissary."

"A papal legate, sort of," Bella grinned. "You payin' with cash?"

"Pound notes only."

"None of that funny money, now, that army scrip yer betters palmed off on us last time. And no notes drawn on the Bank of fuckin' Upper Canada."

Marc flinched, noted no reaction from the two eldest at the obscenity, and forged ahead. "We're looking for pork as well as grain," he said.

"Our pigs aren't doin' so good this winter. Some kinda fever gettin' inta them. The boar's doin' poorly too. Unfortunately, a boar is a necessity, ugly as it may be, eh? Like God and shitty weather."

"Is your husband at home, madam?" Marc said.

"Jeezuz, I ain't been called 'madam' since the time I stumbled inta a hooer-house in Syracuse lookin' fer that arsehole that got me up the stump and had to marry me or take a load of buckshot in the underparts!"

"I can return another time," Marc said, starting to get up.

"Siddown, for Chrissake, nobody's tryin' to scare ya off.

Cassie, bring out the jar of hooch and pour a mugful fer me and Officer Edwards."

"Really, ma'am, I couldn't—"

"You call me 'ma'am' once more and I'll toss ya headfirst inta the fire. Now unhitch yer high horse and relax. I got some questions I wanta ask you."

Cassie did as she was commanded, blushing fiercely as she served Marc and sensed his eyes upon her flimsy dress and what it inadequately concealed.

"Pretty one, ain't she?" Bella said, downing half her drink in one gulp. "Spittin' image of me, though you'd hardly think so now. 'Course I had two eyes to see with back then and still ended up in this shit-hole."

"How may I help you?" Marc said.

"I wanta know why you're really here."

"But I've told you that . . . Mrs. Hislop."

"I hear Monsieur Papineau and Wolfred Nelson're kickin' up shit in Quebec. Colborne, and his Tory ass-lickers think the same trouble's about to start up here, don't they?"

"I am not at liberty to comment," Marc said, swallowing his astonishment.

"Aren't ya, now. Well, that's one of the things wrong with this province, ain't it? The people in power don't feel the need to be at liberty to say anythin' by way of explanation to the wretches who've got no power of their own."

"The people here, I'm told, elected an Assembly in

which the majority of seats are held by members of the Reform party."

"Well, you are up on yer politics, ain't ya?" She polished off her "whisky" and waited until he had at least sipped his. (Jamaican rum, he was only mildly surprised to discover.) "What I am at liberty to say to you and yer limp-pricked major-domos back in Toronto is that my Orville worked as hard as any man to get Mr. Perry elected to the Assembly. He even escorted Mr. Mackenzie on his tour through this district in thirty-four—him and a dozen others, like Wicks and Stebbins and poor young Jesse Smallman that hung himself for grief over the state of affairs. That don't make my Orville a revolutionary. His grandpapa, now there was a true revolutionary. Fought side by side with George Washington at Valley Forge and got his left leg blown to kingdom come. Folks up here don't know chapter one about real revolution."

"I assure you, madam—"

"We got more assurances from your bigwigs than we could use to paper a privy." Her mammoth breasts heaved above the stretched waistline of her dress, but it was the flare of her eyes that held Marc spellbound. "If it was up to me, I'd've organized a posse of Minutemen, marched on Toronto, and done what my countrymen did to it in the War of 1812: jam a stick of dynamite under it and blow it inta Lucifer's parlour." She sighed extravagantly, like a basso profundo at the end of an aria.

"That's treasonable talk, madam."

"Lucky fer you I didn't, eh? You'd have no toy soldiers

to play with. But I'm only a woman, and Orville ain't what he useta be." She chuckled softly. "Poor Orville wasn't ever what he useta be."

"Your husband is ill?"

Bella guffawed, sending a spray of spittle past Marc's knees. "Not as ill as he oughta be! He can still get it up, if that's what you're inferrin'."

"Madam, there are children present."

"Don't I know it. I got eight livin', all of 'em in this stinkin' room. But I've had twelve all told. It'd've been a goddamn good trick if I could've organized a revolution between the ploughin' and the begettin', wouldn't it?"

Marc got up and pulled his coat on quickly before Cassie could arrive to assist him. Buster meantime had sidled up to him and was stroking the brushed wool as if it were ermine or beaver, or a pet that would purr in gratitude.

"I hear tell the new governor ain't a military man," Bella said, still wedged so firmly in the big chair that if she were, on a whim, to have stood up it would have come with her like a monstrous bustle. "That should be an improvement right there."

"Mr. Hislop is not here?" Marc tried again.

"Mr. Hislop is out in the barn somewheres or else skunk-drunk in a snowdrift. Mr. Hislop don't spend much time in his house these days, or nights."

Cassie looked ready to interrupt her mother; her lower lip trembled and tears sprang into her eyes.

"Don't you shush me, girl," Bella hissed at Cassie. "I'm all you got in this world, and don't forget it." She turned back to Marc, who now stood rooted to the doorjamb. "I've had all the babies I'm ever goin' to. I've made that perfectly plain to his nibs." She reached under the horsehair cushion and produced a menacing pair of tin-snips. She snapped the pincers together with an ominous click. "If he so much as breathes on my bed with his hoe-handle at half-mast, it's snip, snip—good-bye and good riddance. And he'll get some of the same if I see him within spittin' distance of my Cassie."

Just before he shut the door behind him, Marc slipped a shilling into his young admirer's grimy palm.

As he walked to the corner of the house where his horse was tethered, Marc noticed a male figure scuttling in his direction. It seemed to have emerged from between the barn and the lean-to beyond it. The figure stopped, appeared to take its bearings, then hailed him. Marc dropped the reins and strode out, not without curiosity, to meet, he presumed, the treacherously sweet Orville Hislop.

"Who the hell're you!" Hislop shouted querulously. He started forward.

Marc continued on towards him. Hislop stalled, uncertain of his ground. His glazed eye had caught the tufted shako and flash of scarlet at the open throat of the military greatcoat. Hislop himself was clad only in overalls, boots, and a bulky sweater, which struggled to envelop a low-slung belly that seemed at odds with his otherwise muscular and work-hardened body. He wore no cap, and the brindled mop of his hair was littered with straw, and worse.

Marc shot out his hand. "I am Ensign Edwards," he said, "on assignment from the quartermaster at York. We're looking to buy surplus grain or pork for the army, as soon as possible."

"Are ya, now? You don't look like no quartermaster to me," Hislop growled. "And what've ya been foragin' at in my house, eh?"

"Your good wife directed me out here to you," Marc lied, with an ease he was growing accustomed to.

"Good wife, my arse," Hislop said, and Marc could see now that he had been drinking—a lot—and that he had become suddenly aware that this uniformed stranger had noticed it. He grinned broadly, exposing three yellowed stumps of teeth, and winked. "You'll know all about it when you're married."

"I understand from Mrs. Hislop that you've had a bad year and that I'm not likely to find what I'm looking for."

"She told ya that, did she, now? Weren't that just splendid of her! Well, Mr. Ensign Edwards, you just come along with me and I'll show you half a dozen of the finest hogs in the county."

Marc followed Hislop into a rickety, shed-like appendage to the barn, trying to keep upwind of him. Inside, the stench was overpowering: the result of a pigsty unmucked for weeks, mixed with a similar stink from the adjacent cattle stalls.

"Takes a little gettin' used to." Hislop chuckled, peering sideways at Marc as the latter thrust a handkerchief over his mouth and nostrils. "Just plug yer nose and take a gander at them barrows. They'll be as fat as my wife's tits by Easter." Marc could just discern the scrawny outlines of several young, castrated hogs, so begrimed it was only their occasional twitch or shudder that distinguished them from the mud and excrement they inhabited.

"Good thing we don't eat the outside of 'em," Hislop said encouragingly.

"Yes," Marc said, and he stumbled back outside. A few yards away was the peculiar lean-to affair. "That where you keep your sick boar?" he said between gasps.

Hislop squinted, coughed, gargled a mouthful of phlegm, and said, "That's right. I been tendin' to the poor bugger all afternoon."

"I was raised on a farm, believe it or not," Marc said. "My uncle worked wonders with sick animals. I'd be glad to have a look at him for you."

Hislop's eyes widened as far as his alcoholic haze would permit. "That's mighty considerate of you, sir, but it's just a touch of colic." He had Marc by the elbow and was ushering him towards his horse. "You be sure to let me know about them barrows of mine. I'll take any price that's fair, especially if you're payin' cash this round. We don't see much minted money in these parts. I can give ya the names of some other fellas in the township—"

"Quartermaster Jenkin will be in touch with you next month, provided those hogs are healthy . . . and clean as a babe in its bath," Marc said, mounting his horse. Then, without a nod or farewell, he rode straight out to the side-road.

At first he headed south towards the highway, but when he came to a path that wandered west through the bush below the Hislop place, he urged his horse onto it. He followed it slowly in a wide arc until he was at the rear of the farm, where he had a sheltered view of the lean-to and the barn behind it. He was just in time.

Glancing around every few seconds, Hislop was skulking his way towards the lean-to. He staggered around to the near side of it, where a rickety door or hatch had been propped up to block the low entranceway. He stood still, as if listening intently. From inside the lean-to came a mewling sound, most unpig-like in its keening persistence. Seemingly satisfied, Hislop jerked the hatch away and flung it aside.

"Stop yer whinin'! Ya want Bella out here with the snips?"

The keening increased, broken finally by a series of hic-coughing sobs.

"Get yer skinny arse outta there, the fun's over."

A moment later a woman's head pushed its way out of the murky interior: first a tangle of red curls, then a pale face.

"Outta there, ya little hooer," Hislop barked. He reached down to grasp the girl—for she was only that—by one thin wrist and heaved her up and out into the nearest drift. She landed on both buttocks, her equally thin legs splayed and one oversized boot ripped off. She was clothed only in a flannel nightgown and a man's sweater that she had not succeeded in getting over her head in time.

"I want my shillin'," she said with a perfunctory whine.

"You almost cost me twenty dollars—if I'd've missed that soldier, out here with the likes of you."

"I'll holler my head off—"

But she didn't. Hislop kicked her in the stomach, knocking the wind and any resistance out of her. She let out a gasp, curled up into a ball of bent limbs, and started to whimper.

Marc was just about to spur his horse forward when the girl leapt up and turned to flee. Hislop whirled around and snatched at her nightgown, and as she wrenched herself away from him, the entire gown with the sweater came off in his hand. Hislop's chin dropped in amazement. The girl saw her chance and sprinted towards the sideroad, stark naked but for one blackened boot that thumped into the snow like a club foot.

Marc realized immediately that she would come out onto the sideroad only a few yards from where the path he had taken met it, so he headed at full gallop back through the bush. As he charged out onto the road, the girl was just coming through the trees. Unexpectedly she turned north and, still bounding like a spooked doe, oblivious of her nakedness or the freezing air around her, she sped towards the end of the road. Marc caught up with her just as she veered back into the bush. Leaning down, holding the reins slack in one hand and guiding the horse with his knees, Marc grasped the girl under her arms at the apex of one of her leaps and swept her up in front of him onto the horse's withers. She let out a surprisingly loud shriek and tried to strike him.

"I'm not Hislop!" he cried. "I've come to help you." The horse kept on going along a faint trail through the bush. The girl's struggles eased—in relief or exhaustion. Marc brought the horse to a halt and dismounted.

"I'm going to take you down from here and wrap you up before you freeze to death," he said. "Please don't scream. There's no need. I'm not going to hurt you." She said nothing. Her body went limp in his arms.

He drew her gently down and, holding her under the arms—his gloved hand crushing one of her small, stiff-nippled breasts—he tugged a blanket out of his saddle-roll and pulled it about her, twice. Tiny shudders racked her wasted body, no more than a hundred pounds in all. Her lips had turned a ghastly purple, her teeth chattered, and her eyelids blinked frantically. She's dying, Marc thought. He'd seen death like this up close, not on any battlefield, but in the alleys of central London where, every morning as he walked from his rooms to the offices of Jardin and Musgrove, he passed the casualties of lust and other hungers: prostitutes with the rags of their trade falling off their ruined flesh, their emaciated faces peering up at anyone foolish enough to bend down to them and venting a final curse or death's-head plea as their eyelids fluttered and closed.

He opened his greatcoat and crushed her body in against his own warmth, cocooning her, willing her to survive. Foolishly he kissed the top of her head, pushing his nose into the thick, reddish curls, as if the least gesture of affection might astonish and resuscitate. Gradually the shuddering diminished, her cheeks went suddenly rosy, her eyes swelled with tears, and a pink sliver of tongue slipped out to lick her upper lip. Then she snuggled farther into the hug that held her.

The girl sighed, closed her eyes, opened them again, and said in a low, sweet, Sunday-school voice: "You gonna poke me?"

HER NAME WAS AGNES PRINGLE, AND they were on a woodsy trail that, as long as she directed Marc, would lead them to her home. With the blanket and greatcoat still wrapped around her and Marc's extra mitts on her feet, she insisted she was well enough to ride up behind him, holding tight with both arms around his chest. The horse moved at a sedate pace.

"You don't mean to say your mother's Annie Pringle?" Marc said.

"That's right, Mad Annie," Agnes said cheerfully.

Erastus Hatch, as promised, had explained to Marc who Mad Annie was, and had sternly warned him to steer clear of her squattery out on the marshland north of the surveyed concessions. The only route into it lay in a maze of trails, the miller had said (not without some admiration), most of which were booby-trapped and life-threatening to the unescorted. What lay at the heart of this mischievously mined moat was the subject of much public speculation and sustained moral outrage. "Just Mad Annie, a still, and her brood of ne'er-do-wells," Hatch had suggested, "but you could get maimed trying to prove it!"

"You can just let me off at the end of this here path," Agnes said. "I know my way up to the house."

"I could make a lot of trouble for Hislop," Marc said.

"And he'll only make more for us."

"But he assaulted you."

Agnes giggled. "He did a lot more'n that to me."

"He owes you a dress," Marc said.

"We take care of our own," Agnes said.

Hatch had warned him also about the infamous Pringle boys, Mad Annie's obstreperous male offspring, and Marc decided not to be nonchalant about this errand of mercy. A military uniform out here could easily be misconstrued.

"Nobody'll hurt ya," Agnes said, sliding off the horse.

She removed the greatcoat with a slow, purring gesture, rubbed it sensuously against her cheek, then held it up to him. She watched him put it on, then said, "What about yer mitts and this here blanket?" She started to draw the edges of the cloth away from her chest in a sad parody of seduction.

"You'll need them if you aren't to freeze," Marc said. "You sure you can make it home?" He was gazing dubiously through a screen of cedars at an uneven open area that was likely a swamp come spring, dotted here and there with scrub bushes, the remnants of cattails, and stunted evergreens. Several hundred yards farther, on the distant verge of the clearing, he spotted several shacks and tumbledown outbuildings. No welcoming smoke rose from any one of them.

Agnes was in the midst of nodding "yes" to Marc's inquiry when her eyes widened and her pale cheeks went paler. "Jesus," she hissed. Then she wailed, "It's Ma!"

From the cover of a nearby cedar stepped the woman known throughout the district as Mad Annie. Marc's initial instinct was to laugh, for she was at first glance not a prepossessing sight. From Hatch's descriptions and cautions, given in detail on their ride to Buffaloville, Marc had expected her to be a female of formidable bulk. But before him now, with her feet planted apart as if she were on snowshoes, stood a tiny woman clothed in a loose sweater, a lumberjack's tuque, woollen trousers fastened at the waist and ankle with binder-twine, and a pair of mismatched boots. Her face was misshapen, like a badly aged apple doll. But it was her eyes that caught Marc's attention. They were large and round—intelligent, belligerent, and curiously vulnerable. At this moment, they blazed with suspicion and imminent aggression. Marc could see nothing lunatic in them.

"Put the girl down," she commanded.

"She is down," Marc said firmly. "I've brought her home—to her mother, I presume."

"Who I am ain't your business, mister," she said, assessing the uniformed rider and his horse with a single cold, bright glance. Then she turned to the girl, as if Marc were now of peripheral interest at best. Agnes wrapped the grey blanket twice around her and shuffled across to her mother.

"What'd the bastard do with yer dress?" Mad Annie said.

Agnes ducked away from a blow that did not come. "Tore it offa me."

Mad Annie smiled with her lips only (she appeared to be toothless). "They do get excited at the sight of tits and a fur-piece, don't they?" When Agnes peeked up to acknowledge her mother's remark, Mad Annie cuffed her smartly on the back of the head.

Marc started forward in the saddle. He was still trying to square the image of this crone with Hatch's colourful account of a matriarch who had "whelped" seventeen times, including two sets of twins, only the first three of her litter being traceable to Mr. Pringle, who had long since vamoosed or died happily by his own hand. Mad Annie caught Marc's movement out of the corner of one eye and wheeled about.

"You stay right where you are, mister. You're trespassin' on Pringle property."

"I suggest you leave the girl be," Marc said. "She's been kicked and abused enough for one day."

"That so?" Without looking, she reached out and grabbed the blanket covering Agnes's shoulder and hauled the girl before her. Agnes collapsed submissively at her feet. As she did so, the fabric parted, exposing her breasts, like two puffed bruises. "He pay you?" Mad Annie barked, glaring back up at Marc.

"It was Hislop, it was Hislop," Agnes whimpered. "He did me every way all afternoon in that . . . that pigsty, and then he rips my dress and throws me out."

Mad Annie ignored her daughter. "You poke her, you pay," she said to Marc.

"Madam, I find you a repulsive and unnatural human being. I recommend you take your daughter, who has suffered an outrage and nearly lost her life, and care for her with any kindness you can muster as her mother and protector. Otherwise I shall have the law on you."

Agnes was shaking her head at him.

"And I recommend you turn that ball-less bag-o'-bones around and hightail it offa my land before I do somethin' beneficial, like blow yer pecker off." From under her sweater, or through one of its several vents, she had drawn a pistol, and she was aiming it at the ensign.

Marc had never before stared into the business end of a deadly weapon aimed at him. His gut went queasy, but the disciplined training he had endured for over a year at Sandhurst held him in good stead. He blinked, but did not flinch.

Agnes took advantage of the momentary standoff by scampering up and away, clutching the army blanket to her throat.

With steely calm, Marc turned his horse and trotted deliberately back down the trail, his broad shoulders providing the perfect target for a bullet. At the first bend he stopped and turned to look back. Mad Annie had caught up to Agnes but was not berating the girl. Instead, the two women had joined hands and were making a rapid, zigzagging dash across the frozen marsh towards home.

Avoiding their own booby-traps, Marc thought. Only now did it occur to him that the pistol appeared to have been neither primed nor loaded. He rode slowly, pondering what further assault might yet be made upon the dignity of the Crown's commissioned investigator. More than that, he was shaken by the raw realities of existence in this savage hinterland. The law and civilized society seemed very far away.

NINE

I know, I know," Hatch said, "back home the likes of Mad Annie and Orville Hislop would be thrown into Bedlam or packed off to Van Dieman's Land on the first boat."

"Hanged at Newgate more likely," Marc said, but in truth he was more disappointed than outraged. Any anger remaining was now directed at himself and his failure to glean any new information.

"The way many folks around here look at it, they really aren't doing much harm to anybody but themselves. Annie's gaggle do manufacture bad hooch from time to time, and once in a while the sheriff catches one of her boys stealing a chicken and they spend a month or two in jail. And those Yankee farmers are just an independent lot by birth and upbringing. You never really stood much of a chance of getting anything useful out of them. Still, I think you did the right thing by carrying on to see Farley and McMaster. Those farmers have been here since before the war and are as tame as brood hens, but they'll soon report that you seemed to be what you claim to be. It'll keep Hislop and Wicks wondering and set you up for the Stebbins place tomorrow. You'll find them quite a different kettle of fish."

Marc and Hatch were seated before a lively fire mulling over the day's events and taking stock of the investigation. Erastus was being as encouraging as his good nature and the facts would allow. They were alone in the house.

After a fine roast-chicken supper, parts of which proceeding seemed to be coldly amusing to Winnifred Hatch, Thomas Goodall had hitched the Percheron team to the family cutter and joined Winnifred and Mary Huggan in the forty-minute drive to Cobourg, where a charity meeting of the Ladies' Aid had attracted the two women and an evening at the pub their driver. According to Mary, Beth Smallman had been invited to join them but had politely declined. Winnifred had dressed for the occasion in a carmine-coloured dress with ruched sleeves and jutting shoulders, of a material that swished like shale ice when she moved.

"It's hard to imagine any of these expatriate American farmers forming so strong a personal hatred towards Joshua that they'd want to see him dead," Marc said. "They all knew who he was, and showed no hesitation in admitting it. Their anger is focused on the government and the leaders of the Family Compact. You'd have to believe that they chose Joshua merely as a scapegoat for the Legislative councillors or the Toronto bankers. If so, then why choose a man who himself had begun appearing at Reform rallies and listening respectfully to what was being said?"

"I agree, though I also think we're looking for one man with some kind of personal grudge. Stebbins is a known hot-head and a very secretive chap. He seems to do an awful lot of hunting for a fellow whose smokehouse is usually empty."

Marc took note of the point, then said, "Most of these people will have known Jesse Smallman better than his father. Jesse was an associate during the period when the alien question threatened the political and property rights of the immigrant Americans, and tempers were naturally frayed. But the question has been more or less settled for a year. Any direct threat to the livelihood of Wicks, Hislop, or Farley is over. They do appear to me to be consumed by the demands of their farms. And, of course, Jesse himself died twelve months ago. It's an unequivocal connection between Joshua and some mad soul out there that I have to establish and understand."

Hatch puffed on his pipe. "We also have to consider the possibility that we may well have a different sort of mystery on our hands—one that doesn't involve a deliberate murder."

It was something they had both been thinking, but, spoken aloud, it seemed somehow more daunting.

ONCE AGAIN MARC ARRIVED LATE FOR breakfast. If Winnifred had slipped past his door last night on her way to another assignation with the hired hand, no hint of it showed in her face or demeanour as she went about helping young Mary serve up helpings of porridge and molasses, followed by pork sausages and boiled eggs, with thick slices of just-made bread and peach preserve. Thomas's chin drooped slightly more than usual below his downcast eyes (too much ale, or some more physical activity? Marc wondered), and Mary Huggan's cheeks glowed from something more than fanning the morning fire.

After breakfast, while Erastus and Thomas went off to the mill to check on some suspected damage to the mill wheel from shifting ice, Marc walked down to Crawford Creek. He could imagine the unerringly straight surveyor's line that permitted one curve of the meandering creek to be included in Hatch's property and another curve, in the opposite direction, to be excluded from the Smallman lands, depriving them of drainage and irrigation. Feeling vaguely impious, he tramped off the worn path and along the bank of the stream, impressing his regimental bootprints defiantly upon the clergy's preserve.

His efforts to revisit the facts of the case this morning,

however, were waylaid by the sudden and disturbing image that popped into his head of Winnifred Hatch and Thomas Goodall entangled and thrashing on that simple plough-man's bed in the January dark. And that lascivious picture turned his thoughts to his own romantic past.

Outside of his early fumbled attempts with one of his uncle's maids, his only sustained and satisfying sexual relationship had been with Marianne Dodds, a ward of their illustrious neighbour, Sir Joseph Trelawney. Theirs had been a passionate affair, chaste at first, but after a tacit understanding of sorts had been reached, it had quickly become a complete meshing of body and youthful spirits. When Marc was sent up to London to apprentice law, letters of confession and promise and eternal steadfastness cluttered the mailbag of the daily coach between London and Kent. Then hers stopped. By the time Marc could get leave to return home, Marianne had been forcibly removed to a distant shire and his love letters had been burned in the great man's grate. No explanation was ever offered for either barbarity. Several months later, back in London, he learned that Miss Dodds had been married off to a vicar with five hundred pounds and a twenty-year-old son. Uncle Jabez, unfailingly kind and meaning to be helpful no doubt, had whispered some unconsoling wisdom in his adopted son's ear: "In this country, class is class and blood is still blood. I can give you everything you need and deserve, except that."

Marc's reverie was interrupted by the sight of a small

figure making its way towards him along the trodden path behind Smallman's barn. He waved. Beth waved back.

In his suffering and bewilderment at Marianne's loss, Marc had plunged back into his work, happy now that lawyering was so hateful to him. And for the first time he had given in to the teasing of his fellow clerks, as young as he but infinitely more worldly, and followed them to the theatre and the fleshpots of London. Only once. The one good aspect of that night, ironically, had been his delight with the play itself, and his subsequent participation in amateur theatricals. His friends later accused him of moral priggery, but his abhorrence of the brothel and the offstage licentiousness of accommodating actresses was a physical revulsion, inexplicable but as uncontrollable as a reflex. There had been no woman in his life since.

Marc started across the untrodden snowscape of the Clergy Reserve towards Beth, who had halted at the edge of her property to wait for him.

It wasn't that there had been no opportunities for romance at balls in the neighbourhood, or later at the Royal Military School. At the suggestion of his "uncle" Frederick, Marc had willingly been sent to the school to "mend his heart and seek the only commendable career for a young man of spirit." Even in Toronto, since his arrival last May, there had been possibilities. So far, Marc had danced, flirted, dallied, and generally enjoyed the company of women, but that was all. He had refused to join the subalterns on their

periodic expeditions to the stews and gambling dens of Toronto that catered exclusively to the needs of officers robbed
of combat by the prolonged post-Napoleonic peace. Despite
his apparent prudery, Marc retained the respect of his mates,
even their affection.

"Good morning, Ensign Edwards," Beth said as he
puffed up the path towards her. "I see you decided to take
the military route."

"DID JOSHUA HAVE ANY SORT OF contact, friendly or otherwise, with any of the extremists out there in Buffaloville?"

They had walked, without predetermination, into the
woods on the Crown land above the Smallman farm, savouring the air, enjoying the challenge of ploughing their
way through the pure drifts.

"None that I know of," Beth said. "Apart from his
evenings with that Georgian crew and our trips into town
for supplies, and the half dozen rallies we went to over
the summer and fall, Father went nowhere. It took every
one of us to keep the farm afloat, even with the mortgage
lifted. The drought was severe. Everybody suffered to some
degree."

"You can remember no altercations at any of the rallies?"

"None. Besides, Azel Stebbins was about the only one
of those people to come to the meetings. After the business

with the Alien Act was over and they got back their rights, most of them lost interest. They had farms to run. Like us."

"But you kept attending," Marc said gently.

"I had my own reasons."

"I suppose Jesse knew more of these people than his father did," Marc said, then he took her mittened hand briefly to guide her over a windfall.

"Yes. They worked together off and on through the election year of thirty-four. And Jesse did some carpentry for a couple of them—corncribs, I think. He was a wonder with his hands."

"And your efforts helped to get Reformers like Dutton and Perry elected in this end of the province, to establish a Reform majority in the Assembly, and even get the alien question settled in your favour . . ."

"But?"

"But even with your majority and Mr. Mackenzie's manoeuvring to get the Seventh Report on Grievances across the Atlantic, even then you were no closer to winning your claim against the injustices of the Clergy Reserve allotments."

Beth stopped so she could read his expression. "So you think our claims may be just, do you?"

"All one needs to do is take a morning constitutional to see that."

"You should've brought Sir John along."

"It's easy now for me to understand how angry and frustrated your husband must have been last year. To have achieved a majority in the House and have so little to show for the effort, and risk."

"And a governor standing on the dock at Toronto ushering in penniless outcasts from the Auld Sod, sure to be grateful voters in the next election."

"From Jesse's perspective, it must have seemed like 'now or never.' In two years' time the entire government might have been Tory."

"With ample means of avenging themselves on so-called traitors and mischief-makers."

A new thought occurred to Marc, and he said, "His father must have learned these things, just as I am beginning to, soon after he arrived here. And Tory though he was, he must surely have built up some feelings of resentment over what happened to his son."

"He was very fond of Jess," Beth said, looking straight ahead.

With mixed emotions, Marc pressed on. "Might he not have drawn the conclusion—as he attended the Reform rallies—that it was all that radical and inflammatory talk that had pushed Jesse to the edge? And could such resentment have resulted in some harboured enmity on Joshua's part towards one or more of the extremists, which, unknown to you, led him to accuse or challenge or even threaten that person or persons?"

Beth seemed to be giving the notion due consideration. After a while, she said, "I reckon it more likely he came to understand exactly why his son did what he did."

"I don't follow," Marc said.

Beth took his arm. "Then it's time I explained."

THEY STOOD SIDE BY SIDE IN the barn. The sun bored through the unchinked log walls and spilled at their feet. From the hayloft at one end of the single, spacious room a square crossbeam ran to the far side. In the shadows, a pair of pigeons cooed amiably. Behind them and under the loft, cows chewed at the clover hay thrown to them earlier by Elijah, their literate caretaker.

"I found him hanging there. Just after noon. I wondered why he hadn't come in for his meal. Thank God I didn't send Aaron after him. Jess knew Aaron and I were spendin' the morning with Mary Huggan's family. So nothing would disturb him."

"I don't need to know—" Marc said, wondering whether his touching her would be welcomed or resented.

"I think you do. That milking stool was tipped over. He'd used it to stand on, then kicked it halfway across the barn. He'd even made a kind of rope-manacle for his hands and somehow tied them behind his back."

"Behind his back?"

"He wanted nothing to tempt him from his purpose."

They stood staring up at the scar on the beam where the noose had rubbed it—one of them imagining, the other reliving.

"You see, I misled you a little last time when I said Jesse wasn't tempted by the radical solutions being whispered throughout the district. In truth, he'd become desperate and depressed."

Marc spoke only because the silence continued longer than he could bear. "Do you know if he actually had contact with any seditionists?"

"He may have. If he did, he didn't tell me. There seemed to be a lot of things he couldn't tell me . . . near the end."

"I'm thinking that he may have learned something that his father might have subsequently come across, something incriminating—"

"But that's what I'm tryin' to show you," she said. "Jess was unlike his father in many ways, but there was one thing they had in common. They believed in the law and the rights it gives us and the duties it demands in return. In any other time and place, my Jesse would've been as conservative as his father. I believe he stared sedition in the face, he may even have let it whisper treason in his ear, and when he realized the rule of law was about to fail him, he had only two choices left."

"To break it—"

"—or take himself out of its reach," she said, suddenly weeping.

Marc held her, and she shuddered against him, letting her hurt and anger pour out.

"There was nothing you could have done," he said as she

wiped her cheek with his handkerchief, then blew her nose in it.

"I know that," she said. "But I can't make myself believe it."

As they were about to leave the barn and the scene of its past horror, Marc paused to stroke the nose of a dappled draught horse in a stall near the door.

"She used to pull our cutter," Beth said, "but we had to sell it last week. Bessie here goes off to a man from our church next Monday."

"But your father-in-law will have left you some money and valuables?" Marc said with some surprise.

"He intended to—that I know—but he left no will," Beth said matter-of-factly. "When Father came back here to live, he engaged Mr. Child as his solicitor. And Father mentioned to him that he had a brother who went down to the States before the war, so there could be nephews and nieces he never heard from. It might be months and months before I know—"

"While your solicitor pursues them as part of the probate," Marc said with a rueful sigh.

"But Father did pay off our mortgage," Beth said firmly, "and sweated behind a plough and harrow." She turned abruptly as if to leave.

At the back of Bessie's stall Marc noticed that the horse had knocked over a bale of straw and exposed the barrel it had been concealing. A barrel with a spigot.

Beth came up beside him and followed his gaze. "Oh, dear," she said, but it wasn't in alarm.

"Whisky?" Marc asked.

"Rum, from Jamaica. Elijah thinks it's his secret cache." She smiled. "And we've never had the heart to let on."

"Was it here when he came?"

The note of levity in Beth's voice evaporated. He felt her grow tense, and wary, as she had been in their first encounter. "Why can't you let him be?" she said. "Jesse wasn't a rum-runner. Or a bootlegger. Such men don't take their own life on a matter of principle."

"You're right," he said. "Please accept my apologies."

She leaned against him and, despite the layers of winter clothing, her womanliness and its effects were unmistakable. "Do you always talk like you're in some duchess's drawing room?"

"Always, ma'am."

"I've never been a ma'am, or even the missus," she said. "Just Beth."

"I'd be honoured if you'd call me Marc, then."

Beth tilted her face towards Marc's, who gathered her close. But the door behind them was jerked open without ceremony or concern for what it was interrupting. It was Aaron, wide-eyed.

"Co-come, quick! You're wa-wa-wanted!"

"Who wants me?" Marc said sharply.

"Mister Ha-Ha-Hatch. He's seen the pe-pe-peddlers!"

• • •

Supernumerary Constable Hatch was waiting in front of Beth's house with his own horse and Marc's. He was flushed with excitement.

"Come on, lad. Durfee spotted the peddlers' donkey clumping onto the ice at the foot of his property."

"Which way were they headed?"

"There was only one of 'em, and he went east, real hasty, up the shoreline."

"Be careful!" Beth called after them.

They swung onto the Miller Sideroad and galloped down towards the highway.

"If he's headed east on the ice," Marc shouted, "we could surprise him and cut him off at Bass Cove."

"By golly, you're right," Hatch replied. "That donkey can't run too fast on the ice, and we'll save the horses by taking the road."

So they wheeled east onto the Kingston Road, galloping apace, and retraced the route they had taken an hour after Marc's arrival in Crawford's Corners on Tuesday. Twenty minutes' hard riding found them on the Indian trail that wound its way up to the scene of the murder and the cave beyond. With no new snow to fill in their previous footprints, they were able to urge their mounts past the deadfall trap before abandoning them and surging ahead without the aid of their snowshoes.

"Christ, he's in the cave!" Hatch cried.

Marc looked up to see the snout and ears of the donkey poking above the rim of the ridge where the cave was situated. Ferris O'Hurley was floundering towards it, apparently spooked by their approach. An unexpectedly deep drift slowed Hatch and Marc just long enough for the jackass and its master to scamper down the far slope and hit the ice of the cove. They were in full flight west.

"Don't worry," Hatch puffed when they had struggled to the top of the ridge. "I've got James watching the sideroad north. If the bugger tries to get back into the Corners he may end up with a buttful of Durfee birdshot."

"My hunch is he's heading back towards Toronto and Lewiston."

"Then why come east to the cove?"

"The cave, you mean."

They went to have a look.

O'Hurley had indeed been making for the cave, for the evident purpose of collecting or destroying materials left there earlier. Ashes from a fire more recent than Tuesday were clearly visible, and papers had been torn and burned in it. Several bottles that had once held what appeared to be contraband spirits or wine had been smashed and scattered, their labels singed.

"They must've been here yesterday," Hatch said ruefully. "Somebody who should know better has told them we've become interested in this place, so the skinny one beetled out here to obliterate whatever they'd left in the vicinity—before picking up his partner in the bush farther down and lighting out for the States."

Marc sighed.

"What's wrong?" Hatch said cheerfully. "We've put the fear of Jehovah into them. They won't be back here for a while."

"Don't you see?" Marc said, sifting idly through the debris. "These fellows are likely advance men for smugglers. They've been using this cave as a hideout, a drop point, and a storage bin for a long time."

"And?"

"And that means that the snowshoe print and broken pipe stem we found on Tuesday could have been left here by one of these peddlers or by any one of a dozen possible confederates."

"And therefore not likely left by the killer of Joshua Smallman?"

"Right."

"But that pipe stem hadn't been here long," Hatch said. "That break on the stem looked fresh, and the thing wasn't completely covered with snow. Even though the ledge here is sheltered, a fair amount of snow would have drifted over it."

Marc nodded. But he was thinking of his conversation with Beth. "What connection, I wonder, could a man like Joshua Smallman have had with vagabonds like O'Hurley and Connors?"

"Maybe that money you found had nothing to do with rum or French wine."

"Perhaps," Marc said, "but have a look at this." In his hand was a strip of paper about twelve inches long whose right half was completely scorched. "See these names down the left side here?"

"Yes," Hatch said. "They're names of various types of whisky and such. Squire Child and I have come across these tally sheets before. Even the writing looks familiar."

"And below each," Marc said with a little more enthusiasm, "is the name of some bay or point along this shoreline, I'd wager."

"And you'd win," Hatch said. "The figures here are dates and times for the drop-offs. All that's missing are the smugglers' names—they've been burned to a crisp."

"Well, we know who Connors and O'Hurley are."

"True," Hatch said. "And you can be sure the alarm will be raised from Kingston to Buffalo. I'll pass this paper on to Sheriff MacLachlan anyway. I may even get promoted," he chuckled.

Marc was still rummaging about the debris, but he found nothing more of any value.

Riding slowly homeward, the two men kept their own counsel for some time. Then Hatch said, "We've got to face the fact that any connection between those sewer rats and Joshua's death is highly improbable. And that means that the cave itself may not have been his destination that night. Maybe the blizzard did confuse him, and he died in a senseless accident."

But Marc said, "I have good reason to believe that Jesse Smallman may have been desperate enough to try to raise money to save his farm by acting as an agent for those free-booters."

Hatch paused before responding. "Have you mentioned this to Beth?"

"Obliquely. But it's a topic she will not talk further to me about. That much I do know."

"Hard to blame her."

"Don't you see, though, it's possible that Jesse had gar-nered vital information about the rum-running trade and that, somehow—in going through Jesse's effects, for exam-ple—Joshua discovered this information. Being an upright man, he might have confronted someone more dangerous than he realized. Or he might have doubted its implications and set out to clear his son's name. In the least, I can't be-lieve he would not attempt to find out more about why his son hanged himself."

"Well now, that makes rough sense, lad. But we're still left with the question of who."

"One thing I did learn yesterday was that most of the farmers out in Buffaloville have been hit hard in the last couple of years. They're desperate for cash, offering me un-derfed pigs and mildewed grain. They're prime suspects for participants in a lucrative smuggling operation. And with Mad Annie's menagerie half a mile away and deep in a part of the bush nobody visits, I'd say the answer to your question lies out there. She's long been suspected of being the biggest bootlegger in the district."

"If there is a connection of some kind—and we don't know what, remember—then this cave is very likely where Joshua was heading the night he was killed."

"Exactly."

"And if the threatened person suspected that Joshua was more likely to be an informer than a convert, Joshua's possession of any incriminating evidence would be all the more dangerous. The chance of it being conveyed directly to the lieutenant-governor and, more important, being believed there without question, would be very high."

"Perhaps bribery was attempted," Marc elaborated, "and when that didn't work, murder was the only option remaining. Joshua Smallman knew too much and had to be stopped."

They rode on in silence. Since Hatch had raised the issue again, Marc felt the time had come to tell him—and him alone—the truth about Joshua Smallman's role as Sir John's official and trusted agent.

"Well, I'll be damned," was Hatch's initial comment on hearing Marc's account. Then he said, "You know what this means, though? If you're going to learn anything at all from Beth about Joshua's motives and behaviour last fall, you'll have to break the news to her as well, and admit that he managed to deceive everyone—except perhaps his murderer. And remember, when she is told the truth, she may be able to interpret past events and words in a far different light."

"I can't tell her," Marc said. "It's too soon."

Hatch was puzzled but held his peace.

As they sighted James Durfee, seated and alone on a snowbank in front of his inn, Hatch said, "Well, at least when you go out to beard the Stebbins couple this afternoon, you'll be scouting evidence of the rum trade: that's a sight more solid than a lot of free-floating political nonsense about secret societies and Hunters' Lodges."

Durfee was waving his musket at them like a bosun's semaphore.

"You're right," Marc said, "but I haven't given up on the political angle. It's in the mix somewhere."

TEN

As it turned out, Marc did not get the opportunity to test either of his hypotheses regarding the motive for Joshua's murder—political treachery or a falling out amongst thieves—on expatriate Azel Stebbins until late in the afternoon of that Friday.

First, he and Erastus stopped to talk to James Durfee outside the inn, where they were informed by the scarlet-cheeked postmaster that he had just discharged his weapon in defence of the realm. "Missed the bugger by a mile, but that mule of his sure got the message!" After a stiff whisky at his own bar (which did little to steady his heart rate),

Durfee assured Constable Hatch that when the noon mail coach arrived, he would forward the news of O'Hurley's flight westward on the ice, and further assured him that if the blackguard were to put so much as his snout ashore he would be taken without mercy. The official alarm would be rung all the way from here to Hamilton and Newark.

After commending Durfee's valour and dispatch, Hatch took his leave, and he and Marc headed for their midday meal at the mill.

"I must remember to tell the sheriff tomorrow about the peddlers' loot Durfee is keeping for me," Marc said as they dismounted and let Thomas see to the horses.

"And you're gonna show him Sir John's warrant and his instructions to you?" Hatch said tactfully.

Marc smiled. "I did agree to do so, but I was hoping then to have a lot more to tell him than I do now. On the other hand, he may be able to interpret some of my observations in ways you and I have not thought of."

"I wouldn't be overly hopeful on that score. Hamish MacLachlan's a fine fellow and a loyal servant, but he got the job because he's a cousin of the attorney general."

After lunch, just as Marc was about to set out for the Stebbins place, a boy sent over from the inn brought a message for the ensign to come there immediately. Marc pulled the boy up in front of him on the saddle and galloped him gleefully down the Miller Sideroad.

Durfee had summoned Marc because, among the

post-luncheon crowd at the inn, there were several noto-rious supporters of the Reform party, men who were not resident aliens and lived nowhere near the Americans in Buffaloville. "I'll just get 'em talkin' and you can sit up here nursin' a toddy with both ears open."

In the two hours that followed, Marc learned about elec-tions, the evils of the Family Compact, the toils of farming, and much else irrelevant and otherwise—but none of it incriminating or pointing in that direction. Everyone had known Jesse Smallman and was saddened by his senseless death. Little feeling of any kind attended the occasional mention of Joshua's name (adroitly dropped by Durfee at in-tervals). Only the bizarre manner of his death seemed of any lasting moment. The most telling consequence of the entire afternoon was that Ensign Edwards was seen weaving his way towards the double-image of Colonel Margison's horse.

A brisk north wind and a steady canter up the Pringle Sideroad, across the second concession, and up the Farley Sideroad into Buffaloville soon sobered Marc for the en-counter ahead. Or so he told himself. The Stebbins farm lay just above the concession line and across the sideroad from the McMaster place he had visited the previous afternoon, following the drama of Agnes Pringle's rescue and return. From Hatch's briefing Marc had learned that Azel Stebbins was by far the youngest of the suspected extremists and the most recently arrived (from New York State). At thirty, and with less than ten years in the province, young Stebbins had established a reputation for himself as a hotheaded republican and an ardent supporter of Willy Mackenzie's oft-stated view that only by annexing itself to the United States could Upper Canada ever be free and prosperous. His wife was reputed to be much younger than he, a child bride brought back like a trophy on his saddle from Buffalo, where he used to go on a monthly bender to the stews and dives of that pseudo-egalitarian Gomorrah.

When Marc arrived, Azel Stebbins was walking towards his barn with a bit and bridle in one hand. When he saw the ensign ride up and dismount, he stopped, took him in with a searching stare, then grinned and shot his hand out to the visitor.

"Hello, there," he boomed from a barrel chest. "I'm Azel Stebbins."

"Good day to you, sir. I am—"

"Ensign Marc Edwards, come to have a gander at the tons of wheat I got lyin' surplus all over the farm." His laugh invited Marc to join in on the joke.

As Marc smiled, he did a quick appraisal of the man he expected to be his prime suspect. Stebbins looked like a quintessential Yankee: tall and ruggedly handsome with blue eyes and hair the colour of bleached hay, big-boned and muscular (features even his coat and leggings couldn't hide), and sporting a hair-trigger grin offset by a calculating tilt of brow and chin, from which drooped a blondish goatee.

"The quartermaster at York has been authorized to

purchase extra supplies in the coming months, grains and pork in particular," Marc said, glancing towards the barn and the coop, smokehouse, and corncrib behind it.

"A mite worried about the ruckus in Quebec, I'm told," Stebbins said as he took the horse's reins.

"That was a factor, I believe."

"And you're the drummer?" Stebbins said.

"Advance agent."

"Seen plenty of drummers where I come from, though not always glad to."

The quick grin telegraphed the joke, and Marc dredged up a weak smile.

"Anyway, I'd like to see whatever you might have to offer. The price will be good, and paid in pound notes."

"Well, I'm relieved to hear that, I reckon—though my Yankee blood hankers after currency you can sink your teeth into."

"Are you new to the province, then?"

Stebbins halted near the big double door to the barn. No grin mitigated his next comment. "I figure you know to the day and the hour precisely when I first set foot on His Majesty's soil, and a good deal of what I've been doin' and sayin' since. You and me'll get along just fine so long as there's no malarkey between us. You look like a sensible young fella to me."

"Erastus Hatch has given me a few details of your stay in the district, but for my part I assure you I am here to reconnoitre grain and pork. There's no politics to a soldier's hunger."

"When you've been here a while you'll learn that everything's politics in this country. As it is in the United States. The difference is, back home everybody's given a chance to join in the game—and win."

The obvious rejoinder—"Then why didn't you stay there?"—was on the tip of Marc's tongue before he reined it in, took a deep breath, and said, "Be that as it may, Mr. Stebbins, I have a simple duty to perform—"

"Now, now, don't get yer garters in a snarl," Stebbins said, hitching Marc's horse to a post, dropping his gear, and starting to haul the doors apart with both hands. "And for Chrissake, quit hailin' me as mister. The name's Azel, though I been called worse from time to time."

"Then you've something to show me?"

"You think we're headin' inta my barn to take a leak?"

The interior of the barn was spacious, well laid out, and scrupulously maintained. Two rows of stalls housed Ayreshire milk cows, a team of Clydes, a roan mare, and a huge bull manacled to a concrete stanchion by a ring in its nose. Fresh straw was evident everywhere. The energy Stebbins was putting into his political activities and unexplained "hunting" forays evidently had not affected his proficiency as a farmer.

"We had a drought last July that hit the wheat hard," Stebbins said, "but I put in a fair amount of Indian corn for pig feed, and it's paid off. The hogs are in the back. Hold yer nose!"

When they'd finished admiring the hogs—robust Yorkies waxing nicely towards slaughtering time—and tallying a potential purchase by the quartermaster's self-appointed legate, Marc said casually, "You've done exceedingly well here in a short time."

"I have done, haven't I? And I've managed a wife and two babes inta the bargain."

"I heard about the fuss over alien rights when I arrived last spring," Marc said in his most empathetic tone. When Stebbins ignored the bait, Marc added, "You must have been concerned you might lose all this."

"You're damn right I was! I built everythin' you see here, and the house, too, with the aid of my neighbours and other Christians who cared not a fig about my place of origin or the way I voted. I put in my own crops with only my woman and a lad or two from the township. Our harvestin' is done together, farm by farm. We got no landlords or fancy squires in this part of God's world."

"And Mr. Dutton was your man for the Assembly?"

"I reckon he didn't need much help takin' this seat."

"Hatch was telling me a neighbour of his suffered terribly from the drought."

Stebbins paused at the bull's stall, seemed to make some sort of decision, and said, "Smallman. Aye, sufferin's an inadequate word to cover what happened to that poor bastard."

"Jesse was a friend?"

Again a brief hesitation, then, "Not really. More like a comrade-in-arms, but when you've fought alongside somebody for the same cause you can make friends pretty fast. Jesse thought we couldn't get a fair shake for our grievances under the present set-up in Toronto, but he couldn't bring himself to cross the line."

"Whereas others did?"

Stebbins grinned cryptically. "Now them are matters I wouldn't know nothin' about, would I?"

"I wasn't implying you did," Marc said lamely. "But we heard rumours of seditious talk down this way and meetings of some secret society."

"The only so-called secret society infestin' this county is the Loyal Orange Lodge, led by that lunatic Gowan."

"At any rate, the alien question's been resolved, hasn't it? Your land is safe and you can hold any office you can get yourself elected or appointed to."

Stebbins said, "You'll also be happy to know I've just applied for my naturalization papers. I been here longer than the seven years they're requirin' for citizenship."

Marc was glad they had turned to leave the barn because it gave him a moment to recover from the shock of hearing this news and the deliberate manner in which it was revealed.

"Yessirree, in a month or so, Azel Stebbins, his wife, and his bairns are gonna be bona fidee subjects of King Willy the Fourth."

Marc was not ready to give up, however, and when Stebbins insisted they seal their verbal contract with a drink, Marc was quick to accept.

"I never trust a man who turns down a free drink," Stebbins said, and winked. He led Marc past the horse stall to a manger below the hayloft, reached down, and drew a clay jug into the weak light of the waning day. He tipped it up, took a self-congratulatory swig, wiped his mouth on his sleeve, and passed the jug to Marc. "That'll tan yer insides."

Marc made a valiant show of duplicating his host's gestures, appending only an explosive wheeze to the set. Stebbins's grin wobbled through Marc's tears. "My God, that's raw stuff," he managed to say.

"Mad Annie's boys ain't too particular, I reckon."

"You wouldn't have something a little less—intimidating?" Marc said.

"Annie's potion's about all folks around here can afford."

"That's probably why I haven't had a decent drink since I left the fort." Marc smiled.

"Well now, I surely wouldn't want a man who's lookin' to buy my crops to go back to his commandant and bad-mouth the local hospitality. Nosirree." Stebbins winked lasciviously, offered a quicksilver grin, and began to brush away at the hay in the manger. "Ahh," he said, and he drew forth a dusty bottle whose smudged label bore no word of English or American. "Bordeaux, older'n my granny's cat. In Buffalo they call this stuff 'French leg-spreader.'"

Marc flinched when he saw Stebbins attack the cork with his jackknife. "There," he said, "all ready for the back of the throat. Be my guest."

Marc had no choice but to hoist the vintage red and let it slide its way, bits of cork still abob, over his tongue and down his astonished throat.

Stebbins then did the same, but continued gulping until the dregs arrived, prompting him to spit furiously. "Jesus, but that's good stuff. A man could do worse'n get pissed on that."

"I haven't tasted anything that good, even in the officers' mess," Marc said, dabbing his lips with a handkerchief, a move that set Stebbins grinning again.

"It ain't available to members of the Family Compact."

"Could an ordinary soldier lay his hands on any of it?"

"You can get almost anythin' fer a price," Stebbins said.

"What else have I got to waste my money on?"

"Well now, if I did know where to find such ambrosia, I'd be sure and tell an ordinary officer like yerself."

"You didn't buy this, then?" Marc forced himself to look suitably crestfallen.

"'Twas a gift, from a friend of a friend. For services rendered."

"Ahh . . . that's unfortunate."

"And we don't tell tales on our friends, do we?" With this caveat Stebbins turned and ambled placidly out of the barn. Perhaps he did not realize how much he had just given away to his interrogator: the confirmation of a direct link to smugglers and a more oblique one to Jesse Smallman and his father.

Buoyed by this thought, Marc was caught off guard when he reached for his horse's reins and Stebbins said heartily, "Where'n hell do ya think you're goin'? Don't ya wanta stay fer supper and meet the missus?"

Marc was most pleased to say yes.

MARC PUT HIS HORSE IN AN empty stall beside Stebbins's mare, removed its saddle, gave it a perfunctory rubdown, and threw a blanket over it. "Sorry, old chum, but that's the best I can do." He chipped the ice off the water bucket in the stall, noted the hay in the corner, and went off to meet the notorious child bride from Buffalo.

Lydia Stebbins was attired in a woollen housedress that hung loosely on her, laceless boots, and a maid's bonnet askew on her brow. She stood before several steaming kettles and pots over a balky fire—ladling what appeared to be stew, intermittently stabbing at the fire logs with a twisted poker, and wiping the sooty sweat from her face like the beleaguered heroine in a melodrama. None of this blurred or diminished her beauty. A two-year-old clung shyly to her dress and stared up at Marc; a crib by the fire held her youngest child.

"Good gracious, Azel, you didn't tell me we was expectin' company," she cried, and she swept the back of a hand across her forehead.

"You got enough stew there fer a herd of longhorns," Stebbins said, shucking his clothes in sundry directions. "Put on a couple of extry dumplin's and set a plate fer Ensign Edwards. Then hie yer pretty little rump over here and shake his hand, like a proper lady."

A proper lady she might have made in other circumstances. Her hair was as black and shiny as ebony and fell in generous, wayward curls over her neck and shoulders and partway down her back. Her face was perfectly heart-shaped, her skin the milk-white hue of the Irish along the windy coasts of Kerry or Donegal. Her eyes were deep pools many a homesick sailor would happily have drowned in. The figure complementing them could only be guessed at, but as she gave her husband a warning glance and moved across the room towards Marc, a dancer's grace and innate control intimated a slim waist and lissome limbs.

"Pleased ta meet ya." When she smiled, her teeth were even, flawless. "You just call me Lydia like everybody else 'round here."

"And I'm Marc," he said, taking her hand and drawing it up towards his lips.

"Jesus!" she yelped. "He's gonna kiss it!"

"That's what they do to ladies over in England," Stebbins said scornfully.

Marc pressed his lips to the back of her hand. Lydia giggled but did not pull away. "You all done?"

"That's all there is to it, girl." Her husband laughed. He was over at the fire now and sniffing at the stew.

"Christ, I been kissed better by a pet calf," she said, her eyes dancing.

THE STEW WAS SURPRISINGLY TASTY AND the dumplings even better. Mr. and Mrs. Stebbins were on their best behaviour, though Marc expected that the elaborate politeness of their "Mrs. Stebbins, would you kindly pass the bread?" and "Certainly, Mr. Stebbins, but not before our guest's been served" was a parody for his amusement or discomfiture—he was not certain which. In light of their performance, and the indignities of yesterday's encounters, Marc began to doubt the possibility of creating in Upper Canada an alternative society to the rabid and reckless democracy south of it—a New World country where decorum, reverence for the law, and respect for one's betters would be the accepted norms. It certainly seemed to be a moot question at best.

While Lydia washed the plates and spoons in a kettle at the fire, Stebbins and Marc sat at the deal table and drank several mugs of coffee tempered with dollops of Jamaican rum. Lydia began to sing, occasionally swivelling around to face them and catching Marc's eye. Her cheeks were scarlet from the heat; tiny pendants of sweat beaded her forehead and trickled down into the hollow of her throat.

"I gotta stay sober tonight," Stebbins said to Marc. Then he lowered his voice to a whisper, and added, "Gotta big meetin' to attend." He laughed out loud, apparently disturbing the baby in the crib. The two-year-old had fallen asleep halfway through his meal and had been tucked into bed in the loft above. Lydia went to the crying infant, clucked over it for a few seconds, then began to rock the cradle with one delicate, booted foot.

"Time for me to vamoose," Stebbins said, and he seemed to shush himself by holding two fingers to his lips.

Marc rose and said quietly, "I'll ride as far as the highway with you."

Stebbins hesitated. "Okay by me. You've been damn good company so far."

Marc bowed to Lydia (he thought he detected an amused exchange of glances between man and wife), and then the two men tiptoed out.

"Not so hard, ya little nipper," he heard Lydia say as the door closed behind them.

Side by side they saddled their horses in the glow of a single lantern. The sky was clear, but the moon had not yet risen. It was a dark winter's evening they would be riding into, along the tree-shrouded lanes they dignified here with the name of "road."

"My God," Marc said suddenly.

"What is it?"

"The horse has thrown a shoe."

"It couldn't have. You rode it in here okay."

"Of course I did. The shoe has to be somewhere around here."

The two men made what both knew would be a fruitless

search through the straw inside and the drifts outside. No shoe was found.

"Well, you can walk him back to the mill without doin' any harm," Stebbins said cheerfully. "Shouldn't take you an hour."

Marc was already leading the animal into the stable yard.

"Hey, he's limpin' a bit," Stebbins said.

Marc swore, then bent down to examine the animal's right front hoof. "He's picked up a nail or something already. I'll have to dig it out and then walk him home very slowly."

Stebbins found a pair of pliers and handed Marc his jack-knife. "Worst comes to worst, you could walk him across to McMaster," he said. "Fancies himself a bit of a horse doctor, he does. Right now I gotta go. Got friends countin' on me."

Marc, angry and suspicious, decided on a single, direct gambit. "Where are you off to?"

"Oh, a small gatherin' of associates who enjoy rollin' the dice once in a blue moon." With that he left.

Marc waited for half a minute and then walked quickly out to the sideroad at the end of Stebbins's lane. From the tracks in the snow, Marc could make out that Azel had turned north and, when the road came to an end up beyond the Hislop place, had plunged into the bush on a line that would take him straight to Mad Annie's. Unless, of course, Stebbins was more subtle in his cunning than he had shown thus far. At any rate, Marc was without a mount and like a duck on ice when fitted out with snowshoes. All that remained was for him to tend to the horse and then trudge home in front of it. At least the roads were well trodden and passable to a desperate man on foot.

He had just removed the nail from the animal's hoof and noted with satisfaction that the cut was not deep when a cry from the house brought him to rapt attention.

"Help! Somebody, help me!"

Lydia Stebbins was standing in her doorway—screaming into the darkness.

APPARENTLY A LIVE SPLINTER FROM THE ebbing fire had been flung beyond the stone apron of the hearth and landed on a nearby pillow, setting it alight. By the time Marc arrived, rushing past a panicked Lydia, the pillow was merely smouldering. Oily ribbons of smoke snaked out of it, but under no circumstance would it have burst into flame or threatened the cabin. Marc picked it up gingerly, sprinted to the door, and tossed it into a snowbank.

Lydia was seated at the table, rocking her youngest in a bunting bag. The two-year-old remained unruffled in the loft. Lydia had made a remarkable recovery.

"Get me a drink of that rum, would you, Marc?"

Marc obliged, eyeing her intently.

"A lady don't drink alone," she said. "It ain't polite."

"I'll sit with you till you've gotten over your fright," Marc said as she sucked impolitely at her cupful of imported rum, courtesy no doubt of Messieurs Connors and O'Hurley. "Then I really must go. My horse has thrown a shoe and I've got to walk it home."

"That won't take you more'n an hour." She pouted prettily. "And don't tell me a big grown-up gentleman like yerself has got to be in bed afore ten o'clock."

"A gentleman doesn't remain alone with another gentleman's wife without his knowledge or permission," Marc countered.

"Now that would depend on the nature of the gentleman, wouldn't it? And the lady." She drained her cup.

"I think it safe to assume your husband would not approve."

"Then he shouldn't go runnin' off and leavin' me to fend fer myself three nights a week. Who am I supposed to talk to? Little Azel Junior?"

"Surely you exaggerate. Where would Azel go three nights a week in this township?"

She smiled and refilled her own cup. "So now you're interested. What's so goddamned attractive about my husband that you gotta give him so much attention? I'm a damn sight prettier'n he is!"

"All I'm saying, Mrs. Stebbins—"

"Lydia."

"Lydia, is that I can't give credence to your statement."

"Christ, what a lingo! Where'n hell'd ya learn that? I bet you wouldn't say shit if ya had a mouthful."

"Azel told me he was going off to gamble," Marc said. He poured himself a cup of the contraband rum.

"And hooerin', fer all I know. He just goes off, I'm tellin' ya, and leaves me here to talk to the walls."

"Well, you may talk to me—for an hour. I've been told I'm a good listener."

MORE THAN AN HOUR LATER, LYDIA Stebbins was still talking. Her dark curls billowed and fluttered as she grew more animated, and the round, black eyes took in less and less of the room and more and more of what they wanted to see.

"I grew up in my daddy's hotel. It had the grandest ballroom in Buffalo, in the whole western half of the state. We had dances and card games that never ended. Two presidents stayed there. Dolley Madison was given my mother's bed fer the night. She sent us a china figurine. Every general and admiral in America passed through Buffalo and not one of 'em but didn't stop to converse with my daddy, the colonel. And he weren't no country colonel neither. When I was eighteen he let me read parts of his war diary. You mayn't believe it, lookin' at me now, with these udders and my bum bulgin' out, that my daddy sent me off to finishin' school in Rochester." She raised her rum cup like a proper lady, took a sip, and batted her black eyelashes. "I can even read French."

She surveyed the cabin skeptically, as if to emphasize the unlikelihood of ever finding a use for French in these quarters.

"In the year before Azel come ridin' up to sweep me away, my daddy was made president of the Loco Foco party in the Buffalo region, and I got to hear some of the most melodious speeches on local democracy ever given, and that includes Tom Paine and Mr. Jefferson himself."

Marc leaned forward. "What I don't understand is how you could give all that splendour up for a man who was already a farmer in a British colony opposed to democracy and who was likely to be more interested in yields per acre than the lofty sentiments of the preamble to the American Constitution?"

She stared across the table at him. "My word, you can talk just like them," she breathed.

"But Azel can't?"

"I don't need remindin' about Azel's foul mouth," she said irritably. Her expression changed as she added, "But the man was a stallion. And when you're a girl of twenty and of a mind to disobey and spite yer daddy, that's all that matters."

Marc flushed, and began to doubt the wisdom of having steered the tête-à-tête into this particular groove. But it seemed too late to turn back now. "Azel kept his nose to the plough, then? Stayed away from speeches and politicking?"

"Oh, he got himself in thick with the Reformers up here

when they tried to take the farm from us just because we come from the States. But he soon got tired of all that."

"Still and all, he's a good farmer," Marc said, aiming for some respectable closure to a strange evening. "You're fortunate to have him." He started to get up.

"Enough of this palaver," Lydia said, a licentious sparkle in her eyes. "Take me to bed."

Marc dropped the jacket he was about to put on.

"You can't go plyin' me with wine and sweet talk and then just march out that door and leave a lady in distress, now can you?"

"But your husband—"

"What he don't know or can't guess can't hurt him, can it?" She hunched nicely over until the rim of her dress slipped perilously close to the outer extremities of her breasts.

Marc realized, far too late, that he had drunk too much— here and earlier at Durfee's—than discretion or common sense or self-interest warranted. And it had been far too long since that brief, passionate encounter with Marianne Dodds in far-off Kent. The room was overpoweringly warm and oddly reassuring, and the heady appeal of this wanton, bright, motherly, vulnerable vixen was not to be resisted.

She reached out for his hand, but it was he who led her towards the bed.

•   •   •

MARC WAS CASTING ABOUT FOR HIS other boot in the dark when Lydia rose up behind him and said, "I told ya, he never comes home before daylight, and he's so stinkin' drunk he'd think you were Father Christmas or the bogeyman." She threw her arms about his neck. They were both stark naked, having performed their feat of lovemaking in that pristine state beneath an engulfing comforter while the fire expired and the air cooled above them. Lydia's engorged nipples pressed into his back and mingling odours floated up from the warmth of their cocoon.

Marc had been prepared for some wanton, wild, or un-coordinated coupling, with pent passions unleashed on either side. It was not so. It was measured and tender and playful. Which of them had initiated this mode and kept it going he could not say, nor did he want to. When she sighed against him, he was not sure whether she had climaxed or was simply expressing her pleasure in advance of the event. They rolled then side by side, still connected. She pressed his head between her swollen breasts in what was undoubt-edly a maternal gesture, or so he interpreted it. He thought fleetingly of the mother he had never really known.

Just as Marc found his second boot and lined it up with the first one on the cold floor, the baby let out a hungry howl.

"Damn," Lydia said, releasing him and flinging herself naked from the bed into the shadows of the big room, illu-mined only by the full flood of moonlight through its narrow west windows. "Don't you move now," she sang sweetly, and seconds later the babe's cries gurgled out.

For a long time Marc lay back under the quilt, savouring his own nakedness and the sensation alive in every inch of his skin, and listening to the suckling sounds of the child. Finally Lydia crawled back in beside him. She shivered deliciously against him.

"I didn't let the little bugger have all of it," she laughed. "I saved a bit for you."

Hours later, it seemed, he fell into a blissful, dreamless sleep.

MARC WAS WAKENED EITHER BY THE sensation of falling or the crack of both elbows on the floor. Whatever the cause, he was certainly awake and unmistakably sitting on his haunches in the dark beside an unfamiliar bed. Lydia, delectably nude, was rubbing the glass of one of the windows at the front of the cabin and squinting out into the moonlight.

"Jesus, it's Azel!" she cried. "He'll shoot us both!"

Marc leapt into action like a recruit caught napping at reveille. He pulled his trousers halfway up, jammed a foot into each boot, and then, flailing at the bed and the floor beside it, snatched at linens, socks, belt, shirt, and frock coat.

"He's puttin' the horse away," Lydia called to him encouragingly. "He'll be a minute yet." She trotted across to the bedroom window and jerked back the gingham curtains. Moonlight poured innocently over their love nest.

"He'll see my horse in there!" Marc gasped as he stepped into the chamber pot and heard it crack once—like a gunshot.

The voice of little Azel Junior drifted down from the loft: "Da-da home?"

"He's too damn drunk," Lydia said. "It'll be okay, once we get you outta here." She was helping him bundle up the clothes he had had no time to put on. "Just pull yer big coat on when you get outside." She tossed it to him, then set about working her shift over the tousled mane of her hair.

"How the hell am I supposed to get out the front door without bumping straight into him?" Marc said as he rolled his uniform into his greatcoat.

Lydia grinned. "We got an emergency exit." Then she leaned over and kissed him gently on the forehead, like a mother sending her tot off to his first day at school. Taking his free hand, she led him across to the southwest corner of the cabin to the big woodbox beside the fireplace. "There's a hatch at the back so's Azel can stuff his chopped logs in without usin' the door."

"But it's half full of wood!"

She began yanking some of the split logs apart, and he soon joined her. In a minute or so they had managed to clear a wedge of space through which he had no choice but to wriggle fundament-first.

"You better hurry, I hear him shuttin' the barn door."

"Da-da home, Mummy?"

The ensign's rear parts had reached the hatch in the wall.

As his legs were pinned underneath him, the only way he could think to open it was to butt it severely. On the third butt the hatch fell. An icy wind took instant advantage. Marc heaved and squirmed and, with a clatter of wood, followed the hatch out into the snow.

Lydia reached down and thrust his bundled clothes after him. "I gotta hop right inta bed," she whispered. "He'll be expectin' to find me warm and ready."

In more congenial circumstances, Marc might have appreciated the irony of her remark, but the first shock of arctic air numbed everything but his brain. Sheer panic kept it functioning. Marc jammed the hatch back into place and leaned against the cabin wall to get his bearings. The moon had risen, and he could see that he was at the rear of the house. Twenty yards to the side lay the barn and outbuildings. Halfway between, the staggering figure of Azel Stebbins aimed itself at hearth and home—towards the front door, a route that would take him mercifully out of sight and allow Marc to sprint unseen to the barn. Even if he made the barn undetected, Marc would still have to pass dangerously close to the cabin to leave by the lane and through the opening onto the sideroad. The impossible alternative was to take his chances on the drifts in the field, where, in the morning, the tracks of his departure would be stamped for all to see and interpret. He took a deep breath and jerked his unsuspendered trousers up to his waist. Stifling a cry with one hand, he reached down with the other and drew a splinter, agonizingly, out of his left buttock.

Azel was carolling a familiar sea shanty with some improvised taproom lyrics as he disappeared along the far side of the cabin. Seconds later, a door slammed. Marc took off for the stables, having the presence of mind to keep to the trodden path between woodpile and barn—no strange bootprints to be found at dawn by a jealous husband with a harquebus. Luckily, the latter had left the barn doors ajar, so Marc was able to slip quickly inside, out of the wind. With teeth chattering, and in the gleam of a sliver of moonlight pouring through the crack in the doorway, Marc trembled and stubbed his way into his remaining clothes. He had just buckled his belt when he felt a tickle of hot breath on the nape of his neck.

Bracing for a savage blow or the plunge of a dagger, Marc instinctively reached down for the sword he had left at the mill. But nothing happened. Slowly Marc forced himself to turn around and face his ambusher. It was Azel's mare, unarmed and amorous.

Stebbins evidently had stumbled into the barn, flung the saddle off, tossed a hasty blanket over his mount, and left it to fend for itself. If he had walked it down to its stall, he would not have missed seeing Marc's horse in the stall beside it. One nicker and the game would have been over.

Marc put his saddle loosely on his own horse, checked its shoeless hoof, and began leading it back towards the doorway. That's when he heard a floor board creak somewhere above him in the region of the hayloft. This was followed by a kind of scritching sound, as if some nocturnal creature were hunkering down or squirming to get comfortable. A rat? A raccoon?

Slowly he made his way farther into the interior of the barn. He stopped and listened. There was nothing but the contented breathing of animals he could hear but not see. Then a creak sounded right over his head, heavily; it could only be a man's footfall. Was someone up there hiding from Marc—or spying on him?

While he was trying to make up his mind whether to lie low or flush out the fellow, the decision was made for him. He heard the hayloft door swing open above him on the wall opposite. His man was on the run.

Marc moved silently along the dark corridor between the stalls. By the time he got outside and trotted around to the far side of the barn, all he could see was the hatch swinging on its hinges and a male figure disappearing into the woods fifty yards away. But he recognized the awkward gait: Ferris O'Hurley, without his donkey.

What would O'Hurley be doing hiding out in Azel Stebbins's barn? Marc was sure it had something to do with the smuggling operation. The Irishmen from the States and their compatriot, Stebbins, were up to their Yankee ears in contraband spirits. But was that all? Connors had been carrying a sackful of brand-new American dollars last Tuesday. And Stebbins was always off hunting without bringing home a deer or a grouse. If it was this gang that Jesse Smallman had been mixed up with last year, it mattered little whether they were smuggling spirits, muskets, or seed money for seditionists: they and the Smallmans were connected in some significant way. Of that he was certain. So, despite the debacle back there in the cabin, Marc felt he had not completely frittered away the evening—if what had taken place in Lydia's bed could be called frittering.

Marc peered over at the Stebbins household. It was dark and quiet. The moon had gone behind a cloud. A few flakes of camouflaging snow had begun to fall. Marc took a lung-chilling breath and began leading his horse along the regular path that led past the cabin and up the laneway to the sideroad. No musket boomed out behind him, no cuckold's cry hailed him back. And O'Hurley was long gone.

Once on the sideroad he was able to pick up the pace. His horse limped slightly but made no complaint. The snow thickened about them. Bruised, sated, dishevelled, splinter-riven, piss-splattered, he trudged homeward. As he turned eastward on the concession line, an ugly thought entered his head. Was it possible that he had been meant to remain in the Stebbins cabin? That Azel was not to be trailed under any circumstances? That someone had deliberately nobbled his horse? No. What had passed between him and Lydia could not have been faked.

Could it?

ELEVEN

Marc missed breakfast (and any speculative remarks on the reasons for his absence from the table), but after an improvised meal of dry cheese, lukewarm bread, and cold tea, he was joined in the parlour by Hatch. Both men lit their pipes, and Marc provided him with an expurgated account of the fiasco at the Stebbins place. Hatch mercifully refrained from comment, then said, "You'll have to fix on exactly what you're going to tell Hamish MacLachlan this afternoon. Our sheriff's a man who appreciates facts." He chuckled and added, "There's not much else he can appreciate."

"Well," Marc said, "we've got this much, I think: evidence

of a note or message calling a respectable Tory gentleman out of his own house and away from his own New Year's celebration into a near blizzard. The gentleman seems pleased about the prospects he's being called to. 'I may have some news that could change our lives forever,' he tells his daughter-in-law, who swore to that under oath. The rendezvous with the summoner was to be at an isolated spot, but one we know now to have been a hideout or transfer point for smugglers, in particular two of their advance men, Connors and O'Hurley. Smallman dies in a freak accident on his way to the cave, said accident having been anticipated or, after the event, conveniently used to collude in the man's death. To wit: no assistance was offered and no report made to the constable of the township or the sheriff or magistrate of the county. Some evidence at the scene indicates that the summoner stood waiting for his victim only a few rods above the death trap."

"My goodness, but you would have made a fine barrister. Perhaps your uncle Jabez was right after all."

"Solicitor is what he had in mind, but I wasn't willing to wait five years while performing tasks an indentured servant would repudiate," Marc said quietly.

"Well, if you go using words that big with MacLachlan, he'll have you clapped in irons on the first charge he can pronounce!"

"I'll tone it down a bit," Marc said dryly, and carried on. "Having established a prima facie case for foul play, I'll lay out the two lines of enquiry we've been pursuing: the political and the contraband. All he needs to know is that malcontents like Stebbins may have suspected that Joshua was an informer—given his past connections, recent arrival, and suspicious attendance at Reform rallies—or that he learned or surmised seditious information from his son while speculating on his activities and suicide."

"You're not going to tell him that Joshua was a spy?"

"Even in telling you, Erastus, I've broken one of Sir John's commandments to me."

"You'll have to tell the girl, sometime."

"But not yet." Marc relit his pipe. "The smuggling angle can be approached in a way similar to the political one. Physical evidence suggests young Jesse may have turned to smuggling to help stave off bankruptcy and the failure of his farm. Half the township appears to have purchased contraband spirits or acted as wholesalers, but only a few of these can be directly linked to Jesse—those who marched beside him at the protest rallies over the grievances and, in particular, those American immigrants whose property rights were endangered by the Alien Act. We can reasonably postulate that somehow Joshua came across information that threatened the smuggling operation. Some ruse was then used to lure him to his death, probably false hopes raised about the reasons for his son's self-destruction. Certainly, the locale points strongly to the latter theory."

"So far, all of this is circumstantial," Hatch said gently, "even though it's damn clever guesswork."

"At any rate, all I want to do is report formally to the sheriff, show him Sir John's instructions to me, and alert him to the fact that I'm going to start using the governor's authority to compel or cow certain suspects into telling something closer to the truth. I've been given full policing powers in the matter. I can hale these renegade farmers, and even old Elijah, before the magistrate and interrogate them under oath. I've just about done with playing games."

"On the positive side," Hatch said, "most of your suspects'll be at the Township Hall in Cobourg later today to hear William Lyon Mackenzie rant and rave. You'll be able to watch 'em close up, stirring their own soup." He got up slowly and added, with the customary twinkle in his eye, "You can hardly see the mend in your trousers, but Winnie was wondering if you'd been reconnoitring grain in a sawmill."

MARC STROLLED UP TO BETH'S PLACE, not only because he needed some bracing air to clear his head, but because he wanted to convey to her personally the arrangements that had been made for the journey into Cobourg and to make sure she would agree to them. No persuasion was needed, however: Beth Smallman wasn't about to miss the opportunity to be roused once more by Mackenzie's fiery rhetoric, even when it meant accepting the charity of a ride with a neighbour and the company of a red-coated infantry officer from the Tory capital.

The Durfees had offered the best seats in their cutter to Beth and her escort, Ensign Edwards. Erastus, Winnifred, Mary, and one of her sisters would be driven by Thomas

Goodall in the miller's four-seater. Another of Mary's sisters would stay with Aaron. The women, with the exception of Beth, would do some shopping in Cobourg, then attend a church committee meeting at St. Peter's, followed by a sleigh picnic. They would all go along to the rally out of curiosity, though Beth was the only declared supporter.

"You don't need to chaperone me, you know," Beth said to Marc at the door. "Mr. Durfee will do nicely."

"Ah, but I want to," Marc said.

HATCH WAS NOT IN THE MILL, but sometimes, Marc had learned, he could be found in the small office attached to it. Winnifred had gone down to Durfee's for the mail and a visit with Emma. Goodall was in the drive shed behind the barn making some minor repairs to the sleigh. The little window in the outer wall of the office was begrimed and frosted over, so Marc just pushed gently on the unlatched door and opened his lips to halloo the miller. No syllable emerged. Through the gap in the doorway, Marc saw a woman's oval face, eyes seized shut, cheeks inflamed with no maiden's blush.

Marc backed away. He didn't pause to close the door.

TEN MINUTES LATER, HATCH SAT DOWN opposite Marc in the parlour. He fiddled with his pipe but didn't bother poking the fire into life.

"It's not what you think, lad," he said.

Marc did not reply, but he was listening with intense expectation.

"I would never take advantage of a servant girl, whatever other sins I may be charged with before my Maker."

"You wouldn't be the first to do so," Marc said, remembering the rumours and whispered gossip that had titillated and scandalized the residents of Hartfield Downs.

"Two months ago she came to me. To my room. It took all my powers and the vow I'd made to my beloved Isobel to push her away. I'd not had a woman since Isobel passed on. I told Mary she didn't have to do this, that it was wrong, that I considered her to be a fine, chaste young woman who would marry soon and raise her own family. She wept, but she did go."

"Why do you think she came to you like that?"

"She was afraid I might send her home. You see, I have a niece in Kingston, and Winnifred's talked about bringing her here, for company and to help out with the chores."

"Mary could get other work, surely." Marc was thinking of the desperate need for decent servants in Toronto.

"Easily. But still, it would mean returning home, even for a little while."

"She was maltreated?"

Hatch grimaced. It was the first anger Marc had seen in the miller's jovial, kindly face. "The father's a drunken brute. He's been in the public stocks half a dozen times. Nothing short of a bullwhip could cure him."

"And if your niece did come, Mary would have to go?"

Hatch sighed. "She came to me again two nights later. This time she slipped in beside me, already . . . unclothed. I promised her she could stay on here as long as she wanted, or else see that she never had to go back to the brute that begot her."

"And?"

"I gave in to my urges. I know it was a terrible thing to do. A wicked thing. She's the same age as my own daughter. And the worse thing of all is, she really seems to like me. And now, though I pray every night for strength to resist, I've gradually, and alas gratefully, come to accept her . . . presence. She's a loving little thing." It took a great effort for him to hold back the tears that were threatening.

"Have you considered marrying her?" Marc knew full well that, in both the old world and the new, older men not nearly as robust and honourable as Hatch married girls half their age in their need for heirs or to satisfy the lusts that were expected to wane with age but didn't.

"I can't find the courage to." Hatch jabbed at the fire as if he might conjure in its flames some image of Isobel that would tender absolution. "And after all, Winnifred has devoted her life to me and our business since her mother died, giving up her own chances for happiness."

"She looks like a young woman who makes her own decisions, for her own reasons," Marc said.

Hatch sighed. "You know, I've even prayed that Mary

would get in the family way, then I'd have to find the courage, wouldn't I?"

That was a wish, Marc thought, that a benevolent Deity might easily grant.

MARC AND BETH SAT IN THE cutter's seat among buffalo robes, and James and Emma Durfee snuggled together on the driver's bench as the team of Belgians followed the familiar road to town more or less on their own. The afternoon was clear and cold, making the runners sing on the snow and sharpening the tinkle of the bells on the horses' harness. Emma Durfee had peremptorily refused to ride in the back with Beth, claiming, with just a hint of humour, that a woman's place was beside her man. Forty minutes of steady progress would see them in Cobourg.

"You've spent most of your time here firin' questions at me," Beth said, drawing one of her furs more closely about her throat, "but you haven't exactly told any of us your own life story."

"There isn't much to tell," Marc said. Their shoulders were touching fraternally through several layers of animal skin. "I was orphaned at five years and adopted by my father's . . . patron."

Beth looked puzzled by the word "patron" but continued to nod encouragingly.

"I soon learned to call him Uncle Jabez. He was

unmarried, so I became the son he never had. I was raised on his modest estate in Kent, among gardens and hedgerows and thatched cottages. Next to us resided the shire's grandest squire, who befriended my uncle and me. Hartfield Downs was magnificent, both the Elizabethan house and the vast farmland surrounding it. I was permitted to play with the Trelawney children, who thought themselves the equivalent of princes and princesses."

"Which kept you humble," Beth said dryly.

"Uncle Jabez brought in private tutors who saw that I learned even when I didn't particularly want to."

"The distraction of all those princesses?"

"Horses, mainly. I loved to ride and be outdoors. I worshipped my uncle Frederick, my adoptive father's younger brother. He was a retired army officer who had fought with Sir John Colborne and the 52nd on the Spanish Peninsula." When Beth made no response to this news, he continued. "Uncle Jabez had been a solicitor in London, but when he inherited his father's estate, he moved back to the country and took up the role of gentrified landowner. He sent me to London to article at law in the Inn of Chancery, which means six days a week with your head buried in conveyancing papers. But I spent all my free time at the Old Bailey envying the barristers in their grand wigs and robes—strutting about the court like tragedians on a stage."

"And poor you with no horses to ride or foxes to assassinate?"

"More or less. What I secretly longed for was action, excitement, some challenge to the manly virtues I fancied I possessed in more than moderate measure."

"Your drudgery left you little time for dalliance, then?"

Marc tried to catch the look that underlined this remark, but failed. "I have seldom found women unattractive," he said.

Beth laughed. "Nor they you," she said.

Emma turned around and, for several minutes, engaged Beth in conversation about a proposed shopping venture and plans for a joint charity clothing drive among the Presbyterians, Congregationalists, Methodists, and, surprisingly, the Anglicans. This interlude gave Marc time to reflect on how he was going to reopen the interrogation of the woman sitting close enough that he could feel the heat of her breath.

"It must have been hard for an upright, honourable, and religious man like your Joshua to have accepted his son's suicide," he said as soon as Emma had turned back to her husband and the road ahead.

Beth shifted ever so slightly away from him. "Of course it was. He loved Jess, even though they weren't together much after we got married. And Jess was no weakling. He was strong and independent, or else he couldn't've left home like he did or started the farm without a lick of help from anybody."

"Did Joshua press you for answers? Reasons? Your own opinion of Jesse's state of mind before he died?"

"Not directly. That wasn't his way. But when I told him Jess was feelin' low, I also explained about the state of the farm and what the future looked like to him back then. One day, Father just asked me to take him to one of the rallies. So I did. And he listened, as I already told you."

"He didn't hint in any way that he thought Jesse might have been tempted by more radical forms of action?"

"No."

"And you have no recollection of him remarking on anything unusual or suggestive that he might have found among Jesse's effects or heard about Jesse from some third party?"

"I was the one that sorted through my husband's effects."

"Still, it's difficult to believe that you and your father-in-law did not have, from time to time, some moments of severe disagreement. After all, he was accompanying you to Reform rallies, and presumably listening to their arguments, but, as you've pointed out, he remained a Tory and a supporter of the government you despise."

Beth didn't answer, but he could see she was deep in thought.

"Cobourg's just over the creek!" Durfee called out.

MARC'S KNOWLEDGE OF THE TOWNS OF Toronto, Hamilton, and London should have prepared him for the village of Cobourg, not yet confident enough to declare itself incorporated. There was a main thoroughfare—King Street, no less—with intersecting avenues and even, Beth told him, two or three concession roads running parallel to it farther north. But to one conditioned to expect cobbled roadways, brick buildings, gas lamps on every corner, tended gardens and stone fences, the rumble of hackney carriages, market wagons, and vegetable barrows, and the buzz and jostle of citizens on the go, Cobourg was a rude shock. The many log cabins and the few frame houses were largely obscured by clumps of untouched primeval forest. The roadbed was rutted solid from the last thaw and only somewhat smoothed out by packed snow. There were no sidewalks along the verges of King Street.

Marc's hosts vied with one another to point out to him the glories of the only stone church ("Presbyterian," Emma added, "up there on William Street"), the simple, frame-built Congregational church (vast enough to entertain two hundred of the faithful), and at the junction of King and Division (the lone treeless intersection) the first stop on their journey: Benjamin Throop's Emporium (a glorified general store). Kitty-corner to this squared-timber, two-storey commercial structure stood St. Peter's Anglican Church.

Hatch's sleigh pulled up behind them a minute later. The women were left to forage through the emporium and, afterwards, walk across to St. Peter's for their committee meeting. Goodall was to pick them up there at four o'clock and drive them up Division Street to the Township Hall for the political "picnic." Sandwiches and cake for afternoon tea had already been packed in wicker hampers, as if it were July and the occasion pastoral. In the meantime, Hatch had agreed to meet the sheriff, not at the new courthouse and jail in Amherst just down the highway, but in the more commodious Cobourg Hotel.

IN THE SHERIFF'S "OFFICE," MARC WAS handed a mug of beer by the smaller of two constables and urged to tell his story. While the sheriff of the Newcastle District, Hamish MacLachlan, rocked back in a chair constructed for his considerable girth and backside, Marc recited his tale much as he had rehearsed it with Hatch (minus all but a dozen arguably necessary polysyllables). The young constables, part-time supernumeraries or deputies like the miller, were so awed they forgot to sample their complimentary beer. But the sheriff himself showed no reaction beyond an occasional pull on his pipe.

"Well, what do you think, Hamish?" Hatch said when Marc had finished.

MacLachlan put out a boot to slow his rocking. "What you've got there, son, is one helluva bowl of beans—and no fart."

Marc was not deflated by the sheriff's summary judgment. Nor was the sheriff offended by Marc's intrusion into local affairs. If Sir John and his successor wished to waste the time of an energetic young ensign on such a fool's errand, then it was no skin off his nose, especially if it meant no effort on his part. Besides, he was far too beset by immediate problems, like the potential firestorm out at the Township Hall.

"I could use another pair of strong arms out there," he said to Marc. "And that flamin' red petticoat of yours won't be a hindrance either. Too bad ya didn't bring your sword, and a Brown Bess with a bayonet."

"He's exaggerating a tad," Hatch ventured.

"You know perfectly well, Hatch old man, there's lunatics on either fringe, and it's a bitch to try and look over both yer shoulders at the same time."

"You're not anticipating a Tory riot?" Marc said with a glance at Hatch.

"No, but Ogle Gowan's Orange Lodgers have been spotted over in Durham County holdin' powwows, or whatever monarchist, anti-papist mumbo-jumbo they get up to when they're well liquored and foamin' at the mouth."

"What about the Hunters' Lodges?" Marc said.

"Never heard of 'em, but they probably exist, if only to keep me from my good wife's bed. You fellas can take your cutter or ride with the constables here, but one way or t'other, I'm gonna need all of ya. I've outlawed all liquor in the hall and, of course, there'll be no weapons of any kind, not even a gardenin' trowel. Transgressors'll be bounced out pronto. I'm also gonna patrol the grounds and privies, and empty every jug and teapot I see."

When Marc looked skeptical, MacLachlan added: "You can be sure Mad Annie's brood'll be somewhere nearby. If you sight any one of them cretins—male, female, or otherwise—I want ya to latch on and hold 'em down till I come with the irons." He took a lusty pull at his beer. "Philander Child's gonna be present to see the bylaws of the last quarter session are strictly enforced."

The young constables had finally noticed that their mugs were still full.

"All right, lads, finish your drinks and be off. I'll trot down on Old Chestnut in a while." He winked. "My whistle ain't quite wetted."

MARC STOOD SENTRY ON THE PORCH of the Hamilton Township Hall, the largest secular structure in the village, and watched with growing amazement the arrival of the Reform party's adherents and detractors. They came by sled, sleigh, and cutter, pony and dray-horse, by shank's mare and snowshoe, toboggan and skid and Norwegian skis; in family groupings, couples, and fraternal cliques. That the backwoods could harbour so many sentient beings without advertising their presence was in itself astonishing, but that somehow these scattered and bush-bound castaways from Britain and elsewhere could discover the date and locale of this political gathering, could find the time to consider its significance, and then arrange for their simultaneous arrival within the hour appointed—this was truly cause for wonder.

For a few minutes Beth stood at Marc's side greeting one

newcomer after another by name, many of whom, to Marc's consternation and concern, were women. "How did all these people find out about the rally?" Marc asked.

"Well, most of us can read," Beth said, "and the *Cobourg Star* gives us some practice once a week."

At five o'clock the front doors were closed. A few torches had already been lit inside under the supervision of Magistrate Child and the fire warden. The brand-new Rochester Pumping Wagon stood at the ready on Division Street. At his own watch, Marc heard the commotion at the rear of the hall as a sleighful of dignitaries apparently drew up in a lane behind the building and entered it via a vestibule presided over by the sheriff and the larger of the two constables. A raucous cheer, punctuated by hoots and catcalls, rose up. Marc hoped that Beth had kept her promise to stay close to the Durfees.

Before going inside to monitor the proceedings, Marc circled the grounds of the hall and checked the privies. All seemed quiet. He lifted each of the several dozen confiscated jugs and jars near the front door: all were now empty. Next to these lay a jumble of wooden handles from farm implements. The smaller constable was instructed to guard these rudimentary weapons, and keep an eye on traffic to and from the privies and the side door of the hall.

Marc made note of the arrival of Azel and Lydia Stebbins, Israel Wicks with his two sons, an unsteady Orville Hislop, and, to his mild surprise, Elijah, the hired man. How had he got himself to town? For the briefest second, Marc's eye caught Lydia's as she brushed past him. She looked quickly away, but not before offering him the hint of a smile—mocking or conspiratorial, he could not tell.

The fifteen or so women stood at the back of the hall near the double doors, not so much because their presence was considered inappropriate but because, in the event of a disturbance or fire, they could get out easily. James Durfee, though not officially deputized, stood watch for the women. Winnifred, Emma, and Beth were close beside him. Mary was with her sister—and many wives and children who had made the arduous trek with their husbands—a block away on King Street. Here, between the Cobourg Hotel and Throop's Emporium, there was much socializing around several bonfires and in the "open-air parlours" of the bigger sleighs.

Every one of the several hundred spectators inside the hall was standing, even though a number of benches were available on the periphery for the infirm or dyspeptic. The torches that lit the smoky, shadowed interior were set high on metal sconces on the walls. As Marc took up his assigned place between the podium and the side door, the first speaker was being introduced: Peter Perry, member of the Legislative Assembly for the nearby constituency of Lennox and Addington. A thunderous roar erupted as he stepped into an undulating pool of torchlight in the centre of the makeshift platform. His companions in the cause, four of them, were seated behind him, hidden in the oily darkness beyond the reach of torchlight.

The crowd's shouted approval rattled the windows and ricocheted into the rafters. Perry, a squat bulldog of a man stripped to his shirtsleeves and in fighting trim, began his speech at full throttle and cranked it upwards from there in carefully calibrated degrees of vehemence and mockery. His target was Sir John Colborne and the news that, in the final days of his regime, he had secretly signed a bill creating fifty-seven additional rectories for the Established Church, thereby adding a thousand or more acres to the already corrupt and bloated glebe lands of the Clergy Reserves.

The crowd roared its disapproval as one. It cheered each note and jab of Perry's defiance. The occasional dissenting "Nay" or "Shame" was drowned out instantly or used by Perry to goad the faithful to further indignation. The heat in the hall—the heat of exhaled rage, of bodies sweating in winter gear, of anticipation—was growing unbearable as Perry soared to the peak of his impassioned flight.

"We shall no longer tolerate the insolence of high office, the flouting of His Majesty's will by petty appointees of the colonial secretary, the hauteur of Rector John Strachan and his Anglican cronies, the daily repudiation of bills passed by the people's duly elected Assembly! We will march through every village and town in this province and tear these ill-got rectories down, board by arrogant board!"

During the tidal wave of applause that pursued Perry

to his seat, Marc slipped out the side door. He breathed in several draughts of cold, fresh air and set about on the first of his half-hourly rounds. It was completely dark now. Marc studied the steady stream of men moving from hall door to privy and back. The glazed excitement in their eyes, like a flame under liquid wax, was not wholly due to the effects of the fiery rhetoric from the platform. Many, he suspected, would have concealed flasks to draw inspiration from as occasion demanded, but such a limited source could not account for the extent of the weaving and yawing in front of him.

Half an hour later, after the third speaker, a failed Reform candidate from Kingston, had finished, Marc noticed a pronounced increase in the level of inebriation. The crowd, somewhat more subdued during the two speeches following Perry's opening salvo, was pacing itself no doubt for the feature attraction yet to come. At the current rate of imbibing, Marc hoped it would come soon.

"Where in Sam Hill are they getting the stuff?" Hatch said to him outside.

"Damned if I can figure it." The two men stared at the three privies carefully. They had been erected in such a way that they were set into a hedge-like row of cedars: to mute their vulgar presence perhaps, or to provide in the cedar fringe a ready alternative for male relief. Only some of the men here bothered to use a privy, but they were the ones for the most part doing the weaving and muttering. Marc took a quick look into each cubicle and in the near-dark could see nothing unusual. No jugs littered the floor or bench.

As he turned back towards the hall, Marc heard a shout that he imagined might have risen from the Highlanders on their first charge at Culloden or King Billy's Protestants at the Battle of the Boyne.

WILLIAM LYON MACKENZIE WAS CENTRE STAGE, the spot marked out for him by Destiny—God's or the Devil's, depending on your politics. The heat and stink of the room was overpowering, but the audience pressed forward so tightly that anyone fainting would remain upright and unnoticed. The double doors were open, the principal effect of which was to have the torches shudder more ominously in their tin calyxes and throw a less reliable light on the crowd below. Marc stood on a bench to better monitor the proceedings.

Mackenzie, the Scots firebrand whose name Marc's superiors had never uttered except in contempt, was surprisingly small. Even though he was swaddled in two greatcoats (of different colours), the thinness of his frame and fragility of his bones was evident—in the delicacy of his fingers, which probed and struck the air in rhetorical bursts, and in the dancer's nimbleness of his feet, which hopped and paused in concert with his words. His head was absurdly large for such a body, as if it had been fashioned solely for the passion of public speech. His blue eyes blazed continuous outrage yet still found moments to dart and judge, or confer brief benediction on those few apostles positioned near enough to receive it. During the first minutes of his jeremiad, the crowd, even those who had been jeering bravely, went quiet, as if some stupefying awe had taken hold. Their messiah did not disappoint.

He reviewed for them the long and sorrowful history of their attempts to gain a legitimate voice in those affairs of state that most affected their lives and the future of their children. There was no need to remind anyone in the room, he said, of the sacrifice already made by a populace comprised almost entirely of outcasts, voluntary exiles, and the dispossessed: ordinary men and women who, like their courageous counterparts in France and the United States, were to be numbered among those first generations of humankind who, in the simplicity of their conviction, said no to tyranny, laid their bodies naked before it, and proclaimed to all oppressed peoples of the Earth: "It shall not pass!"

A rustling thrum and a sustained murmur began to resonate through the hall, wordless but nonetheless coordinated and edged with threat. Marc glanced anxiously towards the big doors but could see no one that mattered. A few souls—exhausted, drunk, or frightened—were slipping out into the night.

The firebrand moved on to catalogue the most recent outrages, pausing between tirades for roars of approval and working the crowd like a seasoned tent-preacher, while his orange-red hair flared about his face like a demonic halo. The throng hooted and participated in his derision of Chief Justice Robinson and Attorney General Boulton and other charter members of the Family Compact who had three times had him expelled from the parliament to which he had been elected and defiantly re-elected. They laughed wildly when he recounted, with apt mimicry, the stunned response of said worthies when, unable to assume his lawful seat in the House, he had subsequently been elected the first mayor of the new city of Toronto. He paused, took a swig of water from a pitcher, ran his fingers through the shock of his hair, and glared out over the crowd as if seeing, beyond them, their common tormentors.

He changed to the subject raised by his fellow legislator, Peter Perry: the fate of the Seventh Report on Grievances. One by one, and in a voice now more terrible for its calculated restraint, he touched on the particular wounds that festered and burned amongst them: the Clergy Reserves, the ruinous lending policies of the Bank of Upper Canada, the rejection by the appointed Legislative Council of bill after bill that would alleviate their suffering, the graft and bumbling of the Welland Canal Company, the low prices of grain manipulated for the benefit of the mother country and its coddled emissaries here among the ruling clique, the greed and venality of district magistrates more arrogant than English squires or the absentee landlords of Scotland and Ireland.

A chant now rose up from the throng, softening whenever

Mackenzie hammered home a point and swelling to occupy even the briefest pause: "No more! No more! No more!"

The rage had become contagious. The parishioners were slowly metamorphosing into a mob, with a mob's unreasoned and overfocused hate, its craving for a scapegoat. Suddenly Marc realized that this kind of collective outrage was potent enough to propel one of its participants to murder, to a sort of political execution whose sole purpose might be release for pent-up anger. The choice of victim could be arbitrary, as long as he represented the party of oppression. Even someone like Joshua Smallman might well do, particularly if he were behaving like a paid agent of the enemy.

Mackenzie had not quite finished. Having stirred their passions and gained their full attention, he began explaining to them, in moderated tones and with didactic earnestness, the importance of their recent success in getting the Report on Grievances a fair hearing in the British cabinet, of their unequivocal victory in the alien question, of their current control of the Assembly and its bills of supply, and, no mean feat, of the Family Compact's acute embarrassment over the abrupt reassignment of the meddling John Colborne. Indeed, a new governor—a man with no military experience to hobble him, a man of letters who penned travel books and poems—was en route from Montreal to Toronto at this very moment. Now was not the time for precipitate or thoughtless action. The recent and sterling example provided by Jacksonian democracy in the republic to the south

proved that, with patience and unceasing pressure and petition, the voice of the people even in remote regions would
be heard and would prevail.

A reverent hush once again gripped the faithful. Hope,
however feeble, had been resuscitated.

"What about my rights?" The voice from the crowd was a
high-pitched, irreverent cackle.

Mackenzie halted in mid clause. Instantly his gaze fixed
the woman twenty feet from him who had spoken. He
smiled and, with a twinkle in his eye, said, "And what rights
have we not yet addressed, madam?"

Heads craned and feet shuffled.

"I wanta know when the land I've been squattin' on
fer twenty-five years is gonna be deeded to me and my
young'uns."

"But squatters' rights have always been protected,
ma'am—unless you're perched upon a bishop's birthright!"

The crowd roared its approval of this quip, but not before
one phrase tittered through it, lip to lip: "It's Mad Annie!"

From his position Marc could see the portly sheriff trying
to force his bulk across the room towards the citizen of his
county he admired the least.

"Then why won't the arsehole callin' himself our magistrate assign me the deed?"

"Have you improved the property according to regulations?" Mackenzie said patiently to Mad Annie over the
derisory howls of the men around her.

"If plantin' whisky trees and harvestin' a bastard a year are improvements, you shoulda had that piece of swamp years ago!" a neighbourly wag suggested.

"You shut yer fuckin' face, Hislop!"

"Madam, there are ladies in the hall—"

"Fuck the ladies! I want my rights! What kinda dickless wonder are you anyways?"

The sheriff and a brace of constables were closing in.

"We got trouble outside," Hatch said to Marc, drawing him through the side door and away from the low comedy. At least Mad Annie had redirected the crowd's attention, and, with Mackenzie's own unexpected shift at the end of his speech, Marc felt certain that the evening would conclude without a riot.

"Behind the privies," Hatch said, hurrying towards an opening in the trees to the right of the outhouses. "Young Farley spilled the beans to me inside."

Marc followed Hatch, and the two soon emerged into the clearing behind the privies. A few yards farther into the bush, they heard a commotion: low cursing, hissed commands, and a clatter of wood and crockery.

"Damn!" Hatch cried. "Somebody's tipped them off!"

By the time he and Marc reached the scene of the crime, Mad Annie's enterprising progeny had scurried into the trees, lugging their paraphernalia with them. Pursuit was unthinkable.

"Well, I suppose the sheriff will appreciate us confiscating

what's left." Hatch chuckled as he held up one of the dozen
or so clay jugs that remained unbroken.

They walked back to the privies, noting a well-trodden
path between the improvised outdoor shebeen and one of
the toilets. "How in blazes did they get the rotgut to the customer?" Hatch mused aloud.

"This way," Marc said. He was pointing to a Dutch door
cut into the upper half of the back wall of the middle privy.
"Not everyone came here to do his business."

"Jesus," Hatch said, "and I bet the ruckus Mad Annie
created in there was a diversion while her lads dismantled
the operation and hightailed it home."

Hatch went back into the hall through the side door,
but Marc decided to go around to the front door for a final
check. He remembered that the shorter constable had left
his post there to assist the sheriff in his pincer movement
against Mad Annie. The uproar inside appeared to have es-
calated a decibel or two, and Marc hoped the crowd had not
begun to view the hapless Annie Pringle as its scapegoat. As
far as he could tell, the pile of potential weapons had not
been reduced. Six or seven of the women had wisely come
outside (Beth was not among them), and several were standing on alert beside their family sleighs. The Reform rally was
nearing its end.

Marc stepped through the double doors—into bedlam.

"I'm gettin' the ladies out!" Durfee shouted at him. "Try
to get to the platform if you can!"

In front of him Marc could see only a seething tangle of arms, legs, and contorted faces, the arms ending with fists, and not a few of them wielding stout sticks or cricket bats. As the weapons came crashing down, the thud and crack of wood upon clothed bone or vulnerable skull reverberated above the cries, curses, and howls of pain. A full-scale donnybrook was in progress. But who was fighting whom? And where had the weapons come from?

Marc plunged in. A berserk fellow was indiscriminately swinging a hobnailed stick at a group of farmers in desperate, jumbled retreat.

"We're gonna bust the heads of every one of you republican arseholes!" the attacker screamed, and he lashed out, striking one of his victims on the shoulder and knocking him sideways. Marc leaped ahead and put both hands on the stick before it could be raised again, ripped it out of the lunatic's grip, and clipped him on the jaw. He dropped in his tracks.

The victim groaned. It was Angus Farley, one of the American immigrants Marc had visited late Thursday afternoon. "Who are these hooligans?" he said, helping Farley to his feet.

"Orangemen from Toronto," Farley rasped. His left arm was hanging limply at his side. "We gotta get to the platform. It's Mackenzie they're after!"

"He'll get out the back way," Marc said.

"They'll be waitin' for him. You don't know these people!"

There was no way that Marc, even armed with a hob-nailed bat, could push through to the platform. From the scuffling and scrambling about him, he got the impression that the invaders were fighting a holding action while the main thrust of the attack lay elsewhere. He dashed to the double doors, where a score of bleeding and battered men were staggering onto the street, picked up a dozen hoe handles, and tossed them back into the fray. At least the odds could be narrowed a bit. Then he sprinted through the snow towards the rear of the hall. And stopped.

Mackenzie's sleigh was occupied by three bat-wielding thugs, lying in wait. Two more commanded the side exit. The honourable members of the Reform party were still trapped inside.

Suddenly the rear door burst open. Six burly men emerged, strung out like pallbearers, and wriggling frantically in their grip was William Lyon Mackenzie.

This outrage, Marc knew, if carried off successfully, would wreak such havoc on the body politic of Upper Canada that the murder of a retired dry goods merchant would seem but a mote in a maelstrom.

TWELVE

The stable boy bringing the sheriff's horse, Old Chestnut, from the livery on Division Street did not recognize the soldierly figure who leapt into its saddle, dug his heels into the horse's ribs, and galloped away towards the rear of the Township Hall in a furious blur of scarlet and grey.

Marc bore down upon his quarry with only the vaguest of rescue plans in mind. Fortunately, the abductors had chosen to indulge in a bit of boyish fun before settling down to their more serious business. To raucous cheers from their three bat-wielding companions on the sleigh, they formed a ragged circle, lifted the helpless Mackenzie above their heads, and began spinning him counter-clockwise—with the intention, it seemed, of concluding the game with a bravura flourish that would see him tossed like a beanbag onto the floor of the getaway vehicle.

"Hurry up, lads," a burly fellow cried from his perch on the sleigh. "We got the tar hot and the feathers itchin'!"

Marc drove the sheriff's horse hard between the sleigh and the abductors, reached down with his right hand, grabbed a thick handful of overcoat, and drew Mackenzie up across the horse's withers. As he charged back towards the road, cries of dismay trailed away behind him. He didn't pause to see whether or not he was being pursued, but he did catch a sideways glimpse of a huddle of astonished women just before he wheeled and galloped south to King Street, with the bundled bones of William Lyon Mackenzie bouncing unceremoniously in front of him.

Marc hurried eastward on the main road, cantered across a bridge over a small creek, and pulled up in front of the Newcastle Court House and Jail. He dismounted, then reached back up and tipped Mackenzie upright. The little Scot slithered down the horse's flank and landed on both feet. He was gasping for breath and struggling unsuccessfully to utter some word appropriate to the occasion.

"We'd better get inside, sir. I am not armed and I have no way of knowing how far those men will go to get you back."

Mackenzie let out a wheeze that resembled a "Yes," which Marc took for consent. Holding his prize by the elbow, he led him into what appeared to be the sheriff's office and anteroom to the jail. A rotund woman of indeter-minate age sat snoozing beside a candle-lantern.

"Mrs. MacLachlan!" Marc shouted. "Does your husband keep a pistol here?"

The woman's eyes opened, and then popped wide. "Jim-iny," she cried, "I ain't Miz MacLachlan, and who in blazes are you?"

MRS. TIMMERMAN, THE CHARLADY, STIRRED THE fire in the stove, got some water boiling, made the tea, and helped Mr. Mackenzie wrestle out of his two mismatched overcoats and adjust the orange-red wig that had come askew. While Marc stood vigil by the window, she poured two dollops of Jamaican rum into Mackenzie's tea. He drank it down like a parched Bedouin at the last oasis. His fingers trembled as he held out the cup for more.

"Are you going to turn around, young man, so I can see your face and thank you properly!"

Marc obliged. "I'm Ensign Marc Edwards, sir, from the 24th Regiment at Fort York."

"The latter I've been able to deduce, Ensign Edwards," Mackenzie said dryly, thrusting out his ungloved hand. His blue eyes glittered with intelligence and unshakable pur-pose. Only the cold sweat that glistened on his craggy face indicated the extent of his fright and the shock of its after-math. "I am Willie Mackenzie."

"I deduced that," Marc said, smiling.

Mackenzie smiled back. "You realize, Ensign, how this will look when the Tory newspapers get hold of the story: radical Reformer saved from a tar-and-feathering he well deserved by one of His Majesty's own house-guards."

"They won't hear about it from me, sir."

Mackenzie eyed him closely. "No, I don't believe they will," he said, and he wiped the sweat from his brow with his sleeve. "Tell me, though, why did you do it? You are unarmed. Those lunatics would have broken your skull as soon as look at you. And I find it difficult to believe that you adhere to many of the sentiments I expressed in the hall tonight."

"I'm a soldier, sir. I know my duty."

Mackenzie smiled again; there was no mockery in it. "This province would be a better place for all of us if every man in it did his duty."

They were interrupted by a commotion outside. Marc opened the door in time to see Hatch at the helm of a cutter drawing up to the jail. Several figures spilled out of it. Sheriff MacLachlan and his two constables pulled a resisting body out of the cutter and began dragging it, kicking and spewing obscenities, across the snow towards the cells at the back of the building.

"Lord in Heaven," Mackenzie said, "that's a woman they're abusing."

"That's no woman," Hatch said, coming up to them and grinning, "that's Mad Annie."

• • •

THE JAIL'S ANTEROOM WAS ALMOST AS crowded as the hall had been—with constables, combatants itching for a rematch, and assorted well-wishers and town gossip-mongers—but space was quickly made for Magistrate Philander Child and his estate manager cum bodyguard, John Collins, who wore a pistol in his belt. Mad Annie's protestations of innocence could still be heard through the stone partition, like howls under water.

Child went right to the seated Mackenzie. "I am happy to say, sir, that none of your colleagues has been injured, and, even now, they are on their way here to retrieve you."

"And I, sir, am happy to report that I am unscathed, except for the wound to my dignity, which is likely to heal in due course."

Child looked relieved, then said with some vehemence, "I am embarrassed, outraged, and indeed mortified by what happened back there. I am a justice of the peace, and the peace of my jurisdiction was broken tonight in a most reprehensible manner. I realize, sir, that there are those amongst your supporters who will conclude that the attack on them and upon the safety of their leader was instigated by the authorities in Toronto, or that, in the least, they turned a blind eye to it."

"I am not among them," Mackenzie said. "I know who did this, and why."

"I believe that," Child said. An anger he was struggling to contain made his cheeks flame and the pupils of his eyes dilate dangerously. "For my part I do not condone public violence of any kind. My forebears have served as magistrates and squires to every king since Henry the Eighth. One of my grandfathers stood with the Royalists against the Antichrist Cromwell. We have taken pride in meting out justice according to its rules, sparing not even ourselves. Hence, I do not condone the barbaric behaviours of the Orange Order or those acting under its direction. They may profess the same cause I do, but he is neither friend nor ally who perverts my cause by committing outrages in its name."

"Well spoken, sir," Mackenzie said. "And I commend this young ensign here. He has loyalties and a sense of duty as powerful as your own."

Child acknowledged Marc with a slight nod. "I will arrange an escort for you," he said to Mackenzie.

"No need," Mackenzie said, pulling on one of his coats. "I hear my fellows coming for me now."

Outside, several sleighs had drawn into the yard, the largest and nearest one filled with cheering Reform supporters, now armed with sticks and clubs. Some of them sported bandaged heads or slings supporting battered limbs. Mackenzie quickly disappeared into their midst, and they drove off, as cheerful as if they had just won the Battle of Lundy's Lane. In one of the other sleighs, Marc thought he saw Beth.

Behind him, in the smoky, sweaty anteroom, Child had

switched from lofty anger to infantile tantrum. "None of this would've happened if that travesty of a woman, that whore of Babylon back there, hadn't primed the crowd with her rotgut liquor and then had the temerity to spew out such malodorous drivel and create the confusion that allowed those maniacs to waltz in through the front door!" He fixed the smaller of the two constables with an Old Testament stare.

"My man left his post only to come to my assistance," MacLachlan snapped. "And we did get the bitch! By God, Child, we got the old harlot in chains after all these years!"

"I say it's time we cleared out the whole rotten mess of them!" Child cried, and he banged on the desk with a fist as heavy as a mace. Mackenzie's teacup bounced.

A dozen heads swivelled and froze. The magistrate's countenance, governed usually by civility and the courtesy of office, was now swollen with a wrath as venomous as Jehovah's before the sins of Jeroboam. His voice was hollow, sepulchral. "I will take away the remnant of that house as a man taketh away dung."

"Mad Annie's, ya mean," the sheriff said helpfully.

Child cast his eyes over the motley crowd in the room. "Yes," he said more calmly, but with no lessening of purpose. "I am hereby authorizing a raid on that squatter's pigsty tonight. We'll go in there with guns and torches and purge every last one of that bastard brood!"

Within minutes, the magistrate's enthusiasm (and legal

warrant) had galvanized those in the room and in the courtyard beyond. A tactical plan of action rapidly evolved. A score of stalwarts from the town would be deputized as supernumerary constables. Four sleighs and teams would be officially commandeered. They would leave town at ten o'clock, proceed along the frozen ribbon of Cobourg Creek to the point where it intersected with Crawford Creek in the thick cedar-and-birch bush immediately north of Mad Annie's squattery. From there they would march on snowshoes through the woods to unleash a lightning assault on its unprotected (and unbooby-trapped) rear. With Madame Tarantula in leg irons, the broodlings would panic and scatter. A discreet torch touched here and there, and Mad Annie's seraglio would no longer offend the public eye, ear, or sensibility—or the liquor laws.

"I've got to go with MacLachlan," Hatch said wearily to Marc. "I'll do my best to see that no one gets hurt out there. Folks are mightily stirred up tonight."

"I'm going back with James," Marc said. "I'm exhausted, and I've got some hard thinking to do." Pieces of the puzzle were now flinging themselves up faster than he could catch and examine them.

"Good," Hatch said. "The women'll need an escort. We didn't nab a single one of Ogle's loonies, so the woods and back roads could be full of 'em. Thomas is gonna drive the Huggan girls and a couple who live farther west along the highway. You could follow them, if you wouldn't mind."

"What about Winnifred?"

"She's helping Dr. Barnaby with the injured. They're setting up in the Common School. He'll bring her home, tonight or in the morning."

Emma Durfee was yoo-hooing them from the driver's bench of the cutter. A light snow was beginning to fall.

"By the by," Hatch said, "I do have some happier news."

"Oh?"

"One of the speakers at the rally told me they'd stopped for refreshment at Perry's Corners on the way down, and the constable there had an Irishman in manacles." Hatch laughed. "And one unhappy donkey."

"So how did you persuade Uncle Jabez to let you quit law-yerin' and head off to military school?" Beth asked.

"I didn't. I persuaded Uncle Frederick and he persuaded Uncle Jabez."

Beth laughed as if she were now part of that happy con-spiracy. A snowflake chose the tip of her nose on which to alight, glisten in filigree, and turn invisible. Emma and James Durfee, wrapped together in a single buffalo robe on the driver's seat, were humming an ancient air suited to the occasion and their feelings and letting the Belgians lead them home.

Although still windless, the evening had grown much colder, and the soft, drifting snow gave only an illusion of coziness. Beth drew the buffalo robe off her shoulders and then did likewise with Marc's. She lifted the separate furs that were shielding their thighs and legs and looped them over one another. Then she leaned in against Marc—shoulder to shoulder, hip to hip—and arranged the upper robes to form a continuous, cozy canopy.

"It's called bundlin'," she explained. "You're allowed," she said, "even if your intentions aren't honourable." She placed her fur-capped head on his shoulder. He could feel her breathing.

"You'd still need money to buy a commission, wouldn't you?" she murmured.

"Uncle Frederick helped. He also wrote to Sir John Colborne on my behalf, and paid my passage to Montreal."

"It must be nice to have friends in high places."

"I've been lucky all my life," Marc said, sliding his right arm around her shoulder and drawing her closer. There was no resistance.

"I haven't told you everythin' about Father," she said after a while, moving only her lips. "I did accept from the very first that you were in earnest and that you could probably be trusted to keep anythin' I told you to yourself. Still, I couldn't tell you all of it, not then. But when I saw what you did back there at the hall, the last of my doubts vanished."

Marc wanted to speak, but he kept very quiet, and very still.

"So much of what you needed to know was painful to me. I save my weepin' for the dead of night, but it still comes and it still hurts. But so does the not knowing. It's so much like the grief I felt for Jess: not knowing why—really, really why—he went out there and hanged himself for me to find him. Why didn't he give me a chance to talk him out of it? I felt alone and betrayed. My love was not enough. And because I didn't really know, I couldn't grieve the way other widows do—and there're plenty of them around here. What was worse, my grieving didn't seem to have any end to it. Every reminder of Jess brought all that pain back instantly. If Joshua hadn't come, if Mr. Child hadn't given us a mortgage, if Elijah hadn't taken on so much of the daily burden, and if dear, sweet Aaron didn't need me to survive, I'd never have made it through the summer."

"You don't have to tell me all this," Marc whispered, brushing her hair below her hat with his lips.

"Then Father was killed. And again I had the not knowing. No one at the inquest believed there ever was a mysterious note calling him away. But, of course, I knew things I couldn't say to them, that I will tell you now. Joshua was obsessed with Jess's death. Every ounce of energy left over from helpin' us save the farm was given over to quizzin' me—oh, ever so gently, for he was a kind, kind man—about Jess's last days. He rummaged through every note and letter Jess ever wrote and searched the house and barn for more. After a while I could tell he'd finally quit blaming me. After that we became truly fond of each other, and then we both needed to know why. So he went along to the Reform rallies with me to hear and see for himself what his son had seen and heard the year before. He knew first hand from the drought last July what the Clergy Reserves fight was all about, what'd made his son mad and drove him to choose death over disloyalty. Then, by the end of October, a strange thing had happened."

Marc withdrew his lips.

"Father began to understand and feel the way his son had, and then he began to believe in the cause itself. Tory though he was, through and through, he came slowly to see that the injustices were unthinkingly or callously caused— and by the very people he so looked up to and revered as the pillars and mainstays of the province. And that they could be cured without the collapse of the state and the ruination of the worthies in the capital."

"He must have felt the conflict terribly."

"He did. He started neglecting his friends. Then he started skipping Wednesdays at the Georgian Club. The day before Christmas he walked over and told Mr. Child he couldn't come anymore."

She had finished. Marc drew her face up to his. She pulled away, reluctantly—or so it seemed to him.

Durfee was about to point the horses north onto the Miller Sideroad when instead he drew them to a sudden halt. "Christ," he said, "the door to the inn's wide open!"

Marc and Durfee leapt from the cutter and rushed into the saloon area of the inn. The door to the inner office hung by one hinge. Durfee found a match, lit a candle, and the two men went in cautiously. The unbreakable safe lay sideways in the middle of the room. Axe marks and dents from a sledge marred every inch of it, the rage and frustration of the perpetrator appallingly evident. In a final fit of frenzy, he had taken his axe to Durfee's desk and cupboard and chopped them to pieces. Papers and spilled ink were everywhere.

"What kinda madman would do a thing like this?" Durfee sighed, leaning against the wall to steady himself.

"Only you, me, and Hatch knew the money was here," said Marc, "as did Connors and O'Hurley."

Durfee knelt down to open the safe, and moments later he withdrew a wad of American banknotes. "Well, they didn't get it, did they?" He riffled through it with some satisfaction.

A slip of paper, not a banknote, fluttered out.

Durfee held the candle while Marc examined the paper. It was about four by five inches and, judging from the torn edges, had been ripped from a larger document.

"Are you all right, James?" It was Emma, in the taproom.

"Stay out there, ladies. We'll be right out."

"It looks like a list of their customers," Marc said.

"For tinware, or somethin' more potable?"

"Can't tell. All we got here is a list of names. The rest of the sheet is missing."

"That paper looks awfully old."

"True. But the writing is similar to that on a whisky list Hatch and I found out at the cave by Bass Cove."

"Ya don't say. Then it's rum-runnin' we're lookin' at for sure."

Marc did not hear this remark. He was staring at a name near the bottom of the list.

"What is it?" Durfee said.

"There's a J. Smallman listed here. And the name's been crossed out."

"An old list for sure, then. You think young Jesse was involved in this business?"

"I don't know, James. But there is one thing I do know for certain. Everything about the death of his father points to smugglers and their doings. It's been about rum-running all along. I should have seen that before now."

"The keg of liquor Hatch said you found in Jesse's barn?"

"Yes. And there's only one place a fugitive rum-runner could hide without fear of discovery."

"Mad Annie's."

"I've got to get there and find Connors before the sheriff and his posse flush him out. And when I find him, I'll thrash the answers out of him."

"You can't go out there into the bush in that costume," Beth said to Marc in the taproom as the men prepared for their mission.

"The lass is right," Emma said. "They'll see you comin' for miles."

"And there may be shootin'," Beth said.

"I'll pick up my pistol and sabre at the mill," Marc said.

"Come to my place first, then. Jess's clothes'll fit you fine."

• • •

HALF AN HOUR LATER MARC AND Durfee were on their way
up Crawford Creek in the cutter. A fresh team borrowed
from Barnaby's place next door moved in sprightly fashion
over the powdered snow on the creek ice. Marc was dressed
in a coonskin cap, grey ribbed wool sweater, plaid mackinaw,
corduroy breeches, and woodcutter's boots.

Marc thought that, with luck, they might arrive at the
junction of the two creeks before the magistrate and his deputies. What exactly they would do after that Marc had not
worked out yet. But Connors held the key to Joshua's death.
Marc recalled with a shudder the viciousness of the blow
that had been meant to send him to his Maker last Monday
night. Connors had even said to O'Hurley, "It's your turn."
How naive, and arrogant, he had been in dismissing out of
hand a pair of would-be murderers and boasting of where
they could find their saddlebag if they had the gumption
to come and get it! Well, if he didn't unearth Connors,
he'd ride thirty miles to Perry's Corners and have a run at
O'Hurley.

"They've beat us to the trough!" Durfee cried.

Four sleighs loomed out of the light snow that still descended peacefully, indifferently upon the countryside.

"Welcome to the show, lads!" MacLachlan boomed as
they pulled up.

Philander Child was standing beside him on the driver's
bench. "All right, gentlemen. Mr. Collins here, who knows

these woods well, is going to lead us through to Mad Annie's. The strategy is to fan out and surround the place. Fire your pistols only in the air. I want no one shot. If they are armed and fire back, well, that will be another story. But I doubt that will happen. At heart, these hooligans are cowards and turn-coats. They'll run like rabbits into our trap and then fall over each other trying to play innocent and cast blame anywhere but on themselves. They are the dregs of civilization. Let's clean 'em out!"

The deputized lawmen jumped down and began snow-shoeing into the woods behind the energetic stepping of Philander Child and his man, John Collins. Durfee and Hatch walked with Marc, offering earnest but contradictory bits of advice on the subtle art of manipulating raquettes. Twenty minutes later, they chuffed up behind the vanguard and peered into the clearing that separated the posse and the wretched cabins of Mad Annie's menagerie.

Marc and Durfee were instructed to follow the sheriff and several constables to the right, while the others shuffled to the left. They stuck close to the verge of the woods for cover, but little activity was visible in the main cabin ahead or the half dozen huts teetering around it. A pathetic droop of smoke from its chimney indicated a near-dead fire. If the Pringles were expecting trouble, or were wide awake anguishing over the capture of their matriarch, they were doing so quietly. By the same token, no constable or magis-trate had ever before come within two hundred yards of the main cabin: the booby-trapped swamp and a general public indifference had kept the Pringles secure for a generation. And, Marc was thinking, what safer haven for a murderer on the run?

The vigilantes spread out silently, then crouched down, awaiting the signal. Five minutes later, John Collins fired his pistol into the air, and each man strode determinedly forward. The only escape route for the besieged would be the frozen swamp to the southeast, and in the dark its leg-hold traps would be as deadly as a bullet in the back.

Several more shots were fired, but the first one had produced the effect the magistrate was hoping for. Half-dressed or nude figures spilled out of every door and hatch of the several hovels—at first shrieking in blind terror, then scrambling in bewilderment and shock as the ring of armed men marched closer and cried out for their surrender.

In front of Marc a naked male Pringle dropped abjectly to his knees in the snow and proceeded to grovel. "Don't shoot! Don't shoot!" he wailed in the singsong chant of a petrified child. Behind him, a girl was darting about in ever-smaller circles, her shift shredded by her own hand, her bare feet pounding the snow, her shrieks piteous and animal-like. It was clear that the Pringles thought they had awakened in the middle of a collective nightmare, with no mother to comfort them.

One of the constables stepped up to the girl and cuffed her smartly on the neck. He grabbed her frail arm and dragged her like a carcass to the periphery, then returned for another victim.

Marc felt sick to his stomach. He found himself kneeling beside the fellow who had dropped into the snow before him. He might have been fifteen or forty, it was impossible to tell. He was skin and bone, his stare goitred, and his face crawling with scabs and pustules. Fear had turned his pleas into babble. Marc lifted him tenderly up and carried him towards a coop of some sort. He glanced around. It was chaos everywhere: shouts, wails, frantic dashing and collision, sporadic gunfire. Marc opened the hatch to the coop. Animal heat radiated from within.

"Slip in there," he said, "and don't make a sound. You'll be all right."

As he swung back towards the woods, Marc noticed two things: several torches had been lit on the far side of the enclosing circle, and a fully clothed male had just popped out of one of the huts. Agnes came tumbling out naked in his wake. Hatch was beside Agnes in a wink, but Marc was already plodding madly after Connors.

Despite his uncertainty on raquettes, Marc easily gained on Connors, who sank to his knees at every step and quickly exhausted himself. A few feet into the woods, he gasped like a spent horse and slumped down.

A triumphant huzzah rose behind them, and Marc arched around to see what it was all about. One of the chicken coops—not the one concealing the wretch

Marc had pardoned—had been set ablaze. The inquisitors were virtuously cheering the conflagration. But something stopped the celebration in its tracks. Even Connors, panting and searching for a curse to fling at the ungrateful gods, looked on, speechless. A dozen hens scrabbled and tottered and attempted flight out of the fireball of their roost, their feathers in flames. Then one by one they fluttered, faltered, and expired, like crepe-paper baubles. The snow hissed at their demise.

The vigilantes stared, awed by the consequence of their own righteousness. Without a word or sign they doused their torches. There would be no more burning. To men for whom the erection even of a log cabin in the bush represented the triumph of the will over a cruel and dispassionate Nature, the deliberate destruction of any beast nurtured by his care and sweat was deeply reprehensible. Philander Child did nothing to urge them further. Three or four of the better-fed Pringles took advantage of the lull and slipped into the bush.

Connors had gotten back to his feet but was still too weary to skulk anywhere. His face was obscenely bloated. He was hatless. His flies flopped open. All the bravado had gone out of him. He stared at the pistol in Marc's belt and the sabre in its scabbard, then looked directly into Marc's eyes. Suddenly he paled and threw both hands in the air.

"Don't shoot me," he rasped. "I wasn't gonna kill ya, honest."

"Your partner was in Stebbins's barn, wasn't he?" Marc said, one hand on the pistol butt.

"We only took the horse's shoe off, I swear to God! He stepped on that nail by himself. Stebbins didn't want ya trackin' us here." Connors took one step towards Marc, bringing his hands down slowly as he did so but holding them well away from his body, as if readying them for the manacles.

So, Connors, O'Hurley, and Stebbins had conspired to keep him from leaving the farm that night. And Lydia had ensured that he was nicely distracted for the duration. What an ass he had made of himself!

"I'm taking you in to jail," Marc said with deep satisfaction.

There was a sharp report and Connors's face widened with astonishment. He opened his mouth to speak, but a bubble of blood flicked out. Then he pitched forward into the snow.

"Jesus!" Hatch cried just behind Marc.

They both turned to see John Collins, pale as a ghost, standing a few yards away at the edge of the woods with a smoking pistol in his right hand.

"I didn't mean to kill him," he stammered. "I thought he was pointin' a gun at you."

"It's all right, John," Hatch said. "You probably saved us the cost of a rope."

Marc had already turned Connors over. Blood was leaping out of a hole in his chest. His eyes were still open. They stared up at Marc in mute appeal. "Father, give me the sacrament . . . please."

"I'm not a priest," Marc said, pressing his fur cap uselessly into the spouting wound.

"I've a confession to make." Connors's voice was a desperate whisper. "Please. I can't go out like this."

Marc leaned closer. "I'm not your confessor, Mr. Connors."

"I killed a man."

Hatch was now at Marc's side.

Blood surged out of Connors's mouth. He choked, coughed, gasped in pain.

"Who did you kill?" Marc said, willing the villain to speak.

The voice was less than a whisper now. "Smallman."

Marc's heart jumped in his chest. He tried to quell the foolish elation, the almost childish sense of triumph rippling through him.

"Joshua?" he said, and waited.

The final two syllables uttered by Ninian T. Connors in this life were crystal clear:

"Jes-se."

THIRTEEN

Marc showed Erastus Hatch the list of names on the slip of paper he had found among the American bills in Durfee's safe. Both men were exhausted, but too much had happened for either of them to entertain the possibility of sleep. The miller's house at midnight was quiet and growing cold. The women were home and safely in bed. Mad Annie and five of her offspring were gracing the cells of the district jail. The cadaver of Ninian T. Connors had been wrapped in a horse blanket and carted off to the morgue in Cobourg.

"I've seen plenty of lists like this over the years," Hatch said. "Could be customers or potential retailers for the rum.

This is definitely an old list: Jesse's name must've been crossed off after he was . . . murdered." Hatch stifled a yawn. "Still, I'd feel a lot better if we had the missing half of this paper. A string of names isn't much in the way of proof."

Marc sighed. "True. Which leaves us with a confessed murderer but no clear or provable motive."

"We have to figure it had something to do with a falling-out over the smuggling business."

"Whatever the exact motive, it's conceivable that Joshua found something among Jesse's papers, either about the rum-running or perhaps even the apparent suicide, and tried to confront Connors or one of his cronies."

"There's still O'Hurley," Hatch said between yawns. "He may be the only one alive who can tell us what really happened in that barn a year ago."

"I've got to tell Beth, of course. The one good thing to come out of all this so far is that her husband did not take his own life. You can't imagine the relief it'll be to her."

"She'll have to know something about the ugly circumstances, though."

Marc sighed again. "I know."

"Anyways, O'Hurley should be safe under lock and key. MacLachlan's sending a courier up to Perry's Corners and another to Toronto. In fact, there'll be couriers galloping up and down the province all night."

"Well, sir, I'm too tired to think straight," Marc said, getting up.

"I quit thinking an hour ago," Hatch replied.

• • •

MARC HAD WILLED HIMSELF TO WAKE at dawn, and he almost did so. Certainly it was no later than seven o'clock when he slipped into Jesse's clothes and padded out to the main room. Mary had the stove going and was humming some Gaelic ditty. In the hearth in the parlour, a fire was starting to warm the air.

"We're to let the mistress stay abed," Mary said. "She worked alongside Major Barnaby until the wee hours. And such a ruckus, eh, among Christian men who oughta know better." The apostasy of Christian males did little to dampen the girl's spirits, as she resumed her ditty with scarcely a missed beat.

Just as Marc finished a hasty meal of bread and cheese, Hatch opened the front door and came in. He set down an armful of parcels on the writing table and brushed the snow off his coat. He and Mary exchanged glances, the latter blushing nicely.

"I got some unsettling news," he said to Marc. "Durfee tells me one of the couriers sent back in the night from Perry's Corners reported that O'Hurley has flown."

"Damn!"

Mary giggled.

"It seems his jailer got overly interested in some of O'Hurley's liquid wares. O'Hurley got clean away. But he left the donkey behind."

"They'll never get him," Marc said. "He'll be in Lewiston by noon."

"There's worse news," Hatch said, with a very unserious twinkle in his eye. "Durfee says MacLachlan's constables came riding up at daybreak and rousted him out of his wife's arms to tell him that Mad Annie and her litter had broken out of their escape-proof jail."

"I can't wish them ill," Marc said, surprising even himself at his sudden sympathy. Last night's brutal raid had left a sour taste in his mouth.

"You heading over to Beth's later?"

"Right away."

"But it's the Sabbath, she'll—"

"I don't want any of this news to reach her before I do."

"Didn't see any smoke up that way."

Marc pulled on Jesse's Mackinaw and the fur cap, still encrusted with Connors's blood. "I'll be back soon. We both have a lot of deep thinking to do." He paused at the writing table. "What are these parcels?"

"The big ones are clothing for the Hislop children. Winnifred collected them at the church yesterday. She's going to drive the cutter out to Buffaloville after the service this morning to deliver them. The others are letters for some of the folks out that way. Durfee gets Winnifred to take them along whenever she can."

Marc was staring, incredulous, at one of the letters. It was addressed to Miss Lydia Connors, Crawford's Corners, Upper Canada.

"Lydia Stebbins . . . is a Connors?"

Hatch's face lit up, then turned a slow, rosy red. "By God, that's right. I remember Winnie telling me something about that last year, but as usual I was only half paying attention. Something about Lydia's mother down in Buffalo refusing to admit the girl had gone and married a fool like Stebbins."

Without a word of farewell, Marc whirled and left the house.

He ran along the path beside the creek and into the rear of the Smallman farm. No one was up or about. Several cows were lowing, as if in distress. Elijah's cabin was sealed and smokeless. Marc hurried by and, rapping once on the summer-kitchen door to announce his arrival, he stumbled inside.

At the door to the big room stood Aaron, surprised and still rubbing sleep out of his eyes. The house was as cold as a tomb.

Five minutes later Beth emerged in a nightshirt and shawl. Her eyes were wide with expectation. Marc had seized the opportunity to change back into his uniform, which Beth had brushed and laid out for him.

"It's all right, I've brought good news," he said immediately to quell the rising anxiety in her face.

"Then we'll have time to make a fire and have a decent cup of tea."

• • •

AFTER THE TEA HAD BEEN POURED, and Aaron had left to split wood in the summer kitchen, Marc sat down beside Beth and tactfully recounted the remarkable events of the evening past.

"Murdered?" she whispered, as if the word itself were tantamount to the deed. "But I saw him there in the barn— alone. I'd watched him grow more troubled and heartsick every day. No one, not even me, thought it was anythin' other than what it seemed to be."

"I understand. You hadn't the slightest cause to think anyone would want to murder your husband. But Hatch and I heard a dying man's confession. He mistook me for his priest, remember. There can be no doubt about it. And when we find O'Hurley, we'll know all the facts."

Beth said nothing for a long time. Marc watched her intently, wanting so much to lay a comforting hand over hers, but knowing there were more questions to come, brutal ones that had to be answered.

It was Beth who finally reached out and folded both of his hands in hers. "You don't know what solace you've brought me this mornin'." Her eyes filled with tears. "I can get on with my grieving for Jess now." She squeezed his hands fiercely, but he knew the passion in the gesture was not meant for him. "And then maybe I'll be able to get on with my own life." A fresh thought seemed to strike her. "I'm only twenty-three years old."

Marc went over to the fireplace and poured more hot

water into the teapot. He gave Aaron a salute through the open doorway, and walked back to Beth.

"I think I know why Jesse was murdered," he said. "And it may also help me to find your father-in-law's killer."

She looked up politely, her mind elsewhere.

"You will need to know why, won't you?" Marc said.

"Yes. I think I will."

"It may be painful."

She smiled ruefully. "I'm growin' used to that."

"I'm convinced that Jesse had some kind of dealings with his murderer in the weeks before his death. We know that Connors and O'Hurley were peddlers of rum and possibly other contraband from New York State. We found Jesse's name on what we're assuming to be one of their lists."

Seizing on the word "assume," she said, "Could there be some mistake?"

Marc placed his hand very lightly upon her wrist and looked straight into her eyes. "Please tell me: could Jesse, in his desperation to save the farm and show his father he could make it on his own, have thrown in with smugglers to get the money he needed to keep up the mortgage?"

Beth did not turn away, but she dropped her eyes as she said, "Yes."

"Did you suspect anything like that at the time?"

"Only that he started behavin' rather odd, comin' and goin' at all hours. He told me he was doin' carpentry work out on the Pringle Sideroad. I asked him about the cask in the barn, and he said Hislop or somebody'd given it to him as payment for a corncrib he built. But why would they want to murder him over a bit of smuggled rum?"

"I'm not sure they did."

"What do you mean?"

"I was told on Wednesday evening that sometimes these peddlers are used as couriers and go-betweens for seditious activities. A secret society called the Hunters' Lodges may have been imported here from the United States, with a view to providing support for Mackenzie's more radical proposals, maybe even insurrection or an invasion in aid of one."

"That's just talk," Beth said. "I've heard nonsense like that for years. Nobody really believes it. You heard what Mr. Mackenzie said at the end of his speech last night."

"If Jesse were even toying with the notion of linking up with these lodges, he could have learned vital and dangerous information. He may even have discovered it inadvertently while participating in rum-running, since the two activities are often combined."

"How long have you been listenin'?" Beth was staring anxiously at Aaron, who was standing by the woodbox with an armful of split logs.

"I just c-c-come in," he said, dropping the wood helter-skelter at his feet.

Beth looked relieved. "It's all right, Aaron. I'm not mad at you."

Marc suddenly had an idea. "Did anyone question Aaron about the night of Joshua's death?"

Beth grimaced. "MacLachlan and Mr. Hatch, both of 'em—in my presence. He was out back for a few minutes and saw Father walkin' past towards the front of the house. He saw no one else."

Marc looked at Aaron, who was following the conversation closely. "Son," he said, "would you think back to the night when Mr. Smallman rode out into the blizzard?"

"I reme-m-member," Aaron said.

Beth couldn't bear to see her brother distressed. She turned to Marc. "Please—"

"I've got to," Marc said. "Think carefully, Aaron. When you saw Mr. Smallman pass you on his way from the barn to the front door of the house, was he carrying anything in his hand or did you see anything sticking out of his pockets?"

Aaron smiled and said without hesitation, "He had a letter."

Aaron stood placidly amidst the scattered wood, but Beth leapt up. "Why didn't you tell that to Mr. Hatch?" she said as gently as she could.

"He d-d-didn't ask me."

"Don't you see what this means, Beth?" Marc said. "You were right all along. There was a written message calling him out there on some pretext. It was a rendezvous. There was foul play. And we must pursue his killer until we find him!"

"Calm yourself. You'll have a fit."

"I'm having more than that! I know who killed Joshua."

Beth's face betrayed her skepticism. "You do?"

"First of all, the motive behind the murder was Joshua somehow discovering among Jesse's effects evidence related to his dealings with Connors and O'Hurley. You said last night that Joshua became obsessed with Jesse's suicide. He may have deduced that Jesse was rum-running. He could have bumped into Connors anywhere about here last fall. He might have learned, from Winnifred or Durfee, that Mrs. Stebbins was Connors's sister and—"

"What?"

"When I left the mill," Marc said breathlessly, his heart racing as fast as his mind, "I saw a letter from Lydia Stebbins's mother in Buffalo: it was addressed to Lydia Connors."

"She was a Connors?"

"That's right. And her father was a bigwig in the Loco Foco wing of the Democratic Party, a group of fanatics who hate centralized government and big banks and go about rattling sabres everywhere. The Hunters' Lodges could easily be an offshoot. And Connors's mate O'Hurley was hiding out at Stebbins's place the day I went there. He hobbled my horse so I couldn't trail Stebbins to some secret meeting out past Mad Annie's."

Beth leaned back, a bit overwhelmed by Marc's fervid narrative. "But I heard he's a gambler and dicer," she offered.

"He tells his wife and everybody else he's going hunting!"

"Most of the farmers hunt—"

"Don't you see, hunting is the code word. And he's never come back with a deer that anybody's actually seen. Gambling at Mad Annie's was just another cover story, like the hunting. Somewhere out in the bush there were secret and dangerous meetings going on."

"But how did Father—?"

"Joshua would've found out from you that Jesse was out in Buffaloville doing carpentry work most of the summer and fall before he died. My hunch is that your father went out to Stebbins's place to confront him with whatever he thought he knew. Remember that Joshua must've had mainly suspicions at this point. If he had had hard evidence, he would have gone immediately to Philander Child with it."

"Come to think of it," Beth said, "Father did go out that way—once—sometime in October, to look at some pigs."

Marc scarcely heard. "As it was, he was probably relying on surprise and conviction. We'll likely never know exactly what Joshua thought he knew: whether it was suspicion that Jesse was a rum-runner whose death could have been linked to those outlaws, or something more sinister, like secret societies and vendettas against turncoats."

"Turncoats?"

"Well, if Jesse joined the Hunters even nominally and then got cold feet, they would have considered him to be a turncoat. In that case, either Connors forced him to hang himself, or he and O'Hurley did it for him."

Beth shuddered. "So you're sayin' that if Connors didn't kill father, then Stebbins did?"

"It could have been any one of the Hunters," Marc said. "Stebbins no doubt denied all the accusations, and, without proof, being an honourable man, Joshua told no one for the moment. But I'm certain he had not given up. Nevertheless, the wind was up among the conspirators. My guess is that on New Year's Eve one of their lesser lights delivered a message to Joshua. The bait would have been information related to Jesse's death. It might well have hinted that somebody knew something to suggest it had not been suicide after all. That would have drawn your father out in a blizzard on any night. It would also have sealed his own silence in the interim. Likely he was instructed to tear up the note and scatter the pieces, or his killer callously came down from the cave and removed it."

Beth was having difficulty with the pace and fever of Marc's monologue as well as with what he was saying. For a moment she had an image of this man in the thick of some battle, eyes ablaze, sword raised in righteousness. "But Azel and Jess were good friends," she said. "We went to rallies together."

"Not everyone is what he seems," Marc said, and the sudden deflation of his voice and demeanour caused her to glance at him in alarm.

Marc took a deep breath. "I should have told you this right at the outset," he said quietly. "You must believe me when I say it was not because I mistrusted you. I trusted you right away, and I've had no cause to regret it."

"What is it?" Beth appeared incapable of bracing herself for more news, good or bad.

"I didn't want to tell you unless it became a necessary part of the investigation. I think now that it is." After the briefest of pauses he said, "Joshua Smallman was a commissioned informant for Sir John Colborne. He sent back monthly reports on suspected incendiaries in this district."

Beth sighed, not with disappointment but relief. "I've known all along."

"You have?"

"Oh, he never told me. But I knew all the same."

"But you took him to Reform rallies, to party meetings!"

"I told you that first day: he was the most honourable and decent man I ever met." Something in her glance intimated that she might have added "until now."

"You see, I knew he would report the truth. And the truth's always been that the farmers of this township are simply fightin' for their rights and their livelihood by electin' members who'll represent their interests. It's not been us who've twisted the laws for our own ends."

Marc wisely refrained from mentioning contraband rum and bat-wielding rallymen. "I've got the last report he ever wrote in my saddlebag," Marc said. "When you read it, you'll see that your faith in him was justified."

"But why is this important now?"

"If the Hunters, or whoever they really are, suspected your father was an informant or even a personal friend of Sir John's, they would be even more desperate to silence him, and to do it quickly."

Beth took that in. Then she said, "But what are you goin' to do about Stebbins? You've got no more proof than Father had."

"Maybe not—not until we run O'Hurley to ground anyway. But I don't intend to wait for that to happen. If Stebbins himself didn't kill your father-in-law, then he knows who did. The answers lie somewhere in Buffaloville. And, Sabbath or not, I'm riding out there as soon as I can get the horse saddled. I'm going to shake the truth out of that conniving weasel and then haul him before the magistrate!"

At the door Beth said, "Be careful. There's been too much death around here lately."

MARC HAD JUST FINISHED SADDLING THE colonel's horse—which showed no sign of lameness, thanks to a temporary shoe and the ministrations of Thomas Goodall—when Hatch came puffing up to him. He had a piece of paper in his hand, but before he could comment on it, Marc launched into a sustained narrative of his theory of the murders of Jesse and Joshua Smallman. Thomas and Erastus stood wide-eyed and open-mouthed.

"So you see," Marc concluded his tale, "it's been about

rum and politics all along. I'm going to tell Stebbins that you and I witnessed Connors's deathbed confession, and that he admitted to Jesse's murder and complicity in Joshua's. That ought to shake him up!"

"My God, but you're a devious fellow for one so young." Hatch laughed. "I reckon you'll be pleased then to see what I've dug up for you." He held out the quarto-sized sheet of paper he had brought with him.

"What's that?"

"All this talk about smuggling reminded me of one of them lists we found back in December. In fact, it's the one we mentioned to you Wednesday night. I took it from Isaac Duffy before we packed him off to Kingston for smuggling. This one's got names, places, and the kind and amount of booze as well. It was enough to nail the bugger in court."

Marc was scrutinizing the information. It covered the full page. Under headings for "Rum: Jamaican" and "Bourbon: Charleston" appeared lists of names and what seemed to be townships or locales.

"It's J. Smallman again," Hatch prompted, with evident satisfaction. "And it's been crossed out—real faint, mind you, but crossed out just the same. We saw it there in December, but with Jesse dead a year, I paid it no heed."

When Marc continued to pore silently over the document, Hatch decided to press on unaided. "Don't you see, lad? Jesse was definitely up to his ears in this sordid business.

And Joshua found out! There's the connection we've been looking for, eh?"

Marc was staring, transfixed, at the heading under which "J. Smallman, Crawford's Cnrs.—6 casks" had been set and then very lightly crossed out: "Hunting Sherry." The word "hunting" had been underlined. And the two names just below it were Nathaniel Boyle and Jefferson Boyle, the Yankee smugglers Hatch and Child had driven from the county. Were they all connected to the Hunters' Lodges? Surely the reference was no coincidence.

Every ounce of blood drained from Marc's face. "My God," he whispered. "This is the second list I've seen with J. Smallman on it. I've had it wrong from the beginning."

"Had what wrong?" Hatch said.

Marc didn't reply, but climbed slowly onto his horse as if in a trance.

"Where're you off to?" the bewildered miller asked.

"To flush out a murderer," Marc said.

FOURTEEN

Marc's first stop was Elijah's cabin. He knew that he would not find the hired man in it, now or ever. He also had a pretty good idea where the old devil would turn up. But for the moment, it was the contents of the cabin itself he needed to examine, something he should have done long before this.

The door opened easily enough. The signs of a hasty departure were everywhere, and it was such haste that Marc was counting on. The table had been cleared of the incriminating newspapers with their religiously underlined accounts of the radical activities in the Cobourg area and beyond. Marc now knew the real reason why they had been singled out, and again chastised himself for having missed the obvious on his first visit here. But the clutter of spilled tobacco, broken quill pens, and pieces of clay pipe remained just as he had noticed them earlier in the week. In less than a minute he had found what he was looking for.

Not wishing to disturb Beth again (it didn't appear she would be riding into Cobourg to church with the Durfees), Marc walked the horse back to the path beside the creek, rode down to the mill and then across the road into the bush that surrounded Deer Park estate. He would have to walk the last few yards, as he intended to approach the grand house from the rear. It was the magistrate's cook he had to see next.

MARC LEFT RUBY MARSDEN IN TEARS, but Philander Child's servant had told him what he needed to know, breaking down rapidly under his quick and intimidating interrogation. He walked around the stone house from the servants' quarters to the porticoed entrance at the front with the confident stride of a man who has the truth in his pocket.

Squire Child's cutter stood beside the porch. As Marc strode up to it, the great man himself came down the steps and boomed a hearty "Good morning" to the sleigh's driver.

"Off to church, are you?" Marc said, coming up.

"Ensign Edwards," Child greeted him, unconcerned and friendly as ever. "Do you wish to ride with me?"

"I wish to talk to you in the privacy of your study, sir, about a matter of some importance."

"Indeed?" Child showed only mild suspicion. "But you can see, young fellow, I am about to set off for St. Peter's."

"The service will have to wait, then."

Child, who had taken one step up into the cutter, halted. He turned a severe face towards the rudeness offered him, the kind he had occasion to practice often on the bench and at the quarter sessions, where his unappealable decisions could make or break a man and his family. "I beg your pardon?" The driver had dropped the reins and was looking on with amazed interest.

"I wish to speak to you, alone and immediately, about the death of Joshua Smallman. I know who killed him."

Child blinked once. "Well, then, we had better find a warm place to sit."

COGGINS WAS HALED FROM HIS MIDMORNING nap to stir the fire and coax coffee out of a distraught cook. When he closed the door of the study discreetly behind him, Child poured out two snifters of brandy next to the coffee cups and raised his glass to Marc.

"To the truth," he said. Then, "Well, don't give me a long rigmarole about it, tell me what it is you have to say to me about poor Joshua's accident that's important enough to keep me from the Reverend Sinclair's sermon."

"Murder, sir. Joshua Smallman, like his son, was murdered."

"Yes, Hatch told me about Connors's confession. Puzzling business, that, but I've sat on the bench for twenty years and I still can't fathom the serpentine convolutions of the criminal mind."

"Jesse was murdered in a dispute with smugglers. Joshua was murdered," Marc paused, eyeing Child intently, "by you."

Child's coffee cup slowed almost imperceptibly, then continued up to his lips. He sipped contemplatively. His brows arched as he said, "By me? Well, then, it's quite a tale you have to tell." He eased his bulk back into the leather folds of his chair. "If you don't mind, I'll just sit here and listen. It's one of the things I do best."

Marc was somewhat nonplussed at the magistrate's calm response, but then he realized he had not laid out any of the pieces of the puzzle that, with Ruby's admission and what he had found in Elijah's cabin, now formed a complete pattern in his mind.

"The tale, as you call it, begins with motive. I surmised long before I arrived here that I would have to discover the motive for Joshua's murder before anything else could come clear. I have already explained to you, on Wednesday evening, how I thought the killing took place that night—"

"And a plausible bit of deduction that was. Though highly improbable. But I interrupt—please continue."

"You decided that Joshua must be killed because you concluded he was a turncoat and because his death would be personally convenient and profitable to you."

Child smiled. "The man was a Tory. When he cut himself he bled blue."

"Quite so. When he came back to Crawford's Corners, you took him into the Georgian Club. You attended the same church. You became his solicitor. More than that, you had already taken an interest in the property of his son and daughter-in-law. You arranged a mortgage on their farm for them so they could build a barn, buy cattle, and diversify, likely using your contacts with the Bank of Upper Canada, which routinely refuses loans to impecunious farmers."

"You've learned a lot about us in eight short months."

"Not enough, I fear. But I suspect you coveted Jess's farm because it borders on the Clergy Reserves section. Given your status and influence with those in high places, you planned to purchase that protected property, a very valuable piece of real estate that would eventually yield a handsome profit."

"It is not against the law to make a profit."

"But you knew that Jesse Smallman was not likely to make a go of his farm."

"Then why would I be foolish enough to bail him out with a mortgage?"

"You had to get him in deep enough to ensure his

complete financial failure, and to have the land revert to you as the mortgage holder. You must have been pleased when he took his own life, as you and everyone else thought at the time."

"It wasn't I who manufactured the drought. Nor did I sit in the Legislature that enacted the Clergy Reserves statute. Even so, I fail to see what this putative bit of melodrama has to do with Jesse's father or cold-blooded murder."

"Following Jesse's death, Joshua Smallman surprised himself and you by packing up and leaving Toronto to come to the aid of his daughter-in-law. He paid off the mortgage, thwarting your designs on the property. Still, with the drought and no government action on the Clergy Reserves, the farm remained a doubtful prospect for the Smallmans. I believe you befriended Joshua not only because he was a conservative businessman but because you hoped you might persuade him to give up the farm as a losing proposition and take his in-laws back to Toronto or over to Cobourg."

"You are employing a surfeit of 'suspectings' and 'believings,' are you not?"

Child appeared to be enjoying himself. Certainly Marc could see no sign that his mounting assault was having any disquieting impact on the magistrate.

"I also suspect," Child continued with a smile, "that you will have to eliminate me as murderer because I happened to have spent New Year's Eve from eight o'clock till two in the morning in this very room with a score of the district's most law-abiding citizens. But do continue. I'm eager to hear how I killed a man I admired while I was several miles from the site."

Marc took a deep breath. "I believe you watched with growing unease as Joshua Smallman began to attend Reform rallies with his daughter-in-law, ostensibly as her chaperone. Every Wednesday evening you and your Tory acquaintances talked a bit of politics between bouts of whist, and it became apparent that the Reform propaganda was having a serious effect on Joshua. I imagine he nodded his head in assent less and less as the summer wore on. I'll wager he began to stay on after the others had left to voice his concerns to a man of some power and authority in the district, and indirectly in the councils of the Family Compact in the capital. He would have been discreet at first, ambivalent even, not knowing himself what was happening to him. I think he found it nearly impossible to accept the dawning truth that the Tories themselves were ultimately responsible for the economic mess the province was falling into, and not the rebellious farmers with their legitimate grievances."

"You can't be a true believer without periods of doubt," Child said.

"But was Joshua Smallman still a true believer? That was the question that tormented you. Beth has told me that her father-in-law started missing the Wednesday soirees in the fall. By early December you two had had a serious falling out. All your subtle attempts to persuade him to sell the farm had failed. Moreover, Joshua's increasing sympathy for the Reform cause seemed to guarantee that he would never sell his son's land—as a matter of principle. I suggest that you quarrelled openly after the others had gone one evening. He may have hinted to you that his own son might have been driven to break the law, and later to take his own life, by the injustices inflicted upon him. However he worded his withdrawal on that day, he left you with the shattering conclusion that he had turned Reformer."

"Good reason for losing a friend, I should think, but hardly provocation for murder." Child poured himself another brandy. The man seemed to be pleased that this droll young ensign had provided him with a ready excuse to miss the tedium of an Anglican sermon.

"Agreed. But it is one thing to turn one's political colours—many gentlemen have done so in the Mother Parliament—and quite another when those colours belong to a nation."

"As our own United Empire Loyalists did in the eyes of the American revolutionaries?"

"I'm talking about treasonous activity, sedition, casting your lot in with your own country's enemies."

"You are not implying that Joshua Smallman was a traitor, a turncoat?"

"No, but I know for a fact that you yourself thought so."

"Indeed. Do you read minds in addition to your military duties?"

"Just before Christmas, Constable Hatch apprehended a peddler named Isaac Duffy and brought him promptly to you. You soon discovered he was up to his Yankee eyebrows in rum-running. On the document Hatch had removed from him, you caught sight of the names of a couple of notorious villains you'd been trying for years to get evidence against: Jefferson and Nathaniel Boyle. The two of you rode straight out to their farms, but they'd already fled back to the States or gone into deep hiding."

"I fail to see where this is going," Child said, but he made no move to rise.

"You took special note of their names, but you also took note of the name just below the Boyles' on that incriminating document: J. Smallman. A very faint line had been drawn through it, so faint that Hatch only noticed it this morning upon close examination. Since the list seemed to be a current one, you assumed that the 'J' referred to Joshua. Hatch assumed it was Jesse and ignored it: what good would it do to speak ill of the dead? But you were so shocked you said nothing. Instead, you went along with Hatch in search of the Boyles. But you couldn't get it out of your mind that Joshua Smallman's name was listed under the words 'Hunting Sherry.' You likely knew from your own sources at Government House that there were serious allegations being made concerning the existence and operations of the Hunters' Lodges—even though you showed only nominal interest in the subject on Wednesday evening. Connors and O'Hurley

used 'hunting' as a code word for the local insurrectionists
they were enlisting. Given what you had observed of Joshua's
leanings over the preceding months, it all fit."

Marc leaned forward in his chair. "I submit, sir, that by
Christmas Day you had reached the sad conclusion that
Joshua Smallman, in his grief over his son's horrific death
and the bitterness he felt at the collapse of his lifelong
beliefs, had gone over to the enemy and that, using the
smuggling operation as a cover, he was actively supporting
the Hunters." Marc practically hissed the next sentence.
"And you yourself said to me in this very room that the
people you despised most in the world were smugglers and
traitors."

"It sounds as though you're well into the second act
of this tawdry little tragicomedy," Child said affably. "Or
should it be called a fairy tale?"

Marc ignored the jibe. "When you gave that heartfelt
speech in front of Mr. Mackenzie last night, I realized just
how fanatically you felt about loyalty and about playing by
the rules. Your family has served eight or nine kings through
thick and thin, dispensing justice and upholding laws even
when they didn't agree with them. You can't be half a patriot any more than you can be half human."

"This is not even news, let alone evidence."

"I also got a glimpse into the depth and vindictiveness
of your temper when, after tolerating the peccadilloes of
Mad Annie for years, you incited a herd of vigilantes to

burn her out. It's also possible that you got wind of Connors and O'Hurley operating hereabouts again. It wouldn't do to have one of them blabbing on about Joshua's involvement in smuggling—raising questions you wanted left alone—so you decided to eradicate the whole lot of them at one fell swoop, despite the dubious legality of the operation."

Child looked abruptly up at Marc, held his eye, and said, "I imagine murder might be viewed in some circles as legally dubious."

"Yes, surely. But not when it comes to the treatment of seditionists or spies, not in circumstances where authority feels itself besieged or in a state of apprehended insurrection. The unobtrusive removal of a dangerous turncoat becomes a kind of noble service to the state, to be sanctioned—lauded even—after the event, should it ever become public knowledge. And when that 'noble' act eliminated a man who stood in the way of your gaining his property, then it was doubly serendipitous."

"You seem to have forgotten that Mrs. Smallman would inherit her father-in-law's estate. If so, why would she sell, eh?"

"But I have not forgotten that you were the man's solicitor. You knew he had no will, and that there were possibly relatives in the States with a claim on the estate."

"The chances of finding them would be slim."

"True, but as a lawyer, you knew you could delay the probate until Beth Smallman was forced to sell her farm—to you."

Child smiled cryptically, poured himself another brandy, and said, "Why did you ever abandon the bar, young man?"

"Words are no substitute for action."

"Agreed. Well, you've established a plausible motive for me, but I must say that I'm still unable to envision my leading a friend-turned-enemy into a deadfall trap while sitting in this chair sipping brandy, much as I am now. Did I have a three-mile-long piece of string to trigger the trap or a siren song only poor Joshua could hear?"

Like the accomplished barristers he had seen in high flight at the Old Bailey, Marc decided it was time to prick the complacency of the witness in the box by playing the first of his trump cards. "I have just come from interviewing Miss Marsden. It didn't take long for her to break down and admit that she had lied to the sheriff when she swore that Elijah Chown spent the whole of New Year's Eve with her."

A corner of Child's left eye twitched once—that was all. "You had no authority to trespass on my property and intimidate my servant," he said, but it seemed more a pro forma objection than righteous umbrage.

"I have Sir John's warrant authorizing this investigation, along with his detailed memorandum of instructions," Marc said, tapping the pocket of his frock coat. "And when Miss Marsden saw the governor's seal, she soon decided to tell me the truth."

"If that is so, then I advise you to interrogate Elijah, not me. I fail to perceive what motive that deranged soul might have had to waylay and murder the man he worked for, whose daughter-in-law he protected as if she were his own child. In any case, Elijah is no concern of mine."

"Ah, but he is. He is in every way your man. It was you who brought him here from Toronto, ostensibly to help Jesse and Beth to survive on their farm."

"Indeed it was. He was the relative of a friend in the capital, addled but good-hearted, and knowledgeable in farming here. It was an arrangement that suited everyone involved."

"And I have no doubt that your motives were less than altruistic. You needed someone you could control close to that scene, and such a gesture would be sure to disguise your true motive. And if need be, Elijah could be persuaded to be unhelpful."

"You are inordinately cynical for so young and inexperienced a gentleman. But remember, when Jesse couldn't pay Elijah's wages, I did so," Child said with serene detachment. "That is, until Beth found out. When Joshua came, she was able to pay the man properly."

"Yes, and by then Elijah had become attached to Mrs. Smallman. But when you needed to, you made sure he realized where his loyalties lay. He owed his living to you. He took a shine to your cook. He spent more and more of his free time over here. Furthermore, I'm certain you have some more tenacious or threatening hold over him, something so compelling that he would do your bidding even if it entailed murdering Beth's father-in-law."

"And precisely how were such an improbable duo able to

execute a scheme to assassinate a harmless dry goods merchant?" Child was looking relaxed and bemused again. No hint of a twitch. "Your fantasies are far more entertaining than Holy Communion at St. Peter's."

"I can only speculate on the details, but from the evidence available, I've been able to set your scheme reliably in outline. What I surmise happened that night was this. You decided that Joshua must be confronted and your suspicions put to him—man to man. Even if he could successfully dispute them, you likely intended to pressure him into selling the farm to you by threatening to ruin his reputation with vicious innuendo. After all, he couldn't prove that the 'J. Smallman' on the smugglers' list you confiscated was not him. You sent a servant with a note that contained some message designed to lure him out, even on a snowy New Year's Eve. Beth thought it was an invitation to your soiree, but it was something more sinister."

"But why did I not merely summon him here into my presence and have it out in this very room?"

"You did not do so because you had already determined that if he could not satisfy you of his innocence of sedition, you would execute him on behalf of the Crown—for its sake and to satisfy your own greed. That is why the double motive here and the explosive nature of your character are so relevant. For you, nothing could absolve a turncoat or exculpate a Guy Fawkes with a grenade in his fist. And your lust for land and status is without bounds."

"And this Elijah chap is supposed to have joined me in my murderous crusade. Just like that?"

"I think you decided to confront Joshua in a secluded spot, interrogate him, and then, if necessary, have Elijah dispatch him—out where no one would think to look. Oh, they'd find his horse, all right, miles from the deadfall, but I believe the body would have been dragged along the lake ice and dumped into the snow half a township away. The bears and wolves would scatter the bones. They might never have been found, or identified."

"You do have a florid imagination. You should take up novel writing: the three-volume Gothic variety."

"As it turned out, you didn't need to do any of that. Elijah established his alibi with your besotted cook, then slipped out and rode one of your horses to the smugglers' cave at Bass Cove, a place you'd likely heard about from Durfee or one of the other longtime residents of the area. His instructions were to wait there for Joshua's arrival, and then to keep him there, by force if necessary, until you came yourself to begin the inquisition. Elijah may appear old and addled, but he's neither. He's a muscular farmhand who can and does read. A knife or pitchfork would be all the weapon required to intimidate the older and weaker man."

"I was in this room until two hours past midnight."

"I'm sure you were, with many worthies to testify so. Your plan was to make some plausible excuse to retire early—a touch of indigestion perhaps—and then sneak out and ride undetected up the lakeshore to the cove at the foot of the ridge. But you did not have to. When you 'stepped out for some air,' say, around ten o'clock, Elijah himself was waiting for you in the stables. He told you that Joshua Smallman had indeed been lured out to Bass Cove but had never reached the cave. The God who anoints and protects monarchs had steered the turncoat into a deadfall trap meant for deer or bear, and thus meted out His own brand of retribution. And that's most likely how you viewed what happened out there, though I strongly suspect that Elijah directed Joshua into the deadfall trap or, in the least, deliberately left him there to die. A personal trial of the man's honour out there would have pleased you perhaps, but it was not to be. Higher powers had intervened and done the dastardly work for you."

"The Lord moves in mysterious ways His wonders to perform," Child said with deliberate irony.

Marc didn't notice, for he was riding the crest of a rhetorical adrenaline rush, soaring along on the wings of his own argument. "At first I thought Joshua had been tempted out there by a note from one of the political radicals suggesting knowledge about Jesse's apparent suicide."

Child was fussing nonchalantly with his snuffbox.

"But that was wishful thinking. Joshua may have been obsessed with his son's inexplicable death, but I don't believe now that he would have been foolhardy enough to venture up there in a blizzard unless he recognized the handwriting

on the note delivered to him by one of your servants, who
doubtless thought he was the bearer of an invitation, perhaps
a peace-offering. Joshua read it in the barn while making his
nightly check, a message from a man he had no reason to
fear, even if he did quarrel with him over politics and land
acquisition. After all, this man was a justice of the peace.
What you put in that note I do not know, because the note
was destroyed by Joshua or, more likely, removed from his
body by Elijah after the fact. Joshua was knocked unconscious: alive but dying. Leaving a man to die and not reporting it is tantamount to murder. And those who seduced him
out there under false pretenses are equally guilty. In the
least, you are an accessory."

"At the inquest, as I recall, even Beth could not swear to
the existence of a note."

"But her brother Aaron will."

A minor twitch of the left eyelid. "I see. So you've been
browbeating helpless cretins, have you?"

"The boy is as sharp as you or me. His testimony will
stand up in court."

"Perhaps. But you have nothing but a falsified alibi for
evidence. You could not bring this within a mile of any
court."

Time to play his second trump card, Marc decided. "At
this moment, I have your accomplice incarcerated in the
miller's office. He has confessed to the salient details as
I've outlined them. Moreover, he has implicated you." This

devastating fabrication was delivered with such élan that Marc almost believed it himself.

Child rocked back, but not from shock or the onset of fear. He was laughing. "Well now, this time you've been too clever by half," he roared. "For a second there you had me damn near convinced that you knew what the hell you were talking about. You might even have swayed a gullible jury envious of the gentry's innate superiority."

"My duty is to report everything I find to Sir John or his successor."

"It'll have to be to Francis Head, I'm afraid. Your mentor and protector is on his merry way to Montreal and obscurity." He let a chuckle ripple to a halt, heaved his bulk forward in his chair, and fixed Marc with a look that blended contempt, complacency, and aristocratic anger. "You are a brilliant fool," he said, "a meddling tyro whose vanity is exceeded only by his vocabulary. You do not have the hired hand in custody at Hatch's. You appear not even to know his last name."

"What do you mean?" Marc snapped.

"Elijah *Gowan* left the district right after the donnybrook last night, with his own kind." The magistrate smiled his patronizing, judiciary smile. "The man is second cousin to Ogle Gowan, grand master of the Loyal Orange Lodge, whose lunatic apostles broke up the rally last night and tried to tar and feather the leading light of the Reform party. Elijah's a more fanatic Orangeman than his notorious cousin. He can track republican sentiment like a hound on the spoor. The Orange Order see any suggestion of annexation or democratization as tantamount to treason against the British crown, which in turn they revere as a bulwark against popery."

Marc was momentarily thrown off stride by the sudden failure of his trump trick and this revelation of "Chown's" true name, but he quickly regained his momentum. "I admit that I do not have him in custody. However, he will not be very far from his cousin; we'll have him apprehended within a day." Marc did not feel obliged to confess that he had inferred from Elijah's obsessive interest in radical newspapers that he was a sympathizer, not an implacable opponent.

"We shall see, shan't we?" Was there a flicker of doubt before the resurgence of confidence? "Anyway, Elijah Gowan is long gone from Crawford's Corners. And I have good reason to believe he will be found only if he wants to be found. You've played your bluff, I'm afraid, without a deuce to support it." The smugness in Child's face was galling, to say the least.

"We'll find him. And when we do, he'll talk. In fact, I see now that you did not really need a hold on the man. All you had to do was convince him that Joshua Smallman was a turncoat who had thrown in with the Hunters' Lodges and arch-republicans. He would have throttled Joshua in his own bed."

"That is quite true. But even if you should somehow find him, he'll never say a word against me or any other loyalist.

You could put him on the rack and crack every rib and he would remain steadfastly silent. You see, for fanatics like Elijah, this isn't a game of politics or conflict of ideologies, it's a holy war, a crusade carried forth with God's own connivance."

"And what does that make the man who uses such fanaticism for his own ends?"

"It depends on the ends, doesn't it?"

Time now for the ace up his sleeve. "I think he'll talk," Marc said, "because I have irrefutable evidence that places him outside that cave in a position that gave him an unobstructed view of, and snowshoe access to, the deadfall trap."

Child maintained the smug expression he had no doubt cultivated on the bench and in the counting house, but his gaze was fixed on Marc as he reached into his jacket pocket and drew out two halves of a clay pipe.

"Hatch and I found this bit of stem on a ledge near the cave. I picked up this other piece a few minutes ago in Elijah Gowan's cabin. As you can see, they are a perfect fit. This evidence and his fabricated alibi will be enough to loosen his tongue. He won't fancy hanging or rotting in prison for a man whose motives had as much to do with greed and personal power as political sentiment and loyalty to the Crown."

"You have no direct proof of my involvement." Child's voice had gone cold.

"But I do have a case: a motive, a plausible scheme of events, a suborned servant, a man in flight without explanation, testimony that a message was received by the victim, and a summary of this conversation."

"You would take all that rubbish to Francis Head?"

"I intend to. Without delay."

Child uttered a world-weary sigh and sat back in his chair. "You are a sterling young man, Ensign Edwards. You showed us incredible courage and a selfless devotion to duty yester-evening when you rescued Mackenzie from that lunatic lot. You are a credit to your regiment. Your actions could well earn you promotion, even in these post-Napoleonic doldrums when such preferment is hard to come by. I observed your kindness out there at Mad Annie's, and the calm and solicitous way in which you dealt with the dying Connors."

"My God," Marc said suddenly, "it was your man who shot Connors. Would you stoop so low to protect your own hide as to involve John Collins in your crimes?"

Child ignored the remark. "My point is this: why are you going to the fruitless trouble of concocting such a report and presenting it, with all its flaws showing, to a lieutenant-governor who will have been in office for less than a week?"

"Until Elijah Gowan is caught and offers up his confession, I may not have proof enough to satisfy a court," Marc said, with more spite than he had intended, "but the evidence I do have, at the very least in these politically sensitive times, will throw serious doubt upon your character and on your probity as a justice of the peace. You are finished as a magistrate and as a pillar of this community."

"Francis Head will laugh you out of his office," Child

said, straining now to maintain his air of unconcern and suppress his rising anger.

"I have no alternative but to do my duty," Marc said stiffly.

"Then you truly are a fool," Child said.

Marc rose. He reached into his pocket and withdrew two letters. "I may know little of politics, sir, but of one thing I am absolutely certain. Joshua Smallman was no turncoat. I doubt even that he was a committed Reformer. What you didn't know, and what you would have learned if you had not been obsessed with seizing control of his farm and had given the gentleman the courtesy of an interview, is that he was a commissioned informant for Sir John Colborne, the governor's personal friend and a trusted confidant."

Philander Child desperately tried to look amused. "Another bluff, Mr. Edwards?"

"Why don't you take a moment after I've left to peruse the last report he ever sent to Sir John? I had it from the governor's own hand, along with this detailed memorandum outlining the reasons why Sir John himself suspected foul play and chose me to come down here to investigate."

Marc dropped the letters on the table beside Child. It took all the moral courage he could muster not to turn at the door and watch the magistrate as he read through the documents—whey-faced, stunned, all the pomp and pride leaching out of him as the contents of each successive page burned itself into his heart.

FIFTEEN

Marc was almost at the end of the winding lane that linked Philander Child's estate to the Kingston Road when he heard sleigh bells. He brought the colonel's horse to a halt and waited. Seconds later, Erastus Hatch's Sunday cutter passed by the entrance to Deer Park on its way to Cobourg, where the rituals and ceremonies of the sabbath would be played out as they had for generations of millers and other ordinary day-labourers. Thomas Goodall manned the driver's bench, cracking his whip above the ears of the horses and trying not to over-notice the erect and proper, but not unhandsome, figure of Winnifred Hatch seated at his side and looking quite ready to take the reins should he unexpectedly falter in his duty. Seated serenely in the sleigh itself, cheek by jowl, were the stout constable of Crawford Township and his one-time scullion, Mary Huggan.

Marc waved but they did not see him.

Well, he thought, there was at least one truly happy outcome of his week in Crawford's Corners. Father and daughter had found someone besides each other to cherish and build a life with.

MARC LEFT A BRIEF NOTE ON the table for Erastus, took a last, fond look around, and left the house. He threw his bedroll and pack over the horse, secured them, checked the saddlebags, and mounted. He nudged the animal around to the mill, then trotted up to the rear of Beth's place. A casual observer might have thought that the ensign, dressed for Sunday parade, was enjoying a leisurely morning ride along Crawford Creek. Not so. Marc's mind had raced and seethed since the confrontation with Philander Child. There was much to sift, assess, decide.

As he led the horse up to the house, Beth appeared at the back door. She ran towards him, hugging a sweater to her small body. "Elijah's gone," she cried. "He never came home last night. I'm worried sick."

Marc took her hand. "He's gone for good," he said. "Let's go inside. I've got a lot to tell you."

• • •

How to tell Beth, and how much, had occupied a good portion of Marc's thoughts since he had left Child. Even now, as they sat sipping tea, Marc was only half certain of what he needed to say. He had been brought up to believe that women were weaker than men, but more delicate, refined, and sensitive—and hence more vulnerable to poetry, music, art, the graces that make the world bearable. But the price of such sensibility was, alas, intrinsic frailty, the constant spectre of psychological disintegration. Here before him was a woman only two weeks into mourning the loss of a "father"; the shocks she had borne over the past year and those rude revelations of the last two days ought to have crushed her, left her emotionally maimed, utterly exhausted, dependent upon the strength of some consoling, masculine arm. And yet here she sat with a teacup on her knee, waiting patiently for Marc to say what she knew could not be kept from her, whatever her own wishes might be. (And, of course, though it would be much later when he had time and the predisposition to ponder the more eccentric aspects of his week in Crawford's Corners, he would be forced to admit that few of the women he had encountered here—Winnifred, Lydia, Bella, Agnes, or Mad Annie—fitted the comfortable cameo of womanhood presented to him by dear Uncle Jabez.)

Marc began. "After I left here this morning, I went straight over to Hatch's and told him my theory. But before I could set off for Stebbins's place, Erastus showed me a document that completely altered my view of what happened to your father-in-law and why. I'm sorry to say that it pointed a finger at Elijah."

"That can't be so. He's worked here without pay. He's been kind to me and especially to Aaron." She looked truly bewildered for the first time since Marc had met her.

He swallowed hard and looked away. "I found a bible in his cabin. It had his name in it: Elijah Gowan."

"Gowan?" She drew out the syllables of the name slowly, as light dawned in her eyes. "Like Ogle Gowan?"

"He's a second cousin, yes. And an—"

"—an Orangeman."

"Apparently he believed that your father-in-law was about to throw his lot in with the annexationists. And to many Orangemen, that is an anti-monarchist act, an act of high treason."

"But how?"

"How and why he came to believe Joshua had gone that far we'll only know when we catch him."

She nodded, still perplexed. Marc told her about the matching pieces of clay pipe.

Beth sat very still, as if absorbing more than words. "Elijah couldn't have got Father out there in that blizzard," she said.

"Yes, that is true. And that's why I'm convinced that a second person was deeply involved in Joshua's death. I believe Elijah was to be made the instrument of murder, but someone a lot more clever and knowledgeable planned it, with cold premeditation."

"Who?"

"I've identified the culprit," Marc said, releasing each word carefully, "but so far I don't have enough evidence, and until I do I am honour-bound to keep the name to myself."

"I understand," she said, implying more than mere agreement.

"But as soon as Elijah is arrested, we'll have the means to establish the whole truth, and justice will be fully served. Joshua's murderers will not go unpunished."

Beth smiled wryly, the hurt hidden in the humour: "It's been some time in this province since justice has been served."

Marc could find no words to deny it.

Putting a hand on his wrist, she said, "It's not your fault— the bush, the politics, the mess we're in. You've done me a great service, so great that nothing I can do or say will ever be enough to repay you."

Marc knew this was not so, but offered no suggestions.

"You've given me answers to questions that would've plagued me—perhaps for the whole of my life. You've given me back the father I loved more than any other, a man who did not wander foolishly to his death in a blizzard but died for what he was, what he stood for. And you've given me back a husband I can mourn and remember as I ought to."

"I did my duty," Marc said, "that is all."

For the moment they both accepted the lie.

Marc shook hands with Aaron, and Beth accompanied him to the back door, where the colonel's horse waited.

"I'll write Erastus and James in detail as soon as I can, but I'd be obliged if you would, in the meantime, extend my sincere thanks to them for their many kindnesses."

"They'll want to know about Elijah."

"Yes. You may tell them anything I've revealed to you."

"Still, they'll be disappointed not seeing you off."

"Yes. I've grown quite fond of them. I have never made friends quickly, but this week has been like no other in my life."

"Your long and interestin' life."

"My short and boring life."

"Till now," she said, smiling.

"You won't be able to run this farm on your own," he said softly.

"I know. But we'll be all right just the same."

"You could come to Toronto. Open up a shop."

"You mustn't talk like that. We're only allowed one hope at a time. You must go back to your regiment. I need time to grieve, and reacquaint myself with God after our recent quarrel, and be a mother to Aaron, who's never had one."

"I understand," Marc said, though he didn't. "But I'll come back, just the same."

"Hush," she said, laying a finger on his lips. "Don't make

promises you may regret having to keep. Remember, you're still a Tory at heart and I am not."

Before he had a chance to argue his case, she eased the door shut.

He waited for the latch to click into place before he took three reluctant steps to Colonel Margison's second-best horse, which was already dancing with traitorous thoughts of an open road and the company of its own kind somewhere at the end of it.

EPILOGUE

Elijah Gowan was apprehended a week later, cowering and bewildered in a pantry off the summer kitchen of his cousin's house. He was eager—proud even—to make a full confession, viewing his actions as righteous and necessary. Moreover, he readily implicated Philander Child. In fact, he had kept the note he had removed from Joshua's body (telling Child that he had destroyed it)—the one in the magistrate's own handwriting. Gowan's trust in his benefactor, it seemed, had not been total: the note was his insurance against betrayal.

It was a clearly worded missive in which Child explained

that he had been approached by a mysterious stranger who wished to remain anonymous and who had information concerning the death of Jesse Smallman. The informant would agree to meet only in a safe, neutral spot—the cave at the end of the old Indian trail beside the lake. It was enough to lure Joshua to his death.

Child was subsequently arrested and bound over at Kingston to the spring assizes.

Marc's own actions and his report to Sir John Colborne, who forwarded it to Sir Francis Head, the newly arrived lieutenant-governor, had two immediate consequences for the young ensign, one happy and one not. Marc was promoted to lieutenant on Sir John's enthusiastic recommendation, for which he was more than grateful, but that gentleman also suggested that Sir Francis put him in charge of security for Government House and make him his aide-de-camp. Both of these honours were regarded as promotions and were the cause of much envy among his fellow officers. Marc, however, saw the new posting as an insuperable obstacle to his being transferred to Quebec, where rebellion and true military action were thought to be imminent.

Ferris O'Hurley, the escaped peddler, never reached the border. He had unwisely decided to circle back to Perry's Corners and liberate his donkey, still in the hands of its captors, and was caught trying—unsuccessfully—to persuade it to accompany him home. O'Hurley soon confessed to having "witnessed" Ninian T. Connors as he "assisted"

Jesse Smallman to hang himself in his barn, following a violent quarrel over the spoils of their rum-running business. And while he admitted that he was aware of the American dollars that Marc had impounded, he maintained that all he was ever told was that it had come from the Hunters' Lodge in New York State and that Connors was taking it to a group of Upper Canadians to aid them in their ongoing struggle against tyranny. Only Connors knew who the contact person was, and that secret died with him.

As Marc sat at his desk pondering these matters, he could not help feeling that his week in Crawford's Corners had been somewhat more than an adventure. He had carried out a successful murder investigation. He had learned much about this odd colony and its extraordinary citizens. He had made some friends. He had met a woman to whom he would shortly send a long and, he hoped, persuasive letter.

He picked up his pen and began to write.

BOOK 2

SOLEMN VOWS

AUTHOR'S NOTE

Solemn Vows is wholly a work of fiction, but I have endeavoured to convey in it the spirit of the period and the political tensions that led to the Rebellion of 1837. The statements, actions, and character traits attributed to actual historical personages referred to herein—Sir Francis Bond Head, William Lyon Mackenzie, Allan MacNab—are fictitious, and readers will have to make up their own minds as to whether such characterizations are consistent with the historical record. (For the record, Head did dissolve the Legislative Assembly abruptly in 1836, he did campaign vigorously in the ensuing election, and he generally ignored advice from the colonial secretary.) All other main characters are the invention of the author, and any resemblance to persons living or dead is coincidental.

While Danby's Crossing is fictitious—as are the taverns and domiciles of the characters—the streets, landscape, and public buildings of Toronto in 1836 have been depicted as faithfully as my research would allow. Of particular value in this regard were: Gerald M. Craig, *Upper Canada: The Formative Years, 1784–1841*; Sir Francis Bond Head, *A*

Narrative; J.M.S. Careless, *Toronto to 1918*; G.P. de T. Glazebrook, *The Story of Toronto*; William Denby, *Lost Toronto*; and Lucy Booth Martyn, *The Face of Early Toronto*. Any errors of fact in the novel, deliberate or otherwise, are my own.

PROLOGUE

In June of 1836, the British colony of Upper Canada was once again in turmoil.

The farmers of the province, still nursing their many unresolved grievances against the ruling Tory elite, had pinned their hopes for reform on the newly appointed lieutenant-governor, Sir Francis Bond Head. There were two important features that recommended him in their eyes: he was a Whig appointment after a long line of Tory nominees, and unlike his predecessor, Sir John Colborne, he was not a military man. In fact, he was an assistant commissioner of the Poor Laws and a travel writer with administrative experience in South America.

But their hopes were soon dashed. Head decided almost immediately that the Reform Party was the real problem, infiltrated as it was by republican sympathizers like William Lyon Mackenzie who were openly advocating annexation to the United States. Head soon offered a drastic solution to the political stalemate wherein a Reform-controlled (and elected) Assembly routinely had its reformist bills vetoed in the Tory-controlled (and appointed) Legislative Assembly. When Reform members of the Executive Council had the effrontery to resign en masse at this thwarting of responsible government, Head dissolved the Assembly. He then called new spring elections, with a view to having Tories elected in the majority in that chamber.

Moreover, he infuriated the Reformers by campaigning on behalf of the Tories, whom he renamed the Constitutionist Party. The implications were clear and were hammered home on the hustings in rally after rally: a vote for the Constitutionists was a vote for the Crown, while a vote for the Reform Party was tantamount to treason. The meddling of the lieutenant-governor in the colony's politics was forbidden by law, but Head justified his actions by claiming that the future of British North America was in peril, especially with rumours of similar, serious unrest in the sister province of Lower Canada.

Whatever the outcome of the election, the process itself was bound to heighten tensions and invite even greater dangers.

ONE

❧ ❧

June 1836

Lieutenant Marc Edwards wiped the sweat off his brow with the sleeve of his tunic, but not before a rivulet had slid into his left eye and two greasy drops had plopped onto the shako cap cupped between his knees. The afternoon sun of a cloudless June day was pouring a relentless heat down upon the hustings and its well-fed, overdressed occupants.

Surely, Marc thought, the grandees of Danby's Crossing (or pompous old Danby himself) could have had the foresight to erect the rickety political scaffolding under the shade of the maple trees drooping at the northwest corner of the square, or at least close enough to Danby's Inn for its two-storey veranda to provide some merciful relief. Such was not the case, however—here or anywhere else in the backwater province of Upper Canada, where, it seemed to Marc, elections were considered life-and-death affairs, and high serious-ness and bodily suffering prime virtues. And such discomforts invariably included a shaky platform groaning with dignitar-ies, each of whom managed to "say a few words" in as many sentences as were consonant with their social standing or the patience of the throngs.

At the moment, Garfield Danby, the self-appointed chairman of the day's proceedings, was droning away at what he took to be a stirring introduction of the guest speaker, Sir Francis Bond Head, lieutenant-governor of the province, who was seated next to Marc directly behind the podium. As Marc gazed out at the dusty square and the several hun-dred people gathered there on a sweltering Tuesday after-noon in the middle of the haying season, he marvelled at their perseverance, their dogged insistence on hearing every word offered them, as if words themselves might somehow right their many grievances against the King's representa-tives, grievances that had bedevilled the colony for half a generation.

Not two days ago, many of these same folk—farmers, shopkeepers, dray men, and their wives or sweethearts—had stood in this same spot to listen to platitudes from politicians of both parties, right-wing Constitutionists (as the Tories were now styling themselves) and left-wing Reformers. And today they had come back to hear the most powerful man in the province, King William's surrogate in this far corner of his realm. They came to listen and, from what Marc had learned about them in the twelve months since his arrival in Toronto, to judge. Hence their willingness to stand quietly during Danby's ill-grammared maundering. Sir Francis would speak, eventually—if the heat didn't liquefy them all before sundown.

Marc could hear the governor shuffling the several pages of notes he had prepared with the help of his military secretary, old Major Titus Burns, and of Marc, who was now his principal aide-de-camp. This speech, like all the others over the past week, would simply repeat his unvarying themes: public order before any redress of acknowledged complaints; a stable government to assure justice and to effect lasting reforms; a purging of extremists of both left and right (Sir Francis being, after all, a Whig appointment in a Tory domain); reiteration of His Majesty's opposition to republicanism and the "American party" led by William Lyon Mackenzie; and a direct appeal to the common sense of the yeomen who peopled the colony and whose roots lay deep in the soil of the motherland. With Major Burns's rheumatism acting up more frequently, Sir Francis had been calling more and more upon Marc, whose days as a law student had left him proficient in English, to help him in speech writing and, on occasion, to draft official letters to the colonial secretary in London, Lord Glenelg.

While Marc had chosen the action of a military life over the tedium of law, he was happy to sit at a desk and write because he was, by and large, in agreement with the governor's sentiments and strategy. Even though Marc knew that the grievances raised by the ordinary citizens were valid, mainly as a result of the winter weeks he had spent at Crawford's Corners and Cobourg where he had carried out his first investigative assignment, he had little sympathy for the Reformers. He believed, as did Sir Francis, that because these grievances were of long standing and had been noisily protested by the "republican" immigrants from the United States, the first priority was to calm the waters, reassert the King's authority with a firm and fair hand, and then one by one deal with the people's complaints in an atmosphere free of partisan rant and rhetoric. This message, cunningly couched in the rhetoric of regal prerogative, seemed to be having a positive effect on the electorate. (That the lieutenant-governor was by tradition supposed to be neutral in election campaigns was being conveniently overlooked.)

On the bench directly behind the governor, Langdon Moncreiff—the newly appointed member of the Executive Council—slumbered noisily. Above Danby's drone and the rush of a sudden breeze through the far maple trees, the councillor's snores rose as strident and nozzling as any hog's.

Sir Francis shuffled his papers again; Danby appeared to be running out of inspiration. The crowd below fidgeted in anticipation.

Remembering that he was on the hustings to ensure the governor's safety, Marc put his shako back on, leaned forward, and scanned the village square. He knew that immediately behind the platform, where the path south began, two junior officers stood watch, their horses tethered nearby. Marc swept his eyes over Danby's Inn, where the entire entourage, like a royal progress, had arrived at midmorning with flags flying and carriage wheels clattering. Ensign Roderick Hilliard, fresh-faced and keen to please, stood stiffly at the entrance and gripped his Brown Bess tightly. The platform dignitaries—including three merchants, a brace of lawyers, and a rotund banker—were less than twenty yards from the balustrade of the inn's upper veranda. Hilliard gave Marc the briefest of nods. Beyond the inn, the wide corduroy road that led west to Yonge Street was fringed on the north with several tall maple trees, now sporting a dozen youngsters who had climbed among the branches to "get a gander" at the vice-regal personage or simply to make a happy nuisance of themselves. Opposite the hustings, the general store and a sprawling livery stable merited only a cursory glance. On the east side, the smithy was now fireless and quiet, and in front of the harness shop next to it, the proprietor and his family stood in the sun, smiling as Danby wound up his introduction. Above the harness shop was an apartment with glass windows and, higher still, a gabled garret. Marc spotted nothing unusual.

Half-throttled by his own snores, Councillor Moncreiff let out a gasp and a purging cough before the snorts started up again. Marc suspected that the other self-invited platform guests were likely dozing as well. It was not yet three o'clock, but everyone here had already put in a full day. For those travelling in the governor's retinue—Ignatius Maxwell, the receiver general and veteran Executive councillor, his ample wife, and his debutante daughter, along with Langdon Moncreiff and the governor's physician, Angus Withers, and their escort, Lieutenants Edwards and Willoughby, and a company of eight mounted and fully armed junior officers—the day had begun at nine o'clock outside the garrison at Fort York. After a lurching ride up dusty Yonge Street, past Blue Hill, Deer Park, and Montgomery's Tavern at Eglinton, they had travelled the quarter-mile east to Danby's Crossing.

Upon arrival, Sir Francis and the Toronto worthies had been greeted by the local gentry and their ladies (from as far away as Newmarket), several of whom had got into the Madeira sometime earlier. Danby had laid on a stultifying midday meal, with wine, several desserts, and cigars. If Sir Francis had been shocked by the presence of the ladies throughout the meal, by the ingratiating speeches of welcome, or by the port-and-cigar aftermath, he was too well mannered to show it. Marc and his second-in-command,

Colin Willoughby, had led the troop into a back room, where more modest fare awaited them.

Willoughby had given Marc a look that said quite plainly, "Did we really leave England for this?" which made Marc grin. He liked Willoughby. The young man had arrived with the governor in January, suffering terribly from a luckless love affair. Sir Francis had taken Colin under his wing and had asked Marc to assist him. Marc found it easy to sympathize with the pain of unrequited love, as his own attempts to win over Beth Smallman, a widow he'd met in Cobourg, had had little success. None of his letters had been answered. Marc now glanced down at Willoughby, whose scrutiny of the crowd in the square was as keen as Marc's had been upon the peripheral buildings. When Marc caught his eye, Willoughby nodded reassuringly and turned his eyes back to the crowd.

"Ladies and gentlemen," boomed Danby at last, "I present to you this afternoon, Lieutenant-Governor Sir Francis Bond Head!"

A gust of wind swept across the platform, and one of the sheets of notes fluttered out of the governor's hand just as he was about to stand. He reached down to retrieve it before it reached the floor, as did Marc. There was an embarrassing collision of heads, followed by a loud cracking sound somewhere beyond them, a muted thud close behind them, then silence. Marc turned to see Councillor Moncreiff sit bolt upright and flick open both eyes—eyes that saw nothing.

The old gentleman was already dead, his blood and lungs beginning to ooze through the gap in his waistcoat.

Marc froze. Then everyone seemed to move at once. Angus Withers threw his bulk over a crouching Sir Francis, the other dignitaries flailed for cover, Willoughby vaulted onto the platform, and Langdon Moncreiff's body slumped to the floor. The confusion of noises struck Marc a second later: women screaming, men shouting, the governor hissing to his protector to get the hell off him.

"He's dead," Marc said to Dr. Withers and Sir Francis as they untangled.

Beside him, Willoughby went pale and the whites of his eyes ballooned. Marc steadied him, then leapt up onto the bench and peered across the crowded square. The throng had not yet panicked; they were either too shocked or too curious to move. The members of Marc's contingent appeared to have recalled the training he had given them before the governor's patriotic rallies had begun a week ago. Several of them were already mounted and scanning the crowd and buildings for the source of the gunshot or some glimpse of a fleeing assassin.

They had not long to wait. A man's cry, sharp enough to carry over the excited mutterings of the crowd, soared out of a treed area on the northwest corner of the square. This was followed by the sounds of branches snapping and a body hitting the ground. Marc looked over in time to see a rough-clad farmer stagger to his feet, gaze around him with brilliant, stunned eyes, and then scurry towards the general store. In his right hand he carried a large hunting gun.

"There he is!" Marc yelled to two of the ensigns who had just ridden up to the hustings. "Apprehend him!"

The crowd now turned to face the latest commotion, and they, too, began screaming for someone, anyone, to block the assassin's flight.

"Stop that man!"

"He's getting away!"

But no one stopped him as the assassin dashed past the general store and down the side of the livery stables towards the trail that led into the back townships of York County. He had tied his horse just behind the stables and now he swung into the saddle and, gun in hand, raced away into the bush.

"Detail! Form up and pursue!" Marc called out to his men. "Willoughby, bring up our horses and we'll follow."

Willoughby was trembling. Marc gave him a furious shake, anxious that the governor not see what looked like cowardice in the face of danger. Willoughby was no coward: Marc would have staked his life on it. "We've got to go, Colin," he whispered fiercely. "Now!"

Fortunately, Sir Francis, Dr. Withers, Ignatius Maxwell, and others on the platform were still crouched around Moncreiff's body, and Marc was able to pull Willoughby away from the hustings. At last the frightened man began to take gasping breaths.

"I'm all right now," he said to Marc as Ensign Hilliard trotted up beside them with the horses in tow.

"Then let's be off," Marc said as he hit the saddle. "We can't let him get away!"

WHEN SIR FRANCIS HAD GIVEN MARC the task of forming a guard for his political forays into the hinterland, he had spared no expense. Marc had chosen eight young and eager subalterns from his regiment at Fort York (Colin Willoughby was put forward by Sir Francis) and armed them with Brown Bess muskets in addition to the traditional sabre and pistol. The horses now galloping along the trail of the assassin, no more than a hundred yards ahead of Marc, were the best that York County could provide. The pounding of their hooves around the next bend could be heard clearly.

"They'll get him soon at this pace!" Hilliard shouted excitedly over to Willoughby.

"If he hasn't swung off the trail into the forest!" Willoughby yelled to Marc.

"I hope they know enough to keep an eye out for that," Marc said more to himself than to Hilliard or to Willoughby, who seemed to be dropping back. But there was no chance of slowing down to wait for him.

A few seconds later, Willoughby came abreast at a rapid gallop. "Some of the townsfolk are following us!" he shouted.

Eager to be in on the kill? Marc wondered. Or hoping to obstruct justice in some way?

"There they are!" Hilliard shouted.

The rumps of the governor's prize horseflesh came into view as Marc dashed around yet another S curve. He dug both heels in, and his mount—a chestnut mare—responded with a burst of speed that brought Marc alongside Ensign Parker and the others.

"Where is he?" Marc cried.

"Still ahead, sir. We can hear the bugger even when we can't see him!"

"We need to be sure he doesn't deke into the woods. If he's a local, he'll know every deer-trail in the township."

"We thought of that, sir, but the trees are too thick on either side for a horse to get through. He'd have to go on foot, and then we'd spot his horse."

"Good thinking, Ensign."

"I think he's panicked, sir. I think he's beating his mount flat out, and it won't be long before it dies under him."

"I hope so. We can't push our own animals much farther at this pace."

As Hilliard and Willoughby joined the main group, Marc took the lead, raising his hand to signal the others to remain nine or ten strides in his wake so that he could listen to the hoofbeats of the assassin's horse up ahead. The cadence of its gallop was distinctly audible, and it was beginning to flag. A minute or two more and they would have him. Marc's heart was racing in a cadence of its own, driven by anger, excitement, and the sheer thrill of the chase. This was what he had abandoned law and the Inns of Court for! Here he was thundering into danger (the man ahead had, after all, just murdered in cold blood and doubtless would not hesitate to do so again), careless of his safety, hazarding all for his monarch.

Coming around a sharp turn in the trail, Marc at last caught a glimpse of the felon: a mane of grey hair flying in the wind, the glint of the sun on the gun barrel, the pinto beginning to fail under him.

"Halt! In the name of the King!" Marc cried, but it was too late. Felon and mount had swerved into the tangled bush.

Marc swore and reined his horse in as brutally as he dare. If he were to follow the assassin into this narrow passage in the woods, those coming up behind might charge on past him, unaware. It was only seconds, however, before Willoughby and the guards arrived.

"He's a local, all right," Marc said, catching his breath and stroking the chestnut's neck. "He's gone in there. There must be a track of sorts or else he's trying his luck on foot."

Marc eased the horse between two stout pine trunks and entered the humid gloom. As he had suspected, they were on a deer-trail that wound tortuously through the dense woods. There was no need to wave the troop into single file.

"We're right behind you, sir!"

Farther back, he could hear the commotion of the camp followers from town as they, too, stumbled into the woods. One of these fellows, with a stentorian bellow, kept calling out "Stop! Stop!" as if mere repetition would shame the fugitive into giving up the chase.

In the dim light, Marc could easily make out the felon's passage, for the trail itself had been unused since heavy rains a few days earlier, and the pinto's hoofprints were registered clearly in the boggy ground, every stricken step of the way.

"That horse can't last more than a minute or two longer in this morass," Marc called back to Willoughby. "You'd better get your pistol ready. We may need it soon."

The trail arced steeply upwards, and with a sidling lurch, Marc found himself out of the forest entirely and partly blinded by the sun. Ahead lay an extensive clearing—the back field of a farm, most likely—lush with timothy. He could not see the fugitive. Then, as his eyes adjusted, he spotted a rocky, spruce-topped ridge on the eastern edge of the field. At the base of it, not more than fifteen yards away, the pinto pony lay on its side, wheezing, dying. Behind it and rising slowly was the fugitive, with his grizzled chest-length beard and wild shock of grey hair and mud-splotched overalls. He was barefoot. All this Marc saw in a single moment, along with the musket that was pointed straight at his heart. He had been given no time to evade or to retaliate, or even to cry out: the trigger was already being squeezed. What he did feel, in the moment before his certain death, was a twinge of animal terror, then an eerie calm. If he had to die here, at least his courage would have been tested, and found worthy.

The shot did not come. Instead, the felon turned, scrambled up a path of sorts towards the top of the ridge—and vanished. Perhaps the troop coming up out of the woods behind Marc had decided him against pulling the trigger.

"Are you all right, sir?" Ensign Hilliard asked as he and Willoughby reined in beside Marc. "I saw him pointing the gun your way. I was sure he was going to shoot."

"He thought better of it," Marc said calmly. "He's on foot now, climbing that hogback."

"Let's get after him, then," Willoughby said. Marc noticed that the young man was now looking flushed. There was nothing like a fox hunt to get a gentleman's blood up, Marc thought.

"I think we'd be better off waiting here," Marc said.

"Why, sir?" Hilliard said a bit too forcefully. "We can fan out on either side of the ridge and run him to ground."

"Some of the townsfolk are coming up through the woods," Marc said. "At least one of them will know something about this terrain that might help us get our man and save us time and energy."

"Whatever we do," Willoughby added, "we need to remember that he's got a gun and is quite prepared to use it."

"Nevertheless, I am ordering every one of you to make every attempt to capture this man alive. The odds are that the murder was politically motivated, and the governor will need to know who was involved and why. Anything less could throw the election, and the colony, into chaos."

"We'll do our best, sir," Hilliard said.

The first of the townsfolk following the official posse now emerged into the clearing. His name, he announced when he had stopped panting, was Alvin Chambers, a farmer from York Township. Marc addressed him sharply.

"Where does this hogback lead?"

"It's the height of land hereabouts and runs up that way for pert near two mile," Chambers said.

"Are there farms on both sides?"

"Here and there, with lots of bush in between 'em."

"If you have any idea where the gunman might be heading, I command you in the name of the governor and the King to tell me."

Chambers winced at the authoritative tone of Marc's voice. "We do better 'round here when folks ask us politely."

"Are you refusing to co-operate with the King's guard, sir?"

"Nope. I wouldn't want to offend Sir What's-His-Name, now would I?"

Ensign Hilliard made a move to thrash the insolent man, but Marc held up his hand. "We'll find the blackguard without your assistance, then." He wheeled his horse towards the ridge.

"There's an old trapper's cabin up there about a half-mile

through the scruff and rock," Chambers drawled. "No need to go straight up here, though."

Marc paused but did not look back.

"Just ride on north along the base of the hogback till ya come to the bush and a small crick just inside it. There's a path there that goes straight up to the cabin. I didn't see who we was chasin', but some of the fellas ridin' behind me figured—"

But Marc had already given the signal to move forward, and whatever the farmer had said was lost in the thud of hoofbeats. Alvin Chambers was soon joined by his friends, and they followed the governor's guard on foot, many of them gesticulating frantically, Marc noted when he glanced back.

"I think we had better keep that rabble well away from us when we catch up to the gunman," Marc said to Willoughby.

"It's hard to tell whose side they're on," Hilliard added.

Less than five minutes later, the troop came to the bush again, and they could hear the creek tumbling down the ridge nearby. "Well, they didn't deceive us about this land-mark," Marc said.

"So far," Hilliard said.

A minute later, Willoughby called out, "I've found the track!"

"Tie your horses up here," Marc ordered. "Ensign Parker will stay with them and make sure these locals don't get any farther than this. The rest of us will proceed with caution, on foot, up to the cabin. Bring your rifles and have them ready to fire. I'll lead the way. No one is to make any move until commanded to do so. Lieutenant Willoughby will walk directly behind me and cover me, should I come under fire."

Ensign Parker sighed theatrically, while the seven other ensigns eagerly followed Marc's lead. After a long winter of gaming, grouse-hunting, and wenching—relieved by endless hours of idling—they were primed for action.

The path was steep and stony, following the line of least resistance. Scrub pine and barbed bushes blocked any view of what might lie above. Ten minutes of laboured climbing saturated the officers' uniforms with sweat. There was nothing in sight except more bush.

"We could be headed into a trap, sir," Hilliard suggested.

Marc did not reply, and the ensign decided he had offered enough unsolicited advice for one day.

A few minutes later, they clambered awkwardly up over a projecting ledge. Marc whispered, "There it is," and signalled for silence.

Perched on a rocky outcrop at the highest point of the hogback was an ancient log hut, windowless and scarcely big enough to confine one medium-sized bull. A hole in the roof was the only chimney, but no smoke drifted out of it into the steamy afternoon heat. The ground immediately around the cabin was bare, making it impossible to approach it under cover. Between Marc and what appeared to be the only door in the hut, the slope was precipitous but dotted with scrub trees or overgrown bushes. With luck he might be able to crawl up close enough to negotiate with the killer without getting shot before he could begin.

A shadow moved in the doorway. Their quarry had come to roost.

Marc turned to his men, who had all come up behind him and were peering anxiously upwards. Several began loading their Brown Besses. Willoughby's pupils were the size of the buttons on his tunic. Half an hour ago he had seen a corpse with a gaping hole in it for the first time; now the muzzle of a loaded gun might well be aimed at him. Suddenly Marc felt the full weight and responsibility of command: decisions that he would have to make in the next few minutes could put in jeopardy both his own life and the lives of those who trusted his judgment. He took a deep breath.

"I'm going to sneak up as close as I can to the cabin," he said quietly. "I want you to cover me in case I'm spotted. But do not fire at the fugitive, merely send a volley over his head to keep him lying low inside, and then only when I give the signal by raising my sabre or uttering a command. If I am shot, then Lieutenant Willoughby will take over the unit and issue orders. Even so, if you must shoot, try to wound him only."

"Understood," Willoughby said, fighting for breath.

"Will he not try to escape by running back along the ridge the way he came?" Hilliard asked timidly.

"Perhaps," Marc said, "but I think he's decided, one way

or another, to make his stand." That such a decision clearly put Marc's life at risk was a grim possibility. They felt it to a man.

Without further ado, Marc set out. He moved quickly between clumps of brush, pausing at each to squint upwards at the hut. Three-quarters of the way there he realized with a sigh that his feathered shako and scarlet tunic would make him visible even if he had had a granite boulder to hide behind. But the gunman had made no move to warn him off or to put a bullet through his head. Perhaps in his exhaustion and remorse, he had decided to wait for Marc's arrival and then throw himself upon the King's mercy.

Marc was now about thirty yards or so beyond his men and no more than fifteen yards from the hut itself. It was, he could see now, a hovel: crumbling and pathetic in its slow collapse. The stench of offal and rotted vegetables was overpowering, even at this distance. Suddenly, the gunman appeared in the doorway, his eyes, deep in their sockets, gleaming feverishly. He still held the gun, an aging hunting musket, in one hand.

"Put the gun down, sir," Marc shouted gently in his direction, "and no one will get hurt. I represent Lieutenant-Governor Head, and I need to talk to you."

The old fellow moved the gun as if to drop it, but it seemed permanently morticed to his right hand, and, instead, it began to rise alarmingly upwards. But something in the man's startled stare caused Marc to relax his guard.

He stood up slowly and, without taking his eyes off the gun, raised his arm and barked out a single order: "Hold your fire!"

Marc took a step forward. "I won't hurt you," he started to say, just before a volley of explosions from below rocked him. He had to grab a nearby branch to stop himself from tumbling back down the slope. The sting of gunpowder filled his nostrils and stung his eyes. What had happened? Had he been shot at? Hit? For several seconds he sat on his haunches beside a bramble bush, in shock.

"Are you all right, sir?" Hilliard was beside him, and Willoughby and the others were staggering past him towards the cabin. There was no one in the doorway.

"I'm fine, Ensign," Marc said through the ringing in his ears. "But why did you shoot? I ordered you to hold your fire."

Hilliard gasped. "We heard you call out 'Fire!'"

Marc stood up and brushed past him, joining his men, who were crowded around the figure on the ground in front of the doorway.

The old man was dead, with half a dozen bullets in him. Willoughby was turned away from the corpse. He spoke to Marc without looking at him. "I take full responsibility for this," he said in a trembling voice.

"But you were the only one who didn't fire," Hilliard said.

"That's because I wasn't sure what you had ordered,"

Willoughby said to Marc with some emotion. "It sounded like 'Fire,' but I couldn't be sure because your back was turned. But with that gun pointing right at you, I gave the signal and the men fired."

"And saved your life, if I may say so, sir," Hilliard said.

Marc sighed. "You may be right," he said. He turned to Willoughby. "It is my responsibility to give unequivocal orders. If I had turned away from the gunman long enough to face you and give the order clearly, this wouldn't have happened. In the circumstances, Colin, your reading of my command was the correct one. Even so, while I was still upright, you had no authority to interpret it either way, and no cause to give independent orders of your own."

Willoughby looked chastened but also visibly relieved. One of the ensigns, not quite as young as Parker, went over to the nearest bush and retched.

"Perhaps we saved the Crown the bother of a trial and the cost of a gibbet," another offered, keeping his gaze well away from the body.

Finally Willoughby glanced down at the corpse. The face had been smashed by one of the bullets, and several others had ripped through the torso and abdomen, which were now an indistinguishable mass of blood and innards. Wherever the man's eyes were, they no longer gleamed.

Willoughby sat down suddenly and put his forehead on his knees.

"Remember, Colin," Hilliard said consolingly, "this

fellow here put a bullet through Mr. Moncreiff, an innocent gentleman who wouldn't've harmed a mite if it was biting him."

Marc was bent over the body, trying with some difficulty to pry the gun out of the old man's death-grip. He stood up with the offending weapon in his hand. The look on his face was grim. "And this man may be as innocent as Moncreiff himself."

"What do you mean?" Willoughby asked.

"This gun has not been fired," Marc said. "Not today and, by the look of the barrel, not in my lifetime."

TWO

➤ ◄

What the hell have you people gone and done?"

It was the man with the troll's bellow. He and six or seven others were scrambling up the last few yards of the slope towards Marc and his men. Their gaze was upon the body, crumpled on its own threshold. The man with the big voice took two threatening strides towards Marc, then stopped, not because Marc's right hand had gone to the haft of his sabre, but because he had caught a close-up glimpse of the victim's smashed face.

"Sweet Jesus," he cried. "You've killed Crazy Dan. You've gone and massacred him!" Behind Marc, his men shuffled and tried not to look—all the fight suddenly gone out of them. They glanced about, more bewildered than angry.

"That crazy old fellow raised his gun and pointed it at Lieutenant Edwards," Ensign Hilliard said, stepping up to their accuser. "His finger was on the trigger. We had no way of knowing it was not primed and loaded. The lieutenant here risked his life trying to talk the man into surrendering. We had no choice but to fire off a volley." Hilliard spoke formally, as if he were rehearsing what he would say in his deposition to an investigating magistrate.

"But Crazy Dan wouldn't hurt a flea. Everybody 'round here knows that."

"We're not from around here, sir," Marc said. "To us he was a man with a gun fleeing a murder scene."

"But the shot came from the other side of the square!"

"What is your name, sir?"

"Luke Bethel. I've got a farm farther up the hogback on the Tenth Concession."

"What happened here, Mr. Bethel, is a tragic misadventure. There will no doubt be a proper inquest, and you and your companions may well be called as witnesses."

"How can we be certain, sir," Hilliard said, "that the old geezer didn't hide the murder weapon in his cabin or toss it away somewhere in the bush? We don't know for sure that this old crock of a gun was the one he had in his hand when he fell out of the tree."

"Yes," said Willoughby, a burst of hope rising in his stricken face. "If he was really crazy he might have—"

Luke Bethel cut him short. "Crazy Dan hasn't taken that musket out of his right hand in the past twelve years."

"What do you mean?" Marc said, glancing down and noting that the dead man's fingers were still seized in a gripping rictus.

"Crazy Dan come into these parts in 1816, after the war with the United States. He homesteaded about a mile south of here. Never married. Kept to himself, but was never un-friendly. He was said to be some kind of hero at the Battle of Lundy's Lane. One day he come into the general store—not in Danby's Crossing but the one on Yonge Street below the tollgate—and said he'd killed fifteen good men with the gun he was totin'. He swore he wouldn't ever kill a livin' thing again, not a steer nor a chicken, and he vowed to carry the musket with him everywheres—unloaded and detriggered—to remind people of the evils of war."

"My God," Ensign Parker exclaimed from the rear where he had been violently sick. "We've shot a hero of Lundy's Lane!"

"He was fightin' on the American side," Bethel said.

"Well, then, if everybody knew this, why were people in the crowd yelling at him to stop and egging us on after him?" Marc said, suddenly confused.

"Only a few of us in this region actually knew Crazy Dan. Even after he gave up the farm and moved out here five or six years ago, whenever he did go to town—which wasn't often 'cause his old neighbours brought food for him up here—he went to the Lansing junction up north on

Yonge Street. Everybody up that way knew the old guy, and knew he was harmless."

"Then how on earth did he get to Danby's and climb a tree while surrounded by a hundred people?"

Bethel shrugged. He turned to the others. "We don't rightly know. Maybe he just followed some of the youngsters and joined them up there in the tree. He sometimes borrowed old Frawley's pinto, so that's how he got himself into town. He coulda been there all night. There wasn't any rhyme or reason to what he might do or what might've got into his head. Me, I figure that gunshot spooked him, made him think he was back at Lundy's Lane."

"But you were there!" Marc said. "Why didn't you warn us?"

"That's just it," Bethel said. "I did. I was yellin' 'Stop' at you from the minute you left the square. But your horses were too fast for us. We couldn't catch up to you."

Marc sighed. "We did hear you, but we assumed you were shouting at the culprit."

"We're used to havin' our advice ignored," someone from the group of farmers remarked. It was Alvin Chambers, who had hung back until now.

"But you, sir," Marc said sternly to him, "were standing three feet away from me at the edge of the bush back there, and failed to inform me of what or whom I might expect to see when I arrived here. I demand that you explain yourself."

Bethel gave Chambers a puzzled look before the latter

replied: "We are not in the habit of takin' orders from the military or the grandees of the Family Compact, especially when they're given in a patronizin' tone. We don't tug our forelocks in this province—sir."

"I could have you haled before a magistrate," Marc snapped.

"And I'll tell him I was in the process of informin' you about Crazy Dan when you hopped on your high horse and galloped away."

"Well, I only hope you're pleased with the results of your umbrage," Marc said, glancing pointedly at Crazy Dan's bullet-ravaged body.

"Sir, I still think we ought to have a look inside the cabin," Hilliard said. "Just to be sure."

"You're right, Ensign." Marc nodded to Bethel, and the two of them went into the old fellow's hovel.

It was a stinking shambles. Marc's gorge rose as they picked gingerly through the detritus and ruins of one man's life. There were no guns or bullets or powder or any indication that there ever had been. No animal skin adorned the floor or walls. No bone had been gnawed and discarded: the rotting food was entirely vegetable. Crazy Dan had kept his vow.

"Look at this, would ya?" Bethel whistled under his breath.

Marc came over to him. On a stump table in one corner lay five pieces of hardwood in various stages of being carved.

Marc picked up what appeared to be the only finished figure: no bigger than a baby's fist, it was an exquisitely rendered bird in flight. He held it up to the light in the doorway. "It's a dove," he said.

"For peace," Bethel said.

As Marc and Bethel left the hut, Willoughby and the others looked at Marc. He shook his head slowly. Then he turned towards the farmers: "I'll report everything that happened here directly to Sir Francis, and he'll take matters into his own hands. Will you see that this man is given a proper burial?"

"We will," Bethel said.

"Damn right," Chambers said. "Out here, we take care of our own."

As THE GOVERNOR'S GUARD RODE BACK towards Danby's Crossing less hurried and much less assured than they had been riding out, Marc's mind was in turmoil. Within the space of an hour, he had witnessed a respected citizen and member of the government murdered; he had organized a pursuit with dispatch and discipline; he had drawn judiciously upon the advice of his men and the local folk (with one forgivable exception, perhaps); he had improvised a plan of attack-and-capture that failed only because no one could have foreseen that the musket aimed point-blank at him was not really lethal and its possessor not really an assassin; he had put his own life on the line twice; and, alas, he had contributed to the death of an innocent man, a harmlessly demented veteran of the wars who carved minia- ture doves.

Marc's heart ached, not because he would soon have to face his superior and make his awkward explanation, and not because he would have to bend the truth just a little to protect his men, whose own motives could not be ques- tioned, but because at the last millisecond before his men fired, Marc had known the old fellow was innocent. That was the tragedy of it all.

Not the least of his problems now was the bald fact that someone other than Crazy Dan had murdered Langdon Moncreiff. Not only was the felon at loose, but in their haste to pursue the obvious suspect they had given the real assassin more than an hour to make his getaway. Moreover, any clues he might have left around the square were certain to have been trampled by the curious spectators. The trail would be stone cold. And because Moncreiff was a member of the Executive Council (and all the controversy associ- ated with that body and its relations with the governor), such an arrogant and outrageous assassination could not go unpunished. What is more, time would be short, for the first polling in the upcoming election was less than two weeks away. Marc dearly wished to curse the Fates, but he knew it would be a waste of good breath: the fiasco of the afternoon had been of his own making.

When they rode up to the hitching posts in front of the Danby's Inn, Marc noticed right away that the governor's carriage was gone. He looked quickly over the square. Fewer than a dozen people remained, most of them moving purposefully from shop to shop or gathered on the wooden sidewalk, gossiping. A few youngsters of indeterminate gender hovered about the deserted hustings: curious and delightfully appalled. Marc waved his weary troop towards Danby's saloon, and then entered the lobby of the inn proper.

Angus Withers rose from one of the settees and greeted Marc with a gruff smile. "Did you catch the bugger?"

"He's dead," Marc said.

"Good. Save us all a lot of trouble."

"I'm afraid not, sir."

Marc led him back to the settee and sketched out the near-farcical events regarding the shooting of Crazy Dan.

"You'll have to tell Sir Francis immediately," Withers said with a snap of his jaw.

"Why did he leave?" Marc said.

"He felt it was his personal responsibility to inform Mrs. Moncreiff of her husband's tragic death. Maxwell went with him—and in such a godawful rush he left the women behind. I stayed, of course, to give the body a careful going over."

"Why did Mr. Maxwell leave his wife and daughter out here?"

"Well, he is Moncreiff's brother-in-law, you know. Mrs. Moncrieff is his sister."

Marc raised an eyebrow.

Withers grinned thinly. His thick, permanently arched brows gave him a look of perpetual surprise—part amusement and part censure. "Didn't know, eh? If you're going to serve the panjandrums of the Family Compact, as I do, then you'll have to get to know who's related to whom on the royal tree and who wants to be related to whom."

"I'm learning, sir."

"Anyway, to answer your question, the receiver general had urgent business in the city, beyond consoling his sister. More to the point, he often finds Mrs. Maxwell and his daughter more ballast than he needs for most occasions. He practically leapt into the vice-regal carriage and into the governor's lap. But don't look so worried. Mr. and Mrs. Danby have been entertaining the abandoned females, in a pathetic effort, I presume, to compensate for the social catastrophe of the afternoon."

"How will they get home?"

"Danby has offered to take us in his barouche to Yonge Street, where, if his horses are as well bred as he claims, we'll arrive in time to catch Weller's coach from Newmarket."

"And the body?"

"Sir Francis will arrange everything in that regard. I shouldn't be surprised if the dear old soul is given a state funeral—considering the circumstances." He raised his brows to their limit. "By the way, even though he assumed that you would capture the assassin, Sir Francis did ask me to convey his distinct wish that you, and you alone, were to be put in charge of all matters pertaining to Moncreiff's death. Furthermore, he wants a full report from you tonight, even if you have to wake him."

"I see," Marc said, though he wasn't sure that he did. There were city and county magistrates and, he had heard, a special Toronto constabulary modelled on the London "bobbies." "This is surely not a military affair, sir?"

"Ah, one more thing you have yet to learn. Although he was barely robust enough to lift a pen or his wife's skirt, Langdon Moncreiff was a major in the people's militia, that vast weaponless fighting force that alone stands between us and pandemonium in the radical townships."

"Well, whatever the reason for the governor's trust in me, I still have a murder to solve, don't I?"

"I'm afraid you do."

"Then I'd better get at it."

"Before you do, Lieutenant, our 'Ariadne' and her offspring desire you to pay them your respects. They're in the sitting room, through that door."

"AH, IT IS SO KIND OF you to see us, under such dreadful circumstances." Mrs. Maxwell beamed at Marc from her reclining position on a sofa. "Chastity, my dear, you will remember Lieutenant Edwards from the governor's ball at the Grange last, ah, when was it?"

"October," Marc said, bowing slightly to acknowledge the younger woman.

"My, what a prodigious memory you have, young man, doesn't he, sweetie?" Mrs. Maxwell turned up the beam in her dark eyes slightly, then dropped her gaze to her extensive bosom in a parody of coquettishness.

"Miss Maxwell and I danced the galliard, as I recall," Marc said.

"So we did, Lieutenant," Miss Maxwell said without a blush or dropped eye.

"In what way may I be of assistance in this tragic business, Mrs. Maxwell?" Marc said with more politeness than he felt. "I have just learned from Dr. Withers that Councillor Moncreiff was your brother-in-law. Please accept my sincere condolences."

"Thank you, sir," she replied, and pulled a lace hanky out of the folds of her elaborate skirts, but it found no tear to wipe away when it reached her left cheek. "And do call me Prudence, otherwise I shall begin to think myself old, and beyond those pleasures reserved inexplicably for the young."

Chastity quickly changed the subject. "We thought you might wish to ask us a few questions about dear Uncle Langdon." Her voice caught in her throat, and cracked. Marc offered her his own handkerchief, and she sat down wearily on a sofa across from her mother. Chastity Maxwell was as lithe as her mother was sumptuous, with pale-grey eyes and flaxen hair. Her angular features, like her father's, revealed more character than beauty. Last October at the Grange she had tripped her way through the intricate galliard with Marc, and though not truly attracted to each other (who knew why in such matters?), they had enjoyed the pleasure of the dance. Unfortunately, Marc's card had been filled, as it invariably was, and they had not danced together again.

Marc turned to Prudence and soon became aware that the blush on her cheek was not only rouge but also the after-effect of drink. Behind her on a tea trolley sat a near-empty decanter of red wine and a single smudged goblet. The Danbys had been entertaining the visiting grandees with vehemence.

"What I need to know, ma'am—"

"Prudence, please—though my mama always said I had none to speak of."

"Do you know of anyone who might wish to kill your brother-in-law? Did he have political enemies? Rivals who might be jealous of his recent appointment to the Executive Council?"

Prudence Maxwell laughed, a snorting sneeze of a laugh that she belatedly turned into a ladylike cough, which gave her a plausible excuse for waving her hanky about. "No, no, you won't find anything in that direction. And even though Chastity and I have seen little of him and his wife Flora in the past few years—now that's another story and one that has no bearing on the dreadful events of this day—I did know him very well in his youth. And it is my considered view that Langdon could never work up an opinion strong enough to make a monkey fart, let alone a decent enemy or two. Now if it'd been my Ignatius shot, God forbid, I could've given you a dozen names."

When Marc looked shocked at this, she added with relish, "How else do you think the man got rich and feared by lesser men?"

"Mother, please stop. You're overwrought."

Prudence turned to her daughter, squinted grotesquely, as if she had momentarily lost her sight or had failed to recognize the young woman across from her. Marc saw now that she was very drunk, but just as he stepped over to offer her some assistance, she winched her eyes wide open and leered up at him. Her voice was a loud slur: "Hell, honey, I ain't been wrought over in a long, long time."

Chastity was up instantly, her tears forgotten. "I'll call Mrs. Danby and the maids," she said briskly to Marc. "We've got to get her to a bed. Our coach arrives in less than an hour."

"You'll be all right?"

"I'm used to it."

MARC WAS SEATED ON THE FRONT bench of the hustings exactly where he had been sitting when Moncreiff was shot. The platform was no more than four feet above ground.

And though Moncreiff had been snoozing upright in the second row, he could have been seen by any marksman at or above the level of the hustings floor. Luke Bethel out at Crazy Dan's cabin had claimed the shot had come from the other side of the square, which must mean the eastern side. The boardwalk that surrounded the square was a foot high, and at least a dozen people had been standing on benches in front of the shops: that extra elevation could have been enough. If so, then anyone near the general store, the livery stables, the blacksmith's, or the harness shop—or in the alleyways in between—might be a witness. He would need to question every merchant and tradesman who had been standing within or near their shops at the time of the shooting. Even then, the presence of so many strangers could easily make any interrogation fruitless. Add to the mix the probability that ninety per cent of the on-lookers were Reform sympathizers who would be disinclined to answer questions from military investigators about the death of a Tory.

While Marc was willing to take Prudence Maxwell's dismissive description of her brother-in-law at face value, she was unlikely to know much about his political or financial affairs—or his personal peccadilloes for that matter. Like it or not, he would have to probe into the man's life in a manner that was sure to enrage the power-brokers in the Family Compact (of which Moncreiff was a nominal member) and ruffle feathers just about everywhere else.

"Would you care for a smoke?" Angus Withers sat down beside Marc and offered him a cigar similar to the one he was puffing on.

"No, thank you."

"I find a good smoke helps me think. Either that or it just anaesthetizes the thought processes to the point where I don't give a damn any more."

"I wanted to ask you, Dr. Withers, about the wound, if you don't mind."

"That's why I came out. The ladies and I—well, only one of them can be legitimately termed so—have to be off for Yonge Street in half an hour."

"What was the angle of entry? It might help me determine the vantage point of the shooter."

"Unless the poor devil was lying sideways on his bench—"

"He wasn't. He was dozing, but otherwise perfectly upright."

"Then the bullet struck him just under the right shoulder, broke through a couple of ribs, ripped out his lungs, and exited through the fleshy muscle above the left kidney. Only the lungs were hit, no other organ."

"So he had to have been shot somewhat from the side, the right side."

"And from a point considerably above where we are now perched."

While Dr. Withers worked on his cigar, Marc scrutinized

the eastern edge of the square. There was only one place the gunman could have been for that trajectory, and, even then, he would have to have been a crack shot. If indeed Langdon Moncreiff had been the target.

"Thank you, Doctor. At least I know where to begin."

And with that, Marc strode deliberately towards the harness shop.

THREE

❊

Good afternoon, Sergeant," the harness-maker boomed cheerily, coming out to greet Marc on the wooden walk in front of his shop. "We been expectin' someone like yerself to come callin', haven't we, Sarah-Mae?"

Sarah-Mae, as tiny as her husband was gargantuan, poked her bonneted pink face out from behind her better half.

"I'm Phineas Kimble, harness-maker to three townships for twenty-two years." He threw out a hand the size of a pig's rump. He towered over Marc, who was himself almost six feet and accustomed to peering downward when he talked.

"How do you do, sir," Marc said. "I'm Lieutenant Edwards, and I've been asked by Governor Head to discover who committed the heinous murder of Councillor Langdon Moncreiff earlier today." Kimble's handshake was surprisingly gentle, the fingers as supple as the leather he worked for a living.

"I don't reckon the governor does too much askin'." Kimble grinned.

"Do you want to come in, Lieutenant Edwards?" Sarah-Mae said in a soft, musical voice. "I've just made some tea."

"Officers in the British army don't sip tea at five in the afternoon, Sari-girl. Why don't you just whisk on into my study and fetch us a bottle of the best brandy?"

"Nothing, please," Marc said. "I merely wish to ask you and your wife some questions about the shooting. It will only take a minute or two."

"Well, sir, we saw it all," Sarah-Mae volunteered. "Didn't we, Phinn? The whole, horrible thing. I near to fainted right here on the walk."

"I caught her just in time, though, as you can see fer yerself, there ain't much to catch!"

"We was standin' here watchin' the proceedin's from about two o'clock onwards, Phinn and me and our three eldest."

"We closed up shop like everybody else on the square," Phineas added. "We got a better view by standin' on one of our benches."

"And a lot of others did likewise," Marc said. "There

must've been about three dozen people around the edge of the square with a bird's-eye view of the murder."

"Surely, then, somebody saw somethin', Sergeant," Kimble said. "All we could see from here is the old fella rear up like he'd been rammed you-know-where with a hot poker and then crumple backwards with a big swatch of blood under his arm. Then all hell broke loose."

"Did you see a man run past the general store with a gun in his hand?" Marc asked quickly, then stared intently at Kimble's raw-boned face as he reached for an answer.

"Well, now, funny you should ask me that," he drawled. Was he stalling? Marc wondered. "Sarah-Mae didn't see a thing fer several minutes, but when I looked up from steadyin' her, I did see the old geezer sprintin' fer Bill Frawley's pinto by the stables. Looked to me like Crazy Dan, though I ain't seen him in a dog's age." He paused and returned Marc's searching stare.

Marc hesitated, then said, "It was Crazy Dan. But he didn't do any shooting."

"I thought not. Still, I found it awful puzzlin' at the time."

"Oh, why is that?"

"Well, Sari here figured she heard a crack like a gunshot somewheres nearby, but the baby'd started to cry back inside the shop and my boys was makin' a considerable racket and the crowd was just startin' to applaud, so she wasn't sure— but then when I seen Crazy Dan doin' his act and everybody and his aunt hollerin' at him to stop . . . well, I just figured she must've been wrong about it."

Sarah-Mae was bobbing her pink chin in agreement.

"Did you not hear the shot?" Marc said to Kimble.

"Can't say as I did."

"Phinn don't always hear too good in June," Sarah-Mae said by way of explanation.

"Hay fever and devilish terrible sinus," Phineas explained. "Plugged up like a constipated cow." To Marc, his ears looked as if they were too big to be plugged by anything.

"Well, you'll not be overly surprised, then, to learn that we have good grounds for believing that the assassin's bullet came from the opening up there in your garret."

Harness-maker and wife looked up slowly, in tandem and in joint puzzlement. "You mean the attic?" Phineas asked.

"Yes."

"But there ain't been nobody up there since Cecil was born ten years ago," Sarah-Mae said in what appeared to be genuine alarm.

Marc turned to Phineas: "Would you be kind enough to take me up there?"

"If that's what you want. We're always pleased to be able to help an officer in King Billy's service. Ain't we, sweetheart?"

Sarah-Mae bobbed her chin, then added, "But you may have to *fly* there."

• • •

As Marc stared upwards at the back of the establishment, he saw the problem. The shop rooms of the business occupied the first floor, and the Kimbles lived in the apartment that comprised the second floor. A rickety ladder led up the outside wall to a small Spanish-style balcony that had long since lost most of its ironwork.

"When Sarah-Mae and me first come here, that ladder was the only way we could get from the shop to our bedrooms and parlour," Phineas explained patiently. "After one arse-freezin' winter, I cut a hole and built a proper set of stairs inside the house."

"What about the attic room?"

"You got in through a hatch in the parlour ceiling. We used to store saddles and extra harnesses up there, but so many bats and raccoons got in that after a while I just sealed up the hatch and plastered over her. And as far as I know, nobody's been up there since. Even the coons seem to have found better spots to batten down in."

"How would you get in if you really had to?"

Kimble looked at Marc as if he thought this were a trick question. After a pause, he said, "Can't ever see why I'd want to do such a fool thing, but if ever I did, I'd use that vine growin' up alongside and hoist myself up to the back window there. The vine's as thick as Sari's wrist and there's never been glass in that window."

"Then that's what I'll do."

"'Course, the balcony could crumble as soon as you put yer big toe on it."

Marc took this as an example of the man's humour. "We are positive that the shot came from that room, so I must examine it carefully."

"Then I better go with you," Phineas said quickly.

"Suit yourself," Marc said.

They moved over to the foot of the ladder.

Marc whistled. "Someone's been on this ladder recently. That break is fresh."

"Coulda been one of the boys, or the neighbour kids."

Marc ignored this and stepped onto a sound rung. Once on the balcony, he immediately spotted, in the inch-thick dust on the plank flooring, unmistakable signs of bootprints, though they were smudged and gave no indication of what boots had made them. But they were man-size, and fresh.

"It wasn't a youngster who made these," Marc said as Phineas crawled up beside him.

"And it sure as hell wasn't me!" Phineas raised a giant boot into a smooth patch of dust to make his point.

"And now we shinny our way up there," Marc said, grasping the vine and giving it a trial tug with both hands. In this sort of gymnastic, he had only to draw upon his innumerable childhood experiences playing pirates or crusaders on his adoptive father's estate. Within seconds he had scaled the wall and hauled himself through the paneless window. Then he turned to give the floundering harness-maker a hand up.

While Phineas was surveying a room he had obviously not seen for some years, Marc went immediately to the opening on the far wall. The late-afternoon sun poured into the weathered room and illuminated every detail. Smudged footprints led directly to the rotting sill. Marc ran his fingers along the ledge and paused.

"Could be a groove left there by a musket barrel," Phineas said, peering over Marc's shoulder. "Or any other kind of tool."

"Perhaps, but this is used in only one kind of tool," Marc said, holding up a wrapping that had been bitten off a paper-sheathed bullet. "And here's the mark on it."

"You can tell the kind of gun from that?"

"That and several other things," Marc said. "The shooter, as you can see, was a good fifty yards away from the hustings as he knelt here and rested the barrel of the gun in the notch on the sill. No smooth-bore gun would be accurate from this distance, so our assassin must have used a rifled bore, which would account not only for its accuracy but for the damage it did to Moncreiff. The marking on the wrapper suggests that the rifle is of French design, a model of some recent make copied by the Americans. I'd hazard a guess that this is a U.S. army rifle manufactured within the past five or six years."

Phineas took a minute to absorb this series of logical deductions. "So you're tellin' me that some Yankee freebooter climbed up into my attic while Sarah-Mae and me were standin' no more'n ten feet below on the sidewalk and blasted the bejesus out of the councillor?"

"I expect that he was counting on the general hubbub and every eye being directed at the hustings. No doubt that is why he waited until the precise moment that the governor was about to rise and make his speech." Or, Marc thought, the owner of these premises had become conveniently and temporarily deaf. "Also, at three o'clock, this window would still be in the shade of the overhang. With dark clothes on and the gun rubbed black, he would be hard to see. And he could be out that back window and down the vine to the ground in ten seconds. I expect he broke that rung in his haste to get away."

"With nothin' but bush behind us," Phineas said.

"And it would have to have been somebody, wouldn't it, who knew this place was here and never used, and was readily accessible."

"With a hundred-dollar Yankee rifle." Phineas began to sound doubtful.

"Well, that does narrow down the possibilities. But fifteen minutes ago I was contemplating the prospect of going house to house in search of a needle in a haystack."

The two men made their way back down the vine and ladder. As he stepped to the ground beside Marc, Phineas said, "Well, at least you found the haystack."

Marc was already studying the thick bush that began not more than ten yards behind the harness shop. For someone who knew the area, it would provide the perfect escape route. The assassin must have known both the terrain and the idiosyncrasies of Phineas Kimble's three-storey establishment. A new thought struck him. "By the way, do you have anyone helping you with your harness-making?" he called after Phineas, who had turned towards the corner of the building.

Phineas paused, or froze: it was hard to say which. He swung his huge body around and by the time he was facing Marc his face was lit up by a grin. "Now there's a good question, Sergeant. I am real happy you asked me that, 'cause somebody along the square would've told you sooner or later, and I'd have looked the darn fool fer not rememberin' it myself."

"Then you do have hired help."

"I did have hired help, and that's why it slipped my memory somewhat just now."

"How long ago?"

"A fella with the odd handle of Philo Rumsey worked as my helper fer two years—up to last winter. He was a dandy worker, mind, but not reliable."

"He drank?"

"No more'n anyone else 'round here, though that's plenty, I reckon. But he wouldn't show up much of the time—'specially when the deer was runnin'."

"He was a hunter?"

"And a damn fine one: he could pick a fly off the wall of the livery stable from this very spot."

"What kind of gun did he use?"

"Well, it wasn't no Yankee bluestockin', I can tell you

that. It was an old musket from one of the wars long past. Rumsey's as poor as a church mouse, with a woman and six kids to feed."

"Yet you fired him last winter."

"Indeed, I done just that. But then I took to feelin' sorry fer his missus and the bairns, so I let him come in now and again and do some piecework for me when I got more orders than I can handle."

Marc asked the next question and held his breath for the response: "Then Philo Rumsey is still hereabouts?"

"Of course he is. He lives in a cabin about a hundred yards that way, straight into the middle of the bush— where he likes it."

"Why didn't you tell me all this at the outset?"

Phineas Kimble grinned again, and this time he let the twinkle remain in place. "Well, now, how can I answer a question before it's asked?"

Trying to contain both his irritation and his rising excitement, Marc peered into the shadows ahead of him in the bush.

"All you gotta do is step between them two birches," Phineas called after him. "The path is as plain as the pestle on a pig. Walk straight on and keep an eye out fer the chiminey smoke."

"Thanks for your help."

"You're welcome, but I oughta mention that Philo himself ain't likely to be at home right this moment."

"What?"

"I heard he went down to visit his dyin' mother—last week."

"Down where?" Marc barked. "Dammit, man, tell me where!"

Phineas was unperturbed by the shift in tone: "Down to Buffalo, where he was born."

MARGARET RUMSEY WAS PERCHED ON THE edge of a log stool like an emaciated sparrow watching an owl measure it for the kill: wary, fearful, resigned. What she was particularly afraid of, Marc wasn't sure. The spectre of an officer in tunic and feathered cap standing—however politely or diffidently—in the sanctuary of one's home was enough to strike terror into the most innocent heart. But, when Marc had first entered the gloomy, smoke-filled single room of the Rumsey cabin, its mistress had seemed more flustered than scared, more embarrassed than awed. The symptoms of her impoverishment and misery were everywhere evident: the grimy, runny-nosed children who clutched at her apron and dared to peek up at the uniformed stranger, the barrenness of the room itself. Marc could see only a few pieces of stick furniture, half a dozen vermin-infested straw pallets, and a charred kettle that had fallen into a sputtering fire.

Between ineffectual attempts at keeping her two eldest from sidling up to Marc and brushing at his jacket as if it were a cardinal's robe, Margaret Rumsey had been, at first, as curious as she was guarded. She had even managed a smile when Marc had reached down and ruffled the hair of one of his admirers. Marc had winced inwardly as he realized with a shock that this woman, gaunt and pale in dirt-streaked rags, had once been pretty—and happy. But as soon as he had begun asking questions about her husband's whereabouts, her pinched brown eyes drew back into their hollow sockets. Did she know? Or was she merely afraid of what she didn't know but strongly suspected?

"You say your husband left for Buffalo to be with his dying mother?"

"Yes, sir, last week. Elmer, don't be touchin' the gentleman's sword!"

"Do you remember the exact day he left?"

Margaret Rumsey paused, as if thinking hard. "I lose track of the days of the week. With these young'uns one day is t'same as the next."

"Was it before or after the last Sabbath?"

"Oh, we don't go to service . . . no more." Her eyes widened. "But they're all baptized! I saw to that."

"I was merely trying to help you recall when Mr. Rumsey left for Buffalo."

"'Twas Tuesday last, I remember now, 'cause Mr. Danby, God bless 'im, had me over to the inn to help with the clean-up. He calls on me when there's a gentlemen's gatherin' or lodge meetin'." Marc looked skeptical, and she added with a blush that brought some colour into her grey pallor for the first time, "I don't go over to the inn lookin' like this. Mr. Danby give me a uniform." Then as if further explanation were called for, she said, "No sense in puttin' on anythin' decent 'round this dump. The littl'uns'd just puke or slobber all over it."

"That would make it exactly a week ago, then," Marc prompted.

Margaret nodded. Then with a trembling lip she said, "But you ain't told me yet why I haveta answer all the governor's questions."

"A man was murdered this afternoon, in the square. Did you know that?"

Some of her fear drained away, and Marc could see that she was relieved, though still wary. "I heard about it. Everybody has. But Philo couldn't have had nothin' to do with that awful thing, he's been gone since Tuesday last."

"And you're certain he hasn't come back?"

"His mama's dyin' of womb cancer or somethin'. All his family lives in Buffalo. He said he'd be gone fer two weeks or more. He's left us no food, and I've gone and spent the last of Mr. Danby's pay on medicine fer the baby. If he'd've come home, these young'uns wouldn't be whinin' fer their supper, now would they?"

Marc thanked her and turned to go. "You will let Mr. Danby know the minute your husband comes home. I will need to talk to him." If Philo Rumsey were indeed in

Buffalo—and until that was verified independently Marc was going to assume that his prime suspect had contrived an alibi for himself—then it was quite possible that before leaving he had passed along crucial information regarding the set-up of his sometime employer's unused attic and was, therefore, at least an accomplice to some degree or other. Accomplice or assassin, Philo Rumsey was undoubtedly the key to solving this puzzle.

At the door Marc thought of a final question. "Did your husband own an army rifle by any chance?"

"Philo's a good huntsman, sir, the best in these parts, else we'd starve. But he uses the Kentucky musket my daddy give him when we got wedded. And he makes his own bullets right here in this room."

"Philo was never in the army, back in New York?"

"No, sir. He was only eighteen when he begun courtin' me, and we left Buffalo to come up here and start a new life. But Philo weren't much fer farmin', and we lost the homestead. That's when he took up harness-makin' and brung us here."

"Well, thank you once again. If you'll be kind enough to inform Danby of your husband's return, he will pass the news along to me."

"Philo's brothers're in the army, though. They're doin' real good, I'm told."

My God, Marc thought, I've found the murderer or murderers in a single hour of careful investigation! He grinned from ear to ear, and the children, seeing this, joined him.

Marc reached into his pocket and pulled out a handful of pennies, then tossed them joyfully upwards. The children jumped up to grab them, giggling and hysterical with delight. Marc bowed to Margaret Rumsey and strode away through the bush towards the square.

His heart sang. Then it sank. Suddenly he was shaken by a surge of helpless, nameless rage.

DR. WITHERS AND MAXWELL MÈRE AND fille were gone by the time Marc got back to the inn. Briefly he asked Garfield Danby to relay any news of Philo Rumsey's reappearance in the township, bade good-bye to him and Mrs. Danby (who looked as if she had suffered shell shock at Waterloo), and made his way to the saloon.

Seven of the young officers were gathered around the bar singing lustily with charged glasses. On Marc's arrival they stopped singing in mid-phrase, until, at an approving nod from their commanding officer, they started up again and continued until the song was satisfyingly finished.

Marc applauded theatrically, then said to the nearest man, "Ensign, please get the horses from the ostler. We've got to get back to Government House before dark."

"Yes, sir!"

"Where's Lieutenant Willoughby?" Marc asked.

Hilliard blanched, then stepped aside so that Marc could see past the bar to one of the gloomy corners of the saloon beyond. Parker and Willoughby appeared to be slumped comatose across a table, their arms dangling like knackered eels. A quart of brandy—two-thirds empty—teetered between them. The rest of the men, feeling chipper, had wisely stuck to watered claret.

"I wouldn't get too close to Parker," Hilliard warned. "He upchucked even before he started in on the brandy."

Marc went over to Willoughby and reached out to touch his shoulder. He was stopped, however, by a low droning that had been emanating from the two men all along but which he heard only now.

"They've been crooning away like that for the last hour," Hilliard said. "That's why we started singing. It got on our nerves."

Marc leaned over and listened.

"Innocent . . . innocent . . . no eyes . . . no eyes . . . innocent . . . innocent . . ." The words were thick-tongued and breathy but nonetheless distinct.

"I guess they just saw today more than they bargained for," Hilliard said helpfully. "Though Christ knows what either of them will do if we ever get into a real battle."

Marc let his hand rest on Willoughby's shoulder. "None of us knows that, Ensign. And maybe it's just as well."

The officer Marc had sent for the horses poked his head in the front door.

"All right, men. Check your gear and get ready to ride," Marc said.

"What'll we do with these fellows?" Hilliard said.

"Tie them to their saddles. A good jarring might bring them around." Marc smiled, and then helped Hilliard haul Willoughby upright. "It's all right, Colin. Everything's going to be fine—just as soon as we get you home."

At least, he hoped so.

SIR FRANCIS HAD RENTED ROOMS FOR Marc and Colin at Mrs. Standish's boarding house on Peter Street, where they would be at his beck and call. And Marc dropped Willoughby onto that good woman's veranda before waving farewell to his troop as they continued towards the garrison. Then he rode up to King and Simcoe, where Government House stood in its six-acre park. He handed the chestnut mare to one of the waiting stableboys, and ran up the steps into the foyer. There was almost an hour of daylight left. With luck he would not have to wake up the governor. For although Marc knew that Head would be eager to hear what he had learned about who might have shot Moncreiff, he was acutely aware that first he'd have to tell the governor about the death of Crazy Dan. He didn't relish reporting this news to a groggy, half-awake superior.

He was met in the vestibule not by the duty-corporal but by Major Titus Burns, Sir Francis's military secretary. The old fellow winced as he grasped Marc's hand.

"Don't mind my rheumatism, old chap, it can't be helped, and what can't be cured must be endured."

"How is Sir Francis, Major? He's had a horrific day."

"So I've heard. But I expect he'll have worse before he has better."

"He commanded me to report on my day's investigative work as soon as I returned," Marc said.

"That would be inconvenient in the extreme." Burns chuckled. "He's gone off to an emergency meeting of the Executive Council."

"Then I'll wait here in my office," Marc said. "I have most urgent news for his ears only."

"I'm afraid the walls have ears in this house," Burns said. "But there's no need for you to wait. Sir Francis explicitly instructed me to send you home to a warm supper and a feather bed. Dr. Withers gave him and me an account of your abortive expedition following the tragic shooting of Councillor Moncreiff. He will want your first-hand version, of course. But there is an election pending, and tomorrow he will be tied up in meetings until eleven in the morning. He wants to see you in the inner sanctum at that hour precisely."

"I'll be there."

"So will I, Lieutenant. I'm never anywhere else."

THE WIDOW STANDISH LET HER PARLOUR curtain drop discreetly and opened the front door of her respectable boarding house. ("My husband, Chalmers, wouldn't have it any other way," she said more than once, "as he was a very particular gentleman, especially when it concerned the creature

comforts of his beloved, God rest his soul." The dear departed had left her a well-built frame residence eminently
suited to respectable boarders.)

"Oh, Lieutenant Edwards, it is you," she said, feigning
surprise. "I was just putting the cat out for the night."

"Good evening, Mrs. Standish."

"My heavens, but you do look tuckered out."

The cat was nowhere to be seen. "It's been a very long
day."

"Your walk from Government House was a pleasant one?"
Widow Standish liked to work Government House and any of
its doings, however peripheral, into any conversation.

"It's a beautiful June evening," Marc said, following his
landlady and self-appointed guardian into the carpeted hallway.

"I've saved you some supper. It's on the hutch in the
dining room. Just some cold beef and bread with a bit of
cheese."

"I'll nibble at it later, if you don't mind."

"Oh, I see," she replied, lowering her voice and whispering, "He's still on his bed where I left him."

"He saw his first dead man today, I'm afraid, and it was
not a pretty sight."

"Oh, I see," clucked Widow Standish. She looked relieved. "I thought it might've been just the drink."

USING A COTTON CLOTH AND FRESH water from the dry sink,
Marc managed to clean up Willoughby's face, and then he

got him out of his uniform (which looked beyond rejuvenation, even by Maisie, Mrs. Standish's very dedicated maid-cook-and-launderer). Willoughby moaned now and again, but his eyes remained resolutely shut. Marc tugged a night-shirt over the young man's lean, well-muscled body and let him flop back on the bed. The night air was humid and still: he would need no covers.

As Willoughby's head hit the pillow, his eyes popped open, then closed again. But in the second or so that they remained open, they took in Marc bending over and the darkening room behind him. And what Marc thought he saw in Willoughby's face was fear.

"My God, old chum, but you've had one hell of a fright this day," Marc whispered.

Willoughby, blind and deaf to the world once more, began to breathe regularly and, from the outside at least, peacefully. His was an aesthetic face, fine-boned with fair skin as smooth as a debutante's. The brow was high and delicately veined, the hair—now matted and repulsive—was blond and curly, as his beard would be if he could grow one. Like this, with his eyes closed, he might have been mistaken for an adolescent, all promise and possibility. But when those grey eyes were open, Willoughby looked more like he had seen too much too soon, and Marc was never sure whether his suffering would erupt in words or action, or turn in upon itself.

Marc knew that Colin Willoughby had not begun his manhood years auspiciously. As the second son of a wealthy Buckinghamshire landowner, he was destined for the army

or the church, but chose instead a more hedonistic life in
the gambling dens and whorehouses of London. Papa Willoughby promptly had him hog-tied and returned to the
family castle, and after a good talking-to, he was shipped off
to military school at Sandhurst. After which Willoughby
père purchased a lieutenant's commission for him in the
army, where fils was pleased to discover that dicing and
wenching were neither uncommon nor unappreciated.

However, this happy state of affairs was spoiled by the
catastrophe of his falling in love with a respectable young
woman of high virtue, ample fortune, and great beauty. As
Willoughby told the story whenever he'd had three mugs
of whisky, his beautifully affluent Rosy ("pretty as a prim-
rose, she was!") had placed unwarranted restrictions on the
recreational habits of her fiancé (it had gotten that far, he
insisted), and then despite his repeated vows to be forever
faithful to her after the nuptials, she had jilted him without
cause, explanation, or remorse—after the second reading
of the banns! And his father, fearing the worst, wrote to
his good friend Sir Francis Bond Head and—presto!—four
months later, Willoughby found himself in Toronto, where,
he had been assured, the climate was a sure cure for romance.

Sir Francis had realized the need to keep young Willoughby from the temptations of barracks life, and so, having
made Marc his chief aide-de-camp on the recommendation
of his predecessor, he had hit upon the strategy of appointing
Willoughby as Marc's assistant, and renting rooms for the two
of them nearby.

From that day late in January of this year, Marc had taken Willoughby under wing, playing the role of older brother and guardian. This arrangement had worked to the benefit of both. So far Willoughby had fallen off the wagon only once—at the governor's Winter Gala when the sight of all those beautiful bare-shouldered young women dancing had reminded him painfully of what he had almost won and then thrown away. He had poured whisky into wine goblets and got himself belligerently drunk before the ball had ended, and it had taken Marc, Hilliard, and two other burly officers to lug him to a carriage and haul him back to Mrs. Standish's, where he further humiliated himself by swinging wildly at Marc in front of their landlady and uttering a lot of gibberish—the only decipherable parts of which were oaths. Fortunately for Willoughby, the next day he had recalled none of the night's more memorable events. Since then, while he was occasionally sullen about the menial tasks given him around Government House (who wasn't?), his youthful high spirits and keen intelligence had made him an enjoyable addition to the tiny complement of officers at the governor's residence. As for Marc, he was beginning to realize that he had found something he had not expected after a year in Upper Canada: a male friend his own age, a kind of brother.

"But I don't know whether you'll make it as a soldier, old chum," Marc sighed and left the room quietly.

FOUR

❧ ❧

The lieutenant-governor rose to greet Marc as he was shown into his office by a shuffling, sober-faced Major Burns. "Do come in, Marc. And take a seat. We have much to discuss, and I have given orders that we not be interrupted for at least the next hour, barring a catastrophe."

"I think we may have already had one, sir," Marc said as he sat down on the edge of a high-backed brocaded chair and let his boots settle into the thick carpet.

"I was thinking more along the lines of Fort York being blown up—again," Sir Francis quipped, indicating his knowledge of that disastrous event in the War of 1812.

Major Burns smiled at the witticism despite the rheumatic pain that had squeezed his numerous wrinkles into
rigid parallels. He turned to go.

"Stay, please, Major. I may have need of your sage advice,
and I wish you to take notes." Head sat down across from
Marc at a gleaming cherrywood desk that occupied fully
a third of the room. Upon it were scattered a dozen thick
tomes punctuated by leather bookmarks and innumerable
papers, graphs, and maps. Marc recognized the one book
that lay open: the blue-bound, 350-page Seventh Report
on Grievances, an anti-government tirade written by a
committee of the Reform-dominated Legislative Assembly.
Major Burns took a seat off to one side beneath a mullioned
window that caught the full force of the midmorning sun.

"As for this business about Crazy Don—"

"Dan, sir," said the major.

Sir Francis hid his irritation in a tight smile. "Crazy Dan,
then—"

"Would you like me to go over the events, sir?" Marc
asked, as several beads of sweat formed between his shoulder
blades and began to trickle down his back. "I made notes on
them before I arrived here this morning."

"Not necessary, lad. As far as I am concerned, the book is
closed on that unhappy adventure."

"But, sir, you have not yet heard my version of the
story—"

At that moment there came a discreet tapping at the

door and, before anyone could protest, the governor's personal servant, in full livery, slipped silently into the room, slid a silver tea tray on the desk before Sir Francis, and stepped silently away again.

"Coffee, Major?" Burns nodded. "Marc?"

Marc was about to decline when Sir Francis said, "Of course, you will. I hear that Mrs. Standish serves only weak tea for breakfast." He poured three cups of coffee and placed on each saucer a tiny, jam-topped scone.

"I do intend to hear all about what happened yesterday from your own lips," Sir Francis said to Marc between nibbles on his scone. "From all accounts, it was an exploit worth the telling."

"And there is a perfectly logical explanation for the tragic consequences—"

"That is true. And you will perhaps be surprised to learn that I already know all I need to know about how and why Crazy Dan was shot."

Major Burns, his fingers stiffened by pain, spilled his coffee into the saucer.

"Major Burns and I—who rise with the sun—have been in this office since eight o'clock this morning, closeted with two sleepy magistrates and a clerk who took depositions from each of the ensigns involved. They were hauled from their quarters one at a time and thoroughly interrogated here. Each of them signed a sworn statement relating his version of the events. We had hoped to include Lieutenant

Willoughby, but Mrs. Standish told my messenger that he was indisposed." Sir Francis frowned over the word, attempted a rueful smile.

Marc was about to explain the cause of Willoughby's indisposition but saw that Sir Francis considered it of no immediate relevance.

"The upshot of those interviews and affidavits is that the magistrates came to the conclusion that the death of this wretched creature was unfortunate but, in the circumstances, justified. No blame is to be assigned, and there is no need to drag Dr. Withers in for a formal inquest."

"Is that wise, sir?"

For a moment Sir Francis looked nonplussed, then said, "It is not a question of wisdom, Lieutenant, but of justice. A man fled a murder scene brandishing a gun. He had more than ample opportunity to stop and explain himself if he knew himself to be innocent. Upper Canada is not the republic to the south of us, where lynching and vigilante action are commonplace and condoned. This same man, as attested to by eight loyal officers, pointed a musket at you from ten paces. Were they to let him shoot you first, then release their volley? Especially when they swore upon this Bible that the order they heard was 'Fire!'"

"I think the young man is referring to the possible political fallout," Major Burns said quietly as soon as he was certain that Sir Francis had finished.

Sir Francis feigned astonishment, though his features

were so nondescript that a casual observer could see only extreme shifts in emotion. Marc had already noted that Sir Francis used the natural calmness of his face and demeanour to telling effect in heated discussions. You had to watch his eyes carefully. "And what political fallout might that be? It was the magistrates who did the questioning, as is proper and customary. The affidavits are public court documents. Later today or tomorrow, you will add your sworn statement to the docket."

"The lieutenant has studied law at the Inns of Court," Major Burns said.

"What I meant, sir," Marc said, "was that the farmers who followed us, and were in a way witnesses to most of the events under question, might wish to have their say at a formal inquest, even though I am fully confident, as you are, that no other conclusion would be reached than the one made here this morning."

"Purely a waste of time," Sir Francis declared with some vehemence, "and you know from our previous conversations and my reports to Lord Glenelg in London that the time wasted here in the past eight years on committees and commissions and grievance petitions and the naming of this member and that in the Assembly has been the principal cause of the current deadlock and the hardening of positions on either side of every issue—petty or important."

"I agree, sir, but my hunch is that these men are supporters of the Reform party, and that they are quite capable of

suggesting to all and sundry in York County that the magistrates, as instruments of the Executive, simply protected
their own by denying an inquest and aborting their right to
testify."

"Let them feed whatever rumour mill they like! You've
seen for yourself over the past week the effectiveness of my
strategy of following the politicians of both parties onto the
hustings no more than two days after their own nomina-
tion speeches or public debates. Grit or Tory, the voters
are getting a chance to see the vast difference between, on
one side, a politician with all his rant and thunder and, on
the other, a statesman who takes no partisan position but,
rather, occupies the same wide ground that King William
himself would, were he to voyage to this colony—which is,
after all, the surrogate terrain of Britain herself. You have
seen first-hand how efficacious my direct appeal for loyalty,
patience, and trust in their sovereign has been and how well
my calm denunciation of all extremism has been received.
The fact that most of the extremists are republican and that
in that quarter also lies the greatest threat to the Crown
does not have to be spoken aloud. Nor would it be proper for
me as the King's representative to do so."

Marc nodded, and finished the last of his coffee. It was
cold.

"And I fully believe that the fact that I was appointed by
a Whig government—and was not automatically accorded
membership in that claque of bankers, lawyers, and men of

property they call the Family Compact—has made it not only more difficult for the fanatics on both sides, the Orange lunatics and the so-called Clear Grits, to label me partisan but also has given me credibility on the hustings and at the levees."

"Quite true, sir."

Sir Francis leaned back in his wing chair and took a deep breath, aware perhaps that he had just delivered a rostrum speech to two seated confederates in a small room. Then with a twinkle he said, more reflectively, "Oh, I know how many of those who now gather round me and cling to the royal hem once sniggered at my appointment: a half-pay major—down on his luck doing a hack job as commissioner of the poor law—daring to replace the dashing Sir John Colborne, high Tory and hero of Waterloo. But their skepticism then and their sycophancy now neither deters nor influences me. I was sent here by Lord Glenelg with a specific mission. And I intend to accomplish it. Let your farmers in York rant for a while. They'll come onside after the election, you'll see."

But would they? Marc wondered. It was imperative that the governor have a less fractious Assembly if he were to begin to address the farmers' many grievances, but a Constitutionist sweep at the polls could have unforeseeable consequences. As Marc had learned in January during his investigation in Cobourg, the Upper Canadian farmer was righteously bitter, politically astute, and increasingly willing to take bolder, riskier action.

"Now, Major, if you'll take up your pen, I wish to sit back and hear Lieutenant Edwards's report on the assassination of Councillor Moncreiff. From what Dr. Withers intimated, you were about to follow up several promising avenues as he left you."

With the tragic business of Crazy Dan apparently closed, Marc recounted in precise detail his visit to Phineas and Sarah-Mae Kimble, his search of the attic room above the harness shop, and his discovery of Philo Rumsey's likely involvement. Sir Francis listened without interruption, his face impassive, while Major Burns scratched away with his quill pen.

"Excellent work, Lieutenant," Sir Francis said when Marc had finished. "Outstanding work. Sir John's opinion of you, I see, was understated."

"Thank you, sir, but I am afraid we're only partway there. Until we apprehend Philo Rumsey and question him, we cannot be certain that what seems obvious is actually true."

"It usually is, in my experience. But I take your point."

"And while I'm pretty certain it was Rumsey who pulled the trigger, or else a close confidant, there is the puzzling question of motive. Why would an out-of-work harness-maker who prefers to hunt deer murder Councillor Moncreiff in such a public place and in such a public manner?"

"A pertinent question, eh? Especially as we are in the middle of an election campaign and the murdered man was a member of my cabinet, so to speak."

"The possibility of this being a politically motivated kill-ing seems likely, does it not?"

"You think the radical Reformers might be behind this atrocity?"

Marc did not reply. While he feared such a possibility for what it might do to the stability of the province, he had an even deeper fear, one that had occurred to him again as he had been making notes this morning in preparation for this interview. "Have you considered, sir, that Councillor Mon-creiff may not have been the target?"

Sir Francis leaned forward and Major Burns dropped his pen. "What do you mean? You've just said this Philo fellow was a hunter and an expert marksman with a rifled weapon. Surely he knew at whom he was shooting."

"Well, sir, it only occurred to me an hour ago as I was re-picturing in my mind the sequence of events just before the shot rang out."

"And?"

"And instead of rising from your seat as you appeared about to do, you dropped a paper and bent down to retrieve it."

No one spoke for several long seconds. Then Sir Francis laughed. "Nonsense! No one would dare assassinate the King's representative. No British governor has ever been put at such risk, even in uncivilized places like the penal colonies of Van Diemen's Land. It is simply unthinkable— a preposterous notion!"

"I agree, sir, that it is difficult to fathom a British subject committing such an act, but the shooter in this case is a transplanted American with brothers currently in the U.S. army. Moreover, he is poor and disaffected; he may even be deranged. God knows who might have put him up to such a desperate business."

"All of which are relevant points, no doubt. But you are barking up the wrong tree, young man. Meantime, we do have a gentleman dead of a gunshot wound. It was Moncreiff who was actually murdered, so surely it would make sense to begin at least with the assumption that he was the intended victim and work out from that not-unreasonable position."

"Yes, sir. I am quite prepared to do just that."

"Good. And let's have no more foolish talk of de facto regicide. It's too early in the morning." His eyes bounced momentarily.

Marc carried on. "What I propose to do, then—with your approval, of course—is to discover if there is any connection between Councillor Moncreiff and Philo Rumsey. Perhaps some action recently taken by your new Executive Council affected Rumsey or his family negatively. Perhaps it was something a previous council did, and Rumsey decided to take revenge at the earliest opportunity. I recall that your itinerary for the York Township address and the names of the accompanying contingent were published in the Upper Canada Gazette a full ten days before the event."

"Yes, that was part of my strategy to win the ordinary folk over to the King's side, even before I officially dissolved the Assembly: to publicize my addresses widely and to include selected legislators to sit with me on the platform and share the limelight."

"Rumsey had, then, forewarning and the time to set up his alibi in Buffalo," Marc said. "In that regard, we'll have to have someone, from Fort George perhaps, slip across to New York State and check out Rumsey's dying mother."

"And try to ascertain whether Rumsey had connections with any republican fanatics over there. He might be a member of one of the Hunters' Lodges, the ones I read about in Sir John's report of your first investigation in January."

"That is always possible. But from the looks of his cabin and the wretched state of his family, I'd say not likely."

"Nevertheless, I'll send a request to Fort George to have the Rumsey clan checked out." Sir Francis gave a little sigh. "I suppose, though, we'll have to face the fact that if he did murder the councillor, he may decide to stay in Buffalo or go farther inland where we'll never catch him."

"I don't think so, sir. His wife and six children are near to starvation. I believe he'll be back in the province within the next few days or so."

"But if he is that indigent, then I suppose you'll have to consider the possibility that someone might have paid him to murder Moncreiff."

"In which case there could be a personal motive."

"And that means you'll have to look into Moncreiff's

private life." Sir Francis grimaced. "An unsavoury task, and one that will demand the utmost tact. Which is why I want you to undertake it. What do you propose to do first?"

"Well, sir, we need to have Rumsey's cabin watched day and night. As a hunter and long-time resident, he knows the area and the bush around it. He won't stroll across the square at Danby's Crossing and wave to his friends. Phineas Kimble, the harness-maker, will need to be questioned again, and anyone else up there who knew Rumsey, to get as much background information on him as we can. I myself will interview Councillor Moncreiff's brother-in-law, Ignatius Maxwell, and discreetly explore the victim's recent personal life and his political connections. And I thought of doing something unorthodox in order to discover how he was viewed politically by the Reformers."

"Unorthodox?"

"Yes. I was hoping to obtain your permission to interview William Lyon Mackenzie."

Mackenzie was the leading Reformer, a rabble-rousing firebrand, and editor of the *Constitution*, a weekly newspaper whose pages routinely excoriated the government and its leadership.

Sir Francis flinched. "That man's a fanatic. What he won't prevaricate he'll equivocate. You'd be wasting your time and putting the investigation at risk."

"I met him back in January, sir. In fact, I saved him from a tar-and-feathering, and we had a brief conversation. I know he trusts me, and I believe he will give us a perspective on the councillor's political status that might prove invaluable."

Sir Francis began to fidget with his coffee cup. The sun had risen close to its zenith and no longer flooded the room. "All right, you may go ahead. And while you're there, I want you to ask him to provide me with the name of a very irritating letter-writer who's been filling the pages of the *Constitution* with tripe and nonsense now for the past month—someone who hides like a coward behind the pseudonym of 'Farmer's Friend.'"

"I'll ask him, sir."

Sir Francis detected the note of skepticism in Marc's response. "Tell Mackenzie that I wish only to discuss the issues raised in these letters with their author— as part of my assiduous and continuing effort to understand the long-time grievances."

"I'll do that, sir."

"More important, it seems obvious that you are going to need some assistance, especially if you expect to carry out your proposed work within the next day or two. And I'm referring to expert help, not the enthused amateurism of your junior officers or NCOs."

"Where would I get such assistance?"

"When Toronto became a city two years ago, the municipal council established a five-man constabulary modelled on the force that was set up by Robert Peel in London in '29."

"The bobbies?"

"That's right. While they are still nominally supervised by the magistrates, they act on behalf of the city council, as a unit, as a kind of independent police force, with specific duties and designated territories. I know the chief constable, Wilfrid Sturges, quite well, as he was a sergeant-major in Wellington's army. He spent three years on the London force before emigrating here last year to help establish the Toronto constabulary."

"And you think he'll be able to help us?" Marc was dubious.

"Indeed. I'm going to send a message to him within the hour and request that he offer his best man to you today, to be attached solely to you and your investigation."

"That is most kind of you, sir, but I feel obliged to point out that the murder took place outside the city limits in the Township of York, where the Toronto constables have no authority."

Head frowned almost imperceptibly. "It is not authority I am interested in, but expertise and local knowledge. I have declared this assassination to be a concern of the military and hence to be placed under the jurisdiction of the military, who in turn take their orders from me."

"I see, sir."

"And, Lieutenant, I hope you can see also that those of us who bear the heaviest burdens of power and responsibility must occasionally ride roughshod over the petty rules and small-minded regulations confected by bureaucrats to keep themselves amused."

Marc smiled. "That is the reason I abandoned the law, sir."

Sir Francis smiled also, but his smile was more like that of the fox that had just surprised himself at his own cunning, as he said, "In the meantime, while we are quietly checking out Rumsey and watching his house in the township—the full hue and cry would send him to cover forever—I will tell the Executive Council, who will in due course tell just about everyone else in the province, that we have a prime suspect in our sights, and that it appears he was a hired killer."

"But why tip our hand in any way, sir?"

"Ah, I see, Lieutenant, that you have not yet mastered the fine art of the politician. If, for the moment, the populace believes the assassin to be a hired killer—and he may well be, do not forget—then who in the current political context is most likely to be suspected of hiring him to shoot a Constitutionist councillor?"

Marc saw, but he was less than impressed. Not only might the investigation be compromised by the premature release of vital information, but allowing the radical Reform group to be obliquely blamed for "hiring an assassin" was certain to harden, not soften, the divisions between left and right, and could severely skew the coming election. "Perhaps we'll have the blackguard in irons within the week," Marc said with little conviction.

"I want you to take all the time you need, Lieutenant. You are to devote every waking hour to this investigation. While there may be some short-term political gain in having the matter unresolved, any failure of the government, and hence of the governor, to apprehend the heinous assassin of a respected privy councillor would undo those gains and begin to cast doubt upon my promise to provide a period of peace and stability as the necessary prerequisite to addressing the people's concerns."

"And you yourself, sir, will need to be circumspect in your comings and goings until we know more about the nature and extent of this business."

Sir Francis leaned back. "Then you don't know me, Lieutenant. Not only do I have no intention of curtailing my public appearances, I have already put in train plans for an expanded trip into the London district, beginning next Monday."

"You can't mean that, sir? Those counties down there are the hotbed of radicalism. Half the populace are naturalized Americans."

"Be that as it may, I intend to lead a delegation of Executive councillors to Brantford, Woodstock, and London— where I shall stand tall upon the hustings and deliver my message of hope and reconciliation."

"But, sir, if I am to continue the investigation, then I'll—"

"—not be able to organize the guard for my protection."

"Precisely."

"I will take Willoughby with me. In fact, starting this afternoon, Willoughby will replace you temporarily here at Government House as my assistant military secretary. I have a mountain of correspondence to get through before I set out next week."

"Willoughby is a good man, certainly. He has done much of the detailed, day-to-day work on security . . ."

Sir Francis caught the reservation in Marc's assessment. He smiled paternally. "You don't have to be coy about Willoughby, Marc. I know all about his checkered past. I am a friend of his good father, and it was I who agreed to bring him out here with me. He is still young enough, I hope, to find himself as a man, and what better means could there be for doing so than taking on a new profession in a new country? In fact, my original intention was to put him in charge of my security and work him in as military secretary eventually. He is, as you know, well educated and highly intelligent."

"Why did you not do so?"

"First, a few days after our arrival, he got himself disgracefully drunk and ran about Government House frightening the maids and throwing wild punches at anyone trying to restrain him—all this while babbling incoherently about his 'faithless Rosy'!"

"The woman who left him at the altar," Marc said.

"Indeed. Then, while I was reconsidering the matter, I

read Sir John's report on your splendid work in the Cobourg investigation and his unequivocal recommendation that I take you on as my aide-de-camp."

"Well, Willoughby has begun to adjust nicely in the past few months, has he not?"

"Thanks to you, lad. And to Mrs. Standish's cooking. There's even a rumour that he may have himself a lady friend." Sir Francis raised one eyebrow.

"Truthfully, sir, I've seen no sign of it, but, until yesterday, he had seemed much more optimistic and friendly, less given to moodiness."

"Yes, I heard about yesterday from Hilliard, who let the cat out of the bag, I'm afraid."

"It was the sight of the body, sir. Crazy Dan was hit with a full volley. The corpse was a mess. Several of the men were sick."

"I know all about that sort of thing, alas. I was at Waterloo—a slaughtering ground. Mind you, I was with the engineers and not in the main battle at all, but I was close enough, nonetheless. He'll get over it, as far as anyone ever does."

"He'll be happy to hear your news, sir. I think keeping him active and giving him more responsibility is just the tonic he needs."

"Then why don't you send him in on your way out."

Marc paused before answering.

"He is at his post, is he not?" Sir Francis narrowed his gaze.

"In fact, sir, I could not rouse him before I left at ten thirty."

Head's blue eyes blazed with a cold, steady fire. "Well, Lieutenant, please return home instantly and inform Lieutenant Willoughby that he is to report to this office by one o'clock ready for duty. If he fails to do so, he will find himself sulking in the brig!"

"Yes, sir!" Marc jumped to his feet, knocking over his empty coffee cup.

The noise woke up Major Burns, who had been peacefully asleep for the last part of the interview—the quill frozen in his arthritic grip.

Sir Francis got up and drew the pen tenderly from the Major's fingers. "I may need both you and Willoughby soon," he said to Marc at the door.

Then, as the governor walked Marc into the anteroom, he snapped at one of his underlings, "Corporal, help Major Burns to his rooms."

Marc ran down the steps of Government House and across the lawn to the winding roadway that led up to King Street. His mind was not bubbling with the details of his new assignment, however; rather, he was wondering how he was going to get Colin Willoughby sober enough to present himself to Sir Francis by one o'clock.

FIVE

❧ ❧

The Widow Standish, a handsome woman in her mid-fifties, for whom the word motherly had been coined, was on the veranda to greet Marc. She was wringing her apron as if to dry her hands, but they had not been near water since the breakfast dishes. "I tried to wake him, sir. Maisie and me both, one of us tugging at either arm, and him in his nightshirt only!"

"It's all right, Mrs. Standish. I'll take over," Marc said as they hurried through the hallway towards the boarders' rooms in back. "If you and Maisie would be kind enough to fill the bathtub and provide some fresh towels—"

Mrs. Standish looked abashed. "Oh, sir, there's not a drop of hot water in the house. It's too warm out for a fire, even in the summer kitchen."

"I think cold water would be more helpful," Marc said, and strode off to Willoughby's room.

When Marc dropped his friend Colin naked and stinking into the bath, one of Colin's arms flapped, then the other, then both legs, and finally the whole body thrashed upwards. His eyes snapped wide.

"Jesus Murphy, where am I?"

"You're in your own bathtub, but if you don't get a grip on yourself you're going to find your accommodations considerably less comfortable."

As Willoughby grumpily tried to get the soap lathering in the cool water, Marc told him about the governor's offer to make him temporary assistant to Major Burns and commander of the palace guard for the duration of Marc's investigation. At first Willoughby had difficulty taking it in, due in part to his monstrous hangover, but Marc sensed there was something else, something deeper perhaps, that made it hard for him to grasp what had happened. He still looked like a man in shock.

"I'll leave you to your toilette, Colin old chum. Maisie is dusting off your spare uniform, and Mrs. Standish has started a small fire in this wretched heat to boil you some coffee. So quit feeling sorry for yourself and buck up! You've only got half an hour to make or break your fortune." He shoved Colin's head playfully under the soapy water and was pleased to see the troubled young man bob back up—with a wan smile on his face.

DURING THE SHORT WALK UP TO Government House, Marc had time to explain briefly to Colin that the governor had taken the depositions regarding the shooting of Crazy Dan and had, pending their own statements, absolved them of any blame. This news did not have the spirit-boosting effect that Marc had expected, so he quickly told Colin about the governor's plans to travel through the London district next week, plans that involved Colin in his new role.

"Do you mean to say that I'll be in charge when we go west?" Colin said, his grey eyes brightening and some colour flushing into his pale cheeks.

"That's right. And what's more, you'll be the governor's secretary in all but name, as dear old Major Burns is able to do less and less each day."

"And you will be fully in charge of the, uh, investigation?"

They were now stopped on the gravel path that wound its way up to the ornate veranda of Government House.

"It's not a job I asked for," Marc said carefully, "and indeed I was surprised that the governor insisted on my taking it after the fiasco up at Danby's Crossing."

"Do you have any idea who might have done it? Any trail to follow?"

Marc hesitated. Despite the governor's own proposal to broadcast selected facts about the investigation, Marc felt that the less said to anyone the better. However, Colin's sense of complicity in the death of Crazy Dan and the sight of the maimed body had obviously left him shaken and vulnerable—just at a time when he would need to be clear-headed and confident. The responsibilities being offered him could well be the making of him, as an officer and as a man. (The quick capture of the real murderer would do much to ease both their consciences.) And a true friend would not stint in such circumstances by withholding information.

"We think it may have been a disaffected American living up there."

"Has the hue and cry been sent up?"

"Not yet. We're pretty certain he's gone to ground over in New York."

"Ah, then there's little chance we'll ever see him again."

"You may be right," Marc said, hoping against hope that he wasn't.

At this point the duty-corporal at the door waved them inside.

MARC AND COLIN WROTE DOWN THEIR separate accounts of the "tragic incident" (as everyone in Government House

had begun to refer to it) and signed them. Marc decided not
to delay beginning his own work a moment longer. He set
off for Somerset House on Front Street to interview Ignatius
Maxwell, who from all accounts was a brutally frank judge
of men. He didn't get far. In the foyer, he was stopped and
handed a message that instructed him to meet with someone
called Horatio Cobb, police constable, at six o'clock in the
Crooked Anchor, a sleazy tavern on Bay Street north of
Market. Marc was due to have supper with Eliza Dewart-
Smythe and her uncle Sebastian at seven and, as he was
beginning to feel he might at last have found a woman who
would help him get over his disappointment with Beth
Smallman, it was imperative he be there on time. Since he
also planned to visit Mackenzie at his newspaper office that
afternoon, he decided to stop briefly at Mrs. Standish's for a
cold midday meal with a glass of warm ale. Then he headed
down the half-block to Front Street and walked briskly eastwards under a pleasant June sun. He began to whistle.

The investigation had begun.

SOMERSET HOUSE WAS BY NO MEANS the only mansion of
note in this prosperous area of the city, where many of its
successful merchants, lawyers, bankers, churchmen, and
privy councillors lived—as well as a few of those less distinguished members of the Family Compact who, by dint of
birth or marriage, managed to maintain both status and the

requisite bank balance. But Maxwell's house was the grandest on its block, with an unobstructed view of the bay and
the islands beyond. The building itself was as pretentious
as it was presumptuous—all stuccoed quarrystone and slate,
neo-Gothic turrets and chimneys wishing they were belvederes, and a carved portico at the entrance to a legendary
ballroom fit for princes (should they ever deign to come).
Marc walked past the portico without admiring its rococo
cherubim, going on to the more plain visitors' entrance
off York Street, which was adorned with a morbidly black
wreath and an ornate door knocker.

A butler in mourning clothes listened as Marc stated his
name and asked to see the receiver general. After waiting in
vain for Marc's card, the butler trundled off down an unlit
corridor. It was a good five minutes before he returned and
wordlessly led Marc down the same corridor. A door was
discreetly opened and, as Marc followed the butler's nod
into the room ahead, the servant said in a low, conspiratorial tone: "Lieutenant Edwards, ma'am, as you instructed."

Before Marc could quibble or retreat, the door was closed
behind him, and he found himself alone in a sunlit sitting
room with Prudence and Chastity Maxwell. Chastity had
either just rushed here or was in the midst of working up a
rage, for both her cheeks were crimson and her eyes were
blazing. Prudence, if she had been engaged in a heated exchange with her daughter, had recovered with remarkable
speed and aplomb, for she rose gracefully, batted her heavy

lashes at Marc, smiled, and said, "Good afternoon, Lieutenant. Do come in. Iggy's out just now, but due back within
the quarter-hour. I've instructed Jacques to let us know the
second he steps through the front door." She put out her
ungloved hand—though the rest of her costume was formal
enough (as befitted mourning attire) and composed of several layers of cloth that shimmered and rustled gloomily. She
turned to Chastity. "You remember Lieutenant Edwards, do
you not, darling?"

Chastity blushed just as her cheeks were cooling from
whatever contretemps she had been having with Prudence.
"Of course, Mama."

"You are not a gentleman who can easily be forgotten,"
Prudence said to Marc, and she motioned him to sit. Marc
nodded and took a chair across the room from his hostess.

Chastity did not sit. "Please excuse me, Lieutenant, but I
was just on my way out—"

"Not to meet that man, you most certainly are not," Prudence hissed without seriously undermining her smile.

Chastity now looked more exasperated than angry. She
gave Marc a sidelong glance that implied, "You see what I
have to put up with" and said to her mother, "I told you I am
meeting Angeline and we are taking her carriage down to
the new millinery shop on King Street. I must have a black
hat for Uncle's funeral on Friday." Then without waiting for
any further remonstrance, she smiled beatifically at Marc
and left by the far door.

"What are we to do with this younger generation, Lieutenant?" Prudence said to Marc, who she had apparently decided was old enough not to be included in it.

Marc smiled noncommittally. "Is there something in particular you wished to discuss with me?" he asked warily, thinking of several dubious possibilities.

But either Prudence had scant recollection of yesterday's encounter in Danby's Inn or had determined to pretend that it had never happened. She was clearly playing the lady and mistress of the manor. "As a matter of fact, sir, I was hoping to ask a favour of you in regard to my daughter. But first, would you like some coffee, or a sherry?"

"Nothing, thank you, ma'am. I will of course be happy to be of service in any way that I can, though I must tell you candidly that almost all of my time is now taken up with investigating the dreadful business of your brother-in-law's death."

The rouged eyelids dropped down for a respectful second. "Yes, I understand. As you see, our entire household has felt its effects. And while Langdon and I were not close in recent years—you know how families can drift apart even when they live cheek-by-jowl—we are grieving deeply for him and for my devastated sister-in-law."

"Please convey my condolences to the family."

"Thank you. You are an exceptionally sensitive young man." Prudence opened her eyes wide and gave him a frank, ungrieving appraisal.

Marc cleared his throat. "Since I have you here now, ma'am—" and sober, he thought unkindly.

"Prudence, please."

"—I was hoping you might give me your insight, as a family member, into Mr. Moncreiff's personality or into any, ah, personal problems he may have been experiencing of late. You see, improper as it is to be probing thus while the family is still in shock, I need to discover a motive for the shooting. People don't kill other people without a powerful reason to do so."

"I understand. And, in fact, I have spent this morning considering what such a reason could be. Many years ago Langdon was a dashing young man, and I was pleased when he married Flora. But for the past ten years he has led what I can only describe as a dull and directionless existence. He has very few opinions and those he has are calculated to offend no one. He does not attend society balls or fêtes and, until Sir Francis begged him to become an Executive councillor or whatever they're called, he had contributed nothing to the province except two daughters and a disheartened wife."

Marc was not sure how to put his next question. "Was she bored enough to, to—"

"—find herself a more accommodating man?"

This time Marc blushed, and Prudence watched him redden and then pale—never taking her eyes off his face. She gave him a rueful smile. "It does happen, you know, even here a long ways from Sodom and Gomorrah. But the answer is no. And I do know my sister-in-law in that regard."

"Thank you for your candour, ma'am." Marc rose. "I'm afraid I have several more urgent appointments this afternoon. Would you tell Mr. Maxwell that if it is convenient, I shall call back at four o'clock. You can send word to Mrs. Standish, my landlady."

Prudence spread one hand across her bosom in either a gesture of modesty or an attempt to call attention to its generous curvature. "But I haven't had a chance to ask that favour of you."

"Oh, I am sorry. Please, there is plenty of time for that." Marc remained standing.

Prudence got up and rustled across to him, but there was nothing predatory in her movement. In her face there was genuine concern: "I am positive that my daughter is illicitly consorting with one of the guardsmen up at Government House."

"Are you suggesting that there have been improprieties?" Marc said, taken aback.

"I only suspect so. I can get nothing out of the girl except self-righteous denials, which of course merely deepens my suspicions."

"Has she been seen with one of my men?"

"Not in any compromising situation, no. But she's been hanging about with Angeline Hartley since that creature came here in January and—"

"Sir Francis's ward? Surely you—"

"I don't think anything, but I know she's a wild thing, not yet out of her teens, she has the run of the governor's open carriage, and the two girls have been seen riding up in College Park with unidentified officers."

"Unchaperoned?"

"Well, not exactly. The governor's elderly coachman and a groom are always with them, but that hardly counts. It's the secret comings-and-goings that are the real problem. Like this trip to the King Street millinery today, and two or three such 'stories' every week. I'm positive Chastity is having clandestine meetings where she may be getting up to all sorts of shenanigans."

"But if it is one of my officers, ma'am, and I have no inkling of any such affair to date, I am certain nothing improper would occur. Indeed, my officers, all of whom I know well, would be honourable and proud enough to present themselves to you and Mr. Maxwell before courting your handsome daughter."

"And I am sure of that, too, Lieutenant. But Mr. Maxwell is very particular about who ought to be allowed to 'court' his daughter, as you so quaintly put it. Mr. Maxwell is very possessive of his possessions, and I am afraid that junior officers are not included on his roster of suitable suitors." The look that Prudence now gave Marc suggested strongly that she, too, was deemed one of her husband's possessions.

"Ah, I see. However honourable this suitor might be,

Miss Maxwell knows in advance that he would be discounted."

"You have considerable knowledge of the ways of the world," Prudence said and, she did not need to add, of women.

"What do you think that I could do to help you in this matter?"

"The first thing I need to know is who. I am willing to intercede on my daughter's behalf with Ignatius, but only if I know who the young man is, and whether he's worth the trouble it may bring down upon my head."

"Then I will make inquiries and let you know the moment I have found anything out."

"Thank you so much."

Prudence held out her hand and, as Marc took it to give it a mannerly kiss, she squeezed his fingers hard. By the time he looked up in surprise, however, she had turned her face away. At that moment Jacques put his head in the doorway and said, "The master will see you now in his study."

"I CAN'T BELIEVE ANYONE WOULD WASTE a bullet on dear old Monkee, let alone pay someone else to do the job." The Honourable Ignatius Maxwell, receiver general of Upper Canada and man of substance, sat in a thronelike leather chair opposite Marc before a flower-filled bay window overlooking York Street. He spoke with the deep voice and easy authority that comes from long years of unchallenged privilege, and every once in a while he took a puff on his cigar, which otherwise he used as a rhetorical prop. He was ruggedly handsome, despite the paunch beneath his silk blouse, with a crop of studiously unkempt reddish-blond hair and a pair of wispy mutton chops that framed his face like pale parentheses. His unoccupied hand rested in the pocket of his moleskin smoking jacket, cut in the latest London style.

"It appears, however, that someone did just that," Marc said, marvelling at how quickly the governor had begun spreading the news of a possible hired gun.

"So I've been told up at Government House. Some Yankee republican by the sound of it." He flapped at the air with his cigar. "Still, it makes no sense. Even if one of the Clear Grit radicals was mad enough and rich enough to arrange such an assassination in the midst of an election, why would they shoot a harmless codger like Monkee?"

"That's what the governor has asked me to find out. Was Councillor Moncreiff indeed harmless? A threat to no one?"

"The man had no political ambitions. I'm sure that you already know that the governor selected Monkee for the council after the disgraceful resignation of those radicals and traitors back in March precisely because, as a nominal Tory but one notorious for holding no fixed opinions, he would be a threat to no cause whatsoever. Nor for that matter would he be of any service to one. He was simply a body to fill up a chair and not open his mouth except to say 'Thank you.'"

"Is that not perhaps being a little too harsh?"

"Harsh, maybe, but true nonetheless. Monkee himself was delighted. That's the whole sad truth of this business. For the first time in years he looked forward to getting out and about. He volunteered to accompany us up to Danby's Crossing." Maxwell stared at his cigar as if he expected it to provide him with an explanation of the inexplicable.

"Then I feel that we must examine the possibility that your brother-in-law was murdered for some personal reason. And since I cannot yet see any connection between him and the man we suspect of actually pulling the trigger, I am forced to explore the hypothesis that someone with a personal grudge did the hiring of the assassin."

Maxwell gave Marc a look of pure contempt, and merely harrumphed. Marc waited patiently. "No one held a grudge against Mr. Moncreiff, unless it was Flora, and she blamed only herself for having been attracted to his good looks when she was old enough to have known better."

"Did he have financial difficulties?"

"No, he did not. He was still living comfortably on the money his father made for him and invested wisely back home."

"Then that leaves the, ah, personal aspect."

Contempt flashed again in Maxwell's eye: "Did he have a bit on the side, you mean? Like, for example, the wife of a jealous husband, who, finding he could not compete with our dashing Monkee, paid a mercenary to vanquish his rival?"

"I take your point."

"It is possible, of course, that he had a doxy of sorts he visited on each second Tuesday of the month—lots of men in this town do—but such women do not have jealous husbands or lovers. They're bad for business."

"I agree."

Marc thanked Maxwell and rose to go. Jacques appeared at the door to show him out. When Marc looked back he saw the receiver general with the cigar clamped tight in his teeth and both hands gripping the arms of the chair—their knuckles white.

MARC WALKED UP YORK STREET TO King, passing several of the substantial homes of those who had prospered in a province that had doubled its population over a decade and in a city where fortunes could still be made in ways never dreamt of in the mother country. A recent dry spell after a rainy spring had left the town's roads passable, especially those sections that had been well gravelled, but here and there puddles of watery mud—courtesy of a weekend shower—awaited the unwary walker. Drays and country wagons heading home from the Market Square in Old Town jostled for right-of-way, and weary teamsters urged their horses on with a lick and a heeya! Shoeless youngsters hooted and shrieked with laughter, their spirits undulled by a long day of labour (or its avoidance). Jauntily dressed chatelaines and ladies-in-training strolled along the intermittent boardwalk, holding their skirts above the muddy swirl, their bonnets fluttering in the late-afternoon breeze.

Turning east on fashionable King Street, Marc passed a dozen or more elegant shops (by Toronto standards), several with multi-paned bow windows displaying wares tailored to the taste of the discriminating lady or gentleman. (Marc, of course, had seen the originals of these makeshift establishments in the metropolis at the centre of the Empire itself.) He touched his cap to several young women with whom he had danced at various official functions, but if they had not first smiled broadly (or coyly) at him, he would have been hard-pressed to recall their faces or names. Two of them, recent debutantes he thought, giggled and clutched their brand-new hats—purchased, he assumed, from the millinery shop near King and Yonge, the one Chastity Maxwell was supposed to be visiting.

Out of curiosity Marc paused to look down the street towards the shop and was rewarded with the sight of Angeline Hartley, the governor's wayward ward, emerging from its front door. She moved smartly towards a barouche, with its hood down, where the governor's elderly coachman and a groom stood waiting with impassive rigidity. The latter helped her climb in and open her parasol. Chastity did not follow. Angeline was alone. The carriage lurched and sped away westward towards Government House.

Marc continued eastwards, and as he passed the alley just

beyond the millinery and the dry-goods store attached to it, he glimpsed, at the far end where it met the tradesman's lane running behind the shops, a blur of taffeta and military red. Chastity and her illicit beau? Perhaps he should ask a few questions around Government House and the garrison on Mrs. Maxwell's behalf, Marc thought. Ignatius Maxwell was reputed to have a quick temper and, as his good woman had remarked, he guarded his possessions jealously.

As he crossed Yonge, barely avoiding an errant donkey-cart, it occurred to Marc that Colin Willoughby had come home very late in the evening several times in the past couple of weeks, yet in the morning he had not seemed hungover, or inclined to talk about the previous night's exploits. Was it possible, then, that Colin had fallen in love? Perhaps, but he was still given to brooding, and even before the disturbing events at Danby's Crossing, Marc had caught him glancing coldly at him for no apparent reason. If Colin was smitten by Chastity Maxwell, he may have chosen dangerously, though it was conceivable that the receiver general excluded pedigreed lieutenants from his caste of unsuitables.

As he neared Church Street, Marc noted the imposing two-storey brick jail. Beside it, but set back about fifty feet from the street and encircled by green lawns, sat the matching court house. (Whether the single design had been chosen by the city fathers for reasons of frugality or a desire to make a public statement about justice in the colony was an open question.) Several carriages drawn by matched teams had pulled up in front of the court house and were busily discharging or collecting dark-suited barristers and solicitors—the backbone and principal prop of the ruling Family Compact. Somewhere nearby, in one of the many offices attached to the jail itself, Marc assumed, would be the modest quarters of the Toronto constabulary, and he wondered vaguely why he had been told to meet the constable with the arresting name of Horatio Cobb in a tavern. Had the man's father read *Hamlet*, or had he been an admirer of Admiral Nelson, Marc wondered.

Turning south on Church Street, he was soon at number fourteen, the building that had housed the infamous newspaper, the *Colonial Advocate*, for many years, and was now home to the even more presumptuous *Constitution*, both of them conceived and produced by the provincial firebrand, William Lyon Mackenzie.

Three times this diminutive Scot with the orange wig had been thrown out of the Legislative Assembly, only to be re-elected immediately by the faithful constituents of York County. The frustrated scions of the Family Compact had dumped the *Colonial Advocate*'s type into Toronto Bay, but had still failed to stop its weekly invective. As soon as the aldermen and councillors of the new City of Toronto had been elected in 1834, they had chosen Mackenzie as their first mayor. He was, by general admission, the de facto leader of the Reform group on the political left, if not always its preferred choice as standard-bearer. He had helped write the Seventh Report on Grievances and had spent a year in England lobbying for the many reforms it recommended. He had come back in fighting trim to sit again in the Reform-dominated Assembly—recently dissolved by Head—and founded an even more radical organ.

Marc studied the plain printer's shop and the bookstore attached to it, whose small front window held a dozen neatly displayed, leather-bound tomes and the advertisement: "Latest titles from New York and London." So this was the den of what, from several platforms, Sir Francis had termed "republican demagoguery." It appeared to be both ordinary and respectable.

But Marc had heard the firebrand at his volcanic best at the Cobourg town hall, where he had roused the crowd of farmers to righteous fury and where Marc, in spite of himself, had begun to see the justness of their cause. However the governor managed to shift the balance of forces in the upcoming election, it was imperative that the festering, legitimate grievances of the farmers, tradesmen, and labourers be dealt with immediately.

"Well, well, I believe it's Ensign Edwards, is it not, come to beard the mangy lion in his den!" Mackenzie stood in the open doorway, wiping ink from one of his hands on a smudged apron and thrusting the other out to greet Marc.

• • •

"SO IT'S LIEUTENANT, NOW. CONGRATULATIONS." MACKENZIE smiled at Marc across the tiny, cluttered office with genuine warmth. From the adjoining room came the metallic sounds of compositors picking and setting type. A bluebottle fly batted against the window-glass half-heartedly in the heat.

"Thank you, sir."

"I presume your promotion was entirely due to the small service you rendered me and the Reform party last winter in Cobourg?"

Marc smiled, as he was expected to—pleased not only that Mackenzie remembered him but that he felt comfortable enough to tease him. Marc had been told that Mackenzie had a sharp sense of humour, observed less in latter years than when he had first come to the colony. Marc turned the subject to yesterday's tragedy.

"What do I make of it, you ask, beyond regret at the senseless death of a harmless old man?" Mackenzie said. "Well, lad, there are several ways of responding to that question, depending, I suppose, on who's asking it and why. I infer from your presence here that the governor is concerned about the effect it might have upon the elections."

"That, of course, as well as the importance of finding the killer."

"Rumour has it that the shooter was an ex-patriot American with a grudge or an empty larder."

"Rumour is reasonably accurate, for a change."

It was Mackenzie's turn to smile. Then his chiselled

features took on a grave, almost sorrowful, cast. He brushed his wig back unconsciously with his right hand. "A rumour like that could do irreparable harm to the Reform cause in this election. As you know, the governor is stumping the constituencies and playing up the loyalty theme. The murder of one of his hand-picked councillors by a crazed democrat from the States would play to the paranoia out there and make credible the preposterous claim that the Yanks are mustering for imminent invasion."

"Which is why the governor wants this man found," Marc insisted.

Mackenzie gave Marc a narrow, appraising glance. "I think you do believe that, lad."

"But surely, sir, you see that, crazed or not, if this killer were hired, he could have been recruited by anyone with a reason to do away with Councillor Moncreiff—including someone from his own, ah—"

"—class?"

"Or party . . . which might suggest to the electorate that the Compact and the Tories do not have their own house in order."

"Yes, I do see." Mackenzie began drumming his fingers on the desk, rustling the papers scattered there. "Are you sure you've chosen the right profession, Lieutenant?"

"What I am leading towards, sir, is the question of who might have reason to have Councillor Moncreiff assassinated?"

"Well, then, I'll save you and Sir Francis some time by stating here and now and unequivocally that no one in the Reform party and no one remotely interested in its welfare would have hired an assassin or shot the old fellow himself."

"But there must have been resentment and some bitterness among Reformers when Sir Francis replaced the protesting councillors with even more unpalatable members? Could a Reform sympathizer, albeit temporarily deranged, have hired an assassin to publicly eliminate one of those new councillors, as a message or a warning to the governor himself?"

Mackenzie gave the question some thought. "Deranged he would have to be, but, yes, it is possible. However, in such a case, Moncreiff could only have been a symbolic target. The old codger had no status as a politician or as a mover and shaker. Remember that Ignatius Maxwell was seated on the same bench as Moncreiff, according to the eyewitness reports my compositors are just now setting to type. If the motive were practical revenge, then that grasping fraud would have been singled out, not Moncreiff."

Marc shuddered. How many of the spectators present at Danby's Crossing yesterday had already relayed their biased accounts of the events there to the radical press? But if Mackenzie had heard details of Crazy Dan's death at the hands of a less than competent British troop, he had decided not to bring it up. Or perhaps the complicity of Alvin Chambers, one of their own, had given the farmers some pause before spreading the story abroad. But the details, twisted beyond all recognition, would come out eventually and the governor's crude attempt to smooth over their ugliness would soon become part of the campaign rhetoric.

Emerging from his momentary reverie, Marc said, "I think you're implying that the 'message' was more likely intended for Sir Francis?"

Mackenzie appeared shocked. "If that is so, then it is profoundly regrettable. The lieutenant-governor is the representative of the Crown."

Marc hesitated, took a deep breath, and said quietly, "But you are accused everywhere, even by some of your own supporters, of being an ardent republican."

Mackenzie smiled wryly. "Thank you for the 'ardent.' That I am. But if you were to read the many back issues of my *Colonial Advocate*, you would see that I have been from the outset a champion of responsible government—whatever form it must take in the particular circumstances of British North America. And even if that form turns out to be republican in nature, it would not necessarily mean any irrevocable break from the mother country. I have admired people like Edmund Burke and David Hume all my life. What we have begged for and then demanded in Upper Canada is that the executive of our government be chosen representatively from members of the Legislative Council and the Legislative Assembly, and that they be accountable in turn to those bodies."

"But where does that leave the governor?"

"It leaves him in the position of vice-regal. For example, to whom is the prime minister and cabinet of Great Britain responsible?"

"To Parliament."

"Precisely—and not to King William. But does that arrangement diminish the traditional and residual authority of the monarch? Not a whit. It's called a constitutional monarchy, and is a uniquely British configuration. That is all we have ever asked for."

"But if the governor could not govern under instruction from the colonial secretary, this province would become a country of its own."

"Something like that, eventually and all in good time," Mackenzie said, somewhat bemused by the drift of the conversation. "And if we are refused that, then . . . well, an independent republic is always possible."

And revolution, thought Marc.

"At any rate, Lieutenant, you do see that it is in the interest of my party to have this assassin tracked down and the truth revealed. You have my word that if I hear—from my innumerable sources—any news of this person or any snippet of gossip pertaining to the tragedy, I will inform you personally."

"Thank you. There is one other thing, sir—the delicate matter of whether Councillor Moncreiff may have had some, ah, personal difficulties—"

Mackenzie chortled. "Sexual intrigue and all that? Low behaviour among the high and mighty?"

"Something of that sort, yes. Naturally his family may be reluctant to discuss such indelicacies, so I was wondering if you, as a journalist, one-time mayor, and long-time resident of the city, if you—"

"Had heard any gossip too salacious to print?"

Marc merely nodded.

"Not a whisper, and I've heard plenty over the years, most of it true, alas. That brother-in-law of his, now there's a man with a peripatetic codpiece, a roué by any other name. But not Langdon Moncreiff."

Marc's surprise showed. "The receiver general? But his wife just assured me he was very possessive."

"As he is. Of her and all his chattel. But especially of her, as it is still her daddy's money propping up that hypocritical façade and Daddy's power in the Compact keeping Maxwell in office. One where graft, nepotism, and corruption are the norm, I might add." Mackenzie looked sadly at Marc in his bright uniform, the feathered shako cap resting confidently in his youthful hands. "You are still young enough, perhaps, not to realize that the innocent perish more often and more tragically than the wicked."

Marc thought of Crazy Dan but said only, "Thank you, again."

They shook hands.

At the door of the shop, Mackenzie said, "As a party,

we are confident that all the legitimate political and legal means still at our disposal will be sufficient to see justice prevail."

Suddenly Marc turned and said, "By the way, the governor made a special request of me when he learned I was coming here."

"And we all know the nature of a governor's 'requests,' don't we? What is it, lad?"

"Sir Francis is eager to know the name of the correspondent in the *Constitution* who signs himself Farmer's Friend."

"Is he, now?"

"He is interested in the stories he tells, despite their implied criticism. He wishes to speak with this person, as he feels such an encounter might be of great benefit to him as he ponders just how to proceed with the grievances."

"I'll bet he does."

"Is that a no, sir?"

"Lieutenant, I would not reveal the name of a pseudonymous correspondent to King William himself. But you can advise the governor that I do indeed know the writer and that his contributions to the *Constitution* are both authentic and voluntary. As such they may be of benefit to him and the future health of the province."

"I'll do that, sir. Thank you for your candour. I expected nothing less."

"Good luck with your investigation."

And it looked to Marc as if luck would be sorely needed.

SIX

❯❯ ❮❮

After returning briefly to his boarding house to bathe, change his linen, and shave, Marc walked to Yonge and Bay, where, as a nearby church bell chimed six times, he pushed his way into the smoky premises of the Crooked Anchor. At the bar, amid the din and wonderfully variegated stink of the place, he had the tapster point out the small figure of a man seated at a table and hunched over a flagon of ale and a plate of trout and onions. When Marc sat down opposite, he looked up, one cheek still plugged with a forkful of supper.

"Constable Cobb?"

"Who would like to know?" Cobb swallowed his mouthful without removing his eyes from the intruder.

"I'm Lieutenant Edwards. Governor Head has arranged, through your superior, for you to assist me in the investigation of the murder of Langdon Moncreiff."

Cobb continued forking his supper upwards as if he were pitching hay into a needy manger. In the silence, Marc sized up the man who looked as if he were more likely to fumble the investigation than help it. Cobb reminded Marc of one of Shakespeare's clowns, several of whom he had seen in Drury Lane: Bardolph or Dogberry, perhaps. His nose met you first, a jutting cherry-red proboscis with a single wart on its left side. Set deep within their sockets, Cobb's eyes were tiny, dark, and hard. The hair, which apparently had never seen a brush and seldom a bar of soap, stood up starkly wherever a finger or palm had skidded through it. Cobb could not have been much more than five feet, but the thick knuckles and muscled neck suggested a powerful physique. Marc noted the navy-blue coat and trousers that passed for a uniform among Toronto's upstart constabulary, this version festooned with dried egg and congealed grease. A stiff helmet lay perilously close to the supper plate. Cobb might have been anywhere between twenty-five and forty years of age: he gave the impression that he was born looking like this.

Cobb, who had returned Marc's scrutiny in kind, finally opened his mouth to speak. "Would ya care fer a bite of supper? A pot of ale?"

"No, thank you, I'm dining out later."

Cobb smiled, though it was hard to be sure because the man's eyes and mouth were not particularly co-ordinated with one another. "Miss Dewart-Smythe is better company, I reckon, than the drubbers and riff-raff in here."

Marc did not smile back. "And what would you know about Miss Dewart-Smythe?"

"I know a lot about a lot of things, yer grace. It's what the city fathers pay me fer."

"I'm not a duke, Constable, I'm a lieutenant, Lieutenant Edwards. 'Sir' will do nicely."

"Well, then, Sir Edward, sir, I observed yer young lady on several occasions in the week past—in the course of me duties, I hasten to add. And a gen-u-ine looker she is."

"Don't mock me, Constable, and do not speak in that flippant manner of the young woman in question. That uniform will not protect you from a good thrashing—"

"Now, now, don't get yer linens in a snarl. If we're gonna work side by side—and I got the orders from the sarge loud and clear on that score—we can't go on callin' each other by ten-syllable sober-quettes. You just call me Cobb, like the wife does when she's speakin' to me, and I'll call you . . . Major."

Marc relaxed slightly. His experience in dealing with native-born citizens in Cobourg last January had taught him to proceed cautiously, to take no offence until certain some was warranted, and to proceed obliquely wherever possible.

"Very well, then. You may call me 'major,' but if you don't mind, I'd prefer to address you as 'constable,' Constable," Marc said, regretting the awkward repetition.

Cobb shrugged.

"Now, please tell me how you came to know of the lady and my, ah, interest in her welfare."

Cobb signalled for another ale, and seconds later the tapster hopped over with a fresh, frothing flagon. "They know me here," Cobb grinned, then said, "The lady may not have mentioned that her uncle's stores was burgled two nights ago. Their home and warehouse are on my patrol, so I went up there to see if I could help. The varmints had skedaddled, of course, with six cases of claret and a tun of port. Shame, too, 'cause it'd just arrived from overseas."

"But I was there Monday evening—"

"I seen ya come out, lookin' particularly satisfied, I'd say. But the old fellow and me was in the warehouse lookin' over the damage at the time. I spied ya prancin' off down Newgate Street through the storeroom window. The lady herself didn't know nothin' about the break-in till later. Things like that tend to scare aristo-crustic ladies, I'm told."

Marc knew enough to ignore what was irrelevant. "Did you find any clues?"

"Nothin' except a jimmied back door. The sarge is in quite a flap about this thievin' of spirits. There's a rash of it goin' 'round. I was called out to assist Constable Wilkie—he's got the east-end patrol—way out at Enoch

Turner's brewery near the Don River last Saturday, it was. A dozen barrels of good beer rolled out and loaded quick as a fart onto some schooner or dory, no doubt. Big shots like Dewart-Smythe and Alderman Enoch tend to make the sarge's breakfast bubble."

"You didn't suppose that I was the thief?" Marc said impishly.

Cobb gave him a curious look. "It did occur to me, Major, but you weren't luggin' any casks under yer arm, and I figured you had more interestin' counter-band in mind."

"And you had observed me there on other occasions?"

Cobb took a hefty swig of ale, brushed the froth away with his cuff, and said, "We work closely with the watch at night. There ain't much about people's comin' and goin' we don't know about—sometimes even before they do." He laughed, spraying ale over the remnants of his dinner.

"Then your observational skills may come in handy during my investigation," Marc said affably.

"Our investigation, Major."

"Have you been briefed on the details?"

"So far, I only know what I hear in the taverns between here and Church Street."

"You spend your time in taverns?"

"Only durin' the day," Cobb said, ostensibly offended.

"But should you not be patrolling the streets assigned to you? In London a bobby's principal function is to prevent crime by providing a visible presence day and night."

"Now, Major, I do venture outdoors once in a blue moon, just to air out my uniform and stretch the kinks out of my legs. But I find I can learn more about evil-doin' by just sittin' here keepin' my rabbit ears open and waitin' fer my many informants—or snitches as we call 'em—to sashay up and tell me what I need to know, fer the price of half a flagon usually."

"But there are disturbances of every kind out there, surely."

"Surely. And lots more in here. We constables are run plum off our feet, or knocked off 'em, by brawlers and drunks and wife-beaters and the like. Why, if I didn't spend half my time movin' smartly from dive to dive, I'd miss the pleasure of a fist in my face or a knee up the nosebag, so to speak, or the pure joy of smackin' a low-life silly before he pukes all over me. Yessir, Major, us constables've got plenty of hours in a day to do a lot of serious investigatin'—in and out of the town's taverns. Not to speak of all the happy hours we put in investigatin' whorehouses and investigatin' inebriated gentlemen home to their good wives and investigatin' some mistress cudgelled black and blue by a bigwig fer the sheer sport of it, and investigatin'—"

"I take your point, Constable."

"To give you a fer-instance, it was whispered to me not five minutes before you come in here that the same thieves did over the wine warehouse as did the brewery. Got no names yet. But I will, if it don't take you forever to investigate a simple murder." He drained his flagon, waved it once at the tapster, and said, "So why don't you start things rollin' by feedin' me the details."

Aware that he was in danger of being late for his supper with Eliza, Marc quickly sketched out what had happened up at Danby's Crossing (censoring somewhat the chapter entitled "Crazy Dan"), and even outlined the theories he was considering. Cobb listened without comment, equally absorbed, it seemed, in making his ale last to the end of Marc's tale.

Marc finished but did not wait for Cobb's response—should he have one—for he felt he had sized up his assistant sufficiently and assessed his potential usefulness. "What I'd like you to do, Constable, is arrange for a surreptitious surveillance of Philo Rumsey's cabin. I'm convinced he will return, secretly, to fetch his wife and children or bring them money. He may even use an intermediary."

"You want me to keep an eye on his place without anybody else knowin'?"

"Precisely."

"Well, the best way to do that, Major, is fer me to have a couple of local types act as our eyes and ears up there. That way, no one'll get suspicious or try to warn off this Rumsey fella. I can set that up tonight. I'll have to loan a horse from the sarge, and take Wilkie with me, 'cause he used to live in that township when he was a tad. We'll ride up there and just pop into the saloon, out of uniform. We'll have yer watch goin' before it gets dark."

"Better still, I'll write you a note to take to the hostler at Government House, and he'll provide you with fast horses—"

"—which'll blow our cover within five miles of Danby's saloon. The sarge's nags'll do just fine."

"Yes, you're right. At any rate, I'll leave the surveillance to you. But we also need to interview the storekeepers on the market square—discreetly—and build up a picture of the Rumseys and Phineas Kimble, the harness-maker. I'm certain he's involved, because he definitely lied about not hearing the shot that came from his own house."

"If you go up there and take one step outside Danby's in yer fancy dress, the jig'll be up, Major. What I'll do tonight is get good and drunk, so's I'll have to sleep it off on the street or the bush. I'll take some pots and pans along and pertend I'm a peddler, and Wilkie'll be my helper. Then I'll go door to door tomorrow, hungover like, and purvey my wares, whilst pokin' about gently fer any gossip about Rumsey or Kimble. Wilkie'll suggest who we can trust up there as our spies, and take care of that end before he comes home."

"Yes, Constable, that sounds like a superb plan." His respect for the man was growing with every passing minute. Marc rose.

"Enjoy yer dinner, Major."

Marc hesitated. "Pardon the personal question, but did your father by any chance name you after Admiral Nelson?"

Cobb flinched. "No sir, Major, sir. My pappy named me after some fella in a foreign play."

Sebastian Dewart-Smythe, wholesale wine merchant, lived on Newgate Street near Yonge, not too far from the stately residence of the influential Reform family of William Baldwin. Mr. Dewart-Smythe had one wing of his spacious (but not so stately) residence devoted to the safe storage of tuns and casks of imported wine. In the other wing he lived in comfortable, unostentatious affluence with his niece, Eliza. Only one servant, a butler-cum-valet, lived in. The Dewart-Smythe family of Kensington, England, operated wholesale wine houses on three continents.

Marc had met Eliza the previous November at a harvest fête held in the sumptuous halls of The Grange a few weeks after she and her uncle had arrived to open yet another branch of the family business. He had danced with her once, and afterwards made polite chatter with her long enough to learn that, while her uncle was her guardian, she had come with him principally as a helpmate—her interest in and knowledge of wines along with her fluency in French, Spanish, and Italian making her, she claimed, indispensable. Marc had been aware of her rich, dark, ringleted hair, intelligent brown eyes, voluptuous figure, and attractive, if not pretty, features. But at that time he had not yet recovered from his youthful affair with Marianne Dodds, the ward of a neighbouring landowner back home in Kent. Last November, all the young women at soirees and balls had seemed to him to be frivolous and self-absorbed.

Then, in Cobourg this past January, he had, he was certain, fallen truly in love. The sudden and mysterious death of Beth Smallman's father-in-law had brought him to her farm, and he had been of material assistance to her. While Beth herself had been noncommittal, she had undoubtedly been drawn to him even though their political outlook and loyalties were opposed. But when Beth did not reply to his letters and even the letters from Beth's friends and neighbours stopped coming, he began to accept that there was no hope for him. It was then he suddenly realized just how different Eliza was from the debutantes and husband-seekers among her contemporaries.

In April he had met her by chance on King Street, shopping, and they took up their November conversation as if six months had not intervened. She shocked him, then, by inviting him back to her house for coffee, in the middle of the afternoon with her uncle absent next door and a befuddled butler serving them. But what was most surprising was that Marc found himself completely at ease in her presence. Eliza said what she meant and meant what she said. There was no need to be on guard or to wonder what was going through her woman's mind: her gaze was as candid as it was kind. The only difficulty—and it was one he was loath to discuss with her—was that she seemed to him much of the time more like an elder sister than a potential lover.

But not all the time, and definitely not this evening. Supper itself was pleasant and predictable enough, with Uncle Sebastian steering the conversation back to wine whenever it threatened to veer towards topics he thought too crude for feminine ears, and Eliza having her say on the most arcane details relating to the business here and abroad—while Marc smiled vacuously and basked in Eliza's knowing, grateful glances. Then, despite a solemn promise to Eliza not to do so, her uncle raised the subject of the break-in late Monday evening and proceeded to expound upon the incompetence of the newfangled constabulary and the superiority of the magistrates and squires of old. Marc decided to remain mum on both themes.

At seven thirty Uncle Sebastian rose with some effort (he was portly in the extreme) and said deliberately, "Well, I'm off to the Shakespeare Club meeting at McBride's. May I give you a lift, Lieutenant? It's not out of my way."

Marc got up. "It's a fine evening, sir, and I feel the need to walk off some of that splendid meal."

"But only when you've finished your cigar and brandy," Eliza said. "You wouldn't be rude enough to rush Mr. Edwards into the street hatless, would you, Uncle?"

"Of course not, my dear. Do stay for a few minutes, sir. I know that my niece gets lonesome with only the day-servants to talk to while I'm working. I'm sure Chalmers will be happy to show you out before he retires at eight." The old man gave Eliza what he assumed was a stern look and headed for the hall.

"He won't be back till ten o'clock," Eliza said with a conspiratorial smile. "They're doing a reading of Act Three of *Julius Caesar* tonight and Uncle, improbably, has been cast as the lean and hungry Cassius."

"Well, I'll certainly stay for a little while. I've had a trying two days, and you're always such a thoughtful listener."

"I'll put my oar in when required," Eliza said.

FOR THE NEXT HOUR MARC RECOUNTED, not always in sequence, the events and emotions and mental debates surrounding the death of Langdon Moncreiff. And though Eliza was not especially concerned with politics, she was fascinated by human behaviour and motive. She interjected, almost tenderly, from time to time to ask a question or to seek further explanation. At last Marc began to wilt, his broad shoulders sagging, and he slumped against one of the pillows on the settee. Eliza, in a simple blue dress with a dark sash accentuating her narrow waist and full bosom, slipped across the room, fussed with a spray of pink roses for a minute, then turned and settled herself demurely beside him.

"Do you think Moncreiff could have been mixed up in some lovers' quarrel?" Marc asked her drowsily, quite sick of all such unanswerable and futile queries.

"No, I don't. An outraged husband or jealous lover would have done the deed himself or else arranged for it to be done in a less public place. You are wasting your precious time and energy pursuing that line of inquiry."

"So you know a lot about love and lovers?" Marc teased.

Eliza frowned briefly, and Marc instantly regretted the remark. "Oh, it's nothing," she said. "I did love someone deeply, and lost him. But don't you think that sort of experience makes one appreciate the troublesome joys of love itself, that one can become the stronger for it? And more capable of genuine affection?"

Marc was about to agree wholeheartedly but was forestalled by the suddenness of the kiss that neither of them could recall initiating. Marc put his arms around her, and the softness of her breasts pressed against him. He let his face drift into her hair as she gripped his back with clenching fingers.

The hall door banged shut.

They sprang apart. Eliza straightened her hair, patted her dress smooth, and leapt to the dining-room door in time to greet her uncle with a cheery hello.

Then she said with genuine concern, "But you're back early, Uncle. It's only nine thirty."

"Gastric complaint, my dear. I'll take some salts and go right to—" Uncle Sebastian stopped in mid-sentence, all thought of his balky stomach forgotten. "Young man, what are you doing here at this hour with my niece—unchaperoned?"

•   •   •

Uncle Sebastian tipped forward in his padded chair, pushed his bewhiskered face over his plump and aching belly, and glared at Marc. "What I want to know, Lieutenant—and I wish the candid answer of a true gentleman—is this: What are your intentions towards my niece?"

It was a fair question, and one Marc had asked himself several times before this evening and a dozen times on the slow walk behind Uncle Sebastian as they made their way in stiff silence to his office.

"I am not sure how I would characterize my intentions, sir. If I knew for certain, I would have approached you before this."

"Are you in love with Eliza, sir? I cannot put it more bluntly than that."

"I may well be—"

"What blather and circumlocution! You should be ashamed of yourself. You've been skulking around here uninvited for the past six weeks, stirring up gossip along Yonge Street from the bay to Lake Simcoe! You had the impudence to linger here on Monday evening while I was attending to my ledgers and then again tonight when I expressly indicated I wished you to leave, as a proper gentleman would have done without having to be reminded. If you do not love her and have no intention of asking for her hand, then, sir, you are a blackguard and I am much deceived."

His jowls shook with anger and chagrin, but there was a kind of pleading in his eyes as he stared steadily at Marc.

"You are not deceived, sir. I am truly fond of your niece, and I am in the process of falling in love. That is the truth, upon my word as an officer."

"Then you are considering a proposal sometime soon?"

Marc hesitated—not too long, he hoped—before saying, "I am."

Uncle Sebastian sat back, winced at his rebellious stomach, and attempted to relax. "Do you wish a brandy? Chalmers, bless him, is still afoot."

"No, thank you. I am exhausted from a—"

"Not too tired, I trust, to be asked a few pertinent questions regarding your suitability as a suitor for Eliza's hand."

My God, Marc thought, I must be having a bad dream.

"I must ask you about your parentage and prospects, Lieutenant, because, whether you know it or not, Eliza is the sole living heir of her generation in the Dewart-Smythe family. She stands someday to become a very wealthy woman."

"I did not know that. We talk of many things, but not money."

Uncle Sebastian gave a skeptical cough but carried on. "Money must be talked of or it will speak for itself. Now I understand that you are the adopted son of a reasonably prosperous country squire named Jabez Edwards—whom you affectionately refer to as 'Uncle.'"

Marc wondered where this was leading. "That is right. Apparently I called him that before—"

"And who, then, were your real parents?"

"Thomas and Margaret Evans. My father was the game-keeper on the estate. They both died of cholera when I was five."

"But you were officially adopted and raised up as Jabez Edwards's own in the County of Kent?"

"I was."

"Adjacent to the lands of Sir Joseph Trelawny?"

"That is so."

"And you are the sole heir to the Edwards estate?"

Marc smiled inwardly. His parentage would have disqualified him as Eliza's suitor except for the fact that he had been given a reputable surname, seemed likely to inherit a minor estate, and had rubbed shoulders with the petty aristocracy next door. "Not quite," Marc said slowly.

"What do you mean, not quite? You either inherit or you don't."

"The land is entailed to full-blooded Edwards' heirs, the sons of his younger brother, Frederick, who lives in France. There was a younger sister, Mary, who would have been my aunt, but she died before I was born."

"So you inherit nothing?"

"Not quite. Uncle Jabez invested his own money wisely in stocks, and I am promised whatever they have yielded, at his death."

"No land, then, and an indeterminate sum of money?"

"That is the case. But you must rest assured that any motive I might have for asking Eliza to marry me—were I to do so in the near future—would not include seeking her fortune."

"Well, we shall see, shan't we?"

"Are you forbidding me to see her, sir?"

"Not at all. But I must insist that you call on her only when invited and then only in the afternoons. There will be no more late-evening tête-à-têtes. Is that clear?"

"Yes, sir." Marc realized that the old tyrant was serious about all this, and that, as a lifelong bachelor, keeping watch on a beautiful and vulnerable heiress (and one he obviously adored) was not easy.

"Now, which of us is going to tell Eliza?" the old man said.

When Marc dragged his exhausted body up the three steps onto Mrs. Standish's veranda, he was greeted by Colin Willoughby peering out the doorway.

"Christ, but you look like a fox who's spent a day in the kennels," Colin said. He was dressed only in his nightshirt, with an expression of immense satisfaction—almost a smugness—masking evident fatigue and strain.

Marc was so tired he could muster only a noncommittal grunt in response.

"Don't shoot the messenger, old boy, but I was instructed by the governor to command your presence at Government House the moment you returned."

"Tell him I'm dead," Marc moaned.

"Now, who'd want you dead?" Colin forced a laugh.

The uncle of a girl I know, Marc smiled grimly to himself.

SIR FRANCIS WAS ALMOST AS EXHAUSTED as Marc, but each went bravely through the motions of doing his duty. Marc gave the governor a synopsis of his activities at Maxwell's, Mackenzie's, and the Crooked Anchor.

"This Cobb sounds like a crude but cunning devil," Sir Francis said with a nice balance of admiration and revulsion. "Chief Constable Sturges assured me that he was his best man, but then that is a relative statement, eh?"

"I feel that almost everything depends upon his apprehension of Philo Rumsey," Marc sighed. "It seems most probable at this point that Councillor Moncreiff was shot by a hired assassin in order to make a political point of some kind. I believe we can rule out any personal motive whatsoever. Which means, I am afraid, that until we get hold of Rumsey alive, we have no way of discovering who engaged him and for what reason—short of interviewing every malcontent and opponent of the government in Upper Canada."

"Perhaps this Constable Cobb will be able to trace Rumsey's recent movements and link him with the sponsor of this crime."

"From all accounts, sir, Rumsey was a loner, a man who disappeared at will into the bush to hunt—or whatever."

"And you would rule out any direct involvement of the radical left?"

"Yes, sir, I would. Mackenzie convinced me that it would be suicidal for Reformers to have been involved. They may be fanatic, but they are a long ways from being stupid."

Sir Francis suppressed a yawn and turned the gesture into a nod of assent. "While you were there, Lieutenant, did you have a chance to inquire about the identity of Farmer's Friend?"

"I did, and Mackenzie refused to tell me."

"I thought as much."

"But he did say that the writer is a real person with an intimate knowledge of his subject."

"That's precisely the problem, alas." This time Sir Francis let the yawn take its full course. "Come to see me tomorrow afternoon, and I'll explain more about Farmer's Friend. In the meantime, if you see Cobb, you might assign him to make discreet inquiries about the matter. I understand these new constables keep an ear close to the boardwalk."

"Or the bar," Marc said. "I think that's a good idea, sir, provided it doesn't interfere with his duties in the Moncreiff investigation."

"That is understood, of course."

At the door of the office, Marc said casually, "How did Colin get on with his new assignment?"

Sir Francis smiled through his fatigue. "Considering he had the granddaddy of all hangovers, splendidly. He took the bit in his teeth and began planning the security arrangements for our proposed swing through the London district next week and, with Major Burns's heroic assistance, got through a mountain of correspondence before dark. Which left me free to deal with the incredible fuss over the assassination. The funeral is to be held on Friday."

"Military?" Marc said with apparent disinterest.

"As a matter of fact, it is," the governor said. "The family insisted."

"Well, I'm delighted to hear that Colin is doing well."

"We may bring him back into the fold yet," Sir Francis said. "If so, his father will be the happiest man in England. And I shall be sure to let him know just who did the most to help his son."

"I'm just trying to be a good friend," Marc said with no attempt to be immodest.

"Something we all need," Sir Francis said.

SEVEN

Marc spent an anxious Thursday morning sweating in his tiny office at Government House, while the place hummed with activity he could take no part in. By eleven o'clock more than a dozen dignitaries—including Chief Justice Robinson, the attorney general, the solicitor general, and the bankers, merchants, and barristers who made up the appointed Legislative Council and the six-member Executive—had paraded into the governor's suite to report on the state of the State, offer unsolicited advice, and propound exotic theories as to the motive for the crime. On several occasions he noticed Colin Willoughby either rushing past

him or else locked in earnest colloquy with Hilliard in the
vestibule. It was just before twelve when word came to him
to meet with Cobb within the hour—this time at the Blue
Ox.

Marc decided to ride down to the rendezvous, as the Blue
Ox was a low-life tavern, frequented by sailors and their colleagues, at the east end of Front Street (still called Palace
by some) beyond the Market Square at Frederick. He could
leave his horse safely at one of the market stalls and proceed
the last block and a half on foot.

As soon as he had stepped into the maelstrom of pipe
smoke, boozy breath, and raucous chatter, the barkeep
caught his eye and pointed to a curtained-off table in the
corner most distant from the light of day. Marc made his
way through the gloom, drew aside a curtain, and sat down
opposite Cobb, who was puffing asthmatically on a short-
stemmed clay pipe.

"Too early for ale, Constable?"

"A tad, Major. But I had enough last night to last me fer
a while."

"But you were on duty last night," Marc said sternly.

"As I recollect, Major, the purpose of my visit to Danby's
saloon was to give the appearance of a drunken peddler too
tanked to make it home."

"I recall that stratagem, but—"

"The hardest body to fool into thinkin' you're drunk is
another drunk," Cobb said, as if conveying an obvious truth

to a particularly obtuse pupil. "And the joint was full of drunks."

"What did you manage to accomplish, then, before you decided to play the drunkard?"

"Wilkie and me spent the early part of the evenin' settin' up our surveillance."

"And?"

"And it's all set," Cobb snapped.

"I require the details."

Cobb arched his eyebrows, thick as a pair of cigar butts.

"I am expected to make a full report to the governor in an hour," Marc said.

"Well, then, you can tell him from Horatio Cobb that it's all set: if that bastard Rumsey so much as shows the end of his pecker up there, we'll know what shade o' purple it is!"

"The governor is not interested in the culprit's append-ages—"

"Figure o' speakin', sir. Give the good governor my re-grets, but tell him if I was to give away the details of my spies, agents, and snitches, no criminal of any kind would ever be caught in this town. He'll have to take the word of a lowly constable, and that's the sum total of it. And so will you. Sir."

"There's no need to get agitated; I'll find a way to explain it to Sir Francis. The important thing is that we're prepared to take Rumsey if he returns to Danby's Crossing. And by tomorrow or Saturday we should have some word on how matters stand in Buffalo."

"You figure that's where he's holed up?"

Marc nodded. "Now what about your morning's work among the shopkeepers on the square? Did you see Phineas Kimble?"

Cobb may have blushed, but it was impossible to tell. "I didn't quite get around to that."

"What do you mean, not quite?" My God, I'm beginning to sound like Uncle Sebastian, Marc thought.

"I only woke up an hour ago. I found I'd been sleepin' in the bush, beside my horse, thanks be to Jesus."

Marc now noticed that Cobb's peddler's outfit was not only rumpled but littered with bits of stick and grass.

"So you've blown your cover already!"

"Not quite, Major. I simply galloped back down here as fast as I could. I knew you needed to know what Wilkie and me did about the surveillance."

"Well, then, I'll just have to go up there myself. We need to get background information on Rumsey because even if we're lucky enough to capture him, there's no guarantee he will talk."

"You could try a little torture, Major. I hear tell that's what they do down in them dungeons you English folk have tucked underneath yer castles."

Marc glared at him.

"But you won't need to make the trip, Major. I'm gonna get myself some ale and a plate of smoked fish, courtesy of the house, and then I'm headin' back up to Danby's.

Nobody's seen me crawlin' out of the bush yet, so that's what I'll do, tryin' my best to look hungover, mind. I'll meet you at the Tinker's Dam way up on Jarvis Street, say, about seven tomorrow evenin'? That is, if you ain't too busy otherwise."

"But that's practically in the countryside!"

"And safe from pryin' eyes, eh?"

Marc smiled reluctantly. "You've done good work thus far, Constable Cobb. I'll meet you there at seven. But there is one other minor matter that the governor wishes you and me to address."

"And what might that be?" Cobb pulled the curtain aside and signalled to the tapster.

"The governor is exercised about a person calling himself Farmer's Friend, who writes a weekly letter in Mackenzie's new paper, the *Constitution*. These letters, Sir Francis feels, might be having an adverse effect on the election here in York County—"

"Where Mackenzie just happens to be runnin'."

"That is irrelevant. What I've found out is that the writer is not Mackenzie or one of the other candidates but a genuine farmer. And this seems to be the problem."

"Ya mean he's tellin' the truth."

"Well, his version of it, I suppose. Anyway, it occurred to me that those sources of yours might be able to give us a name or a lead to the author's identity. Apparently these letters have stirred up a lot of comment locally, so there may be loose tongues about here in the taverns and—"

"You're hintin' that since I spend some time in them, I might be able to call on a snitch or two?"

"Something like that. But, of course, you still must focus your principal attention on the Moncreiff murder. In the meantime, I'll go up to Government House and report to Sir Francis."

"You don't want to eat first?"

The tapster was heading their way with a tray of drink and food.

Marc stood up. "I'll see you at seven tomorrow." As he stepped out of the curtained stall, he let in a glimmer of daylight. "Constable, where did you get that black eye?"

"Got into a bit of a brawl at Danby's," Cobb said proudly. "Had to make it look real, now, didn't I?"

MARC WAS BACK IN THE GOVERNOR'S office at two o'clock. Sir Francis sat behind his desk, looking tired but determined. Major Burns shuffled several papers—notes or reports of some kind—then leaned back as far as he dare to catch the slight breeze from the open window behind him.

"Before I hear your report, Lieutenant, I have some interesting news for you," Sir Francis said. "I have just received a deposition from Magistrate Thorpe up in York Township, taken from a farmer named Luke Bethel."

"He was the man I spoke with after Crazy Dan was shot," Marc said with some surprise.

"That's the one. And according to his sworn testimony, Crazy Dan's gun was still in his grip with his finger on the trigger as he lay dead on his doorstep. Bethel admitted under close questioning from Mr. Thorpe that he saw Crazy Dan raise the gun just as he came over the rise below the cabin, but cannot say whether it was pointing at anyone in particular. He says also that, although attempts were made to warn you that Crazy Dan was harmless and the gun stoppered, these were not successful, and therefore the troops could not have known these critical facts before discharging their weapons."

"That is all true," Marc said, marvelling at Luke Bethel's honesty in the face of much temptation to behave otherwise.

"It seems to me you made quite an impression on Farmer Bethel."

"Quite the reverse, I'm afraid."

"In any case, this affidavit will go a long way to justifying my decision not to hold a formal inquest."

While Marc was relieved at this unexpected turn of events and heartened by Bethel's integrity, he was less than reassured by the governor's cavalier decision not to hold the inquest. Too often, it seemed, the governor dealt high-handedly with volatile political situations that required insight, diplomacy, and judicious decision-making. Marc brushed aside this thought, however, and dutifully brought Sir Francis and Major Burns up to date.

"Thank you," the governor said when Marc had finished.

"That is encouraging. We'll meet again tomorrow before the funeral, if there is anything further to be discussed, and later on after you've talked with Cobb at seven. Now, Major, would you mind giving Lieutenant Willoughby a hand in his office?"

Major Burns nodded assent, rose stiffly, and left the room.

"I have another matter I wish to discuss with you privately," Sir Francis said conspiratorially, and Marc wondered what was coming next.

"It's about Farmer's Friend."

"Ah," Marc said, relieved. "I've put Cobb on his trail. If there is a trail to be found, he'll find it."

"I hope so. But what I wish to do, in the few minutes I have you alone, is explain to you more fully why I think this matter urgent."

"My duty is to carry out your commands, sir, not to question them."

Sir Francis smiled wryly. "Well said. I wish more of the people's representatives felt that way. Nonetheless, I do want to explain to you why I am so serious in my concern over Farmer's Friend. After all, we have an angry, dissolved Assembly, an Executive that resigned in protest, and a contentious election campaign in progress, not to mention a political assassination."

"Well, sir, I did wonder at the timing of your request."

"As any thoughtful human being would have. But it is precisely the timing that is most significant here. As you know, this Reform mouthpiece"—and Sir Francis tossed last Monday's edition of Mackenzie's newspaper rudely upon the desk between them—"this demagogic puffery is the common currency of journalism in this province. Its gross hyperbole—matched, alas, too often by the Conservative press— is so extreme, so distanced from fact or possibility, and so outrageous that readers of every stripe, supporters or detractors, have become inured to it. That is, as you know, one of the reasons that I decided to take to the hustings myself and deliver to the ordinary, loyal Upper Canadian the kind of plain talk he has not heard now for more than a decade."

"I understand, sir."

"Moreover, the so-called 'letters' sent by the quire to the popular press every week are cut from the same hyperbolic cloth and fall upon the same deadened ears. But five weeks ago the *Constitution* started to include a letter each week from this Farmer's Friend, and what has been different about it—and indeed more compelling—is that it, too, speaks in plain language and gives the dangerous illusion that its author has no political agenda except to recite the facts and have them make their own point unaided by bombast or political cant. What is more, each letter is in the form of a story, a kind of parable, which purports to illustrate the effects of various official policies upon ordinary folk. I have had three members of the Legislative Council in here today complaining of the influence these letters seem to be having upon the very moderate majority we are endeavouring to bring over to the Constitutionist side. Someone, most likely Mackenzie, has begun printing these meddlesome parables as broadsheets and flinging them about the hinterland like snowflakes."

"But if they are not distorting the truth, sir—"

The governor's eyes tightened. "Dammit, man, they are telling only one part of the truth. I haven't the slightest doubt that these 'real-life' tales are true—for that's where their power to persuade lies—but to go on and on about the evils of the Clergy Reserves and the failure of the banking system to support the individual farmer or gripe about money being wasted on the Welland Canal that could have been used to improve roads is to ignore the good our policies have also done: we have to have money to support the established clergy, do we not? If they do not get it from the reserve lands, it will have to come from the farmer's own pocket. And if our richest citizens did not selflessly put up their own capital to establish banks, there would be no banks at all!"

"And you feel the letters from a single malcontent could be significant in the election?"

"My task, Lieutenant, is to make certain that by every legal means possible the Crown and the justice it embodies prevails at the polls. I wish to overlook nothing that might be detrimental to our cause. At the moment, for example, the murder of Councillor Moncreiff is working in our favour. There is fear and outrage among people of all classes."

And a convenient Yankee scapegoat, Marc thought, but it was a thought that did not make him happy. "Do we not, sir, have to respect the right of citizens to send letters to the press anonymously, provided they are not libellous?"

"Of course. And as I intimated briefly yesterday, I wish only to invite this person here to have a heart-to-heart talk. I feel that in doing so I may discover, shall we say, more subtle ways in which to frame my plain talk as we head into the London district next week. I have no wish to staunch the flow of the letters themselves."

"May I have copies of these letters, sir? There may be some clue or other in them that could lead eventually to identifying their author."

"Indeed you may. I had Major Burns clip them out for you."

WITH NOTHING TO DO BUT WAIT for Cobb's report tomorrow evening and for any news from Buffalo, Marc sat in his office and read over the letters penned by Farmer's Friend. As described by Sir Francis, they were written in simple, compelling prose. Each was in the form of a story, complete with touching dialogue and an ending pathetic enough to wring tears out of Diogenes. Each parable focused on one grievance and a single example of its devastating consequences.

One letter dramatized the struggle of a farm couple to better their lot by investing their tiny store of hard-won

capital in a gristmill. The mill, already serving their township, was owned by an elderly bachelor with no family in
North America, who promised the couple that they could
"buy him out" when he was ready to retire. When that day
arrived last fall, he moved in with the couple and their five
children and, on condition that they look after his simple
needs until he should die—in addition to a cash payment
equal to half of their life savings—he turned the operation
over to them. The new miller and his eldest sons immediately spent the rest of their savings on needed improvements
to the machinery. What they didn't know until several
months later was that there was a lien on the property.
The original owner had taken out a mortgage with the
Investment Bank of Toronto and had been paying it off in
quarterly sums. He assumed this would be no burden to the
enterprising couple, but what he hadn't done was read the
fine print of the contract he had signed.

On January 1, 1836, the outstanding sum became due
and payable in full within thirty days. All this usually meant
was that the mortgage would be renegotiated at the current
interest rate. But the bank, a well-known institution backed
by a group of wealthy members of the Family Compact,
refused to renew the mortgage and offered no explanation.
The couple desperately tried to arrange a mortgage with the
other two banks in the province but, again, were summarily
and inexplicably rebuffed. A month later the Investment
Bank foreclosed and took over the mill. Lo and behold, a

nearby landowner, with direct links to the Tory faction in Toronto, bought the mill, appropriated the improvements, and set up a thriving business next door to the beleaguered couple. To no one's surprise, the Investment Bank had provided the mortgage money for the transaction. The disenfranchised couple was left with no savings, no mill, and no intention of turning the old miller into the streets (refusing even to take a cent of the money he offered them).

Other letters told similarly heart-wrenching stories, unvarnished by sentiment or anger. One recounted the familiar tale of a farmer whose pond had dried up and whose only alternative source of water now lay in an adjacent property designated as clergy-reserve land. The description of cattle nearly dying of thirst a hundred yards from fresh water—while a weary farmer and his wife carried buckets of stolen water in an effort to save them—was as touching as it was, sadly, true.

The wretched state of the roads—which the province could not afford to maintain because of the hundreds of thousands of pounds that had gone into the corrupt management of the Welland Canal scheme—was painfully illustrated by the story of a sick child being driven in her parents' donkey-cart to the doctor who lived not on some back-township concession but on Kingston Road. Necessary repairs on several sections had not been carried out because government subsidies had been delayed, in part, it appeared, because there was uncertainty over who was to receive the patronage money to do the actual work. Needless to say, the wagon bogged down, the child's condition grew worse, and when a wheel broke off and the donkey collapsed under the strain, the father was forced to run on a shortcut route through swamp and bog—with his daughter whimpering in his arms—in a futile attempt to reach the doctor's house. The child was dead on arrival.

When Marc finished the last letter, he leaned back in his chair and lit his pipe. His hand was trembling, but not because of the obvious tragedies related in these stories and so witheringly told by Farmer's Friend—after all, dreadful deaths among the poor and the abandoned were common-place everywhere on Earth, it seemed, and were, everyone said, the result of God's will. Few people really expected justice from the world. But these tragedies and injustices were preventable, not inevitable: they were the direct consequence of greed, mismanagement, malfeasance, and criminal negligence. And these themes were the flashpoints of the current election. Moreover, the parable-like format made these accounts accessible to anyone who could read, and that included most of the property owners eligible to vote. These letters could be mass produced, and distributed as broadsheets at political rallies and picnics and at the many church socials held during the fine-weather month of June.

It was little wonder that Sir Francis was worried.

•   •   •

MARC'S SLEEP THAT NIGHT WAS INTERRUPTED twice: first by a nightmare in which the scene of Moncreiff's murder was replayed with horrifying verisimilitude, except that the assassin's bullet travelled through the bent neck of the governor before striking Councillor Moncreiff. The second interruption was less fantastic but more disruptive, as a noisy (drunken?) Lieutenant Willoughby clattered and thumped his way down the hall, crashed against the door to his room (next to Marc's), and finally pitched inward to the accompaniment of muted curses and breaking porcelain. After that, there was silence. Widow Standish had, mercifully, slept through the commotion. Then, surprisingly, there came a soft whistling from Willoughby's room: a sprightly air of some kind, lyrical and longing.

WILLOUGHBY'S MOOD HAD SOURED CONSIDERABLY BY morning. Marc met him coming out of his room on the way to breakfast. Colin was understandably bleary-eyed and out of sorts, but the look he gave Marc as they almost collided was quite hostile.

"Sorry, Colin, I'm still half-asleep," Marc lied amiably.

"You're never half-asleep, so don't go pretending you are!"

"Hey, don't take your hangover out on me! I'm an ally."

"You're like all the others," Willoughby said, some unspoken resentment seething though his clenched teeth. "You're looking out for number one. You want everything: advancement, women, glory—"

"If I remember rightly, it was you whom the governor chose to take with him to the London district," Marc said, more puzzled than hurt by Colin's words.

Willoughby's jaw dropped, and whatever he had intended to say was left unuttered. He looked at Marc now as if he were seeing him from another angle. A boyish grin broke across his face. "I'm sorry, Marc. You know I have trouble sometimes controlling my anger. I'm doing my best to forget what happened back in England with my dear Rosy, but every once in a while, all the frustration boils up inside me."

"Apology accepted," Marc said with evident relief. "But you'll need to keep your wits about you around Sir Francis."

"You're right. I think I'll go straight up there now and get the day started."

By the time Willoughby got to the end of the hall, he was whistling.

MARC HIMSELF WAS IN NO HURRY. He had thought of offering to help with the governor's correspondence but decided against it because he wanted Colin to feel fully in charge. As it turned out, Marc did not have to twiddle his thumbs for too long. Before noon, Sir Francis summoned him to his office.

They were alone.

"I've just received a written report by courier from Fort

George," the governor said. Nothing in his face indicated the nature of the news. When he wished to, Sir Francis could play poker with the best. "Major Emery has outdone himself. I must recommend him for an official commendation."

"They've unearthed Rumsey?"

"Not exactly. But in less than a day and a half they have gathered several bits of important information."

Marc simply sat back and waited.

"First, the story from Mrs. Rumsey about her husband's mother being gravely ill was true. The family is well known in Buffalo, and the people over there are, fortunately for us, loquacious busybodies. A cousin of Rumsey's assured our agent, who was accompanied on his rounds by one of the New York sheriffs, that Philo had arrived the previous Thursday and stayed at his mother's bedside until her death on Saturday. She was buried on Tuesday in a private funeral attended only by family members. They all swear that Rumsey was present."

"And if he were in Buffalo then, he couldn't simultaneously be a hundred miles north in Danby's Crossing."

"But he wasn't at the funeral. A neighbour, who is not particularly friendly with the clan Rumsey, told our agent that Rumsey was seen leaving the house on Monday morning—with a packsack on one shoulder and a large rifle on the other."

"A U.S. army rifle—a gift from one of his brothers, no doubt," Marc said with mounting excitement.

"We won't know that for sure until we catch up with him."

"But if we're now pretty certain that he set out last Monday morning for Canada, how could he have reached Danby's Crossing by midafternoon on Tuesday? A courier could do it in seven or eight hours, but only with fresh horses every twenty miles. Do you think he had that kind of help? Are we possibly looking at a larger conspiracy?"

"I think not," Sir Francis said with more confidence than seemed warranted. "He could have ridden up to Fort Niagara and taken a boat across the lake. Fishing vessels and smugglers abound on the lake, as you know from your Cobourg investigation. A small bribe would bring him across in three or four hours—probably on Monday night. That would give him ample time to reach Danby's and plot his strategy."

"If so, it looks more and more as if the harness-maker Kimble was in on the murder. Rumsey is not going to miss his mother's funeral on the off chance that he might be able to take a potshot at Moncreiff."

"Well, he was happy enough to use her as his alibi. And he couldn't have known precisely when she would die."

Marc nodded in sad agreement. "But he definitely has not returned to Buffalo since Tuesday?"

"Not to the family home, according to the nosy neighbours, but it's not likely he would go back there, unless he feels he has been targeted as a suspect."

"Well, let's hope he's still in the province and not yet

aware he's a fugitive." Marc considered the latter possibility doubtful, thanks to the governor's hasty decision to broadcast the notion that an American malcontent was the likely culprit, but he said nothing further on the matter.

"At any rate, we're making progress," Sir Francis said amiably. "And Willoughby and Hilliard are fine-tuning our travel plans for Monday."

"Yes," Marc said, "Willoughby has even taken up whistling."

THE FUNERAL FOR LANGDON MONCREIFF—ONE-TIME major in the local militia, privy councillor, businessman, husband, uncle, and father—was as solemn and dignified as the rutted streets and intermittent rain would allow. There was much pomp and ceremony, and a sea of crêpe and sackcloth stretched for three city blocks, according to later reports in the Tory newspaper, the *Patriot*. Sir Francis rode at the front of the procession, as befitted his station and dignity—proud, grieving, unafraid: "A man of imperial demeanour with the common touch," enthused the *Cobourg Star*. What Langdon Moncreiff might have made of all this hoopla was not cause for speculation in the press, liberal or conservative.

MARC RECEIVED A WRITTEN INVITATION TO have supper with Eliza and her uncle at seven thirty that evening. If Sebastian

had read the riot act to his niece, it had been a mild reading—though Marc had little doubt that he and Eliza would
be chaperoned for the duration. Was it possible that her
uncle had relayed to her, however garbled in the translation,
the nature of her lover's "intentions"? He hoped not. Meanwhile, there was the appointment with Cobb.

The rain had stopped and the sun was shining by the
time Marc left Jarvis Street north and nudged the chestnut
mare onto the muddy lane that he had been told would take
him to the Tinker's Dam. For a moment he thought he was
heading straight into the bush, but the thicket of scrub alder
and hawthorn was short-lived. Beyond it, helter-skelter on
either side of what was now merely a mud path, lay improvised huts and hovels that had never felt a carpenter's square
or an iron nail. Nor was there a level spot of green ground
anywhere, just middens and cesspools. A few puffs of tired
smoke were the only indication that these grim buildings
were inhabited. Marc could see no one around except a
blackened pig or hairless dog rooting in a garbage dump between two huts. Marc was glad he had buckled on his sabre
at the last minute.

Rounding a twist in the pathway, Marc spotted the Tinker's Dam. There was no sign outside, but the fact that it was
the most substantial building on the "street" left no doubt.
Nor did the blast of raised voices Marc could hear pouring
from its paneless windows and one-hinged door. What on
earth was Cobb up to, Marc wondered, as he tethered the

mare to a tree stump where she could be seen from inside the tavern.

In this establishment, there was no tapster primed to point out Constable Cobb, nor was there a bar or table: a wooden plank on two trestles served as the former and three or four tilting stumps provided the latter. The proprietor stood beside an open barrel of whisky, collecting pennies from the customers before they dipped a battered tin cup into the raw liquid. The clientele was a motley collection of men who—from their ragged clothing, slumped posture, and deep-set, sad eyes—looked to be unemployed, unemployable, or simply so far down on their luck that nothing much mattered except the solace of alcohol.

The din of their conversation—vibrant with anger, bravado, pathetic threat—suddenly died. Every eye in the place was fastened upon the uniformed intruder. Marc smiled but kept one hand on the haft of his sabre.

"It's okay, gentlemen, the lieutenant's a colleague of mine. Go back to your business." It was Cobb, perched on a stump-stool, puffing on his pipe, and back in his constable's attire. Several of the barflies made grudging way for Marc.

"Pull up a stump, Major," Cobb said heartily, as if they were in the governor's parlour sampling brandy. "Care fer a dram?"

Cobb's wife must have taken advantage of his absence to clean and buff up his uniform, for the stains had been removed from the coat and a fresh shirt peeked out from under it.

Marc eased himself onto a sawtoothed stool and asked,

"What were you thinking of, calling me out to a place like this? We stick out like a pair of roosters in a fox's den!"

"Now, Major, don't get yer scabbard in a curdle. These chaps may look dangerous, but they'd only stab you if you was alone in an alley with yer back turned, yer flies undone, an' both legs wobbly with the drink."

"But I have to shout to hear what I have to say!" Marc yelled into the general roar.

"May be, Major," Cobb shouted back, "but who's likely to be listenin', eh?"

"Couldn't we go for a walk?"

"An' how then would I be gettin' my cup refilled?"

Marc gave in, but only because he realized that he had adjusted to the noise level and that Cobb would, strangely enough, function better here than elsewhere.

"You may find it hard to reckon with, Major, but it's in this dive and in the Blue Ox—where I dined—that I come up with the details I think you'll find interestin'."

"Be that as it may, Constable, I am most anxious to know what you found out about Philo Rumsey up at Danby's."

Cobb sighed, shrugged his shoulders, emptied his cup, and said, "You're the governor, Major. Do ya want me to start with the point where I crawl out of the bush and gather my pots together?"

"I don't need all the extraneous—"

"I know, I know." Cobb got up and went over to the whisky barrel.

Marc was suddenly aware of being stared at. He turned to his left, and no more than three feet away stood a ragged creature with a walleyed gaze and a drooling lip.

"Don't mind ol' Stony," Cobb said, sitting down. "He likes to look, but he's as deaf as a post, ain't ya, Stony?"

Stony grinned, and drooled happily.

"Here's my report, Major, sir, with the details whittled away."

Marc acknowledged the witticism, and waited.

"I had no trouble gettin' the wives to chatter on about the Rumseys. Seems they're the talk of the town. Rumsey is a loner. He ain't got a political bone in his body. But since Kimble let him go last year, he's been desperate poor. Kept his family alive by huntin' in the winter and sellin' the meat left over. The gossip is he's beat up his missus or the nearest kid when he's been in an ugly mood—but nobody claims they actually saw this."

"Desperately poor enough to take cash for a little marksmanship on the square?" Marc mused.

"Desperate enough, I'd say. But I don't think it was Kimble put him up to it."

"Why not? It was his house the shot was fired from."

"Maybe so. But Kimble's got debts. He's a bit of a poker player, they told me. He may be part of the set-up, but he's not the money man."

"And his politics?"

"A Reformer, but then everybody up in that township

except old Danby and his dame are liberals," Cobb said with some vehemence. "And so are lots of ordinary folk down here." He stared hard at Marc.

Marc carried right on: "Has anyone seen or heard of Rumsey, on the day of the shooting or since?"

"Not up there."

Marc's jaw dropped. Cobb deliberately took a slow draft of his booze, then said, "He was spotted in here on Tuesday evenin'."

"Jesus!" Marc cried. "We could have taken him!"

Cobb smiled. "Not a soul in here would've turned him in—without a fifty-dollar reward."

"Who saw him? Let me question him!"

Cobb sighed. "You don't get it, do ya, Major? I was told by one of my snitches who was told by a pal of the guy who was supposed to've seen somebody who might've been Rumsey."

"My God."

"But he was here, all the same," Cobb sighed again, and began to fuss with filling his pipe. He peered up and said, "He's been spotted in other places, too."

"Christ, man, are the governor and I the only two people in the province who haven't seen him?" Marc was exasperated, but he knew now that in Cobb lay his only hope of solving this crime.

"Keep yer linens dry, Major. I'm just gettin' to the good part. It seems Rumsey was a loner and a recluse up in Danby's Crossing, but down here in town he was quite the dicer and ladies' man. In these parts he went by the name of Lance Carson. His favourite waterin' hole turns out to be the Blue Ox. One of my regular snitches there knew who he really was, though. But in them kinda dives and whorehouses a man is who he says he is."

"And?"

"And so his movements weren't as secret as he figured. Another snitch reckons he may've spotted someone who looked like Rumsey-Carson gettin' off a fishin' boat on the pier down past Enoch Turner's brewery." Cobb paused for a suspenseful puff. "About sun-up on Tuesday. And luggin' a long 'fishin' pole.'"

"I must have that man as a witness."

Cobb said nothing, puffing contentedly on his pipe.

So, Marc thought, Sir Francis was right about Rumsey coming across the lake. And now they had him back in the province on the morning of the shooting and here at the Tinker's Dam a few hours after it. Had he been on his way back to Buffalo? Well, no one had seen him there yet. So there was a chance that he might simply be hiding in the bush until he could figure out how to get his wife and children away with him. But with Cobb's spies watching them closely, that would not be easy. Surely now it was just a question of being patient. There seemed, moreover, no quick way to link Rumsey with whoever had put him up to the deed.

"You want to hear the rest or not?" Cobb said.

"You've got more?"

"A bit, and then some."

"Well, then, get on with it!" Marc snapped in his officer's voice.

But Cobb had got up and was glaring over Marc's shoulder. "Harpie, you get away from Stony or I'll come over there and knock the last of yer brains all over yer face!" He sat back down. "Sorry, Major, where was I? Ah, yes. As I said before, I had supper in the Blue Ox before I come up here. My dinner companion, fer the price of a meal and a flagon, happened to mention that he might've seen Rumsey-Carson here at the Tinker's Dam about a week before the shootin'. In fact, I might've seen 'im myself if I'd've known what it was I supposed to be lookin' at."

"But you've already said that Rumsey-Carson was in the city a good deal of the time he was supposed to be off hunting."

"Ah, but it's who he was spotted with that's downright curious."

"The person behind the assassination?"

"Could be. Could be. Seems that Rumsey-Carson was seen drinkin' here with a stranger—no one'd ever seen him before anyways—and they was talkin' real low and secret-like, and when they finished, some money changed hands. Foldin' money. Big bills you gotta crinkle more'n once."

"This sounds like the evidence we need," Marc said excitedly.

"'Course, it coulda been just a gamblin' debt bein' settled . . ."

"What did this stranger look like?"

"Hard to say. Dressed like a sailor, I was told, with a wool navy cap of sorts pulled way down over his brow—it was ninety degrees in here, I bet—and a bushy black beard."

"But that could be any of a hundred men wandering around the docks." Marc could not hide his disappointment.

"Maybe so," Cobb said, "but he walked an' carried himself like a swell."

MARC'S MIND WAS ABUZZ WITH FACTS and theories and might-be's, as he and Cobb strolled over to the chestnut mare. Two naked children, purple with impetigo, were staring at the great beast with wide-eyed wonder.

"There is one other thing, Major," Cobb said, making a shooing motion with his hand that failed to dislodge the children. "Not a big thing, but you did ask me to look into the business of the letters in Mackenzie's paper."

Marc stood with one hand on the saddle. "But surely you—"

"That was the easiest part, Major. When I dropped into the Crooked Anchor to whet my whistle after my bumpy ride home today, a fella there was in his cups and braggin' that he earned himself a U.S. silver dollar every Saturday mornin', and all fer pickin' up and deliverin' a letter to the *Constitution*."

"Did he say who gave it to him?"

"He wasn't that drunk. And if I hadn't've still been in

my peddler's disguise, he wouldn't've spouted off like that at all."

"Tomorrow's Saturday."

"I believe it is, Major, though we country folk don't pay much heed to the days of the week."

"But that means that—"

"I can kick the old lady outta bed before sun-up and head down to Abner Clegg's place."

"You know this man?"

"He's a dock worker and, if rumour be fact, not always an honest one. I'll track him to your letter-writer like a he-hound on a she-hound's arse."

Marc nodded his approval while failing to hide his amazement. Then he went over to the children and put a three-penny piece in each of their grubby hands. Cobb looked on impassively.

"You've done yeoman's service, Constable. I shall let the governor and Chief Constable Sturges know of your . . . diligence. And, if you'll keep track of any monies you've paid out during the investigation, I'll see that you're reimbursed."

"We ain't allowed to take fees," Cobb said curtly.

"Would you like a ride home?"

"No thanks, Major. It's a pleasant evenin' fer a stroll. Besides, ya never know how many interestin' people you might bump into along the way."

Marc mounted his mare and waved to the children.

"Incidentally," Cobb added, "I managed to sell three of the wife's cookin' pots."

It wasn't until Marc was crossing Hospital Street that he had the unwelcome and disturbing thought that Cobb had gathered an enormous amount of pertinent information in only a day and a half, but not one jot of it had been, or could be, corroborated. Was it possible that he had made some of it up? All of it? And if so, why?

IT WAS ALMOST EIGHT THIRTY BY the time Marc had reached his boarding house, bathed, changed his shirt, and presented himself at the Dewart-Smythes'. The excitement and mental turmoil over Cobb's tidings had made it difficult for him to concentrate on what might lie before him. But it was hard to imagine that Uncle Sebastian's blundering interference could seriously alter the rapport he and Eliza had cautiously established over the past few weeks.

Although he was late, no mention was made of it. Supper was served in the parlour-dining room, and, although Uncle Sebastian kept a watchman's eye on his niece and her suitor throughout the several courses of the meal (the jellied venison was particularly tasty, as were the fresh strawberries), Eliza showed no sign of irritation or concern. They discussed the funeral service, the outlandish dress of this or that country aristocrat, the sadness in the gait of Moncreiff's daughters as they walked from St. James' Church to their crêpe-swathed carriage, and the awful moment when the hearse had heaved sideways in the mud of a rain-slick street and nearly capsized. Eliza remarked how closely related were comedy and tragedy, which brought a reproving glower from her uncle, who then turned the conversation into a monologue on the infinite opportunities for the expansion of the Dewart-Smythe enterprise. "New York, now there's a market, eh?" he sighed. Eliza gave him a curious stare.

When the meal was complete, Eliza pushed her chair away from the table and went over and sat down on the sofa. She patted the cushion beside her. "Come over and have a cigar," she said to Marc. And to her uncle, whose remonstrance never got as far as his lips, she said, "Did you not tell me earlier, Uncle, that you were going to check the new stock before retiring?"

Uncle Sebastian huffed a bit but replied, "I believe I did." And he struggled up out of his chair. Before he was fully upright, Eliza had taken two slim cheroots from the humidor on the table beside the sofa and popped one of them between her lips.

"Eliza! What would your blessed mother say if she were alive to see you behaving . . . behaving like a—"

"—gentleman?" Eliza said, laughing.

"Don't be impertinent," Uncle Sebastian said, but he hurried off so as not to bear witness to the actual lighting of the offending objects.

Eliza blew pretty smoke rings into the still evening air as

twilight descended outside the bay window. "He'll be gone for at least half an hour," she said, leaning against Marc.

For a long minute they were content to let the touch of their bodies speak for itself. Through the open window, the evening breeze perfumed the room with the scent of roses.

"You should know he's been asking me frank questions about what he calls my 'intentions,'" Marc murmured.

"I thought so," she said, but there was only amusement in her face. "He's been trying to find a way to warn me about the dangers of young men without actually spelling them out. I'm not sure he can spell them out, the old dear."

"He was quizzing me about my parentage and my prospects. I'm sure he sees me as a fortune-hunter pursuing your money and your virtue."

"Well, you can't have my money!" she laughed.

"I'm serious. In your uncle's view, both my bloodline and my potential inheritance are suspect."

"You mean he would refuse you my hand in marriage?" The dark eyes danced.

"Yes, I believe he would."

"And would you ask for it?"

"Well, I . . ."

"I'm teasing, silly. Let's not spoil a good cigar with that kind of talk."

Marc sighed with some relief. Eliza was unquestionably a remarkable young woman. But when they had set aside their cheroots and slid comfortably into one another's arms and when Eliza began nibbling at his ear, Marc simply held her close and rocked back and forth—his own lips open in pleasure but not in passion.

Just then there was a sudden commotion in the hall.

"Call out the watch! Fetch the constables!"

Marc and Eliza jumped to their feet, but it was doubtful Uncle Sebastian had noticed their embrace.

"They've been at it again!" he cried.

"Who?" Eliza said.

"The wine thieves, that's who!"

EIGHT

❧ ⚬ ❧

Marc had yet another restless night. This time his nightmare took him to the death of Crazy Dan. In one horrific
sequence the poor devil appeared with his head sundered
from his body and floating above the neck-stump, where it
proceeded to cry out a single word, over and over: innocent,
innocent! This time when Colin Willoughby clumped in,
waking him in the dead of night, Marc was relieved.

Only in the morning, when he found that Colin had
arisen early again and headed up to Government House, did
Marc realize that it had been days since he and Colin had
had a chance to sit down and talk as friends and it seemed

unlikely they would have an opportunity to do so soon. At least the reasons for their distance were all in Colin's best interest: his new duties at Government House and, it seemed probable, a newly awakened love life. Well, when all this trouble blew over or was resolved, he would take Colin out on a well-deserved pub-crawl.

Before going over to Government House to report Cobb's news to Sir Francis, Marc walked briskly through the Saturday sunshine to Eliza's place. There he found Constable Ewan Wilkie, who had taken over Cobb's patrol area and had returned to the scene of the break-in to examine it in daylight. He seemed pleased to see Marc, probably because he provided a neutral party to place between himself and Uncle Sebastian's unchecked contempt. The thieves, whoever they were, had been professional to a fault. A door to one of the storerooms had been jimmied with a minimum of noise or damage. They had chosen an entrance off a shadowy alley and, somehow knowing the merchant's routine, had moved in undetected just after closing time and selected only a few tuns of the most expensive wine. The fresh ruts of a cartwheel suggested they had boldly parked a wagon on the street and, as darkness fell, had rolled the tuns onto it, covering the booty with a sailcloth or such, and then trotting off at a sedate pace for their lair.

Wilkie, a stolid man who blinked a lot, blinked at Uncle Sebastian and summed matters up succinctly: "I reckon, sir, you'll have to get yerself a night watchman."

This advice did little to modify the good merchant's contempt. And Marc decided that it was an inopportune time to ask after Eliza's health. So he and Wilkie left together and walked down Yonge Street. Just before they got to King, Wilkie said, "By the bye, sir, Mr. Cobb wants to see you."

MARC MET COBB AT THE COCK and Bull on York Street about eleven o'clock. For the first time Cobb looked just slightly abashed. Something had gone wrong.

"You didn't find out who Farmer's Friend is, I take it," Marc said, unable to keep the critical tone out of his voice.

"'Fraid not, Major."

"Did this Clegg fellow show?"

"Yup, just like he said," Cobb replied. "I got to his house down on Front Street just as the sun was comin' up over the Don. Out he waltzes a few minutes later and starts headin' west into the city proper. I was able to keep myself well hidden behind bushes until he arrived at Market Square, where the farmers'd already begun settin' up their stalls and barrows. It was busy enough fer me to mix in with the crowd, seein' as I wasn't in uniform."

Marc refrained from pointing out that his beet-sized nose, spiked hair, and bottle shape might provide something less than perfect anonymity.

"Well, all of a suddenlike, he starts to pick up his pace, and I do the same. But there's three dozen stalls around us, and people start jostlin' me, and before I know it, Abner Clegg's vamoosed."

"You lost him?"

Cobb looked hurt. "I don't give up that easy, Major. I circled 'round the Market Square, checkin' all the streets in and out. No sign of him or his shadow. So I head up towards Mackenzie's shop on Church Street, duckin' in and out of alleys careful-like, and pretty soon I spot him comin' out of the printin' place."

"He had delivered the letter?"

Cobb ignored the impertinence of the interruption. "So I follow him down here to this dive. I send a message to you, and then wait outside fer him to leave. But all the time I'm thinkin', like I always do, and I reckoned he wasn't outta my sight after the market fer no more'n a quarter-hour, so he must've picked up the letter from one of the houses or shops within, say, three blocks of Mackenzie's."

Marc made no comment on this unhelpful bit of deduction. Finally, he said, "Why the secrecy? All this cloak-and-dagger manoeuvring? Surely most letter-writers deliver their material themselves or have a friend do it or pay a street urchin a penny to carry it—or, if all else fails, use the mails."

"Beats me, Major. But I don't suppose you're interested in hearin' the actual end to my story?"

Marc heaved a deep and resigned sigh. "I'm all ears."

"Clegg's got a mouth twice the size of his brain, lucky fer us. He starts braggin' in here—in front of my chief

snitch—about how he figures he was bein' trailed this
mornin', and just to make sure it don't happen again, he's
arranged with his client to pick the letter up next Friday
instead of Saturday."

"Well, that's better than nothing," Marc said as kindly as
he could.

"And I'll be there like a—"

"I'm sure you will," Marc said.

WHEN THE DUTY-CORPORAL USHERED HIM into the governor's office, Marc was mildly surprised to find Sir Francis
seated at his desk next to Willoughby, shoulder to shoulder
and obviously putting the finishing touches on one of the
speeches planned for the progress through the radical ridings of the London district. Sir Francis glanced up at Marc
with his usual welcoming smile and impeccable manners,
but Colin was so engrossed in his work that he seemed not
to have realized anyone had entered the room. Sir Francis
directed Marc to the chair usually reserved for Major Burns
(prostrate, apparently, with a rheumatic attack), and the
corporal slid another up behind his commander opposite
Marc.

"I've asked Lieutenant Willoughby to work into the
night if necessary to get the wording of my Brantford speech
exactly right. Tomorrow being the Sabbath, we have only
a few hours left to get everything perfected for our assault

on the western ridings. And as you know, Marc, my success there is critical to the outcome of the election."

"I believe so, sir."

Willoughby's constant scratching and blotting were an irritation, but Colin himself seemed oblivious to the conversation going on no more than ten feet from him. Not once did he look up to greet Marc, and Marc realized with a guilty start that he himself was both hurt and jealous. He wanted Colin to do well, but not well enough to supplant him. He felt that his protégé ought to show some gratitude or at least acknowledge that Marc had played a part in his rehabilitation.

"It is vitally important that we win seats in all regions of the province," Sir Francis was saying. "Our triumph must not be in numbers alone. I want troublemakers like Mackenzie and Peter Perry and Marshall Spring Bidwell driven from the field."

But not humiliated, Marc wanted to say.

"Young Hilliard is doing a splendid job in helping Willoughby with the security of those travelling with me—including my son. You have trained the ensign well, Marc."

"Thank you, sir."

"You'll also be pleased to know that I am taking along in the official party the receiver general, Mr. Maxwell, and Colonel Allan MacNab. I want not merely to show the flag but to flaunt it!"

Certainly the inclusion of MacNab would have that effect.

MacNab was a high Tory, who had been instrumental in having Mackenzie expelled from the Assembly for the third time, in 1832. He was also a symbol of loyalty to the Crown and of the rise to wealth and power of the native-born. He had fought bravely as a militiaman in the War of 1812 and had become on his own merit a successful lawyer, legislator, merchant, and land speculator. The sight of him sitting beside Sir Francis in full regalia would undoubtedly raise hackles and tempers.

"About the investigation, sir," Marc said diffidently.

"My word, yes. Of course, that is why you have come, isn't it?"

When it seemed clear he was to make his report in Willoughby's presence, Marc began. As was his custom, Sir Francis listened without interruption as Marc gave him chapter and verse of Cobb's prodigious discoveries at Danby's Crossing and elsewhere.

"Excellent work, Lieutenant. If all this information proves out, it appears we have identified the man who pulled the trigger and established that he was most probably a paid assassin. This corroborates the edited account I have already released to the public. And when we capture the blackguard, we'll know who is really behind the murder, and why."

"That is what I believe, too," Marc said. "But it begs a more serious question. Should we set up a general hue and cry with a warrant issued and all military and police personnel given a description of the man—"

"What does he look like, by the way?"

"Constable Cobb did not relay that detail to me, sir, but I am sure he could at a minute's notice."

Sir Francis looked thoughtful for a moment. "I sense you do not wish to raise the alarm immediately?"

"If Cobb is right, sir, the odds are that Philo Rumsey has not gone back to Buffalo but is camping out in the bush. Why he would do so, except that his wife and children are still in Danby's Crossing, we don't know. But if the alarm is raised everywhere, he may well panic and cross the border—forever."

"So we might be better off alerting our people along the border—at Fort George, Fort Erie, Fort Henry, and even Fort Malden—and leave it at that for now?"

"I believe that is the more prudent plan, in the circumstances. There is no likelihood of Rumsey assassinating anyone else, as he himself has no political motive."

Sir Francis watched Willoughby's quill-scratching for almost a minute. "All right, Lieutenant, we'll do just that—for a few days at least. But you do realize that our decision is based on our acceptance of the evidence gathered by one lowly police constable."

"I do, sir," Marc said, keeping his own doubts to himself.

"It does seem amazing that this Cobb—who, I was told by Mr. Sturges, comes from a farm family near Woodstock—could have found out so much so quickly."

"Well, he did fail in one respect, sir," Marc said. And he

gave the governor an account of Cobb's misadventure with
the letter courier.

"Well, that's unfortunate. I was hoping to come face to
face with Farmer's Friend before setting off for the west," Sir
Francis said, then added, "Don't you find it odd that Cobb
could tease out so much useful information up at Danby's
and in the taverns of the town, and then allow himself to
be led astray by some nondescript like Abner Clegg—in his
own patrol area?"

"What are you suggesting, sir?"

"Only that these constables were not selected from former militia members, who might have brought some experience to the occupation. They were patronage appointments
made by Toronto aldermen sympathetic to the Reform party
and headed by a Reform mayor."

"You think Cobb may have allowed his political views to
influence his duty in this particular case? Because he owes
his appointment to Mackenzie?"

"I am suggesting that it is a possibility."

"In this business of the letters, you mean?"

Sir Francis sighed. "I hope to God it's in this instance
only."

"I'll do the job myself, then," Marc said quickly, "next
Friday morning. I'll have the letter-writer's name for you by
Friday noon."

"And with any luck you'll have Rumsey in irons," Sir
Francis said warmly. Suddenly he clapped a hand on Marc's

shoulder and began leading him towards the door. "Now I have a much more pleasant assignment for you. The coachman I usually employ to drive my ward about town—and to keep a close watch on her—is ill today, and Angeline has her heart set on a shopping trip. I'll have one of my grooms drive the team, but I would feel more at ease if you were to escort her. It will take less than an hour of your time."

"I would be happy to do so," Marc said, suppressing his chagrin as best he could.

At the door Marc turned around just far enough to catch Willoughby's eye. Colin was smiling.

ANGELINE HARTLEY, THE GOVERNOR'S WARD, WAS petalled entirely in pink, from her floral hat to her frilled and be-ribboned frock to her dainty boots and the bloom of her parasol. Even her face shone pink with the first blush of womanhood—a state she wished, devoutly and often, to enter permanently. She was all of seventeen, and nothing set her heart aflutter as much as a young man in uniform. The image of Lieutenant Edwards—tunicked and tall and handsome—was not so breathtaking, however, as to strike her dumb. Quite the opposite. She babbled non-stop in Marc's ear all the way down fashionable King Street. About what Marc was not able to decipher exactly, but, then, it was the passion and intensity of her girl-chatter that mattered most. When they passed Bay Street, Angeline stopped talking, sat upright (she had been teetering coquettishly towards her escort's shoulder from time to time), arched her parasol jauntily, and with a gloved hand waved to the throng of onlookers she imagined must be watching in undisguised envy.

"Do stop here, Coachman!" Angeline called, and the young groom drew the open carriage to a halt. "This is one of the shops where I purchase my dresses and gowns," she said to Marc, who had stepped down and offered her his hand. She held it as long as she dared, then moved across the boardwalk to Miss Adeline's.

"I'll wait for you here," Marc said, touching the brim of his shako cap.

"I shan't be long, Lieutenant," Angeline burbled, then twirled prettily and entered the shop.

A minute or so later, the shop door opened, but it was not Angeline who emerged. It was Prudence Maxwell. And if Angeline was a spring flower, Prudence was a late-summer rose or gladiola. She had packed the overblown bloom of her flesh into a low-cut bodice and blinding-yellow skirt. All about her hung an air of over-lush ripeness. When she spotted Marc, she stopped abruptly and aimed a thick-lipped smile in his direction.

"Why, Lieutenant, how nice to see you once again."

"Madam," Marc said, bowing briefly.

"My, what onerous duties Sir Francis puts upon you!" she laughed. "How are your ears?"

Marc acknowledged the reference to Angeline with a slight smile. "They have survived, ma'am—so far."

"Well, I do hope they last until next Saturday."

Marc looked puzzled.

"Good gracious, doesn't that old fuddy-duddy up at Government House tell you anything? The whole town is agog with the news, Lieutenant. We are holding a gala at Somerset House next Saturday evening—to welcome Sir Fuddy-Duddy home from the wars and celebrate the coming triumph in the elections. Every officer at the rank of ensign and above has been invited. Your invitation must be on your desk by now."

"That is pleasant news indeed, and I must apologize for not noticing the invitation. But as you can see, I've been kept occupied away from my office."

"Well, so long as you come," she said, feigning a pout. "As hostess I have taken the liberty of placing your name first on my dance card. I trust you do not mind?"

"I would be honoured to have the first dance with the receiver general's wife."

"I'll try to make it a waltz," she said with a leer. "It's so much more intimate than a galop or a reel, don't you think?"

"I'm sure you dance well, whatever the form."

She stared at him as if deciding how she should take this remark, then smiled and said in a more serious tone, "Have you discovered the name of my daughter's secret lover yet?"

"I have one or two suspicions, ma'am, but no confirmation."

"Could you throw me a hint? From the blush on Chastity's cheek these days, I feel it may come too late."

Marc replied quickly, almost priggishly, "I could not, madam, compromise the reputation of any of the good men under—"

Prudence frowned and then stepped onto the road, coming up close to Marc beside the carriage. "Jesus, fella," she hissed, "you don't need to spread that mannerly crap all over me. We ain't in Mayfair." A gust of perfume made Marc gasp, as she stretched up and kissed him on the chin, permitting him a frontal glimpse of her barely harnessed breasts.

"That's for being a naughty boy," she laughed, before turning towards her own carriage, which had just pulled up.

Marc watched her leave, annoyed, because, in spite of himself, he had been momentarily aroused.

Angeline came out of the dress shop, unaware of what had just taken place, though the teenaged groom was still gawking. Marc helped her aboard, and they moved off up the busy street. Angeline's chatter about ribbons and furbelows and the hat she was planning to buy today was now pleasantly diverting. So much so that, as they began to slow down in front of the new millinery shop, Marc did not see or hear the pounding of hooves or the clatter of wooden wheels bouncing wildly until it was almost too late. The rear portion of the runaway vehicle skidded into the governor's carriage and knocked it upwards and over with a jarring collision, pulling its horses to their knees. Marc just had time to grasp Angeline and follow the arc of the carriage as it careened and slammed onto the boardwalk with a murderous thump amid the squeal of terrified animals. He hurled himself sideways and tumbled onto the road, landing in a pool of soft dirt, and breaking Angeline's fall with his own body. Dazed but thinking hard, he peered down the street at the disappearing wagon and saw its driver—in overalls and a straw hat—hauling futilely on the reins and crying havoc. Then surprisingly, the "runaway" team veered neatly to the left down Bay Street, still racing but not without guidance. At least it seemed so to Marc as his head swam and his vision suddenly blurred. As he rolled over to check on Angeline, he saw Ensign Hilliard galloping across King Street towards them. Where had he come from? Had Hilliard been following him? Or following Angeline?

At this point, as a curious and concerned throng began to close in around them, Angeline tried to raise herself out of the only mud puddle on the street, sighed loudly, and sank back in a faint. Marc lunged in time to catch her firmly in his arms, at which her thick lashes opened to reveal pale-blue eyes with just the hint of a twinkle in them.

"Are you all right?" Hilliard panted as he knelt down beside them.

"No bones broken, Ensign. But don't hang about here, get after that wagon!"

Hilliard jumped to the task and hurried away. Marc struggled to his feet with Angeline still limp in his arms. Several sturdy men had freed the horses and righted the carriage. Miraculously, it, too, was in one piece.

"Someone please fetch the lady a glass of water," Marc said just as Angeline swooned again and he had to drop to one knee to catch her. This time she pulled his face down towards her and kissed him lightly on the cheek. The on-lookers applauded.

"Would the lady like to come inside our shop and rest?" said a familiar voice. With Angeline still wrapped around him, Marc looked up to see who the proprietor of the millinery shop might be. There, standing over him with an expression of intense curiosity and amused concern, was the face that had haunted him night and day for the three long months of winter.

It was Beth Smallman.

"Fallen in love again?" she enquired.

NINE

❯❯ · ❮❮

Beth and an older woman—white-haired, sweet-faced—helped Angeline into the millinery shop. At the sight of her mud-splattered skirt, the girl began to weep. Then her whole body trembled, and she started to sob in earnest. The shop door closed resolutely, and the curious had to be content with watching Marc stagger to his feet, more dazed by the mysterious reappearance of Beth Smallman than by the accident.

"Where's the driver?" Marc said, suddenly remembering the groom, who had been sitting on the bench at the front of the barouche.

"Here, sir," the young man said, brushing off his livery. His face was pasty white. "I'm so sorry—"

"It was not you who struck the carriage," Marc said reassuringly.

"But I saw it coming, sir, and my tongue went stiff as a plank. All I could do was jump and save myself."

"And I'm happy that you did, son. There's no need to wring your hands over it. I saw the runaway myself and just had time to latch on to Miss Hartley."

"But the wagon's ruined!" the lad despaired.

"Not entirely," Marc said. Several burly men had arrived on the scene and were sorting out the tangle of harness and gear, while another stroked the noses of the frightened horses. Marc gave the collapsible leather roof a tug. "This rig won't be keeping off any rain for a while, but I think the creature itself will live long enough to get us home."

Someone came out of the dry-goods store with a pitcher of water and two glasses.

Controlling his own shakes as best he could, Marc was about to leave the groom sitting on the boardwalk with a drink in hand and a mothering woman at either shoulder when he saw Ensign Hilliard come trotting up King Street towards him. An even bigger crowd had now formed, and Hilliard had to force his mount through to Marc.

"Were you able to catch him up?" Marc asked.

"I caught up to the wagon, sir. And the horses, poor devils."

"But no driver?"

"Someone saw him headed towards the docks, but I couldn't find him. Nobody knew who he was."

"That's unfortunate," Marc said, and the same thought lay unspoken between him and Hilliard: Was the "accident" deliberate? And if so, who was the target? "Most likely he saw my uniform and realized he had struck an officer, and then panicked and fled."

Hilliard nodded but looked doubtful.

"But surely he'll sneak back for his horses and vehicle," Marc suggested.

"Ensign Parker was with me when we saw the collision, sir. We were on an errand for the governor. I'll have Parker stand watch on the wagon until one of the city constables can take over. We'll find the culprit, don't worry."

"Good idea, Ensign. But don't you leave just yet." With that Marc parted the crowd and entered the sanctuary of the millinery shop.

Inside, the older woman was brushing as much mud off Angeline's skirt as she could while making soothing maternal noises. Beth was holding Angeline's gloveless right wrist gently and rubbing it with some sharp-smelling unguent. The girl's sobs had subsided, and she smiled adoringly at Marc through a scrim of grateful tears.

"She's just shaken up," Beth said. "And bruised her wrist a little."

"I'm fine, really," Angeline said, her eyes still fixed on Marc.

"Are you well enough to travel back to Government House?"

Angeline nodded angelically.

Marc then led her carefully back out onto the street, where few of the spectators seemed to have relinquished their place. Marc called Hilliard over.

"The carriage appears to be drivable," Marc said. "Walk the horses and Miss Hartley back to Government House, inform Sir Francis that there's been an accident, and have Dr. Withers examine her."

"Yes, sir," Hilliard snapped, and leapt to Angeline's side to assist her up into the jittery carriage.

If Hilliard was infatuated with the governor's ward, Marc thought, it was just as well he was heading off for Brantford and farther fields on Monday morning. For it was an infatuation that would do his career little good.

"Are you not coming with us?" Angeline asked.

"No, Miss. The groom will sit with you if you feel faint."

The groom was most pleased to accept this responsibility.

"Where are you going, then?" Angeline said with a little pout that reassured Marc the girl was recovering rapidly.

"I'm going back into the shop to see a woman about a hat," Marc said.

MARC SAT ACROSS FROM BATHSHEBA MCCRAE Smallman in a sparsely furnished room that served as an office and temporary retreat at the rear of the shop—much as he had five months earlier sat in the simple sunshine of her farm kitchen in Crawford's Corners. Now, as then, the sun poured lavishly through a south window and backlit the slim figure and copper hair of the woman he had been drawn to from the instant he saw her and heard her speak, like Cordelia, in a voice ever soft and low. Now, as then, she poured him a cup of tea and served him a scone with homemade huckleberry jam—as if long months of separation and silence had not intervened.

Marc could think of absolutely nothing to say other than to mumble a brief and garbled account of how he and Angeline happened to arrive entwined and dishevelled on her doorstep. She listened politely and observed him with the gentle skepticism that he so admired and out of which flowed her humour and her candour.

When he paused sufficiently, she said almost solemnly, "I owe you an explanation, Marc."

"Not at all," Marc said bravely. "You made me no promises."

"I didn't open your letters," she said.

"Erastus wrote me back. He said he thought you just needed time." Erastus Hatch was her neighbour, who had helped Marc during his first investigation into the mysterious death of Beth's father-in-law, Joshua Smallman.

"That is so. I'd lost a husband and then a man who was a father to me. I needed grieving time. But that's not the real reason I didn't open your letters." She looked across at him until he raised his eyes and held on to her steady gaze. "I was afraid to."

"But after a while everybody stopped writing," Marc said with just a touch of self-pity.

"I am sorry for that: I asked them not to write."

"But why?"

"Because I'd made arrangements to come here and start a new life. I didn't want to complicate yours."

"You've been here since March?" Marc was astonished.

Beth laughed. "Only since April, actually. Oh, I knew we would meet eventually. But you must believe me when I say I have not been deliberately secreting myself away from you."

"Oh, I do."

"You and I do not exactly move in the same circles here in Toronto."

"But I've ridden right past this place a hundred times since April, and I've overheard women discussing the new bonnet shop more than once!"

"But you haven't had occasion to purchase one," she said in her familiar half-teasing way.

"Or, until today, to accompany a lady to do so."

"You didn't notice, then, that this shop was next door to my father-in-law's dry-goods store?"

"My God, so it is!" Marc was delighted that his surprise once again brought a smile to her face. Joshua Smallman had operated a dry-goods establishment on King Street for many years. Since his own arrival here thirteen months ago, Marc had been in the store several times and had met the proprietor. Only now, though, did he remember that Beth—after protracted legal proceedings—had inherited his estate, including the dry-goods store adjacent.

"This shop is part of the same building that Father owned," Beth said, as if reading Marc's thoughts. "We leased out the dry-goods section, set up for ourselves in the smaller space, and moved into the apartment above us."

"But you must have seen me," Marc said.

"Oh, yes, I did. Many times. Mostly from the shop window as you rode or marched on by."

"Yet you did not—"

Beth's reply was barely a whisper: "I wanted to. More than once."

"My God, why didn't you? You must have known how I felt—feel—about you."

Beth looked down as if contemplating what she ought to say next, or how. Neither had touched their tea. "That has never been a problem, though I do hear you've been paying court to a beautiful and intelligent young heiress."

"But no one knows about—"

"I'm afraid everybody does," Beth said with a sad smile. "All the great ladies of the town pass through our doors here. And they're mighty fond of their gossip."

"I see. Well, then, what they don't know is that Eliza

and I are just good friends. In fact, I like her for many of the same reasons I admire you." Marc realized only as he spoke these last words that they were undeniably true. The principal difference seemed to be that Eliza elicited as much brotherly affection and respect as passion, while Beth evoked affection, respect, and something else he could not put into words.

Beth blushed, her pale Irish skin showing every shade of embarrassment prompted by Marc's declaration. Deliberately she picked up her cup and sipped at the cold tea. When she spoke again, her voice was eerily calm: "I also owe you a full explanation of why and how I got here."

"Yes, I've been wondering what happened to your brother and to the farm," Marc said, glad for the moment that the conversation had moved away from its more dangerous direction.

"I'm sure Erastus wrote you that he married Mary Huggan, and that Winnifred got married to Thomas Goodall."

"A double wedding, yes," he smiled.

Mary had been Hatch's housemaid. Winnifred, his daughter, had taken a fancy to Goodall, their hired man. After his experiences in their township in January, Marc considered them all to be his friends.

"Well, the Hatch mill and farm was bound to be a bit crowded with both couples living there," Beth continued. "And so when my aunt Catherine, my father's sister, wrote me from Boston that she had a small inheritance, no living relative nearby, and was looking to start up a ladies' business of some kind, I made the biggest decision of my life. I suggested we set up a millinery shop here in Toronto, in father's building, and run it together. She jumped at the chance. I leased the farm to Winnifred and her new husband—on condition that they let Aaron stay on and help out, like he has since we first moved there. They said yes."

Aaron was Beth's teenage brother, slow of speech and slightly crippled.

"Aaron's very happy. I've been back to see him. And Mary's expecting her baby in September."

At this point Aunt Catherine Roberts poked a round, friendly face through the curtain and said, "Sorry to interrupt, Beth, but Mrs. Boulton wants to know when the black-widow bonnets are due in from New York."

"Tell her sometime late next month," Beth said. "Better still, pick an exact date and make sure to get her order in writing."

Aunt Catherine grinned, and slipped back into the shop.

"You've become quite the businesswoman," Marc said.

"And you've become quite the speech writer for a Tory-tinted Whig governor," Beth retorted with unexpected bluntness.

A deep silence hung between them. What had to be said sooner or later had just been uttered. There was no taking it back.

Finally Marc said quietly, "Will you grant me an opportunity to try and explain?"

Beth said nothing. Her face was turned to one side—her expression implacable.

"Please. You owe me at least that. I've been to hell and back since we parted in January."

"All right," she said stiffly. "You talk, I'll listen." And she remained as she was, half-turned away from him, like a stern priest in a confessional.

"I have not relaxed my determination to see the grievances addressed that you and your neighbours showed me to be real and reversible. You don't know just how far I've come in changing my views because you have only the slightest knowledge of how I was brought up to think and behave. My adoptive father was a landowner, and a good Tory. I absorbed his values and attitudes. My two years at the Inns of Court confirmed and deepened these views, as did my training at Sandhurst. Since my arrival here to serve Sir John Colborne a year ago last May, I have been surrounded by, and taken orders from, the pillars of this community, every one of them a Tory of some stripe or other. But after meeting you and seeing for myself what you suffered as a result of governmental negligence and obtuseness, I came to accept the legitimacy of your complaints. What I told you then about my change of heart was sincere, and is still so."

Marc waited for a response. But none came. The bell

over the shop door jangled. Low voices in the next room discussed embroidery and veils.

"Why, then, you might ask, am I in the service of a governor bent on defeating the Reformers at the polls? First of all, I am a soldier, and as such I was commanded, against my will and better judgment, to become Sir Francis Head's chief aide-de-camp. It took some time, but I slowly became convinced that his strategy of appealing to the moderate majority and of dampening down the extreme rhetoric on both sides was right. And this will be just the first step of a multi-step plan to correct, in good time, all the legitimate complaints."

Beth turned her face to Marc and squeezed out a grim smile. "That sounds like one of the speeches he's been giving on the hustings."

"But don't you see that his plan is at least worth a try? What has been gained since the Reformers took over the Assembly in '34? Even with a Whig governor and a Whig colonial secretary, not one grievance has yet been addressed."

"And you trust this Whig gentleman, this commissioner of the poor laws and glorified mine manager, to right all the wrongs?" The contempt in her voice shocked Marc.

"Yes, I do. He is under orders from Lord Glenelg to do so, and I believe in his sincerity."

"You've seen such orders?"

Marc stiffened. He had gone a lot further than he had intended. That he was privy to some of the exchanges between London and Toronto was a grave responsibility. His probity in that regard must be absolute: he had sworn a solemn oath.

"Well, the governor's letters to the *Patriot* are not state secrets," Beth said. "Did you have a hand in writing the one in today's edition?"

"No, I did not," Marc said sharply. The conversation was not going the way he had hoped.

"Are you helping him with the speeches for Woodstock and London?"

"As a matter of fact, no. Lieutenant Willoughby is. I've been assigned to investigate Councillor Moncreiff's assassination. It seems the governor was impressed with my work in Cobourg and Crawford's Corners in January."

Beth flushed and said softly, "He should be. I'll never forget what you did for me, or how you did it."

"Then, please, let us at least be friends. Let me come and see you."

"No, not for a while. At least, not till the election is over."

"My God, Beth, what in hell does politics have to do with love?"

Beth sighed. "Politics has to do with everything."

Marc stared past her out the window, struggling to control his anger.

"You say you're investigating the murder of Mr. Moncreiff. That is a good and proper thing to do. He was a nice man. He came in here with Mrs. Moncreiff to help her pick out an Easter hat. I liked them both. Most of our customers are Tories or sympathizers, and I do not hate them. In fact, I've come to like and respect many of them. But when I read the governor's letter this morning, I knew why I could never be married to one of them."

"What on earth are you talking about?"

"The governor suggests in so many fancy words that Mr. Moncreiff was shot by a hired killer from the States, in the pay of a disloyal citizen or citizens, and he doesn't have to spell out which party they cleave to, does he? But he goes even further than that! He hints darkly that foreign influences are at work, and this isn't likely to be the last violent act we'll see. You know the rest of the argument."

The rejoinder Marc had planned died on his lips. Was Sir Francis actually using the councillor's murder so blatantly for political purposes? The foreign threat and necessity of unswerving loyalty to the Crown in times of crisis, etc.? Was this the theme the governor and Colin had been weaving into the speech Marc had seen them concocting?

"I had nothing to do with such tactics," he said lamely. "I do not approve of stirring up irrational fears. I thought that's precisely what we were attempting to prevent."

"Then have a look at this poster some concerned citizen left on my doorstep this morning." She handed Marc a rectangle of stiff paper. He read what was printed there.

Farmers!

BEWARE!

The enemies of the King and the People,

of the constitution, and Sir Francis Head

ARE DAY AND NIGHT, SPREADING LIES.

They say Sir Francis Head is recalled—

Sir Francis Head is not recalled,

but is supported by the King and his ministers.

They say tithes are to be claimed in Upper Canada—

Tithes are NOT to be claimed in Upper Canada

FARMERS!

Believe not a word these Agitators say

but think for yourselves

and **SUPPORT SIR FRANCIS HEAD**,

the friend of Constitutional Reform.

"This is the very type of rhetoric the governor is trying to avoid," Marc said with not nearly the conviction he intended to convey. "He would not have approved this. Nor would I."

Beth looked at him sadly, regretfully. "Then shouldn't you do something about it?"

Marc got up. "I am a soldier, not a politician. I must do my duty."

"As I must do mine—to honour the memory of my husband and his father, who both died because of politics."

At the curtains, Marc said, "Do we not have a duty to love?"

"Yes," she said. "That is what keeps us human."

As they parted once again—with the gulf between them apparently wider—Marc was certain only that he loved her.

WHEN MARC ARRIVED AT GOVERNMENT HOUSE—bruised, sore, crestfallen—he found Sir Francis agitated and incoherent. He was pacing up and down the lofty entrance hall, with Willoughby and Hilliard following warily and flinging words after him that were meant to mollify but were having the opposite effect. Had something gone wrong with plans for the journey on Monday? Or worse? Major Burns was looking on stolidly from a nearby doorway, either indifferent or too ill to intervene. It was the sight of Marc that brought Sir Francis to such an abrupt halt that Hilliard and Willoughby tottered right past him before stopping themselves.

"Ah, it's you, Lieutenant—at last."

"I came as quickly as I could—"

"You're not hurt, I hope?" Sir Francis said, halfway between threat and concern.

"Not really, sir. Just a bruise or two."

"Well, Angeline tells me you saved her life." The governor's panic at seeing his ward dishevelled, scraped, and weeping still showed in his face, as if he could not yet bring himself to believe she had not been seriously injured.

"Miss Hartley is recovering?"

"Yes, she seems to be, but I can't tell whether she's crying over her ruined dress or a bruised arm. She just repeats your name over and over."

"Any sign of the blackguard?" Hilliard asked Marc.

"I'll have the bugger horsewhipped and clapped in irons!" Sir Francis cried with such vigour that his eyes bulged. Marc realized with a sinking feeling that Hilliard had not been discreet in his account of the incident.

"It may well have been an unfortunate accident, sir," Marc said. "A runaway wagon is not that uncommon, especially during the Saturday market."

"I have a difficult time believing that," Sir Francis said through clenched teeth, "after what I've been told by Hilliard and my ward and even the groom."

"Ensign Parker has been posted to watch the horses in the event the driver returns for them. The constables will take things from there."

"I want the man brought here! Is that understood, Lieutenant Edwards?"

"I'm sure that Cobb and Wilkie will get to the truth of the matter, sir."

Sir Francis uttered a purging sigh. His anger slowly drained away. He put a hand on Marc's shoulder. "You must forgive me, young man. I am overwrought. I've had a terrible shock, especially after what happened up at Danby's. You deserve nothing but my gratitude and my deepest respect. I should be more concerned for your hurts than for my own wounded pride."

"It's been a trying week, sir—for us all," Marc said, wondering what the governor would say if he were to learn the nature of the hurt now burning its way through his aide-de-camp.

Willoughby and Hilliard looked as if they wanted to say something helpful but had chosen discretion over valour.

Sir Francis began pacing again. Everyone else stood where they were and watched anxiously. "I don't give a damn for my own safety," he said, picking up the shreds of his earlier anger. "I intend to walk tall into the lion's den next week. I shall challenge any citizen to strike down the royal surrogate, if he dare. But to prey upon innocents like poor Moncreiff and now my ward, a mere chit of a girl, for whom I am solely responsible, and who has been most abominably abused. I will not have it, do you hear?"

Everyone in the far recesses of the building could hear.

"Perhaps I could find a couple of reliable corporals from the garrison to watch Miss Hartley while you are away," Marc said, then bit his tongue as he saw Willoughby glowering at him: it was Colin who was now in charge of such matters.

"My God, Lieutenant, you're right. I will be gone for four days, and Angeline will be here alone and unprotected." The implications of this remark had just begun to sink in, for Sir Francis stopped in mid-step and glared at the nearest Athenian pilaster as if he would, like Samson, bring it and the house crashing down.

Willoughby decided it was prudent to put his oar in. "Perhaps you could suggest, sir, that the young lady keep indoors for the duration. After all, it's only until next Thursday."

Sir Francis shifted his glare from the pilaster to Willoughby. "That, sir, is a preposterous suggestion!"

Willoughby's head snapped back as if struck. But Marc was pleased to see that he held his ground. "But you wouldn't willingly put her in danger?"

"I have absolutely no intention of putting my ward's safety in jeopardy. But she has expressly conveyed to me her desire to shop for a gown suitable for the gala at Somerset House next Saturday, and on Tuesdays she always takes the carriage to Streetsville to visit a second cousin of hers of whom she is extremely fond, and on Wednesdays she goes riding in the College Park."

"But surely, sir, these are extraordinary circumstances," Willoughby tried again.

"Miss Hartley, provided she is fully recovered by Monday, will continue with her habitual routine. Is that clear to everyone?" The governor's voice had the ring of royal prerogative in it. No one spoke. "Moreover, she shall be fully protected and armoured against the slightest interruption or irritation. Willoughby, you will choose two reliable men from the barracks to act as bodyguards. You yourself will accompany Miss Hartley wherever she wishes to go, and I shall hold you personally responsible for her well-being as well as her safety."

Willoughby began to tremble, from anger or chagrin, it

was hard to tell, and Marc felt obliged to say, "I would be happy to take on those duties, sir. Lieutenant Willoughby will be needed at your side in Woodstock and London."

"That is a magnanimous gesture, sir, and I know you would carry out those duties conscientiously, as you demonstrated this afternoon," Sir Francis said evenly, but his rage—stoked no doubt by guilt and anxiety over Angeline's mishap on King Street and, probably, by Willoughby's mistimed temerity—was not far below the surface. "But Lieutenant Willoughby has already done me yeoman's service this week: the speeches are written. You, on the other hand, have a murderer to catch. Any pressing paperwork here next week can be handled by Major Burns, whom you and Willoughby will assist whenever you can."

"But what about your own safety, sir?" Willoughby said desperately.

"Hilliard will take over the unit. All the basic arrangements have already been made, thanks to you." Sir Francis looked long and hard at Willoughby, who was in a way like Angeline: a ward and a trust, as well as the prodigal son of a friend. He said, not unkindly, "Colin, I am giving you a very important assignment. You have acquitted yourself with distinction these past few days. I have already written to your father to inform him of your progress and of the potential I see in you. But you are a soldier and an officer: you took an oath to serve and obey your monarch and those who speak in his name—however you may personally feel about the commands given you. What I am telling you by offering you this assignment is that I have enough faith in you to put Miss Hartley's well-being in your hands."

And with that the governor wheeled and strode towards his apartments.

Willoughby stood stock-still, clenching and unclenching his fists, a wild, unfocused anger in his eyes. Four days to be spent as chaperone and nursemaid to an overindulged, babbling, flighty, whim-driven ingenue would have unsettled the most dedicated officer. For Willoughby—who had become, however temporarily, the day-to-day aide-de-camp of a lieutenant-governor—it was a crushing blow.

Hilliard made consoling noises, but Willoughby swore at him or the world in general, brushed rudely past Marc, and stormed out.

Major Burns, impassive in his office doorway, said to Marc, "I think you'd better go after him. He looks capable of anything."

Including self-destruction, Marc thought, and headed for the door.

MARC SPENT THE NEXT TWO HOURS in a fruitless search of every public house and drinking den within a five-block area of Government House. Not only did he not find Colin, he found no one who had seen him. At least his anxiety over Colin was keeping at bay the dark thoughts about this afternoon's encounter with Beth. It had promised so much, had seemed so serendipitous—fated even—that the disastrous outcome was all the more unbearable. It seemed self-evident now that he must give her up. That decision was simple compared with the impossible one: to cease loving her. So he was not surprised to find himself on Eliza's flower-bedecked doorstep—red-eyed, haggard, and seeking any sort of solace. His urgent need for comfort made him blissfully blind to the inappropriateness of wringing pity out of another woman who possibly entertained the notion that he was in love with her.

Eliza took one look and ushered him quickly past a startled butler and her uncle's office into the sanctum of her private sitting room. He slumped onto the sofa there and let Eliza pull his boots off and undo the buttons of his jacket. Seconds later a brandy snifter appeared in his right hand, and he drank.

"Did you get hit by a horse?" she said lightly, but there was deep concern in her eyes. She stroked his brow, and he felt both guilt and ease at the spontaneity of the gesture.

"By two horses and a wagon," he murmured, and realized then that this was the only part of a devastating day he could talk about, the only part of it that he had a right to reveal to this handsome, generous, unjudging woman with the sloe eyes and free-falling, lustrous hair.

"Do you want to discuss it?" she said gently. "Or shall we carry on as we usually do?"

"Let's carry on," he said.

And so they talked about wines and the hazards of shipping and the bad roads that ruptured casks, and about a dozen other idle, tender diversions—always giving a wide berth to the confusions he couldn't talk about and she knew to be more than accidental.

Later on when she kissed him, he kissed her back. And felt like a traitor, though who it was he was betraying most, he could not determine.

IT MUST HAVE BEEN MIDNIGHT WHEN Marc slipped out of Uncle Sebastian's house like a cat burglar and walked home under a star-filled sky. Once there, he eased open the door of Colin's room just enough to note that the bed was undisturbed. He tiptoed back to the veranda and sat down on the bottom step to wait.

He was just dozing off, his chin in his hands, when he heard footsteps. It was Colin, walking deliberately. He was not drunk, Marc was relieved to see as he stood up to greet him. Colin stopped, squinted incredulously at the shadowy figure on the porch, and then came up to Marc until they were face to face—no more than a yard apart.

In the distorting light of the moon Marc could see a sudden rage take hold of Colin's features, then his body, and finally his fists. "Traitor!" he hissed and swung wildly at Marc's head. Marc ducked away easily and watched, with some bewilderment, as his friend wobbled noisily into the hall.

Well, he was alive and almost sober—that was something, Marc thought; then he wondered what in heaven could possibly happen next to make his own life more miserable.

TEN

➤ ◄

At daybreak on Monday morning Sir Francis Bond Head's vice-regal cavalcade trotted out of Toronto onto Dundas Road, with flags flying. For four days the capital would be without its steward, but the countryside west of it would be graced by his presence and treated to the power and authority of his rhetoric. The future of a British colony lay in his hands and in his capacity to persuade. Having a convenient scapegoat—a disaffected Yankee mercenary, for example—was an unexpected boon and too tempting to be resisted. Sir Francis would hammer that plank into every platform on his royal route. And lest the loyal citizens of

Toronto, in his absence, forget the message he had delivered to them daily from the seat of Government House, he left these words on the front page of the *Gazette*:

> *I consider that in a British colony, British interests should be paramount, and that in these provinces we should foster them by every means in our power, by infusing into the country Britain's redundant population, and by giving nothing to aliens but their bare rights.*

MARC SPENT THE MORNING WITH MAJOR Burns, working on backlogged correspondence. About ten o'clock he heard Colin come out of his office (they had not spoken about the incident on Saturday night) and go back towards the living quarters. If Colin was still angry, he was keeping it to himself. But a morning spent on a shopping expedition with Angeline Hartley would soon put any restraint to the test. A few minutes later, the governor's second-best carriage was heard rattling along the east driveway towards Simcoe Street.

About eleven, Marc got a note from Cobb to meet him at the Crooked Anchor. He left Major Burns asleep on his desk and walked quickly towards Bay Street. He was eager to hear any news about Rumsey. Sunday had been a long and tedious day for Marc. The governor was a strict observer of the Sabbath and expected others to emulate his public piety. After church, Marc tried to forget his personal troubles for a while by riding up to the mess at the garrison. Throughout the winter months he had eaten his evening meal in the officers' quarters there at least three times a week—both as a pleasant diversion and as a way of maintaining contact with the regular army. But lately his increasingly onerous duties as aide-de-camp had made these visits less and less common. Last night he had astonished his peers at mess by getting thoroughly drunk and singing bawdy songs he couldn't remember having memorized. But the camaraderie and the drink had worn off by morning, leaving Marc lower in spirits than ever. What he needed most was action—of any kind. A break in the investigation would be just fine.

Cobb was nursing an ale and looking as if he, too, had found Sunday interminable.

"Anything on Rumsey yet?" Marc asked, skipping the preliminaries.

"You don't expect him to pop up in front of us and beg for the leg irons, do you?" Cobb muttered.

Marc waited while Cobb scratched at his wart. His uniform had regained its customary stains. His sweat-soaked helmet and wooden truncheon lay on the table. "His wife hasn't budged from the cabin except to trot off to Danby's to empty the slop pots. The older kids're spendin' a lot of time at Kimble's harness shop. The Kimbles seem to've taken to the Rumsey brood. My spies are suggestin' the Kimbles are just what they seem to be: nice honest folk who vote Reform, as they ought to." Cobb peeked up from his ale to see the effect of this provocation.

"Perhaps Rumsey is content to let the Kimbles take care

of his children," Marc said. "He doesn't sound like much of a father. Unfortunately that means he might well forsake them and join his relations in Buffalo."

"Or he's got another reason to hang about."

"Another assassination?"

"Could be. Or could be he's into some kinda fuss with the people payin' him."

"There are just too damn many 'could-be's' in this case," Marc snapped.

"Downed one too many at the mess last night, did ya, Major?" Cobb asked.

Marc ignored the jibe (while quietly marvelling at Cobb's seeming omniscience in matters local), and said, "Give me something positive, Constable, something definite. God knows, I need it."

"Well, then, I can tell ya fer certain that the little collision on King Street was most definitely an accident."

"And how do you know that?" Marc said abruptly, immediately regretting the doubt in his voice—which Cobb did not miss.

Cobb polished off his ale, then said evenly, "Wilkie found the driver of the cart. Wilkie's just a country bumpkin like myself, but he does know a horse's arse when he sees one, and in fact he recognized both of the horses. Turns out they belong to a butcher on John Street. So Wilkie had them taken home, where said butcher was most startled to see them and even more startled not to see his driver—one

Alfie Foote by name. Seems that Alfie'd lost his regular job as a joiner and talked the butcher into takin' him on as a teamster. Which the kind-hearted butcher did. Only Alfie neglected to tell said butcher that he'd never driven a harnessed team before. He only got a block or so towards the market when the horses reckoned they would go fer a nice trot up Newgate Street. Alfie tried yellin' at 'em, but they figured he was encouragin' them, so they roared along Newgate, wheeled south onto Yonge, and then decided to head fer home back along King Street—where you was foolish enough to get in their way."

"You're certain of this?"

"Wilkie's known Alfie and his folks fer years: dumb, but honest as they come."

"Good work, Constable," Marc said in what he hoped was not a patronizing tone. Then he remembered something. "When did you discover all this?"

"Late Saturday afternoon. We don't walk around with a thumb up our noses, Major."

"Then why didn't you inform me immediately?"

"Now, now, keep yer braces buckled. I left a warm stew and a willin' woman in my house to come all the way to Mrs. Standish's place. But you wasn't home."

"But that was Saturday. You had all day yesterday to get in touch."

Cobb looked horrified. "Major," he said solemnly, "yesterday was the Sabbath."

•　　•　　•

WHILE MARC WAS PLEASED WITH THE news that the collision had not been deliberate—which meant that Angeline Hartley's life was not in any danger—he was annoyed at Cobb for not informing him in time to let Willoughby off the hook and to put the governor's mind at ease before he left. And while it was possible to get a message to Sir Francis at Brantford or Woodstock, he knew the governor well enough to realize that he would want to hear the facts directly from the source. Nor could Marc leave his duties here to ride west himself. In any event, Colin had been given his orders, and Sir Francis, who saw them no doubt as yet another trial by fire for the wayward Willoughby, would be unlikely to reverse himself. Marc finally decided that he would send a note by courier to the commander at London barracks informing the governor that it seemed almost certain that no one was out to injure his ward but that, to err on the side of safety, he would have Willoughby continue to shepherd Miss Hartley according to her whim. Nor would he tell Colin: at least the poor bugger now had some reason to think himself useful as the girl's chaperone. If he were to find out that the whole business had been a mistake, he might go off the deep end for good.

THREE DAYS WENT BY WITH NO word from Danby's Crossing. Marc sent Cobb back to his regular patrol, subject to instant recall should the need arise. Major Burns's fingers stiffened so much that his pen dropped between them. Marc buried himself in paperwork. Colin fumed and boiled by day and avoided Marc in the evenings by heading out somewhere every night. "The blast of his cologne would've brung a donkey to its knees," Mrs. Standish informed Marc, who was grateful for such news, as it seemed that Colin had found some female company to help him cope with his bitter disappointment (as long as that company wasn't the daughter of a possessive and vengeful receiver general). The day trip out to Streetsville had been particularly trying as Angeline's second cousin proved to be an exact copy, and so poor Willoughby had had a giggler at each ear and was paraded about the town like a wooden soldier on display.

"I feel like a goddamn pimp!" he was heard raving to a defenceless duty-corporal.

As for Marc, he avoided Eliza's company for as long as he could, and found more than one reason to pass by the dry-goods store and its adjacent millinery each day. But he didn't go in, and no one he knew came out.

On Thursday evening, the governor's cortège returned, and everything changed.

HILLIARD WAS BUG-EYED WITH EXCITEMENT AS he recounted to the staff of Government House the succession of triumphant speeches delivered by Sir Francis. Colonel MacNab was ecstatic. Receiver General Maxwell predicted a Tory-Constitutionist landslide, with even Mackenzie going down to defeat in the second riding of York. There wasn't the faintest rumour of a threat against the governor. Security had been tight, the crowds boisterous but non-violent. The governor's message had sunk in, and its effect had been palpable.

So when Marc was asked to join Sir Francis in his office after supper that evening he was astonished to find him in high dudgeon. By the time Marc arrived, he had already worked himself into a crimson rage—with the ailing Major Burns as his sole witness. Marc had expected to be asked immediately for a report on Rumsey and another on Angeline and the accident, but the governor had already chosen his theme.

"I want that bastard's name, do you hear?" he shouted at Marc across the room.

"Do calm yourself, sir," Burns was saying. "You'll do yourself some damage."

"I do not intend to be upstaged by some anonymous coward calling himself by the ludicrous name of Farmer's Friend. The people of Brantford and Woodstock and London heard for themselves who is really the farmer's friend!"

"I'm sure they did, sir," Burns soothed, and glanced at Marc imploringly.

"Damn right they did!" Sir Francis seemed for the moment to have lost sight of Marc. "But everywhere we went, everywhere, those damnable broadsheets preceded us. They were even left on church pews, I was told, on the Sabbath! And supporters of that traitorous Yankee and so-called Reformer, Bidwell, had the nerve to move through the crowd in London handing them out like invitations to tea! Giving them out to the people who had come to hear their governor, not to have their minds polluted with that rot!"

"But, sir—"

"And don't tell me to calm down, Titus!" Sir Francis brayed.

"Are you referring to the letters written by Farmer's Friend, sir?" Marc said quietly.

Sir Francis wheeled and caught sight of Marc near the door. He heaved a huge sigh, and struggled to get his anger under control. When he spoke again his voice was low, but still tight. "It is, Lieutenant. And I'm glad you're here. I want you to drop everything and follow this Clegg fellow from his house tomorrow morning. Don't lose him. Let him lead you to the writer of these scurrilous, seditious letters. Find out his name. Then bring him here to me by force if you must. And don't tell Cobb. I don't trust that man."

"What about the investigation, sir?"

"Damn the investigation, Lieutenant! I want Farmer's Friend in this office by noon tomorrow! You can tell me then why you haven't caught Rumsey."

"But, sir, I thought you wanted to speak to the letter-writer before you left for your tour of the hustings, to help you with—"

"I want those letters stopped, Lieutenant. I do not want

anything disrupting what we have accomplished in the past four days. Is that clear? You are to find this traitor and put a stop to his democratic drivel!"

"Understood, sir."

MARC WALKED TOWARDS THE BOARDING HOUSE through the soft darkness with a slow and troubled step. He had never seen Sir Francis so agitated, so lacking in control or perspective. Moreover, what he was contemplating was not legal. Even if Marc were to track down Farmer's Friend tomorrow—presuming, of course, that Cobb had not been deliberately misleading them—there was no lawful means of stopping the flow of letters or coercing the author to visit Government House. That some kind of intimidation was being planned Marc found both distasteful and profoundly unsettling. And a good part of his unease had its roots in the unhappy exchange he had had with Beth Smallman just five days earlier.

He was a block away from home when he sensed that he was being followed. He turned quickly, but could see no one. Perhaps his nerves were more frayed than he thought. He had not slept well all week. Every time the duty-corporal or a courier moved through the hallway outside his office, he had jumped with the anticipation of sudden word about Rumsey from Cobb and the call to precipitate action. It had not come.

Marc felt the breeze of the club descending upon him just

in time to duck, so that the savage blow glanced off his padded shoulder and merely grazed his shako cap, knocking it off.
But the force of the attack spun him sideways and down. He
struck the ground hard, and his bare forehead pitched into
the root of a tree. The world swam. With blurred vision he
saw a black figure raise the club above him, poised for the kill.
He rolled away. The club must have missed him, for he found
himself against the tree trunk, with his skull still intact.

It was several minutes, though, before his head cleared
enough for him to struggle to his knees and peer anxiously
about.

"Sorry, Major, I lost the bugger. Are you all right?"

"Yes, Constable. I think so."

"That was no robber," Cobb said as he knelt down and
helped Marc to his feet. When Marc started to wobble,
Cobb hung on to his elbow, and Marc could feel the tensile
strength in the little man. "He was tryin' to kill you, and
there ain't no doubt about it."

"Then you saved my life, Constable."

"Just doin' my duty, Major."

"But this area's not on your patrol," Marc said.

"So it ain't," Cobb replied, as his attention was diverted
to an object on the ground. "What's this, then?"

"It's a button," Marc said, "from a military uniform."

"You got enemies in the service, Major?"

Before Marc could respond to this unexpected notion,
Cobb attended to the immediate need. "We need to stop

jawin' and get you home so's the widow can have a good gander at yer skull. I can see a lump comin' straight out."

Marc was happy to let Cobb guide him the remaining few yards to the familiar veranda. "Did you get a good look at him?" he asked.

"Not really, Major. I was some ways off. I let out a holler and the bugger skedaddled in the dark. I had to stop and make sure you was all right before I set off after him. By then he'd got clean away."

"What did you see of him?"

"Medium build, big overcoat, and a woolly sailor's cap."

"Not likely a soldier, then. Though that button is odd," Marc said.

"And the fellow had a great bushy black beard on 'im."

MARC SAT HUDDLED IN A CLUMP of lilac a few yards from the house of Abner Clegg, with a thundering headache and a bruised shoulder, staring at the disc of sun just rising over the Don River and thinking about the attempt on his life the previous evening. According to Cobb—who surely must be trusted implicitly from now on—Rumsey had been seen in the Tinker's Dam with a dark-capped man sporting a bushy beard. Could the person who had paid Rumsey to shoot Moncreiff have come after the man investigating the crime?

Cobb had explained that Rumsey himself was thin and

more than six feet tall, so he could not have been the assailant. But why try to murder the investigator when anything he knew or surmised would have been passed along to his superiors? Murdering him would not stop the investigation. This was as far as Marc got with that conundrum, for the front door of Clegg's shack swung open and the courier himself emerged. He looked carefully about him in all directions. But Marc, wearing a simple blue shirt with grey trousers, could not be seen. Feeling himself safe, Clegg—an angular, loping man—moved swiftly down Front Street towards the market.

Marc waited until Clegg was fifty yards ahead before he came out onto the roadside and sidled along, whistling nonchalantly. One advantage he held over Cobb's effort last week was that the market on a Friday was only a quarter the size of the one on Saturday. It would be hard for Clegg to elude him there. When he saw Clegg nearing the market, Marc ducked between two houses and, as he had anticipated, his quarry took that moment to glance around for anyone following on his trail. Satisfied that he was home free, Clegg strolled in among the stalls.

Meantime, Marc raced up George Street to the lane that ran behind the row of houses on the north side of Front Street, then wheeled west onto it and reached the market in time to see that Clegg had similar notions—except that he had sprinted past Colborne Street and then deked into the lane that backed the stores on the south side of King Street.

Marc followed. But when he turned into the lane, no one was in sight. Stacks of boxes and crates and rotting refuse lay everywhere. A rat waddled from one pile to the next. Then Marc heard the crack of wood breaking, about thirty yards ahead and to his left. Clegg had slipped into an alley and was headed south back towards Colborne. Marc decided to take a narrower alley to the same destination. Stumbling over debris and scattering rats as he went, Marc emerged not on Colborne but farther south on Market Street. As he peered around the building at the end of the alley, he saw Clegg gazing his way, scrutinizing every bump in the road. Again satisfied, the courier began a more leisurely pace west on Market.

By now Marc knew exactly when Clegg was most likely to turn and stare back behind him. What puzzled him still, though, was the motive behind all this clandestine movement. Despite the governor's intemperate ranting, there was nothing in any way seditious about the letters. If anything, they were muted and rational in comparison with the regular press on either the left or the right. Why, then, would Farmer's Friend go to such melodramatic lengths to maintain his anonymity? He felt he was very close to finding that out.

Marc trailed Clegg west along Market, across Yonge, and then north to the tradesman's lane that again backed the businesses on the south side of King. The courier suddenly slowed down, and Marc slipped behind a tall packing crate.

There was no one else in the lane at this time of day. Few people would be up yet, and no business opened before eight, if then. It was just Marc and Clegg and the empty lane.

Marc watched with some amusement as the courier flattened himself against the wall of a brick building, then edged along towards a door at the back of one of the businesses. He eased one hand around the jamb and rapped—once. A few seconds later, the door was opened slightly, a beige envelope appeared and was grasped, then a large coin followed suit. Clegg tucked the envelope inside his shirt, scoured the lane both ways for the enemy, then moved past Marc at a brisk trot—heading no doubt for Church Street and the *Constitution*.

Marc did not follow. With his heart now thumping more vigorously than his head, he walked up to the door and knocked quietly. When it opened, he merely said, "Hello, Beth."

"YOU MUSTN'T BLAME ABNER CLEGG FOR leading me here," Marc said. "He did everything to lose me but turn himself inside out."

They were in the small back room again, but this time there was no tea or scones, and they had to keep their voices low because Aunt Catherine was still asleep and unaware of the identity of Farmer's Friend.

"My letters must be having more influence than I

thought," Beth said. "The governor's put his top investigator on the trail."

"I didn't ask for this assignment. And I had no inkling that you could have been the author. I still can't believe it."

"Thanks very much."

"No, I didn't mean to imply that—"

"—a woman isn't smart enough to write letters like that?"

"I don't know what I thought when I realized Clegg was at your door," Marc said lamely, as a stab of pain struck him between the eyes.

"You've been hurt," Beth said with concern.

"It's part of being a soldier. But this bump had nothing to do with you or Clegg. Besides, I've been told I've got a thick skull." He smiled warily.

"Tell me more about my letters. Please."

"Well, they've stirred up quite a lot of admiration and an equal dram of umbrage and condemnation."

"I think that's about right, don't you?"

"When the governor got to London, Mackenzie's people had printed your individual letters as broadsheets and sprinkled them like hailstones all over the political landscape. Sir Francis was not amused."

"Well, that is praise enough, is it not?"

"He was enraged, actually, and ordered me to bring him the name of Farmer's Friend or the perpetrator himself by noon today."

"Have you read them?" Beth said softly.

"Yes, I have."

"And?"

"And I think they are telling and true and written from the heart."

Beth caught her breath, and looked up at Marc for a long moment. "Thank you," she said. "That means a lot to me." Then in a different voice, she added, "So what are we to do now? Are you duty bound to turn me in?"

Marc did not answer right away. The question had been clawing at his heart. "Why not let the world out there know who you are? Let them be astounded to learn that the author is a woman who was also a farmer, who suffered exactly as those in her stories suffered, or whose sufferings she took on, on their behalf? Don't you see how much more power and authority could be gained?"

"That isn't possible . . ."

"What is the worst that could happen? You've done nothing illegal. The governor can rant and rave, but then he'll be just like the rest of the politicians he despises." The words were just flowing out of Marc before he was fully aware of the deep forces propelling them. "It might do him good to feel powerless for a change."

"But I can't, don't you see?"

"No, I don't."

"It's got little to do with me and everything to do with Aunt Catherine."

Marc was baffled and, as it showed in his face, he could

feel Beth beginning to withdraw, and he suddenly felt cold, very cold, in the pit of his stomach and in the region where his heart stammered and stalled.

"How many customers do you think we would have left if they found out I was the author of those letters?"

"Then to hell with them! They can go—stuff themselves!"

"Be quiet. I won't have her wakened. And try to think of someone besides yourself for a minute."

"Marry me, and I'll get transferred back to England and—"

"You must not talk such foolishness. I was the one who encouraged my aunt to sell everything, leave her friends, and come up here to start a new life. I never should've written those letters, but my husband, who could've written them in blood, isn't here to do it. So I had to take the chance. And now only Abner and you know who Farmer's Friend is. And it must stay that way. It must." She was on the verge of tears, and she fought them back fiercely.

"But I swore an oath," Marc said, "to serve my king and obey my superiors. I made a solemn vow."

"Then the time's come for you to choose between love and your duty," she said in a voice that chilled the air in the cramped room.

Marc got up and, without looking back, walked out into the alley. A pair of rats eyed him till he was safely out of sight.

● ● ●

MARC WAS STILL IN A DAZE when he got back to Mrs. Standish's. He was barely aware of changing into his uniform and making polite conversation with the widow and Maisie over late-breakfast tea in the parlour. In walking out on Beth—forever, unless he could conjure some morally dubious compromise—he had instinctively, reflexively, chosen to do his duty as a soldier, and that meant giving Sir Francis Beth's name. But when he arrived at Government House, he found he was not prepared to do so and came up with a plan of sorts to delay the inevitable. Unable to equivocate face to face with Sir Francis, Marc wrote him a note explaining that he had tracked the courier to King Street and Bay, where he had temporarily lost him, only to meet him returning with the letter in hand. Hence, the writer was located in that block of King Street between Bay and Yonge. Therefore, all he had to do was place himself there next Friday or Saturday and wait for Clegg to come to him. His fingers shook as he penned the lie and saw it staring back up at him.

With the polling about to begin on Monday and with last-minute rallies to be arranged—as well as the grand gala tomorrow night—Marc was hoping that Sir Francis might have his attention redirected long enough for him to forget about Farmer's Friend or, in the least, downplay its significance. That was all Marc could think of at the moment. Even so, he was so torn with conflicting and irreconcilable emotions that he had to get out of Government House entirely.

He soon found himself walking in the afternoon sunshine down to Bay Street and the Crooked Anchor. Perhaps

Cobb would be there. He desperately needed someone to talk to. To his disappointment, the constable was not in. Marc stood at the bar anyway and sipped on a dark ale. No one spoke to him.

He was just turning to leave when Cobb stumbled through the doorway, out of breath and wide-eyed.

"What is it?"

"Rumsey," Cobb said. "He's been spotted near the Tinker's Dam—headin' due north. On foot. For Danby's Crossing."

At last, Marc thought.

ELEVEN

I'll get a horse and come with you," Cobb said.
He and Marc were in the stables of Government House,
and a groom had just finished saddling Marc's chestnut mare.

"Not right now," Marc said as he swung into the saddle.
"I want you to go up to the house and alert Willoughby and
the governor. Have him call out as many troops as he thinks
necessary. I'll need some backup at Danby's, but we've got
to be prepared to initiate a pursuit and a full search if the
bastard gets away on me."

"If he does, Major, then he'll head fer the wharf. I'm sure
of it."

"I'll leave that part to Hilliard or Willoughby. But if Rumsey's making for his cabin on foot, he's only got a half-hour head start, so I'm certain I can get up there about the same time as he does."

"Don't underestimate shank's mare," Cobb said.

But Marc was already on his way.

He rode furiously north up Simcoe Street, shouting and waving aside donkey-carts, drays, vegetable wagons, and cheering youngsters. He swung briefly along Lot Street and then onto College Avenue, where he was suddenly alone with the horse-chestnut trees on either side and the vista of the university park ahead. He urged the mare to her best gallop and, pounding east again, reached Yonge Street in a blaze of speed and sweat.

But the mare soon began to flag, and he was forced to pull her back to a sustainable canter. At the Bloor turnpike, he let her drink a little and had to pull her roughly away before she did herself some damage. A dead horse under him would be an ignominious end to his second investigation. In fact, he thought, it was time to start using more brains than bravado. He couldn't just blunder into the square at Danby's Crossing and announce his military presence to all and sundry. He still had no idea how many allies among the locals up there Rumsey might actually have, despite Cobb's repeated assurances that the fellow was a loner. And Rumsey would be armed with a long-range rifle and a sharpshooter's eye.

With a start Marc realized that he might be riding into true danger for the first time. This was not the case of a panicked man in pathetic flight, as Crazy Dan had been. Rumsey was a cold-blooded killer. He had hidden himself successfully for ten days, living off his wits, no doubt. He knew every stick and stone in the woods around Danby's. As a celebrated deer hunter, he would have stealth and patience on his side, should he need to call on them. You didn't fell a twenty-point stag by letting him see you first.

Marc did not slow down at the Eglinton tollgate, and was in full gallop as he passed the startled onlookers outside Montgomery's Tavern. He decided to approach the hamlet from the north, where he would be least expected to arrive. So he rode on past the crossroad to Danby's. A quarter-mile farther on he veered east into the woods. It wasn't thick or swampy here, so he made good headway and soon came to the rugged trail that he had ridden in pursuit of Crazy Dan. Only this time he followed it south until he could see smoke rising from the chimneys of the hamlet just ahead. He eased the exhausted mare a few yards off the trail into the brush, dismounted, and tethered her. He took down his Brown Bess musket, bit the paper off a bullet, and loaded it. For good luck he touched the haft of the sabre that Uncle Frederick had given him upon his graduation from Sandhurst (a weapon Frederick himself had used at Waterloo). Then he picked his way through the trees towards what he hoped was the vicinity of the Rumsey cabin.

Marc was soon soaked with sweat, which he attributed entirely to the heat of the overhead sun. Surely Rumsey would not stump boldly into his cabin, even if he felt there had been as yet no general alarm raised against him: his instincts would lead him to scout the near environs first, and only then would he slip safely home. At this very moment Rumsey could be on the prowl nearby—quiet as a cat, deadly as a rattler. Every four or five steps now, Marc stopped, stood still, and listened intently, while making certain there was always a thick tree trunk between him and what he took to be the path to the cabin. His progress was much slower and more erratic than he had intended, and for a moment he was certain he was lost. While he had been inching his way southwards, he might well have passed by the cabin to the left or the right. He stopped walking and leaned against a birch tree. He was dizzy. He couldn't keep the sweat from stinging his eyes and blurring his vision. His bladder throbbed with the residue of the ale he had drunk at the Crooked Anchor. There was no sound anywhere except his own laboured breathing.

Then he saw it: a mere thread of smoke curling up into the humid haze and lolling there just above the treeline to his right. The cabin could be no more than thirty yards away. He was still trying to decide whether to sneak up on it or simply march through the front door and trust that the sight of a uniform and a primed musket would do the rest when he heard a shout and then a cry. Running low and as swiftly as he could, Marc made directly for the source of those very human sounds. One had been uttered in rage, the other in distress. And they were now being repeated, louder and more terrible.

The cabin came up so quickly before him that Marc almost ran right into it. He found himself at the windowless wall opposite the entrance on the west side. He sped along the north wall and swung around into the clearing in front of the cabin. Rumsey was already in full flight towards an opening in the woods to the south—the path he no doubt used to get him to the Tinker's Dam. Marc raised his gun, caught the blue blur of Rumsey's overalls in his sight, and fired. Rumsey stumbled at the abrupt blast of sound, twisted briefly in Marc's direction, started to raise his own gun, then whirled and fled.

Marc cursed and began reloading. He knew it was hopeless to pursue Rumsey on his own terrain, a tactic more likely to prove fatal to the hunter than the hunted. But then he realized that Rumsey could have stood there at the edge of the woods and dropped the meddling soldier like a fawn frozen in fear. Rumsey must have assumed that the soldier was not alone, for they rarely were (few being as foolhardy as this one, Marc thought). So, he was more likely to flee than to counterattack. All Marc had to do, then, was follow after him as noisily and clumsily as he could—calling out as if to comrades and perhaps even firing off a shot or two for dramatic effect. If Rumsey continued south, Willoughby or

Hilliard would be able to intercept him at the Tinker's Dam or at the city docks, his most probable destination, where Cobb was sure to be waiting with a squad of deputized constables.

Marc never got to put his plan into action.

"My God, somebody help me! Please!"

It was Margaret Rumsey, calling out from inside the cabin. Marc put his gun down and rushed in.

MARGARET RUMSEY LAY WHERE SHE HAD fallen under her husband's savage blows—on the dirt floor next to a rickety bedstead. One side of her face was already beginning to swell, and her lower lip was split open and bleeding profusely. Her right arm hung limply at her side, bruised or broken. She had apparently used it to ward off Rumsey's fists. Her pathetic grey shift was torn down the front, and when Marc came up to her in the smoky light, she clutched its shreds together to cover her breasts.

"It's all right, Mrs. Rumsey. I'm Lieutenant Edwards. I was here last week. I'm here to help you. Don't be alarmed."

The terror in Margaret Rumsey's eyes began to fade, though the tears—now able to flow—made it difficult to determine what other emotions might lay there. She was trying to speak through blooded spittle: "Elmer . . . Elmer."

"Your boy?"

She nodded, then groaned and closed her eyes.

Marc looked around for the children. Up in the loft at the east end of the big room, he saw the whites of a pair of eyes. "It's all right, Elmer. You can come down now."

Slowly, a boy of ten or eleven descended the ladder and stood, unmoving—traumatized either by the violence he had witnessed or his mother's sobbing. Marc went over to him. "You must try to be brave, Elmer. Run quickly to Mr. Kimble's shop and bring Mr. and Mrs. Kimble back here right away."

The boy simply stood and trembled.

"Your father has gone off into the woods. He won't come back."

The boy began to shake his head, but whether yes or no, Marc could not tell. "It's all right. I'm a soldier. I've got a sabre and a gun. Nobody will hurt you or your mother. But your mama needs help. Now go!"

At this curt command, Elmer Rumsey dashed out the door. He did not look at his mother.

Marc found several cloths and a pail of ice-cold well water and began daubing at Margaret's cuts and welts. Gently he raised her right arm and rotated it. She winced but did not cry out.

"Good," he said, "it's not broken. Now hold this cold cloth against that swelling on your cheek. He may have cracked it, but we'll wait for the doctor's opinion on that."

Despite the pain it caused, Margaret shook her head vigorously.

"It's all right. I'll pay the doctor. You've suffered enough."

She began to weep, though the sobbing had stopped, and Marc sensed that these were not tears of pain now but of a deeper anguish no physician could touch. Marc managed to create a soft place for her to lie down by arranging every threadbare blanket he could find to form a sort of nest on the bedstead. He lifted her up and placed her down upon it, covering her nakedness with a grimy sheet.

"Are the other children safe?"

"Yes," she said huskily. "At Mrs. Kimble's."

"Mrs. Kimble will be here in a minute. Then I'll arrange for the doctor to come. Now, can you tell me what happened?"

Margaret pushed herself up onto her good elbow. Her eyes widened, as if her mind had unexpectedly cleared and she had remembered things she must say, pain or no pain. "He went crazy. He was out of his mind. He never hit me before, never. But he was so angry, so angry. 'I killed a man fer nothin',' he kept yellin' and screamin', and I couldn't stop him. 'I killed a man fer ten dollars,' was all he said."

"Did Philo shoot Councillor Moncreiff in the square last week?" Marc asked.

"That man told him he'd make us rich. Philo said he could earn us fifty dollars, we could move back to Buffalo, buy us a house, and I said, 'But how can you get fifty dollars?' and Philo said, 'You'll see,' and when that old feller got shot out there and Philo sneaks in here the next day with his mama just dead and then sneaks out again and tells me to say he's still in Buffalo, then I knew how he was gonna get us fifty dollars."

"Then why was he so angry, Mrs. Rumsey?"

"He was screamin' like a wild man that the rich fella paid him ten dollars at first, but then wouldn't give him the rest of it."

"Did Philo know who this man was?"

"Fella with a big black beard, Philo said. Someone pretendin' to be what he wasn't. But Philo found out who he was, and he said he was gonna get his money, one way or t'other. But he was so angry, so angry. He was writin' the fella a letter. 'This'll make the bugger pay,' he yelled, but I kept tryin' to get him just to up and leave now fer Buffalo, and be satisfied with ten dollars, and he goes all purple in the face and his eyes bulge out somethin' terrible, and I'm real scared, and he up and hits me, and when I get up he hits me again and again, and all the time he's yellin', 'I'm gonna take my gun and get my forty dollars, you hear!' Then he throws the letter into the fire and runs out, and I hear a gun go off, and I don't know what's happenin'."

Marc eased her back down just as the door opened and Mrs. Kimble came bustling in. She had a basket of salves, bandages, and a towel full of ice. "There, there, luv, it's gonna be okay."

Marc moved away to let her minister to Margaret Rumsey. As he did so he noticed for the first time the fire smouldering

in the grate of the big stone fireplace. He crouched down and
with a thumb and forefinger lifted free a crumpled sheet of
paper. It was singed around the edges, and smudged with soot
and ash. Marc blew off as much of this as he could, then unfolded it and walked out into the sunlight to read what Philo
Rumsey had been writing by way of threat to the man who
had instigated the murder of Langdon Moncreiff.

This is what remained for him to read:

> *tried to carrie out my part of the*
> *pay me in full fer doin yore*
>
> *not my fallt Guv Head dropt hi*
>
> *or I'll go to the magistra*

Marc was deeply disappointed that the person being
threatened was not named, but the substance of the rest
of the letter was stark enough. Rumsey had been given an
initial payment of ten dollars, with another forty promised,
no doubt, when the deed was done. But Rumsey had shot
the wrong man! Sir Francis—as Marc had relived the action every night in his dreams—had bent down to pick up
the notes for his speech, and the bullet had missed him and
struck Moncreiff. In the letter Rumsey was pleading that it
was not his fault that Sir Francis had bent down without
warning, and was demanding full payment or else he would

go to the magistrates. That seemed a hollow threat, however, and Rumsey must have realized it as he wrote it, and
decided in a rage to take more direct action. Perhaps they
would be lucky enough to trail him to the doorstep of the
real villain of this affair. Besides confirming Rumsey's guilt,
the note explained also why he had been hanging about
York County since the shooting instead of seeking asylum in
Buffalo: he wanted his forty dollars.

Most important, in Marc's view, was the confirmation
of his initial hunch that Sir Francis had been the assassin's
target. The unthinkable had almost happened. And Marc
himself must bear the grim news to the governor as soon as
possible. Head's life might hang in the balance.

Marc picked up his musket and poked his head into the
cabin. "I have urgent business with the governor," he said to
Mrs. Kimble, still at Margaret's side. "I must leave."

"Everythin'll be okay here. Mr. Kimble'll see to it."

"Have him bring a doctor. I'll take care of the fee."

Margaret Rumsey sat up, stared hard at Marc, and cried,
"You won't hurt him, will you?"

WHEN MARC FINALLY FOUND HIS WAY back to the spot
where he had tethered the mare, he discovered only a pile
of fly-ridden horse-dung. The branch to which she had been
tied was not broken, so it appeared someone had stolen her.
Philo? No, he had headed south, where his only chance of

escape or revenge lay. But it was still possible that Philo had an accomplice. Possible also that Cobb's assessment of Phineas Kimble had been premature. Sarah-Mae Kimble seemed a genuinely kind person, and she had readily admitted hearing the shot that had killed Moncreiff. But her husband had not. Moreover, he had given Philo occasional work long after he had had to fire him for the good of his business. Why? Did he, like his wife, feel sorry for the Rumsey children? Or was there a darker ulterior motive?

These thoughts occupied Marc as he crashed through the bush back towards the square and the livery stables. There he would commandeer the best horse in the name of the king, and ride on to Government House. Sir Francis must be shown Rumsey's letter and told the unsettling truth. By the time Marc managed to find the trail and make his way to Danby's, he estimated he had lost close to an hour since the initial encounter with Rumsey. In a state of near-panic he stumbled into the livery stables and gasped out his royal command.

The proprietor—a sandy-haired old gent—gave Marc a gap-toothed grin, spat out a gob of tobacco juice, and said, "Well, now, I could do that, sir, but I don't reckon that'll be necessary."

"I am on the governor's business, sir."

"I don't doubt you on that score. But yer own mare is restin' comfortable in one o' my stalls. I corralled her on the road after some fool run her ragged an' just left her to catch her death in her own sweat. I figured you'd want to ride her back to town."

It was late afternoon, with shadows lengthening across the streets, when Marc at last rode up to Government House with the scrap of Rumsey's alarming letter in his pocket. He expected to find the place alive with bustling troops and excited clerks, but only the duty-corporal greeted him in the hall and, with no especial concern, ushered him into the governor's office. There he found not only Sir Francis but also Willoughby, Hilliard, and Titus Burns. They were in the midst of a toast, and it looked as if it were not the first.

"Come in, come in," Sir Francis beamed, all smiles. Willoughby and Hilliard looked like a pair of cats who had just shared a canary. "We were beginning to worry about you, Lieutenant. In fact, I sent Parker and a unit up to Danby's to make sure Rumsey hadn't shot you before we got him."

"You got him?"

"Not I. It is Willoughby and Hilliard here who deserve the credit."

"But it had to have been Lieutenant Edwards who flushed the blackguard out and sent him scuttling our way," Colin said generously.

"You did encounter him, then?" Sir Francis asked Marc.

Marc was still trying to take in what was happening here. He had news that surely superseded anything else, but his instincts told him that it was Sir Francis alone who should hear it. "Yes, sir. I took a shot at him near his cabin, and he was fleeing south. I got down here as fast as I could to raise the alarm."

"Then once again you have done me and the province a great service," Sir Francis said, choosing to ignore the obvious question as to why it had taken Marc almost two hours to make a forty-minute journey.

"Has Rumsey confessed?" Marc asked.

"No, he hasn't," Hilliard said with a curious grin on his face, somewhere between a smug and a smirk.

"Well, it doesn't matter," Marc said to Sir Francis. "I've got proof that he did it."

"We won't need it," Hilliard said.

"He's dead," Colin said.

"Dead?"

"Yes, Lieutenant," Sir Francis said. "That's what we've been toasting: the just outcome of a heinous crime. Hilliard and Willoughby were led to a pier near Turner's brewery by Constable Cobb. They and their platoon hid in the long grass down there and simply waited. About an hour ago, Rumsey arrived and, thinking himself unobserved, started to make his way towards an old fishing boat tied up at the dock. When challenged by Hilliard here, Rumsey turned and fired, wounding an infantryman in the leg. A moment later, the villain went down in a hail of bullets."

"And good riddance," Hilliard said.

"The rifle that killed poor Moncreiff was found in his hand," Sir Francis said.

"And that's the end of it," Colin said.

"But now you'll never know who hired him," Marc said.

"But we don't know for sure that anybody did," Hilliard said.

"I agree," Sir Francis said. "As far as I am concerned, the whole sorry business is over. We have an election to deal with, and the fact that the killer turned out to be a malcontent Yankee will certainly not work against us. And now we have the extra fillip of having brought him to justice—swiftly and remorselessly."

"And we have a gala tomorrow night to spread the good news and celebrate," Hilliard said.

Marc held his peace.

IT WAS EARLY EVENING BEFORE MARC was given his private audience with the governor. The parade of well-wishers traipsing in to congratulate him on his triumph in the London district and upon the quick and tidy resolution to the "Moncreiff business" not only prevented Marc from seeing the governor alone but made the revelation he had to make all the more distressing.

Marc began by saying, "Sir, I wanted most urgently to see you alone the minute I arrived here from Danby's Crossing. But it has proved impossible—"

"Don't blame yourself, young man. Just get on with what you seem to have an incurable urge to say." Sir Francis was still in a euphoric mood.

"I'll get right to the nub of the matter, then. I have incontrovertible proof that it was not Langdon Moncreiff whom Rumsey was hired to kill."

"I thought that missive might be a letter of promotion, as you've been squeezing it to death for the past minute."

"Rumsey was hired to kill you, sir."

"You must be joking," Sir Francis said, but the twinkle in his eye had already dimmed. "I told you last week that no one would dare assassinate the King's representative abroad."

Briefly, Marc outlined what had happened earlier that afternoon. He repeated Margaret Rumsey's words verbatim.

"I see why you are so agitated, Marc. But, even so, we must take a long, objective look at this evidence. I'm sure Mrs. Rumsey had no cause to lie to you about her husband's claims. After all, they were incriminating, not exculpatory, and a woman in that dreadful state is not likely to be dissembling. However, how can we be sure that Rumsey did not feed her such false information in order to justify his own seditious actions?"

Marc held out the charred letter. "I found this in the fireplace, where Rumsey tossed it before running off."

Sir Francis took the scrap of paper and read it carefully—growing paler by the second. He read it again, and the paper trembled in his grip.

"You do recall dropping your notes, sir? And Moncreiff was almost directly behind you along the line of fire. I checked these details last week. There can be no doubt that as you bent down suddenly, the bullet meant for you struck Mr. Moncreiff."

Sir Francis sat down stiffly in the wingback chair beside his desk. All colour had drained from his face. His eyes were glassy, and for a second Marc was afraid the governor was going to faint. But he drew in a single, gasping breath to bring himself around. Both hands still shook in his lap.

"There is more, sir."

"Then spit it out, dammit!"

The governor's sudden anger shocked Marc, but he gritted his teeth and carried on with his duty. "This letter confirms what Rumsey's rantings to his wife implied: that he was a paid killer, and that the one who engaged him appeared in disguise. What is more, he was seen by a witness to have given money to Rumsey, and that witness described the man as having the posture and bearing of a swell or a bigwig—by which we may infer that he meant a gentleman."

"Somebody in the government? Or the Family Compact? That's . . . absurd. It has to have been some Reformer with the bearing of a gentleman."

"Perhaps, sir. But we must consider both possibilities. I hate to say it, even to think it, but we may well have a traitor amongst us. And we do not know but that he may try again."

Sir Francis stared at the letter as it lay on his desk before him. The truths that it bore were inescapable, and that reality had taken a cold grip upon him: anger, fear, confusion, indecision, brief bravado—all were clearly readable in his posture and expression.

"Shall I leave you alone, sir?"

"No, Marc, I think not." A cunning, calculating look had come over his face. "You see, don't you, that I cannot make this evidence public. I dare not tell even my most trusted allies in the Executive and Legislative councils. Such news would create panic on a grand scale—a traitor among the upper echelons of government or respectable society? The governor's life in jeopardy and no way of dealing with it short of a witch hunt through the ranks of the social register? Or posting a regiment of troops around Government House?"

"But would this news not stir up sympathy for you . . . and your cause?" Marc had intended to say "our" cause, but the thought had come out otherwise.

"Maybe so, but the confusion and alarm among our own supporters would be disastrous. I've run the entire campaign around the notions of loyalty, lawfulness, and peaceful public order."

"What are you suggesting, sir?"

Sir Francis rose and strode as bravely as he could to the window. With his back turned to Marc, he said with chilling calculation: "Only you and I know the contents of this troublesome letter." The paper crackled in his grip.

"That is why I waited so patiently to see you alone, sir."

"And once again your judgment was unerring, Marc. And so, if I were to destroy the evidence—as I am doing now—no one outside this room would know any different, would they?" Slowly and deliberately Sir Francis ripped Rumsey's letter to pieces. They fluttered to the floor like dust off a dead moth's wings.

"But, sir, your life may be in danger—"

"I do not really think so. Rumsey botched the initial attempt. He is now dead. The public will be fully satisfied that Councillor Moncreiff's killer was himself justly killed. The momentum we have gained in the campaign is now self-evident, and the Moncreiff business—sad as it may be—has already worked to our advantage and will continue to do so. Why would anyone risk another attempt on my life so near to the election?" As he spoke, Sir Francis seemed to be trying to convince himself of what he was saying as much as he was Marc. A residual and persistent fear still lurked—like a bright, throbbing thorn—in the corner of each eye. "The political motive, you see, has been virtually eliminated. And since you and I know that it was not a lone madman who tried to kill me, but rather an intelligent if misguided gentleman, then it follows that I am in no imminent danger."

The governor's gaze narrowed. "In fact, there will be nothing to stop us now—not Mackenzie, not Bidwell, not Perry, not the demagogues from the American republic, not even Farmer's Friend and all his ilk."

Marc did not reply.

"So you see, Marc, we cannot ever divulge what has just passed between us," Sir Francis said quietly. "The Moncreiff affair is closed."

"You know you can count on me," Marc said. "My loyalty to the King is absolute." Well, almost absolute, he thought, even as he prayed that the governor's obsession with the identity of Farmer's Friend would be forgotten.

"Yes, yes I can," Sir Francis said, as he went over to his bookcase, fumbled with some books, and came up with a Bible. He slapped it on the desk, face up. "Put your hand on this Bible and swear a solemn oath that you will never reveal the contents of Rumsey's letter to a living soul." His eyes danced maniacally.

"But, sir—"

"Swear it! Now!"

Marc did as he was told.

THE SOLSTICE SUN HAD SUNK DOWN somewhere beyond Fort York, but there was still light in the sky: hazy, insubstantial, ghostly. Marc walked and walked. He had no idea where he was going or why. A day that should have been replete with triumph and satisfaction had turned into a nightmare whose images floated unmitigated before his mind's eye—taunting and terrible: Beth's face as he had turned and left her sitting in that cramped room, stunned and alone; the battered face of Margaret Rumsey and her pathetic plea for her worthless husband's life; a hired killer shot to pieces by a soldier's volley, just as Crazy Dan had been; the gloating visages of Hilliard and Willoughby; the half-mad stare of Governor Head, who was, it seemed, dangerously unstable.

It had been a day that had begun with the wrenching argument at Beth's over vows of love and duty, and it had ended with yet another vow that was just as compromised and conflicted as the others. For he had had more than enough time to march into the governor's office and admit that he had done his duty by discovering who had written those telling and true letters on behalf of the voiceless citizens of the province, and then confess that he could not reveal the name because of a matter of honour that was more compelling than duty, a trust too solemn to be broken. In short, it came down to a choice between loyalties. But, of course, he had not done the honourable thing; he had taken the coward's route and had been rewarded with the unforeseen possibility that the governor had lost interest in his vendetta against Farmer's Friend. With luck, he would soon abandon it entirely—letting Marc wriggle off the hook like a pusillanimous worm.

Of course, he could still crawl back to Beth in a week or so and boast that the governor had not forced the author's name from his lips and never would, implying craftily that her lover had, with passing nobility, chosen her over his soldierly duty. But just minutes ago he had put his hand on the Holy Bible at the irrational behest of a man he no longer respected and had sworn yet another binding oath of allegiance—when he ought to have turned and marched from the room. So, even if he were now to go back to the crazed governor and openly refuse to betray Farmer's Friend, it would be an act of supreme hypocrisy. He could not do it. His tongue would turn to stone.

He walked on and let the last of the twilight settle around him, blurring the painful edges of everything before him. Only one thing was now certain: he could never look Beth Smallman in the face again.

ELIZA OPENED THE FRONT DOOR BEFORE he reached the top step. She laughed softly. "I've been watching for you since supper." The fragrance of night flowers hung about her as she reached down to him.

They entered the unlit vestibule, and when she took his hand to lead him into her sitting room, he was so grateful he almost burst into tears. "Is your uncle at home?" he managed to ask.

This time Eliza giggled, a rippling little-girl laugh that cut through Marc's misery as a baby's smile might mellow a cynic. "He's taken the steamer to Kingston. We have the whole place and what's left of the evening to ourselves."

He sat down on the sofa in what had become over the past few weeks their intimate room. She took a candelabrum off the mantel and brought it over to the table beside the sofa. "This is more comfortable than the settee in the parlour," she said, sitting down and patting the cushion beside her. She was wearing a simple pale-linen dress over her chemise, and the flickering gleam of the candles caught the tender hollows of her neck and shoulders and highlighted the darkening surge of her unbound hair. No stays reconfigured the sensual droop of her breasts.

The light shone also upon Marc's face.

"My God, what's happened? You look devastated."

"I am," Marc said, and when she drew his head consolingly to her breast, he did not resist.

"Then you must tell me why."

So he did. In rushed, incoherent phrases he poured out the day's disappointments and humiliations, editing out only those portions sanctified by oath. Farmer's Friend was "someone dear" but, in this version, resolutely male. The Moncreiff case had not been properly concluded, but, of course, it could only be hinted as to why. The sad episode at Danby's Crossing could be fully exhumed and recounted, including even the chagrin at losing his horse and being patronized by a hostler.

Eliza fetched the brandy decanter and poured them each two fingers. "Sip slowly, darling, you'll singe your tonsils." She ran her fingers through his hair with such casual caress that it seemed as natural as breathing.

Marc looked up from his nestling place and said, "Will you marry me?"

Eliza uttered a tiny laugh—half-nervous, half-amused.

She pulled back so that his head came up and she could look at him directly. "You've only had one brandy."

"But I'm serious, darling." It was the first time he had used the word in her presence. He took her hand formally in his and said, "I want you to be my wife. Now. As soon as we can arrange it."

Eliza looked at him with a solemn, almost wistful, expression on her face. "But I can't," she said softly. "Please, believe me, it's not that I'm not genuinely fond of you. I am. The time we've shared these past weeks has been the best thing that has ever happened to me."

"Then, why? I don't understand."

"Well, for one thing, there's Beth Smallman."

Marc showed his amazement. "You know about her?"

"Enough. This is a very small town." She smiled as best she could and added, "And those candid descriptions of your exploits in Crawford's Corners in January left little to the imagination."

"But that's over," Marc said, feeling foolish at having dropped to one knee. He got up awkwardly to sit beside her. "It's finished."

"Perhaps. But I do wonder if such things are ever finished." Her expression darkened. "The man I tried to leave, back in England, followed me here."

"He did? Why didn't you tell me? Has he been bothering you?"

She stroked his cheek in a decidedly motherly gesture.

"He's managed to keep his distance—so far. But I am more than a little afraid of him. He's unstable, perhaps even mad, though he has tried to change his ways."

"You must tell me who he is!"

"So you can play guardian?" she said, not unkindly.

Marc sat back. "You won't marry me, then?"

"I don't think I'll marry anyone, so don't feel sorry for yourself."

Marc reached for her hand. "It's Uncle Sebastian, isn't it?"

"In a way, yes."

"Then there's nothing to worry about. I'll just—"

"We're going to New York," Eliza said, not letting go of his hand.

"I don't follow—"

"Uncle Sebastian is on his way to Montreal to meet Uncle Samuel and escort him and a shipment of port to Toronto. Uncle Samuel is going to take over the business here. Uncle Sebastian and I are moving to New York to set up shop there."

She let go of his hand. "It was Uncle Samuel who was supposed to go to New York, but Uncle Sebastian suddenly changed the plans. He says I may stay here if I wish . . ."

"But?"

She looked him square in the eye with a glance that conveyed pain and resignation in equal measure. "I won't leave him," she whispered. "He cannot do without me."

Marc was pretty certain why Sebastian Dewart-Smythe had altered their plans. "When do you leave?"

"In a week or so. As soon as Uncle Samuel gets settled in."

Marc was numb. There was nothing to say.

Eliza said, "But we don't have to marry. You could come with us to New York. I could teach you the wine business. We could travel to the continent, to France, to Italy—" She stopped. She reached out again and ran her fingers down one side of his head and cupped them about the nape of his neck. She sighed. "That was foolish of me. I'm starting to sound like the little girl who wants to eat her cake and have the baker, too."

She knew, as he did, that he could not leave the army any more than she could leave Uncle Sebastian and the wine business she was born to.

"This is good-bye, then?"

"You could come again tomorrow. He'll still be away."

"I've got to attend the gala at Somerset House," Marc said, "and you've already refused to come with me."

"I'm sorry, but there may be someone there I don't wish to meet."

"Oh, I see," Marc said, not sure that he did. "Your rejected suitor?"

She smiled cryptically. "So we've got only tonight to ourselves. I want you to do one thing for me, if you will," she said with mock solemnity. "A sort of last request."

"Anything."

She pulled his face into the hollow between her breasts. "I want you to make love to me. Now."

And there in their intimate room, in the uncertainty of candlelight and its insubstantial shadow, Marc made love to the woman who had just refused to marry him. The discovery that she was not inexperienced in conjugal matters was, initially, somewhat disconcerting, but she left him scant opportunity to mull over such moral niceties.

It was dawn before he found the will to leave.

TWELVE

On Saturdays Marc often went over to the garrison to take part in the morning parade, not because he had to—as aide-de-camp to the governor and attaché to Government House he was excused such routine manoeuvres—but because it made him feel more of a constituent part of the regular army. On this particular Saturday morning, he needed the tonic of military ritual and rigour more than ever. The prospect of filling the idle hours between breakfast and the gala at Somerset House in the evening with nothing but replays of the images and events that had happened since Thursday was intolerable. After the parade,

Marc lunched with Colonel Margison and Quartermaster Jenkin in the officers' mess, where talk of his heroic exploits in flushing out Philo Rumsey was both flattering and galling. At midafternoon, he made his way back to the boarding house, and there he found a note waiting for him, from Horatio Cobb.

IN THE CROOKED ANCHOR, COBB SEEMED uncharacteristically eager to tell Marc about Rumsey's death at the pier near Turner's brewery. He had barely touched the fried trout in front of him. "It was me that led the troops down there and told 'em where to hide in the grass so's them ridiculous costumes wouldn't show," he was saying.

"I know, and I'm sure you'll receive due credit," Marc said.

Cobb was anxious to talk, but he was also eyeing Marc closely, as if sensing that there had been some sea change in his outwardly unflappable superior. "That don't matter a pig's arse," he said and jabbed a fork into his plate. "So, like I was sayin', after I talk them into skulkin' down there like a pack of bird dogs, I start to sneak back up the embankment to see if I can spot Rumsey before he gets too close to all them pop-guns. I know it's important to take Rumsey alive as he's got a lot of talkin' to do before we hang him, but, dammit-all, the bugger'd already outcircled me. The first thing I know, I turn to see him almost on the wharf and scuttlin' fer a fishin' boat with a little cabin on it. So I give out a holler, but the troop is already liftin' out of the grass like flushed pheasants, and Rumsey of course sees 'em."

Cobb took a deep breath but did not raise his flagon. "I swear to God, Major, one of them crazy soldiers shoots before Rumsey can say shit or surrender. Naturally, he misses, but Rumsey ups and fires back, and I hear a mighty yelp and see one of the soldiers grab his leg and go down. Then there's a roar like a ten-gun salute and the poor bastard flies backwards with the guts shot out of him before he hits the water."

Cobb now hoisted his flagon and drank greedily. "I ain't ever seen anythin' like it, and I hope to Christ I never do again."

Almost absently Marc said, "Any idea who fired that first shot?"

Cobb picked up on the tone instantly. He looked at Marc for a long second before answering. "Could've been any one of 'em. They ain't got a brain to divvy up amongst 'em."

"Rumsey's dead," Marc said. "And that's all that seems to matter."

Cobb picked at the bones of his trout. "Well, it ain't really none of my business, I suppose, but I recall you figured Rumsey couldn't've been actin' on his own. Don't we have an instigator of some kind maybe runnin' around loose somewheres? Or don't that matter no more either?"

"As far as the governor is concerned, the case is closed."

"And as far as you're concerned?"

"I do what the governor commands me to do."

Cobb flashed Marc an enigmatic grin. "Well, then, I best get back to my humble patrol."

Marc rose and held out his hand. "It's been a pleasure working with you, Constable."

Cobb did not respond, but he watched Marc as he slowly made his way out of the tavern.

MARC RETURNED TO MRS. STANDISH'S AFTER eating supper at the officers' mess, where all the talk was about the upcoming gala at Somerset House, the life-and-death decisions regarding dance cards and partners, the relative merits of one colonial beauty over another, and the irresistible allure of the British officer in his ceremonial accoutrements. There was much teasing of Ensign Rick Hilliard, who, having won inestimable favour in the governor's eye during their trek through the western hustings, had been rewarded with the honour of escorting Angeline Hartley to the ball and dancing both the lancers and the galop with her. It was almost eight o'clock when Marc stepped onto the veranda and greeted his landlady, who was sweeping the dust of the day off her threshold.

"Is Colin home?" Marc asked her.

The Widow Standish leaned forward with both hands on her broomstick. "He was, Lieutenant. But he's left—and in such a state!"

"He'd not been drinking?"

She sighed: "No, sir, I could not say he had. But he was unforgivably rude to me, he threw his clothes all over his room, and on his way out he give Maisie such a snub as left her sobbing for an hour in the laundry shed."

Marc was beginning to tire of defending the young man he had taken under his wing, but he said, "Colin's had a frustrating week chaperoning the governor's ward when he was promised better things. Then yesterday, as you've heard, he was part of the heroic troop that tracked down and shot Mr. Moncreiff's killer. Now he has nothing before him but returning to his routine duties at Government House on Monday morning. And he tends to get upset over such disappointments—"

"More like a little boy throwing a tantrum, I'd say."

"And I daresay you are right, Mrs. Standish."

As he began dressing for the gala, Marc realized that he had sleepwalked through the day's events. His failure to live up to Beth's expectations, Eliza's rejection of his proposal (did she know more about him and Beth than he had supposed? Could she herself have arranged to leave because of what she knew?), his abject behaviour before a superior whose ethics (not to speak of his dubious sanity) he found repugnant, and his cowardly acquiescence in the whole sordid cover-up of the Rumsey affair—all these less than sterling actions had left him benumbed, devoid of passion and commitment.

Even worse was the fact that both his superior officers and those he commanded viewed him as an exemplary soldier, and could not stop pouring praise in his direction. It had been his efforts, they had said repeatedly, that had pointed the finger at Rumsey on the very day of the murder, his strategy that had set up the spy system at Danby's Crossing and the Tinker's Dam, leading to Rumsey's being spotted yesterday (Cobb was a mere cipher in all of this), his quick thinking and courage at the cabin that had spooked the fugitive and sent him scuttling to the docks, and his intuition that had forecast the precise pier to which the villain would flee. He might even be made a captain.

It was little wonder, then, that Marc found he was unable to concern himself with Colin's moods, perceived slights, and childish disappointments. Willoughby would just have to face the stern realities of being adult and conscionable like everybody else. After all, what had he to complain about compared to someone like Beth Smallman, who had lost a husband and a much-loved father-in-law in the same year, who had been left with a farm and a crippled brother to raise alone in the semi-wilderness? Or Eliza Dewart-Smythe, rich heiress that she was, who had been orphaned at three and raised by a succession of uncles more attached to the wine business than parenting, and who had been bitterly disappointed in love (had it been a fortune-hunter pretending to be a lover?) and had come two thousand miles to an outpost of civilization to learn a man's business and compete in a man's world? To hell with Willoughby! Let him take care of himself.

On his way out, he gave Maisie a warm smile, and was rewarded when her face lit up and she blushed prettily.

THE PROVINCIAL ARISTOCRACY WAS OUT IN full force and gay panoply. Tory gentlemen and their wives from London, Brantford, Cobourg, and every place in between had come into the capital a day or two before the event and set themselves up in comfort at the best Toronto hotels and inns or had descended upon wary relatives with spacious abodes in town. In one way or another, all this had been part of Sir Francis Head's strategy for the elite to take back the political powers of which they had been indignantly deprived in the elections of 1834 and upon which they had hereditary claim.

Every carriage and horse-drawn vehicle in York County and beyond had been commandeered for the purpose of conveying the eighty-some guests to the magnificent residence of Mr. and Mrs. Ignatius Maxwell (and daughter) along a route that would give them the widest exposure for their ostentation and the least discomfort for their behinds. Most of them connived to promenade at least part of the way westwards along fashionable King Street, where the hoi polloi cheered and jeered them with equal vigour. And since more than a dozen handsome officers of the 24th Regiment of Foot had been included in the guest list and since such officers were necessarily resplendent in scarlet or green and gold with high, feathered shako caps, those with the most important carriages and the showiest horses contrived to pick up one or more of these trophies, adding both colour and sex appeal to their equipage.

Marc chose to walk. He went down Peter Street to Front, where, dangling from a flagpole in front of the Toronto Hotel, was a crude effigy of Philo Rumsey, his neck well wrung by a hangman's noose. They would, it appeared, be celebrating more than a patently successful electoral campaign tonight. For a block around Somerset House, the streets were bustling with stomping horses, beleaguered grooms and footmen, and of course gorgeously arrayed women and rigidly handsome gentlemen moving in stately file up the stone steps of the great neo-Gothic house. Sir Francis stood beside Prudence and Ignatius Maxwell on its lush portico and accepted fealty in the form of curtsy and bow from the guests. All this house needs is a moat, Marc thought uncharitably. He was surprised to see several moderate Reformers among the guests, including Robert Baldwin and Francis Hincks.

As he made his way politely along the reception line, Prudence Maxwell leaned over to him and whispered, "I've put you down for the waltz later on, Lieutenant—when the party's had a chance to warm up."

•   •   •

Marc was a natural and, on most occasions, an enthusiastic dancer. He was glad this was so, for it enabled him to coast through the main part of the evening in a not-unpleasant, near-narcotic state. Riding the rhythms of the music (the orchestra in the ornate mezzanine of the enormous, tall-windowed ballroom was the best money could assemble) and tripping through the formal configurations of the set-piece dances, he was able to smile and utter brief, meaningless pleasantries as fingers touched and hips brushed and eyes locked—while his thoughts and feelings floated free in their own misery-laden ether. Indeed, it was only by reference to his dance card that he could be sure he had actually partnered Angeline Hartley, Chastity Maxwell, and half a dozen other belles whose names he was expected to remember. When he somewhat reluctantly went over to Prudence to fulfill his commitment to the waltz, he was surprised that she glided out onto the floor like a proper chatelaine, made light but coherent conversation, and barely looked him in the eye. Her own eyes, however, were beginning to sparkle like the Champagne fuelling them, and Marc hoped for her sake that she would make it through the evening with her hostess's dignity intact.

When the requisite and preordained dances were complete, the orchestra took a break, and the grand ladies and gentlemen repaired variously to the sweetmeats-and-

Champagne tables or to the powder rooms tucked away behind a huge screen of intersecting Persian rugs. Within minutes, natural groupings had formed and were from time to time reformed as boredom or more avid passions took precedence.

Without a lot of real interest, Marc stood well aside and observed the to-ing and fro-ing. He noticed that Willoughby (who had arrived late and scrupulously avoided him all evening) was paying much attention to Chastity Maxwell. Could Colin have been the officer secretly courting her? It was possible. Colin had definitely been seeing some woman or women in the past week or so: Mrs. Standish's instincts in that regard were near infallible. Hilliard, who had arrived with Angeline, had danced with her at least three times and was now plying her recklessly with Champagne while the governor's gaze was averted. Marc decided to keep his own watch on the couple. He liked Hilliard, who was as ambitious as he himself was, and did not wish to see him jeopardize his career so foolishly. Prudence Maxwell, tulip glass in hand, was chatting with Chief Justice Robinson and his sturdy wife, while her own husband was in a far corner, his mutton chops caressing the cleavage of a debutante from the hinterland. When the justice and his spouse took their leave, Prudence made a wobbly beeline for the drinks table.

When the orchestra returned and struck up a lancers tune, those guests with youthful energies took up the challenge. Without the strictures of the dance card, men and women were free to partner as caprice propelled them.

Liaisons or the promise of such were made, coyly retracted, then reinstated with a coquettish smile or an extra squeeze of hip or fingertip. Hilliard stuck close to Angeline (or she to him, it was hard to tell). Willoughby had disappeared but not, Marc was relieved to see, with Chastity—who was keeping a daughterly eye on her mother. For Prudence, still counting herself among the vigorous, had tottered into a square, tumbled against a startled ensign, and, in breaking her fall, had latched on to a part of him generally reserved for his own use. Chastity and another woman—whom Marc took to be Flora Moncreiff, her aunt—assisted Prudence towards the powder rooms, but she put up such a fuss that they had to be satisfied with sitting her down on a chair, where she slumped like a punched puppet. Ignatius Maxwell was nowhere in sight. Nor was the debutante.

Marc wanted very much to leave all of this—the superficiality and the melodrama and the picayune rivalries. But he was genuinely concerned about Prudence, and Chastity too. God knows where Maxwell had spirited his young woman or what he was planning to do with her. Prudence was undoubtedly aware of her husband's philandering, but the humiliation of his carrying on at a gala of which he was host and which the governor himself had sanctioned as a celebration of sorts could well prove too much. He expected her at any moment to start proclaiming her mate's apostasy before the assembled pillars of the community. And with a voice like hers, the deafest dowager in the hall would soon know all.

Fortunately, the frolic was almost over. The last dance

had been announced. Marc took the opportunity to sidle over to Chastity and say quickly, "If you need any help with your mother, please call on me. I'll stay till the end, if you like."

Chastity smiled gratefully. "Thank you. She's almost asleep in her chair, thank God." Marc moved a discreet distance away, and noticed that Chastity was looking anxiously around the ballroom for someone—her truant father, or Willoughby?

The dance was now over, and the revellers began to make their way to the vestibule with its dazzling chandelier and majestic oaken doors. The commotion of footmen, grooms, and restless horses could be heard outside in the summer air. The butler, Jacques, and his conscripted underlings were busy sorting out wraps and hats and gloves, and bowing curtly at increasingly rapid intervals. Several of the regular servants had begun snuffing out the candles, and the big room began to darken by degrees. Looking weary and bored, Sir Francis stood on the porch and bade farewell to all and sundry. Marc hung back until he saw Chastity and her black-robed aunt lift the near-comatose Prudence towards the rear exit, which led to the women's apartments beyond.

He was just about to depart when Ignatius Maxwell clapped him on the shoulder and said heartily, "Do join the governor and me for a nightcap and a cigar, young man. We hear you are the toast of the town!"

• • •

IF SIR FRANCIS WAS WORRIED ABOUT his eccentric behaviour yesterday evening, he showed no sign of it during the twenty minutes or so that he and Marc and Maxwell spent in casual conversation in the receiver general's den in the wing of Somerset House reserved for his use—and any privacy he might require from time to time. Obviously, the governor still had full confidence in his aide-de-camp. Marc endured their compliments as best he could, taking refuge in the French brandy and a West Indian cigar.

"And I must tell you, Ignatius—confidentially, of course—that I intend to make this young Turk here my military secretary as well as principal aide-de-camp. Poor old Burns will be ready for half-pay within the month. But Marc here—"

Marc was on the verge of a protest—just how he might have worded it he would never know—when Sir Francis suddenly pitched forward in his chair. Maxwell caught him before he toppled to the floor.

"It's nothing, nothing," the governor mumbled. "A bit too much Champagne and one too many cigars."

"You're sure you're all right?" Maxwell said with some alarm.

Marc's alarm was as real as Maxwell's but had more sinister sources: was this another attempt? Was the madman still loose and determined to have his way? Marc cursed himself for having been so caught up in his own personal problems that he had not bothered to keep a close eye on the very man whose safety was his foremost responsibility. How simple it would have been for an assassin to slip something poisonous into one of Sir Francis's drinks amid the noise and bustle of the gala!

They both bent over the stricken governor.

"I'm just . . . very tired," he said in a voice suddenly weak. He was also grey around the gills.

Maxwell nodded at Marc and said to Sir Francis, "You'll stay in my apartments tonight, Governor. I'll ring for Jacques, and we'll have you tucked in, in a wink. One of the officers can escort Angelina back to Government House."

Sir Francis made no protest, and Marc was relieved to see the colour returning to his cheeks. Fatigue, drink, and the exertions of the evening seemed to be the worst of it.

"Would you mind informing the governor's footman, Lieutenant, that his master will not be needing the carriage tonight?"

Marc agreed, then quietly withdrew. He put on his jacket and shako cap, and made his way through a maze of hallways towards the ballroom. He had just stepped into it when he met a concerned man in livery, looking for Sir Francis. He seemed much relieved at the news Marc conveyed, and trotted out through the massive doors, still manned by two stout servants. Otherwise the vast space was empty, silent, and growing dark as the final few candles burned themselves out. Marc had taken just one step back towards Sir Francis—the governor's safety was still his responsibility—when he heard Jacques's voice behind him.

"Excuse me, sir. Mrs. Maxwell's in a bad way. I've been summoned to the master's rooms. Would you mind just keeping an eye on her till I am able to get back to her?"

"Where is Miss Maxwell?"

"She has gone to her room, and my knock failed to rouse her, sir. I'm afraid she is fast asleep. And Mrs. Moncreiff has gone home with her daughters."

"Should I go for a doctor? Is she seriously ill?"

Jacques actually blushed, then stared at his shoes as he said, barely above a whisper, "Not exactly, sir."

Dead drunk and about to stir up a ruckus of some sort, he might just as well have said. But the message was clear nonetheless, and Marc had no choice but to temporarily abandon Sir Francis and head in the direction Jacques indicated, while the butler made for the safer domain of the male Maxwell. The corridors were unlit, so Marc had to tiptoe along until he spotted a door partly ajar with a flickering light of some sort behind it. With a mixture of disgust and pity, he eased the door open and stepped inside.

At first he could see little, as the only source of illumination seemed to be a candle-lamp on a small table set against the far wall. Cautiously he edged towards it.

"Over this way, lover." The voice was that of Prudence Maxwell, slightly slurred but showing little sign of physical distress.

As Marc drew nearer, he noticed—with a start—that he was not in a sitting room or antechamber: he was in the lady's boudoir. A canopied four-poster bed stood before him in vivid outline. In the pool of light splashed across it, he could see a rumpled, rose-embossed comforter, and the pale, rougeless face and sprawling coiffure of Prudence herself, who peered up at him with blurry-eyed curiosity.

Marc started to backpedal: "Please excuse me, Mrs. Maxwell, I had no idea you were abed when Jacques asked me to look in."

"Oh, it's you, Lieutenant," Prudence breathed, and blinked sharply, as if that might somehow bring him more fully into focus. "You'll do just fine."

"I'll have Jacques wake one of the maids."

"Jacques has already done what he was told to do. Now be a good lad and come sit beside me. I've a dreadful—"

"Please don't do anything you'll regret in the morning."

"—itch. Way down here!" She threw back the comforter with a single sweep of her hand. "And I never regret anything in the morning."

Prudence Maxwell was as naked as Godiva, though the image she presented upon the silk sheets of her feather bed was more akin to a Rubens nude—all pink and plump and enticingly hollowed. Her prodigious breasts stared up at Marc with their stiff, blind eyelets.

"Climb aboard, sailor. This brig needs her sails trimmed."

The second and a half that it took Marc to avert his gaze was all the time Prudence needed. She lunged halfway off the bed, braced her plummeting weight on one outstretched hand, caught her balance, and seized Marc by the left wrist. Thinking she was about to crash unaided onto the hardwood floor, he had sprung forward to assist her, and the combination of his leap and her seizing precipitated them both back onto the bed. Whereupon she began to tear at his clothes as if she were plucking a warm chicken. He felt his shirt ripping, but the more he tried to find a decent and workable purchase on his assailant, the more he inadvertently stirred her ardour by brief clutches of breast, hip, thigh, or buttock.

"I've got to have you, you beautiful man!"

"But think of your husband—"

"I am thinking of the son of a bitch!"

She had almost succeeded in trapping his thighs in a scissors hold when they heard a noise in the hall (the door was still ajar), as if someone heavy had just stumbled.

"That's him now!" Marc gasped as he attempted to pry her nearest thigh away from his pant leg without having the manoeuvre misinterpreted.

"He never leaves his apartment," she hissed and, to refocus her lover's attention, made a grab for his privates. "He's in there now screwing that little bitch from Brantford!"

The next stumble was not only louder, it was right outside the door. And it was followed by a singularly primal, male grunt.

"Jesus! I thought he'd gone. You better get out of here fast."

"How?" Marc said. He looked wildly about him. There were one door and two windows too high and narrow to be of use.

Under the bed was a possibility, but hiding there could be more daunting than merely confronting a cuckolded husband.

"He gets into such terrible rages," Prudence said, and there was genuine fear in her voice.

Just before blind panic seized him, Marc had one rational thought: at least the governor must have recovered.

"The closet!" Prudence screamed through her teeth. "It runs all along that wall over there. Get inside. Quick! Please!"

Marc sprinted for the closet, deep in the far shadows of the room, pulling his tattered uniform together as best he could. He fumbled about for a door handle, found one, yanked the door open, and practically somersaulted into the silks and brocades and other gauzy attire exclusive to the female sex. He eased the door shut just as the interloper clumped into the room.

"Ah, darling. You see how ready I am for you? What took you so long?"

Marc had to admire the lady's aplomb.

Maxwell—no doubt thwarted earlier in his pathetic attempt to seduce the young woman from Brantford—had apparently decided to offer his favours to his long-suffering wife. Marc heard a thick body thump onto the bed, followed quickly by a slurred moan, then a muffled male gurgle: "My God, you are ready!"

Well, Marc thought, as he thrashed softly among dresses and shifts and petticoats like a bumblebee in a web and tried not to listen to the groans and wheeze of the aging fornicators: this is surely the ultimate humiliation. It was at that moment that he realized the latch on the outside of the closet door had slipped back into place during his frantic entry. He was trapped.

"Ah, yes, lover, yes, yes!"

The room beyond fell suddenly and blessedly silent. Moments later a pair of mismatched snores vied for supremacy.

Desperately, Marc searched along the length of the closet, trampling on dresses as he did, but none of the other doors had been left unlatched, and none could be opened from the inside. He could force one of them open, but the noise might waken one of the spent lovers, and with his luck he knew which one it would be.

He was here for the night. Or longer.

Deciding that he might as well try to sleep—at least it would be Prudence or her maid who would open one of these doors in the morning—he sat down and lay back against the rear wall and was just beginning to take note of the fact that his bladder was alarmingly full when the wall abruptly gave way. He found himself lying flat on his back and staring up at what had to be the ceiling of another room. The adjoining room! He nearly laughed aloud for joy! Prudence's closet obviously served the occupants of both chambers. He had fallen through an unlatched door on the opposite side.

A tight but definitely female squeal brought him upright and twisting around to see whose privacy he had now invaded. The squeal erupted again, as if a maid had just identified a mouse in her bed.

Marc slammed his eyes shut, but not before—in the light of several candles—they had taken in the essentials of a young woman standing naked in front of her four-poster bed.

"I'm sorry, Miss Maxwell," Marc whispered, though he wasn't sure why. "I can explain everything tomorrow, if you'll just pull a robe on and show me the door."

There was no answer. Was she terrified? With good cause, he thought. Finally he detected a faint rustling noise, waited for thirty seconds, then opened his eyes just a slit.

Chastity Maxwell remained frozen not ten feet away, her youthful beauty caught nicely in the candle's glow. She was staring at him. There was fear or concern of some kind in her gaze, but she made no move to cover her breasts or the golden thatch at the vee of her thighs. What on earth did she want? Marc's heart sank. Not again!

Still she said nothing but began to jerk her head furiously and roll her eyes to a low window on the outer wall, which was wide open to the midnight breeze. On the third or fourth swivelling of head and rolled eyes, Marc got the point. She wanted him to go out through the window quietly, afraid no doubt that her mother might have heard her suppressed shrieks and taken it upon herself to come staggering in from the hall to beat back the barbarous threat to her daughter's maidenhead. Marc smiled his understanding, and Chastity continued to watch him silently as he crept over to the window, hoisted himself up onto the wide ledge, twisted around so that his legs hung down outside, ready to cushion his drop to the ground, and began to lower the trunk of his body over the outside sill—while trying not to stare at the beautiful young woman standing there like Galatea, nude before Pygmalion. Just as Marc was about to drop, Chastity moved back to the bed. At the same time, a second un-clothed figure unfolded itself from under the flounce around the lower part of the four-poster and rose up over her.

It was Hilliard.

Marc was so shocked he forgot to brace his legs and feet, and as a result he crashed heavily to the ground twelve feet below.

A needle-sharp pain shot up the length of his right leg, and he collapsed in a heap. The unmuted scream he let out might have awakened the soundest of sleepers. Grimacing and cursing silently, he listened for any signs of disturbance within the great house, but all was quiet. He rolled over into a sitting position. He was in a garden, and somewhere close by he could make out a street lamp. He was home free. But when he tried to get up, his right ankle rebelled, and gave way under his weight. It was seriously sprained. He was not sure he could walk, or even limp. My God, was this the final humiliation? Was he going to have to crawl to Mrs. Standish's on his hands and knees?

"Require some assistance from the local police?"

Marc looked up into the shadowy face peering down at

him. The nose glowed like a beacon, and never had Marc been so happy to see it. "Cobb!"

"That's what the wife calls me when she's in the mood," Cobb said, tucking his truncheon back into his belt. "I pert near split yer noggin with this here, Major. Took you fer the burglar that's been upsettin' rich folks down here."

"Would you mind helping me to my feet?" Marc said. "I've turned my ankle."

Cobb leaned down and pulled Marc up, then held him as he tottered and swayed.

"I don't think I can get home on my own," Marc said.

Cobb was appraising the dishevelled state of Marc's clothes. "You do this often, Major? Drop out of strange windows in the middle of the night?"

"Only when I can't find the door."

"Why don't you just put an arm around my shoulder and we'll see if we can find the door to the widow's place."

"Thank you, Constable."

"'Course, with me gone, the burglars down here'll think Boxin' Day's come early."

They had barely shuffled half a block when Cobb paused to catch his breath, then said, "Say now, Major, where'd you leave yer hat?"

THIRTEEN

I t was nine o'clock on Sunday morning when Marc woke
up after a deep, dreamless sleep. Even so, his whole body
ached. He realized now how utterly exhausted he had become in the ten days since the governor had narrowly missed
being assassinated. The throbbing in his right ankle reminded him, despite his best efforts to blot out the memory,
of the débâcle at Somerset House, and his astonishment
that it was Hilliard, not Colin Willoughby, who had been
courting both Chastity (the second misnomer in that family) and disaster. With a supreme exercise of will, Marc raised
himself up and stepped down onto the rug below. His yelp

was piercing enough to bring both Mrs. Standish and Maisie flying to his rescue.

"It's all right," he insisted, not a little abashed at being observed standing at his bedside in his cotton nightshirt. "I twisted my ankle last night."

"That must've been some dance," Mrs. Standish said. "Maisie, run down to the wharf and buy some ice." To Marc she said, "You'll have to ice that swelling for a couple of hours at least. You should've had it looked to when you come in last night."

"I didn't want to disturb you—ouch!"

Mrs. Standish had both hands on his wounded ankle. "Well, it ain't broken—just sprained. So we won't need the doctor."

"Did Colin come in after me?"

"Ain't put his head to the pillow yet," Mrs. Standish said reprovingly, and waved Maisie off on her errand.

Marc was not unhappy with that news: whoever Willoughby's lover was, she would provide some necessary consolation, diversion, and, possibly, perspective.

Later, Marc was served breakfast in bed by an enthusiastic Maisie, who peered up at him with worshipping eyes whenever she felt he was not looking. Then the two women dressed and went off to St. James' to hear "the dear Reverend Strachan" fulminate against the enemies of the Mother Church. Marc fell asleep again.

By midafternoon he felt strong enough to limp gingerly

about the house and, eager to find something to occupy his mind so that he would not start mulling over "what if's" and "might've been's" in regard to his feelings for Beth and his attraction to Eliza, he decided to go to the officers' mess at the garrison and while away the Sabbath in the pleasure of male companionship. He had initially considered going over to see Eliza, as her uncle was still away, but remembered in time his solemn promise to her Friday night that he would see her only once again: on the day of her departure. Anything else would have been unbearable for her, and probably for him. So, Maisie was sent to Government House to arrange for the chestnut mare to be brought down to him, and to enquire after Sir Francis. The governor had fully recovered from his temporary dyspepsia and was safely at home. At four o'clock, with minimal assistance, Marc mounted and rode off towards the fort, less than a mile from the city.

It was dusk when he mounted again and, pleasantly drowsy with good wine and serviceable food, trotted east along Front Street towards the town. In fact, he had fallen into a doze in the saddle, and the mare, without specific instruction, headed up John Street for the stables, and her stall. When Marc was finally jerked awake, he looked up to see that he was in front of Government House.

"Good girl," he murmured. "You took yourself home." He nudged her around towards the stables, where he hoped to find a groom to lead the horse to his boarding house and return with her here. But just then the duty-corporal came hustling down the front steps to intercept him.

"An urgent message for you, sir!" he puffed, holding out a sealed envelope.

"From whom?"

"I think it's from Lieutenant Willoughby, sir. A lad from the city was paid to run it up here, and he says it is very urgent. I was just about to send a rider down to the garrison to find you."

"How long ago did it arrive?"

"Maybe half an hour ago."

"Thank you, Corporal," Marc said, taking the note and dismissing the messenger. As he opened the envelope and recognized the handwriting as Colin's, Marc speculated as to the nature of any "urgency" his wayward friend might have got himself into: an irate husband with a primed pistol was the best bet. He read the note, but it was not what he expected. Not at all.

Marc:
Wilkie and Cobb are down at Enoch Turner's brewery.
They apprehended three thieves breaking into the premises.
While they were questioning them, one of them, a fellow
named Campbell or Kimble, suddenly said that he had some
knowledge of Rumsey and the Moncreiff shooting. When
Cobb pressed him, he clammed up and swore he would

only talk to somebody high up with more authority. Cobb
suggested you, and the villain agreed. Wilkie was dispatched
to fetch you immediately. When he appeared at the widow's
house, he found me coming out. I told him I would go up to
Turner's while he went looking for you—and scribbled this
note for him. Come as quickly as you can. This may be our
only chance to find out who was behind the assassination.

Colin

Marc did not hesitate. He urged the mare to a full gallop
and was soon speeding east down Front Street towards the
brewery. The sun had almost set, but there was still plenty of
misty, high-summer light.

So, Rumsey had had an accomplice after all, Marc
thought. He was not surprised, as he had suspected Kimble
from the outset. Cobb had reported that Kimble had money
troubles, and so his involvement with the murder and with
these break-ins was no doubt driven by the need for cash.
And it seemed certain that the information he could provide would lead to the naming of the instigator and the
discovery of his motive. That this person was in all likelihood a member of the elite class, whatever his politics,
would explain why Kimble was demanding to speak to a
high-ranking official: the knowledge he possessed was deadly
dangerous. For a brief moment, Marc felt a pang of jealousy:
what if Willoughby—also a member of the governor's staff—
should prove to be that high-ranking person and get credit

for solving the murder? Marc shook off the thought and dug his good heel into the mare's left flank. Justice was the paramount concern.

As Marc galloped past the last houses on Front Street, he looked up to see the great Gooderham windmill that marked the eastern entrance to the capital. It was turning slowly and steadily, a symbol, Marc thought, of humanity's persistence and quest for permanence in an otherwise inhospitable wilderness. Marc was almost beginning to feel at home here. Soon Turner's brewery stood before him, shadowed and unlit anywhere inside or out. It was Sunday, and no one would be about—except the police and the thieves they had caught in the act. Good old Cobb: he had proved himself yet again. Marc felt a twinge of guilt at having ever doubted his loyalty.

The brewery offices faced the road, and beside them was the warehouse complete with large double doors, where the teamsters would park their wagons for loading casks of beer and unloading barley, hops, and other supplies. On the far side of the warehouse, Marc knew, there was a platform that served as a pier on the Don River, where shipments of beer were loaded onto barges and drifted down to the Gooderham wharf on the lake. There they could be hauled aboard steamers or schooners bound for Cobourg or Burlington. To the west, and rising up two or more storeys, was the brewhouse proper, with its half-dozen chimneys above the malting kilns. Marc assumed that the thieves had been caught in the warehouse section, where they could, as soon as darkness came, load casks and kegs onto a boat of their own with little fear of being disturbed. Marc tied up the mare and hopped up onto the platform facing the river. It was very dark here on the eastern side of the brewery, even though in the west there was still light in the sky. He pushed open one of the doors and limped in, one hand on his sabre. His ankle throbbed like a headache but held his weight.

"Cobb!" he called out in a loud stage whisper.

No answer.

He limped farther inside, but saw little except the blotchy outlines of kegs stacked one upon the other. Perhaps they were in the office section where there were lamps and chairs to aid interrogation. He tried to walk faster, but the pain in his ankle meant he was barely able to hobble down the dark hallway towards the owner's office. When he finally got there, he found the room empty and silent. Which meant they must be in the brewhouse, where, he recalled, there were spacious windows that provided both sunlight to work by and cool air to make the men's labour tolerable in the summer. Cobb must have taken them up there for the interrogation for some reason.

With his limp growing more agonizing at every step, Marc made his way to the brewhouse doors and eased them open. A hazy mote-filled light permeated the vaulted room around and above him. Marc could make out the enormous oaken vats where the beer, in its final stage, was fermenting on its own time, and the series of wooden catwalks that connected them and allowed the brewmaster and his assistants to observe the progress of the wort. In behind them, but not visible, were the kilns—now cold and dark. The air was musky with the odour of yeast and hops, and the pleasant sting of fermentation.

"Up here!"

It was Willoughby. Marc breathed a sigh of relief, and headed for a ladder that would take him up to the first level of the catwalk system, where Willoughby's voice had come from. Climbing up caused him excruciating pain, but he was determined to be in on the conclusion of this investigation: it had cost him more than any honest man should ever have to bear.

"We're up here, Marc. Everything's under control."

Oh, no. Had they already got the information they needed? If so, then why was he being asked to climb up there? He got the answer a second later when something hard, blunt, and angry struck him on the forehead. He gasped, felt his limbs turn to water, and crumpled on the catwalk.

WHEN HE WOKE UP, IT WAS dark. The light from a single lantern swayed a few inches before his eyes, making whatever was behind it blacker still. He was propped up against something wooden. His head now throbbed in concert with his ankle. His feet were tightly bound together with twine, and his hands likewise, in front of him.

"I knew you'd come," Willoughby said. "And come alone. You'd never pass up a chance to further your overweening ambitions—at the expense of those you have the effrontery to call your friends." The disembodied voice was hoarse, at the edge of exhaustion or uncontrollable excitement. It was seeded with incalculable bitterness and something far more feral, far more lethal. It was scarcely recognizable.

"What the hell is happening?" Marc moaned and twisted futilely at his bonds. "What have you done with Cobb and Wilkie?" he asked softly and, for the first time, fearfully.

"They're a long way from here, you'll be pleased to know." Willoughby laughed, a low chortle. "And there are no thieves here. Just you and me. And in a few minutes, there'll only be me." Willoughby moved the lantern so that it illuminated both his face and Marc's, as if he wanted to make sure that Marc could see the cold derision in his eyes that was already so vivid in his voice.

Marc had no more doubts as to his fate. He was staring into the face of a madman, of one who was past all reason, all caution, all caring, of one who, for whatever perverted motive, had deemed revenge the only course of action that would satisfy.

"Why have you tied me up? What are you planning to do?" Marc tried to keep the tremor out of his voice but failed.

"I'm going to kill you, Lieutenant. I'm going to tip you into that vat there, bound hand and foot, and then I'm going to watch you drown, second by second."

"You're mad! You can't expect to get away with this!"

"Oh, but I will. And this time the right man will die." Again he laughed, holding up the lantern so that Marc could see his tormentor's enjoyment.

Marc couldn't believe what he had just heard, but then understanding dawned. "You hired Rumsey to shoot me?"

"That was my only mistake. The son of a bitch missed and killed dear old Moncreiff. But that was your doing, too, wasn't it? You bent down, like the fawning sycophant you are, to help the almighty governor pick up a scrap of paper!"

"And it was you who took that first shot at Rumsey down on the docks."

"I only had to fire my gun. The others did the rest."

"You're mad."

"And you're repeating yourself, Lieutenant. But I'm not mad, you see, only angry. And twice as clever as you, you who've set yourself up as regimental know-it-all. Otherwise I wouldn't be here listening to you whine and beg. You'll be astonished to learn that I've known every pathetic move you've made in your so-called investigation—sometimes before you yourself did. You made it particularly easy for me to have Crazy Dan killed: it was you, remember, who failed to give the proper order, not me."

Marc's mind returned to that horrible episode and to the

events that followed. Willoughby certainly had been in a position to clarify the order, and had chosen not to—a deliberate scheme to have Dan blamed for Moncreiff's murder and then conveniently silenced. When Rumsey was fingered, Colin must have been in quite a panic, even though he'd taken pains to disguise his identity in his dealings with him at the Tinker's Dam. But with Rumsey dead and the governor happy, Willoughby would be in the clear. Only Marc stood in his way. And all that "remorse" he'd suffered had been for the inadvertent murder of Moncreiff, not the mangled corpse of the innocent and harmless Crazy Dan.

"You're the fool," Marc said, realizing that his only hope of survival was to keep Willoughby talking until some plan or other suggested itself to him. "I hadn't the slightest suspicion it was you who hired Rumsey. I even had evidence from Rumsey that seemed to point to the governor as his target. You've risked this charade for nothing!"

Willoughby merely laughed. "So you think that's what this is all about, do you? I can't for the life of me see why the governor chose you to investigate a murder."

"Why am I here, then?"

"Because I hate your guts, that's why. I hired Rumsey to blow your brains out, and when he failed I thought of nothing except how to do the deed myself. But first I had to make sure I wasn't found out. Then, when the chance of taking your job for a week came up, I thought, well, perhaps I can show Sir Francis Bonehead that I am your superior in every way after all, perhaps I'll even get what I was promised when the old fart took me on back in London: I was to be his aide-de-camp! He made a promise to my father! A solemn vow! And he reneged on it."

"You cannot blame Sir Francis—"

"I blame you! That's why you're trussed up like a capon for the pot! I want you to know exactly why I hate you, what I have suffered at your hands, and why I need to watch you cringe and cower and beg like a dog for your miserable life, and then watch you die slowly like a fly in porridge."

The odour from the vat that Marc was resting against was suddenly overpowering. He felt his stomach heave. "All this just because I was commanded to take your job—against my will?"

Willoughby did not answer. He pushed the lantern forward into Marc's face so that his own features were obscured. Only his voice—bitter, enraged, irrational—now carried his venom to its target. "You really have no idea, do you? Well, then, sit back and listen while I tell you a story. It'll be the last one you'll ever hear."

"But I've tried to be your friend, I—"

"Quite true. My anger over the governor's betrayal was intense when I arrived with him in January. He told me you were recommended by Sir John and his hands were tied, and so on. But I was already suffering, and it took little to drive me back to drink and whoring. It was you who kept me from going under when you got back from Cobourg."

"And I knew you'd had a bad love affair in—"

The lantern was drawn back marginally so that only the sleep-deprived, whisky-slitted, bloodshot eyes could be seen. "But you didn't know, Mr. Investigator, did you, that the woman who jilted me was here in Toronto?"

"That's impossible, you came—"

"I came out here, four months after she abandoned me and left me to perish in the sewers of London. She herself came out here in November—to escape me!"

Marc could hear the maniacal chuckle deep in Willoughby's throat as he watched the truth register in his victim's face.

"You can't mean Eliza?"

"She might've been Eliza to you, but she was Rosy to me—always."

"You're making this up, you're—"

"—mad. So you've said. But it was Miss Dewart-Smythe, my darling Rosy, my dear, dear pink rose."

Eliza, who was forever surrounded by flowers, by pink roses, Marc remembered with a start.

"You will be amazed to learn—arrogant fool that you are—that she was besotted with me even when she suspected me of being dissolute and unfaithful, even when I came to her bed stinking of other women. It was her meddling uncle who undid me, who found out what I was up to in the stews and opium dens—and that my father was threatening to disinherit me. Well, that news put paid to the engagement, after the second banns had been publicly proclaimed! I was ruined."

"That's why your father arranged for you to come out here." Marc continued to twist at the rope binding his hands, as he strove to keep Willoughby talking. The pain in his ankle prevented even the slightest attempt to loosen the bonds around his feet.

"He didn't know, but I did, that Rosy was heading this way also."

"But why did you—"

"Because I still loved her, you fool! You insensitive fool! And as soon as my feet hit the wharf here, I made straight for her house." A chilling, brutal tone took over the voice and its twisted narrative. "You can't begin to imagine how that cold bitch treated me! She made me stand on the porch in the snow, she ordered me to stay five blocks from her house or else she would go directly to the governor and destroy any hopes I had of advancement here."

"And you managed to keep away, even though—"

"I had to! But, Christ Almighty, how I hated and loved the bitch at the same time. I wouldn't expect an egotistical bastard like you to understand, but I loved her from afar more than ever, even as I plotted ways to avenge her snub." He chuckled softly and added, "I found a couple of scoundrels at the Tinker's Dam only too willing to burgle St. Sebastian's precious wine cellar."

Willoughby had no idea just how closely Marc could identify with the remark about loving from afar.

"Then back you come, taking my job away from me, and then, suddenly, in April I see you with my Rosy, and I see the looks you give each other, and I can't believe my eyes: you rob me of my rightful appointment and then you steal the only woman I've ever loved."

"But I didn't know, you should have—"

"Shut up! I don't want to hear another word from you or I'll dump you into this vat right now."

Marc said nothing, but his mind was racing. Willoughby could be no more than three or four feet away. He had been crouching low so as to stare his victim down and reap the rewards of his slow, mental torture. If Marc could get him talking again, perhaps he could use his bound legs as a battering ram—painful as that might be—and topple Willoughby off the catwalk. It did not seem likely that he could free his hands: already he could feel blood trickling down his palms.

"Taking my Rosy was the last straw. I began to plot my revenge. I heard about this Rumsey fellow at the Blue Ox and I sent a note to him in a roundabout way, and we met at the Tinker's Dam. He had no idea who I was, but when he saw ten dollars in his palm, he came on board. I sent him the information about the governor's trip to Danby's Crossing. A murder on the hustings, I calculate, will throw everything into confusion: people will naturally think the governor was the target. Who'd want to kill a no-account like you, eh? And the beauty of it is, I will be standing near the platform when the shooting takes place, so I can't be suspected. I'll even get to turn around and pretend to be shocked at your face blown apart, while I'll be laughing inside. But you always find a way to bugger things up, don't you? You even managed to get your buggy tipped over on King Street and that foolishness got the governor all sweated up about Angeline—who's no angel, by the way—and that got me assigned to guarding the little ball-breaker for a week instead of leading the governor's guard and showing him I was better at the job than you, the incompetent that got Crazy Dan killed. If you hadn't tried to play Sir Lancelot on King Street, I might have gotten what I truly deserved. I might've even tried to forget about Eliza. So, you see, in your own blundering way, you ensured your own death."

Willoughby started coughing. And Marc noticed that some of his words were slurred: he had doubtlessly been awake since yesterday, and had probably been drinking rotgut whisky in some dive. That meant he was beyond exhaustion and, most likely, in that state of final euphoria just before the mind and body collapse around each other. If only . . .

"And here's the best of it, you conniving, immoral bastard. Angeline's driving me crazy with her juvenile chittering, and she won't let me near her, so I go looking for solace elsewhere, and I remember Lady Maxwell batting her lashes at me in February at the Grange, so I sneak into her bed and she goes off like a bombshell, and I'm feeling so mellow I even begin to think maybe you're not a hypocritical arsehole after all."

"But you tried to club me to death!"

"I got myself drunk at some blind pig and went a little crazy. And I damn near got caught—it gave me quite a fright. I discovered a button missing on my tunic when I got home. But not before I snuck back to Lady Lascivious, and she wraps those fat stumps around me and lets me stay till morning. I begin to feel generous again, the world doesn't seem so bad when you're getting it regular—I even have thoughts of replacing Hilliard between Chastity's thighs. But then you go and do it again—seal your own fate. For what do I find when I slip back into Somerset House last night after everybody's gone and the master's tucked away with his own doxy, but a hot-blooded woman already primed for her lover. Except when I wake up in the morning, there's something interesting on the floor beside the bed—"

"My shako . . ." So it had been Willoughby at Prudence's door, not her husband. "But, Colin, I was only—"

"I told you to shut up and listen! What I want you to know—to take with you as the muck clogs your throat—is that the hardest part of all this was not outfoxing you. That was easy because your arrogance knows no bounds and blinds you to what's right in front of your nose. No, the hardest part for me was having to pretend, day in and day out, that we were friends while the very thought of having to smile at you made me want to retch."

Marc braced himself for the one chance that remained. He heard Willoughby begin to stand up, so he swung his legs together in a vicious arc, hoping to catch Willoughby behind the knees. They cracked into the vat, and Marc screamed with the pain of it. Willoughby had leapt nimbly out of the way.

"Nice try, Lieutenant. There's no use struggling. You're a dead man. But if you beg a little, I might let you live a minute longer. If you've got a final prayer, you'd better start saying it now."

Marc said nothing. His prayer was fervent but wordless. His hands went up to his shirt, where he had tucked away Willoughby's note. If he was to die, so be it, but when the brewers fished him out of the vat, they would find the murderer's incriminating message.

Willoughby laughed, and there was nothing human left in it. "Looking for this, Lieutenant?" He dangled the note between his thumb and forefinger in the patch of light from his lantern. Then he set the lantern down and tore the paper to shreds. "It'll make a fine addition to the brew, won't it?" And he laughed again: an hysterical cackle. "And so will you. I'm going to get away with the whole thing. As soon as I've seen you suck in your last breath, I'm going down to the warehouse and roll a few casks off the dock, so when they find your body contaminating their beer, they'll think you surprised the booze burglars and got surprised yourself. And who knows, some people may even think you died a hero!"

Marc felt Willoughby's powerful, vengeful arms begin

to lift him up, as one does a cripple. He twisted feverishly, and even tried to bite his tormentor. He felt his injured foot strike the iron edge of the open vat, the wort bubbling and lethal just below.

"Stand where you are, sir! You're under arrest!" The voice was loud, coming from somewhere in the darkness below.

Cobb's commands struck Willoughby with the force of a truncheon, and he dropped Marc in a heap onto the catwalk. Willoughby wavered as if he had been stunned, or perhaps the effects of sleeplessness, rage, and drink were taking their toll. Marc rolled away towards the vat. He didn't relish tumbling on his own off the catwalk and cracking his skull open on the stone floor of the brewhouse. Cobb was climbing the ladder with the aid of a lantern, making him an easy target for Willoughby, who, seeing exactly who the challenger was and that he was alone and unarmed, staggered towards the spot where the ladder met the catwalk floor. On his way, he knocked over his own lantern, and it shone upwards, allowing Marc to see that he was drawing a pistol from his belt and cocking it.

Marc could hear Cobb's feet clumping on the rungs of the ladder as he climbed bravely and foolishly upwards. In desperation, Marc started rolling over and over towards Willoughby. At any moment he expected Colin to wheel and put a bullet into him, but he seemed fixated like a snake, waiting for Cobb's face to rise up above the ladder before shooting him point-blank.

Marc struck Willoughby just behind the knees. He top-pled instantly: first forward, then, in trying to right his balance, sideways—kicking the lantern as he did. There was a short, pathetic shriek, a splash, and then silence. Marc hauled himself up—two-handed—to the rim of the vat into which Willoughby had pitched. He reached down for the lantern, fumbled with it, got its handle between his hands, and held it up over the surface of the vat. He could see nothing. Cobb could be heard huffing up the final few steps of the ladder.

Suddenly there was a whoosh and a frantic splashing, as Willoughby broke through the murky surface and began flailing in the froth. Marc could make out only the hollows of his eyes and mouth.

"Reach your arm up this way!" Marc cried, realizing as he called out that he could not raise his bound wrists above the iron edging of the vat. However, the sound of Marc's voice—the familiar ring of its command—seemed to cut momentarily through the absolute shock that had gripped Willoughby, and he stopped thrashing about for a second and stretched out his right hand—still gripping the pistol—towards the safety of the vat's rim. At the same moment, Cobb thumped up beside Marc. In the unsteady gleam from Marc's lantern, the constable thrust his arm out over the bubbling wort. As he began to sink back down, Willoughby managed to clutch Cobb's wrist in a death-grip, and the pistol plopped harmlessly away. Cobb grunted, and then started to haul Willoughby slowly but surely towards him.

Willoughby's head and shoulders rose up out of the yeasty mass, like a stag out of quicksand.

"Hang on, Colin! Everything'll be all right!" Marc shouted.

And it looked as if it should have been, for Cobb, with his breath coming in great gusting pants, was in the act of clasping his left hand over Willoughby's wrist so that he could lever him up and over the rim. But at the sound of Marc's voice, Willoughby let go of Cobb's wrist. The whites of his eyes flared in their dark hollows, and their pupils seized upon something directly before them, widened with recognition or dismay, and squeezed shut against whatever could not be borne. Cobb's other hand clutched at air. Willoughby drifted down into the comforting ooze, his Byronic curls floating in the froth for a long second before they, too, vanished.

Marc groaned and slumped to the catwalk floor, reaching down in a vain effort to coddle his throbbing ankle.

Cobb picked up his lantern, turned its light fully upon him, and said, "Well, Major, you seem to get yerself into the goddamnedest predicaments."

FOURTEEN

As it turned out, Cobb had to carry Marc down the ladder, while juggling his lantern, and through the brewery to the door that opened onto the road. There stood a two-wheeled, tumbledown donkey-cart and a grizzled donkey, who looked as if he hadn't been separated from it since birth.

"You must have quite a story to tell, Major," Cobb said dryly as he unhitched the donkey and stroked its muzzle. "Lean on the butcher-cart fer a second—I'm goin' 'round the back to fetch yer horse."

The sky above Marc was pitch-black, but the full moon

had arisen already in the southeastern sky, shimmering far out on the lake and bathing the landscape with a surreal light. Strangely, Marc felt that, despite the trials of the past two weeks and the horror of watching Colin Willoughby let himself drown, he was, against all odds, being blessed. Then a cloud passed briefly over the moon, and he felt his heart darken with the suddenness of night.

Cobb returned, leading Marc's mare. "I'll put you in the cart, Major—where ya aren't liable to fall out—and do my best to walk this donkey gently home."

"The mare will follow along," Marc said as he allowed Cobb to hoist him into the box of the cart. There was no driver's bench, as the butcher who owned it simply led the donkey through the narrowest of alleys in the town, delivering his wares to the back doors of inns and taverns. Cobb grasped the halter, and the tiny entourage started down the road towards the city limits.

"So, Major, how in heaven's name did you succeed in comin' all the way out here to try and get yerself killed?"

"Your story first," Marc said. He was still too numb to talk with any semblance of coherence. "How did you manage to arrive just in time to save me—again?"

"It's a bit of a tall tale, Major, but at the rate this ass is hoofin' it, we got all the time we need." Without turning his head, Cobb told his story. "It all started around five o'clock. Me and the missus and the little Cobbs was just tuckin' into a joint of rare beef when Wilkie comes poundin' on our door.

'Mistress Cobb,' I say, 'we're in fer trouble, mark my words.' And so it come about. Seems that young Maisie Pollock'd come rushin' into the station house with her hair a-flyin' and her eyes as big as a guinea hen's, and when she catches her breath, she sobs out a tale of terror and violence."

Cobb paused to give Marc the opportunity to say sharply, "Has anything happened to Mrs. Standish?"

"Calm yerself, sir. Everybody's okay—now. Seems that Lieutenant Willoughby come home about four thirty in a wild and unmannerly state, which is a polite way of sayin' he was pissed and belligerent. He was swearin' like a Trojan and talkin' to himself, and when the widow tried to calm him down, he pushed her into a laundry hamper and called Maisie a lewd name, which she refuses to repeat, and then stomped off to his room. And just when they think he might be gonna sleep it off, they hear the most godawful crashin' sounds and the most dreadful cursin'—mostly yer name bein' taken in vain—and by the time they get up a nerve to have a gander, he comes staggerin' out of there like a ravin' loonie, knocks Maisie on the cheek with an elbow, and roars out of the house. The room is a shambles—bedclothes ripped and scattered, drawers pulled out and smashed, feathers tore out of the mattress. Wilkie and me saw this fer ourselves when we got there. So there's nothin' to be done but to give up the best part of our Sabbath and go huntin' fer the lunatic."

"Is Maisie all right?"

"Nothin' a kindly nod from yer direction won't cure," Cobb said, still looking ahead at the moon-washed fields between them and town. A few paces later, he took up his story again. "In the state he was in, we thought Willoughby could do some awful harm to anyone in his way. We know most of the taverns he frequents, so Wilkie and me divvy them up and go lookin' in them one by one. But there's not a whiff of him anywheres, and nobody admits to seein' him. So we finally give up, and Wilkie goes home to his family, but I figure I ought to take one more peek to see if the widow's okay, figurin' that Willoughby might've circled back there. But everythin's calm, the women're tidyin' up the room, and they mention you're up at the barracks, so I plan on hikin' out there to let you know what's happened and ask you to keep a close eye on the widow and Maisie.

But, of course, I spot you gallopin' past me like a runaway colt, and I holler after you, but you're spooked or some-thin'—and I start thinkin' maybe you and Willoughby have been bad boys together, so I commandeer the nearest vehi-cle, this butcher-cart parked outside Gandy Griffith's house, and I light out after you. Except it's damned hard to get a donkey to trot and to steer him whilst jouncin' in the back. I see you're keepin' to Front Street, so I tag along as best I can. Then I lose sight of you, but when I get to the end of Front Street, I can see yer dust way down the brewery road, and I figure you're headin' fer Turner's or the wharf. When I get here, with half my teeth loose, I mosey about and finally spot yer horse tied up behind. I go in, and hear voices. I light a lantern and head fer the noise. And that's about it."

"Thank you," was all Marc could say, knowing it was not half-enough.

"But you ain't heard the best part yet," Cobb said, and Marc could hear the wink in his voice. "The widow found this while she was tidyin' up."

Out of the big pocket of his coat, Cobb drew a bushy, black beard.

"Well, that's the precise piece of physical evidence we need," Marc said. His mind had miraculously cleared, and he was thinking hard—despite the drum roll of a colossal headache.

"It's an actor's beard," Cobb added. "You can feel the glue 'round the edges. I'm told you gentry-men back 'ome are given to puttin' on theatricals."

Marc decided it was time to fill Cobb in on as many of the details about the murder as he could ethically reveal. He began by describing Willoughby's certain but unprovable complicity in the death of Crazy Dan. He then explained— to Cobb's intermittent "ums" and "ahs" of surprise or confirmation—that he himself had been the target of Rumsey's bullet, but that when he and Sir Francis had both bent down to retrieve his speech, the bullet had struck Moncreiff instead. Marc did not mention that he had assumed, for a day, that the governor had been the intended victim, nor his misreading of the scorched remnant of Rumsey's note.

"I thought you two was friends," Cobb said when Marc's narrative stalled.

Marc told him about Willoughby's jealousy, touching briefly on his reluctant romp with Prudence Maxwell and not at all on his encounter with the misnamed Chastity. He also let Cobb know that Sir Francis was the one who had ordered the investigation closed, being happy with the results as they stood and pooh-poohing any suggestion that Rumsey was a paid assassin.

"Well, now we know he was paid," Marc concluded, "and by whom. And we have all the proof we need in that regard, and the attempt on my life here will confirm that it was I who was the target all along. We shall go together to Government House, wake up Sir Francis, and give him the complete story, the whole unvarnished truth."

Cobb was silent for a long while. They were drawing near to the first houses on Front Street, where windows glowed with the warm light of the lamps within.

"I don't see that we got proof of anythin'," Cobb said at last.

Marc was flabbergasted. "But you are my witness, Constable. You saw Colin Willoughby try to kill me. You found me bound hand and foot with this goose egg on my skull!"

"What I seen, Major, and what I believe are not quite the same."

"In what way? What on earth are you driving at?"

"Just this, Major. All I actually saw from the floor of the

brewery was someone who might've been Willoughby standin' wild-eyed over you. You were tied up, as I found out
when I got up there. I yelled at everybody to stop whatever
they was doin'—until I could climb up and see fer myself.
Then I start up the ladder and I can see nothin' but the ladder and the dark. Nobody up there is sayin' a word. Just as I
start to peek over the top rung, what do I see but you rollin'
like a croquet ball and smackin' Willoughby a crack on the
legs that sends him tumblin' into the brew."

"But he had a pistol out and was going to shoot you. I
saved your life!"

"I believe you, Major, and I'm grateful, too. I won't forget
it."

"But?"

"But all I really saw was the black shape of Willoughby
fallin' over the rim of the vat. We'll probably find the pistol
with him when they drain the vat in the mornin'. Which'll
only go to show that he had his officer's pistol with him—
not who he was aimin' it at."

"All right, Constable," Marc said coldly. "Tell me what
point you're really trying to make."

"There's no cause to sulk, Major. But what I'm thinkin'
is this. You and me have a pretty clear notion of what happened, then and now. But how might all this look to other
people? The widow sees Willoughby in a lather and cursin'
you by name. That suggests there's bad blood between you
two. I see you racin' off to the brewery so het up you don't

hear me hollerin' at you from thirty feet away. When I get here, half an hour later, I find you two up on the catwalk. You're tied up: by Willoughby or by the robbers you may've surprised. Maybe Willoughby was plannin' to get revenge on you, but it's only your story that he intended to toss you into the vat: maybe he was aimin' to tickle you within an inch of yer life—in a manner of speakin'. What I do know is only what I seen: and that was you whiplashin' Willoughby inta the beer-mash where he drowned."

Against his better judgment Marc was beginning to understand where Cobb was taking this scenario. In a curious way he was perhaps trying to protect Marc—the man who had, as he well knew, just saved his life at the risk of his own. Nonetheless, he felt compelled to say, "But it was Willoughby who had the motive. I had no reason to kill him."

"Well, I expect Miss Dewart-Smythe will back up that part of the business—should ya want to involve her in this mess—but what about the scrap over Mrs. Maxwell? Would it be wise to air all that dirty laundry? And someone with a suspicious mind might think it was you who was worried about Willoughby takin' yer job and yer woman away from you. You said yerself that Willoughby pleased the governor while you was off investigatin'."

"But nothing happened with Mrs. Maxwell. I've told you that as an officer and a gentleman."

"And I believe you, Major. Still and all, there's a good chance yer fancy hat is lyin' somewheres about Somerset House."

"Prudence Maxwell will deny everything. Her husband is possessive and easily enraged. I think we have little to fear on that score."

"Maybe so. But I've also heard his missus is quite a spiteful lady regardin' matters of the heart. After all, you've gone and killed her lover."

Marc felt a sudden pang of pity for Prudence Maxwell, for her despairing gambits into lust, for her loveless existence. He hoped that Chastity might manage to make something more satisfying of her life.

"And it's said she holds the purse strings in that particular household," Cobb added.

Despite his aching ankle and throbbing head, Marc found Cobb's arguments aroused the latent barrister in him. "But all of this assumes that some person out there with influence or motive will press these matters. Is there any reason someone in authority should not believe the sworn testimony of a policeman and a British officer? I can assure you that the governor himself will be enormously relieved." Of this Marc was certain, knowing as he did that Sir Francis still thought he himself might have been the target and that his mortal enemy might yet be plotting a second attempt on his life. The news that his aide-de-camp had been the intended victim and that the motive had been personal jealousy would come as a great relief. He would be able to get on with winning the election.

"It's the governor I'm anxious about," Cobb said. They were now stopped where the brewery road met Front Street.

"Well, you needn't be. I can't tell you why, but he'll be relieved when I tell him the truth."

"Maybe so. But think of this, Major: the polling starts tomorrow, and in most places goes on fer a couple of weeks. The governor wants nothin' more than to crush all the folks who don't agree with him. And so far, everythin's gone his way. Law and order and loyalty've been his watchwords. Then along comes the cold-blooded shootin' of Councillor Moncreiff, a man beloved by all, they say. Then, lo and behold, the governor's personal investigator unmasks the killer, one Philo Rumsey, and he—oh lucky stars!—turns out to be a Yankee. Barely a week goes by before the governor's own troop puts enough lead in him to sink a three-master—a perfect endin' to this sorry tale. The assassin from Buffalo, where democratical demagogues're as thick as herring, is hunted down and given rough justice by the wit and grit of the governor himself, the King's very own representative."

"Go on," Marc said, but he already knew what was coming, and his heart was turning to ice.

"So along you come, draggin' him out of bed to tell him he's got the story all wrong. It ain't the splendid one he's been proclaiming from a dozen hustings and feedin' blow by blow to the Tory papers. Oh, no, it's a messy saga of love and jealousy between two officers. And these officers, oh my, turn out to be two of his own aides, and one them, alack-a-day, is the chief investigator of the Moncreiff murder, and what does he find out? After Rumsey is gunned down and hanged in effigy in ten counties, he finds out, long after the governor's fairy tale's been heard and conned by heart, that, by golly, there was no political connection at all. Rumsey was just a poor man with a big family who needed money to feed his starvin' bairns. And these two aides of the governor—hand-picked by Sir Francis himself—have been hoppin' in and out of the same beds, and end up facin' each other down in a brewhouse, till one of them is tipped into the booze and drowns like a river rat."

Cobb was right. The only physical evidence left was an actor's beard, and that by itself meant nothing. Many of his fellow officers kept such props and, as he had once been, were enthusiastic thespians. The note that had brought him here was in shreds. Suddenly he thought of something he had overlooked. With rising hope, he said, "But the duty-corporal was given the note by a youngster and told it was from Willoughby and directed to me personally."

"And where will we find this lad?" Cobb said, almost apologetically. "And the corporal didn't actually see what was in the letter, did he? So as far as he's concerned, it may've been a message to get you up to the brewery fer a gentleman's showdown: a duel of honour—in a manner of speakin'. Besides, you're still missin' my point. Yer governor ain't gonna want to hear what you got to say."

Marc felt he had no choice but to break his oath to Sir Francis. "You must swear never to tell a soul, Constable, but the governor received evidence, now discredited, that he might have been the target. And he still thinks so. You are right in surmising that he does not want the Moncreiff-Rumsey version of the murder disturbed in any way. But for his own personal well-being, I feel obligated to tell him—with as much conviction and with what scant evidence we have—that he was not the target. I know him well enough to realize that he will not simply accept my word on that score: I shall have to lay out the full story, sordid as it is, and call on you to assist me. Please understand that I am not asking you to tell Sir Francis anything but the absolute truth—no more and no less."

Cobb appeared to think about this remark for a moment, then said, "And he may believe us. All I'm sayin' is he will never let such a story get out to the voters—or the Reform press."

Again, Cobb was right. Sir Francis was aware of the erratic nature of Willoughby's character and would certainly give Marc the benefit of the doubt regarding the nature of their conflict and its deadly outcome. But he would never, in the present circumstances, allow such tawdry details to become public knowledge. Mackenzie would have a heyday with it. He would no longer need Farmer's Friend.

"And knowin' the governor," Cobb was saying, "he'll probably make us swear on the Bible never to tell a livin' soul."

Yes—another solemn vow to withhold the truth in the

cause of the common good. But Marc could not do it. He had had enough of vows to last him a lifetime. And what was an honest man to do when loyalties clash and cannot be resolved? "But we've got a dead officer drowned in a vat of beer with a cocked pistol," he said wearily, as if such dilemmas were too vast or too minute to be bothered with.

Cobb was stroking the donkey's nose. "I been considerin' that," he said. "If you decide not to tell the governor what really happened, it wouldn't be hard to set up a story to explain Willoughby bein' at the bottom of a vat."

"And just how would we go about that?"

"Well, Major, after I help you home, return this butcher-cart, and take yer horse up to the stables, I could go back to the brewery, jimmy the warehouse doors a bit, and roll a couple of kegs into the river."

"What on earth for?"

"You'll report Willoughby missin' in the mornin', and as this brewery is part of Wilkie's patrol, he'll be up here to look into the break-in, and whenever Willoughby's body decides to float to the top or the brewers give the wort a good stir, it'll look like Willoughby, drunk or not, came up here, fully armed, and surprised the robbers. And paid fer it with his life. He'll be hailed as a hero. And the governor'll have another officer to brag about, and Willoughby's poor ol' dad'll be saved the grief of findin' out his son was a perfect monster."

"But what about Willoughby's actions at the widow's

place? His movements tonight will be investigated, surely. Chief Constable Sturges will have heard of Maisie's complaint. And the duty-corporal will remember my taking the note, even if he knew nothing of its contents."

That made Cobb stop and think for a moment or so. Finally he said, "All you gotta do is say the note was an apology to you and Mrs. Standish. I'll say, if anybody bothers to ask, that neither Wilkie nor me found Willoughby in our wanderings, but I did run into Lieutenant Edwards lyin' in a field at the edge of town, a little drunk and a lot woozy from fallin' off his horse. I then dash back to town fer help, borry the donkey-cart, and deliver ya safe to yer bed and board. Ain't that the way it happened, Lieutenant Edwards?"

Despite his amazement, Marc managed to say, "But how would an officer like Willoughby get wind of a robbery?"

Cobb smiled. "I hear tell he spent a lot of time on the King's business in the Blue Ox and other such waterin' holes—where loose talk is as common as loose bowels. Even so, I can't see any of this stuff really bein' necessary. You've got to remember, Major, the folks that run this province are fond of takin' the most agreeable and least irksome story as the truth."

Once again Marc had underestimated the pure cunning of the native-born Upper Canadian. He was too exhausted to work out any specific rationalization for his decision, but he knew, deep down where most things in life really mattered, that he had no choice but to choose as he did. "All right, Constable. Let's do it."

The donkey started up again, matching his pace to Horatio Cobb's.

"I guess now that you and me's started to trade secrets—in a manner of speakin'—I ought to confess somethin' else. Abner Clegg didn't get away from me last week. I tracked the bugger right up to the milliner's door and watched the lady there hand him the package."

"But why did you not tell me this right away? You must've known I'd find the letter-writer eventually."

For a moment only the donkey's harsh breathing was heard. "I knew you was kinda soft on the lady," Cobb said with a blush in his voice.

Marc yawned, but not because he was not intrigued by Cobb's omniscience and, more impressively, by his sensitivity. "Then you must have known she was living here before I did."

"Well, I got kinda chummy with her aunt Catherine the day after she set up shop on my patrol," Cobb said by way of explanation. "The old gal likes a cup of tea and a good, gossipy chinwag."

"I see. Well, thank you, anyway—Cobb," Mark said. The constable's name on his tongue felt good, and proper. "But I think I have blown my chances with that particular lady."

"That ain't the story I been told, Major."

But Marc did not hear this comforting response: he was asleep.

The little procession had turned now onto Front Street—donkey, constable, cart with lieutenant, and chestnut mare. In the eerie half-light of the solstice moon, the entire city lay open before them.

Cobb leaned over and chuckled. "Good night, sweet prince."

BOOK 3

VITAL SECRETS

AUTHOR'S NOTE

Vital Secrets is wholly a work of fiction, but I have endeavoured to convey in it the spirit of the period and the political tensions that led to the Rebellion of 1837. Actions and characterizations attributed to actual historical personages, like Sir Francis Bond Head and William Lyon Mackenzie, are fictitious. All other characters are the invention of the author, and any resemblance to persons living or dead is coincidental.

There were theatres, amateur acting groups, and touring companies from New York and elsewhere in Upper Canada during the late 1820s and throughout the 1830s. While details are sketchy, the first permanent playhouse is reputed to have been the Theatre Royale, located on the upper floor of Frank's Hotel in Toronto. The Regency Theatre described herein is a much more elaborate one than actually existed—though establishments like it were flourishing by the 1840s—and my Mr. Frank is fictitious. For details see Murray D. Edwards, *A Stage in Our Past*. Information on the theatres in New York City during the period may be found in Mary C. Henderson's *The City and the Theatre: New York Playhouses from Bowling Green to Times Square*.

Finally, by 1835 the new city of Toronto boasted the first municipal police force in North America, a five-man constabulary headed by a chief constable and modelled on the London "peelers."

PROLOGUE

It is March 1837, and Upper Canada is as restive as ever. There had been high hopes when Lieutenant-Governor Sir Francis Bond Head engineered victory for the Tories in the election of June 1836. It was expected that a period of stability would be ushered in, and that the many grievances of the farmers and their representatives in the Reform Party would soon be addressed. It was not to be. Head proceeded to enact repressive legislation and thwart the efforts of the Reformers in the Legislature. Drought had gripped the province, and the banks, safe in the hands of the Family Compact, refused to grant credit. Moreover, the clergy-reserves question still rankled. One-seventh of all the usable land was set aside for the established Anglican Church and was being held uncleared until land prices improved. More grating was the deadlock in the provincial parliament, where the unelected legislative councillors vetoed legislation put forward by the elected Reformers that might favour the suffering population.

As a result of Head's machinations, unrest had become increasingly widespread. A more radical wing of the Reform Party evolved under the strident direction of newspaper editor and politician William Lyon Mackenzie, who had lost his parliamentary seat in the 1836 election. Secret meetings and rallies took place throughout the countryside, and rumours of impending civil strife and the smuggling of arms from the United States were rampant. In a few months a new queen, Victoria, would be crowned, but she would bring no peace to the troubled colony.

PART ONE

MARCH 1837

ONE

For the second time since his arrival in the New World, Lieutenant Marc Edwards was setting out on a winter expedition to Cobourg and, this time, to places eastward to Kingston. On this occasion he was not alone, for at his side, cantering contentedly on a sleek, bay gelding and puffing coils of pipe-smoke into the air along with his frozen breath, was Major Owen Jenkin, quartermaster of His Majesty's 24th Regiment of Foot. The newly risen sun floated above the horizon-line of the forest ahead of them like a disk of burnished brass, as the duo swung up the long curve of King Street towards Scaddings Bridge and the Kingston Road.

Behind them, the capital city of the province lay rumpled and quiescent in its coverlet of snow.

"By Christ, but it's good to be on the road again, eh, Marc?" Jenkin said without taking his teeth off the stem of his pipe.

And it was. Ever since he had resigned his post at Government House—on a matter of principle—and returned to the spartan barracks at Fort York after his second investigation, Marc had suffered the boredom of peacetime military routine. He didn't regret his decision, but he had jumped at the chance to go foraging with Owen Jenkin.

"It was kind of you to invite me along, sir. I'm sure you could have managed quite well without me."

Jenkin emitted a rumbling sort of laugh, one that began in his substantial belly and rose up through the smoky realms of his throat till it met the clamped jaws and had to wheeze its way past. The older man had the face of a fallen cherub, with rubicund cheeks so bulging they pinched against his thick eyebrows and made the dancing orbs of his eyes all the more prominent for having to operate in such a confined sphere. The lips, had they been visible beneath the flourishing and unfashionably grizzled beard, would have shown themselves fleshy and sensuous. Evidently the quartermaster was a man who had feasted upon the fruits of life and found them satisfactory.

"Since you've had the impertinence to question why I brought you along, lad, I'll tell you. I'm told that when you came this way last winter on special assignment for the former governor, you passed yourself off as an agent for the quartermaster searching out reliable suppliers of pork and grain."

"There are few secrets in a garrison, I see," Marc said.

"I'm told also that your eye for quality and your nose for the bogus were as keen as a horse-trader's."

"You forget, sir, that I was part of that large foraging party you led two summers ago into the western region," Marc said.

"I do not forget that at all. I was quite aware of you watching me and taking note of every detail of the operation. I also know you were raised on a country estate in Kent, where matters agricultural were close to hand and as natural as breathing air uncontaminated by London soot."

"You know a great deal about me indeed," Marc said in what he hoped was a respectful tone.

"Don't look so worried, lad! I haven't been spying on you. With a mug like mine, espionage would be a hazardous occupation, to say the least."

Marc wondered how much, if anything, the major knew about what had happened last June when Marc had tried, and failed, to win the hand of Beth Smallman. Surely he couldn't know that Beth had left her millinery shop in Toronto last January to return to Crawford's Corners, near Cobourg, to nurse her ailing brother Aaron.

"To tell the truth, I've admired you and your deportment

since the day you arrived here. Your exploits and actions are well remarked among the officers of the regiment."

"I'm flattered, sir, but—"

"You're too quick with a 'but,' lad," Jenkin chortled. "The chief reason I rescued you from a death by boredom was entirely selfish: I can't ride a mile unless I have someone to laugh at my witticisms."

Any further talk was forestalled as they clattered across the planking of Scaddings Bridge, which spanned the frozen curve of the Don River. To their right they could see on the flats below the snow-softened outline of Enoch Turner's brewery and Gooderham's distillery with its giant Dutch windmill, whose broad appendages were utterly still in the windless winter air. Beyond these familiar signposts of civilization, the great lake sprawled frozen and silent to a far horizon. A few rods past the bridge, they entered the bush, through which meandered the only highroad linking Kingston and Toronto.

To his surprise, Marc found himself relaxing as the forest drew them into its infinite precincts. The irregular twenty-foot span of the road itself was now the only indication of a human presence. Invariably Marc had entered the bush—winter or summer—with nothing except a shudder and a prayer. But today the sun was shining as if it mattered. The rolling drifts and powdered mantle on bough and branch glistened and beckoned. It might have been England, except that here in the New World, he had begun to realize, bush and stream, insect and beast, lake and ice were the primary datum. All else was secondary. Once you accepted this irreversible fact, Marc thought, you could begin to feel the power and awful beauty of the wilderness.

The Kingston Road, for example, was a fanciful name attached to what was a wagon-track winding through the pine, fir, birch, and maple of the great boreal forest. It provided easy going for the pair of soldiers, as the rutted mélange of mud and corduroy was still frozen stiff, and the recent flurries had been packed down by constant coach- and foot-traffic. And where the odd tree had been downed and blown across the right-of-way, diligent farmers had hauled it aside and cleared away any accumulated drifts. With no wind and not a cloud anywhere in the blue vault above, they expected to travel the sixty miles or so to Cobourg easily. There they could seek out a welcoming hearth and a feather bed. And should their horses flag, they could stop for luncheon and a rest at the hamlet of Perry's Corners. As Marc well knew, much land had been cleared in Northumberland County around Cobourg, and the quartermaster would be planning to visit the many farms there to make arrangements for the purchase of hogs and grain. The actual deliveries would be made later in the fall when the harvest was in and the sucklings fattened.

They rode a little ways along the track before they rounded a bend and the road behind them vanished. The quartermaster took the pipe out of his mouth and picked up the conversation. "I knew your uncle Frederick, as it happens. I've known him for most of my adult life."

Frederick Edwards was the brother of Marc's adoptive father, Jabez Edwards.

"Ah, I see," Marc said with a rush of feeling he could not quite control. "You and Uncle Frederick fought together, then?"

"We did indeed," Jenkin said, knocking the ashes out of his pipe against the pommel of his saddle. He sat back, loosened his grip on the reins, and let the bay find its own trotting pace.

"Where did you meet?"

"At Sandhurst. We were both striplings, really, not yet twenty, but puffed up with the arrogance of youth and spoiling for a chance to unseat General Bonaparte."

"You didn't have to wait long," Marc said with a meaningful sigh. "Those were momentous days for an army officer."

"Don't get me started on *that* story. Once I get going in that direction, only a cannonball can stop me."

After an hour's stop at the inn of Perry's Corners to feed, water, and rest the horses and to refresh themselves with what the quartermaster called a "traveller's toddy," the duo set out again. For a long while neither spoke. Jenkin returned to the pleasures of his pipe, and Marc let the vast silence of woods and sky settle serenely where it wished.

"Lieutenant Fred Edwards, your uncle Frederick, and I fought side by side for eight years in Spain," Jenkin said, as if their earlier exchange had not been interrupted. "We crossed the Pyrenees and walked all the way across France to the gates of Paris. We helped bring the Corsican bastard to his knees."

"It was Uncle Frederick's stories that encouraged me to withdraw from the Inns of Court, give up the law, and join the army," Marc said. "It never occurred to me then that Britain might not have any more wars to fight or tyrants to depose."

"There will always be wars somewhere, lad. Of that you can be sure. And I'm not certain one should wish too hard to have them visit us again. Your uncle Fred may have left a few of the less glorious particulars out of his fireside tales."

"It's true, I must admit, sir, that I did wish for some modest insurrection to break out when I first arrived here, with just enough skirmishing for me to prove myself to myself and to my country."

"From what I hear at the garrison, you've gone some ways in that direction already."

Marc made no reply to the compliment. After a while he asked, "Did you know Uncle Jabez?"

"We met, yes. He spoke of you as his son."

Marc smiled. "I call him uncle, to everyone's confusion, because that is the term of endearment I used for him before he adopted me when I was five."

"I know. I met your real parents once. Fine people they were."

"Thank you, sir. I myself have only the vaguest recollection of them, a few memories of my father as he took me about the estate, and of course my mother knitting in front of a huge stone hearth. But the feeling of once having been loved and cared for has never left me."

"You were the only child that Thomas and Margaret Evans ever had." It was a statement, not a question.

"Cholera is a terrible form of the plague," Marc said, alluding to the disease that had felled his parents within days during the summer of 1815. But he was thinking now of young Aaron McCrae, Beth's brother, struck down by typhoid fever, yet another of the recurring pestilences sent by God, it was said, to keep His people humble and in their proper place.

"Did you meet *me*, then?" Marc asked, that odd possibility having just occurred to him.

Jenkin laughed and said, "My word, no. You were not yet born. I came down to the estate with your uncle Fred sometime before ought-six, it must have been, because it was in September of that year that we were ordered to Devon to defend our sovereign soil against invasion by the French. From that day until we reached Paris in 1814, we were soldiers and little else."

"You didn't fight at Waterloo with Uncle Frederick?"

"No. That was the only battle we didn't stand side by side. I was wounded near Paris, nothing serious—until gangrene threatened to set in. The surgeons cut out half of my left buttock, and I was ordered home, standing at attention all the way!"

"But you remained in the army?"

"By then it was the only life I knew. I was thirty-some years old and looked fifty. But I took up a less hazardous line of duty, thanks to Sir John Colborne, as quartermaster of the 24th, a post I've occupied with some satisfaction now for over twenty years, at home and abroad." And here he rubbed a gloved hand across his ample paunch.

"I think it was about ought-five when Uncle Jabez gave up his law practice in London and returned to manage the estate his father had left him."

"And you were not yet a gleam in your father's eye."

"So it was likely that summer that you came down to Kent with Uncle Frederick."

"Most likely. What I do remember clearly is that we were treated like royalty by Jabez. I think he missed the bachelor parties and goings-on in London, and we were gay company, as I recall. Your neighbour, Sir Haughty Trelawney, condescended to invite us to a county fête where Fred and I got regally pissed and made inappropriate advances towards a pair of ageing debutantes."

"I've always suspected Uncle Frederick liked the ladies."

"They weren't all ladies," Jenkin roared. Then, in a more serious tone, he added, "But don't get me wrong, lad. Once Captain Edwards met Delores that year in Paris, he never looked twice at another woman."

"Which is why he's stayed in France all these years."

"Indeed."

"He came over for wonderful extended visits about every second year. But I've never met my cousins, nor my aunt Delores."

"Nor your other aunt, of course," Jenkin said casually, then stopped abruptly.

Marc's horse, an all-purpose mare borrowed from the garrison stables, stumbled on a rut and lurched against the quartermaster's gelding before righting herself. Marc reached out and put a hand momentarily on Jenkin's pack. "It's all right, sir. I know about Uncle Jabez's younger sister."

Marc was relieved to see the smile return to Jenkin's face, where it was a near-permanent feature. Whatever horrors lay locked behind it—and there must have been many during his service in the long, mad Peninsular War—they did nothing to diminish its affable glow.

"I met dear, sweet Mary that same summer," Jenkin said, more warmly than sadly. "She couldn't have been much more than fifteen. A regular sprite, she was, a lively woodland nymph, racing over the hills between your place and the great Trelawney estate like a leggy colt just out of the chute. All blond tresses and freckles." Jenkin squeezed his eyes shut with a slight wince of both cheeks. "I can see her limber and wholesome, as if she were here before me at this very moment."

Marc did not interrupt the major's reverie for several

minutes. Then he said, "She died before I was born, or so I was led to believe. Uncle Jabez would never tell me much about her, even when I grew old enough to be more than curious about a young woman who might well have been a surrogate mother to me, as Jabez was my father. All I've ever known for certain is that she went up to school in London and died there suddenly and tragically."

"Would you like to know more, lad?"

"You know what really happened?"

Jenkin nodded.

Marc said, "Please. Tell me about Aunt Mary."

"Well, lad, I got the story in bits and pieces from Fred over the years we served together. Mary grew up on the estate under the easy but kindly care of her father, while her brother Jabez sought his fortune in the law courts of London and, a little later, Frederick went off to Sandhurst and glory. When old man Edwards, many years a widower, died, Mary was alone there and, as I understand it, lived with the Trelawneys next door for a while, until Jabez finally decided to sell his share in the London firm and occupy the Edwards farm, modest as it was. While Fred was too discreet to say so openly, I gathered that Mary had become—how shall I say it delicately?—a free spirit."

"Somewhat wild, you mean?" Marc said. "She seems to have had little adult supervision or discipline."

"Spoken like a genuine trooper." Jenkin chuckled. "But true, nonetheless, and alas. However, Jabez soon took her under his wing and—of this I am certain—formed a power-ful filial bond with the sister he hadn't really seen much of in recent years."

"That is what I've always assumed to be the reason be-hind his inability to speak of her to me or anyone. Even the inadvertent mention of her name could stun him into silence and, occasionally, tears."

"So when she was seventeen," Jenkin continued, "he persuaded her to go up to London to Madame Rénaud's fin-ishing school. She was an exceptionally bright girl, and he felt that three years of music, French, and the domestic arts would make a lady out of her. There were, I believe, even hopes that she might prove a suitable match for one of the Trelawney tribe next door."

Marc shuddered: his teenage affair with the young ward of Sir Joseph Trelawney had ended disastrously, and was an emotional wound not yet completely healed. "How did Aunt Mary take to the business of being 'finished'?" he asked.

"Like an unbroken yearling to the bit and bridle," Jenkin said, with evident approval. "But she stuck it out for almost two years, according to Fred, though by this time—it had to have been about 1809 or '10—we were both in Portugal and dancing a jig or two with the Iron Duke."

"Until . . ."

Jenkin sighed, a heaving belly of a sigh. "Until word came to Jabez from Madame Rénaud herself that, just days before the end of the winter term, Mary Edwards had fallen gravely ill with a fever and the bloody flux."

"Yes: Uncle Jabez told me that much, once. He said he'd had no warning, and when he rushed up to London by express coach the next morning, she was already dead."

"Well, if it's any consolation, Frederick insists that she was still breathing when Jabez arrived. She died within the hour, in his arms."

"It's no wonder he doesn't want to remember. But surely he had words with Madame Rénaud; he was a lawyer after all," Marc said.

"I'm sure he did, lad. Fred says that Jabez was torn between anger and remorse. Your uncle Frederick had many letters from him during the subsequent year. They moved him so deeply he could barely bring himself to open them. He burned each of them immediately afterwards."

"I'm glad I wasn't alive to see Uncle Jabez in such a state. By the time I was old enough to be aware of him and who he was, I found him the gentlest soul on the face of this earth."

"I'm sure he came to accept her death eventually. Apparently he did try to sue the school, but his heart wasn't in it after the initial rage had subsided and simple grief had taken over. The old lady must have known the seriousness of Mary's illness long before she wrote to Jabez. But what could he do, really?"

"Just bring her home for burial," Marc replied.

Jenkin sighed again. "The poor man was not able to

make even that small gesture. There was suspicion she'd died of typhus, and the authorities apparently compelled him to have her interred in that great stinking maw of a graveyard in central London."

"But, sir, I saw her grave-marker in our garden every time I headed up into the west woods." And even now he could picture that slim, white tablet with the tersest possible inscription: "Mary Ann Edwards, 1789–1810"—as if Uncle Jabez could not bear to add one syllable more.

"Aye, lad. The marker is hers all right. But she's not under it."

As they rode into the clearing that presaged the hamlet of Port Hope, Marc said, "Thank you for telling me all this, sir. It fills in a lot of the gaps in the story of my adoptive family. In a strange sort of way, I now feel as if I actually had an aunt. Perhaps someday soon I can persuade Uncle Frederick to give me more details. After all, he was closer in age to his sister than Uncle Jabez, and they must have played together often as children."

"But you won't tell Jabez about . . . what I've just told you?"

Marc smiled. "No, sir, I shan't. The last thing in this world I want to do is bring pain to my uncle."

They rode in silence for a while, and Marc reflected on the strange and surprising story he had just been told. He wished he could have known Aunt Mary, wished Uncle Jabez had been more forthcoming. That he was related to such a determined and unfettered spirit both alarmed and intrigued him.

BY THE TIME THEY DREW NEAR to Crawford's Corners, a winter moon hung like a silver saucer above the tree line in the southeast and cast a swath of shimmering light across the roadway ahead. The cold black sky around it was studded with stars as bright as a newborn's eyes. Neither had spoken for the past hour and now, in the mysterious calm of evening, it seemed almost profane to do so.

Fourteen months before, en route to his first investigation, Marc had travelled this very road in the dark of a winter night. Memories of that time flooded in. As they approached the crossroads that marked the centre of Crawford's Corners, Marc could feel the presence of the houses and cabins he knew were camouflaged by the bush and the darkness.

"That must be the light from Durfee's Inn," Marc said quietly.

It was a warm, orange glow on the right, no more than twenty yards away.

"We'll be made most welcome there," Marc said. "James and Emma Durfee are good people, salt of the earth."

"They'll be surprised to see you back here," Jenkin said. Then, without warning, he brought his mount to a halt in the middle of the intersection. "And that light over there," he said, "must be from Erastus Hatch's place. I can see the outline of the mill just behind the house."

Hatch had helped Marc with his first investigation, and had become a friend. Just to the north of the miller's land lay the farm of Beth Smallman, leased now to Thomas Goodall and his wife, the former Miss Winnifred Hatch. Beth's house, which Marc knew well, could not be seen from this vantage-point, but he knew Beth was there, nursing her brother Aaron.

Marc urged his mount straight ahead. The quartermaster's hand on his elbow stopped him. "I will go on into Durfee's," he said gently to Marc. "You are to turn left and make your way up Miller Sideroad."

"I don't understand," Marc said.

"I will carry on to Kingston, and then work my way slowly back westward, doing business with the farmers en route, as I normally do. I should be back in Cobourg in about a week. If you find yourself at leisure here, feel free to make any arrangements with the locals as you see fit, and I'll endorse them when I get here. But should you find more pressing and pleasant things to do, I will cover this region on my return."

"But I assumed you brought me along so we might work as a team," Marc said, genuinely puzzled, though a bizarre and not unsettling notion was now suggesting itself to him. "I still have things to learn from you."

"I will do nicely on my own, lad."

"Sir, I must protest—"

"Marc, my boy, you have unfinished business here in Crawford's Corners, not a hundred yards from where we are presently stalled."

My God, Marc thought, was there anyone left in Toronto who did *not* know about his on-again, off-again romance with Beth Smallman?

"If the lady's answer is no," Jenkin continued, "you can always catch me up."

"Is that an order, sir?"

"It's the true reason I asked you along. Now go."

With that curt command, the major wheeled his horse to the right and trotted off towards Durfee's Inn, leaving Marc alone in the intersection.

Very slowly he made his way north along Miller Sideroad.

TWO

Marc realized that he dare not arrive unannounced at Beth Smallman's door at seven o'clock in the evening, when the entire household would be present: Beth and her brother Aaron, Winnifred, and Thomas Goodall, her tenants, and probably a servant girl. He found himself quite relieved at the thought. Although he had been mulling over in his mind how he might arrange matters so that a brief encounter with Beth would be both possible and plausible (to Major Jenkin), the quartermaster had preempted him most unexpectedly and, incredible as it seemed, with a generosity of spirit that now left Marc feeling almost ashamed. The major had given him a week, free of any commitment or duty, to put his personal affairs in order, to "woo the lady" as the amateur thespians among his fellow officers might have put it.

But he was no Galahad and Beth was certainly no fawning princess. She and her late husband had hacked a farm out of this unforgiving bush, working side by side in the fields and in the barn. She had suffered the violent deaths of two men she adored: husband and father-in-law. She had taken an active part in local politics as a staunch Reformer, and after her husband's death had become more radical and more vocal, risking her status as a "respectable" woman and widow in a society where men were likely to see her more as a threat than as a suffering soul in need of understanding and sympathy.

Unable to run the farm on her own, and with an inheritance from her father-in-law, she had pulled up stakes and moved to Toronto to start a new life as proprietress of a millinery shop on King Street. She had been joined in that venture by her aunt Catherine from the United States. In fact, ever since Beth's rejection of him last June, Aunt Catherine had been his ally, lobbying on his behalf and sending him encouraging notes from time to time during the fall.

Marc dismounted and led the mare up the lane to the miller's house, planning to put the horse in Erastus Hatch's barn and settle her down for the night before approaching the back door. But that door suddenly swung open, and Erastus himself emerged, coatless and excited.

"By the Lord, it *is* you!" he cried, striding through the drifts in his slippers. "I saw you turn into the lane, and when I recognized the uniform, I said to Mary, 'There's only one soldier I know who's six feet tall and walks like a duke!'"

Marc reached out and grasped the hand of his friend, who had been so helpful in the Cobourg investigation and had put in more than one good word for him with Beth Smallman. "Yes, it is me, sir, and I've come to stay for a few days, if you've got room for me."

"You shan't get past the doorway, Marc, unless you quit calling me 'sir.' I'm Rastus to my friends, and I number you among them."

"Rastus it is, then."

"What's brought you all the way out here?" Hatch said, clutching his loose sweater more tightly about him. It was a straightforward question with no hint of suspicion or concern, but that was typical of the man.

"I'll explain the whole thing as soon as I've bedded down the mare here for the night. And if you don't get back inside, you'll catch your death."

"Well, son, you know your way about in the barn, eh? There's enough moonlight to work by if you use one of the stalls on the south wall. Meantime, I'll go tell Mary to put the kettle on and rouse Susie and the little one."

"I'll be as quick as I can."

"By the Christ, but it's good to see you!" Hatch cried, then began to brush the snow off his slippers, gave up with a

chuckle, and turned back towards the house. "And I'm not
the only one who'll think so!"

The miller glanced to the north, towards the log house of
Beth Smallman.

MARC AND ERASTUS HATCH SAT IN the two padded chairs
before the fieldstone fireplace and a blaze whose roaring had
just begun to die down to a steady, amiable murmur. Two
tendrils of pipe-smoke rose drowsily and intermittently into
the warm ambience of the miller's parlour. It was nearly ten
o'clock. Mary Hatch—who, as Mary Huggan, had served
the miller as cook and housekeeper long before she married him—had cobbled together a supper for their guest of
cold beef, bacon, eggs, and fried potatoes. Her sister Susie, a
carbon copy of her older sibling (red hair, translucent Irish
skin, freckles, a wisp of a figure), then brought tiny Eustace
Hatch out of the nursery to be admired and cooed at. Marc,
of course, said all the appropriate things, but inside he felt
an uncharacteristic pang of envy and a sudden intimation
of the inexorable passing of time. Then, with the babe returned to its slumber and Mary excusing herself, the two
men settled into their port and pipes.

Although considered by the local farmers he served to
be a "merchant," Hatch still helped his hired hands with
every aspect of the mill's functioning and the working of the
land surrounding it. His large, peasant fingers were callused,

his face had the red, raw look of the active yeoman, and his modest paunch was well muscled. For a while they traded harmless bits of gossip about their different locales, reminisced about Marc's investigation here fourteen months earlier, then lapsed into a silence that was not uncomfortable.

"So you've given up being a supernumerary constable," Marc said.

"That was not a hard decision in the least. After what happened here last winter, I kind of soured on the law. I try now to mind my own business, do an honest day's work, and treat my customers fairly. Of course, with Mary and the little one, all that's been made much easier."

"You look like a man blessed."

"That I am, though I'd be hard-pressed to say why the Lord's chosen me," Hatch said solemnly, then added quickly, "But I'm not fool enough to keep on asking Him why!"

"Wisely said."

"But I'll tell you truthfully, Marc, I'm one of the few souls in this county who *is* happy."

"It's been a grim year everywhere in the province," Marc said. "Bad weather, lean crops, falling prices, paper money losing value by the month, the banks reeling. Made all the worse, I suspect, because so much was expected after the Tory victory in the election last spring and the governor's promise to bring about real change."

"I've given up on that, too." Hatch turned and looked directly at Marc.

"Being a Tory?"

"Not quite as blunt as that, but something close to it." He leaned back again and spoke between hefty puffs on the pipe. "I've given up on politics, at least for the time being, and I used to make all the right noises whenever asked to, as you know."

"Noises in favor of the governor, you mean?"

"Exactly. I believed in the rule of law and I still do. But what has happened around here since last June is downright frightening."

"How so?"

"The ordinary folk—who are suffering the most, as they always have since the beginning of things—have begun to give up on the political process, too. Myself, I've decided to do what I can in my own bailiwick. I've extended credit where I shouldn't, ground grain for free when there was no other remedy, and doled out my own flour so some of the kids in the township won't starve. But many of the others, with no resources to fall back on, are growing desperate. And to make matters worse, many of my Tory acquaintances, who wouldn't ordinarily tip their hat to an Orangeman, are starting to spout their fanatic heresies. Both sides have hardened their positions since the election. It's almost impossible to stand anywhere in the middle, or be nonpartisan or even a simple, caring Christian."

"Sir Francis has much to answer for, I'm afraid. Instead of using his majority in the assembly to redress the complaints of the farmers and work towards reconciliation, he has ruth-lessly pursued his own agenda."

"You were wise to get as far away from him as possible." Hatch looked at Marc, put his pipe down, and added, "No-body hereabouts was surprised to learn about your resignation as his aide-de-camp. We knew what kind of man you were."

Marc tried not to look affected by this kind remark. "Then why don't the conservatives repudiate the governor?"

Hatch laughed. "Believe it or not, they blame the actions of Willie Mackenzie's radicals for making Governor Head the way he now is: erratic and spiteful."

"And have there been *actions?*"

Hatch paused, drew noisily on his dead pipe, glanced at it balefully, and said, "I'm afraid there have. People aren't just ranting and raving anymore: they're organizing and holding secret meetings. There's been talk—right here in Hamilton township—of arms about to be smuggled across the border, of trunkloads of American dollars and coinage on their way—to be used for God knows what dastardly purpose."

"But we heard that sort of fear-mongering gossip last year, remember?"

"That is so. But this is not talk. Just last Thursday a gang of Orange thugs discovered a meeting of Mackenzie's follow-ers in progress about a mile east of Cobourg, and decided to break it up. But it was no Reform rally they were disrupting. The conspirators were armed with pitchforks, sickles, axe-handles, and, they say, a dozen or more pistols. There was a regular donnybrook. Dozens were injured on both sides. And by the time the constables arrived, the worst of it was over, and everyone fled who could still walk. Of course, the wounded suddenly contracted lockjaw. Nobody would lay a charge. What I'm saying, and what I fear every time I look into little Eustace's eyes, is that these desperate men are planning an insurrection or show of force sometime soon."

"But they'll be slaughtered, don't they know that? They can't fight the British army with hoes and pistols."

"That may be the only thing holding them back."

Marc heaved a huge sigh. "You mean soldiers like me?"

"Yes, at least until they get guns and training. And they'll need the Yankees for that." Hatch tried to light his pipe with a flaming stick from the fire, without success. "If I were you, I wouldn't wander around the back concessions of Northumberland County with that uniform winking in the noonday sun."

"But surely an offer to buy their grain or hogs at a price well above the current market will have to be welcomed. The army is not their enemy."

Hatch smiled. "They'll certainly let you in the front door, but don't expect a cup of tea. I think the poor buggers are desperate enough to sell their produce to anyone." Hatch chuckled ruefully.

Marc yawned but, fatigued as he was, he did not want to fall asleep here in the cozy security of the Hatch parlour. Instead, he reached down between the two chairs, picked up the decanter, and poured himself a tumbler of port. Erastus declined Marc's offer of more.

The fire, ebbing rapidly, snapped and crackled intermittently.

"Well, lad, there's one subject we seem to have been avoiding, eh?"

Marc turned to face his friend. "Tell me everything I should know about what's happened next door."

"I thought you'd never ask. Let me start with the good news. My daughter and her husband are quite happily married, even though they are very different people. Certainly, I was as surprised as anyone when Winnifred announced she had selected Thomas Goodall, my hired man, as her husband. Thomas is a fine farmer and a good Christian, but he hasn't said more than a dozen words a week since birth—less than that if you deduct the Lord's Prayer every Sunday. Winnifred—well, you know her—she has two opinions on every subject and ain't shy about conveying them to anyone within earshot. When she lived here she was more or less lady of the manor, but now that she and Thomas have their own farm, she's pitched in and done more than her share of the outdoor labour." He paused and lowered his voice. "And she's in the family way."

"That's wonderful news," Marc said sincerely, for he liked and admired this proud, intelligent woman, and wished her well.

"And just in time," Hatch said cryptically. To Marc's

puzzled look, he said, "Well, believe it or not, Winnifred's been getting involved in politics this winter, too. Radical politics." This last remark was whispered, as if the walls might have ears.

"But she's an independent thinker and a conservative like her father, surely."

"Indeed she was. But the bad news is that the farm has not prospered. With last summer's drought and the available water being tied up on the clergy-reserve land next to them, they had a poor harvest, despite their effort and the expense of hiring extra help. And what they did take off the fields was sold at prices that didn't cover their costs. They're desperate to get enough cash to pay the leasehold."

Marc was astonished. "But surely Beth wouldn't demand payment or turn them out? After all, they're looking after Aaron for her. And she's got plenty of money."

"All true. She refused to take any payment on the lease. She's offered to pay for any hired help to do Aaron's share of the work until he's fully recovered."

"I'm told by Beth's aunt that the boy has made remarkable progress."

"Yes, he has, and we thank the Lord daily for that."

"But?"

"But Winnifred is . . . well, proud, too proud I'm inclined to think. But she says—and Thomas agrees, according to her—that they ought to be able to make a decent living out of their farm or else abandon it. And when she found that most of the farmers in the county were in the same boat, in spite of the backbreaking work and heartbreaking effort, well, she began to blame the government—and quite publicly. When Beth came down to nurse Aaron in January, she soon discovered that Winnifred was slipping off to gatherings of Mackenzie's malcontents, spouting their slogans, and behaving strangely. Eventually Beth told me."

"Did you succeed in stopping her?"

Hatch sighed. "No," he said with a wry smile that conveyed both regret and acceptance. "My attempts to dissuade her simply encouraged her to become even more committed. When I heard about talk of violence and outright sedition at these rallies, I became worried. I did manage to persuade Thomas to go with her to protect her, and him without a political bone in his body. This she readily agreed to, to my surprise."

"And now that she is expecting?"

"She's stopped going. On her own account, we assume, unless Thomas found enough words to assert himself in the privacy of the boudoir." Hatch smiled at the notion.

"But she hasn't changed her mind about the lease or the success of the farm? Surely, with a child on the way—"

Hatch looked suddenly grim, the customary laugh lines of his face collapsing around his eyes. "She says they'll give it one more year. The babe is due in September. If the fall harvest fails, they'll wait out the winter here, then—my God, I can barely say it, Marc—she, Thomas, and the child will sell everything they have, go down to Buffalo, buy a Conestoga wagon, and head west across the Mississippi to the Iowa Territory."

Marc took this in, then said evenly, "I don't think that will happen, Rastus. There's every chance the governor will be recalled and a new one will follow the British government's policy of conciliation. There are moderate, decent men on both the left and the right: their voices will be heard."

Hatch tried to smile his gratitude. "And you count yourself among the moderates," he said.

"I do," Marc said with some conviction. "It's taken me a while, and I'm still learning, but I've come a long way, I think, in less than two years."

"And we all know it."

Marc was well aware whom the "all" was meant to include.

"But Winnifred's luck hasn't changed," Hatch continued glumly. "Last Friday, Thomas was chopping wood out behind the house and damn near sliced off his left hand. Dr. Barnaby had to stitch it together like a rip in a glove. He's got it wrapped in a great bloody bandage, with a splint on his wrist to keep him from using the hand for anything. He can't even pick up a spoon to stir his tea with it."

This was more serious than Winnifred's political leanings, Marc thought.

"The man has chopped a thousand cords of wood in

his lifetime. But he's exhausted and worried to death," said Hatch. "Fatigue will lead to such accidents."

"Thank God for Barnaby," Marc said. Charles Barnaby was a semi-retired army surgeon who lived across from the Durfee Inn but kept a surgery in Cobourg several days a week or whenever it was needed in emergencies.

"He's a splendid gentleman. They don't come any better than Barnaby. In fact, you won't get to see him tomorrow because he's been in and out of his surgery since the fracas last Thursday night—setting bones and lecturing the participants on their foolishness. I lent him my cutter and Percherons on Saturday so he could transfer some of the wounded home, if necessary."

"I wondered why I didn't see them in the barn."

"That pair can haul a sled through anything. And we've had a bundle of snow this winter. The drifts are six or seven feet in the bush."

Hatch yawned. There was little time left. Marc cleared his throat to ask what had to be asked.

"Beth is fine," Hatch said suddenly. "She nursed Aaron night and day all through January, and for a while there we were very concerned for her own health—"

"But she's—"

"Fine now, as I said. As soon as Aaron began to regain his strength, she did, too. And since Thomas became helpless last week, Aaron's been strong enough to chop firewood and help Winnifred and Beth with the chores in the barn."

"Has she—"

"Ever mentioned you? Not by name. But you've come up in the general conversation several times this winter, and Beth's been an avid listener. I'm sure she knows how much you've changed and that you still love her. But—"

"There's always a 'but,' isn't there?"

"But she's just been too busy with Aaron and with the problems of the farm to turn her attention to her own future. You know how faithful she can be to a task she feels is important, and how selfless she is when it comes to helping those who need it."

Marc nodded.

"Even if she *is* a Congregationalist." Hatch smiled. "What I'm trying to say is, I think you've come at the right time to make your pitch."

"Let's hope she feels the same way," Marc said.

But how far could he hope? How far did he deserve to?

MARC WAS AWAKENED SLOWLY AND LUXURIOUSLY by the mid-morning sun slanting across the counterpane. By the time he had completed the most rudimentary toilet and donned the scarlet, green, and gold of an officer of the 24th Regiment of Foot, the Hatches' dining-room was well warmed by the fire in the wood-stove and suffused with breakfast aromas: bacon, frying eggs and potatoes, and fresh-baked biscuits. The chores had been completed: cows milked, fed, and watered; stalls mucked out; hens relieved of their night's labour; kindling chopped; and the day's supply of firewood lugged indoors. Marc tried not to look abashed when he was greeted by the household as if he were the prodigal son being treated to the fatted calf.

"Sit down, lad, and dig in," Hatch said as he settled into his captain's chair, then took Mary by the hand to stop her fussing with Marc's plate and utensils, and eased her down to her own place next to him. Susie arrived promptly with a steaming platter of food.

"I apologize for sleeping so late," Marc said.

"Nonsense," Hatch said. "You've got a difficult day ahead of you, eh?"

Marc acknowledged the reference to the task at hand with a tight smile.

"How is the babe this morning?" Marc asked Mary.

"He's as healthy as his papa," Mary said.

Suddenly Marc felt his heart lurch. Seeing Erastus Hatch, so long a widower and so lonely just a year ago, happy and at ease here in his home made Marc realize how badly he wanted to change his own life, and how much depended on what might happen or not happen in the next few hours. He decided that he would need to take a long walk and consider carefully what he might possibly say to Beth that would make a difference. He knew also that he needed an hour or so to regain the courage he had imagined for himself when he had played out the reconciliation scene with Beth at least a hundred times since last summer.

Hatch was halfway through his request for more bacon

when he was interrupted by the sound of the back door opening and closing. Susie Huggan set down a plate and hurried to answer the door. Seconds later she reappeared with a big grin on her face.

"It's our neighbour," she cried, "and she's brung us a basket of duck's eggs!" Susie stepped aside to reveal both the visitor and her gift.

It was Beth Smallman. She glanced at the figures seated around the table, and stopped when she came to Marc.

The basket fell to the floor, and the duck eggs with it.

THREE

S o, you're in our neighbourhood again—scoutin' hogs and whatnot?" Beth said with that touch of colloquial teasing in her voice that Marc found irresistible. She was alluding to his visit the year before and to his rather inept attempt to pass himself off as an assistant quartermaster. The "whatnot" suggested that she knew full well the true purpose of his abrupt arrival this time.

"And duck's eggs," Marc said, "when they're not broken."

"Things've changed a lot here since last June."

"Little Eustace, you mean, and Winnifred and Thomas?"

"I think you know what I mean," Beth said.

They were walking slowly northward along the snow-packed

path that linked the miller's house with the Smallmans'. It meandered its way more or less beside the frozen creek on their left and the cleared ground on their right. The snow was so deep that no stubble showed through from the fall's meagre harvest. Only uprooted, charred stumps marked the crude outlines of pasture and wheat field.

"Fewer pigs and more radicals?" Marc said, struggling to keep the tone of the conversation light. It felt so good just hearing Beth's voice once again that he found himself torn between wanting the dialogue to continue at any cost and the fear that one wrong turn in its progress would kill it outright. And her physical presence here beside him—their footsteps in lazy unison, the breeze crisp and clean in their faces, the sound of their voices the only sound anywhere, the delicate frost of her breathing mingled with his own— left him so intoxicated that he was sure to blurt out some foolishness or other. He was tempted to reach over and take her elbow, as a proper gentleman should, but he dared not.

"Winn an' Thomas had to keep what grain they took off last fall to feed the oxen, the three cows, and our pigs."

"Erastus told me about their troubles."

"They haven't had it worse than any others in the township." Marc caught the edge in her voice, but when he glanced over, she was staring resolutely ahead.

"Rastus also told me how well you've nursed Aaron through his illness."

The low morning sun blazed through the fringe of Beth's

hair below the tuque and transformed it into a russet halo. It took all of Marc's willpower to resist pulling the tuque away.

"I'd have even prayed to the Anglican God if I'd thought He could help," Beth said.

"Ah, but you know perfectly well He's always been a Congregationalist."

Beth laughed, and for the first time glanced sideways at Marc. The force of her gaze, the infinite blue intelligence of her eyes, struck him like a blow. He felt numb and then, strangely, invigorated. His blood hummed.

"Whichever gods intervened," Beth said, guiding him briefly around a submerged stump, "Aaron's made a wonderful recovery. In a minute you'll hear him chopping wood out behind the summer kitchen."

"Chopping wood? But—"

"Oh, I see that he naps every afternoon. But I figured he needed to get outdoors as soon as he could. He lives for the animals and his chores around the barn."

"And he'll be needed more than ever now that Thomas has a battered hand."

"Seems we just get through one trial when a new one comes on."

"Who'll help with the spring ploughing and planting?" Marc said, trying his best to make the question sound disinterested.

Beth slowed her pace, for which Marc was grateful, as it suggested she was not overeager to arrive at the cabin. In the distance he could now hear the staccato *chunk* of an axe on wood.

"Well, Winn won't take money, from me or her father, so it'll have to be mainly me and Aaron and Winn. Winn and me have done some sewing this winter, so we'll have a few goods to trade for a bit of hired help. And we can work the ox-team together if we have to."

Of that Marc had little doubt, even though, under the bulky mackintosh and cloth trousers, Beth was tiny and trim and not much more than a hundred pounds.

"But that means you might be stuck down here until June or later?"

"It's not a matter of choice. We often get 'stuck' where we ought most to be."

Marc winced at the reproof. And he realized with a sinking heart just how difficult and possibly hopeless a task lay before him. How could he plead a lover's cause in the face of such competing exigencies, of such overriding moral claims? There seemed for him, equally, to be no choice: he, too, was where he "ought most to be." So he plunged recklessly ahead: "But surely your aunt Catherine will be needing you at the shop? Spring and summer are your busiest seasons."

"I hadn't realized you were so well acquainted with the millinery business."

Ah, that teasing tone again, but he persevered. "Your aunt did pull up stakes in New England, as I recall, to join you in Toronto. Surely you can't—"

"Your 'recall' is as keen as it's always been. But I can do without your 'surelys.'"

"I'm sorry."

"No, you're not. But it doesn't matter because I've taken care of Aunt Catherine and the business."

"You haven't sold it?"

Beth laughed for a second time. "No, we haven't. When I left in January to come here to nurse Aaron, we hired a young girl from the town to help Aunt Catherine with the seamstressing side of the business. And next month a distant cousin from her husband's side of the family is coming up to Toronto from Rochester to stay with her."

"Can she sew? And help run the business?"

"He certainly can't sew—"

"He?"

"A great-nephew. About your age, I think."

"And what help could he possibly be in a millinery shop?" Besides being a male presence, and possibly a handsome one to boot.

"Since you're so curious, he's really interested in starting a business of his own. Things've been bad in the States since the dollar went crazy down there, and he wants to start a new life. He'll live in and keep his aunt company, help with any heavy work, and learn how to operate a shop. Any further questions, counsellor?"

For Beth's benefit, Marc managed a smile at this reference to his aborted law career. They walked a few paces in silence, but neither seemed in any hurry to speed up. Something remained to be said.

"How long will it be before Thomas is able to work again?"

"Well, it was his left hand he cut, thank God, so he's still able to do quite a bit with the right. Dr. Barnaby says it should be completely healed in a month, six weeks for sure, if he doesn't tear it open or let it get infected."

"Barnaby should know if anyone does. He's repaired a thousand sword cuts in his time. But what about Winnifred?"

"I see the good news is out."

"Due in late September, Rastus tells me."

"She's as strong as an ox. You'll see quite a change in her."

"Her father was extremely worried about her."

Beth stopped. The axe-blows were much sharper. Along the northwestern horizon a bank of black clouds curdled the otherwise pristine blue of the winter sky.

"You know about her going to the meetings?"

"Not much. But enough to realize how much her thinking must have changed since I last saw her. Moving from church bazaars and social teas to smoky barns and questionable associates is quite a shift for anyone, and incredible for a—"

"Woman? I think we've had this conversation before, haven't we?"

"Surely she won't take such risks now."

They were still face-to-face: assessing, gauging, probing.

"Surely not," Beth said.

"Well, then, I'm glad she's being sensible. And Thomas, too."

Beth put a mittened hand on Marc's arm. She smiled wanly, and he noticed now the dark shadow under each eye and the vexed wrinkling at the corners of the mouth he wanted to press against his own and breathe into comfort. "I haven't been to any of the meetings," she said. "I've been too busy with Aaron."

Marc's relief was palpable.

"I listen to what Winn and Thomas are saying, which isn't a lot—at least not outside their bedroom. But I say nothing."

"It's hard to believe you've given up," Marc said, turning with her and walking, slowly again, towards the ring of Aaron's axe.

"Oh, I haven't given up. But after we lost the election last June, after all our effort and after all the promises made and not kept by the governor, I couldn't summon up the energy to protest—even though I was raging underneath my numbness. Auntie and I worked hard at the business all summer, and hard it was—dispensing bonnets and frippery to the very people that engineered us out of the Assembly. Then, when the bad harvest hit and the Yankee dollar collapsed and Sir High and Mighty reneged on his solemn word, just when my blood was starting to boil like it did when Jesse was alive and we were up to our necks in Reform Party politics, I discovered that everything had changed."

"In what way?"

"The open talk of violence. And I don't mean the vicious talk we've all got used to."

"Talk of revolt, you mean?" Marc could have bitten his tongue, but it was too late.

Beth stopped and looked searchingly at the man who had done so much for her last winter and who had more than once declared his love for her.

"Damn it, Beth, I'm not here as a spy!"

She stared at her boots. "I'd not be honest if I didn't admit that when I dropped those eggs at the sudden sight of you, that was my first thought." She peered up. "But I haven't thought it since. Nor will I again."

"But I'm still in this uniform?"

"Yes, you are, aren't you?" She started walking again, as if afraid to hold his gaze any longer for fear of what she might detect in it and preferred not to see.

"I think we've had *this* conversation before," he said.

They had turned onto the path that wound between the barn and outbuildings towards the back-shed of the split-log cabin ahead. Marc stopped and quickly placed one hand on each of Beth's shoulders. He held her gaze for several long seconds. She made no attempt to look away. He saw what it was he had to know: her feeling for him had not diminished, in spite of everything that had happened over the past fourteen months.

"We've spoken about everything except the thing we

really need to speak about," Beth said softly, her eyes misting over. "I haven't been avoiding it. After lunch, when it settles down inside, we'll sit by the south window like we did last year and have a long cup of tea."

He leaned over and brushed his lips across her cool forehead.

She pulled back, reluctantly he thought, and said, "Now, let's go and say hello to Aaron."

MARC REMEMBERED AARON MCCRAE WITH VIVID painfulness: a tall, gangling sixteen-year-old with one lame leg that he dragged behind him and slurred, stammering speech. But he was no simpleton to be patronized or mocked by his fellows, though Marc had little doubt they had done so more than once. He had his sister's blue eyes that, like hers, saw much more than they conveyed. In fact, it had been Aaron's observation and reliable memory that had helped solve the mysterious death of Joshua Smallman last winter. But Marc wondered what might have been wrought upon that misaligned frame by typhoid fever and eight weeks of agonizingly slow recuperation.

Aaron spotted Beth and the uniformed gentleman at her side, and put down his axe. A quarter-cord of hardwood lay scattered about him. A big grin spread across his face as he recognized Marc.

"H-h-h-ello, Mr. Edwards."

"Hello, Aaron. I'm so happy to see you are recovered, and back helping run the farm." Marc made a point of admiring the lad's handiwork.

"Lieutenant Edwards has come for a visit," Beth said. "He's going to stay for dinner."

"G-g-good."

Marc, too, was pleased to hear this, then remembered that "dinner" was sometimes the local term for luncheon, to which meal he had already been invited.

"Just finish up that log, Aaron, and then come inside. We don't want you overdoing it, do we?"

Aaron frowned, then smiled his agreement. Marc was astonished to see that Aaron had grown another two or three inches, bringing him close to Marc's six feet. Moreover, he had "filled out," as they said here in the colony, putting on muscle around bones that had thickened and toughened. His pale face and a telltale hollowness around the eyes hinted at the earlier ravages of the fever, and underneath the loose sweater and denim work pants that new bulk would likely be a bit flaccid and toneless, but the big-knuckled, bare hands and masculine jut of the chin intimated that he was soon to be a full-fledged, powerful man.

"I'll see you inside, then," Marc said.

Aaron grinned again, and gave his sister a curious look before turning back to his work.

At the shed door, Marc stopped for a moment to watch the operation at hand. Aaron gripped the axe with both hands, raised it over his shoulder, braced himself as best he could on the lame leg, then drove the axe downward, using his strong leg for leverage and balance. For a second it appeared as if he must topple, given the angle at which his body was tilted laterally, but at the point of impact everything straightened itself—axe and axeman—so that the plane of the blow ended flush with the propped log. The wood split with a ruptured cry, followed instantly by the lad's grunt of triumph.

"He's learned to adapt," Beth said as she opened the back door. "Now let's go in to lunch."

Like so many of those around him, Marc thought.

THE MID-DAY MEAL WAS OF THE pioneer farm variety—roast venison, potatoes, turnip, fresh bread, slices of cold ham, and several pots of hot tea —cooked by Winnifred and Beth, and served by young Charlene, yet another of the innumerable Huggan clan, before she herself joined them. Quaintly referred to as the "hired girl," Charlene received no pay. ("But I'm keeping track of wages owed," Beth had said, "and I'll settle up with her some day when she may really need the money.")

Arriving late to the table, Thomas Goodall seemed startled to see Marc, then greeted him abruptly. Marc noticed the large leather mitt on his left hand and offered commiserations. Thomas merely nodded in acknowledgement and carefully removed the mitt to reveal a hand bandaged from fingertips to wrist and immobilized by a pair of splints.

"So they've made you quartermaster again," Winnifred said to Marc with a smile, deflecting his gaze as she passed him the bowl of steaming mashed potatoes.

"To be honest, ma'am, I was asked along by Major Jenkin more or less to keep him company between the capital and Cobourg."

"And he lost track of you somewhere near Crawford's Corners?"

"He suggested that I had some business to transact in this vicinity."

"Whatever those transactions might be, I'm sure we wish you every success." And here she glanced across at Beth in time to catch the full bloom of her blush.

Beth recovered quickly enough to say, "The lieutenant has come to reconnoitre hogs for hungry soldiers, I believe."

Marc laughed, as he was meant to. He was delighted with the banter and quite pleased to be the butt of it. He had been afraid that the travails of the past months and Winnifred's flirtation with Mackenzie's cohorts might have soured her quick wit and frank appraisal of the world—qualities he had both admired and been wary of on his visit here last year. But there *had* been changes. Marriage and impending motherhood had apparently softened the edges of her cynicism and, if her father's account were accurate, had cooled her anger at the injustices meted out to her and her kind.

"I *am* authorized to issue contracts for grain and hogs on behalf of the quartermaster," Marc said in a more serious vein. "It occurred to me that I might be able to help you out in that regard."

"We decided last fall that it was better to hang on to what we have rather than sell it at a loss. Since then the price of grain's gone lower and paper money of any colour is shrinking."

"The army is offering a price well above market value—with the blessing of the lieutenant-governor."

That remark brought a moment of meditative silence, during which the only sounds were the click of forks and scraping of knives.

"P-p-please, pass the—"

Thomas Goodall, anticipating Aaron's request, slid the bowl of turnips over to the lad with his good hand. The other he kept out of sight below the table. Aaron nodded a mute thank you, but in spooning out a second helping, he tipped the bowl over. Beside him, Thomas instinctively reached out to right the bowl with the nearest hand—the swaddled one—then jerked it back in pain.

"Are you all right?" Winnifred asked anxiously. The danger of sepsis was ever present in such circumstances, and Thomas's reflexive wince was cause for alarm.

Thomas nodded and tried to smile. But smiling was no more natural to his craggy, ploughman's face than talking was. He looked up at Winnifred with an expression she alone read as reassuring. "Won't be shootin' no more deer fer a while."

Winnifred beamed. "This one'll last us till spring," she said to Marc. "Thomas bagged it in January."

"I'm not so sure you should be trying to work at all until Dr. Barnaby is ready to remove the stitches," Beth said. "Outside of splitting wood for the stoves, there's really not much in the barn that can't wait awhile or be done by Winn and me."

"So stupid . . . so stupid of me," Thomas muttered while keeping his eyes on his food and tucking the injured left hand into the safety of his lap.

"If you need cash, then," Marc said disingenuously, "perhaps you could spare a portion of the grain you've stored, provided it is in good condition."

"I'm a miller's daughter," Winnifred said. "I do know how to store grain." She turned towards Thomas. "What do you think, love, can we afford to sell some of what we've saved for feed and seed?"

Thomas put down his fork and peered ahead in thought. There was definitely a smile in the dark recesses of the eyes. "I figure about half," he said, and brought the fork back up to his mouth.

"That's what I thought as well."

"We can do business, then?" Marc said, but his glance was more towards Beth than Winnifred.

"If the price is right," Winnifred said lightly, but her

relief at the prospect of generating some cash out of their failed harvest was clearly evident. "Thomas and I will take you out to the granary later this afternoon, and we'll talk turkey. We'll be expecting you back here for supper. I'll send Charlene over to Papa's place to invite them to join us as well."

"Are you not worried about having a uniformed officer as your house-guest?" Marc said with a broad smile around the table, then realized, too late, the clumsiness of the quip.

Winnifred was the first to break the awkward silence. "You mustn't believe all the rumours buzzing up and down the back concessions," she said. "You're welcome to stay with us as long as you wish to." Then, glancing at Beth, she added, "Or need to."

Sitting here in the welcoming warmth of this Upper Canadian farmhouse among people who had without doubt suffered both hardship and injustice, Marc could not bring himself to believe that these farmers would resort to armed resistance or open rebellion against the Crown. Their capacity and willingness to adapt to circumstance, with imagination and perseverance, was everywhere to be observed and marvelled at by newcomers like himself.

Under his present misgivings, then, a deep calm prevailed. He even felt ready to face Beth, alone and unprotected by sword or uniform.

FOUR

Marc and Beth were together in the sitting-room. The pot-bellied stove glowed cordially in the corner, a pale winter light ebbed through the window in the south wall, and the two cushioned chairs faced one another at an amiable angle. A little while earlier Beth had led Aaron to her own bedroom for his requisite afternoon nap. There, Marc noted once again the small library of political and religious books left to her by her clergyman father, one of them open on her pillow. Thomas had gone out to work in the barn and Winnifred had accompanied him, Marc suspected, to make certain he kept the makeshift mitten on and had any help he might require to otherwise preserve his dignity. Charlene Huggan had been dispatched to the mill to invite the Hatches for supper and to fuss over her sister's baby.

For a long while Marc and Beth sat quietly and sipped their tea, content for the moment to enjoy the presence of the other in the exact place where their eyes had first made contact, and where they had discovered the wordless covenant that quickens love and sweeps it beyond the reach of reason.

Beth put down her empty teacup with a resolute gesture, then leaned forward in her rocker and placed both hands on Marc's knees. "I want to talk, and I'd like it very much if you'd just listen. I need to explain what's in my heart, to you and to myself, and I won't know whether I can find the right words till I hear myself saying them. Do you understand?"

Marc nodded, and gave her his full attention. She averted her gaze, however, as if looking directly at him might cause her to falter. Instead, she stared at the window and the drift of snowflakes now whispering there.

"One thing I know for sure, and so we don't ever have to doubt it, is our love for each other. I used to think that was the hardest part. I was barely eighteen when Jesse came courtin' the minister's daughter. For the longest time I thought he was a nuisance I could do without—go ahead, you're allowed to smile."

Marc did.

"I didn't know I was supposed to feel flattered or have my

stomach go queasy whenever he came into a room. Then after a while we got to know one another a bit, and began to talk some, and I started to like him very much. But it was only when he turned up one day in the back pew of the Congregational church that I knew he loved me. He seemed to be saying he was willing to switch gods for me."

The Lord of the Anglicans had lost more than Jesse Smallman lately, Marc thought.

"We went for a long walk, and I was held by a man for the first time, and we never looked back. I'm telling you all this, I think, because I want you to understand that I know what love is and what it asks us to do. You have the same look in your eye—you had it the first day you came here—that Jesse did, and I feel about you just like I did when Jess and I went for that Sunday stroll along the river flats. No, please don't say anything, not yet."

She stared longingly at the wisps of snow against the windowpane. Marc waited.

"First of all, let me say that I know what you did last June during the election, I know why you left the governor, and I know what you did for me and what it cost you not to betray a trust."

Marc started to protest but Beth raised her hand. "I got it from the horse's mouth." She smiled wryly. "Your policeman friend liked his cup of tea and a good gossip with Aunt Catherine."

"Constable Cobb."

"He was your staunch defender and ally, and convinced Auntie to take up your cause—daily. She argued, and I came to believe, that you'd become as weary of politics and hypocrisy and broken promises as I had."

"Then, if I'd come to you before—"

"Before January and Aaron's illness? Maybe. At least I'd have had the chance to look into your eyes myself. But you'd have come, as you have now, wearing that uniform—*please*, let me finish or I'll lose my nerve."

No battle-nerves could be as agonizing as this, Marc thought.

"You know, I hope, it isn't the uniform itself. I believe passionately in law and order and justice and equality. I've read bits of Paine and Rousseau and Locke and Burke. Jess and I worked for the Reform Party because we believed we could change things, get justice for the ordinary folk through politics and lawmaking. So, I wanted you to find the men responsible for my father-in-law's death last January and bring them before the law. To me, a soldier is an arm of the law or ought to be, and so should be nothing to fear. But when the governor himself corrupts the parliament and bends the law to suit him and his rich friends and ignores direct orders from London—then the law becomes something to be feared, and so do those sworn to uphold it."

Even though Marc was keenly aware of where this argument might lead and could feel a chill slowly seizing him, he could not help but marvel at the eloquence and

clearheadedness of this tiny, beautiful woman. Little wonder, then, that she had been such a disruptive force in last
spring's election. Nor was the irony of the present situation
lost on him: the very qualities he loved most might ultimately drive them apart.

"There's lawlessness on both sides now. The secret meetings are no secret. I don't know for sure but it's a good guess
that some of the treasonous talk is already more than that.
You can't imagine the terror I felt this winter, the endless
nights as I sat beside Aaron coaxing him to breathe, praying
like a sinner to any god who'd listen, and worrying myself
sick that Winnifred—proud, loyal, law-abiding, churchgo-
ing Winnifred—was miles away in some snowbound barn,
cheering and clapping at some sermon of rage and desperation, and all them torches waving away no more than two
feet from the nearest bale of hay."

Marc could think of nothing to say.

"These gatherings are still going on, and sooner or later
it'll be the troops who'll have to put a stop to them." She
glanced across at Marc's tunic, and he was grateful that he
had not worn his sword. "Do you know what my recurring
nightmare has been?"

"I think I can guess," Marc murmured, and looked away.

For a minute Marc thought she was not going to answer
her own question, but finally she said in a hollow voice,
"Winnifred and Thomas are running through the woods,
being pursued by a dark shadow. Exhausted, Thomas turns

around, steps in front of Winn, and faces his pursuer. It is you. You raise your musket, call out 'I'm sorry!' and fire. The noise wakes me up."

Marc shifted his chair so that it was directly facing Beth's. "Then I'll rip this uniform off my back! I'll buy out my commission—"

With the tenderest of gestures, she reached over and placed a finger against his lips. "Oh, you dear, dear man. I knew you would say that, I knew you'd promise to fetch me the moon if I asked you to. You're still a romantic, and it's hard—oh, so hard—not to love that part of you. But think what you're saying. You're only twenty-seven years old, and already you've tried the law to please your uncle and quit it, and then chose the army—your boyhood dream—and here you are offering to throw that away to marry me. Then what? Help me sell ladies' hats? Live off my inheritance like an English gentleman? Return to the law and hope you don't hate it too much?"

She paused to swallow the lump in her throat. "No, if we're going to come together as man and wife, it's got to be on equal terms: the burden of our love's got to be parcelled out fairly. Surely you see that?"

Marc summoned up all his courage and said as calmly as he could, "So, *I* can't quit the army and *you* can't marry an officer: you're telling me, then, there is no hope for us."

Beth's face brightened, filled suddenly with the gentle mockery Marc loved so much. "Not at all! Let me finish. I did have doubts, but now I believe there's *every* hope. For a start, neither of us has any intention of un-loving the other, despite all that might divide us. And more recently, Aaron almost dying and Thomas's horrible accident have taught me a lesson. Any of us could be carried away at any time. We should not deny ourselves love or happiness—not for politics or religion or want of the perfect moment. The madness that's going on now can't last much longer, and you have your duty and I have mine, but in the meantime . . ."

"In the meantime, what?" Marc scarcely dared ask.

"If you ask me to marry you," Beth said with a slight tremor, "I'll say yes."

Marc took a moment to find his voice, then a wide grin spread over his face. "Can I believe what I've just heard?"

"Is that a proposal?" Beth countered, her blue eyes dancing.

"It certainly is."

"Then yes, you can believe it, and yes, I accept."

Marc held her tightly while his mind raced.

"Say when," he demanded eagerly.

"You must go back to your garrison—there is no question about that. And I must stay here for some time."

"With Aaron, of course."

"And with Winnifred. I promised that I would be with her through her confinement and see the babe safely into this world."

Marc stepped back, calculating. "That means September or October at the earliest."

"I know. But I think she needs watching over."

Marc did not need to ask why. "Then we'll get married tomorrow and just live apart for a few months."

Beth thought about that for a bit. "I'd like it done proper," she said, though he saw the indecision in her face and wished he were ruthless enough to take advantage of it. "I need to prepare Aaron. And I promised Aunt Catherine that, should I marry again, she would be my matron of honour." So, marriage had not been a taboo topic at the King Street shop, Marc thought.

She looked at him with a sudden, solemn intensity that brought him up short. "What's important is that we declare our love openly and publicly. We are engaged, and you can shout it to the world if you like. You can even have the banns read by the archdeacon in that stodgy old church of yours. Our wedding *will* happen, if God chooses to let us live till October. Nothing else can prevent it."

Marc leaned over and gave her a kiss on the lips. "You shame me," he said. "And I love you the better for it."

PART TWO

OCTOBER 1837

FIVE

I'm in love, Marc."

Marc put down his copy of the *Constitution* long enough to glance across at Ensign Roderick Hilliard, who was sitting on the edge of his cot in the spartan officers' quarters they had shared now for seven months. Hilliard had served under Marc at Government House during the hectic days of the election a year ago last June. "Not again!" Marc exclaimed in mock surprise.

"This is the real thing," Hilliard said, leaning forward intently, as if to forestall Marc's return to William Mackenzie's seditious weekly "rag" in favour of matters of greater importance. "I know you have every reason to be skeptical, given

my past history, but I have found the sweetest, most beautiful, most *ethereal* creature God ever created."

Last year Hilliard had made a play for Receiver-General
Maxwell's daughter, but when the minister discovered their
affair, he threatened to emasculate the young ensign, then
shipped his daughter off to Kingston to be properly married.

"It's hearing you use such language that keeps me skeptical," Marc replied. "Do I not recall similar epithets employed
to describe the goddesslike charms of one Chastity Maxwell?"

Hilliard looked as if he had been skewered by an épée in
a friendly duel. "That was uncalled for. You know I loved
Chastity and made her an honourable offer of marriage."

But not before you had hopped into her bed, Marc
thought uncharitably before relenting. "You're right, Rick.
I do apologize. And I have to admit she was well married
and away before you decided to work your way through the
debutante rosters of Toronto and the County of York." Marc
smiled broadly to let Rick know he was teasing.

"Well, my stock went down considerably among respectable society when Sir Francis cashiered me." He grinned the
boyish grin he so often used to set a young woman's bosom
aflutter. "But I did try, nevertheless."

Marc had once thought Rick Hilliard to be too brash and
overly ambitious to be a friend, until he realized that under
the handsome exterior and sometimes impertinent manner
lay a keen intelligence and a good heart. And since he, too,
had been told that he was forward and ambitious, he could

hardly hold these character flaws, if flaws they were, against Rick. When Hilliard followed Marc out of the governor's retinue to the purgatory of the Fort York barracks, Marc had taken pity on him. Rick had actually hoped that he, and not a lackey like Barclay Spooner, would take over Marc's position as aide-de-camp to Sir Francis. The two agreed to share quarters and so far Marc had not regretted it. Although not interested in politics or economic affairs (his father being a very rich mine owner in Yorkshire), Hilliard was a lively and witty conversationalist and a born raconteur. Most significantly, Marc sensed that Hilliard would be a valuable officer on the field of battle, for there was mettle under that mantle of charm and bonhomie.

"And who's the lucky woman this time?"

"Tessa Guildersleeve," Hilliard announced. When Marc did not immediately respond, he added with a sudden burst, "Isn't that just the most mellifluous-sounding name you've ever heard?"

"Sounds Dutch to me."

Hilliard frowned briefly, uncertain as to how he ought to take this riposte. "Her father was a Knickerbocker from New York, but her mother was English," he said, as if that explained all.

"How did she get here?" Marc said helpfully, knowing that, since there was no way he could prevent the whole story from being told, he might as well hurry it along.

"She's with that acting troupe that came to town last Friday."

"Three days ago?"

"I know what you're thinking, but I've spent every spare moment for the past two days in her presence."

"Well, then, two entire days is certainly time enough, and here I thought you were ice-fishing off the island or supervising the road detail."

"There's no need to be sarcastic."

"There's every need. You're telling me that you're deeply, irrevocably in love with an actress from the United States who, if I've correctly read the handbills littering this garrison, is in town for precisely five more days?"

"I thought you would understand," Hilliard groused, crestfallen. "After all, you are a man very much in love yourself, and one who has suffered greatly for it."

"Perhaps it is because I *do* have some notion of what love is about that I ask such impertinent questions, Rick. But at the same time I would be a hypocrite to imply that one cannot fall in love at first sight."

Hilliard brightened at this admission. "I know what respectable people think of actresses, but they would be horribly mistaken in Tessa's case."

"Well, then, you must tell me all about such an exceptional soul."

Hilliard's expression went suddenly dreamy. "The Bowery Theatre Touring Company arrived here last Friday from Buffalo. Their engagement down there was cut short for some reason and the lady who runs the operation decided to come up here a few days early. They don't open until tomorrow night at Frank's Hotel, but Ogden Frank adores the theatre, and he's put them up in the best rooms above his playhouse for the whole week. In return, they've agreed to assist some of the amateur players in town by letting them watch the professionals rehearse and get up fresh scenes and do proper elocution, and so on. Mrs. Annemarie Thedford is the company's proprietor, a very famous actress from New York City and every inch a lady, and so generous with her time and advice."

"And Tessa is a member of this illustrious troupe?"

"Oh, yes. There's six of them in all, seven if you count the black fellow who does the heavy lifting. Tessa plays all the ingenue roles, like Ophelia and Miranda."

"And *is* she an ingenue?" Marc asked, knowing what Rick's answer would be.

"Yes, she's brilliant. I watched her do Ophelia's mad scene from *Hamlet* last Saturday afternoon. There wasn't a dry eye in the audience. Even the old farts from the Shakespeare Club blubbered shamelessly. Afterwards she was very gracious, and we spent above an hour talking. She seemed very impressed that I had done amateur theatricals since I was a youngster. We hit it off immediately."

"So I gather. And of what age might this extraordinary ingenue be?"

Hilliard seemed momentarily puzzled by the question, but said quite proudly, "Eighteen."

Marc sighed but said nothing.

"What does age matter? I'm only twenty-five, and she's a beautiful woman. And you wouldn't believe the tragic story of her life."

"Oh?"

"She was orphaned at fifteen when both her parents died of the cholera and she learned that all her father left her was debts. She was an only child, without relatives in America. But her parents had always loved the theatre, and she had been taken to plays and musicals since she was six."

"You found out a lot in a little more than an hour."

"Ah, but our own York Thespians were invited by Mrs. Thedford to put on scenes from our spring production of *The Way of the World* on Saturday evening just for her company. Imagine the pleasure we had in performing before true professionals! And how they did laugh. But best of all, Tessa was thoroughly taken with my Mirabell, and invited me up to her room for a nightcap, the most exquisite sherry I've ever tasted."

"And you returned for a further engagement yesterday?"

"We couldn't really do anything on the Sabbath, but with everybody else in the troupe off to see the sights of the city and take up dinner invitations from several of the more distinguished members of the York Thespians, Tessa and I were able to spend the entire day together. The only unpleasant bit was the dressing-down Tessa was given by Mrs. Thedford for not showing up at the Grange for tea, which, I'm embarrassed to say, I was the cause of. But I turned on the charm, and before I left all was once again sweetness and light."

"Thank God for charm."

"But to get back to Tessa's life: as I said, she was alone and destitute—"

"And loved the theatre."

"—and out of the blue Mrs. Thedford arrives at her house just as the bailiffs do, and spirits Tessa away to her Bowery Theatre, of which she is part owner. It turns out that Mrs. Thedford had been a friend of the Guildersleeves, and so more or less adopted Tessa on their behalf—then and there."

"Sounds suspiciously like those three-decker romance novels you find so enthralling."

"There's more, of course. It soon becomes apparent that Tess has a knack for acting, and is gradually worked into plays requiring the ingenue role."

"What else?"

"By the age of seventeen, she's the talk of New York, and being pursued by every cad and roué in that nefarious town."

"So she and the company run off to "

"I know this all sounds incredibly romantic, Marc, but it happens to be fact. The reason the troupe is on the road is that the Bowery Playhouse burned down last spring, and as the new one won't be ready until this coming January, Mrs. Thedford formed a touring company for this fall. They've been to Rochester and Buffalo, and from here they're going on to Detroit and Chicago."

"And when they do?"

Hilliard stared at the floor. "I haven't been able to think about that," he said gloomily.

"The good news is you've got five more days to find out just how deep your love really goes. And believe me, Rick, that will prove to be a necessary part of the process."

A grateful smile lit up Hilliard's face. "That's true. And the reason I wanted to tell you all this is that we've been invited again to watch a rehearsal of some scenes from Shakespeare—things they've done before but not for some time. It's a chance to see how they whip an act into top shape."

"I'm sure you'll find it interesting, but—"

"I want you to come with me. I want you to meet Tessa."

Marc was surprised, then touched, by Hilliard's request. Of course, Rick did not know that Marc, too, had been briefly intoxicated by the acting scene in London five years ago. He merely wanted to show off his girl to—what?—his best friend.

Thinking that Marc was about to demur, Hilliard said quickly, "Owen Jenkin is coming along, too. He's been in musical hall revues in his youth, and I think he's got the itch again. We'll be the only three there, according to Tessa."

Marc and Major Jenkin had developed a firm friendship ever since their foraging trip last March, with the latter enjoying the role of confidant and avuncular guide. Since then, his fund of stories about the Peninsular War, the Duke of Wellington, and Uncle Frederick had kept Marc entertained through the long, difficult months following his separation from Beth, who was still in Crawford's Corners. Beth wrote to him faithfully every week—rambling, newsy letters about everything that was happening on the Goodall farm and in the township around them. Winnifred's baby was overdue, but no one was worrying. Thomas's hand had healed, though he was left with a dreadful scar.

Some of the news was as alarming as it was tantalizingly vague. Organized gatherings of political resistance were undoubtedly being held, though, thank God, Beth had kept a close watch on the malcontents in her own household. Moreover, the situation in Lower Canada was deteriorating rapidly. Nonetheless, the wedding date had been set, as planned, for Sunday, October 22, now just thirteen days away. Aunt Catherine, who had expanded the millinery shop to include dressmaking, had had one of her new seamstresses make a bridal gown, which had been duly shipped to Cobourg, tried on, and declared perfect. Marc, Hilliard, Jenkin, and three other officers, including Colonel Margison, were planning to ride in state, as it were, to Cobourg two days before the ceremony, where they would provide colour, pomp, and revelry before, and most likely well after, the service at Beth's father's former church. And Aaron would be standing tall beside the other guests, his contribution to the reviving fortunes of the farm well appreciated.

"I'd be honoured to join you and Major Jenkin this afternoon," Marc said. "Maybe I'll get the itch myself."

Normally when they went to town, officers and soldiers made the thirty-minute trek on foot. Just as often, after a hectic round of taverns and less savoury attractions, the more affluent would hire a trap or buggy to drive them back to the fort in comfort. But today Quartermaster Jenkin had arranged for horses to be provided, and he, Marc, and Hilliard rode in leisurely fashion eastward along Front Street in the cool sunshine of an early October day. They arrived at Frank's Hotel, on the corner of West Market and Colborne, just after two o'clock.

The Regency Theatre, constructed the previous June by Ogden Frank, was merely an unprepossessing extension of the hotel itself. From the south wall of the original two-storey inn, which faced east onto West Market Street, he had erected an unadorned brick rectangle so that it fronted onto Colborne Street, where a false balcony and a sign in Gothic letters provided the only visual enticement to would-be playgoers. The theatre itself was located in the lower storey of the new structure, and entered via two wide, oaken doors. On the floor above the theatre, and separate from the main hotel rooms, were situated several spacious chambers that served as additional space for hotel patrons or, when visiting troupes arrived, as comfortable quarters for the players. Frank and his wife, Madge, lived in four rooms attached to the rear of the tavern but otherwise discrete and private.

"We're here by special invitation this afternoon," Rick reminded them when they had delivered the horses to the ostler and were about to enter the theatre through the main entrance. He did not need to reiterate who in the company had interceded on their behalf. "They haven't done their 'Selections from the Bard' show since last winter, so we're going to be privy to a truly professional rehearsal."

Marc endeavoured to look impressed.

"Well, it'll all be new to me," Jenkin said affably. "I did a bit of song-and-dance stuff in my salad days, but nobody dared call it *thee-ay-ter*."

The oak doors swung open at the first touch, briefly flooding the dark, cavernous room inside with sudden light.

"Get the hell out and shut the bloody door!"

The voice came from a raised platform about forty feet away at the far end of the cavern, where the flickering glow from a dozen candles and a single, overhead chandelier exposed five or six individuals. All had apparently been fixated on a tall male figure, downstage centre, but had decided that the novelty of an open door and sunshine was more worthy of their attention.

A very blond wisp of a girl padded quickly over to the imposing male and whispered something up into his ear. He appeared to smile as he turned towards the intruders and said in a stentorian but not unfriendly tone: "Welcome, good sirs. I mistook you for those ragamuffins who've been harassing us all morning. Please, take a seat in one of the far boxes. And be kind enough to keep your lips buttoned. We are engaged here in a serious undertaking."

"You shan't see or hear us, Mr. Merriwether," Rick called

out to him, and then nudged his companions towards a set of crude steps at the top of which was perched a plain wooden box with the front open, like a sort of elevated kiosk.

"Ah," Jenkin whispered, "seats for the mighty."

They ascended, carefully, found three hard-backed chairs in the semi-dark, propped their elbows on the railing in front of them, and prepared to observe the serious proceedings on the stage, now a foot or two below them and about twenty-five feet away. When their eyes adjusted to the interior light, they found that they could see and hear everything before them.

The stage itself was rudimentary: two wooden pilasters and a faded velvet curtain that might have once been crimson composed the proscenium arch, in front of which the playing area extended another five or six feet. Canvas "wings" of a mucus-green hue were set back in receding fashion at each side to effect a sense of perspective. Two small chandeliers on long cables could now be seen beside the large one that was presently lit, and arrayed along the curved edge of the thrust-stage were half a dozen Argand lamps, which, when fired up, would provide ample foot-lighting. Along the side walls, that were about fifteen feet high, iron candelabra were inset in the brick to illuminate the pit below, the six boxes, and the gallery teetering across the back wall. A single door, locked and barred, along the wall to the left opened onto the alley outside and a nearby pair of privies. Two small windows, high up, offered the only natural light and ventilation. No wonder theatres burnt down at regular intervals, Marc thought as he turned his attention to the action onstage.

"We'll start with the death of Lear. I'd like the scene to run right through. I want everybody watching—you're the critical audience, remember. But when we've finished the scene, I don't want to hear a peep from the cheap seats, understood? If I wish to avail myself of your comments—after I've made my own—I'll ask for them."

"Jason Merriwether, the director," Rick whispered.

Merriwether appeared to be very tall, almost Marc's height at six feet, and perhaps in his mid-forties if the graying sideburns were not the result of makeup. But there was no middle-aged paunch or slackening of the skin around the mouth or under the jutting chin. His bearing was imperial, a man of parts who commanded any stage he chose to grace with his presence. His hair was a tawny shade, his chin and upper lip bare, and his nose of ordinary length, but the eyes were coalblack and penetrating, even at a distance of twenty-five feet.

"Annemarie, *ma chère*, would you please give the king your shawl. It may help Mr. Armstrong get in role." The latter half of this remark was spoken with spitting sarcasm and directed at a bent, gnarled man who hobbled forward at the mention of his name. While he could not have been sixty—the dark swatch of unkempt hair was merely speckled with gray—he looked Lear's age without need of makeup or costume. For he had once been a big man, perhaps five foot seven, large-boned and full-fleshed, but the skin on his face, neck, and wrists now drooped as if the flesh had been sucked out from under it without warning. The eyes were murky dots in smudged sockets, and the lips hung loosely in what seemed to be either a permanent sneer or a perpetual whimper. He looked to Marc like a man who wished to hide from himself.

"I don't need your advice to tackle a scene I've played on two continents," he muttered at Merriwether, but did not look his way.

"I think the shawl may help, Dawson," said a tall woman who stepped under the candlelight and gently laid her knitted shawl over the hunched actor.

"Annemarie Thedford, the boss," Rick whispered again.

"It's a bit drafty in here, and you know how easily you catch cold and lose your voice."

"All right, then," Armstrong said sullenly, but he did glance up at Mrs. Thedford like a dog both surprised and grateful that he had not been kicked.

Mrs. Thedford, the owner-manager of the Bowery Touring Company, was also exceptionally tall, near five foot seven or eight, which left her looking down at almost every woman and three-quarters of the men in the colony. Her thick, honey-coloured hair was neatly coiffed, and though her fair complexion would require makeup to project her expression across the footlights, the face itself was the picture of elegance and inborn grace. Her walk could only be described as regal, the consequence of an upright posture and confident carriage. Here was a woman of the world, unbowed by its travails, whose lean and handsomely proportioned figure commanded your attention first, then drew you on to the gaze that held and appraised and fascinated. Marc could not take his eyes off her.

"Where in Sam Hill did Thea get to?" Merriwether roared, making Lear recoil and drop his cloak.

"She was here just a second ago," piped a male voice from the upstage shadow.

"I think she went to puke again," said a sweet and timid female voice.

"That's my girl," her suitor mouthed in Marc's ear.

"I'd better see to her," Mrs. Thedford said with evident concern, then strode quickly across the back of the stage to the right and disappeared.

"Well, she can't very well lie dead in Lear's arms and then start puking at the audience," Merriwether growled after her, but she was already too far away to hear.

Lear himself at that moment began to cough, an uncontrollable hacking that continued for a full minute. When it finally stopped, there was an awesome silence.

"You've been at it again, haven't you? I can smell your stinking breath from here!" Merriwether said with withering contempt.

Armstrong's jaw quivered as if it were expecting a word to emerge, but at that moment Mrs. Thedford swept back in, and Merriwether looked to her expectantly.

"Thea will be here in a few minutes. I've asked Mrs. Frank to prepare her a tisane," she said, as if she were remarking on the pleasantness of the weather.

"But I wish to do the Lear first, *ma chère*. It needs the most work, obviously."

"*I'm* ready to go," Armstrong said with a pathetic sweep of the cloak about his stooped shoulders.

"He's been drinking again."

"That's a lie!"

"Smell his breath."

"I had one mouthful, for my rheumatism."

Mrs. Thedford took Armstrong's hand in hers and pulled him up to face her. "When we're finished here, old friend—and I expect you to stay till the last word is uttered—I want you to accompany me to your room and give me the bottle. God knows where you managed to hide it."

"I'm sorry, love. It won't happen again. I promise."

"For the love of Christ, can we get on with this farce?"

"I think we're doing that tonight," Mrs. Thedford said dryly, and drew a giggle and a chortle from the back of the stage.

"Am I the director here or not?" Merriwether said somewhere between complaint and petition.

"You are, Mr. Merriwether, and a damn good one."

Merriwether looked mollified. Then with a sly grin he stepped under the candlelight and into the shadows upstage. "Then I am making a casting decision that should have been made weeks ago." Into the spotlight he drew by one tiny white hand a young woman, barely beyond girlhood, but nonetheless stunning for all that.

"Tessa," Marc murmured before Rick could.

Tessa Guildersleeve had the white blond hair of an albino, and it fell where it wished in flowing coils over her bare shoulders, its native lustre merely enhanced by the meagre light above it. Her Dutch skin was unblemished and uniformly alabaster from the brow to the rim of her bosom that winked enticingly from the low-cut, frothy shift she wore—which resembled either a priest's frock or a courtesan's nightie, depending on the angle of observation. Her diminutive feet were caressed by ballet slippers, and she moved her slim, pale arms with the impetus and delicacy of a prima ballerina's grand entrance. She was all elfin innocence in movement, but out of the translucence of her blue eyes shone pure desire.

"Tessa, my pretty, you have understudied the role long enough. Tomorrow night you shall step onto this stage as Cordelia."

"You're not going to wait for Thea, then?" Mrs. Thedford said evenly, but there was an edge behind the remark.

"Thea's getting too old and fat for the ingenue, *ma chère*. She'll be laughed off the stage like she was in Buffalo. We don't want that to happen again, do we?"

"What about Juliet, then?"

"Well, I thought Tessa did splendidly at short notice during the entr'acte in Rochester, didn't you, Clarence?"

At this, a young man in his mid-twenties stepped into the circle of light that now illumined five of the six acting members of the troupe. He was handsome in a feminine sort of way that contrasted sharply with the aggressive masculinity of Merriwether. He had curly red hair, pale freckles, and a pallor to match, and languid blue eyes that most directors would have instantly labelled a poet's. He peered towards Mrs. Thedford, but she was staring intently at Merriwether. "Tessa always gives her best," he said guardedly.

"Thea will play Juliet tomorrow night, if she's well enough," Mrs. Thedford said.

"You *could* let her take the role of Beatrice," Merriwether said, staring straight back at her with his intimidating, black gaze.

Mrs. Thedford smiled cryptically. "Meaning that I myself am somewhat too advanced in years to play the part?"

"Not at all, my dear. You'll be acting Beatrice and Cleopatra when you're eighty, should you wish to. What I'm suggesting is that, outside of the farce, there are not, in the makeup of our current program, any roles now suited to the peculiar talents of our Miss Clarkson. That is all."

"I would be more than happy to let Thea play Beatrice, Jason, but then it would be incumbent upon us to find a Benedick young enough to be credible."

"I wouldn't think of it—" Clarence Beasley said, looking abashed at both the director and the proprietor.

"But I'm ready to play Juliet! I *am*!" There was no

sweetness in the ingenue's statement of fact, only the petulance of a child approaching tantrum. Tessa's pretty features were suddenly contorted, and flushed with an unbecoming rush of crimson pique.

"If you carry on like that, missy, we'll have to put you in the Punch-and-Judy show with a slapstick." Mrs. Thedford spoke in the way a mother might in gently reproving a much-doted-on daughter. "Be content with Cordelia, for the time being."

Rick Hilliard stirred beside Marc, who put a restraining hand upon his friend's arm and one finger to his lips. It was obvious that the actors, in the intensity of this interplay, had forgotten they were being observed, and Marc was thoroughly enjoying his invisibility.

Tessa's face lit up instantly, and all traces of tantrum vanished in the unrepressed joy of her response. "Oh, Annie, you are such a dear! I could hug you to death!"

When she threatened to do so, Mrs. Thedford held up a hand and said, "Save that ardour for Cordelia and Miranda tomorrow night." She turned to Merriwether. "Get on with the scene, then, Jason dear. I'll just go and see how Thea's getting on. We'll need her for the farce tonight."

"We'll need *everybody*," Merriwether said, glaring at Dawson Armstrong, who had taken advantage of the diversion to squat on his haunches and drift into a doze.

Mrs. Thedford left, and the director clapped his hands for attention, as if he were orchestrating a cast of hundreds. "All right, Dawson, you know the routine. Tessa, my sweet, while you have no lines for this particular scene—we'll rehearse your other scene later—it is vitally important that you lie absolutely limp in the old man's arms. I suggest that you let the arm facing the audience droop—like this—and your head should be tilted back so your beautiful, long tresses hang down to almost touch the floor, and you can let one slipper dangle from your toes, and contrive to let it fall just as Lear moves from his 'howls' to his speech."

"Must I wear Thea's costume?"

"I think not. We'll try something gauzier that will let your figure show through—in a modest way, of course. Thea's figure, alas, has to be disguised wherever possible: that was the point about her age I was attempting to make."

"I do hope Thea won't be too upset. She's a very nice woman."

"Dawson! Wake up and take your place!"

Armstrong glared at Merriwether's knees, got up, and strode manfully back into the shadows upstage. Tessa padded after him. Clarence Beasley came and stood as close to Merriwether as he dared, anticipating the action to come. A moment later, Lear began his escalating sequence of howls.

Marc felt a chill down his spine. Lear's cri de coeur was heart-wrenching: a deep animal howl bred in the flesh and bone of love and loss. Armstrong might be old, but he was not past his prime as a tragedian. Slowly the howls came nearer and the ruined old king staggered forward with the hanged Cordelia in his arms and floating, it appeared, on the cloak. Tessa looked lifeless, one arm adroop, the body arched but limp, the hair lifting and falling with the cadence of Lear's step, as if something of her was yet living and not ready to die. Marc was moved deeply, and braced himself for the speech he knew by heart.

It was at this critical point, and just as Cordelia's slipper struck the floor like a severed appendage, that Dawson Armstrong staggered, careened, and toppled sideways. Then, in a pathetic effort to maintain his balance, he dropped Cordelia upon the boards with an ugly thump.

"What the fuck are you doing, you goddamn moron, you drunken pig, you stinking excuse for an actor!"

Marc leaned forward in alarm, as did Rick and Jenkin.

But having spewed this venom at the toppled Lear, who lay semi-comatose where he had fallen, Merriwether dashed to Tessa's side, almost colliding with Clarence Beasley.

"I'm fine, I'm fine," Tessa said, whipping her dress down over her prettily exposed knees and scrambling to her feet. "I fell on my derriere." She giggled, and gave that part of her anatomy a reconnoitring rub. "An' there's nothin' much to hurt down there!"

Beasley insisted on taking her hand, as if she were still on the floor, and giving it a gentlemanly tug.

Tessa rewarded the effort with a dazzling smile. "What'll we do now?" she asked Merriwether.

"First, I'll drag this intoxicated sot into the wings, where he can sleep it off. Then you and I will do this scene properly."

"I'll see to Dawson," Beasley said. He went over to the

old man, spoke softly into his ear, then helped him over to the wings on the left, where he collapsed peacefully.

"We better wait for Annie," Tessa said nervously.

"I'm the director, love."

Just then Mrs. Thedford returned. "Well, Jason, you were right. He's found a bottle somewhere and downed it. I've searched his room, but when he sleeps this off, we'll have to watch him every minute until the show opens at eight thirty."

"He'll never make it," Merriwether said.

"Now, you know he's an old pro. If he's awake and no more than half drunk, he can outact any of us."

"Jason says he's going to play Lear tomorrow night," Tessa said with just a hint of little-girl mischief in her voice.

"We'll cross that bridge when we come to it. Right now I'm more concerned with Dorothea's health. She's taken a tisane to help her sleep. She insists she'll be ready for the farce tonight. And I believe her. She made no objection when I told her Tess was going to play Cordelia—to lessen the load on her till she's feeling herself again."

"Oh, thank you, Annie. Thank you!"

"So, whether Dawson does Lear tomorrow night or you, Jason, Tess needs a couple of run-throughs right now. Clarence and I will observe."

"Just remember what I told you a few minutes ago and you'll be fine, sweetie," Merriwether said to Tessa as they walked back into the shadows, Merriwether looking very Promethean beside the slight, five-foot figure of the girl-woman.

"They've edited out the other parts, so there's just Lear

and Cordelia," Hilliard whispered. But Marc's attention was riveted on the stage.

There was a collective intake of breath in expectation of the five howls. Out of Jason Merriwether's mouth they came, but this time they were more bellowed than uttered, more impressing than impressive. From the upstage shadows emerged this other octogenarian with the rag doll of his daughter draped across his outstretched arms. Merriwether was nothing if not the consummate actor, for, despite his height and imperial bearing, he looked now the bowed and broken monarch, his every wearied step a defeated trudge. Moreover, his hunched bulk rendered the slender, unbreathing Cordelia that much more vulnerable and pitiable. And when he laid her down and began his great speech of self-insight and contrition, there was no anomalous thump, only the cadence of the bard's pentameter. But, scarcely noticed except by the quickest eye, the old king's left hand, as it slipped Cordelia's lower half stageward, lingered a split second more than necessary on the curved clef of her buttocks and, just possibly, gave them an impertinent squeeze. The girl herself gave no sign, not even a blink.

Marc heard the rasp of Rick's breath and felt him rising from his chair. With well-coordinated movements, Marc pressed him back down with one hand and placed the other over his mouth in time to throttle the cry of outrage there.

"They're only acting," he hissed, and Rick reluctantly sank back.

Someone else had noticed the king's incestuous touch,

for Marc saw Mrs. Thedford's eyes widen in disbelief, then fix upon the girl while Merriwether completed his series of lamentations over her prostrate form, and made a fine, rhetorical demise. Beasley began applauding, but Tessa turned her newly opened eyes upon Mrs. Thedford and smiled—knowingly, Marc thought. Owen Jenkin began to clap as well, and when Tessa rose to take her bow beside Merriwether, Rick joined him lustily. Marc felt obliged to clap politely, but Annemarie Thedford did not.

Well, well, Marc thought, the acting business hasn't changed much since I dipped my toes into its roiling waters five years ago.

THE NEXT HOUR AND A HALF unfolded less contentiously. The company showed a predilection for death scenes, with the demise of Antony, Cleopatra, Romeo, and Juliet being added to that of Lear. All of this gloom was leavened only by the razor-keen repartee of Annemarie and Jason as Beatrice and Benedick from *Much Ado About Nothing*. As far as Rick Hilliard was concerned, and he made his concern quite vocal, Tessa as Juliet (standing in, for today only, in place of Thea Clarkson) was the show-stopper, despite a less-than-satisfactory Romeo (Clarence Beasley), whose Yankee twang nearly ruined the balcony scene and certainly depreciated the glowing iambics of the beloved above him. And while all of the actors essayed some sort of approximate English stage-accent, Marc detected a trace of genuine English dialect in Mrs. Thedford's speech, even when she wasn't in character. Her performances as Gertrude and Lady Macbeth, opposite Merriwether's Claudius and Macbeth, were the highlights of the afternoon.

The various bits and pieces usually taken by Armstrong or Thea Clarkson were merely read by one of the other players, and Mrs. Thedford agreed with the director's suggestion that the scenes from *The Tempest* be dropped from the bill due to the comatose condition of Prospero. Rick groaned at the patent unfairness of a decision that would deprive him of seeing Tessa play Miranda, the quintessential ingenue. Miranda herself seemed blithely unconcerned.

Just as they were finishing, Thea Clarkson made a dramatic entrance, pale and fevered, and insisted on taking her part as Juliet, even though this set had already been run through twice with clear success.

"How nice of you to make an appearance, love," Merriwether said acidly. "You look more like Lady Capulet or the Nurse than a fifteen-year-old virgin."

Thea seemed about to burst into tears. Illness or not, she no longer gave the illusion of a woman in first bloom, for though she had a pretty, moon-pale face and striking almond eyes, she had put on weight that did not sit on her bones attractively. Moreover, her expression was that of one whose confidence has been shaken by the discovery of some knowledge still too daunting to admit.

"There's no need for gratuitous cruelty," Mrs. Thedford said to Merriwether. "Thea, dear, you and Clarence can rehearse the *Romeo and Juliet* scenes tomorrow afternoon. You need to rest now so you'll be fresh for the farce tonight. After all, it is *you* who must carry the piece."

Thea beamed her a bright smile, then began to weep quietly.

At this point in the proceedings, Dawson Armstrong woke up. "Where in hell did my Cordelia go?"

"Don't you just love theatre people?" Rick exclaimed.

SIX

"Tessa has offered to give us a tour of the facility," Rick called down to Marc and Jenkin, who were standing by the pot-bellied stove warming their hands. "And Mrs. Thedford has invited us to stay for the supper the Franks are laying on for the company in the hotel dining-room."

"We'll take the tour," Marc said, "but this is my night to have supper with Aunt Catherine at the shop."

"Speak for yourself, young fellow." Jenkin laughed. He winked at Marc: "That Thedford woman's a fine specimen of her sex."

Rick hopped down, and they followed him through a curtained doorway to the left of the stage and into the gloomy space beside it, where the actors could rest between entrances. Tessa was waiting for them, her blond hair shimmering in the near-dark. She led them down a long, narrow hallway, on either side of which were several cubicles that Tessa, still leading the parade, referred to as dressing-chambers. Rick insisted on exploring the one assigned to Tessa and Thea Clarkson, professing his amazement at the drawerful of makeup paints and glues, the wig-stand, and the bedraggled mannequin with the evening's costume in place upon it. Marc peered into Merriwether's carrel, where several playbills caught his attention. One of them, an advertisement for *Hamlet* at the Park Theatre in New York, featured a sketch of a younger Merriwether as Claudius, with a wig of curly black hair, bushy brows, and a trim Vandyke of similar hue—looking very much the smiling villain of the piece. Having exhausted the wonders of the airless, windowless dressing-rooms, they retreated as they had come in, and Tessa pointed up the steps to the stage itself, indicating that they were to cross to the other side.

"Where does that door go?" Rick asked, glancing to his left.

"Oh, that takes you into Mr. Frank's quarters," Tessa burbled, reaching down for Rick's hand. "The Franks've got the most beautiful furniture you've ever seen. It's just like a doll's house!"

They crossed the stage—the chandelier was now extinguished—and, through the wings on the right, down into another unlit space. There was a door to their left and a set of steep stairs straight ahead. The door appeared to be the only link between theatre and tavern. Tessa eased it open. They could see the bar just ahead and beyond it a room full of boisterous patrons, not of the drama but the bottle. Tessa eased it closed again.

"Show us *your* rooms," Rick suggested slyly.

"Oh, wait till you see them! We had nothin' like this in Buffalo!" Tessa testified, and skipped up the stairs with Rick on her heels. The party paused on a landing, and then continued up again to the second floor directly above the theatre.

"Is this the only way in here?" Marc asked anxiously. The upper storey of Frank's addition appeared to be self-contained and separate from the original building.

"That's right," Tessa said. "Unless you want to go through that window at the far end of this hall and jump off the balcony onto the street."

"I could call for you like Romeo from underneath the balcony out there," Rick teased.

"What if there's a fire?" Marc asked.

"My, would you look at this!" Rick cried, ignoring Marc's question. He pointed through the partly opened door to the first room on their right.

Tessa blushed, giving the effect of a white carnation magically transformed into a red one. "That's our bathroom. You ain't supposed to peek in there!"

But peek they must.

An elephantine copper tub squatted ostentatiously in the centre of the room, around which, on clothes-horses, were arrayed a dozen bath towels of varying pastel tints. In a far corner a Chinese folding-screen offered privacy to the diffident bather. On top of a pot-bellied stove, spitting and aglow, sat a kettle big enough to swim in.

"The Franks have a maid who readies the bath whenever we wish," Tessa said.

"Looks like that tub could hold more than one person," Rick said, and was rewarded with another full-petalled blush.

A guttural cry directly across the hall from the bathroom interrupted this bit of by-play, as if someone had muttered a curse while stumbling over a coal-scuttle or bag of nails.

"What on earth was that?" Jenkin asked.

"Oh, that's just Jeremiah's babble-talk," Tessa said. "Don't pay him no mind."

At this, the three men turned to the open doorway of a storeroom, where a huge black man was staring at them with white-eyed, menacing curiosity.

Tessa made what appeared at first to be several flirtatious gestures with her hands and fingers across the top of her bosom. Jeremiah, if that's who he was, relaxed immediately, and greeted the newcomers with a gleaming smile that consumed most of his large, round face and bald head.

"He doesn't speak English?" Rick wondered.

Tessa laughed, a bubbling little-girl laugh. "He don't speak at all."

"He's mute, then?" Jenkin said.

"Aaargh," Jeremiah said forcefully, with a painful contortion of both lips.

"He's deaf and dumb," Tessa said matter-of-factly. "But he can read and write and read lips a little—can't ya, Jeremiah?" Here she flashed him a sign, and he nodded vigorously.

"He does the haulin' and settin' up of the flats. Annie— Mrs. Thedford—picked him up off the street and gave him a place to sleep. I told her he was probably a runaway slave but she don't bother listenin' to anyone, especially when it comes to pickin' up strays."

Like you, Marc thought, and raised his opinion of the imperial Mrs. Thedford another notch.

"What's that?" Jenkin asked, indicating a slate that hung by a rope from the man's neck.

Jeremiah smiled, and Marc could discern the intelligence in that face, whose age might have been twenty-five or forty. He realized that the overly demonstrative facial gestures and hand movements were an attempt to communicate almost physically, but might easily lead people to assume he was a simpleton. Marc thought of Beth's brother Aaron and winced inwardly.

Jeremiah drew a piece of chalk from a big pocket in his smock and wrote something on the slate: "My name is Jeremiah Jefferson." Then he held the slate out to Major Jenkin, who erased what was there with the sleeve of his tunic, and wrote: "I am Owen Jenkin."

"Jeremiah, get back to your work!" Tessa ordered suddenly, and accompanied her command with several intimidating hand-signs. "You got props to get ready for the farce tonight."

Jeremiah did not seem to take offense at this rude outburst. He merely bowed his head and backed into the storeroom, but what lay behind the mask of his eyes and his practised public demeanour could only be guessed at. In the room behind him, they saw a straw pallet surrounded by half a dozen steamer-trunks.

"You brought all this with you?" Rick said with enough interest to have Tessa pause and lean against his nearest shoulder.

"Those are trunks with the props and costumes we're gonna need in Detroit next week but not here. There's one or two more downstairs somewheres that Mr. Merriwether's plannin' to send back to New York—stuff we used in Buffalo but don't need no more."

"But how on earth do you haul all of this stuff?" Jenkin asked, his quartermaster's curiosity piqued. "Not over our roads?"

Tessa gave him an indulgent smile, glanced at Rick, and said, "Our stuff comes down the Erie Canal on a barge and then up from Buffalo by boat on the Welland Canal. That's what we got Jeremiah for—to ride with it. And, of course, to protect us from dangerous strangers." She batted her near-invisible lashes at Rick.

"But he's deaf," Rick said with real concern.

"He sleeps right there at the top of them stairs with the

door open all night. The teensiest vibration will wake him up straightaway."

Jeremiah was busy opening one of the trunks as they turned to move farther along the carpeted hallway.

"We each got a trunk in our rooms. We're responsible for our own costumes once they get here, though we do help each other dress." She checked out Rick's response to this double entendre, and was not disappointed.

"Who does the repair work?" Jenkin asked, ever interested in the care and deployment of uniforms. He stumbled for a second over a decorative spittoon near one of the doors, righted himself, and continued: "You must have a lot of it with all the costume changes."

"Thea does the little bits of stitchin' an' patchin'. She's real handy with a needle. But if we're stayin' put for a week or so, like here, Mr. Merriwether finds us a local seamstress." They were moving down the hall now, where doors on either side indicated the sleeping chambers of the cast. Tessa revelled in her role as tour-guide, with Rick at her elbow endeavouring to bump against her at every opportunity. "This here's Clarence's room and that one's Mr. Armstrong's," she said, pointing to the next two rooms on the right, and then putting a forefinger against her pretty lips. "They like to have a snooze after the afternoon rehearsal."

"And where is *your* room?"

"Here at the end," Tessa said, "across from Mr. Merriwether's."

As Tessa opened the door on the left, Marc glanced out the dusty window onto Colborne Street, and noted that the balcony which adorned the front of the Regency Theatre was indeed a false one, making it a dubious escape mechanism for those fleeing a sudden fire and a precarious perch for would-be Juliets.

"The maiden's bower!" Tessa gushed as they followed her inside.

Marc had to admit that the room was nicely decorated, with lavender wallpaper aflutter with sprites and fairies, a thick carpet in some neutral shade, a commode-and-vanity with tilting oval-mirror, a quaint Swiss clock, a settee embroidered with daisies, and a four-poster bed swathed in pink. On a night-table, a decanter of sherry winked at the interlopers.

"Mrs. Thedford insisted I take this room. Usually I have to share with Thea."

"Where does Thea sleep?" Rick asked. "With Mrs. Thedford?"

"Lordy, no. Annie always stays by herself. Thea's sleepin' on her own in a little room in the Franks' place. Annie's afraid the rest of us might catch whatever she's got."

"You've a fondness for sherry," Jenkin said with a smile.

"Oh, that. It's somethin' Mrs. Thedford taught me—to have one or two small glasses after a performance to help me sleep." Giving Rick a sidelong glance, she added, "'Course I do *share* it once in a while."

"Well, that leaves us with all but Mrs. Thedford accounted for," Jenkin said in what he intended to be a disinterested tone.

"We've gone past her rooms," Tessa said.

"Rooms?" Jenkin asked, intrigued.

Tessa led them back into the hall and pointed to the door next to her own room. "I'll just give a tap an' see if she's still up."

"Oh, please don't disturb her," Rick said.

But Tessa, who apparently liked to have her own way whenever it could be arranged, had already rapped, and a moment later the door opened.

"Oh, do come in, gentlemen," Mrs. Thedford said. She stood tall and elegant in the doorway, clad only in a satin kimono, her coiffed hair almost touching the lintel above her. "I heard you in the hall and was about to step out and invite you in."

Jenkin demurred. "We don't wish to disturb you at your . . ."

"Toilette?" She laughed, giving the word its French pronunciation. "Don't worry, sir, you're not invading milady's boudoir."

As they followed her in, they realized that the owner-operator of the Bowery Touring Company had a suite of rooms befitting her status. After introductions were made and requisite courtesies completed, Mrs. Thedford offered them sherry, sat them on her comfortable chairs and settee, and regaled them with witty tales of theatre life in New York. Marc noticed two things: Owen Jenkin was quite taken with the woman, and she herself appeared as regal, confident, and genuine as the image she had projected from the stage. Nor did she seem to be playing a role, of which she was perfectly capable. And if she were, it was one she believed in.

At one lull in the conversation, she looked at Marc and said, "Edwards . . . my, what a fine English name."

"I can't take credit for having applied it to myself," Marc said, and it was plain from her approving expression that Mrs. Thedford—who slept alone in the adjoining bedroom and was, according to her story, long a widow—appreciated the witticism and the lineaments of the man who'd made it. Good Lord, Marc thought, surely I'm too young for her attentions. Besides, it was Major Jenkin who was paying court to her with all the Welsh charm he could muster.

"I noticed the lovely lilt of your accent," the major said gallantly. "Do I detect a shadow of English in it?"

Mrs. Thedford gave him a smile worthy of Cleopatra.

"The merest shadow, Mr. Jenkin. My father was English, but he brought me to Philadelphia when I was still a toddler. I have, alas, no memory of my birth-country, only a few of the unconscious traces of its glorious speech."

"Which is no drawback in the theatre," the major replied.

"Those pieces on your commode there look very English," Marc remarked, admiring a pair of silver candlesticks. "I remember seeing something of that design in London."

"You are very observant, Lieutenant. In fact, the hair-brushes, hand-mirror, and the candlesticks were especially made for my parents as a wedding gift, a matched set. Or so my father told me when I was old enough to understand. They are all that I have left of them—or England—and I bring them with me everywhere."

"Aren't you afraid they'll be stolen?" Rick asked.

"Not with Jeremiah nearby, I'm not. And as he's been complaining of a toothache all day, I expect he'll be more vigilant than usual at his post tonight."

"And we've got policemen patrolling our streets," Rick said, as if he himself were native-born and a major contributor to local improvements.

As they were getting up to leave, Mrs. Thedford said, "I hope you all plan to come to the farce tonight, as guests of the company. And, of course, you're welcome to join us in the hotel for supper."

"Thank you. I wouldn't miss either for the world," Jenkin said with a brief bow.

"I'll be here every night this week," Rick said with an artful glance at Tessa, who had sat through the polite chatter without saying a word, though she and Mrs. Thedford had exchanged cryptic looks, and the latter had given Rick what could only be described as critical scrutiny.

Tessa beamed him a conspiratorial smile, then turned to determine its effect upon Mrs. Thedford. But that lady's gaze rested on Marc.

"And how about you, Mr. Edwards?"

"I must decline, ma'am. I am engaged to dine with my fiancée's aunt this evening."

"Ah, I understand." Mrs. Thedford's eyebrows rose in interest. "But you'll come later in the week, to the Shakespeare, perhaps?"

"Yes, I will," he said, and realized with a start that he meant it.

Rick accompanied Marc back through the gloomy theatre to the front doors. "Isn't Tessa just the most darling thing you've ever set eyes upon?" he asked imploringly.

"You've got quite a girl there, Rick," Marc replied, and left it at that.

CATHERINE ROBERTS WAS BETH'S AUNT, HER mother's sister, who had grown up with the McCrae family in Pennsylvania. After Beth's mother died, her grieving father had taken his children to a new Congregational ministry in Cobourg. Aunt Catherine married and went to live in New England, where her affection for things English had taken root. So much so that when she herself was widowed just two years ago, she had readily accepted Beth's offer to come to this British colony and invest jointly in their millinery shop on fashionable King Street. Ever since his engagement to Beth had been announced ("proclaimed" would be a more accurate description), Marc had arranged to have supper with Aunt Catherine on the second Monday of each month.

"Right on time, Marc." She smiled as she led him through the shop towards the stairs that would take them to her apartment above. "It must be the military in you."

"Or the lawyer," Marc said. He loved to watch the soft gray eyes light up in their bemused way behind the gold-rimmed spectacles. Like Beth, she was a diminutive woman with an Irish complexion and sunny disposition. Without ostentation, she always dressed and carried herself with a spare dignity that impressed her wealthy customers and helped to account for the success of the enterprise—that, plus her Yankee business acumen.

"What's going on in the back room?" Marc asked at the sound of strange voices.

"I've had to hire a pair of extra girls," she said, "to handle the dress-making side of the shop. It's doing very well for us, and the girls do like to talk while they're sewing."

"That's not a girl's voice."

"Oh, that's George. He's just come in the back door. He's been away every time you've come for supper not deliberately, you understand."

"I find you incapable of subterfuge."

"George, stop teasing my girls and come in here for a minute!"

As the giggling died down behind him, there emerged from the door to the workroom a man of twenty-five or so, of medium build, with a baby-faced handsomeness that would appeal to a certain breed of undiscriminating young woman. His dark eyes were still dancing with the charm he had just loosed on the seamstresses. But when he spied Marc, he stopped in his tracks, and glowered at him with undisguised disdain.

"George Revere, wipe that frown off your face and shake hands with Lieutenant Marc Edwards." There was an edge of authority in Aunt Catherine's voice that Marc had not heard before.

George Revere glanced at his aunt—slyly? fearfully?— and dredged up a smile. "Pleased ta meet ya," he said with a noticeable New York accent. His handshake was limp.

"George, as you know, has come up from the States to help me here until Beth comes back. After which he hopes to be in business for himself."

"Sorry, Auntie, but I gotta meet someone in a few minutes."

Aunt Catherine gave him a knowing nod, then added, "But not before you take that costume on up to the Regency Theatre and pick up the others we've promised to mend."

George Revere muttered something rebellious under his breath, wheeled, and ran out the back way.

"Thank God he's not a blood nephew," his aunt said.

BY SIX THIRTY THEY HAD FINISHED supper, and while one of the girls from the shop came upstairs to clear away the dishes, Marc and Aunt Catherine repaired to the sitting-room, where a low fire was keeping the early-evening chill at bay. Usually, they sat comfortably here for several hours, conversing when they felt like it, sipping a sherry or not, reading or reading aloud, whatever the mood of one or the other dictated.

"George is a good lad at heart," Aunt Catherine said suddenly. "But I'm afraid he has it in for anybody in a British uniform."

"Oh?"

"His maternal grandparents had their plantation and home burned to the ground by the English army in the War of Independence. And, like a good republican, he's taken up the resentment with the zeal of a convert."

"What's he doing up here, then?"

"Ah—he only hates the English when they're in tunics." She smiled wryly. "And I think he feels that Upper Canadians will soon come to their senses, throw off their shackles, and join the Union."

Aunt Catherine was fiddling with something in the pocket of her apron, and when she caught Marc noticing it, she stopped abruptly. "But he's got a head for business, and if he settles down and proves himself, Beth and I plan to buy into a haberdashery down the street on his behalf."

"What *is* that you're toying with?" Marc asked, more amused than irritated.

Aunt Catherine looked suddenly solemn. "I went to the post office at noon and saw a letter there for you from Beth."

"Well, for heaven's sake, let's open it and read the good news together."

"I—I wasn't sure it would be good news and so, very selfishly, I decided to wait till we'd finished our supper."

Marc smiled assurance, and took the letter from her trembling hand. He began reading it aloud, editing only those parts obviously intended for his eyes only. As was her custom, Beth wrote her weekly missive in installments as things happened around her or came into her mind. Hence the first two pages were detailed accounts of the harvest (healthy yields, ruinous prices), Aaron's improving health, Winnifred's brave front in respect to the baby's being overdue, Thomas's occasional stints on annual road-duty, the fancies and foibles of the unmarried Huggan girls, and so on. At the top of page three came the news they were both hoping for: Winnifred was delivered of a baby girl, mother and child having come through their mutual ordeal in fine shape.

"Wonderful!" Aunt Catherine cried. "And that means all the plans we made for the wedding are actually going to happen! It's hard to believe."

Marc seconded that.

"Is there more?"

"Yes. The babe's been named Mary, and Beth says, 'When Winn told me that she and Thomas had called the girl Mary, after his late mother, I burst into tears, and quite alarmed Thomas. Then, without thinking, I told them about the story you related to me last March in Cobourg about the Aunt Mary who died before you were born and whose sudden death so upset your uncle Jabez that he could never speak about her in public or private again. I hope you don't mind me telling that bit of family history, for I consider it part of our history now. Anyways, the Ladies Aid of the church are now moving straight ahead on the details of the ceremony a week from next Sunday. I expect you and Auntie will be getting more than one letter a week from now until that wondrous day. All my love, Beth.'"

"Well, such news as this calls for a celebratory drink," Marc said, reaching for the sherry. Included among the "good news" was the fact that Thomas Goodall was too busy with the harvest, road-duty, and a new babe to be involved with Mackenzie's rabble-rousers. "What do you say?"

"Oh my, Marc, I forgot to tell you, but I've been anticipating this letter so much it slipped my mind."

"Not *bad* news?"

"No, no. Quite the opposite. As part payment for mending their costumes, the theatre people have promised me two box seats for tonight's play. It's a French farce of some sort, so it ought to be mildly diverting."

Marc grinned. "It'll take a lot to divert my thoughts tonight, but let's give the theatre folk a chance to try."

SEVEN

Marc took Aunt Catherine's arm and they strolled eastward along King Street in the cool twilight of the Indian summer that the city had enjoyed for several weeks: warm and dry in the day and frosty and dry during the lengthening nights. As a result, streets and roads were amazingly passable, and conditions for the fall harvest were the best in recent memory.

The play was to start at eight thirty, so they stretched their fifteen-minute walk to Colborne and West Market Streets to half an hour, pausing to enjoy the window displays of the many shops along King. At Church Street they

admired the way the white stone of the courthouse and the
jail seemed to have absorbed the last of the sun's light and
were now radiating it back into the semi-dark. Reluctantly,
they turned south to Colborne, and swung east again towards West Market, a short block away. They were greeted
by a scene that was anything but pastoral.

"Well, I didn't expect this!" Aunt Catherine said.

Neither had Marc. Ogden Frank had pulled out all the
stops for the four-day run of the Bowery Touring Company, the first professional troupe to grace his Regency
Theatre. He had set bright candle-lanterns on stanchions
all along the boardwalk in front of the building. Into their
pools of light spilled a dozen carriages and their stamping,
fretful teams. The rutted but dry streets had tempted the
more prosperous citizens to drive to the Regency in style,
though the reception was nowhere near as orderly as they
might have wished. Frank had evidently hired a number of
stable boys to act as grooms, footmen, and greeters—a few
even wore some sort of ill-fitting crimson livery—but the
lads, eager enough, were occasioning more confusion than
courtesy. A team of matched grays and their vehicle was
being hauled towards the stable yard with one outraged
gentleman still in it, while his bonneted lady stood in be-
fuddlement under the canopy of the false balcony. Another
extravagantly attired chatelaine had her brand-new, imported boot stepped on by an anxious greeter, and in jerking away in pain, she managed to put the other boot into

a puddle of fresh horse-dung. Farther down at the corner, a lead-horse had taken offense at the strange hand on its bridle and bolted, the vacant carriage clattering behind like a rudderless skiff. The sidewalks on both sides of Colborne were now jammed with couples and parties jostling and otherwise enjoying the drama on the street.

Aunt Catherine laughed out loud. "It's like a dance at the Grange run by the inmates of Bedlam!"

Ogden Frank himself was oblivious to these minor lapses of organization, for he stood proudly in front of the oaken double-doors, accoutred in the military uniform his father had worn at the Battle of Lundy's Lane. He exclaimed his welcomes so effusively that no one except his wife had any idea what he was sputtering at them. Madge Frank stood just behind him and took tickets from those few people she didn't know and tried her best to smile on those she did. The three Frank children were acting as ushers inside, guiding patrons to their boxes or pointing others to the gallery above or the benches in the pit.

Marc boosted Aunt Catherine up the final step and into their box at the back-left of the main room. He held out a chair for her, then sat down beside her. There were two other chairs in the box, but no-one else came to join them.

"*Milady Surprised*," Aunt Catherine read from the hastily printed program. "A *Farce in Two Acts*. I think we'd better brace ourselves."

Marc was looking at the transformed theatre around him.

Candles, which had been lit in candelabra along the walls, threw a wash of pale light over the hundred or so people who were now filling the available seats. The stage area itself was brightly lit from above by three chandeliers and from below by six Argand lamps that served as footlights. Several flats had been erected at the rear of the stage to give the illusion of a windowed interior, and the most prominent feature of the various domestic props within it was a gigantic bed—Jeremiah's handiwork, no doubt.

"I see what you mean," Marc said.

To the left of the stage, near the curtained door, the enterprising Franks had set up a bar, behind which was temptingly displayed a tapped keg of ale. The interval should prove lively, Marc thought, even if the play doesn't.

"Oh, there're your friends, I think," Aunt Catherine said.

In a box on the wall opposite but right next to the stage itself sat Owen Jenkin and Rick Hilliard among several other officers from the garrison. Rick was leaning on the railing, the better to stare into Tessa's eyes during the performance. Jenkin waved at Marc and smiled. In the other two boxes across from him, Marc noticed many familiar faces from among the members of the Family Compact, along with two ardent Reformers, Robert Baldwin and Francis Hincks. Those in the pit and the gallery at the back looked to be a cross-section of tradesmen, small businessmen, and local farmers out on the town.

"My God, I don't believe what I'm seeing!"

"What is it, Marc?"

"Over there, in the front row of the gallery. It's Constable Cobb."

"Why, so it is," Aunt Catherine said cheerfully, and waved a hanky until she got Cobb's attention. In turn he waved and smiled, as did the woman seated beside him.

"And he's brought Dora. How nice."

"You've met his wife?"

"Oh, yes. Horatio brought her along one day last August, for a new hat. She's a very interesting woman."

Constable Cobb had been a significant and courageous partner in the investigation Marc had led into the death of a privy councillor, during which the policeman had had occasion to visit the millinery shop and, thereafter, to stop in on his patrol regularly for tea and gossip. Since then, Marc had bumped into Cobb on the street from time to time, and always spent a few minutes reminiscing about their joint adventure. But the rough-edged constable's appearance in the audience of a French farce surprised him. Was he here on some sort of official business? Nothing more could be said about the matter, however, because the players had now arrived onstage to an enthusiastic welcome from the drama-starved citizens of Toronto and York County.

Mrs. Thedford had assured them earlier that what they would see this evening would not in any way reflect the fractious goings-on of the afternoon rehearsal. And she was right. These were professionals through and through. Tessa's

French maid, in black satin and crocheted cap-and-apron, was sprightly, and her staccato dialogue and double-takes delivered with a speed and confidence that belied her youth and inexperience. Even the Yankee twang and dropped *g*'s had vanished. And, as Mrs. Thedford had insisted, it was Dorothea Clarkson who did have to carry the play as the paramour of the philandering husband in the piece. As such, she was plopped in and under and behind the big, adulterous bed at stage-centre, in addition to being stuffed into a trunk and made immobile behind an arras, all the while emitting a series of aborted shrieks, cries of surprise, and wails of uncorrectable regret set amongst sympathy-gaining appeals to the capricious gods of love. She gave no sign of illness or fatigue and, in fact, her energy seemed to feed on the laughter she drew in raucous waves from every corner of the theatre.

Merriwether played the ageing, and alas married, roué with stolid good humour, while Mrs. Thedford shone as the outraged wife, even though her scenes were few in Act One. Clarence Beasley played the hapless bumpkin from the country in hopeless pursuit of Mistress Thea with much body-wit and mugging of face, qualities that Marc would not have inferred from the young man's somewhat wooden attempts at Shakespeare. Here the dreadful nasalities from south of the border were deliberately deployed to great comic effect. Finally, if Dawson Armstrong had unearthed another bottle of whiskey, it did nothing to diminish his polished performance as the innkeeper who is the ostensible friend and co-conspirator of the cheating spouse but at the same time lusts after his chum's wife when he isn't ogling the maid.

The first act ended with a burst of applause and approbation that was sustained for a full minute. In the midst of which it occurred to Marc that here in this simple chamber was represented a cross-section of Upper Canadian society, including the staunchest members of both the Tory and Reform parties, and they had just joined together, spontaneously, in a kind of communal laughter in which social boundaries and political divisions had been magically dissolved. It was hard to believe that at this moment treasonous rallies might actually be taking place within a mile of where they were sitting.

"You can bring me up a glass of wine if they have any," Aunt Catherine said to Marc as he started down the ladder from their box. "I don't fancy risking those steps again."

Marc nodded and stepped down into the crush below. After he had handed up a glass to Aunt Catherine, Marc nudged his way through the throng and thickening pipe-smoke to where Cobb and Dora were standing at the foot of the ladder to the gallery, munching on apples they had brought with them. They had not spotted him yet, so Marc stopped for a second to have a long look at Cobb and gain some first impressions of his wife.

Cobb looked much the same as he always did, a sinewy troll of a man with a face that could have played Nym or

Bardolph on the Regency's stage without makeup, and an incongruous pot-belly that had no forewarning slope to it, top or bottom: it was as abrupt as a butte on a prairie. To-night, though, it was partially camouflaged by the waistcoat of the suit he was wearing, one that had probably been his wedding attire, with the trousers now let out several inches and lapels that were a good foot from meeting each other. A bowler hat concealed the uprising of his soot-black hair. And while the angular features were softened by shadow, the mellow but flickering candlelight accelerated the glow of his big nose and the wart blinking nearby.

Mrs. Dora Cobb was something else again. Marc thought instantly of Mr. Spratt and his missus, for Dora was as round as she was high (which wasn't more than four foot ten), but her obesity was modulated by the perfect neatness of her dress and person, by the tightly curled black hair, by the Indian-bead necklace placed just so, by the exact meridian of her wide leather belt, by the creaseless fit of her blouse and skirt, and by the trim shoes on surprisingly tiny feet. She so resembled a child's bulbous top that Marc was chary of bumping against her for fear he might set her rolling out of control. Her expression peered out at the world from a penumbra of cheeks and chins that merely accentuated the cheerful kindliness of her whole demeanour, while the eyes alone signalled that here was a woman who, when chal-lenged, would brook no nonsense and give no quarter.

"How nice to see you again, Constable," Marc said heart-ily.

"Evenin', Major," Cobb said, using his nickname for Marc. "Enjoyin' the carryin's-on?"

"And this must be—"

"Dora Cobb," said Mrs. Cobb in a rich alto voice, amplified no doubt by her diva's lungs and bosom. She darted a critical glance at her husband for his lapse of manners.

Cobb winced, but kept his smile going.

"Pleased to make your acquaintance, ma'am." Marc reached out to take her hand preparatory to bussing it. Before he could accomplish this standard gesture of courtesy, Dora latched onto the offering with both of her ample palms and began levering it up and down, as if she were trying to prime a balky pump.

"Well, it's bloody well time we met," she boomed. "I was beginnin' to suspect Mr. Cobb was deliberately keepin' you to himself. Either that or you had two heads an' three eyes!"

"Now, Missus Cobb, you know that ain't—"

"Truth is, you're as high up an' as handsome as the ladies of the town—if I may defer to them as such—have been tellin' me. You're enough to make a gal's knees buckle."

"Now, Missus Cobb—"

"I'd be pleased, Mr. Cobb, if you'd desist and decease from 'Missus-Cobbing' me like some woodpecker with his peck jammed!"

"Are you enjoying the play?" Marc said quickly.

"A powerful lot of jumpin' in an' outta bed, wasn't there?" Dora said approvingly, "accompanied by a great deal of 'pleasure inta-ruptured'!" She shot a teasing glance at Cobb to be sure he had caught her mimic of his habitual play on words.

Cobb was about to protest but thought better of it.

"I am pleased to see so many people come out to the theatre," Marc offered.

"And I see you're a mite surprised to spot the likes of us here?" Dora said with a wry grin.

Marc denied any such thing, while silently remarking that little in the behaviour of those around Dora Cobb would go unnoticed or unappraised.

"In my case, curiosity, more'n anythin' else," Cobb said.

"Nonsense, Mr. Cobb, an' you know it!" She turned to Marc, pivoting her entire person to do so. "Why, old James Cobb was a regular *thesbian* in his day. He'd rather jump on a stump an' recite a bawdy ballad than he would haul it away to make room fer his corn. And at our weddin' in Woodstock, the old rapscallion hopped on a table durin' the toasts an' spieled out every last verse of Mr. Gray's 'Eligible in a Country Church'!"

"Now, Missus Cobb, do not *eggs-agitate*—"

"An' this crab apple here—warts an' all—didn't fall far from the tree."

Dora began a chuckle somewhere deep within, and while it worked its way out, Cobb said to Marc, "Funny, but we ain't had a *gen-u-wine* murder in town since you an' young Hilliard skedaddled off to the fort last year."

"Then I must be sure to stay put."

"So, when are you gonna come to our place for supper?"

Dora said loud enough to turn heads ten feet away. "All I get is feeble excuses from Mr. Cobb, but now I'm lookin' right at the flesh-an'-blood—"

"You're embarrassin' Marc," Cobb said, part plea and part warning. "Ain't she, Major?"

"Not in the least. I'd be pleased to come," Marc said, initially out of politeness and good breeding, but then with a growing sense of enthusiasm. Why shouldn't he have supper with these good people? Who was he, pretending to be a gentleman, when he himself was the offspring of a gamekeeper and his peasant wife, and one who had had the undeserved fortune of being raised up by a lonely bachelor and member of the petty aristocracy?

"How about Wensd'y? Say, six o'clock? I'll hide the chickens an' make the pig stay outside till we're done."

"*Missus* Cobb!" The constable's wart ignited.

Marc laughed. "I'll be there with bells on."

"Long as they don't wake the goat!"

At this point Cobb was spared any further discomfort by the reappearance of the players upon the stage, announced by three blasts of a trumpet from the wings. Jeremiah Jefferson making a wayward, joyful noise, perhaps?

WHEN THE PLAY ENDED AND THE last of six curtain calls was gracefully acknowledged, Marc led Aunt Catherine towards the exit onto Colborne Street. "I'll walk you home, then come back here for my horse," he said.

"Sure you won't come up to Mrs. Thedford's room for a nightcap?" Owen Jenkin called out just behind them. "We've all been invited." He looked imploringly at Marc, who suddenly got the message.

"Both Aunt Catherine and I have had a long day, Owen. And some personal excitement I'll tell you about later."

"Yes," Aunt Catherine said agreeably. "It's past ten thirty and I've a full work-day tomorrow. We're mending some costumes for the company here."

"Where's Rick, then?" Marc said.

"Probably in the ingenue's boudoir, if I know him."

"I sincerely hope he behaves himself."

"I'll see to it, Marc."

"I'll wait for you outside when I come back from the shop in about half an hour, and we can all ride home together."

"That should work out well for everybody. See you then." And he trundled off to throw himself at the feet of the prima donna from Philadelphia and New York.

Just as Marc and Aunt Catherine started along Colborne, Cobb popped out of the alley leading to the stables. He had his bowler in both hands. "You don't haveta come," he said with acute embarrassment. "Dora gets carried away sometimes."

"I'm coming on Wednesday because I want to, old friend," Marc assured him.

• • •

MAJOR JENKIN WAS WAITING AT THE livery stable with two horses in hand.

"Where's Rick?" Marc wondered, a rhetorical question in the circumstances.

Jenkin nodded up towards the theatre. "He swore to me as an officer and a gentleman that he would have one drink with Miss Guildersleeve and leave when she asked him. Mrs. Thedford was very gracious with me: I was utterly charmed by her. But I'm afraid I may have inadvertently misled her into thinking Rick was going to leave when I did. Tessa is really like an adopted daughter to her, and it's hard enough for actresses to gain respect without having foot-loose soldiers dallying in their rooms. But I wasn't going to go barging in on the youngsters like an outraged papa."

"I think Rick believes he's truly in love with the girl. The odds are he won't do anything to harm her reputation. But you're right: Rick's a grown man, and I'm sure he realizes that Tessa's guardian is next door. Come on, let's be on our way."

The two men, so recently and unexpectedly friends, rode out together towards the garrison a meandering mile or so west of the city centre under a splendid moon and a back-drop of stars. They fell into easy conversation.

"I thought the days of this old war-horse dreaming about a particular woman were over, Marc. But Annemarie is re-ally something."

"So I gather. I must say she impressed me tremendously.

In a motherly way, of course," he added with an appropriate chuckle.

"I asked her about Merriwether, for example, because the man intrigues me. Unlike her, I got the feeling he was acting out a role for himself, perhaps because he wasn't happy with who he really was. Well, she told me the whole story. Seems he was a great star of the Park Theatre for twenty years, before his wife died and he hit the bottle. By the time Annemarie arrived in New York from Philadelphia and established herself, about fifteen years ago, Merriwether was on the way down. She'd met him while she was doing bit roles at the Park and admired his talent. Five years later she had become a star and part owner of the Bowery, and took it upon herself—when everyone else in the theatre world of New York was shunning him—to take a chance on the man, on condition that he give up the drink and attempt to regain his former lustre."

"As Tessa remarked, the woman has a weakness for strays."

"That's an approach I'll have to consider."

"Well, it's obvious she succeeded in rehabilitating him."

"Almost. But she admitted to me, after assuring me they had never been, ah, intimate, that while Merriwether did regain much of his lost talent, he remained a difficult and often unattractive human being."

"I expect she did what she could. And as professionals, they have certainly worked well together, as the mounting of the farce tonight showed. I've seen pieces like that botched many times in Drury Lane itself."

"She seems a very giving person to me. She was kind enough to ask me about my experiences in the war, knowing full well, I trust, that such an opening is in danger of never being closed thereafter. Anyway, I did chatter on about Sandhurst and Portugal and Paris and the exploits of the Iron Duke."

"I envy you that," Marc sighed.

"Please, don't, son. War is tolerable only when you're well away from it."

MARC WAS IN THE MIDDLE OF a dream in which Beth was floating somewhere just above the foot of his bed, beckoning to him as her nightdress sailed away behind her, when a cold finger on his chin brought him reluctantly awake.

"Beth?" he murmured.

"It's Corporal Bregman, sir. Sorry to wake you up at this hour. I've come straight from Colonel Margison."

Marc sat up, shivering in the cold room. It could be no more than 2 a.m. Why would one of Margison's orderlies be rousing him in the middle of the night?

"What is it?"

"Instructions, sir. For you."

"At this hour?"

"I'm afraid so. A fast horse is being saddled for you right now. You are to proceed at once to the Regency Theatre."

"What's happened?"

"One of the actors has been murdered."

Mark glanced quickly at Rick's cot. It was empty.

"Is Hilliard all right?" Marc asked.

"Not quite, sir." Bregman had turned white.

"What do you mean, 'not quite'?"

Bregman gulped hard, and said almost in a whisper, "They're saying he done it."

EIGHT

Marc did his best to shut down his naturally speculative mind as he rode furiously towards the city from the fort, soon leaving behind the young messenger who had brought the disturbing news. But until he knew which actor had been murdered and whether Bregman's comment about Rick Hilliard's being an accused killer was itself speculation or fact, there was no point in fretting unnecessarily. Nonetheless, there was no denying that something terrible must have happened for Colonel Margison to have become involved and issue commands in the wee hours of a Tuesday morning. It was with a genuine sense of dread that Marc pounded up Colborne Street towards Frank's Hotel.

He was about to wheel into the alley that led to the stables when he spotted someone in uniform waving at him from under the false balcony in front of the theatre. It was Ogden Frank, still in his militia outfit. Though the street was silent and utterly deserted, Frank was motioning him to dismount quickly, while glancing left and right as if he expected shutters to be flung open all along the thoroughfare.

In a hoarse, frightened whisper, he said to Marc, "My boy'll see to your horse; just leave it here and come inside right away. Nobody else knows what's happened upstairs, and we'd all like to keep it that way."

All? Who else had arrived ahead of him?

"They're waitin' fer ya inside."

Marc followed Frank through the double-doors, which Frank was careful to secure with a bar, and into the theatre itself, now steeped in gloomy shadow. The proprietor seemed able to navigate without benefit of light, and led the way through the curtained door at the right side of the stage and up the stairs towards the actors' rooms above.

"I don't know what I've done to deserve such a calamity as this," Frank was muttering ahead of him. "If this news gets out, I'll be ruined. I'll have to store hay in the pit."

On the landing—with a candle-lamp in hand, a uniform more dishevelled than usual, and hair rearing up at all angles from a helmetless head—stood Constable Horatio Cobb.

"Thank Christ you're here, Marc. This is the worst bloody mess I've ever seen. It's like an abattoir up there."

"Where's Hilliard?"

"He's in the tavern, through that door at the foot of the stairs, in the charmin' arms of General Spooner."

"Spooner?" Lieutenant Barclay Spooner was the governor's current aide-de-camp, the man who had succeeded Marc in Bond Head's office. "Sir Francis is in on this? What the hell has happened?"

"I'll show you in a minute, though it ain't pretty. Doc Withers is upstairs an' Sarge is in the tavern herdin' all them *hyster-ect-ical* actors an' makin' sure General Spooner don't set off another war with the States." "Sarge" was Cobb's colleague, Chief Constable Wilfrid Sturges.

So that was it, Marc thought: one of the American actors had been murdered and one of ours—a British officer—had been accused of the crime. That would be more than enough to bring the governor wide-awake with his political antennae twitching.

"Go on back to the tavern, Ogden," Cobb said not unkindly to Frank, who was dry-washing his hands in futile frenzy, "an' help Sarge keep a stopper in Spooner's gob, if you can."

Frank nodded, thankful to be doing something other than contemplating his imminent financial ruin.

"Who is the victim?" Marc asked as he and Cobb reached the hallway on the second floor. The name he had been repressing for the last half-hour now forced its way into his consciousness: Tessa Guildersleeve.

"The fella who played the whorin' husband," Cobb said, pointing the way towards the far end of the hall.

"Jason Merriwether?" Marc asked, astonished. How in the world could Hilliard have been involved in murdering Merriwether?

"That's the fella. Stabbed through the chest with Hilliard's sword."

Yes, Marc recalled, Hilliard had strapped on his sabre before leaving earlier in the day in order to impress the girl. "I can't believe that, Cobb."

"Me neither, Major. But they claim he was found with both hands on the haft."

Marc froze in his tracks. Whatever he had been steeling himself for, it was not this.

"In here," Cobb said, easing open the door to Tessa's room. "Brace yerself."

Someone had brought one of the Argand lamps from the stage to illuminate Tessa's room, in addition to several other lit candles. Marc was unprepared for the sudden light that greeted him when he entered. He blinked, then slowly directed his gaze towards the horrors on the carpeted expanse before him.

Jason Merriwether lay flat on his back, as if he had just made the perfect theatrical pratfall and was waiting for a burst of applause before popping up to take a bow. But the famous tragedian and farceur had taken his last curtain call. Like a stake driven through a vampire's heart, Hilliard's battle-sword was sticking straight up out of Merriwether's chest and, in the unsteady candlelight, appeared to be still quivering from the force of the blow. The details surrounding this pièce de résistance Marc took in at a single glance. Blood had geysered out of the wound, splashed indiscriminately over the victim's nightshirt from throat to crotch, trickled down his bare thighs, and was still seeping into the beige carpet. Angus Withers, physician and surgeon to the rich and highborn, the governor's personal doctor, and county coroner, was crouched beside Merriwether's head. With his fingertips he was probing a vicious wound at the base of the cranium. That area of the skull appeared to have been crushed by a blow made either by a heavy, blunt object or something lighter delivered with tremendous force. From his vantage-point several feet away, Marc could see pieces of bone protruding through matted hair and blood. Had the man been attacked twice?

Dr. Withers looked up and flashed Marc a grim smile of recognition and welcome. They had met briefly during Marc's second investigation and taken an instant liking to each other. "Looks like somebody wanted to make sure he went straight to his Maker," Withers said, and picked up from the pool of blood on the far side of the body a large, bronze ashtray. "This could've been used on his skull, but I can't be sure. It was already covered with blood when I found it here."

But Marc could not take his eyes off Hilliard's sabre.

There was no doubt that it belonged to Rick: the initials *RH* were visible even through the gore smeared all over it. Had the killer dipped his hands in the victim's blood? Surely the founting of it from the wound could not have reached the haft on its own.

"I'm damned glad you and Cobb are here. That jackass Spooner roused me from a rare erotic dream to inform me that the governor was near apoplexy—again, I must add—over the murder of some prominent American by one of his officers in a den of iniquity. Spooner had orders, duly passed along to me, to keep this mess contained. What he didn't know was that Frank panicked after visiting Government House and beetled on down to the police station and blabbed it all to Chief Constable Sturges, who had fallen asleep in his office."

"An' that's like disruptin' a hibernatin' bear," Cobb said gleefully. "It was me who took the brunt of his temper when he come fer me, though Missus Cobb herself was just comin' home from one of her customers an' managed to keep him from poppin' the buttons off his vest."

"Which blow killed Merriwether, then?" Marc asked, suddenly hoping that there might be some explanation other than the obvious.

Withers gave the question careful thought before answering. "Well, it seems certain the blow to the back of the head stunned him, and he must have tried to stand up before collapsing onto his back right here where you see him. That blow alone would eventually have resulted in his death, but

I am compelled to say honestly—and will have to testify so—that the sword to the chest was the immediate cause of death. I can say this with certainty because the heart was still pumping blood when the sword-blade cut the aorta. You can see the consequences for yourself. In fact, the sword is imbedded in the floor under the body."

"But why would anyone crush the man's skull and then savagely drive a sword through him?"

"That's for you to discover, lad," Withers said.

"What do you mean?"

"Looks like the governor may have forgiven you your apostasy. Among the orders he issued to Lieutenant Spooner, who as we know will obey them to the letter no matter how repugnant to him personally, was that you are to lead the investigation. Spooner's charge is to keep things contained until you catch the murderer."

"That explains why my colonel was involved." Marc was trying to take in what he was seeing and being told, while still trying not to think the unthinkable. "But how could all this have been managed in such a short time? Major Jenkin and I left Rick here with Tessa Guildersleeve no later than eleven thirty or so."

"Whatever provoked this carnage didn't take long to develop because we know the precise time it took place," Withers said. "The actor who found the body—"

"The fella who played the country bumpkin—Beasley," Cobb said.

"Yes, Beasley. He heard the scream and came running in here at twelve thirty, according to that clock in the corner."

"What scream?" Marc said.

"Tell Marc what we think we know," Withers said, getting up and moving over to Tessa's bed. As Marc watched him, he noticed several things he had not observed before: droplets and smudges of blood were scattered on the carpet in an irregular trail from the feet of victim to the settee, where more blood was smeared, one patch of which appeared to resemble a handprint. Had the killer wallowed in Merriwether's gore, then gone back and sat on the settee to admire his handiwork?

"I've only had a chance to talk to Beasley, so we've got just his version of what happened," Cobb said. "But I gotta say he's the only one of that whole bunch who ain't gone *bear-serk* on us. The women are squallin' like heifers with their teats tied, an' that fella Armstrong's as drunk as a skunk. The mute seems fine, but he ain't sayin' much, of course."

"Beasley heard Tessa scream at twelve thirty?"

"Well, you'll need to *interro-grate* 'em yerself, but what he told Sarge an' me when we got here a while ago, was a woman's scream woke him up, an' by the time he got himself awake an' figured out where the scream'd come from, he found Ensign Hilliard standin' over the body with both hands wrapped 'round the handle of the sword."

"But what was Merriwether doing in Tessa's room after midnight?"

Here Cobb glanced beseechingly at Withers, who grimaced and said, "It gets worse, laddie. Hilliard was seen going into the girl's room with her about eleven o'clock, laughing and carrying on like lovebirds."

"That's right," Marc said. "Owen Jenkin left him there shortly thereafter and we rode home together. But Rick had promised the major he would do nothing dishonourable and, in fact, would stay no more than half an hour for a single glass of sherry."

"And he may well have kept that promise," Withers said solemnly. "We found Tessa comatose on the bed there, and it's possible Hilliard may have dozed off. The room was quite dark when Beasley entered it with a candle in his hand, except for the little swath of moonlight coming through the window and that stub of candle beside the bed. Cobb and I speculate that Merriwether must have come in a bit later expecting Tessa to be alone, probably with evil intentions on his mind."

"That makes sense," Marc said, thinking hard. "We spent yesterday afternoon watching the actors rehearse, and all three of us saw Merriwether make an improper gesture while carrying Tessa in his arms. And, I must admit frankly, she seemed to approve of the assault, though her guardian, Mrs. Thedford, did not."

"And if it was almost dark in here," Cobb added, "he mightn't've spotted Hilliard dozin' on the settee an' . . ."

"And forced his attentions on the young lady," Withers said as delicately as he could.

"And you think Rick heard Tessa scream for help, woke up, grabbed the ashtray—"

"Or the butt of his sword," Withers said. "It's smeared with blood, too, so we can't be sure."

"In either case he smashed the villain on the back of the head to prevent his ravishing the girl," Marc said with a rush. "Which means he was justified in his actions. Tessa did scream, did she not? That's the critical point."

"Loud enough to wake Beasley up at the other end of the hall," Cobb said.

"But why not any of the others?"

"That's easy," Cobb said. "Armstrong was pissed to the gills in his room. When Frank got up here shortly afterwards, he went in to check on him and the old sot couldn't remember what country he was in."

"But Mrs. Thedford's room is next to this one, a thin wall away."

"That's so," Cobb said, "but she was asleep in that little bedroom on the far side of her . . . whaddycallit—"

"Her suite."

"—with wax plugs in her ears, accordin' to Beasley, who woke her up," Cobb finished.

"And Jeremiah is deaf."

"An' the other woman, the one who played the connivin' mistress, was stayin' downstairs with the Franks."

"So you figure Hilliard bashed Merriwether's brains in, probably because he had been wakened suddenly, was confused, heard and saw a young woman he was desperately in love with being assaulted by a large stranger clad only in a nightshirt—remember, Merriwether was almost six feet tall and powerfully built—and simply reacted as any officer and gentleman would have in the circumstances?"

"I wish that were so," Withers said sadly. "Then there would be some hope for Hilliard. But when Beasley got here, no more than two or three minutes after the girl screamed, Hilliard was stooped over the blackguard about to pull his sword out of Merriwether's chest. And that, in any court in the kingdom, is premeditated murder."

It was simply impossible for Marc to accept this version of events. Hilliard's passion and romantic folly might account for the reflex action of defending his lady's honour by any means within his reach. But then to have drawn his sabre and, looking down into the face of Tessa's disabled assailant, raise it above his head with calm deliberation and drive it through Merriwether's chest—well, that was something he was absolutely certain Rick Hilliard would never do. Not even in the heat of battle. The very thought of such an ignominious act was monstrous.

"I figured at first," Cobb said, "that maybe one person banged on the noggin and another put the sword in. But there wasn't enough time. Beasley come runnin' from the end of the hall where the stairs are, so nobody could've dashed in an' done the stabbin' an' run back out again without Beasley seein' him."

"And the girl couldn't've done it," Withers said. "Even if she was faking being unconscious, she isn't strong enough to have driven that heavy sword into Merriwether, not even in a rage. Besides which, she would've been covered in blood."

"Like the ensign was," Cobb felt obliged to add.

"Well, I'm going to question Clarence Beasley very closely, you can be sure. We've only got his word for all this."

"It seems the mute was on the scene shortly as well," Withers said. "And Hilliard, of course."

"Has Rick said anything about this? Surely he's denied it."

Withers fielded that query with reluctance. "He's said very little. He's fanatically worried about the girl, but I've given her a sleeping draught and put her into Madge Frank's care for the night."

"He hasn't admitted anything?"

"All he says is that he fell asleep while he and the girl were sparking on the settee, and when he woke up he was standing over the corpse in the dark and wondering what had happened—when Beasley came in and found him."

"But surely he couldn't have slept through a woman screaming rape and be uncertain whether he had hit Merriwether on the head, waited till he was flat on his back and then skewered him, while the blood gushed all over him? And, don't forget, he also had time to go back to the settee, sit down for a spell, then get up and go over to retrieve his sword. And all this while sleepwalking? I don't believe it for a minute."

Dr. Withers was standing beside the night-table that held Tessa's little candle, a half-full decanter of sherry, and two empty glasses. He ran the decanter, unstoppered, slowly under his nose, then, very carefully, took a minuscule sip and let the wine roll over his tongue. "He may not have been sleepwalking." He pushed his nostrils into each of the glasses. "Laudanum," he said. "A lot of it. Enough, I'd say, to knock an elephant to its knees."

"But that means that both Tessa and Rick were drugged," Marc cried, his hopes rising. "And there's only one reason I can think of why that would happen. It's obvious, isn't it, that Merriwether slipped in here sometime yesterday--everybody in the troupe knew that Tessa took a glass of sherry before she went to bed after a performance—and put laudanum into the decanter. He couldn't have known that Rick would be up here sharing the sherry with her when he first put the opiate into it. Later on, I'm sure he knew Rick was in Tessa's room, and maybe he was inflamed with jealousy, and came across the hall, peered in, and found both of them comatose. And I'd lay odds that he decided then and there to have his way with the girl, and when she woke later, she would assume Rick had been her assailant. How she might have reacted, we don't know, but Merriwether certainly knew how Mrs. Thedford would have taken the outrage. So the blackguard would be able to enjoy Tessa and have Rick take any consequences. All he had to do was snuff the candles out and set about the dastardly deed."

"Well, that's plausible," Withers said. "But how will we ever know what really happened if Tessa and Hilliard were indeed unconscious? And if they'd had more than a mouthful of this stuff, they would have been. Neither of them can give us rational testimony."

"In the meantime," Cobb said, "we got a witness who swears he saw Hilliard with the murder weapon in his clutches an' with the whole front of his tunic covered in blood. You'll see it for yourself."

"And, alas," Withers said with a sad shake of his head, "with his flies wide open."

"You're not implying that Rick was the girl's attacker? That's preposterous."

When neither Withers nor Cobb responded to that assessment, Marc continued. "There must be blood on Merriwether's privates!"

"There was blood everywhere—on both men."

"Well, if there's a court-martial, I'll argue that Rick was drugged, dazed, provoked to his actions by the noblest of motives, and was therefore not wholly responsible for what he may have done."

"You gonna take out yer *law-yer's* licence again?" Cobb enquired.

"Even so," Withers said, "it's a stretch to claim that a befuddled man with altruistic intent pulled a battle-sword out of its scabbard and drove it unerringly through the centre of Merriwether's chest so forcefully that it stuck in the floor under him."

"Damn it all, that's what I'm saying!" Marc shouted. "Dazed or sober, my friend Rick Hilliard could not have done that. He had already saved the girl he loved from harm. He had maimed the assailant. What could possibly have incited him to such a senseless, despicable act?"

"Maybe it was this," Cobb said, holding his lantern high over Tessa's bed.

There on the white, freshly starched sheet was a blood-stain, no bigger than a virgin's fist.

NINE

Having covered the body with a sheet and snuffed the candles, the three men went out into the hall.

"I don't want the corpse moved or anything else touched in there," Marc said. "I'll need to examine the room in the morning light. And we can't have anyone who might conceivably have been involved going in overnight to tamper with the evidence."

Dr. Withers reached into his medical bag, pulled out a wad of sealing wax, softened it in his fingers, and pushed it into the slim crack between the door and the sash near the floor. "How's that?" he said with a wink. "You'll know if a mouse tries to break and enter."

Cobb was leaning over the sill of the hall window that overlooked Colborne Street. "Nobody's come in here," he said, dragging a finger through the thick dust. "Least not since the invasion of Muddy York."

"Unless the interloper was part monkey, able to climb vertical brick walls," Withers added, "you'll have to devote your attention to those people who were in this building from eleven o'clock onward."

"And if they'd tried a ladder under the girl's window, it'd've been stickin' out on Colborne Street like a roofer's thumb," Cobb said. "But I'll check the alley an' street fer any signs just the same."

"Someone could have hidden around the stage area and waited for his chance," Marc said, grasping at straws.

"Then how did the bugger get out again?" Cobb said. "Frank swore to the God of all Orangemen that the front doors an' privy-exit were barred from the inside right after Major Jenkin left. And when he lit out fer Government House, he went out through his own quarters with his wife standing watch. Anybody leavin' that way couldn't've barred the door after them from the outside: when Sarge and I got here, those theatre doors were still barred."

Marc sighed.

"An' there's no other way out of the theatre," Cobb continued, "except through the tavern, an' that door was locked with a slidin' bolt by Frank before he went to bed, as usual."

They were now heading down the only stairs towards the stage and the tavern just behind it.

"All right, all right," Marc said testily. "It's a long shot, I confess. Certainly we've got to focus on the actors first, though I'm not going to rule out Ogden Frank or his wife, or even Thea Clarkson: any one of them could have left their quarters, slipped through the barroom, unbolted the door behind the bar on this side of the stage, sneaked up the stairs, and been a party to murder."

"An' sneaked back before Beasley got out into the hall, I suppose," Cobb said. "An' drippin' blood all the way?" They had spotted no bloodstains on the hall carpet, but only a thorough examination in daylight would settle the question.

"They could have been in it together! The lot of them!"

Withers pushed open the door to the tavern. "Might I suggest that we begin by looking at the obvious evidence first, then move on to the fanciful speculation?"

They emerged into a well-lit room and peered over the bar at a most arresting tableau: two rather shortish men of a middle age, each uniformed, were wrestling over possession of a set of leg irons.

"You are *not* gonna put this man in chains unless *I* say so!"

"I bear the authority of the governor, and this man is now my official prisoner! I order you to release these shackles so that I may secure the felon."

Wilfrid Sturges, erstwhile sergeant-major in Wellington's peninsular army and chief constable of the five-man municipal police force, gave a sharp pull on his half of the shackles and almost succeeded in wresting the whole from Barclay Spooner's grip. Without outside intervention, there was no doubt as to which combatant would eventually triumph. Although both men were of slight build, Lieutenant Spooner, aide-de-camp to Sir Francis Bond Head, was a man whose aggressive movements and gestures could only be described as rigidly crisp but otherwise ineffectual, while Chief Constable Sturges was slimly muscular and deceptively quick, a tough little beagle of a man. Behind them, slumped in a captain's chair with his chin in his hands, was Rick Hilliard. He looked like the sole survivor of a sanguinary battle.

"Gentlemen, would you please drop those shackles," Marc barked at the belligerents. "No one is going to put Ensign Hilliard in chains. I'm in charge of this investigation, and I'll determine who's to be labelled a prisoner and a felon."

Marc's outburst distracted Spooner long enough for Sturges to recover the leg irons and stuff them into his overcoat pocket. "Thank you, Lieutenant. I was just attemptin' to persuade Mr. Spooner 'ere on that very point."

"You are interfering with the Queen's business," Spooner spluttered, whether at Marc or Sturges was not clear, as his moustache, ruthlessly trimmed, twitched at one end and then the other.

"Are you suggesting that I am not in charge of this investigation?" Marc demanded.

"Not in the least, sir. You deliberately misapprehend my intentions. I made the not unreasonable assumption that a man brandishing a murder-weapon smeared with the victim's blood—and his roger hanging out—was, in the least, a prime suspect. Further, as the officer designated to contain the political consequences from this catastrophe, I was endeavouring to put this upstart policeman in his place."

"We'll see who's the upstart," Sturges said, his face reddening. "As far as I can see, we have a civilian murdered, possibly by an army officer, in a buildin' clearly under my jurisdiction."

"And this civilian, as you so quaintly put it, just happens to be a foreign national, making this potentially an international incident. In any event, the governor has seen fit to put Lieutenant Edwards and me exclusively in control of matters here. Mr. Frank had no authority to invite you to interfere. Do you wish me to report your insolent insubordination to my superior when I return to Government House?"

Sturges glared at him.

Marc decided to take full control. "I'll be the one to decide who I might require to assist me. Right now I wish to speak to Mr. Hilliard, without further comment from either of you. Where are the others?"

"Mr. Frank's put them over there in the dining-room," Sturges said to Marc. "I 'aven't been able to get a single, sensible sentence from any of 'em," he added with an accusatory glance at Spooner.

Marc walked to the open archway between the taproom and dining area, and peered ahead. Ogden Frank was seated at a large table, around which the remaining members of the

Bowery Touring Company were arrayed. An open bottle of port and half a dozen glasses, kindly supplied by Frank, sat untouched. Marc made a quick survey of the actors, one of whom he believed had ruthlessly slaughtered another of his or her fellows. After the initial tears and incredulity, it appeared as if deep shock had taken over. Thea Clarkson, in a pink robe thrown carelessly over her shoulders, looked seriously ill. Her skin was rippled with cold sweat and she was trembling uncontrollably. Annemarie Thedford's reaction was registered in the sudden appearance of lines and wrinkles that one did not notice when she was smiling and in command of her surroundings. Her eyes, bloodshot with weeping, were kindled by more than one kind of pain; after all, she was enduring the knowledge of her ward's violation and the simultaneous loss of a professional partner in her life's work. The financial and personal loss would be both acute and irreparable.

Clarence Beasley was staring straight ahead with a glazed expression that was unreadable, but exhaustion was telegraphed in every aspect of his collapsed posture. Leaning on his shoulder, unremarked, was Dawson Armstrong, who, having sobered up enough to have realized the severity of what had happened, had then promptly fallen asleep. Lastly, Jeremiah Jefferson lay with his head on the table, holding his left cheek and moaning softly. His bloated countenance was not likely due to any remorse or particular sorrow over Merriwether's demise.

Unfortunately, Armstrong seemed to have the most obvious motive for doing away with his rival while having the
least capacity for doing the deed. Thea Clarkson appeared
too ill to have wielded that bloody sword, even if Marc were
able to discover a motive for her. While he could envision
Mrs. Thedford defending her ward against attack from any
quarter, she would have to have been mad or bent on self-
destruction to have plunged a sword through the heart of
her own enterprise. His best bet seemed to be Beasley, although if he had smouldering depths, they were ingeniously
disguised. The mute was a possibility, but a slim one. Marc
wanted to sit them down one by one right then and thrash
the necessary truths out of them, but he realized he would
get nothing coherent from any of them until morning.

Poor Frank looked worse than any of the actors. His eyes,
very far apart in his moon-face, seemed to be searching for
each other without much success, and his hand-wringing
was pathetic to behold. Though he was a known Orangeman who might conceivably hate Americans, it was not
plausible that he had built a theatre worthy of attracting
professional troupes from abroad, only to murder the first
bona fide star to step onto his stage.

"What do you want us to do now?" Frank asked. "Miss
Guildersleeve's asleep in our spare room and my missus is
beside herself with worry."

"I'll decide what to do with everybody in a few minutes.
Try to keep from despairing, sir." Other than this vacuous

advice, Marc could think of nothing to say that might be remotely consoling.

"Lieutenant, it is now nearly three o'clock in the morning. The governor will be frantic—"

"Please leave me alone with Hilliard," Marc said curtly to Spooner.

"I think we should do as the lieutenant suggests," Withers said with a barely suppressed yawn.

"Five minutes, that's all!" Spooner said to Marc with a lopsided twitch of his moustache, which simultaneously activated a similar twitch of the left eyebrow. "And I'll be standing beside the bar, where I can keep an eye on you."

"Do you want me to help?" Sturges said.

"May I have Constable Cobb to assist me?"

"Well, what do you say, Cobb?" Sturges said to his favourite constable.

Cobb had been standing aside in deference to his superior, but not without periodic, baleful glowerings at Spooner when loyalty demanded such. "Ya mean fer the rest of the time it takes us to finish the job?" he enquired.

"I do," Marc said.

"But you have no authority to deputize anybody!" Spooner bellowed from his post at the bar.

"I believe the governor will back me up," Marc said. "And this way, the local constabulary will have a say in what is at least partly their affair."

"What a fine solution," Sturges said, and moved across to join Spooner at the bar some ten paces away.

Marc took a deep breath and drew a chair up beside Rick, who had not raised his head once since Marc and the others had entered the taproom. It was doubtful if he'd even heard a word of the conversation around him. Cobb placed his generous profile between Rick and the men at the bar.

"Rick, it's me. I'm here to help you."

"Marc?" The voice was shrunken, scarcely recognizable; the eyes remained downcast. Merriwether's blood had begun to dry in ugly brown smears on his scarlet jacket with its green-and-gold trim. His flies were still untied, but the flaps had been closed. There was blood on his pants, on the backs of both hands, and on his head, where his palms had rested in despair or remorse.

"I need to talk to you, man-to-man."

"They won't tell me what happened to her."

"Tessa is resting. She's had a terrible shock, but I don't think she's badly injured."

"They won't let me see her."

"I'll talk to her the second she wakes up in the morning That's a promise."

Rick's next statement was nearly a sob: "I'm not sure she'll want to see me."

"A lot depends on what you can tell me now, Rick. I realize that it must be horrific to think about what happened up there, but I've been sent by the governor to find the truth, all of it. Don't worry about that trumped-up martinet Spooner; I am in charge. You can trust me." Marc leaned over and whispered into Rick's ear: "And I don't believe for one moment that you drove your sabre through an unconscious man."

Rick Hilliard raised his head slowly, peering up at Marc with round, enquiring, frightened eyes. "What can I tell you?" He looked away with a sigh, but when his gaze fell upon the bib of blood on his tunic, he looked back up at Marc and kept his eyes steadily upon his friend.

"Tell me everything you can remember about tonight, starting with what Tessa and you did when you went into her room shortly before eleven o'clock."

Rick seemed puzzled by the question, or else was just more deeply in shock than Marc realized. But when Marc merely waited, he said at last, "We just laughed and talked . . . about the play . . . and how wonderful she was in it . . . and how much the audience loved it . . . just talk . . . *you* know."

"Yes, I do. But think carefully now. When did you or Tessa take a drink of the sherry?"

"Not for a while. She was bubbling with excitement. Her eyes were like saucers. It must have been about eleven thirty or after—there was a clock in the corner chiming the quarters, I remember—when I suggested we have a drink. I did promise Owen I would not stay long . . . I wanted to, oh, how I did, but I know that he . . . he saw us go into Tessa's room—"

"Merriwether?"

"Yes, and Mrs. Thedford, too, but she smiled and told

us to be careful. I didn't want to let Owen down, or Mrs. Thedford either, and I didn't want to harm Tessa's reputation . . . but look what I've done. Oh, God, this is awful . . . this is unbearable."

"Get on with it, Edwards! I'm not going to listen to this blackguard blubber and wail all night!"

Cobb looked as if he were about to take five giant strides to the bar, pick Spooner up, plop him over the curve of his belly, and snap his brittle pomposity in two like a tinderstick. But he stayed put.

"You can't hold me here! I'm an American citizen!" Apparently Dawson Armstrong had risen briefly to the surface.

"Shut up in there!" Sturges yelled.

"So you had your toast to success," Marc prompted. "Just one?"

"Tessa had one, then insisted I have another . . . just one more for the road, she said, and laughed so deliciously my heart melted . . ."

"Then what happened? You must tell me everything."

"We were sitting on the settee. I don't know how she managed it, but suddenly there was only one candle lit in the room, over by the bed, and a shaft of moonlight came in through the window and laid itself over us . . . we were in each other's arms . . ."

"Go on, Rick. How far did things go?"

"Too far. She was so young, but so beautiful there in the moonlight . . . and she wanted me. I started to feel very drowsy. I thought 'How odd,' because I was getting very aroused, you see, even as my eyelids started to feel like lead . . . I swear to God, she opened my flies."

"Was she getting sleepy, too?"

"I don't think so . . . it's hard to remember because everything was starting to get fuzzy in the room, but I did see her get up, like a ghost in her white dress, and sort of drift over to the bed. I couldn't see clearly, though, because of my grogginess and the shadows on the bed. I remember her dress floating to the floor . . . she was in her shift, that gauzy thing she wore in the *Lear* scene. She was sinking back onto the pillows . . . I heard her giggle . . . I started to get up . . . and oh, Christ, I knew what I was going to do, and she was there—I swear it—with her shift raised above her knees . . ."

"And then?" Marc could hardly breathe as he waited for the answer.

"My legs went rubbery and I started falling backwards and the last thing I recall is the settee hitting the backs of my knees, and I sank back onto it. Then the room went away."

"Listen carefully. Both you and Tessa were drugged. If you've remembered these details accurately, you took twice as much drink as Tessa. You're sure Tessa drank her glassful?"

"Oh, yes. We clinked glasses and watched each other drain them. But who would do something like that?"

"I need to know exactly when you came to, and what you saw. Your life may depend on your answer."

Rick paled, checked Marc's face for signs of duplicity,

found none, and, struggling for the right words, said, "I heard Tessa cry out. I thought I was dreaming it, but my eyes opened. The room seemed dark except for the strip of moonlight over the settee and a bit of candlelight somewhere. I turned towards the bed, but all I could see—I was still groggy—was the white crumple of something on or under a sheet. I felt a sort of black panic . . . Tessa was hurt or in trouble, was all I could think, then nothing. I've been sitting here for an hour trying to remember what happened during those blank seconds. But I can't."

"But you did come to again?"

"Yes. I was sitting on the settee, something wet and sticky all down my front . . . I knew it was blood, I don't know how, and there in the moonlight I saw my sword sticking up out of the carpet. I walked slowly over to it and that's when I saw the body, Merriwether . . . ghastly. I thought, 'I've stabbed Merriwether.' I was reaching to pull the sword out when I remembered Tessa and I was just about to turn towards the bed when the door swung open, and Beasley, I think, was standing there with a candle in his hand and a horrified look on his face. One of us screamed. I was rooted to the spot, couldn't move a muscle."

Marc waited while Rick struggled to control his emotions and Cobb dared Spooner to disrupt the proceedings.

"I could hear Beasley banging on doors and creating havoc, but it was nothing compared to the havoc in my mind. Then Beasley was back with Mrs. Thedford and

Jefferson . . . I heard her shriek and I thought Tessa was dead and my heart stopped, but Mrs. Thedford picked Tessa up off the bed as if she was a doll and ran out of the room with her, Jefferson following. Beasley pulled me aside . . . sometime later the room was full of policemen."

With the aid of Cobb's lantern, Marc carefully examined the bloodstains on Rick's jacket, breeches, and boots. The smear patterns on the jacket appeared to have been caused by Rick rubbing his hands over the splotches there, but there was a curious and unexplainable absence of blood spatters. If Merriwether's ruptured aorta was spouting blood, surely there should have been spots of it where it had sprayed and landed.

Marc knelt down in front of the distraught ensign. "You could only have blanked out the second time for a minute or so at most," he said calmly. "Beasley's told Cobb he heard Tessa's cry, too, and reached the room as soon as he could. It appears, and I say *appears*, that Merriwether was struck and stabbed in the time between Tessa's cry and Beasley's arrival. Now tell me: you say you've concluded that you murdered Merriwether, but you have no actual memory of doing so?"

"I have no memory of killing Merriwether. I had no idea he was even in the room."

"Then, until you do remember it, I am going to assume you are innocent, and look for the killer elsewhere."

Tears of gratitude welled up in Hilliard's eyes. "But I must've done it, Marc. Tessa had to be saved from—"

"Stuff and nonsense!" Spooner cried, prancing across the room with a sequence of stiff manoeuvres found in no training manual. "I've heard enough of this drivel!"

Cobb stepped out in front of him, but Marc drew the constable gently away. "Lieutenant Spooner, I intend to report to Sir Francis in the morning that the case is still unresolved. Ensign Hilliard is a prime suspect, but there was, patently, a rape or attempted rape engineered by the victim with the aid of drugged wine, something I need to know a lot more about before laying any charge of murder."

"You have no evidence for that assumption!" Spooner tipped up on his toes, but the effort merely brought his bristling gaze level with Marc's chest.

"I intend to get it, sir."

"The girl'll be able to tell us more in the mornin'," Cobb added.

A smirk spread across Spooner's narrow face, he jutted out his receding jaw, and his metallic locks shook. "Mrs. Frank says the girl is saying nothing. So how do we know that it wasn't your friend Hilliard who attempted to violate the young lady, was interrupted by Merriwether, who heard her cry from his room just across the hall and came running to the rescue in his nightshirt, only to be butchered by this scoundrel?"

Rick flinched, but said nothing.

Marc was seething inside, but he realized the deceptive plausibility of this version of events. "So Ensign Hilliard drugged himself as well as Tessa in order to facilitate his purpose?" he asked sarcastically.

"Attempts at drugging have gone awry more than once," Spooner sputtered, tipping up on his toes to drive his argument forward like a puff-adder seeking the insertion point. "And if you don't inform the governor of this possibility, I shall take it upon myself to do so."

"The only thing you're gonna take on yerself is my fist!" Cobb hissed.

"Gentlemen!" Dr. Withers chided, coming across the room.

"We all need to put a damper on our tempers," Sturges said with a sharp look at Cobb. "It's the middle of the bloody night an' we're all damn near bushed."

"What in hell're we gonna do with all these people? And a dead body?" Cobb said, back in control.

Without diluting the venom in his smirk, Spooner said, "I'm taking the 'prime suspect,' as you call him, with me to Government House, where he will be placed under twenty-four-hour guard."

"Not in irons, you ain't!" Sturges snapped.

"Then I'd like you to accompany me, sir. I don't want this disgrace to a uniform making a dash for the woods."

"Okay," Sturges said with a resigned sigh.

"What about everybody else?" Cobb said.

"The governor wants this mess contained at any cost. I'm using his executive authority to order this establishment quarantined—"

"You can't do that!" Ogden Frank rolled his rotund body into the room from the dining area. Sweat beaded his hairless dome. "I'll be ruined!"

Spooner ignored him. "I want all these actors placed in their rooms upstairs and a guard posted. Mr. Frank, you will see that they are fed and watered. No-one is to have access to them without permission from me or from Lieutenant Edwards. I want no loose-lipped chambermaids near that upper floor—"

"But who will—"

"Your good woman, Mr. Frank: she already knows what's happened. But no one else must get the slightest inkling of the grotesque events here tonight. No one. Lieutenant Edwards will remain here to question the witnesses in the morning. And I'll be back with fresh instructions from Sir Francis." He gave Marc the courtesy of a final nod.

"I'll prepare sleeping draughts for these people before I leave," Withers said through his fatigue. "They're in pitiable shape. The black fellow's got a wicked toothache, but if he can't get to the barber tomorrow, I'll try and pull it before I leave."

"I'd like a sleeping draught for the wife," Frank said.

"I'll make up two," Withers offered.

Marc took Rick's arm. "You'll have to go with Lieutenant Spooner and the chief constable to Government House. Dr. Withers will come along as soon as he's finished here. I'll see you again before noon tomorrow. Tessa's going to be all right. Try not to worry."

Sturges helped Rick across the barroom, and he was escorted out the front door of the tavern onto West Market Street, more like a man trudging off to the gallows than to the relative comfort of confinement in Government House.

But as badly as he felt for Hilliard, Marc realized that he must bring matters to completion here immediately, and start afresh in the morning. He went over to the entrance to the dining-room. Five pairs of glazed eyes looked up at him as if he were perhaps a kindly executioner come to put them out of their misery. "Dr. Withers will give you each something to help you sleep. Mr. Beasley, take Mr. Armstrong to your room for the night. Mrs. Thedford, would you be good enough to let Miss Clarkson share your room? And would you convey to Mr. Jefferson that he may return to his sleeping-place, where the doctor will attend to his aching tooth."

"Are we under arrest?" Mrs. Thedford said, and the sudden resonance of her deep, authoritative voice seemed to revivify the others, who now turned to stare at her, then at Marc, with something resembling self-interest.

"No, you are not. But I will not be satisfied that Ensign Hilliard is guilty until I have questioned each of you carefully tomorrow morning. Until then, at least, the lieutenant-governor has ordered that all of you are to be held as material witnesses. Food will be brought up to you and maid-service supplied—"

Ogden Frank groaned behind him, wondering how he was to inform his "good woman" of this disquieting news.

"A police guard will be posted at the bottom of the stairs, but largely for your own protection," Marc said unconvincingly. He saw Mrs. Thedford shake her head slightly.

"What about our Tuesday evening performance?" she asked with steely calm.

"Surely you can't be thinking of continuing?"

Mrs. Thedford smiled wanly. "We are a theatre company, Mr. Edwards."

Ogden Frank tugged at Marc's sleeve. "Wouldn't it be best to carry on as if nothing has happened?" he suggested, hope rising improbably for the first time since the mute had pounded on the tavern door and he had crawled out of a warm bed to answer its grim summons. "If the tavern and theatre don't carry on normally, folks'll start to get mighty curious."

"He may be right, Major," Cobb said to Marc.

"We could tell the customers Merriwether took sick." Frank looked to Mrs. Thedford for support.

But Marc said, "We'll make those kinds of decisions after I've interviewed all of you—including you and your wife, Mr. Frank—in the morning. Now please take your sleeping draughts from Dr. Withers."

Withers had set a number of glasses of frothing liquid in a row along the bar. "Come and get it," he called, tapping a spoon against the nearest glass.

When Cobb and Marc were left alone at last, Marc gave his comrade-in-arms a weary but welcoming smile.

"Constable Wilkie'll likely be sent along when he comes on duty at seven," Cobb said. "Who'll watch that lot till then?"

"I'm going to curl up in a blanket at the foot of the stairs through there. You trot on home to Dora now. I'd like you back at ten to sit in on the interviews."

Cobb looked amazed. "But I'm just a 'peeler,'" he said, "not an *interra-grater*."

"You'll come anyway?"

"I'll be here, providin' Missus Cobb rolls me outta bed an' props my eyes open with pipe-stems."

"In the meantime, I've got to give Merriwether's room a thorough going-over. There isn't a scintilla of doubt that he put the laudanum in Tessa's sherry, but if Spooner goes to the governor with that ludicrous story of Rick being a rapist, I've got to have physical proof to counter it. There's bound to be a vial somewhere up there. And if he didn't bring the stuff with him from Buffalo, we may be able to trace it to one of the chemists in town."

"That Spooner!" Cobb snarled. "He's like a banty-rooster in a harem o' hens with its cock in a knot!"

Marc could have hugged him.

WITH EVERY CELL IN HIS BODY crying out for rest, Marc let Cobb out the main tavern door, barred it, and with the aid of Cobb's lantern made his way around the bar and through

the door into the dark recesses of the theatre. He heard
Frank slip the bolt into place behind him. All was quiet on
the upper floor. Jeremiah was asleep on a mat with the storeroom door ajar, a bloody handkerchief tied in a sling for his
jaw. He did not stir.

Merriwether's room was very tidy—Marc wasn't sure why
he should have been surprised—and with several candles
to aid his search, Marc combed through the drawers and
cupboard of a high wardrobe, peering under linens, cotton
vests, and silk stockings, and rummaging through the pockets of shirts, waistcoats, and frock coats. The man must have
rented a barge on the Erie Canal for all this. Marc found no
vial or stoppered apothecary bottle. Behind the door sat a
large costume trunk, a fine wooden piece with copper straps
and fittings and the initials *JDM* stamped on the top for all
the world to admire. It was locked, but Marc had already
found a key in one of the drawers. It opened the trunk on
the first try. Inside, neatly packed in layers separated by
swaths of fine paper, were costumes that appeared to belong
to the Shakespearean program scheduled for Tuesday evening. Meticulously, Marc searched every pocket and sleeve,
without success.

He stood up, frustrated, then stepped back and studied
the trunk from a distance. He peered back inside, reached
down, and stretched out his fingers till they touched the
bottom. He repeated this crude form of measurement on
the outside of the trunk. And smiled. It had a false bottom,

there being at least a five-inch discrepancy between the depth inside and outside. Excited now, he ran his fingers lightly over the surface of the lid and then the sides. Often there was a hidden trigger to release any latch holding a false bottom or secret drawer in place. But he found none. So he lifted the costumes out of the trunk until it was empty. He ran his fingers around the edges of the false bottom, but they seemed to fit the rectangle of the trunk neatly. Then, on the table that Merriwether used as a writing desk, Marc spotted a thin letter-opener. He slid it between the edge of the false bottom and one side of the trunk, and lifted. The false bottom came up towards him far enough for him to grasp it with three fingers and pull it all the way out. He held the lantern above the trunk and peered down.

There was no secret vial of laudanum, but something far more arresting: two brand-new French Modèle rifles—U.S army issue and the most sophisticated infantry weapon in the world—and a box of ammunition. And tucked under the polished hardwood stock of one of them was a folded note. Marc drew it into the light and read:

We understand that you have the merchandise with you. We have the money you require. Please bring a sample with you after the performance on Wednesday evening. Using the same means of communication, you will be supplied at that time with a map showing you the rendezvous point. In the meantime, we will be watching. Vigilance is the byword. Destroy this note.

Several thoughts raced through Marc's mind. These two guns were a sampler: Where were the others and how many were there? By what clandestine system of communication had this note been delivered? Was Merriwether a lone gunrunner among the Bowery Company? To which group of treasonous dissidents were these weapons destined? With Merriwether dead, what chance would there be of setting a trap for the insurrectionists? And finally, did this discovery have anything to do with Merriwether's murder and the fate of Ensign Hilliard?

Marc found himself incapable of further thought. He closed up the false bottom of the trunk, then pulled two blankets off Merriwether's bed, trudged to the other end of the hall, stretched his six-foot length across the opening to the stairwell, and fell asleep.

TEN

While Ogden Frank supervised breakfast for the "material witnesses," Marc decided to begin his interrogations with Tessa Guildersleeve. He wanted to get as much accomplished in this regard as possible before Spooner returned and was necessarily apprised of what Marc had discovered in Merriwether's room—a discovery that was certain to throw Sir Francis into paroxysms of one kind or another. He rapped discreetly at the door in the tavern that led to the Franks' quarters. Madge Frank opened it a mere crack, grimaced, then opened it wide. She was a lean, angular woman who could have used her elbows, shoulders, or hips as weapons, with chestnut hair indifferently tamed, sallow skin, and dark, mistrusting eyes that seemed forever to be seeking something they didn't want to find.

"Whaddya want?" she said.

"Please take me to Miss Guildersleeve. It is imperative that I speak with her now."

"People in fancy getups are always imperative about somethin' or other," she grumbled, but stepped aside to let him in. "I'll see if the poor creature's awake," she said.

"If not, I'd appreciate it if you'd wake her for me."

She glared at him, then heaved a woman's deep sigh that clearly conveyed a message about the incurable callousness of the male species. "Come with me."

Tessa was sitting up in bed, dipping a piece of dry toast in the mug of tea on her lap. She was wearing one of Madge's flowered bathrobes three sizes too big for her. Her face seemed no paler than usual, but her eyes were puffy and her lips drawn tight with tension. However, there was no sign of lingering shock or the kind of trauma that might have been expected from the ordeal she had suffered. She gave Marc a smile with her eyes, much to the disgust of her nurse.

"Tessa's gone through the most horrible thing that can happen to a young lady," Madge Frank said with a twist of her features to indicate that she was vicariously experiencing the horror of it.

For a moment Marc thought that Tessa might have winked at him, but her general expression was one of intense concern as she gave him her full attention.

"I'd like to speak to the girl alone. You wouldn't mind, would you, Tessa?"

"I ain't leavin' this room," Madge Frank declared through clenched teeth as she set her arms akimbo and took her stand in the doorway.

"Suit yourself, then," Marc said civilly, and sat down on the edge of the bed. Tessa showed no sign of being afraid, but he heard Madge suck in her breath. "I'm here as the governor's appointed investigator into the tragic events that took place in your room last night."

Tessa's expression clouded over, and Marc could see a flutter at her throat where the robe parted. Even in distress she was incredibly beautiful in an innocent, unfinished sort of way. "I'll try to help you if I can," she said bravely, though it was clear she had questions of her own she would like answered.

"First of all, I must inform you that both you and Rick were drugged last night. Someone put laudanum in your sherry decanter."

Tessa seemed about to lose her carefully constructed composure, but whether it was the result of hearing the word *laudanum* or the name *Rick* couldn't be determined.

"Who would do that?" she whispered. "An' why?"

"I intend to get answers to both of those questions. And you can help by telling me what happened after you and Rick went to your room."

Tessa blushed a deep peony red, Madge Frank cleared her throat threateningly, but something in Marc's steady, unjudgemental gaze encouraged the girl to begin her story. As she recited it, she kept her eyes on the tea-mug in her lap most of the time, peeking up only once a minute or so to make sure this handsome, kind-eyed officer was still listening and approving. In her own accented vernacular, Tessa's narrative jibed with Rick's at every essential point.

"So you were both seated on the settee, and you asked Marc to stay for one more drink?"

"Yes, I did. I was feelin' so mellow an' cozy and I didn't want things to end."

"I forbid you to take this improper conversation any further!" Madge Frank had started towards the bed, her eyes black with indignation.

"Mrs. Frank, please stand outside the door and observe if you must, but if you say one more word, I'll remove you and shut the door."

Madge huffed indignantly, but did as she was bidden. Marc hoped that he would not need her as an ally anytime soon. "Please go on, Tessa. I know this is very hard, but every detail you can remember may help Rick."

He could see she wanted to ask him about Rick but dared not—yet. "I started to feel real sleepy and I saw Rick yawn, so I went over to the bed an' laid down on it, and I was so groggy I thought I was about to faint, but, still, I really wanted Rick to stay, so I . . . I started to lift up my shift—"

Madge Frank was heard clattering down the hall.

"And?"

"Nothin'."

"Nothing?"

"I must've passed out."

"But you woke up later?"

"Yes." The memory of that wakening flooded back, whole and hurting. "But I was only half awake. There was a huge weight on top of me and a raspy breathin' in my ear. An' before I could say or see anythin', I felt a sharp jab between my legs and I cried out with the pain of it."

"Did you know who . . . was doing this thing to you?"

"No," she said, barely audible. "I fainted dead away again."

"Part of that was due to the drug, Tessa." Two perfect teardrops had slipped out of her pale blue eyes and now sat, one on each cheek, glistening. "Could it have been Rick on top of you?" Marc asked quietly.

Amazement, then fear, filled her face. "Oh, no, it couldn't've been Rick. He would never do anythin' to hurt me. You can't think Rick did this?"

"No, I don't. But I had to ask."

"Rick saved me from bein' murdered!" she cried with passion and a kind of defiant, childlike pride. "Mrs. Frank's told me about . . . about Jason."

"Did you *see* Rick . . . save you?"

Tessa shook her head and shuddered. "I don't remember anythin' except cryin' out at the pain. Then I was driftin' in the dark, and all kinds of nightmares were scuttlin' through my head, and I saw Rick with a knife stuck in him an' he was all bloody and I screamed so loud I woke myself up—here in Mrs. Frank's bed."

Marc sighed. "So you're telling me that you were unconscious from the moment you first cried out in pain, and thus can tell me nothing of what happened in that room after that point?"

"I only know what Mrs. Frank told me: that Jason was stabbed by Rick because he did that awful thing to me." At this, she began to sob softly, and Marc went to the door and called Madge, who appeared instantly from around a corner. "She needs you, ma'am."

"What's gonna happen to Rick?" Tessa cried out from the bed. "What's gonna happen to the company?"

"I don't know yet," Marc said honestly as Madge bustled by him and took the girl in her arms, stroking her hair and murmuring in her ear.

As Marc left, he heard Tessa say like a lost child, "Get Annie. Oh, please, Madge, I gotta see Annie!"

As MARC EMERGED FROM THE FRANKS' quarters into the tavern, Ogden Frank was just unbarring the street-door across the room to let Cobb in.

"I hope nobody spotted you," Frank said fretfully as he slammed the bar back into its slot.

Cobb ignored him, and brushed by towards Marc so

abruptly he sent the roly-poly little man a-wobble. Cobb looked as if he had dressed in the dark with one hand: his coat buttons were misaligned, his shirt was inside out, and his helmet sat precariously on one side of his head. But he smiled gamely at Marc, who himself would not have passed muster at parade.

Before Marc could speak, Cobb said, "I've checked the alley: there's no sign of footprints or a ladder bein' underneath the windows."

Marc nodded and said, "I've got news."

"I've never known you not to," Cobb said.

They sat down at a table, and Cobb removed his coat to reveal a portion of Dora's breakfast preparation on his vest.

"Do you want to tell us something?" Marc called out to Frank, who had stopped wobbling and was now loitering near the door to his quarters.

Frank came close enough to say with a certain spiteful glee, "I heard him an' the woman shoutin' at each other yesterday morning."

"Who and what woman?" Marc said.

"That Thea creature an' Merriwether—jawin' away at each other in the dining-room when they thought nobody was listenin'."

"What were they arguing about?"

"I couldn't tell fer sure, but I'd say it was a lovers' quarrel."

"And how did it end?"

"The woman screamed somethin' like 'I ain't gonna take

it no more!' an' she come streakin' past me bawlin' her eyes out."

"Thank you, Ogden. I appreciate your assistance. Is everything all right with those upstairs?"

Frank looked pitiably grateful and flashed Marc a fawning smile. "They've had their breakfast, but it's put Madge in a fearful rage. Do you think we'll be able to go ahead with the show tonight?"

"I'll let you know right after noon," Marc promised.

"I gotta open the taproom at one o'clock," he said. "Lucky fer us, nobody's stayin' in the hotel rooms above us except my two housemaids."

"Let's keep it that way, shall we?"

Frank nodded as if he were a co-conspirator, then waddled away to deal with his much-put-upon wife.

Marc proceeded to give Cobb a brief account of what he had found at the bottom of Merriwether's trunk.

Cobb arched an eyebrow, whistled through his teeth, and said, "Couldn't we ever get us a plain an' simple murder? Now we got politics muddled up in it."

Cobb was alluding to last year's investigation, and Marc was reminded of a remark Beth had made then that in Upper Canada everything was politics. "But politics or not, Cobb, we've still got to find evidence to clear Rick of this crime."

"Assumin' he didn't do it."

"I'm assuming that," Marc said, staring at the constable.

Cobb didn't react, but merely said, "Ya had a chance to talk to the girl yet?"

Marc gave him a summary of his interview with Tessa.

When he had finished, Cobb said, "Well, Major, that don't seem to be a lotta help to Hilliard."

"It's worse than that. She's convinced he did it in defense of her honour—such as it is, or was. And he's still besotted with her."

Cobb frowned. "Then we better keep her away from him."

"Right now I'm anxious to interrogate the rest of that bunch, but you can see the immediate problem we have."

Cobb nodded. "Ya gotta tell Sir Francis Bone Head about them guns."

"Yes. And I'm positive that what I saw last night was only the sample referred to in the note from the buyers."

"Where would the rest of them be, then?"

"My best guess is that there are more trunks with false bottoms. The one in Merriwether's room was improvised—handmade, I'd say."

"Well, Major, I saw this crew come off the boat from Burlington last Friday with enough baggage for a regiment or two."

"They were planning to try out a number of playbills, here and in Detroit and Chicago. Where would they be storing the props and costumes not in use?"

"Frank's got a big shed and ice-house out back."

"Then let's have a peek." Marc rose stiffly out of his chair.

"You look like ya slept on a sack of potatoes," Cobb said.

"They're all locked." Marc sighed, surveying the six steamer-trunks they had found in Frank's storage-shed.

"I've never found that a problem," Cobb said. He fished about in his greatcoat pocket and drew out a ring of keys of varying shapes and sizes. "This one usually does it fer these kinda trunks." He bent over the nearest one, jiggled the chosen key as if his fingers had suddenly developed palsy, muttered what was either a curse or an incantation, and then, with a decisive twist, exclaimed, "Aha!"

The trunk yawned open.

Over the next fifteen minutes, the two men opened each of the trunks in turn, carefully removed the contents, pried up the false bottoms in three of them, and found what they were looking for. There were twelve U.S army rifles in addition to the two in Merriwether's room, and several boxes of ammunition. They replaced the contents with equal care and relocked the trunks.

Back inside, Marc said to Cobb, "It's possible the others know nothing about the rifles. But we can't be sure. God knows what the governor will decide to do. In any case, I want some time to question the actors before Spooner gets here, so I'm going to give you this incriminating note and

have you go up to Government House with it. That and the
news of the guns out there in the shed should occupy Sir
Francis and Spooner for a little while, time enough for me to
see what I can do to help Rick."

"You're not worried about the guns?"

"Of course I am. We are probably facing some sort of
planned insurrection—high treason for those involved. But
I'm just a soldier now, Cobb, and I'm content to leave these
entanglements to the governor and his aides."

Cobb's grunt indicated his skepticism about the latter
claim, but he did not comment further. "I'm on my way,
Major."

"Would you mind asking Wilkie to bring Jeremiah Jefferson down here to the dining-room before you go?" Constable Wilkie had arrived late at seven thirty to rouse Marc
and place himself on the landing with a stool, a candle, and
a copy of this week's *Constitution*.

"The mute? I thought you'd want to see Beasley first.
Seems to me he's the one that's got the goods on Hilliard."

"Very true. But Beasley's already outlined his account to
you and Spooner. I need to question the others closely to see
if I can find the discrepancies in it. If I don't, it's going to go
badly for Rick."

"I'll wake up Wilkie an' put him to work, then," Cobb
said, pleased with this modest attempt at levity.

• • •

JEREMIAH JEFFERSON SAT OPPOSITE MARC WITH the air of a man who was concerned with the unpredictable turn of events but innocent of any direct involvement in them. Nonetheless, his past experience with authority had left a residual wariness in an otherwise open and unsuspecting face. Mrs. Thedford had apparently done more than merely shelter him from the slave-catchers, Marc thought: there had been some kind of miraculous rehabilitation.

The interview was conducted by a combination of questions and answers being written on the slate placed between them, and of gestures, lip-reading, and accompanying facial expressions.

Your tooth is better?

Vigorous nod and display of gum-gap.

It kept you awake after the play?

Yes. *Couldn't sleep.*

Did you see anyone come up the stairs after the others were asleep?

No.

Did anyone come back down the hall and go down the stairs?

No.

Did you see Mr. Beasley come out of his room?

Yes. *He scared me.*

He looked frightened? Worried?

Yes. *Running.*

You followed him?

Not right away. He started banging on doors.

What did you do?

Clarence and I banged on Mrs. T's door.

Did she answer?

No. We went into her bedroom.

Was she awake?

No. Earplugs. Shook her.

Then you all went to Tessa's room?

Yes. Terrible.

Marc then took Jeremiah detail by detail through what he saw there: Rick still holding the sword, Tessa unconscious, blood everywhere, Mrs. Thedford running out with Tessa in her arms and Jeremiah following, then being sent to rouse the Franks, helping Madge and Mrs. Thedford get Tessa downstairs and away from the dreadful scene.

Thank you. You've been very helpful.

Say thank you to the doctor for me.

THE INTERVIEW WITH JEREMIAH HAD BEEN helpful, perhaps, but not to Rick Hilliard's case. So far, the various accounts meshed in every important detail. Marc decided to see Dawson Armstrong next, not because he expected the dipsomaniac actor to provide credible evidence about the crime, but because he was the most likely among the members of the troupe to have detailed knowledge of Merriwether's background and behaviour. Despite what he had told Cobb, Marc was eager to discover all he could about the

gunrunning operation. In addition to being a loyal subject of
the newly crowned Queen Victoria, he had a personal stake
in seeing that no citizens' revolt erupted in Upper Canada—
with farmer and soldier staring each other down, weapons at
the ready.

As he motioned Armstrong to a chair across the table
from him, Marc noticed, behind the crumpled features and
depleted expression of the veteran actor, Madge Frank walking slowly across the taproom with Tessa on one arm. They
shuffled into the theatre, en route to Mrs. Thedford no
doubt.

"You were drunk when all the fuss broke out?" Marc
asked, hoping to get this part of the interrogation over with
quickly.

"You won't believe this after what you saw yesterday afternoon on the stage, but I've been sober most of the time
since we left New York last month," Armstrong said wearily,
as if he were beyond caring about anything anymore.

"Yet, according to what I heard Mrs. Thedford say, you
managed to bring along a contraband supply of booze."

Armstrong's posture stiffened, and the creases in his face
did their best to express umbrage at the accusation. "I did
nothing of the sort."

"Then how did bottles of whiskey mysteriously appear
whenever required?"

Armstrong blinked. "I've begun asking myself that very
same question. At first when I found a half-drunk bottle

in the bottom of my trunk, I thought it was left over from a trip I took to Philadelphia last fall. But yesterday after lunch, when I began pulling out my Lear and Prospero outfits, I found another part-bottle in one of the pockets, and I've been so upset lately with Merriwether's putdowns and insinuations, well, I just started in on it. And you saw what happened after that. Annemarie was furious."

"Could Merriwether have planted those whiskey bottles deliberately?"

"That bastard would do anything to destroy my career!" Lear's anger flashed in the tragedian's eyes.

"Did you hate him enough to kill him?" Marc asked quietly.

Armstrong was not surprised by the question. "Of course I did. But after the fiasco of the afternoon, I went up to my room and thought mightily about finishing the bottle I'd hidden well. We had a play to put on, and I managed to resist. But after the play, I came straight up here and started in on it. I took it down in three or four swigs and passed out. When I woke up, it was pitch dark. I felt like hell. I puked all over the rug."

Marc knew he had to ask the next question: "Did you hear Tessa cry out?"

Armstrong did not answer right away. He looked down at the table, and when he raised his eyes again to face Marc, they were brimming with tears. "Yes, I did."

"What did you do?"

"I am ashamed to say I did nothing. My door was ajar. So was Tessa's. I heard her shriek, like she'd been stabbed. I knew she was in some sort of danger. But I was sick, I was woozy, my head was pounding, I was filled with self-loathing."

"Did you see Clarence Beasley come running towards Tessa's room?"

"Yes. And I felt a wave of relief."

Marc hated himself for continuing, but he did his duty: "Do you remember how long it was after the cry that you saw Beasley pass your doorway?"

"It wasn't right away, I know that, because I started crawling towards the hall. Then I heard Beasley's door open and saw him coming to help."

"Isn't it possible that Beasley may have come out of Tessa's room, slipped quietly back to his own room, and then pretended to be the rescuer by running noisily past your door?"

Armstrong was genuinely puzzled by the question. He gave it due consideration before answering. "I see what you're driving at but, no, that's not the way it happened. I heard Tessa scream. My door was open about a foot, and from where I was lying in my puke I could see Tessa's doorway across the hall. Nobody came out after the scream. Then, maybe a minute or two later, I saw Beasley come past."

Marc tried to suppress the discouraging implications of Armstrong's testimony and concentrate on his next task.

"While I have you here, Mr. Armstrong, I'd like to learn a bit more about Merriwether. I assume you've known him for some years, as both of you have starred on the New York stage, as rivals and colleagues."

"What do you need to know other than the fact that the man was a monster with an ego the size of Manhattan Island?"

"Was he interested in politics?"

Armstrong snorted derisively. "That would have meant giving some thought to the welfare of others or the future of America, and Merriwether was obsessed with only his own appetites and satisfying them as often as possible."

"He belonged to no political party or organization that you know of?"

"He didn't vote and even bragged about it."

"He was attracted to women?"

"And they to him. But Annemarie kept him in his place. I'll give him his due there: he seemed to sense, like any cunning beast will, that his recovery and his progress in the world were bound up with Mrs. Thedford and her good grace. He was pathetically afraid of her, though he tried not to show it."

"And yet he raped her ward?"

Armstrong winced at the word *raped*. "The son-of-a-bitch stepped over the line, didn't he? And got what he deserved. I hope they hang a medal around young Hilliard's neck."

A noose was more likely, Marc thought.

• • •

"How is Tessa doing?" Marc asked Mrs. Thedford, who now sat across from him—fatigued, concerned, but with no loss of poise or inherent authority.

"She is recovering remarkably well. The drug that knocked her out kept her from seeing any of the horrors perpetrated in that room. The loss of her virginity appears to have been a physical trauma only. Nevertheless, I have insisted she rest in my room with Thea until this afternoon's rehearsal."

"The show must go on," Marc said, recalling that phrase from five years ago in his brief flirtation with summer theatre in London.

"If it is allowed to," she said simply, holding his gaze in hers.

"But you've already rehearsed the Shakespeare program."

"Yes, as you observed yesterday. But one of our characters has played his death-scene too well, and cannot be replaced." Despite the natural beauty of her deep blue eyes, lustrous skin, honeyed tresses, and regal carriage, a profound sadness enveloped her. "Jason was a troubled and difficult man. Few people liked him. I made the effort to find the best part of him and have it take possession of the whole person. I thought I was succeeding."

"I hate to be so blunt, but the man betrayed you by ravishing your ward."

"I know," she said angrily, "and I'd've picked up the nearest heavy object and brained him with it if I'd caught him at it—or clawed his eyes out as Cornwall did Gloucester's, and with as little remorse."

"But you didn't?"

"Someone beat me to it."

"You believe Ensign Hilliard did it?"

"All I know is that Clarence and Jeremiah shook me awake and dragged me in my nightdress down to that room, and your ensign was still standing over the body, clutching the sword. Everything else is a blur, because once I saw Tessa lifeless on the bed, I seemed to go blind with panic. Somehow I got her out of there, and I don't know what I was thinking of, but I didn't feel she would be safe till I got her as far away from there as I could. Madge Frank calmed me down, and I was persuaded to leave Tessa in her hands."

"But why would Hilliard drive his sword through a man he had already disabled?"

Mrs. Thedford seemed to find the question disingenuous. "Surely you know the young man was in love?"

"But you loved her, too, in your way. Would you have driven that sword through Merriwether's chest as he lay, in all probability, dying?"

"That's very difficult to answer, Mr. Edwards. Each of us has the capacity to love and hate, and either quality has the potential to incite us to actions we would normally consider beyond us. But you saw what Tessa was up to during her scene with Lear? The girl is young and ambitious and feel-ing the urgency of her desires. What happened to her was almost inevitable, though I've done everything I could to forestall it. But to answer your question: I think that in the fury of seeing the deed being done, I'd've cracked the villain on the skull. But why would I then, with forethought and in cold blood, kill a man I admired and whose loss to the Bow-ery Company will likely prove ruinous?"

"Thank you for your candour, ma'am. I'm trying to un-derstand the degree of hatred and moral outrage that must have propelled that sword through a man's torso into the floor underneath it. According to statements already made by Mr. Beasley and Mr. Armstrong, no one entered that room after Tessa's cry at the moment of the . . ."

"Penetration?"

Marc flushed. "Yes. And no one came out who hadn't been in there already."

"Well, I'm relieved to hear that."

"There is one other important matter you can help me with."

"Please, name it."

"Who arranges for the disposition and delivery of your many steamer-trunks?"

"An odd question, but one easily answered. I looked after all the financial aspects of the company, Jason and I shared the artistic responsibilities, and Jason alone handled the travel arrangements for us and the disposition of the baggage. Jeremiah does most of the actual lifting. Why do you ask?" She seemed more amused than anxious by this turn in the conversation.

"You have six trunks in Frank's storage-shed."

"Probably. Only Jason and Jeremiah would know for sure. Have you counted them personally?"

"Humour me for a while longer, please. I take it that the contents of these trunks are not required here in Toronto?"

"Jason told me that he had put all the materials we no longer needed into three trunks and was arranging to have them shipped to New York City."

The three with the rifles in them, Marc thought, and they would have been mysteriously "lost" en route. But exactly where would they have been "lost" if Merriwether had not been prematurely murdered? And who would have "found" them?

"Did anyone other than Mr. Merriwether have keys to those trunks?"

"No. We each have our own trunks, but only Jason had keys for the others." Suddenly she lost her composure for the first time, and with a breaking voice said, "He kept them in a secret pocket inside his King Claudius robe. He thought I didn't know where they were, and I went along with it."

"Please, don't upset yourself over the matter, Mrs. Thedford. I only asked because it might be necessary at some point in the investigation to have access to anything which might have belonged to him."

If she were puzzled by this lame explanation, she had the good manners not to show it.

"Do you know if Mr. Merriwether had any money troubles?"

"Not really," she said, back in control of herself once more. "No actor ever has enough money, but Jason had no one to support but himself, and I was the one risking my meagre capital in the quixotic venture of owning and operating a theatre in New York."

"And you were counting on his return to star status?"

"Yes. That was the main reason we were trying out so many different plays and playbills. I had hoped that Jason would also do some directing at the new Bowery, but now . . ."

"Thank you for your co-operation. I'll let you know after the noon-hour whether you'll be able to carry on this evening."

"Thank you. As I started to say earlier, if we can, we will substitute our musical and recitation program for the Shakespeare. It's something we have done on rare occasions when one of us is too ill to go on: it's a simple series of 'acts' we can mount and adapt with an hour's notice."

"I am amazed at the resilience of actors."

"Would you do *me* a favour?" she said, getting up to leave.

"Of course."

"I promised your friend Mr. Jenkin that I would have

luncheon with him today in the dining-room at one o'clock. He's riding in from the fort. I know you want to keep the news from getting out—"

"Yes, but we also need to do nothing out of the ordinary to arouse suspicions. I'm sure you and Mr. Jenkin will find many more pleasant things to talk about."

And, Marc thought, it'll give me a chance to make up a cover story for being in town and for Rick's unexplained disappearance—and have Owen take it back to the garrison.

"Thank you. Whatever we might say in our anger and our grief over the next few hours, please believe me when I say that we appreciate your kindness and courtesy." With that she walked across the taproom and into the theatre.

Marc was about to send Wilkie to fetch Thea Clarkson when he heard the front door to the tavern slam open, and turned to see Lieutenant Spooner strut in and put an end to both kindness and courtesy.

ELEVEN

Lieutenant Spooner marched to the middle of the barroom with epaulets bristling, executed a teetering two-footed halt, and, regaining the perpendicular, whipped his shako-hat down to his thigh with an intimidating strop. Then he swivelled his head like a horned owl with a fixed stare, as if he expected to discover a cache of Yankee rifles under every table. Constable Cobb followed close behind but walked towards Marc.

"I think Mr. Spooner would like a word," he said.

"Ah, there you are, Edwards. Why didn't you reveal your position at once?"

"It seemed to me that I might actually be observable," Marc replied.

"Constable, please leave this room. What I have to say to the lieutenant is strictly confidential."

"I'll stand out here by the bar an' watch the doors," Cobb said with a helpless shrug in Marc's direction.

Spooner waited until he thought Cobb was out of earshot, then sat ramrod straight opposite Marc.

"I gather that Cobb has shown the note to the governor and mentioned our discovery of the contraband weapons?"

"Don't patronize me, Edwards. You could be court-martialled for revealing that note to an illiterate bobby who may be sympathetic to the enemies of Queen Victoria himself. But the milk has been spilt, and Sir Francis is extremely agitated."

"Has his agitation prompted a plan for us to deal with the situation?"

Spooner appeared momentarily flummoxed, both eyebrows in a regular tantrum of indecision. Then he managed to snarl, "The governor does not have enough information to formulate a response, as you know perfectly well."

"Well, then, Lieutenant, let me lay out the situation as I see it—for you and the governor."

"The guns must be secured before anything else is considered."

"They are secure, sir. You have my word as an officer on that score. I'll have Cobb show you their location, if you like, but my advice is to leave them where they sit."

"To what end, sir? Leaving them open to unlawful appropriation by Cobb or one of his cronies?"

"I am assuming that Sir Francis, being an astute gentleman, is more concerned with tracking down the rebels to whom the rifles were heading than he is in impounding the guns themselves."

Spooner's face went as scarlet as his coat.

"Am I right?" Marc asked casually.

"Yes, damn you. He decided not to accept my advice that the weapons be seized and every known radical be rounded up and interrogated until the last dram of truth was squeezed out of him."

"Please inform Sir Francis, then, that my preliminary investigation into Jason Merriwether's untimely death has pretty much excluded assassination by any political fanatic. The killer is almost certainly one of the other actors. Whether more than one was involved or why there was a falling-out, I don't yet know. But I intend to find out."

Spooner was first astonished; then mocking. "Have you gone mad? The assassin is safely locked away at Government House. Sir Francis wants a full written report on the matter from you before noon tomorrow, after which Hilliard will be charged with murder and thrown into military prison to await trial. You are under direct orders from your supreme commander to concentrate all your efforts upon the business of discovering whom these guns are meant for."

Marc took a deep breath. It appeared he had about

twenty-four hours to find the real killer and save Rick from the noose. But there was a way in which he might be able to buy more time and simultaneously ingratiate himself with Sir Francis: a plan to flush out the seditionists was forming in his mind.

"Have you gone catatonic, sir?"

"Not yet, Lieutenant. But I want you to take a proposition back to Sir Francis for his approval."

"I'd refuse if I could," Spooner sighed.

"Explain to Sir Francis that if the news of Merriwether's death can be contained within these walls until Wednesday night—and so far you've been successful in doing that—then the final contact for the guns may still be made, and the identity and whereabouts of the traitors disclosed."

"But Merriwether was an actor and—"

"And this is what I have in mind," Marc smiled, and outlined his proposal to a speechless aide-de-camp.

When Spooner had left on his mission to the governor, Marc went over to Cobb. "Did you get all that?"

"Every *silli-babble*, Major."

COBB, WHO MADE NO COMMENT ON the audacity of the proposal, now joined Marc for the interview with Thea Clarkson. Of all those questioned so far, Thea appeared to be the most personally devastated. It could have been the consequence of her recent ill health, but if Ogden Frank had been telling the truth, it was almost certainly due to her relationship with the victim.

She really did appear physically ill: haggard, pale, and loose-fleshed, her hair unkempt, her eyes swollen from weeping. Could she have killed Merriwether in a fit of jealous rage upon discovering him with Tessa, then regretted it? But how could she have managed it? Marc mulled over these questions as he sought the best and least cruel way to approach her. Last night she had been asleep in the Franks' quarters, where no sound from the floor above the theatre could be heard. Hence, if she had somehow slipped by Jeremiah Jefferson, awake with a toothache, and stumbled upon Merriwether at the very moment of the rape, would she have had the strength to strike him unconscious with the ashtray and the wherewithal to drive Hilliard's sword through him? Moreover, Armstrong now claimed to have seen Beasley answer Tessa's cry several minutes after it pierced the night, but he had not seen Thea. Further, Armstrong had seemed sure that no mad-eyed assassin had come running out of Tessa's room and down the hall to the only exit. Could both Jeremiah and Armstrong be lying? If so, to what end?

At any rate, one glance at Thea's devastated face and fragile composure caused Marc to begin obliquely and gently. "Miss Clarkson, we have been told that you were in love with Jason Merriwether."

She surprised them with a smile, and for a fleeting second they were privy to the beauty and warmth that had made her attractive to playgoers and suitors alike. "Not everyone has been kind enough to put it like that," she said in a low but steady voice. "But yes, Jason and I were lovers."

"For how long?"

"Our liaison began last winter when I joined the Bowery Company after a year away in Boston. We tried to keep it secret—Mrs. Thedford does not approve of affairs among her actors while they're sharing a stage—but I'm sure everybody in the company knew of it. I think Annemarie realized how much Jason and I needed each other."

"Everyone so far has spoken highly of Mrs. Thedford."

"Everyone will—she's the finest human being I've ever met."

Marc cleared his throat. "And yet Mr. Merriwether was found in Miss Guildersleeve's room—in compromising circumstances," Marc said quietly.

"Jason was attracted to young women, *very* young women, probably because they were attracted to him. And I've found most men cannot resist sustained flattery." There was no coyness or the least irony in her remark: it was simply a statement of what was and is.

"But you quarrelled loudly with Mr. Merriwether yesterday morning? Over Tessa, I presume?"

For a moment Marc was certain she was going to deny this, but all she said was "yes."

"When did you learn that something dreadful had happened upstairs?"

"I was awakened by the commotion in our quarters. Mr. Frank ordered me to stay put, but I did hear them bringing Tessa downstairs and placing her in Mrs. Frank's bed next door. Mrs. Frank told me what had happened. Then the police came."

"Thank you for being so candid, Miss Clarkson. If it is any consolation to you, I intend to find Jason Merriwether's killer and bring him to justice."

"Are we going to be allowed to carry on tonight?"

WHILE THEY WERE WAITING FOR WILKIE to bring Clarence Beasley down, Marc said to Cobb, "Miss Clarkson certainly had motive enough to brain him and passion enough—even in her weakened condition—to put a sword through his body. But there's no way she could have got up there and, even if she had, her timely arrival takes coincidence beyond credibility."

"Ya mean it's too good to be true."

"Precisely. Unless, of course, they're all lying and in this thing together."

"Well, Major, we gotta remember these folks are actors."

Marc sighed. "And I can't see Thea Clarkson being a gunrunner or fire-breathing republican."

"But she might've been jealous enough to've helped somebody else do him in."

"Like Beasley, who also had his eye on Tessa, I'm sure."

At this point the latest potential suspect arrived, and the last of the interviews began.

SINCE BEASLEY HAD ALREADY GIVEN COBB, Sturges, and Spooner an account of his actions and reactions last night, Marc saw his task as having Beasley go over the narrative and flesh it out with details, details that might indicate a lie or an uncertainty. If Beasley's account and corroboration of it by Jeremiah and Armstrong went unchallenged, Rick Hilliard would hang.

Beasley was maddeningly co-operative, forthright, ingenuous almost. He listened to each question with the care he would have offered a director giving notes, paused to take it in, then answered in plain and unambiguous language, keeping eye contact throughout. If this were acting, then Beasley was destined for stardom.

"The number of minutes between Tessa's cry wakening you and your reaching her room are critical to our understanding of what happened," Marc said. "Tell me exactly what you did when you awoke."

"I sat upright. I recognized Tessa's voice, and there was terror in it. That's the first thought I had, and then that I must go to her as quickly as possible."

"And did you?"

"No. My bed is partly under the roof-line and, in my panic, when I went to jump out of bed, I bumped my head against a rafter. I did not black out, for I was aware of falling back onto the bed and then onto the cold floor. But I was dizzy and momentarily confused."

"You heard no further cry or other sounds from Tessa's room?"

"No. And I remember being very worried that I did not. 'Has she been murdered?' was my thought, and I staggered to my feet into the pitch dark, feeling about for my tinderbox and not able to remember where I had left it. I was cursing myself all the time and knocking things over."

"But you found it?"

"Yes, where it was supposed to be: on my night-table. My hands were shaking so badly, it took twenty or thirty seconds for me to get it working and light a candle. By then, my head was throbbing—right here—but I was no longer dizzy."

Cobb put his pipe down, came around, and dutifully inspected the lesion and modest bump on the top of Beasley's head.

"I half ran and half staggered out into the dark hall, but I could see a tiny wedge of light coming out of Tessa's doorway at the far end. I hurried up, and stubbed my toe on that spittoon near Armstrong's door—I think it was ajar, but I can't be sure—righted myself, and crashed into Tessa's room. What I intended to do I do not know. I am not a brave man. I had no weapon except the saucer holding the stub of candle. But its glow and the candle near Tessa's bed were enough light to show me the situation."

THE REBELLION MYSTERIES

"So, if you did not black out when you bumped your head, the time between your hearing Tessa's cry and your arrival could not have been less than, say, a minute, and not more than, say, two minutes?"

"That is my own estimate, yes."

Beasley then repeated the description of the scene that was now depressingly familiar to Marc: Hilliard standing over the victim with both hands on the haft of the bloodied sword.

"Why didn't you go to Tessa immediately? You ran out of the room like a madman, hollering and banging on doors."

"I did not see Tessa, or if I did, the horror of Jason's body stuck like a pig, and blood everywhere, and this soldier standing over him—all that blotted her out. I ran, like a coward, to get help."

"Leaving Tessa, to whom I believe you are strongly attached, with a vicious killer?"

Beasley coloured. "Yes," he whispered. "I am ashamed to say I did. But I will not lie to you. I stumbled back into the hallway and headed across to Dawson's door. It was already open and I saw him lying inside in a pool of his own vomit, still drunk or hopelessly hungover, and I just carried on to Mrs. Thedford's door, and pounded on it like a child trying to waken its mother. The racket alerted Jeremiah, who joined me, and we went in there together."

And the rest they already knew.

Beasley was about to get up when Marc stopped him with

another question: "Do you know any reason why Mr. Merriwether would be in need of money? Desperately in need, perhaps?"

Beasley sat back down and thought about the question, giving no sign that it might have some malign purpose or raise matters that could implicate him personally. "Yes, now that I think back on it, he did."

Cobb removed his pipe and leaned forward.

"Please, go on," Marc said. "Strange as it may seem, your response to the question could be vital to this investigation."

"As you wish. I don't want to speak ill of the dead—even though I did not like Jason or his arrogance, he gave me professional advice and was not unkind in his way—but just before we set out on this tour, I overheard him talking with a theatre manager named Mitchell, a rival if you will, and they were discussing the possibility of opening a new theatre on Canal Street as joint owners. But it was obvious that, at that time anyway, Jason did not have the kind of capital required. Nor would he ever, I thought, if he stuck to acting for his livelihood."

"Was this not a betrayal of Mrs. Thedford, who had given him a second chance when nobody else would?"

Beasley was amazed. "You don't know the theatre world in New York, sir. Mrs. Thedford might have been disappointed in him, but in the end she would have wished him well. When it comes to the crunch, every actor, director, and manager is ambitious for himself. In that regard, Mrs. Thedford is the miraculous exception. But she understands the world she's lived and survived in now for twenty-five years."

Beasley was thanked and went back to the actors' quarters.

"Well, Cobb, we now have a motive for Merriwether's pathetic attempt at gunrunning: money."

"Least it ain't politics," Cobb rumbled.

"True, though it would be simpler if some crazy Orangeman had broken into the rooms up there looking for the gunrunner, found him already knocked senseless on the floor, stabbed him with Hilliard's sabre to finish the job, and bolted."

"Ogden Frank's an Orangeman, ain't he?"

"But not a rabid one. And why would he risk ruining himself financially with such a messy assassination in his own nest when Merriwether could have been killed more conveniently elsewhere? Or merely turned over to Sir Francis. Besides, no one seems to have been snooping around the guns but us."

"Plus the fact none of them actors saw Frank up there till he was summoned."

"Nor any other Orange lunatic."

Cobb sighed, accidentally sucked in the putrid contents of his pipe-stem, spat furiously, and said, "We been at this all mornin', Major, an' we ain't found much to *ex-culprit* your friend Hilliard. I'm beginnin' to think things'd be a sight easier if it turned out he done it."

• • •

Marc and Cobb were sitting in the taproom with a nervous-looking Ogden Frank, drinking a draught of his best brew, on the house.

"I gotta tell them actors pretty soon if it's okay for them to start gettin' ready for tonight. An' my tapster an' assistant'll be comin' through that door in fifteen minutes to help me open the premises an' get some heat an' light into the theatre. And if I don't let one of the maids up to the actors' rooms soon, questions'll be raised about what's goin' on. An' we can't let that corpse fester an' stink up there much longer."

"You serve a good ale," Cobb remarked affably.

"We must wait for word from the governor," Marc said, "and, if I'm not mistaken, I can hear the martinet tread of Lieutenant Spooner approaching at this moment."

Spooner obliged by pushing open the tavern door, eyeing Frank and Cobb with distaste, and strutting over to their table. He remained standing.

"Is it yes or no?" Marc said.

"It's yes," Spooner hissed.

Every person in the building who knew something about what had happened in Tessa's room had been summoned to the stage area of the theatre. Here they were seated on stools and a bench hoisted up from the pit, all facing Marc. To his evident relief, Wilkie had been posted beside the bar in the tavern to ensure that no one entered through the door there. Frank had instructed his staff to carry on with the regular opening of the pub, then joined his wife and the others onstage. Spooner stood aloof and rigid in the wings, making it clear to anyone who cared that he was not a party to the insane scheme about to be proposed by Lieutenant Edwards and inexplicably approved by an increasingly unpredictable governor.

It was nearly two o'clock. Cold sandwiches had been delivered to the actors by Madge Frank at twelve thirty, Mrs. Thedford had been permitted to keep her luncheon date with Owen Jenkin and, then, in a plan worked out between Marc and Spooner, everyone necessary to the scheme had been brought here. It was Marc himself who had led Mrs. Thedford from the dining-room, then returned quickly to explain to Jenkin that he and Hilliard had been given a special assignment by Sir Francis, and would be absent for the next few days. The fact that both Marc and Rick had worked as security officers for the governor last year mitigated the quartermaster's surprise at this news. Rumours of rebellion had been sweeping through both provinces for the past week or more. Jenkin's ready acceptance of his explanation was also the assurance Marc required that Mrs. Thedford had kept her word and said nothing about Merriwether's death. Marc said good-bye to his dear friend, unhappy to have lied to him, but determined to do his duty by uncovering the would-be rebels and their attempt to arm themselves with Yankee rifles.

"I know you are all wondering why I've brought you here," Marc began. "You've been through hell and its chambers since midnight. You are grieving the death of a colleague. You are puzzled why I have not been content to have Ensign Hilliard charged with murder. Perhaps you are even looking at one another and wondering. And to my great astonishment you are eager to carry on with your theatrical commitments. First of all, let me say that the governor himself has asked me to inform you that he wants you to continue your performances, at least until Wednesday and possibly to completion on Thursday evening."

"You might have told me sooner," Frank said. "I been pullin' my hair out since breakfast." The fact that the only hairs on his head were in his ears did not diminish his dudgeon.

"Sit down an' keep yer trap shut," Cobb said. "Any questions'll come after the lieutenant's done."

"But there are conditions attached," Marc continued, "absolute conditions that must be obeyed to the letter. First, for reasons which have to do with affairs of state and therefore are no concern of yours, Sir Francis Head does not want anyone to learn of Mr. Merriwether's death until Thursday at the earliest. Do not assume that there will be any attempt to protect his assassin: the prime suspect is in custody and I am to submit my report on the investigation at noon tomorrow. The killer will be charged and hanged. Secondly, you are to be confined to your quarters as you have been today, in particular because we cannot take a chance that any stray remark you might make in the tavern or dining-room or elsewhere might give away the secret we are endeavouring to maintain. In a short while, after I have examined the murder scene, Mr. Merriwether's body will be taken out to Mr. Frank's ice-house and kept frozen there until Thursday, when it will be released to the company."

Marc paused to study those before him. There was genuine puzzlement on the faces of the actors and a stoical veneer over the strain and fatigue, but nothing beyond expected curiosity. Thea was signing the information to Jeremiah beside her. Tessa, oddly, looked less strained than any of the others, much of the innocence still aglow in a face designed for it.

"You wish us to present our programs tonight and tomorrow night?" Mrs. Thedford asked, staring at Marc quite intently, it seemed. "We will be happy to do so, as it will provide some relief from the tension and doubt we are now suffering. We also need the funds that such work will bring us."

"Does this mean I must play housekeeper for another two days?" Madge Frank demanded, aghast.

"I'm afraid so, Mrs. Frank, for two reasons: Mr. Merriwether's absence is sure to be noticed and Tessa's room is covered with dried blood. The carpet will have to be removed and burned. But I'm sure the actors will co-operate by doing their own tidying up. They have a bathroom up there and a water-closet. It's mainly their meals we're talking about."

"But Thea hasn't got a room up there, she's been stayin' with us," Frank said on behalf of his wife.

"Mr. Armstrong can move in with Mr. Beasley, and Miss Clarkson can have his room. I want to keep the murder room and Merriwether's empty for the time being. Tessa can bunk in with Mrs. Thedford."

"Now, see here—" Armstrong protested.

"Button yer lip!" Cobb said.

"I ain't emptyin' no chamber pots!" Madge cried.

"What'll I tell my housemaids?" Frank said.

"Tell 'em actors are finicky an' *temper-mental*," Cobb suggested.

"That should do it." Marc smiled.

"There's still a problem, though," Mrs. Thedford said.

"I know," Marc said. "You are due to perform excerpts from Shakespeare tonight, a playbill in which Mr. Merriwether was heavily committed. And tomorrow night you are to repeat the farce, where, again, Mr. Merriwether is not only a principal player but the entire company is required to make it work."

Mrs. Thedford beamed a smile at Marc that discomfited him more than he let on: "You seem intimately acquainted with the ways of the stage."

"I have done some amateur acting years ago in London," Marc said, "and I hung about the wings and back rooms of the summer playhouses and, once or twice, Drury Lane."

"You will know, then, that we are capable, at short notice, of rearranging our playbill."

"I was counting on that, ma'am." Mrs. Thedford made a moue at the word *ma'am*, but Marc continued. "If you could come up with that potpourri or oleo you mentioned earlier, we'll spread the word that Mr. Merriwether is ill and incommunicado and delay the Shakespeare till tomorrow night, then—"

"But I have patrons to think of!" Frank cried, almost rolling off his stool. "I've put notices in the papers an' tacked up handbills everywhere."

"And I'm sorry for that," Marc said. "And I'm sorry you've got a murdered actor upstairs. But you have little choice. I am relaying here the explicit orders of the governor. If you refuse to co-operate, which is your right, then the Bowery Company will be sequestered elsewhere as material witnesses to a crime, and your brand-new theatre will be darkened, leaving your patrons free to speculate on your reliability as an impresario."

"You bastard!" Mrs. Frank exclaimed on behalf of her husband, who winced a smile at her and patted her hand. She jerked it away.

"We'll do whatever Sir Francis requires," Frank said.

"On Wednesday, then," Marc said, leaning forward, "and

this is crucial, the Shakespeare program must go ahead in some fashion."

There was a perplexed pause. "We can most assuredly put together a program of short scenes from Shakespeare using the five remaining members of the company," Mrs. Thedford said, "but they will not have the power that—"

"But you miss my point," Marc said, savouring the drama of the moment. "Sir Francis, for reasons of security that I am not at liberty to reveal, wishes the public not merely to believe that Mr. Merriwether is alive but to observe him in action on Wednesday evening."

"Do you intend to bring Old Hamlet's ghost on stage with us?" Dawson Armstrong snorted.

"Not at all. Jason Merriwether will, to all those in the audience, be performing as usual. But the body inside the costume and the face under the makeup will be mine."

TWELVE

Marc himself supervised the surreptitious removal of Merriwether's corpse. He emptied the trunk in the actor's room of its costumes and, leaving the rifles secure beneath the false bottom, dragged it into the hall. There Jeremiah and Cobb were waiting with the body wrapped tightly in a canvas sheet supplied by Ogden Frank. They squeezed the near-six-foot figure into the five-foot trunk in as dignified a manner as possible, shut the lid, and then locked it with the key Marc had used Monday night.

Wilkie was called up from below to help Cobb and Jeremiah lug it downstairs and through the tavern. Fortunately, while blissfully uncurious and lacking entirely in ambition, Wilkie was as loyal as a spaniel. He simply did as he was bid, happy to be relieved of the tedium of sentry duty. The bar-room was crowded, but the regulars, having witnessed the comings and goings of such trunks since Saturday, paid them little heed. Then, with Marc keeping watch, the trunk was slipped into the small ice-barn behind the stables. Blocks of ice were freed from the straw and chopped up, and the pieces packed around the corpse. Poor Merriwether would keep until Thursday. The ice-house was then padlocked.

Marc and Cobb repaired to the dining-room, where they sought out a quiet table in one corner, ordered a flagon of ale and some cold meat with cheese, and reviewed the events of the day.

"Well, Major, you left them *thisbe-ans* without a word to spout, that's fer sure."

"Do you think I convinced them that I can pull this off?"

"Dunno. But they ain't got a lot of choice, have they?"

"Thanks for the vote of confidence."

Marc had done his best to persuade Mrs. Thedford and the others that, at five foot eleven inches, Merriwether was a man to be noticed; indeed, he had been noticed during the troupe's social activities on the weekend. But Marc was just as tall, with a similar build: muscular without being heavy-set and very wide across the shoulders. Their colouring was roughly the same except for Merriwether's dark eyes, but then Marc would be seen, even by those who might have

dined with the tragedian on Sunday, only as a costumed figure up on a distant stage under flickering candles and above
the glare of footlights, bearded and bewigged. He would
have to make a conscious effort at lowering his voice to the
basso range, but the declamatory style of delivery and exaggerated gesturing currently in vogue would assist in the deception. And Tuesday's announced "illness" would be used
as an excuse to forestall impromptu requests for backstage
visits. It was Mrs. Thedford herself who suggested that the
absence of company members from the environs of the theatre be attributed to the news of a death in her family. Her
fellow actors would naturally go into mourning in deference
to her sorrow.

It had been at this juncture that the only serious question regarding Marc's scheme had been raised by Lieutenant
Spooner from the wings. Could Mr. Edwards actually act and,
if so, could he memorize and sufficiently rehearse his lines
and cues well enough to deceive the playgoers of Toronto? To
that, Marc had replied. "I'll know the answer at dinner-hour
tomorrow." And before he had left to oversee the removal
of the body, Mrs. Thedford said she would put together the
pages of script he would have to learn by rehearsal time at
one o'clock the next afternoon. In the meantime, the actors,
surprisingly animated, set about preparing something to entertain the sophisticates of the colony later in the evening.

"I'll be upstairs while the rehearsal is in progress, having
a close look at Tessa's room and doing a thorough search of

the other rooms. Though any evidence there will likely have been hidden or destroyed," Marc admitted to Cobb.

"Well, they couldn't've taken it very far. Wilkie's kept them cooped up there tighter'n a maiden's purse, an' he tracked Madame Thedford all the way to the dining-room when she went to meet Major Jenkin."

"There are stoves in each room for burning whatever might need to be."

"You could grovel through the ashes."

"If grovelling will help Rick, I'll do it," Marc said, and Cobb, to be polite, chuckled.

AFTER ASSURING HIMSELF THAT THERE WAS no microscopic trail of blood along the hall carpet—a trail that would have led him to the killer's room—Marc went to Tessa's door. The wax plug, replaced by Cobb after he had removed the body, had not been dislodged or tampered with. The room was as they had left it last night, minus Merriwether's remains.

The beige carpet had acted like a blotter, recording each spill of blood in blurred but indelible outline. The position of the body, on its back with legs splayed, was thus limned except for the head area. There a ghoulish brown ripple indicated where the skull had been smashed and bled thickly. The slash in the carpet where Rick's sword had stuck in the wood below was clearly visible, surrounded by a dark crimson parabola.

What interested Marc much more, however, were the smudges between the feet of the corpse and the settee about eight feet away near the window overlooking Colborne Street. According to the corroborated testimony of Beasley, Rick was standing over the corpse, holding the sword in his hands. Presumably, his jacket, breeches, and boots had been sprayed with blood from the victim's still-pumping heart, and in order for it to have got all over Rick's hands and the haft of his sword, he would have had either to bend down and immerse himself in it or to rub it all over himself in some sort of ritual triumph. Neither act befitted the man he knew as Rick Hilliard.

But the smudges between corpse and settee, indicative of footprints, however indistinct, were very curious indeed. They had been made by a boot, though the size and nature could not be determined. Without question, however, they went in only one direction: from the settee to the corpse. Only toe-prints were unambiguously visible and he could find none of them pointing the other way, though there were, to be sure, enough random smudges here and there to make any firm conclusion problematic. Beasley and the police had regrettably contaminated the scene while the blood was still fresh. Still, if Rick had done the deed, he would have had to rise from the settee at Tessa's cry, knock the villain down, and skewer him—after which he would have been more or less bloodied, especially around the boots. Then, presumably, he had staggered to the settee, where there were blood-smears on the edge of the seat. The killer had sat down: two fully outlined boot-prints and a palm-print attested to that. Why? To savour his murderous act? Weather the aftershock? Suffer remorse? Whatever the reason, this pause could have lasted mere seconds because when Beasley arrived—say, two minutes after Tessa's cry— Rick was already back over the body and was still there when Mrs. Thedford and Jeremiah appeared on the scene.

Looking now at these toe-prints, one must conclude that Rick had staggered backwards after being bloodied, then staggered forward again, leaving more prints in the same direction. Possible, Marc thought, but not probable. There just didn't seem to be enough prints to satisfy this inter- pretation. And as far as he could make out, the backward staggering depicted here did not resemble the way any man would actually have done it: the print-pattern was simply too regular. Moreover, Rick had told him that the first thing he remembered upon waking was noticing blood on his tunic. If that were true, and Marc believed it was, then Rick would have struck and stabbed Merriwether while un- conscious and with no memory of either act. Besides which, Rick's jacket had seemed to Marc, when he had examined it closely last night, to be too free of splashes and splatter. The smeared patterns were inconsistent with spouting blood. What that portended he could not guess. All he knew was that, despite the contrary eyewitness testimony, there was reason to doubt that Rick Hilliard had committed murder.

Until he could come up with a more plausible alternative, however, he recognized that he had little chance of convincing the governor or the magistrates of Rick's innocence.

MARC NOW BEGAN TO SEARCH THE other rooms. He opened each actor's trunk, finding no more false bottoms, went through the pockets, sleeves, and cuffs of every costume, and sifted through any ash left in a stove. Merriwether, Armstrong, and Beasley had obviously not lit fires yesterday evening, so that only a residual ash remained from fires earlier on the weekend. And nothing was to be found there beyond the ash itself. Mrs. Thedford, however, had put on a small fire in her parlour room, and as Marc rummaged about he did find several charred bits of what appeared to be linen paper or the cloth cover of a book. At the moment, though, he could find nothing sinister in the discovery. Mrs. Thedford would have many papers, playbills, script pamphlets, cue cards, and the like as part of her business. What he was searching for specifically was the container for the laudanum that had been poured into Tessa's sherry decanter, even if it had been shattered into shards. Chances were it was somewhere on this floor. He even opened Mrs. Thedford's perfume bottles and sniffed, precipitating several sneezes but no clue. He picked up a candlestick and shoved a forefinger up the hollow stem of it. No vial there.

Discouraged, Marc went back out into the hall. He put himself in Merriwether's shoes for a moment: he waits till the others have gone down for supper or later perhaps when they've headed for their cramped dressing-rooms to put on makeup. Then he slips across to Tessa's room, vial in hand, pours the contents into the decanter, and slips out again. He can't very well leave the vial there, and he would not be foolish enough to hide it in his own room lest something go awry with his plan. But where else? Maybe he had taken it down to the theatre with him; Marc would have to search the dressing-rooms at least.

It was then that he noticed the ornamental spittoon sitting near Armstrong's door. It was not used as a spittoon up here, but its brass filigree, when polished, would gleam handsomely. Gingerly, Marc pressed his right hand into the narrow opening and down into the wider body of the piece. He struck sand. Frank had probably filled it with sand to act as ballast. Wriggling two fingers, Marc managed to delve down far enough to strike something harder than sand. Seconds later he drew out a glass apothecary bottle, its stopper in place. He turned it upside down and there, on the bottom, in very tiny type, he read: *Michaels*. Ezra Michaels operated a chemist's shop near the corner of King and Toronto Streets. And while this empty unlabelled bottle didn't guarantee that the laudanum had come from Michaels, containers often being re-used, it strongly suggested that the narcotic had been purchased somewhere in the capital.

Marc sighed. If only he had found the vial in Merri-wether's room. It could have been placed out here by any-one—including Rick. However, if it had been purchased at Michaels's, there would likely be a record of the sale and perhaps even a physical description of the buyer. Old Michaels, he knew, boasted that he never forgot a face. He would put Cobb onto this immediately. Remembering a pencil sketch of the actor, out of costume, on Merriwether's desk, Marc returned to retrieve it. He would have Cobb take it to Michaels and, if necessary, to every apothecary and quack homeopath in the city. He might not be able to prove Rick was innocent of murder, but he'd be damned if he'd let the young man go to the gallows as a rapist.

WHEN MARC CAME DOWN TO RELIEVE Cobb and send him off to make the rounds of the chemists, the rehearsal for the impromptu evening ahead was in full swing. Marc took up a stool and sat unobtrusively in the wings to watch. He had little fear that any one of the five actors would suddenly decide to sprint to the double-doors at the front of the the-atre, fling back the bar, and make a run for it down Colborne Street.

On the stage in front of him, illumined only by a single, half-lit chandelier, stood Dawson Armstrong in top hat and tails, surrounded by the three women in old-fashioned bonnets and Beasley, with a carter's cap on his head. They

were in the midst of a dramatized reading of Cowper's "The
Diverting History of John Gilpin." Armstrong, as the hapless Gilpin, who cannot control the horse he's borrowed to
ride with his wife and family to their seaside holiday spot,
was miming to perfection the struggle and strain of the runaway, even while he narrated the tale. The chorus around
him added the comic commentary of his wife and various
bystanders. The whole thing was highly professional and
very funny. Certainly, in a town where runaway horses and
wagons were not infrequent, this piece should go over well
tonight. Marc himself was impressed by the intensity of
concentration that these five managed after the trials of the
past fifteen hours, but only Jeremiah had noticed his arrival,
offering a brief smile of welcome. When "John Gilpin" came
to its risible conclusion, Marc announced his presence by
clapping out his approval.

Mrs. Thedford turned, caught his eye, and said with
amusement, "I hope those watching this evening are so
easily entertained." Then, addressing the others, she said,
"Dawson, I think you didn't come in quite soon enough
at 'The dinner waits, and we are tired.' Your response here
should draw the biggest laugh of the piece, so we don't want
to mistime it."

They re-did the middle section of the poem, agreed
among themselves that it was improved if not perfect, then
Mrs. Thedford said, "Tessa and I will now do 'Lenore.'" Jeremiah stepped smartly forward with several bits of costume
for the next number. Tessa, pale but remarkably composed,

shook out her blond curls, draped a gossamer wrap over her bare shoulders, and sank to the floor in a lifeless pose. Mrs. Thedford donned a black lace shawl that covered her head and shoulders. Staring sorrowfully at the still, beautiful form at her feet, she began to recite one of the most haunting laments Marc had ever heard. Who the poet was he had no idea, but the grief of the speaker for the dead Lenore was agonizingly real:

> See! On yon drear and rigid bier low lies thy love, Le-
> nore,
> Come! Let the burial rite be read—the funeral song be
> sung!—
> An anthem for the queenliest dead that ever died so
> young—
> A dirge for her doubly dead in that she died so young.
> By you—by yours, the evil eye—by yours, the slander-
> ous tongue
> That did to death the innocence that died, and died so
> young.

Then, partway through, the sobbing diminuendos of a violin joined the grieved speaker, and Marc tore his gaze from the heartwrenching scene of woman and girl to glance over and see Clarence Beasley with the instrument under his chin. Tears welled up in the woman's eyes as the poem neared its mournful conclusion:

The life upon her yellow hair but not within her
eyes—
The life still there, upon her hair—the death upon her
eyes.

Marc felt the surge of his own emotion catch in his throat,
and realized he had been thinking of Uncle Jabez and the
sister lost to him forever. Just as Mrs. Thedford recited
the final phrase, she sank to her knees with the grace of a
swan settling over her eggs while Tessa simultaneously rose
through the gauze of her garment till she was almost sitting
up. Freeze. Tableau. Music fades. Finis.

No one moved. For a full minute all thoughts drifted inward. The ghost of Jason Merriwether was palpable.

"Well, it's time to liven things up a little," Armstrong
said in a voice clear, strong, and uncontaminated by drink.
He signed something towards Jeremiah, and the black man
grinned and went over to the far wings. In the shadows there
was a pile of what Marc had taken to be scenery-flats covered
by a piece of sailcloth. Jeremiah whipped this cover away to
reveal, not a stack of flats, but a gleaming pianoforte, which
he began to push out onto the stage. Well, Marc thought, no
wonder Ogden Frank had scratched himself bald worrying
about the future of his investment. But who would play the
instrument?

It was Dawson Armstrong who sat down before it on a
stool and struck a thundering introductory chord. "Ready,
ladies?"

The three women came down to the footlights. With
Tessa between Mrs. Thedford and Thea Clarkson, they
linked arms. Then, to Armstrong's zestful accompaniment,
they entertained Marc, enthralled him really, for the next
twenty minutes with a series of trios, duets, and naughty
ditties from *The Beggar's Opera*, mixing male and female
roles willy-nilly. Mrs. Thedford sang in the rich alto range,
throaty and vibrant; Tessa's note was descant, tremulously
sweet. Thea's voice was contralto, haunted and rippled with
the shadow of longing and regret. The latter concluded this
set with a solo, an aria in Italian about the heroine's sorrow at the loss of her lover. That was all that Marc could
decipher, but there was little need for lyrics here: Thea's
voice, her posture, and the sonority of the song itself were
sufficient. How she contrived to complete it in such circumstance Marc did not know, but he hoped that somehow the
effort was cathartic. When she finished, the women curt-
seyed and the four men applauded.

Without warning or ado, Armstrong now banged out a
single cacophonous chord. Beasley and the women retreated
to a bench upstage. Then Jeremiah Jefferson, barefoot and
stripped to the waist, leapt into stage-centre. From the pianoforte there now came a steady, rhythmic beat from the
lowest keys only, a cadence somewhat like the panic of a
heartbeat but not quite, for there was the thump of bravery
and bravado in it and an intimation of the erotic.

Under the chandelier's flickering cast, Jeremiah's skin
glistened as the muscles beneath tightened and released

in response to the primal obbligato of the music. His eyes were closed and his whole face upturned as if anticipating a benediction of rain. But it was the legs and bare feet that fascinated. Their dance was so intricate, so alien, so intrinsically staccato that it was impossible to tell whether it was animated by the piano's beat or was simply a coincidental and parallel harmony. As the rhythm-thrums progressed in intensity and dissonance, Jeremiah's feet became a gray blur, sweat shimmered and shook free, both eyes were wide open and gazed sightless before the music stopped in mid-beat and his body froze as if it were abruptly bronzed.

"Wonderful, wonderful," Mrs. Thedford said to him as all the tension in him was instantly relaxed and he became Jeremiah Jefferson, escaped slave, once again. She signed her pleasure as well, and he smiled his acceptance of her approval.

"But how can he hear the music?" Marc said to Beasley, who was nearest him. "He's deaf."

"Oh," Beasley said, "he can feel the vibrations, especially if the notes are low."

"I've never seen or heard anything like that."

"Then you've never spent any time in the United States," Beasley said.

Mrs. Thedford came over to Marc and handed him a sheaf of papers. "We're all through here now, Mr. Edwards. We're going up to rest before supper and the show at eight thirty. I've put together, in sequence, the scripts for tomorrow with your parts marked."

"With all this ahead of me, I won't have time to attend the performance this evening, so I am glad I was able to sit in on your rehearsal."

"We look forward to your being part of it tomorrow." Again, she kept her gaze steadily upon him. He could feel in it an intense curiosity and something much more ambivalent and inaccessible. It unnerved him.

"Cobb will look after you when I leave shortly," he stammered.

"I find that immensely comforting," she said with an enigmatic smile.

When the actors had withdrawn, Marc sat on the vacant stage, waiting for Cobb and staring out at the vast space where a hundred or more spectators would be scrutinizing his every twitch and stutter when he made his debut as Jason Merriwether. But his overriding concern at this moment was not the distinct possibility of stage-fright or being prematurely unmasked but, rather, a simple question: How could any one of the people he had just observed in the fullness of their generous talent have committed a brutal murder? And if not one of them, then who?

COBB ARRIVED HALF AN HOUR LATER.

"Did you get to Michaels?" Marc asked at once.

"Good day to you, too," Cobb said, staring at the pianoforte. "We gonna have some song an' dance?"

"Yes. And since I will be at Mrs. Standish's boarding-house memorizing a dozen pages of script tonight, you'll have the pleasure of humming along with it here this evening. You might want to bring Mrs. Cobb—I'm sure I can arrange for a box seat."

"I'll have her get the family gems outta storage."

"What did you find out at the chemist's?"

"Several vials of laudanum were bought there last Saturd'y afternoon by people Michaels didn't know."

"Did you show Ezra the sketch of Merriwether?"

"Yup. But Merriwether wasn't one of 'em."

"Damn. Did you get a look at any of the buyers' names?"

"I did. An' one of them was very familiar. Hang on to yer hat, Major: it was Thea Clarkson."

"My God." Marc had not been prepared for that information.

"Want me to haul her down here? Yer idea that she might've been teamed up with somebody to do the cheater in seems *applause-able* now, don't it?"

"Yes. But I'm going to wait until morning before confronting her. I can't take any chance on disturbing the equanimity of the troupe before the performance tonight. And I'm even reluctant to do so in the morning: this ruse we're attempting must not be compromised."

Cobb sighed. "I think you're more afraid of a rebellion in this province than Sir Francis Swell-Head himself."

"Well, at least it looks now as if we'll be able to

demonstrate that Rick didn't drug Tessa in order to have his way with her. What possible connection could there be between Rick and Thea Clarkson?"

"I'm sure that knowin' the world don't consider him a despoiler of virgins will give the lad a lot of comfort as the noose tightens 'round his gullet."

Marc ignored the remark. "It's still possible that Merriwether bought his own laudanum."

"Possible. Michaels ain't the only chemist in town, just the richest."

"It would be so helpful if I could make a direct link between the drugged sherry and Merriwether. Keep looking, will you?"

"In my spare time, ya mean?"

"Whenever you can. Please."

"You headed to yer old boarding-house, then?"

"Yes. Have Wilkie return to guard duty, then go home to your good wife for a few hours."

"She'll be thrilled."

MARC HAD LIVED AT WIDOW STANDISH'S boarding-house for the six exciting months he had worked at Government House in the service of Sir Francis Head. He had been happily mothered by Mrs. Standish and coddled by her live-in maid-servant, Maisie. He knew he would be welcomed there without question or comment. Moreover, he would have a quiet place to learn his lines and begin to think about the report on the murder he was to present to the governor at noon.

Right now he wanted very much to walk all the way up to Government House on Simcoe Street and visit Rick. But he had so little in the way of good news, he felt he would most likely leave Rick more anxious and depressed than he already was. At least Cobb had got a message to him that Tessa was fine and concerned about him. But Marc would certainly demand to see him before completing his report. If Spooner had not requested a written statement from Rick, then he would get one himself, though he knew Rick well enough to realize that his initial account would be unchanged. However, some small detail overlooked might well prove to be the missing piece to the puzzle. To this point his own investigation had done little but suggest that only three people were in that room when Tessa's cry started a chain-reaction of events and that, short of a massive conspiracy, the window of opportunity for anyone else to have committed the crime and escape undetected was about two minutes.

Since he had to pass Aunt Catherine's shop on his way westward to Peter Street, Marc decided to stop in and say hello. He felt a stab of guilt as he walked through the alley that led to the back door and the stairs up to her apartment. Not only was the wedding set for a week from Sunday in Cobourg, but Aunt Catherine and Beth were now plotting the fine details and, at the very least, he was expected to show some interest and give nominal approval. Daily letters could now be expected. He should have been free to participate fully in the exchange and, further, should have been allowed the luxury of leisure hours to dream, anticipate, and indulge his fondest fantasies.

Beth had insisted they not worry in advance over insurmountable obstacles or impossible decisions. Thus they had not yet worked out where they would set up house other than that Beth would remain with Aunt Catherine and entertain conjugal visits whenever Marc's normally insignificant duties let him loose from the garrison. Only when "things settled down," in Aunt Catherine's polite phrase, would they turn their attention to the question of whether Beth would move into officers' quarters with him or whether they would rent or buy a house he could only occupy intermittently. And the spectre of his being transferred to the Caribbean or India or Van Diemen's Land was not acknowledged at any level.

Hearing a footstep on the back stairs, Aunt Catherine bustled in from the shop. "Oh, it's you, Marc! I was expecting George back."

Marc was quite happy to miss the sullen George Revere.

"Come on upstairs, I've got news from Beth."

Marc wanted to ask "good or bad?" but dutifully followed Beth's aunt up to her parlour, where she fetched a freshly opened letter from the mantel. She smiled broadly, then looked a mite sheepish.

"Beth has ordered me to confess to a little conniving behind your back."

"For my own good, I assume?"

"I couldn't put it any better. But since you've done nothing but dither about arrangements for a honeymoon—using
that god-awful army of yours as an excuse—we've gone
ahead and done it ourselves."

"A month in New York or London?"

Aunt Catherine laughed, quite at ease now and more
certain than ever that her niece had found a man to match
her own spirit and particular humours. "Three days and four
nights at Sword's Hotel on Front Street—the bill to be sent
to me."

Marc was touched. "That is more than kind," he said.

"Well, it isn't Paris, but at least you won't spend your
honeymoon being interrupted by the silly chatter of seamstresses and the loud complaints of over-indulged dowagers
looking for the perfect hat!"

"May I see Beth's letter?"

"Certainly. And you'll see there that you and your bride
are booked on the mail packet out of Cobourg that'll get you
to Toronto before supper time. Now I've got to get back to
the shop. Can you stay for a meal?"

"I've got a lot of work that can't wait. Sorry."

"No need to be. Drop in tomorrow if you can." With that
she headed down the stairs. "Ah, George," he heard her say,
"just take those things right through to the girls."

Marc read eagerly through Beth's letter, written several days after her last one but, not surprisingly given the state of the mail service, nearly overlapping it. He was searching for the slightest negative remark, but the only one that even remotely qualified was a reference to Thomas Goodall's depression over the low commodity prices tempered, Beth assured him, by the healthy progress of Baby Mary and the decision that they had just taken to store their grain and wait for better prices in the spring. According to Beth, the cash they had received from the army as a result of Marc's visit in March and Owen Jenkin's generosity had made the decision possible. Hence, the chances of Thomas, Winnifred, and child pulling up stakes and rushing off to the edge of the earth beyond the Mississippi had been temporarily forestalled. All the other news was upbeat, some of it bordering on the naughty, the letter ending thus: "Auntie, stop reading here. Darling, I long to be in your arms, anywhere but most especially in bed. I count the days and the hours therein. Be well. Your loving wife-to-be, Beth."

Marc found himself trembling. It was actually going to happen. And that knowledge immediately gave him the strength he knew he would need to face the morrow.

THIRTEEN

When Mrs. Standish and Maisie ceased fussing over him, Marc retired to his former room and opened the package of scripts that Mrs. Thedford had given him to study. All three of his scene-sequences were with Mrs. Thedford, which simplified any rehearsal required, and left the rest of the cast and their contributions more or less intact. First up were the two excerpts from *Macbeth* wherein Lady Macbeth tries to drive her waffling mate towards the assassination of King Duncan, followed by the murder scene and its aftermath. These scenes had not been rehearsed yesterday but were obviously ones that Mrs. Thedford and Merriwether had performed often. Next up was a series of excerpts from *Antony and Cleopatra*, cleverly selected, edited, and sequenced to trace the tempestuous affair from its inception to final farewells, concluding with Cleopatra's suicide at stage-centre. Lastly, there was the closet-scene in *Hamlet* where Hamlet beards and upbraids his mother.

Marc was puzzled by this selection because Merriwether was famous for his role as King Claudius, not the younger Hamlet, usually played by Beasley. Hamlet's role here had been clearly assigned to Marc, but as far as he could tell from the program notes scribbled hastily by Mrs. Thedford, in the other scenes from the play surrounding this one, Beasley would take his customary role and Armstrong would do Claudius. Besides being an unusual and potentially confusing arrangement, it seemed to Marc to be exceedingly risky since, as Hamlet, he would be beardless and made up to look like the young man he actually was. The odds of someone in the audience recognizing him or guessing that this Hamlet was not the forty-five-year-old Merriwether were surely increased. But he had little choice. His morning would be taken up with interviewing Thea about the laudanum, writing a report for Sir Francis, and talking to Rick before handing it in. So he sat himself down and began to commit the Bard's iambics to memory.

At ten o'clock the next morning, with his report sketched out and under his arm, Marc slipped past Ogden Frank into the empty taproom. He opened the door to the theatre, startled Wilkie awake, and asked him to bring Thea Clarkson down to the hotel dining-room. Moments later, Thea, Wilkie, and Cobb arrived simultaneously. Wilkie scuttled back to his sentry post. Marc mouthed the word *laudanum* at Cobb, who shook his head slowly. Marc then turned to Thea, who looked very nervous, wondering no doubt what new calamity was about to strike. He got right to the point. "We have discovered, Miss Clarkson, that you purchased a quantity of laudanum from Ezra Michaels's shop on King Street last Saturday afternoon."

Thea went white, then red. She stared at the table and said nothing.

"As you know, Tessa Guildersleeve and Ensign Hilliard were drugged with laudanum. The empty bottle, which is unquestionably the one you purchased, was found in the hall upstairs near Tessa's room. We know you couldn't have committed the murder yourself, but as the supplier of the drug, you must be considered—"

"I had nothing to do with that!" she cried. "Nothing! Why are you doing this to me?" She laid her head in her arms and wept wearily.

"All we need to know," Marc said soothingly, "is whether you have any plausible explanation for why you purchased laudanum last Saturday."

Thea's tears slowed and stopped. Summoning her strength, she raised her head and faced her tormentors. "I bought the laudanum in order to kill myself."

"I don't understand," Marc said lamely.

"I'm carrying Jason's child, and the bastard refused to marry me. He wasn't even man enough to admit it was his." Her voice was thin, but very cold.

"But you couldn't go through with it."

"I would've," she said. "But when I got back here, I found I'd lost the stuff somewhere. You can believe me or not. I don't give a damn anymore."

"Oh, I believe you," Marc said. Cobb could only look at him in astonishment.

WHEN THEA HAD BEEN PUT INTO the solicitous care of Madge Frank, where she was to remain for the time being, Cobb lit up his pipe and said to Marc, "You sure she didn't just happen to drop that *loud-numb* near somebody who didn't like Merriwether any more'n her?"

"What I think is that Thea Clarkson is much more likely to harm herself than anyone else. What we know for certain, though, is that we still have a vial of laudanum unaccounted for."

"She could've dropped it anywheres between here an' Michaels's place."

Marc sighed. "And there's still no way to link it to Merriwether himself. By the by, did you and Mrs. Cobb enjoy the performance last night?"

"Yes, we did, though I kept thinkin' I was gonna fall outta that apple-box an' land on somebody I oughtn't to!

But them Yankees can sure sing an' dance! I figured Missus Cobb's foot-tappin' would wake the dead at Lundy's Lane!"

"Well, I want you up there again this evening, and Dora, too, if she so wishes. I want you as my eyes and ears in the theatre proper. I'll assign Wilkie to watch the dressing-room area."

"Even if we manage to fool the traitors inta believin' you're Merriwether, how're you gonna know where an' when they'll get a message to you about a *round-a-view?*"

"That's the Achilles' heel of my plan, I'm afraid. But the rebels or whoever they are know the guns are here in Toronto, and they believe for now that Merriwether is alive and waiting for the second message: they'll deliver it all right. I've just got to be alert enough to recognize it when it comes."

"You gonna take that report up to the governor?"

"Yes, but I'm going to see Rick first. There has to be some detail he's forgotten: I've got to try and help him recall it."

"I better come with ya."

They slipped out the back entrance to Frank's quarters into the alley there.

"You don't haveta come to supper, ya know," Cobb said. "You got more'n enough on yer plate as it is."

"I wouldn't miss it for the world."

Set back from King Street among the autumn vermilion and gold of maple trees and with its cozy gables, its homely chimney-pots and rambling verandahs, Government House looked more like the estate of a country squire dozing in the Dorset sun than it did the seat of power and nerve-centre of a troubled British colony. The duty-corporal recognized Marc and led him and Cobb into the foyer.

"Where are they keeping Hilliard?" Marc asked.

"In the old pantry at the back, sir," the corporal replied, then added in a lower voice, "but it ain't locked."

"Good. Cobb, would you mind waiting here with the corporal? When I'm finished with Rick, I'd like you to accompany me when I present this report to the governor. Your corroboration will be helpful."

"I c'n manage the 'helpful' part," Cobb said, and the corporal smiled.

It was now about eleven o'clock. Before leaving the theatre, Marc had gone upstairs with Cobb and reviewed with each of the actors a written summary of the testimony they had made to him during the interviews on Tuesday morning. He then had each sign the document, with Cobb as witness. Marc knew he wasn't a surrogate justice of the peace, but he needed the semblance of notarized legality if he were to lay out for Sir Francis the apparent scenario of the murder and then point out the anomalies, such as they were. (Thea had been resting and so was excused, but since Cobb had been present during both interviews with her, Marc was not concerned.) He had hoped to have linked Merriwether to the laudanum, but that was now a lost cause. Though the villain most likely had found or purloined it from his distraught mistress, there was no proof of this. Marc realized also that, distracted as he was by the gunrunning business and the deteriorating situation in Quebec, Sir Francis would not give Rick Hilliard's case his usual close attention. Rick would simply have to help himself.

"And where do you think you're going?" Lieutenant Spooner had popped out of his office next to the governor's and sprung to a quivering halt in front of Marc.

"I have a report to deliver to Sir Francis, after which we have details to work out regarding this evening."

"Well, then, I will be happy to accept your report on behalf of the governor."

"I must hand it to Sir Francis in person, Lieutenant. There are additional explanations and comments that are necessary to his full understanding of the situation."

"Be that as it may, Lieutenant, you will not be able to see the governor today. He's gone down to the Legislature for emergency meetings with the Executive and the Legislative Council. You have no choice but to give the report to me. Moreover, I have been placed in charge of tonight's operation."

Marc was not prepared for this. While he knew Sir Francis had never forgiven him for what he took to be a personal betrayal, he also knew that the governor liked to be informed directly of matters that concerned him and would, despite everything, be willing to accept Marc's word in regard to statements of fact and reasoned judgements. "All right, then," he said graciously, suppressing his rising anxiety, "I'll give it to you just as soon as I have interviewed Ensign Hilliard. His testimony was given while he was in a state of exhaustion and not yet recovered from having been drugged. It would be unfair to him, and improper of me, not to have him corroborate my notes."

"Oh, I don't think anything as elaborate as that will be necessary," Spooner said with a smug smile.

"Are you refusing me access to him?"

"No, you may see him anytime you like." The smirk oozed and widened. "And you may put any gloss you wish upon the ensign's actions; it won't matter a fig."

Marc felt a sudden alarm. "What in hell do you mean, sir?"

Spooner, who had been teetering heel to toe with hands locked behind his back for balance, now brought the latter into view. In his right hand he held an official-looking document. "I have here an affidavit, duly signed and notarized just minutes ago before Magistrate Thorpe."

"An affidavit signed by whom?"

"By your Ensign Hilliard, of course. Who else?"

"You interviewed him without my permission? Sir Francis put me in charge of the investigation, not you."

"I didn't say boo to him. I didn't need to. He called me in and asked for a magistrate."

"That's not possible." But, of course, it was.

"It seems our young swain was materially moved after his visit with that little trollop from the theatre."

Marc heard Cobb gasp behind him. "Tessa?" he asked, dumbfounded.

"She came flying in here a short while ago, wide-eyed and demanding to see the man who had tried to save her from a fate worse than . . . whatever. What could I do? My heart is not made of stone. I let her have a few minutes alone with him. Then I had her escorted back to the theatre: you must have passed her en route." Spooner was enjoying himself immensely.

"You had no authority to do so!"

"Perhaps not, but I doubt very much if Sir Francis will quarrel with the result of my decision."

Marc knew Hilliard well and was not surprised when Spooner delivered the coup de grâce. "He signed a confession. It's all over."

Marc's furious glare rocked Spooner back on his heels, but he gave no further ground. "I still want to see him." Marc struggled to control the anger building in him: this was no time to lose his composure.

"If you attempt in any way to have Hilliard withdraw his sworn statement or otherwise obstruct the course of justice, sir, I'll have you court-martialled."

"Are you questioning my honour, sir?"

Spooner took a step back, the flush of triumph fading from his face: images of a foggy meadow at dawn, pistols poised, and "seconds" holding their breath flitted before him. "Go in there and do as you like, then. It won't matter. He's finished. And then present yourself in my office—without your henchman. We have more important business to discuss."

IF MARC HAD EXPECTED TO FIND his friend haggard and anxious after his ordeal, he was soon disappointed. Rick was sitting on a stool in the windowless room reading what appeared to be a novel by the light of a single candle. When Marc entered, Rick looked up and grinned a welcome that might have been meant for the happy arrival of a delinquent brother. "Marc, I'm so glad you've come. The most wonderful thing has just happened, and I need to tell it to the world!" He was beaming. The lines and pouches deposited on his face from two sleepless nights and endless hours of unceasing worry had been drawn into the service of a smile that, however transitory, was nonetheless genuine.

"What in Christ's name have you done?" Marc said before he could stop himself.

"I told you she was an angel, didn't I? Did you see her leaving?"

"You've as good as written your signature on a gibbet," Marc said, still boiling, "and I've been working my balls into a sweat over you for the last thirty-six hours."

Rick looked wounded, but rallied instantly with another

ingratiating and infuriating smile. "But I killed him to save her, don't you see?" The smile turned beatific.

"Are you telling me that you now have remembered smashing Merriwether on the skull and driving your sword through his chest while he lay stunned and helpless on his back?"

"I have no memory of doing either. But I must have, mustn't I?"

"Then, for the love of God, tell me what you *do* remember."

"I've put it all down in the affidavit."

"Humour me." Marc's emotions were oscillating between anger and fear, and he fought to keep his mind clear and focussed on the task ahead.

"As I told you Monday night in the tavern, I fell asleep on the settee with my flies open. When I woke up, I felt something sticky all over me, like blood."

"You couldn't see it?"

"Not till I stood up in the moonlight."

"Beasley swore he saw some light coming from the doorway."

"Well, I think the little candle on Tessa's night-table was still lit, but I was staring straight ahead at what I had done."

So much for that discrepancy. "But how do you *know* you did it if you have no recollection of it? Could you stab someone so forcefully and have no inkling that you'd done it?"

"Ah, but I'd been drugged, Marc. I was confused. Some

part of my brain must have seen that blackguard on top of my darling and brought me strength enough to smash him on the head with my sword-butt and then—this is what I wrote in the affidavit—I must've seen what he'd done to her and gone a bit crazy. But I was under the influence of the opiate, you see, and my motive was the purest one that any gentleman could have had."

Looking into the guileless and callow face of his young friend, Marc recognized that Rick was assuming he would be released eventually because of the laudanum and the chivalric impulse behind the homicidal deed. "Neither of those defenses will stand up for one minute in a court. You must face the truth, Rick. I know: I've studied the law. And unless you recant and withdraw your confession immediately, using Tessa's visit to explain your quixotic behaviour, your affidavit alone will propel you straight into the hangman's noose."

Rick peered up at Marc, suddenly serious. "I don't wish to die, unless it's in battle. But other than that kind of noble death, to die defending the honour of an innocent is surely a close second." Rick's eyes lit up again, pulling the sagging flesh of his face with them. "And you weren't here, Marc, you didn't see her, you didn't hear her. She got down on her knees and thanked me from the bottom of her heart. She said I would live there forever. She wept for me—oh, they were the most beautiful tears of love and gratitude! And when she left, she gave me her favourite book to read and cherish. Look at the inscription. Is it not the most moving poetry you've ever read?" Rick held out the book and quoted from the inscribed flyleaf: "To my darling hero, Rick Hilliard; yours forever, Tessa."

Marc noticed the title on the spine: *Ivanhoe* by Sir Walter Scott. He wasn't surprised. He needed something sharp, cruel even, to shock Hilliard—the normally intelligent and ambitious ensign—back to reality. "You realize, Rick, that Spooner has suggested to Sir Francis that it was you who drugged Tessa for your own nefarious purpose and then savagely murdered Merriwether when he intervened? And so far, I have not been able to find evidence to wholly refute the charge. You will be hanged as a rapist and a killer, not as a hero out of the pages of Scott or Malory."

Rick took this in. "The corporal told me about Spooner's theory. But Sir Francis knows me: he'll never believe a story like that. And with my confession, why would he bother anyway?"

"Because Merriwether is an American citizen. It just might suit Sir Francis's political interests at present to have the American made the victim."

"But he painted them all as Antichrists during the election!"

"That was then. Right now the governor may be more concerned to keep the U.S. government from financing the local rebels he sees under every bush." Marc was improvising this argument as he presented it, but he had to do something, even if it was underhanded.

"I'll take my chances on that score. Besides, I have Tessa's judgement here in writing, and I'll take the sight of her clutching my knees and weeping for me to my grave."

While Tessa herself will be on the steamer for Detroit tomorrow afternoon, Marc thought, but knew better than to try to tarnish the saint's halo in the eyes of the idolater. Instead, he turned and left without another word. Spooner was right. It was finished.

MARC ASKED COBB TO RETURN TO the theatre and make sure that Tessa was there. Wilkie was due for a tongue-lashing, but there was little point in chastising the girl or her warder: the damage had been done, and Hilliard was, after all, the author of his own fate.

Marc then spent one of the most difficult half-hours he could remember in the service of his country. He and Spooner had to establish the ground rules for their attempt to ensnare the rebels in quest of Yankee rifles. Spooner began by admitting that he had surreptitiously placed a watch on the storage-shed and ice-house. While Marc was annoyed that such a move might already have alerted the rebels to the presence of the military and thus spooked them, he grudgingly accepted the necessity of ensuring that the guns were not simply carted off. Spooner wanted to surround the theatre with troops and have mounted officers nearby, but Marc convinced him to have both groups at least a block away and well hidden. An agent secreted in the loft of the livery stable, with Frank's help, would be able to observe both sheds, the rear entrance to Frank's quarters, and the alley beside the tavern. A second agent could be hidden in a market-stall directly across the road with a view of the tavern-entrance and of Colborne Street in front of the theatre.

If and when contact had been made, word would be relayed by Cobb or Wilkie to Spooner, who would be in the audience and remain in the pit after the play was over. Because they did not know when or how the contact would be made, much had to be left to chance. If there was no time for Marc to consult or relay details, a small group of mounted officers was to follow Marc to any rendezvous, maintaining a safe distance, since the rebels would be very wary of being caught or betrayed. Marc would be unarmed— to Spooner's horror—because he was certain to be searched and wanted nothing to frighten off the plotters. He stressed, with only moderate success, that his principal task was to try to identify them, not capture them. They could be rounded up easily, but only if the ruse was complete and undetected. Spooner provided Marc with a canvas tote-bag for the two rifles—to be secretly marked—which he was planning to take as bait. The exchange of even one dollar for the sample would constitute high treason. The two men nodded agreement, and Marc left for the theatre, determined to get at least one thing right before the day ended.

• • •

As both he and Cobb had been doing all day, Marc slipped into Frank's place through the back door because Marc's exceptional height and distinctive tunic made him an easily recalled figure, as did Cobb's uniform and eccentric profile. If the rebels were keeping an eye on the theatre and hotel, then the frequent arrivals and departures of officers would have raised more than suspicion. Of course, if the rebels had engaged one or more of Frank's stable boys to act as scouts, then the jig was up anyway. He would only know for sure sometime this evening when "Jason Merriwether" hit the boards with his inimitable presence and panache.

FOURTEEN

The rehearsal went much more smoothly than Marc had anticipated. Mrs. Thedford had arranged that only those actually involved in the scenes shared by her and Marc be present: that meant Dawson Armstrong, who delivered the famous "barge" speech describing Cleopatra, cleverly placed at the beginning of the sequence, and Thea Clarkson, who played Charmian, the great queen's confidante, in the death-by-asp scene at the end. For most of the two hours they spent together, Marc and Annemarie Thedford were alone on the Regency stage. The other scenes in the program, well rehearsed on Monday afternoon, had been reviewed earlier for any changes necessitated by the star's absence and the cast was then sent upstairs to rest.

They'd begun with *Antony and Cleopatra*. As Cleopatra, Mrs. Thedford seated herself upon a low stool near the unlit footlights. Antony was to stand off to her left and gaze soulfully at her as Enobarbus (Armstrong) introduced the Egyptian queen to him and to the audience. Armstrong had barely begun when Marc felt a chill run up his spine. Without costume or makeup, Mrs. Thedford had transformed herself into the figure described by the Bard's poetry. Moreover, it seemed to Marc that many of the phrases described Mrs. Thedford herself.

> I saw her once
> Hop forty paces through the public street,
> And having lost her breath, she spoke, and panted,
> That she did make defect perfection
> And, breathless, pour forth breath . . .
>
> Age cannot wither nor custom stale
> Her infinite variety: other women cloy
> The appetites they feed, but she makes hungry
> Where she most satisfies . . .

As Armstrong finished, Cleopatra gave a flick of her right hand and Enobarbus withdrew. Marc heard him clumping offstage towards his room upstairs. Then Cleopatra spoke her opening lines:

If it be love indeed, tell me how much . . .

Antony, besotted with her lethal beauty, found himself replying:

There's beggary in the love that can be reckoned . . .

The scene unfolded, speech and counter-speech, as the ageing lovers bantered and probed, swore fidelity and recanted. The lines which last night had been words on a page and vague phrasings in the head now came readily to Marc's tongue, and he felt the emotion behind the rhetoric when he declaimed:

Let Rome in Tiber melt and the wide arch
Of the rangèd empire fall! Here is my space,
Kingdoms are clay . . .
                    The nobleness of life
Is to do thus.

Yes, he was thinking—even as he flinched under Cleopatra's scornful, teasing ripostes—there is truth here: kingdoms *are* clay, and love is . . .

"I am amazed," Mrs. Thedford was saying, "and it takes much to amaze a woman of my years and experience. You did that as well or better than Jason, who always made too much of himself as Antony to be a credulous dupe of the queen's charms." There was a catch in her voice and Marc realized that the mention of Merriwether's name had unexpectedly upset her.

"He was a fine actor," Marc said. "He will be missed."

"Yes, he will."

"And I feel like a fraud and a cad pretending to be him, but what we're doing tonight is an urgent matter of the province's security. I would not be part of such a scheme if it were not so."

"No wonder you can play Antony with such ease." She smiled, her composure regained. "Let's work through the rest of these scenes, then I'll have Thea come down for my grand exit."

The next two scenes went more haltingly because they involved a range of suddenly shifting emotions as the conflict of sensual love and moral duty, personal commitment and public politics, the power of love and the love of power played itself out. Cleopatra's death-scene, with Thea's assistance, was a moving and grandiose bit of theatre, and only an actress of deep character and subtle sensibility, like Annemarie Thedford, could rescue it from mere melodrama. With period costumes and stronger lighting, it would bring the audience to its knees.

"Now, let's see if you can switch to Macbeth," she said when Thea had left. "I've seen few actors under thirty-five years of age who can do the part justice. However, in the three scenes we're doing together, Lady Macbeth is the dominant force—goading, wheedling, and bolstering her weak-willed husband, who, nonetheless, is an impressive military man."

"What do you suggest? I've got the lines down and I've seen the play at Covent Garden in London, so I can visualize this part of the play leading up to the murder and the moments just after it."

"Well, perhaps you could think of me as a mother figure. Lady Macbeth is often played as an older, haglike virago—bossing you about and taunting you over your lack of courage and questioning your manhood when *you* believe you're a grown-up boy who can think for himself. That should give you the tenor of these scenes and put some vigour into the lines."

This stratagem took less practice than either of them imagined, for so quick and cutting were Lady Macbeth's barbs, so mocking and sardonic her tone, and so convincing the fury in her face that Marc found himself reacting viscerally. Macbeth's pathetic and ineffectual replies popped out with the requisite cowardice firmly attached. It was only the speed of the exchanges and their pacing that prompted repeated run-throughs. Marc found it very difficult to re-establish his role during such repetitions, but Mrs. Thedford, to his wonderment, was able to recapture the intensity of a dialogue even when it was restarted in the middle. He soon acknowledged to himself that, in the *Macbeth* sequence at least, Mrs. Thedford would have to carry the audience: his amateurism would be on full display. Fortunately, the concluding piece of the *Macbeth* sequence was to be Lady Macbeth's hand-washing scene with Thea as the gentlewoman and Beasley as the doctor, which had been rehearsed to perfection earlier. She would be cheered to the echo.

By the end of the *Macbeth* rehearsal Marc felt drained. The post-murder scene, with its multiple references to blood and seas being incarnadined, stirred up images of the carnage in Tessa's room and a soldier's sword steeped in gore. Mrs. Thedford seemed to be capable of charging her lines and gestures with legitimate passion and then simply withdrawing to whatever constituted her own personality with its separate virtues and feelings. But then, of course, here was a woman something less than fifty years of age who had succeeded in a man's world against insuperable odds. Extraordinary emotional strength, self-confidence, and perseverance, in addition to intelligence and talent, would have been necessary. To own and manage a theatre and theatrical troupe would require the ability to motivate and supervise people who were inherently competitive, envious, and insecure, to navigate the shoals of financing and legal contracts, and to weather the inevitable economic setbacks and personal betrayals that were the thespian's lot. Undoubtedly, it was such strength of character that had carried her through the crises of the past two days. If she had wept or lost her nerve or entertained despair, she had done so in private and alone.

"Now, then, Marc, let's do the *Hamlet*. It should be child's play after Antony and Macbeth."

"But why not let Clarence play Hamlet in this scene as well as the others?"

"In order to keep our audience happy and unquestioning, I felt we needed to find a third piece for you, but Beatrice and Benedick would have been impossible for us because it's all tempo and tone, and our complete *Hamlet* sequence is too long and involves too much blocking. So I just picked out this edited version of the bedchamber scene between Hamlet and Gertrude—one we could rehearse alone."

So they proceeded as before. The lines and speeches came easily, as Mrs. Thedford had foreseen, in part because Hamlet was closer in age and temperament to Marc and in part because Marc had been compelled to memorize copious swatches of the text during his home-tutoring period with Dr. Crabbe. But he found it much harder to be on the attacking side than the receiving end, as he had been in *Macbeth*, much harder to be shaming his mother with lines like,

Nay, but to live
In the rank sweat of an enseamèd bed,
Stewed in corruption, honeying and making love
Over the nasty sty!

and to watch in horror as the proud and confident Mrs. Thedford reduced herself to a cringing, mortified creature, defenseless against her son's moral tirade. With the ghost's appearance edited out, the scene wound down with the queen utterly abashed and Marc having to mouth epithets that caused his gorge to rise, but apparently made young Hamlet feel purged and righteous:

> by no means . . .
> Let the bloat king tempt you again to bed,
> Pinch wanton on your cheek, call you his mouse,
> And let him for a pair of reechy kisses
> Or paddling in your neck with his damned fingers,
> Make you ravel all this matter out . . .

When Mrs. Thedford had concluded the piece with "I have no life to breathe / What thou hast said to me," she took a deep breath, reached over, and caressed Marc's wrist. It was a simple gesture, wistful almost. But it struck Marc like a jolt. He felt himself physically aroused—attracted and intimidated at the same time. There seemed to be something mysterious and taboo in her appeal that left his feelings in turmoil.

"Are you all right?" she asked, her concern now taking over. "I've pushed you too hard, I believe. I've forgotten that this ordeal has had a personal meaning for you as well as us."

"I haven't slept well, but I'll be fine."

"Your friend, Mr. Hilliard, stands in the shadow of the gallows?"

"I'm afraid he does. And there is nothing I can do to help. He has confessed."

Marc could see his own pain mirrored in her eyes, and some of his confusion. "Was it Tessa's visit?"

Marc nodded. "He is under the illusion that he has killed for love, even though he has no recollection of doing the deed."

"That sounds Shakespearean, doesn't it?" she said lightly. Then her face became grave. "But I *am* sorry that Tessa escaped us this morning. She went out through the tavern. She's still a child in many ways, but she has done Mr. Hilliard a great wrong."

"And he has wronged himself also," Marc said. He smiled with some effort and said sincerely, "Anyway, I would like to thank you for helping us with this enterprise tonight. I may not get a chance to do so again."

"Oh?"

"You are free to make arrangements to leave tomorrow, if everything works out as we expect this evening. Unless you want to stay and complete your schedule."

"Tempting as that is, I think it best for the others if we get on to Detroit as soon as possible. I'll give you an address in Buffalo where you can ship the body, if that is all right. Jason has an elderly aunt there, his only relative."

"I'm sure the governor will approve that."

"And Major Jenkin tells me you are to be married soon."

"Yes. A week this Sunday."

"Lucky young woman," she said. She paused and went on: "This . . . enterprise tonight, will it put you in danger?"

"Not if my acting skills hold up."

Mrs. Thedford smiled. "They'll do just fine." It seemed for a moment that she might take him in her arms and . . . what? But she didn't, and for that Marc was grateful beyond measure. If she had, he had no idea what he might have done or what irrevocable train of events he might have set in motion.

"Break a leg," she said.

IT WAS FIVE O'CLOCK WHEN HE left Merriwether's room, where he had been mentally rehearsing his roles, and started walking towards the Cobb residence. Using the key that Ogden Frank had given him, Marc left the theatre by exiting through the door that led directly into the owner's quarters (thus avoiding the tavern altogether) and then out the rear door into the alley. Frank, with his hand-wringing now more anticipatory than despairing, had even supplied him with a key to the outside door so that he could slip in and out by this means whenever he wished.

On the bed in Merriwether's room Marc had laid out a suit of the dead actor's clothes from cap to boots. If he were called out to a rendezvous tonight after the performance, then he would have to go in Merriwether's guise, not his own. But for now he was just another soldier strolling east along King Street towards the "old town," where Cobb lived.

Marc felt somewhat guilty that he had not visited the constable before now. Despite the differences in background, life experience, and class, Marc had developed a comfortable rapport with Cobb, without either of them having to resort to pretense or false formality, or move an inch away from who they were. Marc respected Cobb's native cunning and hoped Cobb's admiration of his intelligence was not misplaced. He soon found the clapboard cottage on Parliament Street just above Front. He was delighted to find a neat little house freshly painted or whitewashed and, around it on three sides, the vestiges of the summer's vigorous vegetable garden. Bean-hills, withered tomato plants on stakes, yellowed cucumber vines—all attested to care and diligence. He almost tripped over a fat pumpkin-squash beside the stone path that meandered up to the front door.

"Kickin' 'em won't make them ripen any quicker!" Cobb called from the doorway.

"A bit like us, then?"

Cobb chortled. "Glad ya could make it, Major. I figure a solid meal and a restful pipe or two should set us both up fer the ruckus later on."

"I needed to get away from that place—and Government House. Thanks for inviting me."

Cobb led Marc inside, where he found himself in a cozy parlour with cushioned chairs, a throw rug, a stone fireplace, and a deal table set for supper. The remains of a log in the hearth radiated a welcoming warmth.

"It may be 'umble but 'tis h'our h'own," Cobb said in his execrable imitation of a Cockney accent.

"It's very comfortable. Your missus must be a conscientious homemaker."

Cobb looked decidedly uncomfortable at this compliment. "Most times, I'd agree with ya, Major. But not today."

"Is Dora ill?"

"Healthy as a horse," Cobb snorted, as if this state were somehow sinful. "Healthy as two horses!"

"What's wrong, then?"

"She ain't here, that's what."

"Oh," Marc said, confident that Cobb would get to the point sooner or later.

"Off on one of her calls—again."

"I don't quite understand."

"She's a midwife," Cobb said in a tone that was both boastful and accusatory. "An' the women of this town arrange to have their *off-springers* at the most *inconvening* time they can think up!"

"I didn't know that," Marc said, casting about for an appropriate place to park himself. "But surely you are proud of her: she plays a most important role in the community."

Cobb looked as if one cheek or the other would soon burst. "But *she* was the one that went an' invited you!"

Marc just laughed, and sat himself down in one of the

two cushioned chairs. "You're worried about a breach of manners? Well, don't be. Besides, I smell something delectable cooking in the other room."

"Well, as long as you're not upset, then I guess I can't be, can I?" Cobb smiled, sat down opposite Marc, and offered him his tobacco pouch. "I just figured the English *gentle-tree* was a stickler for good manners."

Marc took the pouch, packed his pipe, and soon both men were smoking with meditative satisfaction. The aroma of some kind of meat stew grew more enticing.

"You didn't get the lad to change his story, then?"

"No. And now it's too late. We can't keep the troupe here any longer when there's a confessed murderer already in custody. I've talked Spooner into waiting until the morning before taking Rick down to your chief and the magistrate. Thankfully, Sir Francis has been incommunicado all day and Spooner, I suspect, is afraid to have Rick charged without the governor's explicit approval."

"You still think one of them actors did it?"

"That seems less and less likely. But one of them knows more than he's saying."

"Shall I bring in the supper, Dad?"

Marc turned to see a girl of nine or ten years standing under the curtained archway between the parlour and the kitchen. Marc blinked and stared. She was beautiful: tall and willowy with long brown hair, large brown eyes, and a freckled grin. How she had contrived to be born from the union of

Horatio and Dora Cobb was a mystery, Marc thought, one of those miracles of generation that keep humans humble and awe-struck.

"This here's Delia," Cobb said proudly. "My first-born. Say hello to the officer, girl."

Delia performed a brief, under-rehearsed curtsey, blushed, grinned, and said, "How d'ya do, sir?"

"Now that you've gone an' *inter-ruptured* us, ya might as well bring the other one in fer viewin'," Cobb rumbled with mock annoyance.

"Fabian wants to see the soldier," Delia said, and rolled her eyes.

Fabian was duly ushered in so that he and Marc could carry out a mutual inspection. The boy was a masculine copy of his sister: bright-eyed, handsome, and shy without being self-effacing.

"And what do you want to be when you grow up?" Marc asked him.

"A grenadier," said Fabian smartly.

"And you?" Marc said to Delia.

"A grenadier's wife," she said promptly.

"I warned you kids not to start yer teasin' ways 'round our guest," Cobb said. "Now get out there an' bring in the food."

Brother and sister exchanged grins, bowed theatrically, and pranced out of the room.

Amused, Marc said, "You disapprove of grenadiers on principle?"

"They do that just to *aggra-grate* me, Major. They're both smart as a whip on a bare bum! The common school up the street ain't seen nothin' like 'em since it opened."

"And you don't need your sums and Greek declensions to be an officer in Queen Victoria's glorious army?"

Cobb gave an invigorating pull on his pipe. "I wouldna thought so," he said.

Supper consisted of a tasty venison stew, replete with vegetables from the garden and cellar—turnips, parsnips, potatoes, onions, carrots—and crowned with dumplings. On the side there was bread baked earlier in the day and butter from the market. An apple pie capped off the feast. The children served the meal, mimicking and perhaps mocking their notion of what waiting on high table entailed, but they ate quietly on their own out in the kitchen.

When he had finished his pie, Marc said, "I'm still puzzled about how that bottle of laudanum got from Thea's possession into the spittoon where Merriwether or the killer left it. If Rick is to hang, then the least I can do for him is to prevent his being thought a rapist."

"Well, Major, if that silly actress was befuddled enough to try an' do herself in with *loud-numb*—I figure she'd've needed two or three bottles fer the job—then heaven knows what she might've—"

"What actress're you talkin' about, Mr. Cobb?"

The two men swung around to face Dora Cobb, who now filled the lower portion of the curtained archway. Her round cheeks glowed red from an exertion she had not yet fully recovered from.

"You wasn't supposed to hear that, Missus Cobb."

"Well, Mr. Cobb, I could stuff me thumbs in me ears, but it wouldn't wipe away the words. Now, tell me, what actress an' what laudanum?"

"Now, you know, Missus Cobb, we agreed to keep our oars outta each other's canoe—"

"Or else you'd've known I had one of them actresses here in the house last Saturd'y."

DORA COBB DEMANDED TO BE FED and watered before she would elaborate on a remark that had elicited gasps from her husband and guest. So they waited patiently until she wiped the gravy from her lips with a delicate pinky, gave Cobb a reproachful look, and started in on her tale.

"This Dorothea person comes knockin' at my back door about two o'clock in the afternoon. She looks like Death's daughter, so I ask her in. Even before she starts talkin', I recognize the symptoms, so I ain't surprised when she tells me she's pregnant."

"We already know that," Cobb said.

"An' that's all you'll be knowin', Mr. Cobb, if you have the impudence to butt in one more time."

Cobb flushed, but decided not to risk retaliation.

"Please, go on," Marc said soothingly, but he, too, found his heart beating with anticipation.

"'Well,' says I, 'it'll be a few months down the road before ya need my services.' At that, she busts out cryin'. An' pretty soon I get the whole sad story. Seems this actor fella got her in the fambly way an' then, havin' had his fun—like most men—he tells her to bugger off. Seein' her life is now ruined, she decides to do away with herself an' the unborn child, so she goes to old Ezra fer some 'poison.' When she gets outta the shop, she changes her mind—goes back in and asks Ezra's wife if she knows of a midwife in town. That brings her here. What she wants now, of course, is to do in the bairn but not herself, an' she reckoned I'd know how to go about it—fer a fee."

"Missus Cobb don't have nothin' to do with that sort o' sin!" Cobb said. "Do ya, sweet?"

Dora acknowledged his defense of her integrity with a dip of her chins, and went on. "I told her just that, an' she sets inta bawlin' somethin' terrible. I was glad the kids was out. Anyways, I set her down an' let her talk and talk. An' by the time she left, she was feelin' a whole lot better. I told her that men often reacted that way at first, but if she gave him a little time an' space an' was real patient, he'd probably come around. 'Course, that was a wad of malarkey, but I didn't want the woman's suicide on my hands."

"You obviously did well for her," Marc said. "She is

suffering, but I believe she'll be all right." He didn't think it prudent to mention the brutal death of the child's father.

"I know, luv. Me an' Mr. Cobb saw her last night: she was warblin' like a robin after a good rain."

"Missus Cobb's the one fer curin' any ailment that's female," Cobb boasted.

"Just to make sure, though," Dora said, "I did sneak that bottle outta her pocket before she left."

"WELL, MAJOR, WE NOW KNOW THERE was two vials of that stuff," Cobb said as he fingered the bottle of laudanum that Dora had taken from Thea. The children had gone out to play, and Dora was getting herself "prettied up" for the theatre later on.

"And the only person with any motive for drugging Tessa's sherry is Merriwether. I figure he put it there in the afternoon and hid the bottle in the spittoon when he came out of Tessa's room, expecting to dispose of it permanently at a more auspicious time. But, damn it, Cobb, that vial had Michaels's name on it, just like this one. I'm convinced that Merriwether bought the drug here in Toronto, on Saturday or perhaps Monday morning."

"But I showed that picture of Merriwether's head in every place that might peddle the stuff."

"And you saw the names on Michaels's ledger that neither he nor his staff nor you recognized?"

"I did. Besides Thea Clarkson, there was only three of 'em, mind you, 'cause we was only lookin' at Saturd'y an' Monday, right?"

"That's right."

"And I even took them names along with the picture inta the dives where my snitches hang about."

"You have the list of names Michaels gave you?"

"Right here, Major." Cobb got up, went over to his great-coat on a nearby chair, rummaged through one of the deep pockets, and fished out a crumpled piece of paper. He handed it skeptically to Marc, who scanned its contents:

Chas. Meredith

Martin Acorn

Claude Kingsley

"What is it, Major?"

"Merriwether was at Michaels's, all right. In disguise."

"How do ya figure that?" Cobb was amazed, as a child is before a magician.

"Claude Kingsley is King Claudius— Merriwether's little joke."

"But Ezra never forgets a face."

"True, but he didn't see the face in the sketch you showed him. He saw the one on the playbill: Claudius with his black wig, bushy eyebrows, and beard. I'll bet Merri-wether even hunched over to lessen the effect of his height." Marc looked at Cobb. "You did mention his height, didn't you?"

Cobb took offense. "I said he was a big bugger about so high, but I didn't think I needed to go on an' on about the body parts when Michaels had a picture of the fella's mug starin' up at him!"

"It's still two hours till the show starts at eight thirty," Marc said. "That should give you time to fetch that portrait of Claudius from Merriwether's dressing-room and show it to Ezra. But I have absolutely no doubt that we've traced the drug to the villain who violated Tessa."

"I can do that, Major. Dora'll be some time gettin' herself harnessed up."

"Don't you see what this means, Cobb? We have incontrovertible proof that Rick Hilliard is not a rapist."

Cobb grimaced. "That oughta make his mama feel a whole lot better."

FIFTEEN

The third evening of performances by the distinguished Bowery Touring Company began much as the first two had. Carriages ferrying the self-proclaimed gentry from their august domiciles to the distinction of a theatre-box with padded seat and unobstructed view started to arrive shortly after eight o'clock. By eight fifteen there was a crush of tardier arrivals along the north side of Colborne Street and, on the south side, a similar crush of gawkers offering gratuitous comment. Under the false façade of the balcony, Ogden Frank, rotund and obsequious, greeted friend and stranger alike and passed them along to Madge, who checked their bona fides with steely-eyed precision.

The air of normality was deliberate. Marc was certain that those seeking to make contact with the gunrunning tragedian would be scrutinizing the situation from within and without. Spooner's scouts and spies had, so far, kept a discreet distance. By 8:25 the box seats, the gallery, and the pit were full. The Regency was abuzz with anticipation. An evening of the Bard's best comic and tragic bits performed by seasoned actors from New York City was an experience not to be missed in colonial Toronto, one you might wish to tell your grandchildren about, should they be so polite as to listen. For the next two hours or so, the rumours of rebellion and rumblings of discontent could be forgotten.

Marc was with his fellow actors in the dressing-room area to the left of the stage. On a rack next to his mirror hung the two costumes he would need after his initial role as Hamlet: Antony's imperial Roman togs and Macbeth's royal robes, the latter complete with wig, chin-beard, and ersatz eyebrows. Thea Clarkson graciously assisted him with his makeup for Hamlet. There was no wig or full beard, but his own sandy hair and eyebrows were powdered to look as blond as a Viking's, and a small goatee of similar hue depended from his chin. He hoped that these changes and the costume would be enough to deceive whoever might be watching for reasons unconnected with the stage. At least he would be tested early on. And if his cover were blown, his assumption was that the rebels would merely vanish, smarting but unlikely to risk exposure by exacting any revenge.

Just how the contact would be made was still anyone's guess, as Merriwether was supposed to know its nature and Marc did not. Nevertheless, he felt he had to try to anticipate it. His intuition told him that the most obvious opportunity for receiving instructions for a rendezvous would be during that fifteen-minute period after the performance ended when well-wishers pushed onto the stage to meet the stars and press gifts upon them. One such gift could easily contain the clandestine message. But just in case a surreptitious entry to the dressing rooms was attempted, Marc had Wilkie placed where he could keep an eye on them as well as upon the door that led to the Franks' quarters. On the other side of the stage, Chief Constable Sturges stood guard over the tavern-entrance and the stairway to the upper rooms.

Marc checked his Hamlet image in the watery mirror, then joined the others in the wings.

"No need to be nervous, Marc," Mrs. Thedford said, touching him on the forearm. "I can't imagine you requiring a prompt, but if you do, watch my lips." She leaned across and gave him a phantom peck on the cheek, exposing, as she did so, the upper-halves of her unmotherly breasts. Then she was sweeping onto the stage as the first scene from the play got under way to welcoming applause.

From his position in the wings, Marc could see the boxes on the far wall of the theatre. Dora and Horatio Cobb, along with Owen Jenkin, were in the one most distant, which afforded the constable a wide view of the pit, the gallery, and

the other boxes. On the opposite side, Marc knew, Lieutenant Spooner and his guests occupied a middle box. There
was nothing any of them could do now but allow the drama
to unfold.

Dawson Armstrong delivered Claudius's soliloquy at
prayer with such spit and verve that the audience brought
him back for two bows. Marc cooled his heels and trembled
in the wings. Mrs. Thedford, as Gertrude, stood beside
him again, but she was fully in role now and said nothing.
He could hear her taking deep, rhythmic breaths. Then
it was their turn and Marc, feeling as if he were stepping
into the cauldron of battle for the first time, walked with
knees aquiver into a blaze of light. When he turned to the
audience to deliver his opening lines, the words, mercifully,
came out. The hundred pairs of eyes appraising him in his
nakedness—for so he felt—were, with equal mercy, invisible, drowned in the sea of black set up by the footlights.

HAM: How now, what's the matter?

GERT: Hamlet, thou hast thy father much offended.

HAM: Mother, you have my father much offended.

The quality and pitch of their long rehearsal yesterday was
instantly rekindled, and Marc soon forgot the audience,
himself, and why he was doing this. He was the Prince of
Denmark excoriating his faithless mother. The applause, as
their scene ended, came more as a shock than an expectation, so engrossed was he in Hamlet's angst. On the other
hand, Gertrude dissolved immediately and Mrs. Thedford

took her formal, practised curtsies as a matter of right, while tugging him into his hesitant bows. Then, as they were leaving the stage, the adrenaline of praise struck: he felt as if he might float down the steps to his dressing-room.

"Well done," Mrs. Thedford said. "You were to the manor born."

"I've still got Antony and Macbeth to negotiate," Marc said with a modesty he didn't actually feel. "Oh, here's your looking-glass: I know what it means to you."

During the *Hamlet* scene, when Hamlet holds the hand-mirror up to his mother and her sins, Mrs. Thedford had insisted that they use the one she kept in her room upstairs, "for good luck," she had said. He was happy now to return the treasure intact.

"Solid work, young man," Armstrong said, and meant it.

Apparently Marc had passed more than one test out there on the boards.

MARC HAD NO MORE SCENES UNTIL after the interval, but he did return to his dressing-room to change into Antony's toga and sandals. Although unbearded, Antony sported a close-cropped black wig and charcoal eyebrows with artfully darkened skin, effectively camouflaging Marc's fair complexion and light brown hair. As he waited anxiously for the interval to begin, he could hear laughter and spontaneous applause as the scenes from *Twelfth Night* completed the first half of the evening. Wilkie came over to report that no one had tried to enter the premises under his watch. Minutes later, the other actors hurried past to their individual cubicles to rest and prepare for the second half.

Meanwhile, Ogden Frank and his assistants made sure no spectator got backstage from the pit through the doors to the left or right, but they did not discourage the relaying of messages and bonbons under the auspices of Madge Frank. Tessa, whose performance of Ophelia had brought audible sobs from the viewers, received a box of sweets and a proposal of marriage. Thea Clarkson as Cordelia was rewarded with a bouquet of chrysanthemums, and Mrs. Thedford with an array of cards and billets-doux. There were no messages for either Hamlet. At one point before they resumed, Cobb managed to catch Marc's eye from his position near the refreshment stall, and shook his head slowly. Perhaps no contact would be made, either because the rebels had simply got cold feet or they had begun to suspect subterfuge and betrayal.

While Marc flubbed a line or two as Antony, as he had predicted, Mrs. Thedford's Cleopatra was so sensual, sardonic, and touching, with quicksilver shifts in mood and tempo, that few in the audience cared what kind of Antony provoked such a complex woman into being, so long as he had. Mother and whore, wanton lover and calculating bitch, goddess and little lost girl—she played them all within a single body with a singular voice. When she rose from her death-scene to accept the approbation raining down upon her, Antony, long dead and forgotten nearby, remained where he was.

Marc returned to his dressing-room to change into his Macbeth costume, but sensed something amiss as soon as he stepped inside. It took him several seconds to realize that there was an extra costume on the rack beside the other two. He reached into one of the pockets of the tunic and, unsurprised, drew out a plain envelope. Inside was the note he had been expecting, printed by hand in block capitals:

IMMEDIATELY AFTER THE PERFORMANCE,
GO TO EAST MARKET STREET, NORTH END.
MOUNT THE HORSE THERE. RIDE EAST
ALONG KING TO SCADDINGS BRIDGE. TWO
MILES UP THE KINGSTON ROAD YOU WILL
BE MET. BRING SAMPLE. DO NOT ALLOW
YOURSELF TO BE FOLLOWED. YOU WILL BE
WATCHED ALL THE WAY. DESTROY THIS NOTE.

So, this was it. His ruse had worked. Now if he could only remember his lines as Macbeth, all might yet be well. Then, with a guilty start, he remembered that he had not thought of Rick Hilliard once in the past two hours. But there was just too much to do here and now. He went down to find Wilkie. Someone had delivered this costume and was, most likely, part of the conspiracy.

"I found an extra costume in my cubicle," Marc said to Wilkie.

"No mystery there, sir. I put it there myself," Wilkie offered cheerfully.

"And who delivered it to you?"

"Oh . . . I see. It was the same fella that's been here a coupla times before, bringin' costumes from some repair shop in town."

Marc froze.

"They usually let him come in through the tavern, but seein' as the play was goin' on and all, the barkeep took him through Frank's place and in this here door. But I didn't let him get more'n a foot inside here. I told him to halt, an' said I'd be the one to deliver anythin' that needed deliverin'."

"Medium height and build?" Marc said, dreading the response. "Sort of baby-faced and fair-skinned? Big smile?"

"That's the fella all right," Wilkie said, nodding his large head. "You seen him too, have ya?"

Unfortunately he had: it was George Revere, bringing another mended costume from Aunt Catherine's shop, except that this one contained a message which could send all who had handled it to the gallows. Marc sat back on the bottom step below the wings. He could hardly breathe. Incurious as ever, Wilkie drifted back to his post. Surely it was Revere, recent arrival from the United States and boisterous republican, and not Aunt Catherine, who was involved. Even so, Beth's aunt was herself a recent immigrant from New England and, Marc grimly concluded, might well be tarred with the kind of broad brush he had seen wielded by members of the establishment here. Was there no end to the entanglement of politics and his personal life? Perhaps Revere himself was innocent, a dupe of treasonous types around him.

Marc had little time to rationalize further, for Clarence Beasley touched him on the shoulder and said, "Lay on, Macbeth."

THE MACBETH SEQUENCE DID NOT GO well. Marc felt sorry for Lady Macbeth, who did her best to carry the scenes beyond his missed cues and omitted lines, including one entire speech, in addition to his pathetic attempt to deploy volume and basso profundity to compensate for his lack of timing and passion. Fortunately this sequence was first up after the interval, giving the audience plenty of time to forget it in favour of what followed. The public knowledge of Merriwether's indisposition (that, alas, had begun to affect the great man's performance) would have made his fans more sympathetic than critical. In any event, it concluded with Lady Macbeth's sleepwalking scene, and as Mrs. Thedford had nicely arranged, thunderous applause greeted her effort.

Marc went straight back to his dressing-room. There were still thirty minutes remaining in the show. He needed to think about what lay ahead the moment it ended. It appeared that the rebels had taken every precaution. Under the moonlight, the Kingston Road would be visible for its entire length, while the forest on either side remained impenetrably black: if anyone tried to follow Marc—a lone, moonlit horseman on an empty road—they could be observed easily by those standing watch in the woods. Moreover, any such followers would easily be seen if they attempted to cross the Don River via the only bridge, while a midnight fording by inexperienced, mounted infantry officers was too hazardous to contemplate. He had little doubt that the horse waiting in the shadows of the market would be on its own, tethered loosely, and untraceable. If he were met some two miles or so east of the bridge, he would be spirited away to a predetermined rendezvous so quickly that any loyalist who managed to trail after him would have no chance of finding him. Thus, he would be on his own, having to convince the rebels of his authenticity, effect an exchange of sample guns and initial payment, and, presumably, arrange a drop-point for the rest of the rifles. Somewhere along the lakeshore, he speculated, where three trunks of costumes destined for New York City would inexplicably go missing.

As he waited out the agonizingly slow minutes left in the evening's performance, Marc tried not to think too much about his dismal failure to help Rick Hilliard, who was certainly not guilty of murder, only of misguided chivalry. Cobb had earlier confirmed Marc's theory about Merriwether's purchase of laudanum, but he now felt much as Cobb did about such a minuscule triumph of detection. He also tried not to think of the consequences of having to arrest George

Revere for sedition, with his wedding into the family a mere ten days away.

The loudest roar of the night told him that the show was over. Within minutes the stage-area would be overrun by enthusiasts eager to touch the garments of the great. He walked quickly through the shadows at the rear of the stage to the far side, past a startled chief constable, and up the stairs to Merriwether's bedroom. There he stripped off his Macbeth robes, but left the wig, eyebrows, and beard in place. He got into Merriwether's street clothes and boots, and then removed the two rifles and the ammunition from the trunk. Earlier in the afternoon he had marked the stock of each rifle, using an awl to drill a tiny hole, filling it with a single drop of ink, and rubbing the surface smooth again. He tucked them into the canvas bag Spooner had supplied, wedged open the window overlooking the alley below, and dropped the bag into some bushes. He waited, breath indrawn, for thirty seconds, but the noise had attracted no attention. Then he went back downstairs. Cobb was waiting for him, with Sturges.

"Jesus!" Sturges cried. "Fer a second there I thought you was Merriwether!"

Marc drew them up to the landing, where, by the glow of Sturges's lantern, they read the rebels' note.

"Spooner's out there tryin' to look casual, but nearer to a conniption fit," Sturges said with some satisfaction. "Should I take this note to him?"

"What do you make of it?" Marc asked Cobb.

"Damned clever, I'd say. But I do know exactly where they're gonna take you."

"Two miles up the Kingston Road is scarcely a precise co-ordinate," Marc protested.

"But it's where there's a path of sorts through the bush towards the lake, used by trappers an' hunters mostly. It's an old Mississauga Indian trail with a bunch of deer-runs off of it, a perfect maze if ya don't know the terrain."

"Perfect for them, disastrous for us."

"Maybe so, but there's a log hut at the end of the path— been there a donkey's age—about a quarter of a mile from the lake."

"Which gives them more than one means of escape."

"Still, if Spooner knows what he's doin', he might be able to catch one of 'em comin' outta the bush onto the highway or makin' a run fer it by boat."

"You're right, Cobb, but only if he stays at least half an hour behind me. Our only chance is to catch them *after* I do the deal, whatever it is, and not before or during it. There's no mention of guns in either note, and no way to prove one of the rebels actually wrote them. They could claim they thought they were buying Yankee whiskey or cigars."

"I see yer point, Major. Want us to tell Spooner all this?"

"Yes, please do," Marc said, and gave the note to Cobb.

"He'll wanta know where the note was found," Sturges said.

"Later," Marc said.

"Here he comes now!" Cobb said.

Marc threw Merriwether's cape over his shoulders and disappeared into the tavern, leaving the policemen to face the onrushing Spooner.

THE MOON WAS IN FULL PHASE and the Kingston Road, mostly dried mud and vestigial logs at this time of year, stretched out before him. Marc had retrieved the gun bag from the alley, manoeuvred undetected through the market to its northeast corner, found a horse tethered there, mounted, and rode in splendid isolation towards Scaddings Bridge. Once on the other side of the Don, he looked back, but no one was trailing him. That eyes were watching him intently from several hidden eyries, he had no doubt. He also felt exposed without his sword and pistol. But he knew he must remain Jason Merriwether throughout the meeting ahead and after. There would be no heroic attempt to make a citizen's arrest: he planned to carry on as if he were indeed a Yankee gunrunner, then walk or ride away, leaving the arrest or any follow-up gambits to Spooner and the governor. He would do his bit, then withdraw and try his damnedest to marry Beth Smallman before the sky fell.

"Stop right there, Merriwether."

Marc did as he was bid by the deep voice from somewhere to his right.

"Now get off the horse an' lead him over here."

Marc walked the horse into the shadows, and waited. Two men suddenly appeared in front of him. They were farmers by the look of their overalls and boots, but each wore a battered top hat from which a chequered kerchief dropped down over the face.

"Merriwether?"

"I am he," Marc said, trying out his New York twang. "I've brought the sample with me. Do you have the money?"

"It ain't that simple. Follow us. You can leave the horse and ride it back as far as the bridge, providin' everything's on the up-and-up." The one who spoke was very nervous, and struggled to keep his voice, deep as it was, from skidding upward.

"Whatever you say," Marc replied with deliberate nonchalance. "If you people're buyin', I'm sellin'." He tethered the horse to a tree and unslung the canvas bag.

They walked in silence. Marc could not actually see the path they were using, but his two companions moved along without hesitation or impediment. Soon they were confronted by a blunt shadow blocking the way.

"We're here."

Marc ducked low and followed the men inside. The hut was windowless, floorless, and, except for the glimmer from a candle-stub on a stump-table, nearly dark. The two who had led Marc here sat down beside a third man, his face also hidden behind a kerchief. Marc squatted down on a log across from them. Between them on the stump lay a saddlebag.

The third man spoke first. "This shouldn't take long. We need to see the quality of yer merchandise. Then we'll show you the colour of our money. If both are satisfactory, I'll hand you written instructions about how and where to drop off the remainder of the goods an' pick up your full payment."

"The price has gone up ten percent," Marc said.

After a tense pause, the third man said, "It's fifty per rifle or no deal."

Marc smiled. "No harm in tryin' a little Yankee horse-tradin', now, is there? Fifty it is." Marc sighed with some relief: he felt he needed to know what price had originally been agreed upon when he came to count out the cash in the saddlebag.

"Let's see the goods, then," said the one who had spoken to him beside the highway. The other man who had accompanied him had said nothing as yet, and appeared to be very jittery, jerking his head from side to side at the least tick of sound.

Marc pulled one of the French Modèles out of the canvas casing into the dim light. While the jittery one held the candle uncertainly in his hand, the other two rotated the weapon over it as if they were roasting a piglet on a spit. One of them gave a low whistle of approval.

"An' you got ammunition an' twelve more in addition to these two?"

"Yessiree. But first I need to see the silver." This was it: once the exchange had been made, the treasonous act would be palpable and irreversible. If any one of these three were caught with the marked rifles, they would be fodder for the executioner.

"It's all there: U.S. silver coins. You may need a mule to carry it."

Marc reached for the saddlebag.

"Lemme see the other gun first."

"Whatever you say. The customer's always right." Marc hoped he wasn't putting it on too thick. He reached for the canvas bag. As he did so, he saw the spokesman for the rebels reach into his cloak and begin to pull out an envelope: the drop-off instructions. We're almost there, Marc thought with the tiniest flush of triumph.

At that moment, all four of them froze at the sound of a clatter just outside the hut. A second later, a fourth man dressed like the others stumbled inside and cried out breathlessly, "They're comin' through the bush from the lakeshore! Soldiers! A whole pack of 'em!"

"What the hell is goin' on here?" demanded Deep Voice.

Marc stood up. "Nobody followed me! Some bastard's tattled on us."

"The deal's off, Yankee!" shouted the one in charge. "You're damn lucky I don't shoot you on the spot." He snatched the saddlebag up in both hands and barked at the others, "Leave the guns. When they find them here and then pick up this arsehole wanderin' around lost in the bush, they'll know who to hang!"

With that, they scrambled for the door and the safety of the woods. They could never be caught once they had a running start. But the jittery one did not immediately follow. He got up as if to go, but suddenly swivelled towards Marc, who had stood his ground. In a quivering, two-handed grip, the man held a cocked pistol. Marc felt its muzzle like an ice-pick under his chin. For an interminable half-minute, it trembled there: Marc could feel the man's indecision. He didn't know why, but he closed his eyes. His life, incomplete as it was, did not flash before him.

Then something prompted him to open them again. The pistol was being lowered, inch by agonizing inch. The candlelight from the table was reflected in the barrel and, then, unexpectedly it illuminated the back of the gunman's left hand, an all-too-familiar hand that bore a throbbing, thick scar. Then the hand, the pistol, and the gunman were gone. There was much commotion in the bush, then all was quiet. Ten minutes later, Marc heard the mad crashing of infantrymen as they staggered into trees and pitfalls.

Marc smashed both fists on the stump-table, furious at Spooner's blundering intervention, but also gob-smacked by what had just been revealed to him. Thomas Goodall, in his desperation, had thrown in with the would-be insurgents. And that scar on his left hand was the result of no accident: Thomas had no doubt been injured at the donnybrook with the Orangemen the previous spring near Crawford's Corners. At this very moment he would be skedaddling back home to lay his disappointed body beside that of Winnifred Hatch, and both of them no more than five yards from the woman he was destined to marry. He tried to move, but couldn't. He was numb. His heart kept pumping, but his brain had given up.

He had no idea how long it was before Lieutenant Spooner careened into the hut, burred and nettled and otherwise beaten about by the Canadian bush. Without ceremony, he teetered in front of Marc and shouted in a furious squeak, "Can you identify any of them?"

There was the slightest pause before Marc heard himself say, "They were all masked."

"Damn it! Did they take the rifles?"

Marc pointed at the marked samples.

"Damn it! Did they give you money?"

Marc shook his head.

"Damn it! Damn it! Damn it!"

Marc brushed by him out into the shadows.

"And just where do you think you're going, Lieutenant?"

Marc did not reply. He found the path and strode steadily back towards the Kingston Road. Several shots rang out: the soldiers shooting at one another, no doubt. He found the horse where he had left it. He mounted and galloped away towards the city. Spooner could clean up the mess he had made. The operation was a total failure. None of the rebels had been caught or identified. And none ever would be.

SIXTEEN

Marc's first thought was to keep on riding right through the city to the fort, where he could stable the rebels' horse (stolen surely) overnight and then find himself a warm, safe bed, preferably a long way from the arrogance of authority and the desperation of those without it. In refusing to name Thomas Goodall, he recognized that he had crossed a line, had committed an act that could not be undone. But what precisely that was he did not at this moment care to know: something other than his mind was now directing him willy-nilly where it wished. So be it.

Thus it was that he did not question the horse when it

swung down West Market Lane and stopped outside the entrance to Frank's Hotel. The upper windows of the rooms above the tavern and those above the theatre were all dark except one: the parlour room of Mrs. Thedford's suite. Something was nagging at him, a vague feeling that he had seen or heard something whose significance he had overlooked. He nudged the horse back into the alley that led to the hotel stables. With the motions of a sleepwalker he found an empty stall, unsaddled the beast, threw a blanket over it, and then, stepping over a comatose stable boy, made his way through the dark to the back door of the Franks' quarters. Using Frank's key, Marc eased the door open and felt his way along the hallway that eventually brought him to the theatre entrance. The stage area was pitch black, except where a single shaft of moonlight sliced through one of the upper windows and across the pit. There was no tragedian to take a bow in its mellow beam. Marc crossed the stage, pausing to take in an echo of applause, and tiptoed up the stairs to the hallway above. Jeremiah Jefferson was fast asleep with the storage-room door ajar.

Marc headed for Merriwether's room, where he had left his own boots, tunic, and accoutrements, but halted outside the door with the wedge of light under it. Perhaps Mrs. Thedford was sitting just beyond it at the little davenport-table that served as her desk, working on the company's books or revising the playbill for Detroit or completing the travel arrangements that her murdered colleague would have handled. He felt she was someone he could talk to about matters too painful and complex to be uttered to oneself. He raised his hand to give a one-finger tap on the door, but as his palm brushed it on the way up, it swung silently open. The room was fully lit, but empty. Surely she had not gone to bed in the other room and left half a dozen candles blazing here? But, then, perhaps she had merely gone into that room to fetch something and, overcome by physical and emotional fatigue, had put her head on the pillow and fallen into a deep sleep. He decided he would just take a quick peek inside, then snuff the candles and leave quietly.

He was almost at the bedroom doorway when he heard the sound: a giggle—muted, smothered perhaps, but clearly a giggle. The hair rose on the back of his neck. He listened intently, but did not move. There was a rustling, as of starched sheets. Then a sigh that had no sadness in it. He should have wheeled and bolted, but he didn't. Like a moth to the flame, he was drawn into that doorway and a sight that first mystified and then seared him.

No candle lit the scene on the bed, but the last of the moonlight bathed it visible and shimmeringly surreal. At first blush, it was a silken knot of tawny limbs, intertwined and serpentine. Then a flash of toe, a whipped wisp of hair, a bulb of surprised flesh confirmed the human form—or forms. The willful moans of surrender, the muzzled grunts of pleasure-pain, the yip at forbidden touch would have conjured in any viewer's imagination the lustful conjunction of male and female in the oldest act. But what Marc saw, and his mind at first rejected, was the sexual entanglement of woman and woman: Tessa Guildersleeve and Annemarie Thedford.

They were far too engrossed to notice Marc's shadow fall across the bed, then retreat. Marc did not realize until he had backed across the outer room and sat down on the settee there that he had neglected to take a breath. He was sure they would now hear him gasping, but the moans and sighs continued apace, slowing and receding gradually as the minutes ticked by. Mrs. Thedford's voice became distinguishable: a sequence of soothing sounds above the grateful mewling of the girl. Marc sat stunned. Yet despite the almost visceral revulsion he felt, the tenderness and consolation in the sounds from that room were undeniably those of love's afterglow—not the satiate wheezes of lust's exhaustion. That Annemarie Thedford loved Tessa Guildersleeve was unashamedly revealed.

His mind began to work again. He found himself staring across the room at the commode where Mrs. Thedford kept the only gifts her father had bequeathed her. In a flash, he realized what he had overlooked the day before, and he knew what instrument had stunned Merriwether and made the horrific stabbing possible. Before him was a plausible motive for what he had known all along was a murder committed in the white heat of rage and recrimination. He did not know entirely how the crime had been orchestrated, but he knew for certain who had committed it.

"Ah, Marc. I thought that was you in the doorway. I'm glad you decided to wait."

Mrs. Thedford was standing across from him, her nakedness swathed in a satin robe, and she was smiling a welcome at him, as if he had arrived a bit early for tea and had happily made himself at home.

"Where are the silver candlesticks, the ones you claimed were so dear to you?"

"I was sure you'd notice sooner or later; nothing much gets past you," she said, and it sounded for all the world like a compliment.

"There was one here when I searched the room yesterday. If I hadn't been so obsessed with finding the laudanum, I would have realized it then."

"Ah, so it was you who'd been in here. You didn't quite place the hand-mirror or the candlestick back where I always leave them."

"You hid the other one, didn't you?"

She smiled warmly. "Silly of me, wasn't it? I should have tucked them both out of sight." There was no bitterness in this remark: it was a plain statement.

"You have no idea how much I've admired you . . ." Marc said, his voice nearly breaking.

"And I, you," she said, pulling a padded chair over beside the settee and sitting down to face him. "And now you've come to accuse me of murdering Jason, and I can see the pain it is causing you."

"I don't know how you did it, but I know it was you,"

Marc said softly, looking away, afraid of what might next be said or done.

"Don't be so disconsolate, Marc. Of course I did it. And I was positive it would be you who would find me out." She was gazing upon him with admiration and a plaintive sort of fondness.

"You admit it, then?"

"I do. And now I'd like you to wipe that disappointment off your handsome face and relax, have a glass of sherry with me—sans laudanum—and we'll discuss everything."

All Marc could think of replying to this unexpected invitation was, "What about Tessa?"

Mrs. Thedford laughed. "The minute I've finished making love to her, she starts snoring like a hedgehog."

THEY WERE SITTING VERY CLOSE TOGETHER, almost knee to knee, sipping sherry like two old friends after a long absence. Mrs. Thedford did not take her eyes off Marc, even as she tipped her sherry glass to her lips. Her seeming unconcern and aplomb were as unnerving as they were incredible.

"I suggest that you go first, Marc. Tell me all you think you know." She sat back, smiling encouragement. Marc collected his thoughts.

"I believe you heard Tessa cry out when she was attacked by Merriwether, and thinking logically that it was Rick Hilliard behaving abominably, you grabbed a candlestick and ran down the hall into Tessa's room. There you discovered Merriwether in his nightshirt on top of a helpless Tessa who, already drugged and disoriented, had mercifully passed out. You did what any responsive person would have done: you struck Merriwether on the back of the skull with the only weapon you had, the candlestick. He reared up, still conscious for an instant, spun around, then collapsed on the carpet, faceup and legs splayed, but still breathing. Enraged by his actions—after all, he had just violated in the most reprehensible manner possible a young woman who was not merely your ward but your . . . paramour—you decided to finish him off. This was a decision taken in a fury, totally irrational and utterly unlike anything you had ever done or thought to do."

"You are very generous." She seemed amused by this quaint narrative.

"You could have struck him again with the candlestick, but I suspect the fact that he was facing you may have caused you to hesitate. It was then that you spotted Rick slumped unconscious on the settee. There was only one candle lit beside Tessa's bed, and in your fear for Tessa you had not seen him. He had foolishly strapped on his sabre to impress Tessa. You pulled it from its scabbard, gripped it with both hands, steeled yourself, and plunged it into Merriwether's chest. Then, the deed done, you were suddenly horrified at what you'd done. Tessa was unconscious and breathing regularly. You had to place the blame elsewhere if you were to survive and help her through this crisis. Somehow you smeared blood all over poor Hilliard, picked up your candlestick, and ran. I'm certain that the weapon is still in this building and can be found.

"But, of course, Tessa's cry had been heard by both Armstrong and Beasley, something you hadn't had time to consider. Fortunately, Armstrong was too drunk or hungover to respond. His door was ajar, so he must have seen you, in the weak light from Tessa's room or his own. The bloody candlestick was in your grip. Beasley claims it was no more than two minutes between the time he heard Tessa cry and his arrival there, so he, too, must have seen you in the dark hall. How you contrived to have them lie for you and do it so consistently I can only guess. But it was midmorning Tuesday before I began my questioning. You had ample time before that to intimidate and coach your colleagues, who are after all your underlings and dependents."

"And you believe me capable of that sort of bullying hypocrisy?" She looked genuinely hurt at being accused of this latter, more venial, transgression.

"Not at first and that was my mistake. I thought from the beginning that this was a crime of passion—I could not get the image of that steel stake through Merriwether's body out of my mind. But having watched you rehearse on Monday, having worked with you alone here yesterday afternoon, and performed next to you last evening, no, I could not believe you capable of organizing and manipulating such a conspiracy."

"Thank you. Because, you see, I did nothing of the sort."

"But Beasley and Armstrong must have seen you. There wasn't time for you to hear the cry, realize its significance, pick up the candlestick, stumble into Tessa's room, strike Merriwether down, discover Hilliard, draw his sword, stab Merriwether, decide to set up the young lothario as the murderer, find something to dip into Merriwether's spouting blood, smear Rick's jacket, breeches, hands, and boots, pick up the dropped candlestick, and flee back to your room. All of this in two minutes? No."

"The reason you believed their testimony was because all of them were telling the truth. What they say they saw is what they did see." She said this proudly, and still there was a twinkle of amusement in her steady gaze.

"It is not possible."

"Well, let me tell you what *was* possible and what *did* happen. More sherry?"

Marc shook his head. Mrs. Thedford leaned forward again, allowing the top of her robe to slip open several inches. She didn't appear to notice, however, for she had suddenly become quite serious, narrowing her gaze and appearing to visualize the actions as she narrated them.

"I knew I would lose Tessa someday. Men were increasingly attracted to her, and I could see her trying out various responses to their overtures. She never stopped loving me, never left my bed except when it was imprudent not to. I'm sure you're worldly enough to realize that our love is considered by most to be unnatural."

"But you were also her mentor," Marc protested. "She must have been terribly confused. And as the older adult, you bore full responsibility for the . . . the situation."

"Again, you are right, and wise beyond your years. But, you see, I, too, was confused. Tessa was not the first woman I had loved, and I knew when she came to me that I should not approach her on those terms. She needed a mother." Her eyes looked away. "All children do." She covered her momentary distress by refilling her sherry glass from the decanter beside her on the floor.

"You lost your own mother when you were very young?"

"I never knew her. Still, I missed her. Odd, isn't it?"

"Not at all," Marc said, having known such a feeling himself.

"Ultimately, we became . . . involved, and though I tried several times to end it, Tess wouldn't hear of it and I was miserable at the thought. We convinced ourselves it was right."

"Surely you were risking everything, the company, the—"

"Perhaps. But I was determined that Tessa not become entangled with any other members of the troupe. So when I saw Jason pursuing her, I read him the riot act. And for a while everything was fine, until Tessa—"

"Started showing an interest in him."

"Yes. You saw for yourself, though, on Monday afternoon how she used the attraction to get back at me because I refused to favour her over Thea in the distribution of parts. She is too young to understand the difference between personal and artistic decisions. Besides which, Thea has been a loyal member of the company and a good friend since joining it."

"You planned to help her through her pregnancy?"

The smile returned briefly. "My, you *are* good at this detecting business. Thea came to me after Jason's death. If only she'd come sooner."

"You might have got them safely married?"

"Something like that."

"It must have been you who talked her out of killing herself after his death."

"I certainly tried. Anyway, when I saw Tessa and Ensign Hilliard hitting it off so well, I was not only not concerned, I was actually pleased. I was sure he would take her in the way of a man—she was shamelessly testing her seduction techniques on him—and that she would then have some better notion about that sort of love, with the certainty that we would be on our way to Detroit by week's end and any emotional connection would be broken permanently."

"You were willing to let Tessa make a choice? Was that not dangerous for you? You might have lost her affection for good."

"That is true, and I thought I was strong enough to carry it off. I even pictured myself as noble and self-sacrificing, a mother letting the child choose the world over her." Her face clouded over. "But, alas, I was not that brave. When Tessa and Hilliard went into her room, I assumed the worst, and braced for it. I went to my bedroom, where I could not possibly be privy to any of the goings-on through the wall. I even put my infamous earplugs in. But not for long. Soon I found myself standing, naked and fearful, right over there with my ear pressed to the wallpaper. I could hear their giggling and the clink of glasses. Then nothing for a long time. I became alarmed. Before I could make up my mind what to do—perhaps get dressed and try a discreet rap on their door—I heard Tessa's cry. It wasn't a scream. It was a sharp yelp of surprise and physical pain. That's all. But I knew what it meant." At last she looked away, abashed.

Marc understood at last how the crime had been accomplished. "There were two cries, weren't there? The first one heard only by you."

She swung her head around to face him, the glorious ropes of her sandy hair swinging sensuously in the variable light. She was smiling through a scrim of tears. "Ah, you are far too young to be so clever. You must come from exceptional stock."

Marc was flattered, unaccountably, but pressed on. "That's how you and you alone were able to get down to that room, kill Merriwether, entrap Hilliard, and get back here."

"That's right. Of course, I had no conception of what was actually going on in there, you understand. I was out of my mind with jealousy and anger at Tessa and at my own foolish weakness: I simply ran out into the hall without a stitch on, the candlestick in my hand. I just assumed that it was the soldier on top of her. Then I was shocked to see the candlestick suddenly smeared with blood and hair, even more to see Jason on the floor, staring up and dazed, his eyes slowly closing. I had hit him a savage blow, but had no memory of it.

"It must have taken me a minute or so to comprehend what I had done. Then the rage took hold, pure and unstoppable. The violator was not young Hilliard, whose amorous pawings I could understand, but Jason Merriwether, a man to whom I had given a second life. I put my trust in him, was about to make him a partner in the Bowery Theatre. And I had specifically warned him away from Tessa. You can't imagine how betrayed I felt. In that moment, I hated all men, monsters who had done nothing but betray me all my adult life. I saw the gleam on the sword, I don't think I even knew it was Hilliard's, but I pulled it out, walked over to Jason, and plunged it through the son-of-a-bitch's heart."

The recollection of that grotesque act had brought sweat to her brow and a tremble to her lip. In a quieter tone she continued. "The blood began spouting everywhere, and I instinctively jumped aside. Some splattered me, but I was naked, so no harm done. I went over to check on Tessa, but I was shaking so hard by then I could not properly detect her pulse. She began breathing regularly with that little-girl snore I know so well. I was sure now that she was all right, and had seen nothing. I took a large handkerchief of hers and dipped it in Jason's blood and smeared it on Hilliard—it took several trips to soak his uniform. And I knew, as you said, how it would go when the two of them were discovered. Then I came back here, unseen."

"That explains why I could find no evidence of blood being splattered on Rick's tunic: you smeared it with a cloth. And there was a set of boot-prints approaching the body because Rick never did stagger back to the settee. You or Jason must have knocked the ashtray onto the floor after he was struck. But you still had a bloody handkerchief and a candlestick to dispose of."

"Yes. I had put on a little fire in the stove earlier, so I started it up and burned the hanky."

"I found traces of it in the ash in your grate yesterday."

"Did you?"

"But the candlestick would be harder to hide. Why didn't you just wipe it clean?"

"I intended to. It took a few minutes for the fire to get going, and I also realized that I needed to wash myself thoroughly—I had some blood on my hands and arms. So I did that, praying that neither Hilliard nor Tessa would wake up too soon, and praying also that it would be Hilliard first so Tessa might be spared the scene in that room. I was more anxious about that than making sure I wasn't caught. I had just dried myself and slipped into a nightgown when I heard Tessa scream loud enough to wake the dead. My heart turned to ice. But the die was cast. I grabbed the candlestick, ran into my bedroom, threw myself down, jammed the candlestick under the blanket, stuffed in my earplugs, and tried to calm myself. It seemed like an eternity before Clarence and Jeremiah came rushing in to fetch me. And the rest you know."

Yes. Rick waking when Tessa screamed, not at the gory sight of Merriwether on the floor, but rather at her handsome young soldier, apparently mortally wounded on the settee. For her, it had been the nightmarish image of a stabbed and dying lover: she didn't yet know that one of her nightmare cries had been real and had sealed Rick Hilliard's fate.

"Tessa didn't see Merriwether," Marc said. "She saw only Rick. Being drugged, she has no recollection of the rape except for the initial jab of pain. She doesn't even know she screamed aloud that second time. And now the blood on Rick has become a hero's badge of devotion."

"Tessa has come through this ordeal better than any of us. I have committed murder, killed a man I once admired and respected. I can never forgive myself for that. Nor will any rationalization justify it or mitigate the remorse I feel. What's more, and just as bad, I have allowed an innocent, even noble, young man to be falsely accused. But I have suffered much before this, and gone on. I hope I have the strength to do so this time."

Marc's head jerked back as if struck. He had assumed that this voluntary and detailed confession had been done as a form of expiation prior to her surrendering to the authorities. But she had just informed him that she expected to carry on with her life, chastened perhaps but unpunished.

"Mrs. Thedford," he began in what he hoped was a severe tone, "you are aware that I admire you and that I abhor the violence done upon Tessa by Merriwether. But I represent the lieutenant-governor and the Crown in this matter, and I have no choice but to do my duty. I intend to wait while you get dressed, then escort you to Government House. There you will be incarcerated, and I will wake up my friend, free him from the fantasy he has been living, and return him to the world."

She smiled. There was true warmth in it. Then she frowned. "You must believe me when I tell you I am truly sorry for what I've put your friend through. I regretted what I had done the moment I saw him again in that room, dazed and self-accusing. But there was no turning back. And I knew it would only be a question of a day or two before he was exonerated. But then, when I learned he was your friend, I felt dreadful."

"You're telling me that you intended to confess all along? And yet you expect to get on a steamer tomorrow and sail off for Detroit?"

"Yes. That is what I have just done, confessed my guilt. And, yes, at noon tomorrow, my company and I will be bound for Detroit." She seemed amused, though there was an edge of solemnness in her gaze as well.

"Then you don't know me very well."

"On the contrary, I know more about you than you can imagine."

"That's as absurd as your thinking I won't take you to the governor."

"You will not do so, not because of what I've said or may do, but because of who I am."

"You're Annemarie Thedford."

"Am I?"

"That may be a stage name, I realize, but what does it matter to me if you have another?"

"A great deal, I hope."

She leaned over and laid a hand on his knee. "My real name is a variant which I adopted many years ago—after I left England. Look at me. I am tall and fair and blue-eyed."

Annemarie Thedford. A name from the past flashed before him. But it was impossible. That person was long dead. Dead before he had been born. Yet, just as she whispered the words to him—as if speaking them too loudly might annihilate what they named—he said them silently to himself.

"Mary Ann Edwards."

She gazed steadfastly at him, waiting for the shock to pass and the implications to sink in. Finally, he was able to say, "You are my aunt Mary."

"Not quite," she said. "I am your mother."

SEVENTEEN

When Marc had recovered enough to find breath and voice, he heard himself say, "But that's not possible. Mary is dead, I've seen her grave. And my parents were Thomas and Margaret Evans. They are also dead."

Mary Ann Edwards took Marc's hands in hers in a grip that was both tender and firm. "I'm sorry that I could find no gentler way to convey such news to you. But I was as stunned and bewildered by it as you are now."

"But how? When?" Marc stammered as the chilling implications of her claim began to take hold.

"'How' is a very long story. 'When' was yesterday at luncheon."

"When you met Major Jenkin."

"Yes. Such a dear man. I took an immediate liking to him. He loves to reminisce, so I encouraged him to tell me about the wars in Europe. Well, he kept mentioning his best friend Frederick. To be polite, I asked a question or two about this Frederick."

"And you discovered his name was Edwards."

"Yes. My brother, whom I last saw leaving for Europe in 1805 or '06."

"But surely you were not surprised to hear his name mentioned by Jenkin?"

"When I first met you on Monday, I noticed your name, of course, but Edwards is a common enough surname in southern England. It occurred to me that you might be a distant cousin—your height and colouring were right—but that was all. I was more concerned with your bearing and intelligence. But when I realized that Owen knew Frederick well, I began to pester him with questions about the family, about my nephews in France, and he eventually got around to Jabez and the estate in Kent. Then I was certain. It was both strange and exciting to hear about my brothers after twenty-seven years of pretending they didn't exist."

Marc began, vaguely, to sense where the story was heading. "And at some point, my name was mentioned."

"Yes." She gave his fingers a squeeze. Part of him wanted to tear away from her grip and this scourging narrative, but another part admitted that he must know the truth, whatever the cost. "Owen, dear soul, was going on about how wonderful Jabez was—it was all I could do to hold my tongue—and how he'd adopted a five-year-old lad whose parents had died and, he said, this was all the more admirable because the boy's father was a mere gamekeeper and the mother a tenant-farmer's daughter. He must have thought me mad, the look I had on my face, when I demanded to know their names. It took him a minute or two, and I thought I might faint waiting, but he finally said Thomas and Margaret Evans. And then I knew for certain. I let him babble on—oh, how grateful I was for his garrulousness. But the child who was ripped from my breast, who I never would have abandoned for the world, was alive, was thriving, and close enough to touch."

She released his hands, as if perhaps she had said enough to hold him there while she wept quietly and composed herself.

"But I stood over your grave-marker in the garden by the big house, and wished you had lived that I might have an aunt . . . and a kind of mother."

"Bless you for that."

"Uncle Jabez thought you were dead. He grieved over you for years. I was forbidden to speak your name because it hurt him so much."

A series of expressions passed across Mary Ann Edwards's face in quick succession: contempt, anger, sorrow, regret, resignation. She took a deep breath, pulled the lapels of her robe tightly together, and said in a low, sad voice: "I thought I had worked out all my anger towards Jabez—after all, it's been twenty-seven years—but you never do, not when the betrayal is so great."

"Uncle Jabez betrayed you?"

"Yes. But you'll need to know the story from the beginning to understand what happened, if you are to forgive him. I cannot, but you must."

Marc realized that she was as exhausted as he was, but the adrenaline was running strong in both, and he sat back, bracing himself for the secrets that were about to be revealed into a new day's glare.

"When I was almost eighteen, Jabez decided I should go up to London to Madame Rénaud's finishing school, after which I would 'come out' and be matched with a suitable husband. I was a tomboy around the estate, I fought against the plan, but when I was forcibly removed to the great metropolis, I soon discovered I liked it very much. Not the ladies' school, of course—Madame Rénaud was about as French as Yorkshire pudding—but the nearby theatres. I sneaked off every chance I got to one or another of the summer playhouses. During vacations I stayed with an elderly cousin who didn't keep close tabs on me, so I was soon landing bit parts and getting to know many of the actors. Eventually I met your father."

Marc waited, fearing the worst.

"Don't worry so: he wasn't a syphilitic pimp. He was a tall, handsome young man of twenty-five, the youngest son of a country squire who had once been a renowned barrister in the city. His name was Solomon Hargreave.

He was a talented actor, but his father disapproved of his
chosen profession, cut off his allowance, and impounded his
grandfather's legacy. Solomon thought me talented as well
as beautiful, and before long I simply abandoned the school
and moved in with him. He was very much in love with me.
I was still young and naively romantic. I was surprised and
confused when I was told I was pregnant."

"You did not marry?"

"No. It didn't seem to matter, though Solomon was willing, I believe. We were quite happy as we were but, of course,
when Jabez learned I had abandoned school, he came up to
London in a perfect fury. We had a great row, but he left,
saying he would be back. I was very frightened, but managed
to hide my pregnancy from him. Solomon was off on a trip
up north with a touring company, so I moved to a cheap flat
where Jabez couldn't find me. Solomon was due back in a few
weeks, but Jabez discovered me first by bribing someone at
the theatre. I went into labour two months early."

"So I was—"

"A bastard, yes. But a beautiful, blue-eyed babe, nonetheless, wee and shrivelled and underweight at seven months,
but kicking and screaming for the teat. I must say that Jabez's concern for my health and that of the baby was genuine and took immediate precedence. He sent for Margaret
Evans from the estate, and had her nurse me and take care
of you. But when Solomon arrived a few days later, everything changed. After Jabez took a couple of swings at him,
he calmed down and settled on a quick wedding. Solomon

was, after all, a gentleman, if also a blackguard in his eyes. But I was defiant. I wanted to be an actress, to make a life for myself on the stage. I told Jabez that we would marry when we were ready to and that I would raise my son backstage. Actresses were then, and still are, regarded as no better than whores. But looking back on that moment now, I believe I suspected even at that youthful age that I preferred women to men: something was urging me to resist marriage."

"Yet you became Mrs. Thedford?"

She smiled wryly, but continued her tale. "I did not understand how determined and how cruel my eldest brother could be. When Solomon had gone off to the theatre, Jabez exploded in a fury of curses and recrimination. So towering was his anger that I feared for my life. But it was my baby's life he was after." Her expression darkened at the memory, as lines of bitterness twisted at her mouth.

"Surely not. Uncle Jabez was—"

"Kind and considerate, yes. As he had been to me. But ever since our mother's death when I was myself a baby and our father's death a few years later, Jabez saw himself as responsible for me, for my upbringing, my education, even my morals."

"What happened?"

"Jabez left in a huff. But two days later, after a long nap—I was still weak and not fully recovered from the birth—I awoke to find Jabez standing over me, and Margaret Evans and my unnamed son gone. 'The bastard has been taken to an orphanage,' Jabez said in the coldest voice I'd ever heard in a man. Then he handed me a large sum of money—in cash—and announced that I was no longer an Edwards, and was to have no contact with him or Frederick or anyone else we knew: I was, in his words, 'dead to the family and to the world.' He left before I could think of a reply. I have not seen him since."

"Then how did I get to the estate?" Marc asked after a long moment. He was sure he knew the answer. Even so, Jabez's heartless abandonment and shunning of his own sister was a devastating truth, whatever the mitigating circumstances might have been. Marc had literally been stolen from his mother.

"I only learned the bare details of that much later. You see, when Solomon returned to find the child gone, I thought he would fly into a rage of his own and confront Jabez, demand the return of his son, and scour the alleys and byways of London until you were found."

"But he didn't."

"No. He was, in his way, attached to the notion of a child, but he had only seen you for a short while, squalling for food and attention, and he soothed me by saying it was all for the best, we were destitute, we both wanted to have careers in the theatre, we were young, we would have legitimate children of our own, and so on."

"And he won you over?" Marc said.

"You must believe this if nothing else, Marc: I did not

abandon you. As soon I could walk, I went to every orphanage in central London in search of you. I was frantic, but you were nowhere to be found."

Their eyes locked. "Yes, I believe you," Marc said, "because I've watched you with Tessa, Thea, and the others. You do not let go easily."

"Soon we started to spend Jabez's blood-money. I felt that without Solomon to back me up, I could not go down to the estate and demand you back. As an unmarried Englishwoman, I had no legal right to my own child: you were Solomon's or Jabez's to fight over. So when Solomon suggested we flee to America to start over again, I said yes. And we did. And except for the child I left behind, I have had no regrets about that."

"But you still thought I had been left with an orphanage?"

"Yes. Solomon and I arrived in New York late in 1810, and having some capital, we managed to do well. I blossomed as an actress, soon outshining him. We lived together as man and wife, but my proclivity for female company and companionship was becoming blatant and undeniable. We quarrelled often. Finally, he decided to return home. His father had died, and he hoped his oldest brother would give him a second chance. I stayed and prospered.

"Then about a year later Solomon sent a letter, the only one he ever wrote to me, saying that he had made a search for our son, and after much effort had located a woman who admitted being the wet-nurse for you at a rented house overseen by Margaret Evans and sponsored by Jabez Edwards. At some point, they had taken you back to Kent and represented you as the child of Thomas and Margaret Evans, who had no child of their own. Solomon didn't know, nor did I, that they had christened you Marcus. But at least I knew you had survived and were being raised by good people on the family estate. That's the last I heard about you—until yesterday. I had no idea that Jabez had adopted you and given you our name. I wanted to dash into the theatre and embrace you till I dropped. But I could not do so. You were investigating a murder I committed."

Neither said anything for a full minute.

"But you 'prospered,' as you say. You became Mrs. Annemarie Thedford."

"That's another long story, but yes, I did. I moved to Philadelphia, where the theatre business was booming. I re-invented myself in a country that encourages a fresh start and admires it when it works. I invented a Mr. Thedford, alas deceased, presented my hard-won capital as an inheritance, played the merry widow, fell in and out of love many times, and finally moved back to New York as that 'widow from Philadelphia,' eventually buying into the Bowery."

"And helped reclaim one or two others like yourself along the way."

"Yes. Including poor Jason."

Marc felt suddenly drained and utterly exhausted. The candles were low and flickering. "What do we do now?" he asked, seeing no way forward. "Either my best friend hangs for murder . . . or my mother does."

"Ensign Hilliard will be freed tomorrow, one hour after our steamer departs."

"But how?"

"You do not think I would have left your friend to pay for my crime? I sat down after our rehearsal yesterday—when I got to spend two hours alone with my son—"

"You deliberately arranged for those scenes, didn't you? Including my playing Hamlet to your Gertrude?"

She smiled. "I knew those hours and our brief moments together on the stage last night would be all that would be allowed me. But listen: I have prepared a detailed confession for the police." She got up, went over to the davenport, and picked an envelope out of the papers there. Marc's mind lingered for a moment in the past.

"That hand-mirror, the one I held up to Gertrude's face, it came from home, didn't it?"

"Yes, as did these brushes and the candlesticks. They were left to me by my father, part of a matched set given to my parents as a wedding gift. All three of their children have pieces of the set."

"I remember seeing that design now, on Uncle Jabez's hair-brushes in his room."

She gently but resolutely brought him back to the present. "This letter of confession is unsealed and undated."

She removed one of two sheets and gave it to Marc. "Can we trust Constable Cobb?"

"Of course." Marc scanned the letter and the signature at the bottom.

"Then bring him with you to the wharf at noon tomorrow. We depart for Detroit then on the *Michigan*. I'll date the letter today, and seal it. I'll ask Cobb to take it directly to his chief. I'll make sure to leave a few papers in here with my handwriting and signature on them. By the time the magistrates have perused the letter and determined its authenticity, I'll be in the United States."

"But they still might not believe you. Barclay Spooner is determined to see Rick hanged."

"On this second page I tell the police exactly where they can find the candlestick. You mustn't see this page: I don't want you compromised. When they find the candlestick, they'll discover Jason's blood and hair still on it. I decided to leave it as it was when I devised this plan. And Owen Jenkin was in this room on Monday afternoon and evening: he can verify that the candlestick was one of the pair he saw here."

"And with the explanation of the two screams laid out in this letter, the sworn testimony of the others makes perfect sense."

"Nor am I underestimating the persuasive powers of my son."

There was nothing left to do now but hold each other. Neither would let go. From the other room, Tessa let out a contented snore. Marc did not shudder.

• • •

THE MID-OCTOBER DAY WAS BRIGHT WITH sunshine in a high, cloudless sky whose deep blue mirrored the unrippled surface of Lake Ontario. On such a day as this, it was hard to imagine the province could be anything but prosperous and peaceful. The weather had made the harvesting of crops seem almost a leisure activity, and an improved harvest it had been throughout the broad countryside. And here on Queen's Wharf at the foot of John Street, Lieutenant Edwards stood bare-headed in the plaintive breeze and bade good-bye to Mary Ann Edwards. Beasley, Armstrong, Jefferson, and Tessa and Thea had already boarded the *Michigan*, and were leaning against the rail, waving or otherwise acknowledging the farewell plaudits of the several dozen fans who had come to see the Bowery players off. An hour earlier, Jefferson and three bulky draymen had muscled a number of steamer-trunks aboard—four of them inexplicably lighter than they had been upon arrival. Constable Cobb stood a few yards away, impassively observing Marc and Mrs. Thedford.

"Will I ever see you again?"

"Only if you come to New York."

"But you will write?"

"Yes. But you must promise to send me long and loving letters about the wondrous woman you are going to marry, and tell me everything about each child as it arrives. I must know that you are happy."

"I will. I'll bombard you with paper and ink."

"And you must promise me one other thing."

"Uncle Jabez?"

"Yes. He must never know about me, or that I have found you. The dead ought to remain dead."

"But not always, surely?"

"Not always," she conceded. "I cannot forgive Jabez, but I can't hate him either now that I see what he's helped you become. It is better for him and you to go on as you have been. I couldn't bear to be the cause of any unhappiness between the two of you. I have more than enough on my conscience already, and I'm afraid I've severely compromised yours."

The steamer blew two peremptory blasts of its brand-new whistle.

"It's time," she said, drawing the sealed envelope out of her reticule.

Marc waved Cobb over. The constable had been given the bare outline of what was to take place, but in order to spare him any improper involvement in the business, he had been told that the letter contained evidence pertinent to the investigation, and it was only in these specific circumstances that it would be passed along. Cobb took the envelope—sealed and addressed to the chief constable—without a word, but his glance at Marc said: I know there's something odd going on here, but it's your affair.

"I'll get this to Sarge right away," Cobb said, and left.

Marc took his mother's gloved hand and kissed it.

"You make me feel like a lady."

"You *are* a lady."

Marc had almost missed the *Michigan*'s departure. He had fallen into a fitful sleep at Mrs. Standish's and had continued to wrestle with the various demons in his nightmares until almost eleven o'clock. When he returned to the Regency's guest quarters, all the doors were open and the rooms empty. Merriwether's trunk and clothes were gone. The Bowery Touring Company had departed. A few minutes later, he found Ogden Frank in the tavern, counting the take from last night's performance.

"That Spooner fella was here at daybreak with a squad of goons, rippin' open trunks an' haulin' away guns. He was mad keen to find you, but I told him I hadn't seen hide nor hair of you."

Marc thanked him, went to the stable to check on the horse (Spooner had got it also), then sent a stable boy with an urgent message to Cobb at the police station just up the street. Looking dishevelled and very unmilitary, he started to walk west towards John Street at the other end of town, but got less than a block away down Colborne when a familiar female voice hailed him. He turned to find Aunt Catherine running towards him at a most undignified gait. She seemed in worse shape than he was: her coat and bonnet were askew, her hair unpinned, her eyes red with weeping.

"My God, Auntie, what in the world's happened?" His only thought was of Beth.

"It's George," she said. "He's gone."

"Gone?"

"When he didn't come in for breakfast, I went to his room, and he wasn't there. His bed hadn't been slept in. He's packed up all his belongings and vanished in the middle of the night!"

Marc was not surprised, but could not say so to Aunt Catherine. At least her deep anxiety confirmed for Marc that she herself had not been involved.

"What'll I do, Marc? I'm beside myself. I feel responsible for the boy."

"First of all, he's a young man, not a child. And, secondly, I have some reason to believe that he may have been mixed up in some dubious, possibly illegal, political activities."

"Oh, no, he couldn't be!" she protested, but he could see her conviction on this point was not strong.

"I'm positive he's safely over the border by now, Auntie. Most likely he'll write and let you know within the week."

"He's in no danger, then?"

"None that I know of, at least not imminently. I suspect he's fled more out of prudence than alarm."

"Oh, Marc, I'm so relieved."

Not as much as I am, Marc thought.

"I do hope this doesn't upset our plans for the wedding."

Marc gave her a peck on the cheek. "Nothing can upset those plans."

•   •   •

Two hours after the *Michigan* had departed, Magistrate Thorpe and the police had taken note of Mrs. Thedford's unexpected confession, discussed the case with Marc, and sent Wilkie off to find the candlestick sewn into the mattress where she had said it would be. A writ for the formal release of Ensign Roderick Hilliard was issued, and Marc having declined the privilege, Cobb begged to be the one to serve it on the governor's staff—hopefully in the presence of Lieutenant Barclay Spooner.

"I figured you'd be dyin' to waltz in there an' strut out with Hilliard on your arm," Cobb said as he and Marc headed west on King Street towards Government House.

"I did, too. But suddenly I found it didn't matter. Don't mistake me, I'm delighted Rick is being freed. He's gone through hell. But he also helped put himself there."

"That blond thing, ya mean?"

"Yes. And I suppose you ought to give this billet-doux from Tessa to him, though I considered tossing it in the lake." He gave Cobb a pink, perfumed envelope.

Cobb accepted it with two fingers, sniffed it in disgust, and dropped it into the maw of his overcoat. "You gonna walk all the way back to the garrison?"

"Yes, I am. I've got a mountain of thinking to do." They were nearly at Simcoe Street. "I want to thank you, Cobb. I couldn't have survived the past three days without you."

"I'm awful sorry about the lady. I know you liked her a lot."

"You're very observant."

"Maybe so. But I never once thought she could be a murderer."

MARC DID HAVE MUCH TO THINK about as he left the city and walked pensively along the road that wound its way towards Fort York. He had a life-history to rewrite in his dreams and in those waking moments when the hours of the days could not be numbed by action. The simple, honest couple, whose deaths he had mourned and whose lives he had honoured as only an orphaned child can, were now something less than father and mother. The yeoman's blood he had felt sturdying his veins was diluted blue-blood after all: he was an Edwards and a Hargreave with a birth-father he might never set eyes upon, with faceless cousins somewhere sharing his genes but not his life. He was also a bastard, conceived—in society's pitiless eye —in sin and born irredeemably out of wedlock.

But he had a mother who had delivered him gladly into her world, fought for his freedom and her own, had been abominably used and declared dead, before resurrecting herself alone in a brave new land. Yet the man she had every reason to hate was the man he himself loved more than any other. True, Uncle Jabez had not abandoned him outright, but until his adoptive parents died unexpectedly, he had been content to watch him grow up as another's son. Could such behaviour be forgiven? Could it outweigh the happy years he had spent, after the age of five, as the "lord" of the estate, coddled and fussed over and supported through life until he became a man? He did not know.

And there were other matters pressing in upon and disturbing the conscience of the man he had supposed himself to be. He was still wearing the Queen's colours and he had not yet heard himself recanting his oath of allegiance. But in the space of a few hours he had contrived to let a killer escape to safety in the United States, had lied to a fellow officer when asked if he could identify any of the would-be insurgents out there in the bush, and had failed to inform his superiors about a young man acting as the messenger between the rebels and the gunrunners. He was also deliberately avoiding the governor's aide-de-camp and his attempts to debrief the man who knew the most about the whole sordid business.

What was most surprising to him, however, given the number of times he had tumbled these quandaries in the cauldron of his mind, was that he seemed to be caring less and less that there were no answers, no pat resolution, no reconciliation of any kind. What he invariably ended up with, regardless of any particular configuration of the problem, was a single-word conclusion: Beth. Of course she did not provide an unambiguous answer to any of these ethical dilemmas: she merely rendered the questions irrelevant.

By the time he walked through the gates and aimed himself at the officers' quarters, he could think only that he had survived the past three days. He was alive and Beth was alive. In nine days they would be married. Then, perhaps, like his more famous Roman namesake, he would be able to stand up and shout, "This is my space, kingdoms are clay!"

Corporal Bregman hailed him. "Welcome back, sir. You've come just in time."

"In time for what?"

"I'm not sure, sir, but Colonel Margison has called a meeting of all his officers for three o'clock And he asked me specifically to have you go to him the minute you arrived back."

"Thank you, Corporal," Marc sighed. It was conceivable that Spooner had sent someone out here looking for him, armed with a list of complaints about his behaviour and deportment as an officer. It was the last thing he wished to talk about, but he had no choice.

Major Jenkin was standing beside the colonel when Marc entered the office, both looking grave. He steeled himself for a serious dressing-down.

"I'll come right to the point, Lieutenant," Colonel Margison said. "I'll be informing the other officers in fifteen minutes but, as you have made plans of a personal nature for next week, the major here and I thought it would be kinder to tell you now—as friends as well as fellow officers."

"Tell me what, sir?"

"Governor Head has ordered every regular soldier, officers and men alike, out of the province and into Quebec. Insurrection there is imminent."

"But that's suicidal! We've got a countryside full of rebels right here!"

"It seems that Sir Francis considers himself invulnerable."

"Our orders are to leave immediately," Jenkin said. "This afternoon."

"But I have a wedding to—"

"It'll have to be postponed, I'm afraid," the colonel said.

"You'll have time to write Beth before we embark at five o'clock for Kingston," Jenkin said. "Our company is to be the advance unit. You can drop it off at Cobourg when we stop for supplies."

This is it, Marc thought, incredulous. What I have wished for since my first day at Sandhurst: to stride into battle to preserve the honour and integrity of crown and country. And Beth, bless her, had given him leave to do his duty.

Why, then, was it all ashes in his mouth?

EPILOGUE

Saturday, October 21, 1837
Dearest Marc:
I received your brief note the day after your ship left
Cobourg on October 13. By then we had already heard
the disquieting news. I have waited a few days before
writing back in order to marshal my thoughts and, in view
of what has been happening here, offer you what comfort
I can. First of all, you have nothing to apologize to me for.
Our wedding, which we had every hope would take place
tomorrow, has merely been postponed, not our love. I
am twenty-five years old, and I have lived long enough in

this world to know that we are not wholly responsible for
what happens to us. Nor, I'm beginning to realize, is God.
We are responsible only for what we feel and how we act
upon what we feel, insofar as we are allowed to in a land
simmering with hate and aggrieved hearts. I have come to
know many of the ideals you hold and how bravely you try
to act upon them. Those are the things I love in you. So,
please do not be sorry that the mad governor has sent you off
to fight in a war you did not make.

You may find it strange to hear me speak like this. I am
finding it strange myself. But we are living in difficult and
treacherous times. Forgive me if I burden you with matters
close to home when you are—I shiver at the thought—
bracing yourself for battle, but you must know that Thomas
and Winnifred are in some serious trouble, possibly even
in danger. I was shocked to discover that Thomas has not
been off doing his road duty at all, but still attending radical
meetings in the township and consorting with people who
are talking and acting as if a farmers' revolt is inevitable.
That is, an armed insurrection. I do not know whether
Winnifred knew or, if she did, whether she approved: she
says little and broods much. But last week, Thomas came
home quite shaken, and swearing that he was finished with
politics for good. I overheard him telling Winnifred that he
had almost shot some American fellow before he came to his
senses and he fled. But now the poor man is terrified that
one of his cohorts will betray him. Several of them—you

remember Azel Stebbins, don't you?—have been hauled
in by the magistrates for questioning about subversive
activities, and he fears one of them will rat on him to save
his own skin. He and Winn are talking again about going
west across the Mississippi to the Iowa Territory. But their
grain is unsold, they are too proud to ask me for money,
and Erastus would not lend them a farthing to abandon him
and their home. Then, three days ago, we heard that a gang
of Orangemen ambushed and beat up a dozen young men
near Perry's Corners, claiming they were "drilling"—with
hoes and forks for guns! To top it all off, Aunt Catherine
writes that her relative, George Revere, has run off to the
States without explanation and that, this week, the windows
on our shop were smashed by vandals.

Enough. I will write only happy news from now on.
The thought of what you may have to do there, if there is a
war, fills me with dread, but am I unforgivably selfish for
thinking mainly of your safety, or your coming through such
horrors whole and still able to smile at me? Believe this, my
darling: I will be waiting for you when you come back. I
live for your return. What I ask of you is equally simple:
survive. Please.

All my love,
Beth